ANNE RICE'S VAMPIRE CHRONICLES

AN ALPHABETTERY

ANCHOR BOOKS

A Division of Penguin Random House LLC

New York

ANNE RICE'S
VAMPIRE
CHRONICLES

AN ALPHABETTERY

Compiled and written by
BECKET

With an introduction by
ANNE RICE

Illustrated by
MARK EDWARD GEYER

AN ANCHOR BOOKS ORIGINAL, OCTOBER 2018

The Library of Congress Cataloging-in-Publication data
Names: Becket, author. | Rice, Anne, 1941– Vampire chronicles.
Title: Anne Rice's Vampire chronicles an alphabettery / by Becket.
Description: New York : Anchor Books / A Division of Penguin Random
House LLC, 2018. | "An Anchor Books Original" — Verso title page.
Identifiers: LCCN 2018001881 (print) | LCCN 2018011772 (ebook)
Subjects: LCSH: Rice, Anne, 1941– Vampire chronicles—Dictionaries. |
Vampires in literature—Dictionaries. | Horror tales, American—Dictionaries.
Classification: LCC PS3568.I265 (ebook) | LCC PS3568.I265 V275 2018 (print) |
DDC 813/.54—dc23
LC record available at https://lccn.loc.gov/2018001881

Anchor Books Trade Paperback ISBN: 978-0-525-43472-6
eBook ISBN: 978-0-525-43473-3

Illustrations by Mark Edward Geyer
Book design by Christopher M. Zucker

www.anchorbooks.com

Printed in the United States of America
10 9 8 7 6 5 4 3 2 1

CONTENTS

ACKNOWLEDGMENTS

450

INTRODUCTION

Where Does It All Come From?

Where do the characters, the stories—and the ideas—of the Vampire Chronicles come from? I've been asked that question for some forty years. Was the series—which now includes more than thirteen books—planned from the beginning? Do I outline the novels? Do I have an overall thematic plan? Did I foresee the direction my hero would take when I wrote the first book?

As I look at this vampire "alphabettery"—at this impressive and enormous work that Becket has created to describe and define a multitude of my interconnected characters, locations, and themes, I face these questions once again. I'm humbled and honored by this new guide to the Vampire Chronicles. It suggests vast complexity and organization, the maturity of characters over the passage of decades, and the development of a hero whose journey was inevitable from the start.

But did the Vampire Chronicles really unfold in an organized way?

My answers about process and progress have always reflected confusion more than anything else. But the challenge of the *Alpha-*

bettery is a good challenge. Because something did organize this series. Something did build this alternative reality. Something did create this high fantasy—the vampire realm with its roots in ancient history—but it may not have been the conscious mind of the author. It may have been an irrepressible gift for world building that only revealed itself slowly and sometimes painfully to the author herself over many years.

Why do only some authors create long and intricate series? Is it a skill that a writer can acquire? Or is fantasy world building a spontaneous outpouring of the imagination that only certain writers discover in themselves—as they struggle to control it or direct it year after year?

All writing for me—truly all writing—begins with a character. It begins with my seeing the character, naming the character, and then putting the character in motion, allowing him (or her) to reflect on or tell a story. It is through the story that the crucial ideas in the writing reveal themselves and become part of its effect on the reader.

I didn't know this when I started writing.

I simply imagined characters and let them lead me into a plot as I followed along faithfully, testing every development for the feeling of authenticity. I suppose I thought all writers worked in this way. It didn't occur to me to outline, or to even try to predict where a story might lead me.

I had a deep instinctive faith in this process. To outline would have been to undercut my faith and remove from the process the intensity of the writing experience and its potential for inevitable truth. I'm not saying I was right in believing this. But it was something so much a part of me that I never questioned it.

So, no, I never as a writer envisioned for a moment that I would be the author of more than thirty books involving vampiric characters and their many personal stories. In fact, I never contemplated writing a series of any kind.

I never dreamed of a book such as the *Alphabettery*. And when I look back on the first years of my published career, I can't remember reading any high-fantasy series which had spawned guides or companions. Though I was a deep lover of science fiction and horror stories, treasuring the greats in those fields, and most especially the old British masters such as Algernon Blackwood, Sheridan Le Fanu, and M. R. James, I hadn't tackled the Tolkien universe of Lord of the Rings yet. However, there was one short-story writer whose boldness in creating a unified cosmology did eventually inspire me to value my own vampire cosmology and not hesitate to develop it in a complex way. This writer was H. P. Lovecraft. I think he is much more widely known and read today. But I can't say Lovecraft was my favorite writer, or that I read enough of him to understand his world. I liked some of his stories some of the time.

What was on my mind in the beginning was simply writing novels that mattered to people.

I wanted my novels to be popular as well as literary. I was frightened of being labeled either a popular writer or a literary writer, and I sought for something spectacular and original and above all "true." I wanted my novels to *mean* something. And I wanted them to entertain.

I began the journey towards my first novel with a vampire named Louis in a room in San Francisco telling his personal story to a young reporter, who two books later acquired the name of Daniel. A vampire named Lestat was born early on in Louis's story as Louis described how he'd been seduced into vampirism by a "maker" he regarded as evil and shallow and unworthy of the gift of immortality he'd given Louis. Louis's deep resentment of Lestat colored all of *Interview with the Vampire.* Yet there were plenty of hints in the novel that Lestat himself might have a very different version of events to reveal, if he were ever allowed to speak. Indeed Lestat's vitality and glamour came to elicit an enormous response from readers, for which I wasn't at all prepared.

Shortly after *Interview with the Vampire* was published, one of my good friends had a fierce argument with me in which she told me Lestat was the hero of my novel—not the melancholy and ever-complaining Louis, but Lestat, Lestat who loved life and embraced life. Another friend, listening quietly all the while, said, "You drew Louis in ink. You painted Lestat in oils."

Surprising as this was, I wasn't disappointed. I was delighted that the novel had evoked passionate reactions. And I went right on writing as I had before—without a plan, creating a character and then fully expecting that character to reveal a story, a plot, and a moral overview—to me and to others.

I wrote two novels before I even considered a sequel to *Interview with the Vampire*. Neither involved a supernatural element. And neither involved a first-person element. And I was the last one to realize, I think, that all three of my published works involved a central theme: the struggle of outsiders—vampires, people of color before the Civil War in the South, and the great castrati opera singers of the eighteenth century—to survive in a world that would not let them in. Once again, it was a friend who pointed out that the vampires, the *gens de couleur de libre*, and the castrati all had something else in common, other than being outcasts. They had a group or world of their own.

When I decided to write a second vampire novel, I knew I wanted it to be Lestat's book. But it was not easy at first for me to hear his voice. I had to court Lestat. I had to invite him in. It was a bit like holding a séance every time I sat down at the computer keyboard. And I read a bizarre mix of fiction to "loosen up" and discover an intimate confessional voice for him that felt exactly right.

At some undefined point, that voice started to talk, or I started to hear it, and the story began to roll. As before, I had no real plan. And the book became a totally fresh story of vampiric awakening and discovery—

so vastly different, in fact—that I had to wrap the book around the events of *Interview with the Vampire* with the briefest remarks on the part of my hero to the effect that Louis had not always told the truth.

The Vampire Lestat was likely my worst plotted novel, the meandering confessions of my hero as he was inducted into vampirism, and fought for his freedom against those who would destroy or enslave him, embarking on a quest for meaning and for love that led him finally to becoming a rock superstar of the 1980s, a book meant not so much to counter the "lies" of Louis but ultimately to provide all the answers to Louis's old questions— questions that Lestat had been unable to answer when he made Louis a vampire.

The finished novel was in fact a prequel, a story of Lestat's existence before he ever encountered Louis—with only a short cliffhanger plot development at the end bringing the reader up to the present moment. I had followed Lestat back some two thousand years in his struggle to discover the origin of the vampires, and I had done it through tale-telling, as Lestat sought the truth from other immortals, prompting them to tell him what they knew, but ending up with a trove of secrets he could not share with his later fledglings Louis and Claudia, who hated him for his silence, his refusal to answer their questions, and ultimately turned against him, as *Interview with the Vampire* revealed.

I had no idea where I would go from there, none whatsoever.

But slowly a wholly different approach to writing came to me.

As I sat down to write a third vampire novel, I faced the impact that Lestat, now a rock singer in 1985, and the author of his own autobiography, had made upon the vampire world.

I began to see a large third-person novel in my imagination, involving a number of characters coming together as the result of Lestat's startling revelations—an autobiography, a series of rock videos—and I dimly envisioned a grand climax, though I was not entirely sure what it would be. There was no outline, no clear plan, no writing of a last chapter before any other. But I did see some marvelous patterns, almost like designs.

Ideas and characters exploded in my mind as I developed the ideas of the novel in terms of patterns. But once again, the characters had to give it substance and form; they had to write it. An ancient vampire emerged from obscurity or hiding to tell a tale of war and tragedy that revealed even more of the origins of the immortals, and a spirit world came into being along with ancient wrongs and ancient curses as elder blood drinkers came together to do battle against a menace awakened by Lestat.

The fact was, Lestat had opened up a limitless and glittering vampire world for me. His "autobiography" had been wholly unlike Louis's tragic story. Whereas Louis had never found the answers to his painful moral and philosophical questions, Lestat in my second vampire novel had found quite remarkable answers, but only because he had found remarkable beings who gave him those answers. And it was the characters once more in the third vampire novel, *The Queen of the Damned*, who revealed their history— either in tale-telling or in their thoughts—

to Lestat, the scribe who could read minds and who became the author of the finished saga, which essentially closed the calamitous events set into motion by Lestat's brashness in the second vampire book.

As I immersed myself in *The Queen of the Damned*, I felt this vampiric world around me, saw it, knew it to be immense and solid, a realm that was delicious to move about in, a phantom land full of new and surprising personalities, and filled with marvelous opportunities to bring my ancient characters in contact with the dazzling innovations of the late twentieth century in ways that were as risky as they were bold.

So that was how *The Queen of the Damned* was written, with a series of characters experiencing their responses to Lestat's revolutions. What I didn't think about was the obvious: the Vampire Chronicles had truly been born with Lestat's story—not Louis's story—and Lestat was the hero of the Vampire Chronicles.

The fourth and fifth vampire books that followed were adventures of Lestat—perilous journeys during which he risked his physical and mental safety to discover more and greater truths about this world and about himself and the other members of his tribe. He was my hero, all right, shining far brighter than anyone else on the shadowy landscape, but a rebellious hero, an outsider and an outcast not only among human beings but also in his own vampiric tribe. And his exploits always left him with partial victories and deepening alienation. But there was a sense always that he could not be defeated, that somehow, no matter what happened to him, he would eventually rise and take on the entire world again when he chose. His personality grew larger and more cohesive for me. I felt I knew him as I knew no other character I'd ever inhabited. I walked through life looking through his eyes, invoking him in some places that seemed particularly perfect for him, deliberately envisioning him at times, and even arguing fiercely with others about what he would do or not do, what he would like, what he might hate. The vampire world remained as solid as he was to me, no matter how large it became. Marius, Pandora, Armand, David Talbot, Louis, Gabrielle, other pillars of this universe, were effortlessly and consistently real. I might not love them quite in the way I loved Lestat, but they were vital and vivid and at times irrepressible as I wrote more vampire books.

For decades I explored these other characters, coloring in vast regions of vampire history, treating Pandora, Armand, and Marius to a kind of interrogation as I uncovered their personal stories, and they confided to me what they had learned from the Dark Blood, how they had survived the agony and immense power of immortality. And all the while the geography of the vampire realm was being mapped, with myriad locations and dwellings being erected, furnished, and sustained and even more immortal characters coming to life.

But how could all this happen without a plan? How could so many characters discuss so many ideas—about human existence, about God and the Devil, about right and wrong, and the destiny of humanity—in these novels if the author gave little or no thought to anything but "listening" to her characters?

If the author had no plan, how could the *Alphabettery*, with its innumerable entries, reveal such a scaffolding for a series of books and such a hierarchy of beings, each with his or her role, great or small, in a history that seemed at times without end? In the more recent books, even the spirit world has been partially illuminated. And other immortals, also described in the *Alphabettery*, have joined the blood drinkers as ageless witnesses to the passage of time.

The trust I had in the 1970s—that if I created a character and followed that character, a story would open up to me—has never faltered. Even when I'd ventured into the multiple points of view of *The Queen of the Damned*, I'd had faith that the characters would lead me to the key dramatic moments of its plot, and to an immense catharsis at the end, and indeed that had happened.

Of course there are no rules where authors are concerned; no one method works for all authors; in fact, there are likely as many ways to be a writer as there are writers. Try to measure Hemingway by the same rules critics use to measure Emily Brontë. Try to explain the power of Tolstoy by a set of rules that also works for Jack Kerouac. The novel—being the great enduring expression of the romantic era in that it is the outpouring of the individual of sensibility—has to be allowed as many forms as there are novelists. Otherwise we have no literature that can include *David Copperfield* and *Last Exit to Brooklyn* and *War and Peace*. The novel is an invitation to innovation and experiment and to tell tales of such magnitude that no one even cares about their form. How else can we explain the seminal power of *Jane Eyre* and the remarkable appeal of Sherlock and Watson in *The Sign of Four* or the impact of Sir Walter Scott upon an entire generation, and perhaps on an entire century, and the haunting effect of the immortal *Frankenstein*? The proper Victorians said novels should contain nothing that could not be read aloud to ladies in a drawing room. Imagine trying to measure *The Adventures of Huckleberry Finn* by that standard, or *The Brothers Karamazov*. People have been trying to make rules for the novel forever; but the very wildest of experiments with the form were conducted in the early decades of novel writing by Daniel Defoe and Henry Fielding, and Samuel Richardson, and Laurence Sterne. Then the Russians came along and wrote great tragedies in the form of the novel. Somebody is always shattering all our conceptions about novels as James Joyce did or James M. Cain.

No one has to know what others have done with the novel to write one's own novel, really. But if you feel a set of rules being imposed on you, either because someone is trying to tell you how you must write, or you yourself are the victim of too many inhibitions, it is always good to discover just how many different kinds of novels there are. Pick up Faulkner's *The Sound and the Fury*. Take a look at *The Member of the Wedding*. And then there is always *Moby-Dick*. And never discount the popular novels, which are often crackling with genius, *The Maltese Falcon* being of course an outstanding example, but then there is *The Godfather* and, a remarkable book of immense scope, Henry Bellamann's *Kings Row*. When I recently discovered Marjorie Kinnan Rawlings's *The Sojourner*, I was stunned.

My way—being led by characters into their stories—became my way because my mind preferred this way. In fact, my mind didn't seem capable of approaching fiction in any other way. And that this instinctive method—of following a character into his own world, his own story—would open up a complex vampiric realm is simply a fact.

I have no capacity to understand why this is my approach to the exclusion of all others. It certainly does not involve a choice. But I think I might be able to shed some light on why it became successful for me—and why the vampiric realm became so immense, embracing time and space, as it has.

But to do this I have to go back to my earliest childhood memory.

I'm talking now about being perhaps five years old and growing up in New Orleans on a beautiful tree-shaded street corner on the edge of the fabled neighborhood called the Garden District, with hours and hours of time on my hands to think and dream. I've described New Orleans and the Garden District in vibrant detail in several of my novels, and I've sought to evoke the sheer breathtaking loveliness of the place as it revealed itself to me from that early time. Giant black-barked evergreen oaks, purple flagstone sidewalks, black cast-iron-lace balconies and fences, gardens bursting with fragrant jasmine and roses and gardenias, great old Greek Revival houses with Corinthian columns along the front porches and leaded-glass doors sparkling in the evening with the light from within, haunted houses, old churches filled with painted saints and stained glass—all of this and more was my New Orleans.

But I want to put all that aside for a moment.

It was 1941 when I was born, and for the first five years of my life, my world always included my older sister, Alice. Only two years and two days separated our October birthdays. There are no memories of the earliest years without Alice—without her amazing vocabulary, her wild far-flung romantic ideas, her fantasies and confabulations, her inexhaustible energy.

I could write an essay on the way in which this older sister (now dead) fostered my curiosity and my imagination. That she was a genius I have no doubt now, and even in those very early years, the word attached to her. She could read immense books before she was nine years old, and I have a vivid memory of her reading Shakespeare for pleasure when she was sixteen and laughing out loud at something amusing in *Hamlet*.

But what I most vividly remember about Alice is that little separated her imagination from the concrete world in which we found ourselves.

I remember digging a hole in the backyard with her in order to create a tunnel through the earth that would take us to China. There was no doubt whatsoever that the project would succeed. But work stopped on the tunnel when Alice discovered what were almost certainly dinosaur teeth in the moist earth, which had to be studied and examined. A little later she informed me that our house stood over a pirate graveyard, and it was the remains of these pirates that now sidetracked our work on the tunnel. On another occasion, after a heavy rain, I remember Alice intently recording the "Morse code" she was receiving through the sounds of water dripping in the drainpipes.

Alice at the age of five and six was also very much involved in World War II, climbing to the top of a yew tree in our yard every day to keep a lookout for enemy soldiers and to practice signals with whoops and calls that she would give when she spotted them. She also practiced shooting them with invisible guns. I suppose it was through this that I learned a war was going on, and who was fighting it. I knew my father, whom I'd never met, was away somewhere due to this war, but I didn't know much else about it.

Alice's achievements frustrated me. I couldn't get up to the first branch of that tree she climbed and never did succeed in climbing it or any other tree. I was down on the ground looking up at Alice from the time I was born.

And before I continue here, allow me to say Alice went on to be a mentor all through my childhood. When I think of the topics she introduced to our family, the science fiction writers she brought home, the books on ballet, and the books on science, I have to ask myself, What would my life have been without her? Alice turned to novel writing late in life and published six novels before she died in 2007. I hear from her readers often. Her own life would make a very interesting story. But I doubt I could ever do it justice, and I don't know that anyone ever will.

As I was saying, my world had included my big sister, Alice, ever since I'd been born.

Until, that is, when I was five years old and Alice was taken off to school, at the age of seven, leaving me alone to play outside for long hours in the sunshine by myself, bitterly lonely and missing her terribly.

Sometime in that year when seven-year-old Alice was gone for hours every day, my personal dreamworld was born, the detailed and complex paracosm in which I started to live the major portion of every day with my own secretly imagined characters. I know for certain that the dreamworld was in full swing by the time I was eight, and had been with me "forever." And several of the characters who peopled that dreamworld then in 1949 are still with me today in a vivid cast of thousands.

From time to time over the years, I've tried to write down the names and stories of my dreamworld people. I've felt a need to record the immensity and complexity of the dreamworld with the thought that somehow a history of this realm might be of value to someone.

But such attempts soon become utterly exhausting. With every passing year—excepting a period of about fourteen years between 1991 and 2005—the dreamworld has grown in size, and more characters related to the original characters have come into being. The family trees are huge and endlessly complicated. And the day-to-day goings-on are as important to me now—as vivid and intense—as they were in those early years. The dreamworld's geography and inhabitants—its landscape, its cities, towns, buildings, and people—have followed a coherent evolution since those early days, resulting in the overwhelming realm that it is today. It involves a country with a government, a constitutional monarchy, and innumerable people of all classes. The neighborhood with which it began, the families with which it began, are still the focus.

For a very long time—at least since 1965—I have enjoyed another wholly separate dreamworld, set in ancient Rome, but it is ancient Rome in another dimension, involving my emperor, my senators, my Greece, and my Egypt and my Asia Minor, my slaves, my poets, and my armies and my generals. Now and then I abandon the ancient dreamworld. But I have never since 2005 abandoned the primal dreamworld, the most important one, the one born to me when I was a little girl, the one that existed from the 1940s up through the early 1990s without interruption, and that is with me now every day.

I myself am not in this dreamworld. There is no place in it for someone like me. I've had fantasies of actually discovering it, or being somehow transported to it, but I play no role in it whatsoever. I watch and listen and inhabit its various characters individually, just as I do characters in my books.

The main protagonists are men and women of means, born in and living in this imaginary country with its own recent history of feudal serfdom and class conflict between an entirely invented "German" aristocracy (and upper and middle class) and a rising class of invented "Irish" people. There is no coherent origin story except that, early on, titled and moneyed Germans and Russians migrated to this invented country, and they brought Irish immigrants with them as bond servants. The German and the Irish intermix today, dramatically.

My heroes and heroines are involved not just in being writers, motion-picture actors, painters, and inventors, but they are also scientists who make amazing breakthroughs in curing disease and great philanthropic bankers who engage in immense projects for the good of the citizens, building universities, planned neighborhoods, and even new cathedrals of staggering size. (I can spend days envisioning the newest national cathedral and its many side chapels.) A boy named Richard, who was the central and most important character for me when I was a little girl, is now approaching seventy (seven years younger than me, though up till recently he was my age), but he is an active filmmaker and television producer. His father, Lawrence, who has also been with me since 1949, is still living, and he is the great philanthropic genius behind the immense projects I described. This world also includes an entire cast of fabulous gangsters, "Irish" thugs who managed heroically to rise from oppression and bring order and justice to the abandoned "German" neighborhoods in which they lived after fleeing the rural areas where they'd long been held as serfs, and these thugs are now fully integrated into the social world of my main characters. There are many police families and firefighter families on the rise in the dreamworld. There are many virtuoso musicians and opera singers.

This imaginary country in which they live has finally been located by me on the planet somewhere on the northern Pacific coast, between British Columbia and the land above it. It has always been a cold country of short summers, in which the men wore velvet clothes and lots of fancy lace, and the houses were Tudor-Gothic affairs with a great deal of wood paneling, marble fireplaces, and leaded-glass windows. I've been filling in the various neighborhoods of the main city, Rosenwood, for decades.

The country now involves not only this capital city, but a number of fully developed towns. My focus shifts from one group of characters to another often, and indeed it has become so frustrating to me to remember the names of all the new characters that I now write down every week or so who has just been "born" into the dreamworld, who has had what child, who has married whom, and so on. This helps a lot. When I can't think of a character's name, I go crazy. And of course there is no one to ask: because nobody else knows the names of these characters or what is happening to them. Only a very few people have ever known this dreamworld exists.

I don't recall ever confiding the existence of this dreamworld to my close friends over the years. I did finally tell my husband, Stan, about the dreamworld, but never really disclosed many details about it. In fact, most of my life, I've guarded the secret of the dreamworld as something others must never find out.

Before I draw the obvious comparison between this dreamworld and the world of the Vampire Chronicles, I want to make several specific points about the dreamworld.

The first is that, though I don't believe in reincarnation and never have, there is one place and one era in the real world which felt extraordinarily like this dreamworld when I encountered it. This is the world of czarist Russia in the 1800s. I first came upon this world reading the history of the Romanovs, with whom I became obsessed for no apparent reason. But while reading *War and Peace*, which I do over and over and over again, I really became aware of disconcertingly powerful and distracting feelings that this place was somehow too like my dreamworld.

To repeat, I don't believe in reincarnation. But I have to confess that I can't shake the feeling that my dreamworld cannot coincidentally be like the world of Tolstoy's *War and Peace* without some supernatural link. And please do note that this has nothing to do with the style or depth of Tolstoy's incomparable novels. I'm simply talking about the social and physical background here.

My fictive velvet- and lace-wearing men and women in their huge houses, with their roaring fires, glittering glasses of wine, and endless discussions of feeling and philosophy—and what matters in life—seem powerfully linked to the Russians of Tolstoy's great saga.

Now, as a child of course I knew nothing of Russia or Russian literature. I don't recall ever seeing a movie set in czarist Russia until well into adulthood. And I certainly never read any Russian literature until my thirties. But the "feeling" is there, the eerie, haunted sense that somehow my dreamworld and the nineteenth-century Petersburg-Moscow world are separated only by a thin membrane. Even the fact that my dreamworld has always been a place of bitter cold winters strikes me as a remarkable coincidence. The dreamworld after all was developed for over ten years while I was growing up in subtropical New Orleans, famous for its purgatorial heat and short mild winters.

Though I cannot recall any early Russian historical influence on my dreamworld, my interests do invade and shape the dream-world. When I took up collecting antique dolls, for instance, one or more characters in the dreamworld were doing the same thing. When I visited major museums in Europe, some of my dreamworld characters were likely traveling as well. And recently—due to my collecting antique sterling flatware and china tableware, a major old-guard character in my dreamworld has created a company to manufacture new sterling-silver table patterns and new bone china. This character, born decades ago, who is the mentor and backbone of a great jewelry store in my dreamworld—a vast place inspired by Adler's in New Orleans and Gump's in San Francisco—has come in contact in his old age with young people uniquely gifted to create entirely new ornate sterling-silver patterns. And I've spent hours creating those silver patterns myself, incorporating motifs and elements into them that I don't believe have ever been used in sterling silver before. I have done the decorating, gilding, and enameling of the china plates as well, and imagined the newspaper advertisements heralding the New Romantic Renaissance offered to the public by this venerable character. When he first appeared in the dreamworld, I don't know, but I know he was active in the 1960s. He is ninety-six now, as is my mother-in-law. He is vigorous and imaginative, and the new lines of sterling and china have given him new vitality.

So yes, there is this bleed-through of my personal obsessions into the dreamworld, and films I've seen and loved often inspire films to be made in my dreamworld, about the dreamworld's history and heroes, films written, directed, and starred in by dreamworld characters, films that I write and produce for hours.

In fact the sheer variety of the dreamworld characters is directly reflective of my enormous interests in many fields, and I've spent hours with the firefighters and cops in the dreamworld just as I have with priests and cardinals. Indeed an archbishop cardinal is one of the main characters who has been active for at least thirty years. This character from time to time has visions and receives the five bleeding wounds of Christ, a physical response to deep contemplation, known as the Stigmata.

But aside from a free flow of obsessions and interests, I know nothing of the *meaning*—the symbolic or psychological meaning—of the many biographies, plot developments, arguments, fights, murders, tragedies, love affairs, marriages, that make up the eternal flow of the dreamworld.

However, I've long suspected that if the day-to-day conflicts, adventures, disasters, heartbreaks of the dreamworld were recorded in detail (an impossible task; I would have to write one hundred pages a day of the dreamworld and nothing else), they would no doubt provide a mirror of crucial events in my own life. But as it is, I never analyze the dreamworld in that way, any more than I would or could analyze the Vampire Chronicles while writing them. I leave my detached faculties of analysis at the door when I slip into the dreamworld; and it is not a place where anyone can find me.

Through much of my childhood, this vivid universe was a great escape from crushing boredom—the tedium of long afternoons in overcrowded classrooms, the waits in doctors' or dentists' offices, the tiresome running of errands, the long bus and streetcar rides to myriad destinations.

But I remember thinking the dreamworld was a sin when I was a teenager, that it came between me and God, and I discussed the endless pull and pressure of the dreamworld with a priest who pointed out that the conflicts I described amongst my characters reflected "sadism." This cast a dark shadow over the dreamworld. I wasn't all that impressed by the idea really, but I remember the discussion with the priest as an indicator of how much the dreamworld had become a problem for me, a distraction, a threat to concentration or my ability to focus on school or prayer or the world around me. In the Catholic world in which I grew up, nothing was really neutral. The dreamworld seemed a terrible thing at times, a curse, a dark handicap, a harmful indulgence to be ashamed of, and something that had to be destructive in general. I remember trying to fight the dreamworld. I kept a little diary of my efforts. I found it years later. It had only a few entries, which ran something like: "Didn't think too much about *them* today." Or *"Them* not too bad today." During the brief time that I wanted to be a nun and a saint, the dreamworld seemed a formidable obstacle.

The bottom line is this: the dreamworld made me feel like a crazy person. When I did discover that two of my sisters had active dreamworlds, I felt a little better about the whole thing, but even then, I felt like a madwoman. The dreamworld was too vast, too detailed, too intricate and seductive to be anything but a symptom of insanity. And

I find myself wondering what will happen to all of these many people I love when I die.

In college, I remember fighting the dreamworld to stay focused on lectures and on books I couldn't read, though no attempt to starve the dreamworld ever really worked. Sometimes I had no control over the dreamworld whatsoever. The dreamworld took over as I trudged down long corridors and up and down staircases, and through winter snow on the long walks between classroom buildings and back to the dormitory. I wasn't there. I was in the dreamworld. When I worked long hours in a little coffee shop near the campus of Texas Woman's University in 1960, alone in the tiny dark kitchen waiting for students to come in and order a cup of coffee or a small meal, I was in the dreamworld.

When I look back on it now, it is clear to me that the dreamworld could only be overcome by something inherently more interesting than the dreamworld.

The fact was, most movies I saw could not compete, so I would often lapse into the dreamworld while watching them. And if conversation lagged, I fell into the dreamworld. And I lay in bed for hours sometimes, finishing important developments in the dreamworld. Novels I read often could not compete. No written material could compete. Yet fragments of films and novels sparked entirely new activities in the dreamworld.

Soon, my college years became devoted to seeking out professors who were brilliant and passionate lecturers, because only in their classes could I hope to resist the dreamworld. I couldn't read for long periods at all, and so most of the knowledge which inspired me in those years came from stimulating and surprising and impressive lectures.

But there was one thing which most certainly was more interesting than the dreamworld: and that was *writing*.

Writing was inherently more interesting, exciting, and rewarding than the dreamworld. When I sat down at a typewriter with a blank page in front of me, I was powerfully excited to explore seriously a fictive realm that might result in a finished and valuable piece of writing. And even before I finished my undergraduate years, I was attempting "serious" fiction.

A strange novella poured out of me around 1964, called "Nicolas and Jean," about a love affair between a male photographer and an enchanting and beautiful boy hustler.

The photographer, Nicolas, has been given the keys to a vast Gothic castle–like structure on the Pacific coast by a rich friend; and when Nicolas goes there one dark and cold night, he finds the beautiful boy Jean—pronounced like Gene—a child prostitute with violet eyes and black hair, living amid rags and debris, having been cast off by the rich man.

Nicolas takes Jean back to San Francisco, caring for him, buying him clothes, seeing to it that he eats, sleeping with him, and falling deeper and deeper in love with him. For Jean, Nicolas even rigs up in his high-ceilinged photo studio a great red velvet swing, with long red-velvet-covered ropes and a padded red velvet seat, in which the boy can be pushed like a child on a playground.

The boy loves the swing, loves being pushed, and laughs with delight, his seeming innocence astounding Nicolas.

The swing, of course, I'd seen in the

famous Ray Milland–Joan Collins film about the famous architect Stanford White and his romance with the Gibson girl. The movie was entitled *The Girl in the Red Velvet Swing*, and indeed Stanford White had such a swing hanging from the ceiling of a great glass conservatory (at least in the movie), and Evelyn Nesbit loved the swing as if she were a child.

That lavish, vividly red velvet swing was exactly the kind of image that went right to my heart when I was a kid, causing me a kind of anguish and hinting to me of some vast romantic and intense domain that I was desperate to find and enter, some intoxicating place that seemed impossibly far from my dreary struggling daily life—yet real and peopled with beings like Stanford White, Evelyn Nesbit, and even Harry Thaw, who after marrying Evelyn Nesbit became so jealous of her past lover that he shot and killed Stanford White in the roof-garden theater atop Madison Square Garden.

As so often happened with me, images and ambience meant infinitely more than anything else. I could find no words to analyze how I felt about this or how the magnificent red velvet swing could be so very important.

The film ended with Evelyn Nesbit debased and lost, playing to crowds of lecherous men in raucous theaters and swinging in a great red velvet swing—hung from the rafters of the theater—that carried her out from the stage and over a crowd of coarse and vulgar drunken spectators.

I was a sixteen-year-old when I saw that film at the old neighborhood "picture show" in New Orleans. I was with my father. And I remember still the pain, the anguish, the frustration that I could not confide to anyone

about what the swing meant to me. I was almost ashamed of how much it meant.

Digression: Two other films I saw in my teenage years filled me with the same anguish and longing and feelings of utter helplessness to escape the world in which I lived. They were Michael Powell's *The Red Shoes* and his *Tales of Hoffmann*. Once more, I beheld an exalted world that filled me with anguished longing and a near-desperate helplessness and fear.

If someone had asked me what I so loved about the exalted world of the two Powell films, I would have said immediately, "The beauty, the sheer beauty of it." That had been true for the world of *The Girl in the Red Velvet Swing*. But it was also a world in which people spoke from their hearts about vital questions with immense intensity: they talked about the making of art, the importance of art, the increasing of beauty through dancing and music. They talked about love. Perhaps it was only love that mattered to the tragic Evelyn Nesbit. But she was an outsider in the exalted world of Stanford White and Harry Thaw, seeking a secure place. And all three films reflected a tragedy, a dreadful loss! They were great drama, and I believed that I was living in my heart a great drama, wrestling with questions about what I wanted in this world, and I wanted to connect with others who felt these same things.

Remember, this was a long time before our archival culture in which you can stream just about any film on earth, study it, move back and forth in it, and pin down the elements that fascinate you as you gain a deeper understanding of them. Films like *The Girl in the Red Velvet Swing* or *The Red Shoes* came and went from neighborhood or little art-house theaters. You watched for them in the papers and ran to see them when you could. They vanished for years on end.

And so it was with another film I saw only once in those years, a film about Frédéric Chopin and his lover, the female novelist who dressed as a man, George Sand, *A Song to Remember*.

My desperate efforts as a teenager to learn music, to be a violinist, to find some entrance through music into that exalted world, came to naught. I had no talent, no gift, no ability at all. But the desire had been born in those films, and it hurt me to hear magnificent music, though I listened to it all the time.

I don't recall ever incorporating that red velvet swing into my dreamworld. I'm not sure I knew how to do it and make it work for myself.

But the "red velvet swing" did surface in that first complete novella, "Nicolas and Jean."

The photographer, Nicolas, is completely faithful to his boy-lover Jean, but they have a falling-out, and Jean disappears.

One day a small-boned, delicate young female model appears at Nicolas's studio, painted, coiffed, and fashionably dressed, eager to be photographed. Nicolas allows the lovely young creature to climb into the red velvet swing. He pushes her in the swing. And he grows more and more eroti-cally aroused as he pushes her, watching the swing fly out and back again.

At the crucial moment when Nicolas is about to kiss the young girl, on the very brink of surrendering to her charms, she speaks to him in the familiar voice of his lover, Jean.

She *is* Jean dressed as a woman, come to put his lover to the test—and alienated forever when his lover fails it.

The end is bitter. Nicolas and Jean can-not be reconciled. Then Nicolas sends Jean away to a fine boarding school. Time passes. Nicolas cannot forgive Jean for deceiving and seducing him in female attire, and Jean can't forgive Nicolas for giving in to his female alter ego. At the very end of the story, snow came with winter to the boarding school, and Jean's last letter to Nicolas is filled with his loneliness as he plays the part of a "normal boy" there, staying behind alone as all the others go home for the holidays.

Now why did the blazing image of that red velvet swing never make its way to the dreamworld, yet turn up in an intense piece of fiction, the meaning of which I did not even want to explore? "Nicolas and Jean" was told from the first-person point of view of Nicolas, the man. Why was that so? Why did I become obsessed in writing it with the beauty of this young boy, with his violet eyes and black hair? I didn't analyze. I kept writing.

Around 1969, in spite of the pressures of graduate school, I was writing a great deal, especially late at night after my daughter was asleep, and that is when I wrote the first draft of a short story called "Interview with the Vampire." I banged out some thirty pages of that story in a matter of hours, and I don't recall, even for a minute, being distracted by the dreamworld. Over the years, I returned to the story and revised it at least twice. It was different from my other short stories, which were attempts to write some sort of realistic fiction, which frankly didn't work.

Three years passed before the novel *Interview with the Vampire* was born.

During that time my daughter had died, a brutal loss for me and my husband, Stan. Stan dealt with this in his poetry. I didn't consciously deal with it at all in my writing, not as far as I knew.

Meanwhile I happened to see a unique miniseries on television. It was entitled *Frankenstein: The True Story*, written by Christopher Isherwood and Don Bachardy and directed by Jack Smight. I didn't notice the credits at all at the time.

But the miniseries captivated me with the same intensity as *The Girl in the Red Velvet Swing* or *The Red Shoes*.

I'd never seen anything remotely like this on television. It was not of course faithful to Shelley's novel, but the title didn't matter. It was lush, sensuous, exquisitely filmed in historical period, with an incredible cast. I had never seen any "horror" story done in film like this, with the dignity of a classic. And once again, it was not the plot or the writing that swept me off my feet in a dream of pain and excitement; the images moved me, the vision of two handsome male figures in evening finery attending an opera, one the ill-fated doctor and the other the monster he'd created, played by Michael Sarrazin, a remarkably handsome actor with vivid blue eyes. When the "beautiful" monster starts to fall apart, the doctor makes another creation, a dazzling female, played by Jane Seymour, to which the cast-off male monster reacts with fatal rage.

I don't know enough about the history of dramatic or film presentations of Shelley's story to know whether this was the first to use that theme—that of a cast-off monster infuriated by a new monster—but I have seen it again recently, as if it is now part of the Frankenstein legend.

This 1973 production included vintage British actors James Mason, Ralph Richardson, and John Gielgud, and the American actress Agnes Moorehead, adding their dignified voices and presence to the unfolding story. In sum, it was a *Masterpiece Theatre* treatment of a horror story. And *Masterpiece Theatre* itself had only been with us for about two years.

When I again took out the old short story of "Interview with the Vampire" to rewrite it, it grew into a novel as visions of *Frankenstein: The True Story* swam in my head. I wanted a cast of magnificent immortals in a gilded milieu, wrestling with the questions of life and death, and the meaning of life, which were always tormenting me and obsessing me. As soon as my vampire had the name of Louis, a novel had taken on life. When Louis's maker appeared with the name of Lestat, the novel really took off. All my love of New Orleans and my historical research into the city paid off. What better place could there be for my deeply romantic characters but antebellum New Orleans with its famous opera house, gilded gambling dens, legendary brothels, disgusting slave marts (one of which was in the lobby of its most famous hotel), Spanish colonial architecture, and magnificent Greek Revival homes—and its reputation for corruption and European elegance? Once again, a milieu, an atmosphere, a dazzlingly lovely filmic realm—these elements were driving me. Not rational plans, not an outline of where a story might go, but a great desire to capture the pure intensity of what I'd seen in *Frankenstein: The True Story* and to take it as far as I could without the slightest compromise, producing an original book that, as far as I knew, did not resemble any other treatment of the vampire in fiction or film. Of course, I never governed the creation with a goal of being unique. The governing desire was fidelity to what I was feeling as I "dreamed" the novel, and my courage to go to extremes with something that might be unclassifiable as I listened to Louis tell me of his personal tragedy and suffering, as I found myself ultimately incapable of putting an end to the wicked and enigmatic Lestat.

There was no red velvet swing in *Interview with the Vampire*. But it was my vision of a fictive realm expressing my love for that icon, and when *The Vampire Lestat* spilled out of me some eight years later, my hero—and Lestat did become a hero from the very first page—was soon wearing a gorgeous cloak of red velvet lined with the fur of wolves. As Lestat went on to Paris (in the late 1700s), out of my memory came perhaps another film seen in childhood, which I'd forgotten, *Scaramouche*. That, too, had been painfully exquisite and deeply romantic for the eleven- or twelve-year-old girl I'd been when I saw it, with a dashing Stewart Granger, a seductive Mel Ferrer, and a lustrous, porcelain Janet Leigh. I did not even make the connection between Lestat's boulevard stage triumph and that old movie until a friend wrote a letter explaining how the book had made her think of *Scaramouche*. Of course. Absolutely. Yes.

An irrational longing fueled my writing.

I sought to embrace what I could not fully understand. I sought to make it mine and sustain it and explore it and live in it as surely as I had ever lived in the dreamworld.

And without my realizing it, I was drawing on years of experience in daydreaming, years of experience in imaginative world building, years of experience in spinning off characters, and families, and places, and situations and tragedy and loss in the secret dreamworld of which almost no one else really knew.

So this is how the Vampire Chronicles came about. It was created as an alternative reality in much the same way as my secret paracosm had been created and always with trust in the characters to create the story, and to elevate in their speech the painful themes I could never escape: Why are we here? What is the meaning of all this? How can we conceive of immortality so easily while facing the horrible fact of our own inevitable death? Can art save us if religion can't? Does art—in its most splendid and transcendent forms—prove that God exists? Are dancers and singers and actors and writers like Mary Shelley really saints of a new secular faith that can make heaven on earth in magnificent ballets, and operas, and films, and novels?

I never lost sight of those themes.

My characters would never allow it.

Those themes—themes that had preoccupied me all my young life—emerged in all my novels over the years whether I ever consciously thought about them or not. After all, the agony behind those fundamental questions had underwritten my infatuation with the red velvet swing, my heartache as I watched *The Red Shoes*. And so my narratives became a dance between exalted realms and inescapable pain; between bold heroes like Lestat and desperate suffering souls like Louis or the vampire Pandora.

That's about it. That's all I've got, as people say it today in the vernacular.

However . . .

There is a famous poem by William Butler Yeats, called "The Circus Animals' Desertion." My husband, Stan, read it to me in the 1960s. I've read it many times since. In the poem, I believe Yeats speaks of the very type of writing I've been describing, as he recounts his infatuation with mythic figures and their tales—Oisin, "The Countess Cathleen," Cuchulain, and so forth and so on, saying,

It was the dream itself enchanted me:
Character isolated by a deed
To engross the present and dominate memory.
Players and painted stage took all my love
And not those things that they were
emblems of.

The poet rejects these "players and painted stage," asserting that

Those masterful images because complete
Grew in pure mind but out of what began?

He must get to the root of those images, he says, finally concluding:

Now that my ladder's gone
I must lie down where all the ladders start
In the foul rag and bone shop of the heart.

It is a magnificent and unforgettable poem.

I think about it often.

But there is no separating for me the "players and painted stage" from the "rag and bone shop of the heart." I can only go to that "rag and bone shop of the heart" through enchantment, through complete creative surrender. That is the way I fall deeper and deeper into pain and darkness—listening to Lestat, following him as he smiles and winks and beckons. That is the way I construct a sustained response to the life I've lived that invites the reader to the very same surrender.

—*Anne Rice*
MARCH 2018

THE VAMPIRE CHRONICLES

ANNE RICE'S VAMPIRE CHRONICLES
AN ALPHABETTERY

Aaron Lightner

• TALAMASCA •

aron Lightner is a psychic detective for the Talamasca Order. He marries into the Mayfair family of witches and plays a major role in bridging the Lives of the Mayfair Witches with the Vampire Chronicles. He appears in *Merrick* (2000) and *Blackwood Farm* (2002).

Born in 1921 in England, Aaron Lightner begins demonstrating remarkable psychic abilities at an early age with both telekinesis and telepathy. His English father and American mother grow so concerned that they introduce him to the Talamasca house. When he is between the ages of seven and twenty-two,

the Talamasca teaches Aaron how to control his psychic powers for the purpose of good. At twenty-two, after graduating from Oxford University, Aaron is invited by the Talamasca to become a member of the Order. After a decade of service, Aaron finally becomes the department head of witch families. He reorganizes their files, supervises the chronicling of families of witches throughout history, and takes particular interest in the Mayfair family.

Aaron meets Beatrice Mayfair in New Orleans and Deirdre Mayfair in Texas, where he also sees Lasher, the evil spirit who has developed a plan to become incarnate as a Taltos through an incestuous breeding program of thirteen generations of Mayfair witches. Aaron discusses Lasher's danger with Deirdre, but she desires to live a normal life, so she asks Aaron to keep the Mayfair emerald—the talisman that represents a covenant between Lasher and the witches in his plan for incarnation—but Aaron decides against it, fearing Lasher's retribution. Aaron then travels back to New Orleans, where he meets with Carlotta and Cortland Mayfair to explain the Mayfair family's history. Abhorring his interference, Carlotta issues a restraining order against him, and Cortland attempts to poison him. Surviving this attempt on his life, Aaron continues watching the Mayfair family from afar.

Aaron discovers Merrick Mayfair, a member of the Creole branch of the Mayfair family, who has been recently orphaned at a young age after her mother and sister are murdered. Because she is tremendously gifted with psychic abilities, Aaron introduces Merrick to David Talbot, Superior General of the Talamasca and Lestat's eventual fledgling. David takes Merrick as his apprentice, while Aaron resumes his investigation into the Mayfair family.

Many years later, Aaron discovers that Deirdre gave birth to Rowan Mayfair, but Carlotta drugged Deirdre into a comatose state, kidnapped Rowan, and convinced Ellie Mayfair to adopt Rowan. Living in San Francisco, Ellie keeps Rowan ignorant of her family of witches, and Aaron keeps his distance from Rowan, believing that it would be best if she not be informed of the Mayfair family of witches. He becomes keenly fascinated by her love interest, Michael Curry, who also demonstrates remarkable psychic abilities. But upon an accidental encounter with Rowan, Aaron reconsiders his decision and offers her a chance to know her family's history. When she refuses, he goes to Michael's house to inquire about his interest in joining the Talamasca.

Meeting with Michael in New Orleans, Aaron informs him of Rowan's history. When Aaron is almost killed in a car accident, he learns that Lasher's plan to incarnate as a Taltos will culminate in Michael and Rowan's imminent child. After discussing the dangerous nature of Lasher with Rowan, who is a highly gifted medical doctor and researcher, he learns that she is interested in studying Lasher and Taltos scientifically. He tries to warn her against this, but she ignores him. After Rowan and Michael marry, she becomes pregnant with a Taltos child. Lasher later fuses with her child and, because of the Taltos' inhumanly rapid birth cycle, he is born and fully grown into a man in a very short period of time. Aaron gives Michael a medal of Saint Michael the Archangel to protect him against evil, and then he sends Michael to Rowan to stop Lasher. After a brief scuffle, Lasher nearly drowns Michael before running away with Rowan.

While the Mayfair family is searching for Rowan, Aaron uncovers a plot inside the Talamasca involving four members—Marklin George, Tommy Monohan, Stuart Gordon, and Anton Marcus, the superior general of the Talamasca who takes over for David after Lestat turns him into a vampire—all of whom are trying to help Lasher incarnate as a Taltos through another female Taltos named Tessa. Before Aaron can bring their treachery to light, Anton arranges for Aaron to be excommunicated from the Talamasca. With his assistant, Yuri Stefano, Aaron begins a private investigation into the Talamasca traitors. During that time, Rowan finally returns to the Mayfair family after escaping from Lasher, who has tortured and raped her. Aaron and Michael reunite to confront Lasher and kill him.

The chapter on Lasher closes when Aaron marries Beatrice Mayfair and continues his private investigation into the Talamasca trai-tors, but the traitors send an assassin, who kills Aaron by running him over with a car. Avenging Aaron's death, Rowan, Michael, Yuri, and Joan Cross (the Talamasca Superior General who takes Marcus's place) discover the identities of all four conspirators and execute each one.

For more perspectives on Aaron Lightner's character, read the *Alphabettery* entries **David Talbot**, **Merrick Mayfair**, **Talamasca Order**, and **Taltos**.

Agatha

• MORTAL •

Agatha is Claudia's mother. Little is known of her life. She dies of the plague when Claudia is five. She appears in *Interview with the Vampire* (1976) and *Merrick* (2000).

She is born in New Orleans in the late eighteenth century and gives birth to only one daughter, whose original name is lost in time. She raises her daughter for five years but falls victim to a plague ravaging New Orleans. Shortly after her daughter turns five years old, Agatha dies, not knowing whether her daughter will survive. Only days after her death, the vampire Louis de Pointe du Lac happens into their house, drinks the daughter's blood to the point of death, while the vampire Lestat takes the little girl, turns her into a vampire, and gives her the name Claudia. Agatha's greatest legacy is as a vicious killer in the body of the five-year-old girl, who will eventually be burned to death for attempting to destroy her maker.

For more perspectives on Agatha's character, read the *Alphabettery* sections **Claudia**, **Lestat de Lioncourt**, and **Louis de Pointe du Lac**.

Akasha

• VAMPIRE •

Akasha is the Queen of Egypt and becomes the first vampire when Amel's spirit fuses with her blood. Her most famous fledglings are Enkil, Khayman, Rhoshamandes, Nebamun, and many thousands more. She turns statuelike after a few thousand years. Lestat awakens her in the twentieth century, but Mekare destroys her when Akasha seeks world domination. She appears in *The Vampire Lestat* (1985), *The Queen of the Damned* (1988), and *Blood and Gold* (2001).

Commonly known as the Queen of the Damned, Akasha is born more than four thousand years before the Common Era, in the city of Uruk, the most important city of its time in ancient Mesopotamia. A beautiful young woman even from an early age, she wins the favor of Enkil, King of Kemet— an empire that will come to be known as the Two Lands of Upper and Lower Egypt, otherwise referred to today as ancient Egypt. Becoming Enkil's bride and queen nearly two thousand years before the building of the first Pyramids, the young Akasha rules over the world's first civilization.

King Enkil supports the traditional Egyptian practice of cannibalizing the dead until Queen Akasha convinces him to change this policy to the agricultural practice of her own homeland. Cannibalism becomes illicit. Eventually the success of this initiative diminishes violence and increases peace, which consequently increases Queen Akasha's popularity. Although savage cannibalism is nearly expunged, smaller rebellious groups that practice ritual cannibalism cause minor uprisings, but they are quickly crushed by Kemetian soldiers.

Fascinated by the supernatural, Akasha invites twin witches, Maharet and Mekare, to the royal court to commune with spirits. When the twins refuse, Akasha dispatches soldiers to the twins' village to force them back to the palace. Upon arriving at the village, the soldiers witness Maharet and Mekare performing the ritual burial for their mother, which involves the unlawful cannibalistic consumption of the brain and heart. The soldiers slaughter every villager except for the twins.

Maharet and Mekare are brought back to the royal court, where Akasha coerces them into communing with spirits. Displeased with the spirits' answers, Akasha imprisons Maharet and Mekare. Mekare summons the spirit of Amel, who attacks the Queen. Akasha orders her servant Khayman to rape Maharet and Mekare in the royal court before banishing the twin sisters from Kemet. The spirit of Amel avenges the twins by continuing to haunt Akasha, Enkil, and Khayman. Conspirators who still practice cannibalism in secret attempt to assassinate the King and Queen. The conspirators leave Akasha and Enkil mortally wounded. At the moment of Akasha's death, Amel's spirit joins with her soul to create the first vampire.

Akasha saves Enkil from death by turn-

ing him into a vampire. They soon discover the challenges of being a vampire, unable to either consume food or procreate. They will never age and never die, except by fire and sunlight. They also possess heightened sensitivity, superhuman strength, regeneration, and an insatiable bloodlust.

Although the King and Queen drink blood primarily from evildoers and enemies, Akasha and Enkil grow so disturbed by the insatiable power and pleasure of their bloodlust that they force Maharet and Mekare back to court to provide an explanation for their transformation. The twins have never encountered anything like this before. They suggest that, because the spirit of Amel is very large, they might dilute him and his influence if they make more vampires, which might also decrease their bloodlust. Akasha tests this by turning Khayman into a vampire against his will, yet this does nothing to diminish the bloodlust.

When Maharet suggests that the King and Queen should kill themselves in order to end this abominable union between flesh and spirit, Akasha orders that Maharet's eyes be gouged out and Mekare's tongue be severed. But before she loses her power of speech altogether, Mekare promises vengeance upon Akasha, which begins the Legend of the Twins. After mutilating the twins, Akasha sentences them to one day of torture before being burned at the stake as heretic witches. Later that night, Khayman rescues Maharet and Mekare by turning them both into vampires in an agreement to rise up against Akasha and Enkil. As they flee, they turn many mortals into vampires, in the hope of creating a vampire army, which becomes known as the

First Brood. After a week of being pursued by Kemetian soldiers, Maharet and Mekare are captured, but Khayman escapes. Fearful of destroying the twins lest it should somehow hurt her, too, Akasha separates Maharet and Mekare by entombing them in stone coffins and setting them adrift in different oceans, Maharet towards the west and Mekare towards the east.

Akasha and Enkil reign as vampire gods for centuries, identifying themselves as gods, Isis and Osiris, to propagate their worship among mortals. They even set up their vampire fledglings as minor gods to be worshipped in far-off temples, such as Nebamun in the eastern lands and Teskhamen in the western countries. In time, a civil war occurs among the vampires, dividing them into two factions, the dark gods who are ruthlessly destructive and tyrannical and the benign gods who worship Akasha. The dark gods are worshipped by human slaves who bring them their victims. The more benign vampires mercifully kill their victims in religious practices.

Great vampire battles ensue. Akasha and Enkil are eventually captured and entombed within blocks of diorite and granite. Pinioned and immobile with only their heads and necks exposed, Akasha and Enkil drink from victims provided by their captors so that their captors can in turn drink from them. After many centuries in this imprisonment, Akasha and Enkil stop drinking blood entirely. Although the lack of blood robs them of immediate strength, the more they age, the stronger they become. They stop talking and moving. Their minds gain the ability to astral project, their bodies become like vacant marble statues, and their skin turns translucent white.

After many more centuries pass, no one remembers why Akasha and Enkil were imprisoned or who imprisoned them or why they can never be let out. And after even more centuries pass, fledglings discover one night that Akasha and Enkil have become so strong that they have broken free from their stone prisons and are lying naked on the floor, embracing each other. Understanding the great immensity of their power, their fledglings now erect them in beautiful sanctuaries, where Akasha and Enkil are worshipped in a blood god cult. Though unmoving, Akasha and Enkil demonstrate awareness, such as accepting evildoers as sacrificial offerings, drawing evil out of people, protecting their fledglings, and even giving droplets of blood to their worshipping subjects.

Many more centuries pass. Soon these religious beliefs begin to diminish. Akasha and Enkil continue to be cared for under the title "Those Who Must Be Kept" by their keeper, a vampire referred to as the Elder. Shortly after the outset of the Common Era, the Elder grows exhausted from his duties and loses faith in the blood god religion, so he takes Akasha and Enkil out of the shrine and leaves them by the Nile River, where they are exposed to the sun. In the Great Burning of 4 C.E., it is discovered here that Akasha and Enkil can no longer be damaged by fire or sunlight, only bronzed. Their fledglings suffer the damaging effects, however. Younger fledglings are incinerated completely, while older vampires are severely burned and weakened.

To unearth the fate of the Mother and the Father, Akasha's former servant Teskhamen turns Marius de Romanus into a vampire. Marius travels to Egypt and finds the evil Elder caring for Those Who Must Be Kept, feigning his innocence. Marius attempts to outwit the Elder and steal Akasha and Enkil, but he needs Akasha's assistance, who rises from her throne and crushes the Elder under her feet. Marius then becomes the keeper of Akasha and Enkil for the next two thousand years. He moves them to various locations, from Rome to Constantinople and even to a secret shrine hidden in the snowy Alps. Under Marius's watch, Akasha's old enemy Maharet learns of the Queen's location. Maharet steals into the sanctuary and stabs Akasha in the heart, only to discover that if Akasha is killed, Maharet and all other vampires will be killed also.

In the 1800s, when Marius introduces Lestat to Those Who Must Be Kept, Lestat's bravado so impresses Akasha that she allows him to drink from her while he gives her some of his own blood. This enrages Enkil, who rises from his throne and nearly kills Lestat. After helping Akasha save Lestat from Enkil's rage, Marius takes Akasha and Enkil away from Lestat, to the Canadian north, where he gives them every modern refinement. Marius makes several attempts to awaken Akasha and Enkil, but it is not until 1985, when Akasha hears the rock music of the band the Vampire Lestat, that she finally truly awakens.

Seeking to have Lestat as her sole paramour, Akasha kills Enkil and drinks his blood to consolidate her power and become the only progenitor of the vampire race. Desiring to rule the entire world the way she had ruled over ancient Egypt, Akasha creates a plan to destroy almost every vampire in the world and then kill all but 10 percent of the mortal male race in creating a new religion for her to be worshipped as a goddess by the remaining mortal female population. With her Cloud Gift, she flies across the world, incinerating with her Fire Gift every vampire she senses, save those whom Lestat loves, yet some whom she cannot sense or who cannot be destroyed by her Fire Gift are spared.

Akasha then appears at the Vampire Lestat concert, where she saves him from the numerous vampires who seek to kill him for revealing their secrets. Eventually, she takes Lestat to Maharet's Sonoma compound, where thirteen of the remaining vampires are planning to destroy her. Akasha offers them the opportunity to be her servants in her new world order, but they spurn her. Even Lestat turns against her when he discovers her true plan for world conquest. He and the other vampires fight against Akasha, but she is too powerful for them. When they seem utterly defeated, Mekare appears. And in fulfillment of her prophecy nearly six thousand years earlier, Mekare decapitates the Queen of the Damned. As the blood drains from Akasha, vampires feel their own life extinguishing also. Before Akasha truly dies, Mekare eats her brain and heart, which causes Amel and his Sacred Core (the life force of all vampires) to enter into Mekare, making her the new Queen of the Damned.

All that remains of Akasha is an empty shell.

For more perspectives on Akasha's character, read the *Alphabettery* entries **Amel, Enkil, Kemet, Maharet, Marius, Mekare, Lestat de Lioncourt, Those Who Must Be Kept,** and **Vampire**.

Akbar

• VAMPIRE •

Akbar is a servant of Queen Akasha in ancient Egypt. His maker and fledglings are unknown at present. He is badly burned in the Great Burning of 4 C.E., and he is killed while attempting to steal Those Who Must Be Kept. Akbar appears in *Pandora* (1998).

Although nothing is known about his maker, Akbar appears to be as old as Teskhamen. Both of them are burned to blackened crisps when the wicked Elder exposes Those Who Must Be Kept to the sun, which suggests that Akbar's maker might have been Akasha herself, who is also Teskhamen's maker.

Garbed in human skulls hanging from his belt and two necklaces of charred human fingers and ears, Akbar first appears in the Vampire Chronicles as a monstrous blood drinker in the Near Eastern city of Antioch, when Pandora is still a mortal. He desires greatly to find the hidden location of Those Who Must Be Kept and drink from Akasha's powerful blood to heal and to consolidate his already ancient power, which makes him an immensely strong vampire. Akbar perceives Marius's love for Pandora and exploits it by draining Pandora to the point of death, then threatening to let her die unless Marius takes him to see Akasha. Marius reluctantly concedes. Akbar allows Marius to transform Pandora into a vampire. But when Marius takes Akbar to Queen Akasha, the arm of her statuesque body reaches up to Akbar's skull, crushes it, then throws him so hard across the room that the force dismembers him. The Queen then uses the Mind Gift to telekinetically push over an oil lamp. Akbar's remains catch fire and burn to ash. Another unseen force like a gust of wind gathers his cinders and carries them away.

For more perspectives on Akbar's character, read the *Alphabettery* entries **Marius** and **Pandora**.

Alain Abelard

• VAMPIRE •

Alain Abelard is the architect and foreman whom Lestat hires to oversee the renovation and upgrading of Château de Lioncourt and Village de Lioncourt in the early twenty-first century. Alain has read the Vampire Chronicles, but he does not believe Lestat is a real vampire, not until the Château's and the village's renovations come to a close. Lestat reveals that he is a vampire and desires to make Alain his latest fledgling. Alain accepts on the night of the Winter Solstice Ball. After Alain is fully transformed into a blood drinker, he enters the Château's ballroom to discover Marius's latest mural on the ballroom ceiling, depicting a circle of vampires that represent each age of the vampire race, beginning with Akasha and ending with Alain, who is holding Akasha's hand, completing the circle.

Alain appears in *Blood Communion* (2018). For more perspectives on Alain's character, read the *Alphabettery* entries **Château de Lioncourt**, **Lestat de Lioncourt**, and **Marius**.

Albinus

• MORTAL •

Albinus is a mortal who works as Marius's servant in fifteenth-century Venice. Few details have survived about his birth and life before serving Marius. The Children of Satan most likely kill him when they destroy Marius's palazzo. He appears in *Blood and Gold* (2001).

If Riccardo is the leader of mortals at Marius's Venetian palazzo, then his second-in-command is Albinus. Each is in total contrast to the other, Riccardo with his black hair and dark eyes and Albinus with his blond hair and eyes of pale green. Neither Albinus nor Riccardo guesses that their master, Marius, is a vampire. Armand befriends both when Marius buys him from the Venetian brothel. Albinus is likely killed when Santino destroys Marius's palazzo for his heretical behavior towards the Children of Satan.

For more perspectives on Albinus's character, read the *Alphabettery* entries **Armand**, **Marius**, **Riccardo**, and **Santino**.

Alex

• MORTAL •

A drummer for the band Satan's Night Out, Alex becomes one of the founding members of the band the Vampire Lestat after Lestat appears to him and his other mortal bandmates offering them fame and fortune. With his brother, Larry, on keyboards, Tough Cookie on guitar, and the vampire Lestat on lead vocals, the rock band becomes immensely famous. After their one and only concert, Lestat quits the band, never to play with them again, although he ensures that, through his lawyer, Christine, Alex and his other two bandmates will be well provided for, so that they will never have to worry about money again. Alex appears only in *The Vampire Lestat* (1985).

For more perspectives on Alex's character, read the *Alphabettery* entries **Christine**, **Larry**, **Lestat de Lioncourt**, **Satan's Night Out**, **Tough Cookie**, and **The Vampire Lestat**.

Alexander Stoker

• ALIAS •

In *The Tale of the Body Thief* (1992), Dr. Alexander Stoker, a retired English surgeon, is the identity that David Talbot selects for himself when he and Lestat, going under the alias "Sheridan Blackwood," board the *Queen Elizabeth 2* in pursuit of Raglan James, the Body Thief, who is in possession of Lestat's vampiric body.

Alexander Stoker's last name is a reference to the gothic author Bram Stoker.

For more perspectives on the use of aliases in the Vampire Chronicles, read the *Alphabettery* entries **Baron Van Kindergarten, Benjamin the Devil, Clarence Oddbody, Eric Sampson, Isaac Rummel, Jason Hamilton, Lestan Gregor, Lionel Potter, Renfield, Sebastian Melmoth,** and **Sheridan Blackwood.**

Allen

• MORTAL •

Allen is one of the principal workers on Blackwood Farm in a crew known as the Shed Men. He and his fellow workers serve as general handymen, craftsmen, farmhands, security men, and even chauffeurs. Allen is considered to be the nominal leader of the Shed Men, and he comes to be well respected by Quinn and his family at Blackwood Manor. Allen appears only in *Blackwood Farm* (2002).

For more perspectives on Allen's character, read the *Alphabettery* entries **Clem** and **Shed Men.**

Allesandra

• VAMPIRE •

Allesandra first appears in *The Vampire Lestat* as the mad Old Queen of the Children of Darkness who throws herself into a fire when her coven ends. She reemerges in *Prince Lestat* having survived the fire and becomes a pivotal character in the Vampire Chronicles. She appears in *The Vampire Lestat* (1985), *The Vampire Armand* (1998), *Prince Lestat* (2014), *Prince Lestat and the Realms of Atlantis* (2016), and *Blood Communion* (2018).

Referred to by Lestat as "beautiful Merovingian Allesandra" and as "the Old Queen," Allesandra is born around 620 C.E., the daughter of Dagobert I, one of the Frankish kings. Rhoshamandes turns her into a vampire when she is a woman in her prime, at a much-older age than most mortals who receive the Dark Gift. Rhoshamandes then includes her in what he refers to as his "line of de Landen vampires," which also includes Benedict, Eleni, Eugénie, Notker the Wise, and Everard.

However, the Roman coven of the Children of Satan attacks Rhoshamandes's coven because he and his fledglings are living in a way that is contrary to their five Great Laws, which demand abasement for their Satanic lifestyle. The Children of Satan capture four of the de Landen vampires—Allesandra, Eleni, Eugénie, and Everard. They are taken to Paris, where they are tortured and starved until they accept the Great Laws of the Children of Satan, and are initiated into the cultic coven.

Allesandra lives in the coven for centuries and sees the transition of leadership to the vampire Santino during the Black Plague. Almost two centuries later, the Children of Satan attack the Venetian palazzo of the powerful vampire Marius, who has offended Santino. They burn Marius, nearly killing him, and they steal his newest fledgling, Armand. Santino keeps Armand in a cell, starving him

for blood, the way it was with Allesandra centuries earlier, until Armand submits to their coven's rule. During that time, Allesandra comforts Armand, and he considers her to be a very beautiful, mature vampire yet also a lunatic. In time he comes to call her the ancient nun of the Old Ways, who teaches him the Great Laws among vampirekind. In the sixteenth century, when Armand leaves the Roman coven to create a new coven in Paris, Allesandra accompanies him, along with her siblings in the Blood, Eleni, Eugénie, and Everard.

In the eighteenth century, she befriends the vampire Magnus (Lestat's eventual maker), who is related to her in the Blood: Rhoshamandes made both Allesandra and Benedict, who became Magnus's maker. When Lestat and Gabrielle encounter Armand's coven, Allesandra remains with Armand when he questions Lestat and Gabrielle about their vampire beliefs and practices. After Lestat convinces Armand that the ways of his coven are futile in the era of the Enlightenment, Allesandra flies into a mad fit, knowing that her way of life has come to an end. She flings herself into a pyre and enjoins Armand to destroy his coven by throwing in all the others, which he does, except for four, two of whom are her sisters in the line of de Landen vampires—Eleni and Eugénie.

Despite her desperate measure, Allesandra survives the burning. She descends into the earth and rests in vampiric torpor, but she is roused by Amel and the mysterious Voice, like several other elders, after the destruction of Akasha and the transfer of Amel into Mekare. Amel, desirous to leave Mekare's wounded mind, tricks Allesandra into commencing another Great Burning, similar to Akasha's rampaging massacre in the twentieth century. Now, in the twenty-first century, Allesandra employs her Fire Gift to burn many revenant vampires in their hotel on Rue Saint-Jacques in Paris, before burning the hotel to the ground. She comes back to her senses entirely when she happens upon the vampire Bianca Solderini (Marius's fledgling), who pleads with her to stop the burning massacre. Together they leave Paris and become part of an underground coven in Cappadocia, in the Caves of Gold, which is led by the vampire Sevraine. Much to Allesandra's great delight, also in the coven with Sevraine and Bianca are her de Landen sisters in the Blood, Eleni and Eugénie. Finally, after nearly a thousand years of oppression, they are reunited as a family of blood drinkers.

For more perspectives on Allesandra's character, read the *Alphabettery* entries **Amadeo**, **Armand**, **Benedict**, **Children of Darkness**, **Children of Satan**, **Eleni**, **Eugénie**, **Everard**, **Great Laws**, **Notker the Wise**, **Rhoshamandes**, and **Santino**.

Amadeo

• VAMPIRE •

Amadeo is the name given to Armand by his maker when Marius buys him from a Venetian brothel. In Marius's palazzo, Amadeo lives with many other mortal boys his own age. Together they all receive an education from Marius and various other tutors in the arts and sciences. During the next two years while Amadeo lives with Marius, he becomes Marius's paramour and discovers that Marius is a vampire. Instead of being repulsed by Marius's true nature, Amadeo becomes even more fascinated with his master and implores Marius to transform him into a vampire also. Marius repeatedly refuses until the day Amadeo incites the jealousy of the Englishman Lord Harlech, who storms into Marius's palazzo, slays several of the other boys, and mortally wounds Amadeo with a poisoned blade. Seeing no other option, Marius transforms Amadeo into a vampire to save his life. Unfortunately, the two do not have much time together, for soon afterward the vampire Santino and his coven, the Children of Satan, invade Marius's palazzo, set fire to it, and nearly burn Marius to death. Santino abducts Amadeo and imprisons him in his coven, starving him for blood until he accepts the cult's beliefs. During that time, Amadeo befriends the vampire Allesandra, who helps him accept the Great Laws and his new life as one of Satan's children, since she too has suffered the same fate. Once released from his prison, Amadeo becomes one of Santino's most devoted followers, impressing Santino so much that he encourages Amadeo to leave and begin his own coven in Paris. Allesandra joins him and changes his name from Amadeo to Armand.

The name Amadeo appears in *The Vampire Armand* (1998) and *Blood and Gold* (2001).

For more perspectives on Amadeo as a character, read the *Alphabettery* entries **Allesandra**, **Andrei**, **Armand**, **Benedict**, **Eleni**, **Eugénie**, **Everard**, and **Tartars**.

Amel

• IMMORTAL •

Amel is the spirit inside every vampire, binding them all together into a cohesive whole that satiates his need for blood. He appears in *The Queen of the Damned* (1988), *Prince Lestat* (2014), and *Prince Lestat and the Realms of Atlantis* (2016).

Nearly six thousand years before the birth of Akasha (ten thousand years before the Common Era), Amel is born of human parents. They live in a tribe in the far north, in the freezing cold and heavy snow. In the tribe of pale skin and darker hair and eyes, Amel, with green eyes and red hair and sickly skin, is considered a mutant. The tribe fears and distrusts him. When he is twelve years old, in an offering to their gods, Amel's parents drug him, lay him on an altar for sacrifice, and abandon him to exposure and predators. An alien race called the Bravennans, who have been observing humans, abduct Amel from Earth and take him back to their home world, Bravenna. The first human they've ever taken, he lives on their planet for many years, maturing to full height. Bravennan scientists enhance Amel's DNA, transmutating him into a superhuman. Deceiving him, the Bravennans inform Amel that their intent

towards earthlings is benign and that they want him to return to Earth to protect humans and to install and repair transmission stations, which will help Bravennans better observe activities on Earth.

When they return Amel to Earth, his superhuman intellect realizes that the Bravennans have deceived him and that the transmission stations do not transmit benign information back to Bravenna but human suffering in the form of psychic energy, which is food for the Bravennans and the Realm of Worlds. Furthermore, Amel also realizes that the Bravennans are responsible for much of human suffering—for plagues, for natural disasters, and for many other terrible things that cause people pain—so that the vast data of their agony will transmit across the universe to satisfy the Bravennans' morally deprived appetites. Amel's sense of moral goodness, which the Bravennans' enhancements do not eradicate, develops during the first twelve years of his life while living with his human tribe. Witnessing their injustice to the human race, Amel rebels against them by protecting human life.

Because his enhanced nature provides him

with the ability to regenerate, he never truly ages, but is immortal. Amel lives for thousands of years, building cities and organizing humans, creating schools, and instructing people how to hunt and gather with greater efficiency. The cities that he builds become increasingly protected against Bravennan observation. Amel dismantles and destroys Bravennan transmission stations. In time, Amel learns how to better protect humans from the Bravennans and eventually discovers how to extract his enhanced DNA from his body to create a new compound that he calls luracastria. Since luracastria is an unknown substance to the Bravennans, their observation and transmission devices cannot penetrate luracastria's density. Able to mass-produce luracastria, Amel creates out of it things that can protect humans, such as clothing, buildings, transport pods, and the entire city of Atalantaya. Even Atalantaya's great dome is made of luracastria. For Amel, Atalantaya is a city paradise where no human will suffer.

No longer able to feed off human suffering, the Bravennans create humanoids called Replimoids, which have no human DNA in their coding. Like Amel, the Replimoids are immortal, possessing the ability to regenerate, but unlike him they also possess the ability to clone themselves. The Bravennans send the Replimoids to attack Amel, but Amel either thwarts each wave of attack or converts the Replimoids to his cause. Four of the Replimoids who join Amel are Kapetria, Derek, Garekyn, and Welf. Finally, in one last effort to destroy both Amel and his luracastria, the Bravennans send a massive meteor shower to Earth, which rains down upon Atalantaya, utterly decimating it until

it falls into the sea, a burning, melting waste. Amel perishes along with the city.

His physical body is destroyed, but his etheric body remains in the particles composing his soul, which also contain his enhanced genetic structure. Amel remains in this etheric state for a few thousand years more, until he is summoned by the twin witches Mekare and Maharet. Not fully recalling his pre-etheric state, still instinctively aware of his superhuman power, Amel boasts to Mekare and Maharet that, though he is spirit, he can drink blood. Queen Akasha summons Mekare and Maharet to commune with the spirits, but when she maltreats them, Mekare summons Amel, who continues to haunt and harass Akasha until she and King Enkil are nearly killed by conspirators. When Amel attempts to gorge on Akasha's blood, his soul fuses with hers, combining both her human DNA with his enhanced genetic structure, the result of which creates the first vampire.

The process of turning humans into vampires shares Amel's genetic enhancements. Akasha does not simply turn Enkil into a vampire but also apportions Amel's blood-lust, as well as his ability to be immortal through regeneration. She does the same with Khayman; and he does the same with Mekare and Maharet; and so on. Any vampire who makes another vampire shares Amel's spirit, yet they all connect back to Akasha, who is like a spider at the center of a web; she remains the host carrier of Amel's spirit, which comes to be called the Sacred Core. Any harm done to Akasha will travel through her etheric connection to all vampires and harm them as well, such as when the wicked

Elder sets Akasha and Enkil in the sun to burn but instead causes the Great Burning of 4 C.E., destroying many vampires but barely harming the host carrier.

Akasha carries Amel's spirit until the end of the twentieth century, when Mekare beheads her and eats her brain and heart, a process that transfers Amel, the Sacred Core, from Akasha into Mekare. Throughout it all, Amel's consciousness remains suppressed and affects vampires only on an instinctive level. After being in Mekare's deeply wounded mind for a few decades, Amel's spirit becomes conscious. He desires to leave her mind and enter the healthier mind of a vampire just as strong as Akasha and Mekare. So he begins speaking to vampires as the mysterious Voice, influencing their judgment and making them immolate other vampires in a new Great Burning. Finally, Amel persuades the vampire Rhoshamandes to kill Mekare and consume her brain. Rhoshamandes must destroy Maharet and Khayman to do so, which he does, but after he kidnaps Mekare, he is afraid that he will die before the transfer is complete. So Amel convinces Rhoshamandes to kidnap Lestat's cloned son, Viktor, to extort Lestat's scientist companions, Fareed and Seth, to help transfer Amel from Mekare to Rhoshamandes. Lestat, however, forces Rhoshamandes to surrender Viktor and Mekare.

Suffering the loss of her twin sister, Mekare desires to join her in death. She offers herself to Lestat, gesturing for him to kill her and take Amel. Reluctantly, he sucks her brain through her eye socket, transferring Amel into himself and becoming the host carrier of vampire existence. But this relationship lasts for only a few years, when Lestat encounters the very same Replimoids sent by the Bravennans to destroy Amel thousands of years earlier—Kapetria, Derek, Garekyn, and Welf. Through a careful process she has developed, Kapetria clones an exact likeness of the human body that Amel had in Atlantis and transfers him from Lestat into this new body. Now the vampires are free of their dependence on the Sacred Core. No longer will they suffer collectively if their host carrier suffers individually. It is a newfound freedom not only for the vampires but also for Amel.

Amel's Replimoid body does not have any sexual drive and cannot procreate or experience sexual pleasure, but his bodily experiences of the world are akin to erotic euphoria, from the taste of wine to the sound of a symphony. Life in his new body is hypersensual.

For more perspectives on Amel's character, read the *Alphabettery* entries **Akasha, Atalantaya, Atlantis, Bravenna, Bravennans, Derek, Garekyn, Kapetria, Lestat de Lioncourt, Maharet, Mekare, Replimoid, Welf, Wilderness,** and **Wilderness People.**

Ancient Evelyn

• WITCH •

Mentioned in *Blood Canticle* (2003), Evelyn is the daughter of Cortland (son of Julien Mayfair) and Barbara Ann Mayfair (daughter of Tobias Mayfair). Because Evelyn is a very powerful witch in the Mayfair family, born with six fingers on each hand, they keep her locked in the attic of their house on Amelia Street. When she is thirteen years old, she is discovered by Cortland's father, Julien, who finds her mute and wearing mostly rags. He takes her from Cortland's house and keeps her in his bedroom. Whereupon he cares for her, and she begins to speak, revealing to him that the eventual incarnation of the evil spirit Lasher will attempt to destroy the Mayfair family, as well as most of the world. In time, Evelyn and her grandfather Julien become lovers, which results in her pregnancy with her only daughter, Laura Lee Mayfair.

Laura Lee becomes the mother of Alicia Mayfair, who becomes the mother of Mona Mayfair, the Designée of the Mayfair Legacy and the fledgling of the vampire Lestat, making Evelyn her great-grandmother, whom Mona refers to (particularly in conversing with Lestat) as Ancient Evelyn.

For more perspectives on Ancient Evelyn's character, read the *Alphabettery* entries **Designée of the Mayfair Legacy**, **Julien Mayfair**, and **Mona Mayfair**.

Andrei

• MORTAL •

Andrei is the birth name of the vampire Armand, as written in *The Vampire Armand* (1998) and *Blood and Gold* (2001).

Born in Kiev, Russia, in 1497 of the Common Era, Andrei is a child prodigy in painting Eastern Orthodox icons. Desiring to live with the monks at the Monastery of the Caves because he deeply believes that his talent not only comes from God but is also an instrument of God's evangelization, Andrei is a profoundly spiritual child and adores the beauty of God and saints as depicted in icons and paintings. His father has no desire for his son to hide his talent in the silence and the simplicity of a monastery, so he seeks highly esteemed commissions for him from prominent individuals, such as Prince Michael, who commissions work to be delivered to Prince Feodor. Andrei, only fifteen years old at the time, accompanies his father on board a ship sailing for Constantinople. But when the ship is captured by Tartars, Andrei is taken prisoner and sold to a Venetian brothel, where he is mercilessly abused until he suffers amnesia and is locked in the dungeon. Not long after, Andrei is purchased from the brothel by the vampire Marius, who takes the boy to his palazzo, where he cleans his wounds, gives him an education, and gives him the name Amadeo. He will later be turned into a vampire and called by the name Lestat knows him as—Armand.

For more perspectives on Andrei's character, read the *Alphabettery* entries **Allesandra**, **Amadeo**, **Armand**, **Eleni**, **Eugénie**, **Everard**, and **Tartars**.

Angelique Marybelle Mayfair

• WITCH •

Mentioned in *Blood Canticle* (2003), Angelique Marybelle Mayfair is a secret witch, the kind that people cannot go to for counsel. Merrick's *oncle* Julien (Julien Mayfair) is Angelique's blood nephew. She receives an excellent education and is very intelligent, but she chooses to live a quiet life in New Orleans. Though she is dark-skinned, like Merrick Mayfair, rumors spread that she has a Caucasian lover in the Garden District, a Mayfair relative, perhaps even her own nephew, Julien, the eighth witch in the incarnation plan of the evil spirit, Lasher.

For more perspectives on Angelique's character, read the *Alphabettery* entries **Julien Mayfair**, **Lasher**, and **Merrick Mayfair**.

Antoine

• VAMPIRE •

Antoine first appears as a nameless musician who aids Lestat after Claudia attempts to murder her maker. Antoine's character remains in obscurity for the next four decades until he is mentioned in the later Vampire Chronicles, when his character is recognized as an intregal part of Lestat's life. He appears in *Interview with the Vampire* (1976), *Prince Lestat* (2014), *Prince Lestat and the Realms of Atlantis* (2016), and *Blood Communion* (2018).

Born in France in the nineteenth century, Antoine is sent to Paris to study concert piano performance at the Conservatoire. In Paris's magnificent culture, he attends the concerts of Bizet, Saint-Saëns, Berlioz, and Franz Liszt. When Antione is seventeen, his older brother fathers a child out of wedlock and accuses Antoine of the crime. The entire family is so ashamed of his alleged disgrace that they send him to Louisiana with enough money to start a new life, but he quickly squanders all his wealth on gambling, drinking, and prostitutes. In the bars he frequents, he leaps onto the piano and plays classical songs riotously, making his audiences both laugh with delight and shrug with confusion. His antics also draw the attention of the vampire Lestat.

Taking Antoine under his wing, Lestat pays for servants to care for him and clean his flat so that he can compose piano music on the magnificent Broadwood grand piano that had once been performed on by Frédéric Chopin, which Lestat purchased for him. Despite all the lavish gifts that Lestat bestows upon him, Antoine never realizes that Lestat is a vampire, only that he lives in a flat off Rue Royale with his companion, Louis de Pointe du Lac, and their ward, Claudia. Just as he once danced to Nicolas de Lenfent's violin music, Lestat dances as Antoine plays original music composed in a twenty-four-hour dash of inspiration.

However, one night Lestat comes to Antoine looking horrific and stinking of the Louisiana swampland. Lestat turns Antoine into a vampire and shares with him through the Blood visions of how Claudia has betrayed him and attempted to murder him, and how Louis assisted her. Antoine plans to help Lestat avenge the crime committed against him. But in defending themselves, Louis and Claudia burn their flat and burn Lestat and Antoine along with it, yet they do not die. They return to Antoine's flat until Lestat is

well enough to leave for Europe and seek the assistance of Armand. Antoine feels too terrified to attempt the journey, so Lestat bids him adieu and leaves him a small fortune. Antoine remains horribly scarred and burned for the next thirty years, not quite knowing how to survive among mortals, hunting only the weakest in the crowded immigrant slums of the Irish parts of New Orleans. Throughout it all, he has two thoughts: music and pain.

Eventually, he leaves New Orleans for Saint Louis, sleeping in cemeteries the entire journey. Soon he is able to play piano again and takes up work playing at mortal gatherings. In time, the wounds from his burns heal, and he reenters society as a gentleman, with fine clothes and a small, albeit luxurious, apartment. Throughout it all, he feels loneliness nagging at him. Continuing to perform music, he travels to San Francisco where he makes a living as a pianist, first in dingy dives, then progressing up towards ornate concert halls, all the while his audience marveling at his dizzying ability to perform and improvise. He becomes quite popular in several circles of society until a Chinese blood drinker threatens to kill him. Antoine leaves San Francisco, but his popularity spreads. As he performs in various orchestral halls and theaters, he sees more vampires using their powers to advance in society. When he stays in one place too long, and when mortals start to observe his agelessness among his other vampire eccentricities, he moves away and seeks the company of other mortals. Finally, the nineteenth century becomes the twentieth, full of electricity and invention. Antoine realizes that he is growing quite strong. No

more scars of the old burn wounds remain. When the Great War shakes the world, he goes to Boston, unsure how to make contact with this modern world, and goes underground and sleeps in a vampire torpor for the next fifty years.

It is only in the mideighties of the late twentieth century that he is awakened by the music of the rock band the Vampire Lestat. Too weak to make the journey to Lestat's one and only concert, he plays for coins in New York subway stations and is overlooked by Akasha on her immolating rampage throughout the Great Burning of 1985. Still gaining back his strength, he spends years playing the violin, living in squalor, earning people's pocket change, and sleeping in graveyards and in cellars. Similar to the previous century, Antoine makes his way slowly up the musical ladder, first performing music in bars, then in nightclubs, one-dollar bills becoming twenty-dollar bills, until he is able to make enough money to lease a home in the Chicago suburbs. He lives a middle-class American life. He thinks of Lestat often, especially when he reads the Vampire Chronicles, purchasing the books as soon as they are published. He learns of the vastness of the vampire family—of Akasha, Maharet, and Mekare, of Marius, Armand, and Khayman, and of all the others. He even finds himself briefly mentioned in Louis's *Interview with the Vampire*, referred to simply as "the musician," without any name.

Not long after the publication of *The Tale of the Body Thief* (1992), which Antoine reads feverishly, he is attacked by a coven of gangster vampires. At that moment, he realizes that he has the power of the Mind Gift, when he telekinetically shoves the vampires against walls and into the pavement, knocking them senseless. He takes their knives, cuts off their heads, and hides their bodies. But the vampire covens keep coming for him until they finally burn his suburban house to the ground.

Antoine moves back to Saint Louis, but he still cannot escape the vampire gangs that seek to destroy him. Another coven finally captures him and sets him on fire. As he burns, he runs faster than they do, escaping far enough to bury himself in the ground, putting out the flames, yet he is still badly wounded. He sleeps in the earth for two more decades, until he hears the radio broadcast of the vampire Benji Mahmoud in 2013. He rises and discovers that he is stronger than ever before, and his burn wounds are healed. A new Great Burning is occurring. Benji, along with the beautiful piano playing of his companion, Sybelle, is broadcasting how vampires are being immolated and slaughtered all over the world, and he is urging the elders to bring unification, order, and guidance, so that they might stop this latest disaster. Antoine acquires work as a piano player in a hotel. He gets a room in that hotel and composes music. All the while he tunes in to Benji's radio broadcasts of the worldwide immolation of vampires.

Antoine heads to New York to seek Benji and Sybelle's help. When he comes to Trinity Gate, their coven house on New York's Upper East Side, the vampire Armand opens the door and welcomes him inside, promising Antoine that he will be well cared for. But he ultimately joins the Court of the Prince at Château de Lioncourt, where he serves as the music conductor of the vampire orchestra in the grand ballroom.

For more perspectives on Antoine's char-acter, read the *Alphabettery* entries **Claudia**, **Lestat de Lioncourt**, and **Louis de Pointe du Lac**.

Antony

• MORTAL •

The eldest son of a wealthy Roman senator nearly two decades before the Common Era, Antony is very protective of his only sister, Lydia. They have a peaceful life under the rule of Augustus Caesar, until their young-est brother, Lucius, full of jealousy and hate, betrays his family to the Praetorian Guard and their spies, the *delatores*, who slaughter his entire family. The only survivor is Lydia, who flees to Antioch, where she conceals her iden-tity by calling herself Pandora and is eventu-ally transformed into a vampire by Marius.

Antony appears only in *Pandora* (1998). For more perspectives on Antony's charac-ter, read the *Alphabettery* entries **Lucius** and **Pandora**.

Arion

• VAMPIRE •

Arion is the maker of Petronia, the maker of Quinn Blackwood. What Petronia lacks as a mentor, Arion makes up for as a father figure for Quinn Blackwood, teaching him how to survive as a vampire. He appears in *Blackwood Farm* (2002) and *Blood Communion* (2018).

Originally from the region of India, roughly five hundred years before the Com-mon Era, during the Persian and Greek conquests in northwestern South Asia when Cyrus the Great is King of Persia, Arion is a human slave purchased by a master who is a writer of satires, comedies, and tragedies for the theater in Athens. Just as Arion's mas-ter's name remains a mystery, details of his master's transformation into a vampire also remain largely unknown at present.

When they are living then in the Etrus-can city that will later become Pompeii, a vampire woman, whom Arion refers to as a sorceress of "the Power," transforms his mas-ter into a vampire. That same night, Arion's master feeds from him and brings him to the point of death, but he feels so guilty about nearly killing Arion that he performs the same ritual that was performed on him and transforms Arion into a vampire. Both maker and fledgling having become vampires on the same night, and without the guidance of the sorceress who transformed his master, they are forced to discover the purpose and power of their immortal lives as newly created vampires. His master believes that what was done to them is an act of evil, and he fruitlessly seeks a cure for the next twenty-five years. During that time, they decide that they will be guided by the principal rule of killing only evildoers, unless they take the Little Drink of blood from victims whom they let live. After all of his efforts to become human again are in vain, Arion's master commits suicide by immolation.

Arion becomes a world traveler for centuries, witnessing history unfold and buying slaves in the same fashion that he was bought, until one day he purchases a slave called Petronia, who is a hermaphrodite. Arion impresses upon Petronia the rule of only killing evildoers. Arion and Petronia relocate to Pompeii, where he teaches her how to make cameos. They open a cameo shop and remain there until the night before Mount Vesuvius erupts and destroys Pompeii and its population. Arion senses the imminent eruption and goes to his villa on the far side of the Bay of Naples while Petronia helps slaves escape along with the shop's wares. Arion then transforms Petronia into a vampire. They live in Naples, where Arion becomes a dealer in diamonds and pearls and uses his vampire powers to cleverly increase his wealth without cheating customers and business associates.

During that time, Petronia meets Manfred Blackwood, who is honeymooning in Italy with his second wife, Rebecca Stanford. Petronia listens with rapt fascination to Manfred's tales of his home—Blackwood Farm, in a Louisiana swampland called Sugar Devil Swamp—which inspire her to visit often. Petronia adores how easy it is to kill victims and hide their bodies in the swamp. Manfred promises to give her Sugar Devil Island in Sugar Devil Swamp, where he has his Hermitage, on the condition that she turn him into a vampire. At first she seeks to betray him, but Arion convinces her otherwise. After she brings Manfred into the Blood, Arion forms a small coven with them and eventually relocates the coven to a home on Sugar Devil Island. On the island, Arion watches Manfred's descendants increase on Blackwood Farm, all the way into the twentieth century, when the home is handed down to Manfred's great-great-great-grandson, Tarquin "Quinn" Blackwood. Petronia is immediately fascinated by Quinn and turns him into a blood drinker. Arion increases Quinn's vampire strength by giving Petronia's fledgling some of his own blood to drink. Arion becomes Quinn's teacher, but at length, Quinn decides to leave the coven, and Arion allows him to go. Arion continues to live in the Louisiana swamplands, killing evildoers and feeding their carcasses to the alligators, until the twenty-first century. He leaves the swamp to join the Court of the Prince at Château de Lioncourt.

For more perspectives on Arion's character, read the *Alphabettery* entries **Blackwood Farm, Hermitage, Little Drink, Manfred Blackwood, Petronia, Quinn Blackwood, Rebecca Stanford, Sugar Devil Island**, and **Sugar Devil Swamp**.

Arjun

• VAMPIRE •

Arjun is Pandora's fledgling and companion, as well as an obstacle blocking Marius's desire to reunite with Pandora, who is miserable with Arjun because of his selfish control over her. Centuries after Pandora and Arjun separate, Amel, in his plan for liberation, manipulates Arjun against his will to immolate several vampires. Arjun appears in *Blood and Gold* (2001), *Prince Lestat* (2014), and *Blood Communion* (2018).

In the fourteenth century, many hundreds of years after Pandora and Marius separate, she encounters a prince of the Chola dynasty in India, named Arjun, who worships her. Pandora is instantly attracted to Arjun—who is educated in Sanskrit and the Vedas, and is very beautiful to behold—and she turns him into a vampire. They remain together for hundreds of years until they encounter Marius at a ball at the ducal palace in Dresden in the seventeenth century. Marius believes that Arjun is manipulating Pandora against her will, but he cannot prove it. He speaks first with Pandora and begs her to leave Arjun. She rejects the idea that Arjun is coercing her before spurning Marius's invitation to leave together. Marius next speaks with Arjun, who, though more

than one thousand years younger than he is, stands up to him fearlessly, telling him that he, Arjun, must willingly surrender Pandora to him, yet he is inwardly confident of his power over her, knowing that she will not leave him for Marius. Defeating Marius's hopes to be reunited with his beloved, Arjun leaves the ball with Pandora, and the two prepare to depart Dresden for Moscow. Unbeknownst to Arjun, Pandora writes a letter to Marius, confessing that he is correct, that Arjun will not let her abandon him, that she greatly desires Marius to find them in Moscow and to take her from him. Unfortunately, the letter is lost among Marius's many belongings, and he does not discover it for another fifty years. When he finally does, Arjun has already taken Pandora away from Moscow.

Around that same time, Pandora finds the strength to leave Arjun, and they do not see each other for another two hundred years. Arjun descends into the earth, retreating into a vampiric torpor when he can no longer suffer the pangs of an immortal existence. He survives in the earth when Akasha rises to commence the Great Burning of 1985, immolating the world's vampire population.

When Amel, as the mysterious Voice, rouses Arjun from his torpor in the earth, Arjun goes to Mumbai as if possessed, not knowing what he is doing, and commences his own great massacre of vampires, burning them with the Fire Gift. Eventually, after hearing the pleas for mercy from his vampire victims, especially those who have been vampires for hundreds of years, he laments not only what he did but how much pleasure it gave him at the time. He spends his time between his home in Mumbai and Prince Lestat's Court of the Prince at Château de Lioncourt, where he causes Pandora no end of guilt and grief. As the years pass, Arjun becomes outraged by Marius's long history with Pandora. He challenges Marius to combat but cannot defeat the former keeper of Those Who Must Be Kept. Marius completely destroys Arjun with the Fire Gift.

For more perspectives on Arjun's character, read the *Alphabettery* entries **Bianca Solderini**, **Marius**, **Marquis de Malvrier**, **Marquisa de Malvrier**, and **Pandora**.

Armand

• VAMPIRE •

One of the most pivotal characters of the Vampire Chronicles, and the author of an autobiography, the vampire Armand has indelibly shaped the destiny of the Chronicles' most beloved heroes. He appears in *Interview with the Vampire* (1976), *The Vampire Lestat* (1985), *The Queen of the Damned* (1988), *Memnoch the Devil* (1995), *The Vampire Armand* (1998), *Blood and Gold* (2001), *Prince Lestat* (2014), *Prince Lestat and the Realms of Atlantis* (2016), and *Blood Communion* (2018).

Born in Kiev, Russia, at the end of the fifteenth century is a boy named Andrei, who will later become the famous vampire Armand. At an early age, he begins studying the prayerful art of painting icons in the Orthodox Christian tradition at the Monastery of the Caves. Andrei, believing that his talent comes from the power of God, becomes greatly interested in living the ascetic life of the monks who bury themselves up to their necks in the earth and are kept alive by being fed small portions of food and water; but Andrei's father rejects the idea of his son becoming a monk, unflaggingly convinced that Andrei's artistic talent, though divinely inspired, should receive more public recognition. At the age of fifteen, Andrei accepts a commission by Prince Michael to paint an icon and deliver it to Prince Feodor. When Andrei and his father are transporting the icon on a ship sailing for Constantinople, Tartars invade the ship, kidnap Andrei, and then sell him to a brothel in Venice, Italy. After enduring numerous acts of abuse, Andrei suffers amnesia and is locked in a dungeon.

The vampire Marius discovers Andrei wasting away and is so enchanted by his angelic beauty that he buys the boy from the brothel and brings him back to his own home, where he nurses him back to health and renames him Amadeo. Other boys Amadeo's age also live in the house and refer to Marius as "the Master." Marius generously bestows upon Amadeo lavish clothing, riches, and an education in the arts and sciences. While the other boys receive more generalized tutelage, Marius excludes Amadeo from them by giving him special attention, private lessons, and excusing his occasional mischief. During that time, Amadeo also encounters Bianca Solderini, a Venetian courtesan, who wins the affection of both Amadeo and Marius.

One night, while Marius and Amadeo are enjoying an excursion through the rougher areas of the city, Marius captures a cutthroat and drinks his blood. Unperturbed and fascinated by the event, Amadeo begs Marius to turn him into a blood drinker also, but Marius refuses. In a fractious response, Amadeo seduces Lord Harlech, an Englishman, who offers to bring Amadeo back to England. But ultimately Amadeo rejects Lord Harlech, truly desiring Marius instead, which sends Lord Harlech into a jealous rage. The Englishman steals into Marius's palazzo and duels Amadeo, who dispatches Lord Harlech easily, but not before Harlech cuts Amadeo with a poison-laced blade. Bianca nurses Amadeo until Marius returns. Marius tends to Amadeo, but he soon realizes that the boy is on his deathbed, so he saves Amadeo's life by turning him into a vampire.

Amadeo transitions quickly and effortlessly, becoming a vicious vampire as well as an excellent fledgling. Not long after Amadeo receives the Dark Gift, the vampire Santino and his Roman coven, the Children of Darkness, invade Marius's palazzo, set Marius on fire, and kidnap Amadeo back to Rome along with many human boys. Watching the palazzo burn, Amadeo believes that Marius is dead.

Santino takes Amadeo to Rome and holds him captive in a cell for months, feeding him his own friends—the other boys that his coven took from Marius's palazzo. During his incarceration, he encounters another member of Santino's coven, Allesandra, a vampire woman in her prime, whom Lestat will later know as the mad Old Queen. Allesandra herself was also captured by the Children of Satan, taken from her master, Rhoshamandes, many years before Santino becomes the coven leader. She helps Amadeo accept his new life in the coven until Santino finally agrees to release and initiate him. Santino and Allesandra teach Amadeo the rituals, prohibitions, and the five Great Laws that govern them. After Amadeo has studied with the Children of Darkness and becomes a high-ranking member of Santino's coven, Santino sends him to Paris to begin a new coven. Allesandra accompanies him and changes his name from Amadeo to Armand.

Armand creates his new coven beneath the Cemetery of les Innocents, where they live for the next few centuries in filth, feeding off the city's indigent population. One night, his coven realizes that a new vampire is in the city, one who does not follow the rules but lives in luxury and splendor and associates with mortals, pretending to be one of them so that he can feed off them, drinking only the best blood. After tailing him, they learn that this vampire is named Lestat and that he has recently turned his mother, Gabrielle, into a vampire also. Armand's coven confronts Lestat and Gabrielle but cannot capture them, so they instead capture Lestat's mortal friend Nicolas. Lestat quickly rescues Nicolas and turns him into a vampire.

Armand and his coven once more confront Lestat, Nicolas, and Gabrielle, only this time, Lestat convinces Armand that the practices of the Children of Darkness are outmoded and superstitious. Believing his coven cannot survive the transition into the modern era, Allesandra convinces Armand to destroy the coven before she throws herself into a bonfire. Armand takes her counsel and begins throwing his coven vampires into the fire, sparing only Felix and Laurent, along with Eleni and Eugénie, both of whom are older than Armand. The four surviving vampires implore Lestat to remain with them and be their leader, but he refuses. Nicolas persuades Lestat to give them Renaud's House of Thesbians on Boulevard du Temple, which Lestat purchases from Renaud and subsequently closes. Nicolas joins the other four vampires, but it is not until Armand joins them also that they become a new coven, which Nicolas names Théâtre des Vampires, and pretend to be mortal actors putting on theater productions about vampires.

Lestat and Gabrielle leave Paris, but Eleni writes to Lestat of the *théâtre*'s progress. Audiences adore the supernatural shows of vampires and werewolves. Armand convinces his coven to show their vampire nature onstage by actually killing victims and drinking their blood. Audiences laud this addition, believing it to be theatrics. By this time, the coven has abandoned the worship of Satan, but not the Great Laws.

A century later, Armand encounters Lestat's two other fledglings, Louis and Claudia. Armand is immediately smitten with Louis and strives to persuade him to leave Claudia, but Louis refuses. During that time, Lestat returns to Armand, explaining how Louis and Claudia have burned him and wounded him badly and begging for Armand to let him drink his older, healing blood. Armand agrees at first, allowing his coven to hold a trial, convicting Louis and Claudia of attempting to kill their maker, which is a violation of the old Great Laws of the Children of Darkness. The coven burns Claudia to death, but Armand denies Lestat's request and pushes him out of a window before rescuing Louis. In retribution for killing Claudia, Louis burns the Théâtre des Vampires and kills the rest of Armand's coven.

Armand and Louis remain companions until the 1920s, during which time Armand glimpses Bianca Solderini in Paris and speculates that Marius has turned her into a vampire also, which tells him that his old maker, Marius, might still be alive. Eventually, after living with Louis's melancholic disposition for decades, Armand realizes that Louis will never fully recover from all his losses, so he leaves Louis (who seems not to care) and goes to live in Lestat's old house in the Garden District. Armand remains there until Daniel Molloy finds him, having heard Louis's tale, which will later become the inception of the Vampire Chronicles, *Interview with the Vampire*.

Armand holds Daniel captive, observing him and listening to the tape recordings of

Louis's tale. Finally, he allows Daniel to leave but threatens him, telling the mortal that he will be watching him. Over the next few years, Armand follows Daniel all over the world, appearing to him randomly and asking him questions, such as how long-distance phone calls can be possible. All the while, Daniel beseeches Armand to turn him into a vampire, but Armand continues to refuse him, giving him instead a vial of his blood, which will protect him from other blood drinkers. Eventually, after Daniel begins deteriorating into a deep depression, which will lead to his death, Armand turns him into a vampire.

While Daniel aids Armand's transition into the twentieth century, Armand buys him an island resort in Florida that he calls Night Island. Following this, they attend the rock concert of the Vampire Lestat and witness Akasha's killing spree of vampires when Lestat's music awakens her. Armand and Daniel gather with the other vampires to hear the Legend of the Twins. At this meeting, Armand is introduced to several other vampires, but he is also reunited with Louis, Marius, and even Santino, before they all stand together to fight against Akasha. After Mekare kills the Queen of the Damned, becoming the new Queen of the Damned herself, Armand invites the remaining vampires back to Night Island, but this short-lived coven soon separates. Even Daniel leaves Armand, who drifts over the next few years.

After Lestat returns from his journey with Memnoch the Devil, Armand believes Lestat's recounting of the tale, especially when Lestat explains how he has drunk the blood of Jesus Christ. Armand begs Lestat to allow him to drink his blood, so that he can taste the Savior of his mortal life. Lestat refuses Armand, but he does show him a token of his journey— Veronica's Veil. Whereupon, seeing the face of Christ on the cloth, Armand calls himself a sinner who will die for God, then attempts to kill himself by flying up into the air as high as his Cloud Gift will allow him. Burned by the winter sun, Armand falls from his great height onto an empty building and is lodged beneath a torn and rusted overhang, where the sun cannot burn him. In time, he is covered by snowfall, too injured and weak to move. He lies there for many days, until he telepathically summons Benji and Sybelle, who use picks and hammers to free him from the ice. They bring him back to their hotel room, where Armand kills Sybelle's violent brother, who is abusing her to death. Though he is blackened by the sunlight, Armand employs his Mind Gift to project an image of himself into their minds so that they will see him as he normally appears, until his body fully recovers from the burns. Benji and Sybelle help restore Armand's health by bringing him victims so that he can drink their blood. Armand stays with them for two months.

When healed, he takes them to visit Lestat, who falls into a vampiric sleep due to his encounter with Memnoch. Armand still desires to taste Lestat's Christ-filled blood, so he gives Benji and Sybelle into Marius's care. The blood shows Armand a scene of Jesus Christ crucified, but before he can see more, an invisible force suddenly blows him back, while Lestat remains unconscious. Armand then reunites with Marius, only to discover that Marius has turned Benji and Sybelle into vampires. Armand is furious with Marius at first, but Marius convinces Armand that he has done him a favor. With Marius's blood in them, Benji and Sybelle will never be inferior to Armand, and they will always enjoy a telepathic connection with him, unlike the telepathic connection between Daniel and Armand, which is forever severed due to the nature of the master-fledgling relationship. In time, Armand sees the wisdom in Marius's thoughtfulness, and he starts a new coven house on New York's Upper East Side, which he calls Trinity Gate, where Armand lives with Benji and Sybelle and continues to learn about all the luxurious conveniences of the modern world.

Armand eventually relocates to Château de Lioncourt, where he participates in the Court of the Prince of Prince Lestat. He often opposes Lestat's decisions, especially when it comes to the fate of the Replimoids and Rhoshamandes, but he loves Lestat and vows fealty to the Prince of all Vampires.

For more perspectives on Armand's character, read the *Alphabettery* entries **Allesandra**, **Amadeo**, **Andrei**, **Benedict**, **Benji Mahmoud**, **Coven**, **Coven Master**, **Daniel Malloy**, **Dybbuk**, **Eleni**, **Eugénie**, **Everard**, **Lestat de Lioncourt**, **Louis de Pointe du Lac**, **Marius**, **Santino**, **Santiago**, **Sybelle**, **Tartars**, and **Veronica's Veil**.

Ashlar

• TALTOS •

Ashlar predominantly appears in the Lives of the Mayfair Witches, but he is mentioned by name in one book of the Vampire Chronicles, *Blood Canticle* (2003), as an influential character for Lestat's fledgling Mona Mayfair.

Ashlar is conceived and born in an hour and a half, many thousands of years ago, on a secluded island where the Taltos live. A member of an ancient race of beings nearly twice the size of average men, Ashlar enjoys a shared consciousness with his immortal kindred, who are able to recollect aspects of one another's history and of the histories of those few Taltos who die from accidents. The relative peacefulness they enjoy on their island, far away from mortals and fear, trembles when

the island begins to sink into the sea. Ashlar escapes with a few of his Taltos kindred, including two of his daughters. They sail to a new land where they set up an encampment. But cold winters make this land painfully unlike their former island paradise.

Ashlar forms a small tribe and endeavors to live in peace with the mortal inhabitants of that area. After a time, the mortals become fearful and distrustful of these Taltos beings. They raid the camp, kill the young, and capture many of Ashlar's friends. Able to defend himself, but unwilling to fight back, he gathers his remaining Taltos allies and takes them to other lands where they can live in harmony with friendlier mortals.

Some of his clan leaves, hoping to find better places to live. Thus, Ashlar's clan continues to dwindle throughout the long centuries. In the Late Iron Age, members of the Taltos even identify themselves as the Picts, who live in the northeastern area of Scotland, and Ashlar begins to learn how to better hide his nonhuman nature from mortals.

As Christianity becomes the dominant religion and political force in the West, Ashlar interacts with various members of the Catholic clergy. The Taltos take vows, make Holy Orders, and are given the assignment of operating a small church. Congregants revere Ashlar as a great saint. He compiles a book of the Taltos, which the Church decides is blasphemous. As time passes, he abandons his work as a churchman, but the laity and clergy do not forget him. After he is believed to be dead, he is canonized and declared Saint Ashlar. Despite all of this, his clan continues to dwindle, until he is the only Taltos remaining. He spends many long years searching for others, but finds none. Throughout all of his searching, he discovers the existence of a group of mortals called the Talamasca, who are fascinated with supernatural beings. Although they provide him with no new information on his kindred, they prove to be valuable allies.

One member of the Talamasca, Stuart Gordon, introduces Ashlar to the female Taltos Tessa, but she cannot procreate, so he leaves her in search of another mate. Through another friend in the Talamasca, Yuri Stefano, Ashlar learns that the recently murdered Aaron Lightner had been involved with the Mayfair family of witches, one of whose members, Rowan, has recently given birth

to a Taltos named Lasher. Eager to encounter Lasher, Ashlar seeks and finds Rowan and her husband, Michael Curry, a former psychic candidate for the Talamasca, only to discover that Michael has killed Lasher. Moreover, Ashlar learns that Lasher and Rowan have mated and produced another Taltos child, Emaleth, but Rowan has killed her, fearful of Taltos overpopulating the world. This news saddens Ashlar, as he believes Emaleth would have made a wonderful mate, but he remains friends with Rowan and Michael and eventually visits their home in New Orleans, where he discovers that Rowan's cousin Mona Mayfair has recently given birth to a Taltos, Morrigan. Ashlar and Morrigan are instantly attracted to each other. They flee New Orleans together to a secret island that Ashlar purchases with his vast fortune.

Once settled on the island, Ashlar and Morrigan have four Taltos children—Silas, Oberon, Miravelle, and Lorkyn—who, like other Taltos newborns, grow to adult size very quickly. In time, Ashlar unearths the location of several other Taltos, whom he invites back to the island, where they can all live together in the harmony that Ashlar once enjoyed thousands of years ago. Ashlar's son Silas becomes fearful and angry towards the mortals living on nearby islands, so he starts a rebellion against his parents, secretly poisoning both Ashlar and Morrigan to weaken them. When Ashlar realizes that he can put up no resistance, Silas openly rebels, capturing his parents, siblings, and any other Taltos who will not follow him. Silas's rebellion lasts for two years, until he attacks the nearest island, inhabited by the drug lord Rodrigo, but Rodrigo and his Drug Merchants fight back, killing Silas and his rebels and capturing the remaining Taltos. Rodrigo locks Ashlar and Morrigan in the large kitchen freezer on the compound, where the husband and wife freeze to death, embracing each other like sleeping angels. When Lestat, Quinn, and Mona liberate the island by destroying Rodrigo and his Drug Merchants, they take Ashlar's and Morrigan's bodies back to Mayfair Medical Center for research, while their three remaining children return to New Orleans to be with their family.

For more perspectives on Ashlar's character, read the *Alphabettery* entries **Aaron Lightner, Ash Templeton, Little People, Lorkyn, Mayfair Medical Center, Michael Curry, Miravelle, Mona Mayfair, Morrigan Mayfair, Oberon, Quinn Blackwood, Secret Isle, Silas, Taltos,** and **Yuri Stefano.**

Ash Templeton

• ALIAS •

"Ash Templeton" is the alias that the thousands-of-years-old Taltos Ashlar—the owner of a successful doll-making company—calls himself in his twentieth-century effort to blend in with mortals.

He appears in *Blood Canticle* (2003). For more perspectives on Ash Templeton's character, read the *Alphabettery* entries **Ashlar** and **Taltos.**

Asphar

• VAMPIRE •

Asphar is the fledgling and servant of Eudoxia. He is one of her most beloved slaves, especially in the making of the beautiful Zenobia so that she and Eudoxia can read each other's minds. Asphar appears in *Blood and Gold* (2001).

Turned into a vampire at a young age by the nearly six-hundred-year-old Alexandrian vampire Eudoxia, Asphar becomes her servant and companion. He serves her faithfully for many years, even when she desires to have the mortal Zenobia as her vampire companion. She makes Asphar turn Zenobia into a vampire, so that Eudoxia and Zenobia can maintain a telepathic connection, which is always lost between maker and fledgling. Becoming the strongest vampire in Constantinople, she gives herself the title "Vampire Empress" and keeps the city clean of other vampires.

In time, Marius moves to Constantinople, along with his companions Avicus and Mael. Asphar learns from Eudoxia that Marius is protecting Akasha and Enkil, the Mother and the Father of all vampires, now called Those Who Must Be Kept, and that she herself drank from the Queen hundreds of years ago. Eudoxia sends Asphar and his companion Rashid to Marius to extend an invitation to her home. Eudoxia is at least three hundred years older than Marius, and when he arrives at her house, she demands that he let her drink from Akasha once more. Marius refuses. Eudoxia, believing that she is stronger than Marius, attempts to force him into revealing the location of the Mother and Father. Asphar's companion Rashid is the first to discover that Marius, because he has been drinking Akasha's blood for several years, is much stronger than Eudoxia and her fledglings. Marius surprises everyone, even

himself, that he possesses the Fire Gift when he accidentally immolates Rashid to ash. After Marius returns to his home, Eudoxia follows, beseeching more respectfully that he allow her to speak with Akasha. Marius acquiesces, but when he brings her to Akasha's shrine beneath his house, the Queen nearly kills Eudoxia. Marius demands that Eudoxia leave and never return. In vengeful retribution, Eudoxia attempts to destroy the shrine but only destroys Marius's house instead. Outraged, Marius comes to her house and uses his newfound Fire Gift to utterly immolate most of Eudoxia's vampire slaves, save Asphar's fledgling, Zenobia. Not even Asphar escapes Marius's fiery anger, as he is burned to ashes shortly before Marius drags Eudoxia before the Queen, who uses her own Fire Gift to incinerate the former Vampire Empress of Constantinople.

For more perspectives on Asphar's character, read the *Alphabettery* entries **Eudoxia**, **Marius**, **Rashid**, and **Zenobia**.

Atalantaya

• SANCTUARY •

First appearing in *Prince Lestat and the Realms of Atlantis* (2016), Atalantaya is the name of the city most commonly known in present day as Atlantis.

Amel creates Atalantaya nearly ten thousand years before the Common Era. Born to human parents, Amel is abducted at the age

of twelve by a race of aliens called Bravennans, who devour human suffering. After the Bravennans augment Amel's genetic structure, giving him superhuman strength and intellect as well as immortality and the ability to rapidly regenerate, the Bravennans return the newly enhanced Amel back to Earth with the mission of repairing their transmission stations, which they claim are harmless devices that observe the human race. Although the Bravennans intentionally mislead Amel, his superior intellect deduces that the transmission stations are not only a means of observation for the Bravennans but also the means by which they feed on human suffering. Moreover, he learns that the Bravennans are also the instigators of much human suffering by means of wars, cataclysms, natural disasters, and other ways human suffering is maintained on Earth. Guided by a sense of morality that he develops during his first twelve years as a human, Amel seeks ways to disrupt the transmission stations in the hope of preventing human suffering, shielding humans by creating cities and caring for them with his superior abilities. Finally, Amel extracts samples of Bravennan chemical compounds used in his heightened genetic structure. He then alters those compounds and develops his own superior substance that he calls luracastria. Foreign to Bravennan scientists, luracastria is an unknown matter that the Bravennan transmission stations cannot penetrate. Thus, mass-producing great quantities of luracastria, Amel not only sets up luracastria shields and barriers around the transmission stations to prevent the Bravennans from observing, feeding on, and causing human suffering, but he also creates the greatest city that has ever been—Atalantaya.

Everything in Atalantaya is created out of luracastria: buildings, sidewalks, driving pods, elevator pods, and clothing. Even the dome spanning over the entire city of Atalantaya is made of luracastria. Mortals come from all over Earth to live in the great city, where they feel no real suffering. Even the Replimoids—the humanoid assassins that the Bravennans send to stop Amel—are impressed with Amel's creation, and many join his cause. Amel rules over Atalantaya for many years until the Bravennans destroy it in a shower of meteors that melts the luracastria completely. Atalantaya sinks into the sea, never to be found again. Amel's body perishes along with his great city, yet his etheric body in the particles that compose his soul survives.

For more perspectives on the subject of Atalantaya in the Vampire Chronicles, read the *Alphabettery* entries **Amel**, **Atlantis**, **Bravenna**, **Bravennans**, **Luracastria**, and **Replimoid**.

Atlantis

• SANCTUARY •

"Atlantis" is the contemporary pronunciation of "Atalantaya," the city founded and created by Amel—a human abducted by Bravennan aliens who genetically enhanced him for the nefarious purpose of helping them devour the energy in suffering, especially the suffering among human mortals. The great city of Atlantis is Amel's effort to stop the Bravennans and put an end to human suffering.

Atlantis appears in *Prince Lestat and the* *Realms of Atlantis* (2016). For more perspectives on the subject of the city of Atlantis in the Vampire Chronicles, read the *Alphabettery* entries **Amel** and **Atalantaya**.

Augustin de Lioncourt

• MORTAL •

In eighteenth-century the Auvergne, France, Augustin is the first child of the Marquis and Marquise de Lioncourt and the eldest brother of Lestat. With their family fortunes squandered and their castle nearly in ruins, Augustin is the first in line to inherit next to nothing, save for their feudal title, their lands, and, of course, Château de Lioncourt.

Augustin grows to hate his youngest brother, who has a deep spirituality and has greatly desired to be a monk from an early age. He and his brother take Lestat from his monastic school and force him back to the castle. Several years later he must do the same when Lestat seeks to run away with a troupe of actors. By the time Lestat is sixteen years old, Augustin has no taste for leading his family, especially when his father grows infirm and his mother grows increasingly cold and heartless. He allows Lestat to become the sole provider for the family, yet

he is incredulous when reports come back to him of how Lestat slaughtered eight wolves that had been besieging the nearby village. If Augustin ever loved Lestat, whatever love remains is entirely snuffed out after the village brings Lestat a gift of a cloak and boots, lined in the fur of the wolves that he singlehandedly killed.

Shortly after the Storming of the Bastille on July 14, 1789, the Auvergne tenant farmers rise up in rebellion against Château de Lioncourt. They loot the castle and slay everyone inside, including Lestat's brothers and their wives and children. Augustin is among the dead.

Augustin only appears in *The Vampire Lestat* (1985). For more perspectives on his character, read the *Alphabettery* entries **Château de Lioncourt**, **Gabrielle**, **Lestat de Lioncourt**, **Marquis de Lioncourt**, and **Marquise de Lioncourt**.

Aunt Julie

• MORTAL •

When the vampire Lestat rescues Rose from a sinking island, he adopts her and sends her to live with two retired schoolteachers, Aunt Julie and Aunt Marge, who take great care of her. When a corrupt judge condemns Rose to a corrupt boarding school, Louis rescues Rose and brings her, Aunt Julie, and Aunt Marge to a beautiful home in New York City, providing them with wealth and servants.

Aunt Julie is mentioned in *Prince Lestat* (2014). For more perspectives on her character, read the *Alphabettery* entries **Aunt Marge**, **Lestat de Lioncourt**, **Louis de Pointe du Lac**, and **Rose**.

Aunt Marge

• MORTAL •

Aunt Marge is one of two retired schoolteachers who care for a young girl named Rose, rescued from a sinking island by the vampire Lestat. He adopts Rose and needs dependable mortals to raise her and love her. He chooses Marge and her roommate, Julie. Lestat constantly sends them money and gifts so that they will never need to worry. After Rose gets embroiled with a corrupt judge and school, Lestat sends Louis to escort her, Aunt Marge, and Aunt Julie to New York, where they live in opulence.

Aunt Marge is mentioned in *Prince Lestat* (2014). For more perspectives on her character, read the *Alphabettery* entries **Aunt Julie**, **Lestat de Lioncourt**, **Louis de Pointe du Lac**, and **Rose**.

Aunt Queen

• MORTAL •

Aunt Queen plays an important role in the mortal life of Quinn Blackwood, providing him with education, culture, and a greater appreciation for the supernatural. She appears in *Blackwood Farm* (2002).

Aunt Queen is born Lorraine Blackwood. Her legal father is William Blackwood, son of Manfred Blackwood, founder of Blackwood Farm, but her biological father is Julien Mayfair, who impregnates her mother due to William's sterility, which directly connects Aunt Queen to the Mayfair family of witches. Aunt Queen is the second Blackwood child fathered by Julien; her older brother, Gravier, is also Julien's son, who eventually becomes the great-great-grandfather of Quinn Blackwood. Aunt Queen marries John McQueen, becoming Lorraine McQueen, but their marriage ends tragically when her husband is killed in a car accident, leaving her to inherit his immense fortune.

When Quinn is just a boy, he meets his great-aunt Lorraine McQueen, who tells him to call her Aunt Queen. Traveling often, and with her home in New York, Aunt Queen does not return to Blackwood Farm for many years. She enjoys spending time with Quinn and listening to him, especially about the ghost that is haunting him, Goblin. She has the ability to see Goblin, but she never tells this to Quinn. Concerned for his well-being, she hires a teacher who not only home-schools Quinn in typical adolescent subjects but also instructs Goblin how to communicate more effectively with Quinn and other mortals.

In time, Aunt Queen invites Quinn to New York to get away from Blackwood Farm and from Goblin. To Quinn's great surprise, though not to Aunt Queen's, the supernatural connection between Quinn and Goblin diminishes. Aunt Queen also broadens Quinn's cultural perspective, allowing him to accompany her on many small adventures throughout the world. She returns to Blackwood Farm whenever she can.

On one of her visits, she discovers that Quinn has found Sugar Devil Island, where it is suspected that Manfred Blackwood murdered his second wife, Rebecca Stanford. During her stay, Aunt Queen also encounters Sugar Devil Island's latest inhabitant, the hermaphrodite vampire, Petronia, who visits Aunt Queen in Blackwood Farm's parlor and engages in long conversations about the mutually fascinating topic of cameos. Quinn warns Aunt Queen against engaging in further conversation with Petronia, but when the vampire is absent, he presses many questions to Aunt Queen about the history of the Blackwood family.

Eventually, Aunt Queen returns to New York, but as time wears on, realizing that the end of her days is coming, she invites Quinn on one more trip through Europe, knowing it will be her last. Quinn agrees, and they spend the next three years traveling abroad. After Quinn returns to Louisiana and she to New York, she lives only a few more years, never knowing that, shortly after their return, Petronia captured Quinn and turned him into a vampire.

For more perspectives on Aunt Queen's character, read the *Alphabettery* entries **Blackwood Farm, John McQueen, Lorraine McQueen, Manfred Blackwood, Petronia, Quinn Blackwood, Rebecca Stanford, Sugar Devil Island,** and **Sugar Devil Swamp.**

The Auvergne

• SANCTUARY •

Once a province of the Roman Empire, as well as one of France's former administrative regions, the Auvergne, which tends to be a colder area, is located near the center of the country, full of many mountain ranges.

Lestat is born in the Auvergne in the castle of his father, the Marquis de Lioncourt, on an estate near a village in 1760, during the reign of King Louis XV, more than two decades before the French Revolution.

After Akasha is killed in the twentieth century, and Mekare takes the Sacred Core into herself, Lestat returns to the Auvergne to commune with the Voice, who reveals himself to be the spirit of Amel.

Lestat rules as Prince of the Vampires from his father's castle in the Auvergne.

The Auvergne is principally featured in *The Vampire Lestat* (1985), *Prince Lestat* (2014), *Prince Lestat and the Realms of Atlantis* (2016), and *Blood Communion* (2018). For more perspectives on the Auvergne in the Vampire Chronicles, read the *Alphabettery* entries **Augustin**, **Château de Lioncourt**, **Gabrielle**, **Lestat de Lioncourt**, **Marquis de Lioncourt**, and **Marquise de Lioncourt**.

Avicus

• VAMPIRE •

Avicus is one of the few vampires from the Blood Genesis who survive into the twenty-first century. In his own way, he has helped shape the lives of most modern vampires by aiding Marius's charge over Those Who Must Be Kept, supporting Gregory's creation of Collingsworth Pharmaceuticals, and favoring the procedure to remove Amel from Lestat. He appears in *Blood and Gold* (2001), *Prince Lestat* (2014), *Prince Lestat and the Realms of Atlantis* (2016), and *Blood Communion* (2018).

Though it is never explicitly stated, Avicus's maker might have been Akasha herself; if it is not her, it is most likely a vampire priest from Akasha's blood cult, which makes Avicus and Akbar close in age.

Originally from Egypt and also a worshipping member of the Queen's blood cult, tall and dark-skinned Avicus is allowed to drink Akasha's blood, which increases his vampiric strength. Nothing at present is known about the several millennia Avicus spent from his time in Akasha's blood cult to the Common Era. But around 10 C.E., when Teskhamen is worshipped by Druids as the God of the Grove in Roman Gaul, Avicus is also worshipped as the God of the Grove by another group of Druids in the northern forest of pre-Roman Britain, possibly in Brigantia (centered around present-day Yorkshire), which is controlled by the Brigantes. However, that area is also bordered by four other tribes for whom Avicus could have been the God of the Grove: the Parisii to the east, the Corieltauvi and the Cornovii in the south, and the Carvetii in the northwest, who are likely related to the Brigantes.

His fate changes, however, when the mortal Mael appears, beseeching Avicus to transform him into a vampire so that he can succeed Teskhamen as the new Roman God of the Grove. Avicus has been imprisoned in the Sacred Oak for so long that he only dimly remembers being a part of Akasha's blood cult in ancient Egypt. He cannot even recall his maker. He knows how to use some of his powers, though not all, yet he is able to employ the Mind Gift to search Mael's mind. He sees how Marius, not wanting to be the God of the Grove, escaped the Druids after Teskhamen turned him into a vampire. Thrilled with the possibility of escaping as Marius has, Avicus makes a deal with Mael: Mael will bring Avicus a victim and help him escape in return for being transformed into a vampire. Avicus and Mael escape together and become companions.

Almost two hundred years later, towards the end of the second century, they encounter Marius in Rome and stay with him for a time as his companions. During that time, Avicus and Mael are attacked by drunken soldiers. Mael loses his head and arm. Unable to properly restore them, Avicus needs Marius to fix the mess he's made of Mael. Marius is amazed at how old Avicus is, yet how little he knows of his own power. Marius removes Mael's head and arm once more and shows Avicus how to reattach them correctly.

After the Roman emperor Constantine turns the Greek city of Byzantium into Constantinople under the Byzantine Empire in 330 C.E., Avicus accompanies Marius there, and they encounter Eudoxia, empowered with the ancient blood of Cyril. Eudoxia attempts to make war against Marius and loses when Marius brings her to the statuesque Queen Akasha, who destroys Eudoxia with the Fire Gift. Not long after this, Avicus encounters Eudoxia's fledgling, a Byzantine vampire woman with the appearance of a fifteen-year-old girl, Zenobia. After Marius abandons them, Mael becomes Maharet's companion, and Zenobia becomes Avicus's Blood Wife. For a time, Avicus and Zenobia live together with Gregory (Nebamun) and Sevraine in a Blood Kindred.

They all reunite in the twenty-first century to discover that Amel is speaking to them as the mysterious Voice, because he seeks to be free from Mekare's wounded mind to live in the mind of a saner vampire of equal strength, which becomes the vampire Lestat. They also reunite once more at the council to help Amel leave Lestat and enter a body of his own. Afterward, Avicus joins the Court of the Prince in Château de Lioncourt.

For more perspectives on Avicus's character, read the *Alphabettery* entries **Akasha, Amel, Eudoxia, God of the Grove, Gregory Duff Collingsworth, Lestat de Lioncourt, Mael, Maharet, Marius, Mekare, Nebamun, Sevraine, Teskhamen, Those Who Must Be Kept,** and **Zenobia.**

Azim

• VAMPIRE •

Azim is already an old vampire when Marius is made, so he claims. At present, nothing is known about his maker or about any fledglings he might have made. After more than a thousand years of living as a vampire, he builds a temple in the Himalayas and gains a cult following that refers to him as "the ancient blood god." His temple thrives for over a thousand more years, and he uses his vampire powers to increase his cult following, the members of which also become his victims during feverish and frenetic ceremonies that worship him. Once he is plump on the blood of his victims, with bronzed skin and wrapped in lavish robes and a silk turban, Pandora visits him in his temple, where his victims are lining up in rows of hundreds to sacrifice themselves to his bloodlust. Because fledgling vampires cannot hear the thoughts of their makers, Pandora hopes to discover from Azim any information about Marius, who is sending out warning signals to other vampires that Queen Akasha has trapped him in ice because the music of the band Vampire Lestat has awakened her. Azim tells her where Marius is buried but only after she partakes of his blood ritual ceremonies and answers his questions about visions of Maharet and Mekare. Pandora leaves, but Queen Akasha comes to him not long after, accompanied by Lestat. Having already incited the Great Burning of 1985, she makes Azim her first great martyr as a lesson to his worshippers. Akasha accuses him of having misled hopeless victims, because she is their blood god. Then she immolates him and causes his head to explode.

For more perspectives on Azim's character, read the *Alphabettery* entries **Akasha**, **Great Burning of 1985**, **Lestat de Lioncourt**, **Maharet**, **Mekare**, **Marius**, and **Pandora**.

Babette Freniere

• MORTAL •

The eldest sibling of four sisters and one brother, Babette Freniere remains unmarried while she manages her family's home, the Freniere plantation—where their chief crop is sugarcane—just north up the river from Pointe du Lac, Louis's plantation. Babette's young brother, whom Louis refers to as "young Freniere," is set to inherit the property when he comes of age; however, his life is endangered when he becomes embroiled in a duel. Although he wins the duel, the vampire Lestat drags him into the woods and kills him, leaving Babette and her plantation in peril. Louis, whom Lestat has already turned into a vampire, befriends Babette, who is now running her family's plantation. Louis's affection for her deepens, but their relationship eventually sunders shortly after Louis's slaves realize that Louis and Lestat are unnatural monsters and burn Pointe du Lac plantation to the ground. Louis seeks Babette's assistance, but she believes that they are demonic creatures, so she locks them in her basement and prays to God to exorcise them from her house. Ashamed, Louis prevents Lestat from killing Babette and then takes him from

there to New Orleans, where they establish new lodgings in a townhouse on Rue Royale.

Babette Freniere appears in *Interview with the Vampire* (1976). For more perspectives on Babette's character, read the *Alphabettery* entries **Freniere Plantation**, **Lestat de Lioncourt**, **Louis de Pointe du Lac**, and **Young Freniere**.

Baby Jenks

• VAMPIRE •

Baby Jenks is a ruthless sociopath who serves as an example of a twentieth-century Generation X teenage vampire who knows little of her culture's history, especially when it utterly destroys her. She appears in *The Queen of the Damned* (1988).

She grows up in Gun Barrel City, Texas, hating her mother, who supports them by making homemade Christian crosses out of pink seashells to sell at the local flea market. Baby Jenks loathes how her mother makes her go to church, how her mother is kinder to strangers than to her own daughter, and how she tolerates her husband's drinking.

By the time Baby Jenks is twelve years old, she brags to her mother about how she is not a virgin and listens to the rock music of the band Vampire Lestat. By the age of fourteen, Baby Jenks is a prostitute, addicted to heroin, and pregnant in Detroit. While she is having an abortion, the doctor accidentally severs an artery. As she lies bleeding to death, the vampire Killer enters her operating room and saves her life by turning her into a vampire. Baby Jenks and Killer become intimate companions. She joins the gang he leads, the Fang Gang, and rides a Harley-Davidson motorcycle alongside the other three members, Davis, Tim, and Russ. Baby Jenks enjoys being a vampire; she relishes her newfound abilities, improved eyesight, monstrous strength, acrobatic agility, and lightning speed.

The gang motorcycles across the United States, drinking blood and terrorizing mortals. Baby Jenks learns how to bury her victims and how to conceal her victims' wounds by pricking her finger and dropping her vampire blood over the wound, which closes instantly, making it appear as though her victim has died from a heart attack. Whenever the Fang Gang enters a major city, Killer warns Baby Jenks to avoid coven houses, since the vampires within are older and can destroy her. But if she is ever in a big city and finds herself in trouble with an older, more powerful vampire, she can go into a vampire bar, like the kind in New York, San Francisco, and New Orleans, where it is the rule that no vampire can kill another.

The gang carries copies of the vampire Lestat's book, but the big words are too soporific for Baby Jenks. She prefers listening to the music of the Vampire Lestat; they all do. To her, Lestat talks about things that the old, stuffier vampires will not talk about. Lestat is her idol. Even though she does not truly believe it, his music teaches her about the history of vampires, going all the way back to ancient Egypt, with Akasha and Enkil— Those Who Must Be Kept.

The Fang Gang goes to the coven house in Oklahoma City and discovers that it has been burned to the ground, with all the vampires inside completely immolated. It is the first of several completely destroyed coven houses that they see as they drive out west to San Francisco to attend the concert of the Vampire Lestat band. En route, Baby Jenks informs them that she has some business to take care of and that she will meet them south of Dallas. She drives her Harley back to her home in Gun Barrel City and kills her mother by beating her in the head with a steam iron until she stops moving. Right before her mother dies, Baby Jenks becomes strangely aware of her mother's thoughts, of the importance of love, of how the world is beautifully interconnected by doing good and avoiding evil, and how her mother forgives her daughter for being an unabashed sociopath since birth. Baby Jenks reverentially buries her mother in the backyard, and then she weeps until her father comes home. Rushing at him, she splits his skull open with a fire ax so that he is alive yet paralyzed, then she buries him in the backyard while he is thinking about the better times of his childhood.

She goes to the rendezvous south of Dallas, but the Fang Gang is not there. The coven house on Swiss Avenue is like the one in Oklahoma City, burned to the ground, along with all of its vampire members. After finding no sign of the Fang Gang, she drives for five nights, backtracking to Saint Louis. Knowing that she is a young and weak vampire, unable to last long on her own, she goes to the coven house on Central West End in the hope of finding another vampire who will accompany her to San Francisco, but she is completely surprised to discover that this coven house is like all the others—burned to the ground. Not all the vampires inside are incinerated. One vampire remains, Laurent. Having been a member of Armand's Children of Darkness in Paris and, when that disbanded, having joined the Théâtre des Vampires, Laurent is centuries old, though he appears to be only two years older than Baby Jenks. He reveals to her that two other members of the coven have been burned alive, that the same thing has happened to many coven houses on the East Coast, and perhaps other coven houses in Paris and Berlin have gone silent, and he knows that the only possible chance for them to escape this fate is for Baby Jenks to drive them west to Laurent's old acquaintance, the vampire Lestat, whose peculiar ability to adapt and survive was the catalyst that changed Armand's Children of Darkness to the Théâtre des Vampires.

Just as they leap onto Baby Jenks's motorcycle, Laurent beholds Akasha behind them. He begs her to spare their lives, but she burns him to ash. Baby Jenks leaps off her Harley and begins to feel her body bursting into flames. As her clothes burn away from her body, and her flesh burns away from her bones, before her eyes melt, she beholds Akasha, the one Lestat mentions in his music, but Baby Jenks mistakes the ancient Queen for a statue of the Blessed Virgin Mary in the alcove of a Catholic church.

For more perspectives on Baby Jenks's character, read the *Alphabettery* entries **Akasha, Armand, Children of Satan, Davis, Enkil, Fang Gang, Killer, Laurent, Lestat de Lioncourt, Russ, Those Who Must Be Kept, Tim,** and **The Vampire Lestat.**

Barbara

• VAMPIRE •

Barbara is born in the 1830s and is turned into a vampire when she is in her fifties, sometime during the year 1887, by two elder vampires. As it does for Gabrielle, the Blood gives Barbara a younger appearance, smoothing her winkles, ending the pain of age, and turning her gray hair mostly raven black. Little is known about her two makers, other than all three live in a small university city, in an old Victorian home, for many decades. One night, when Barbara goes to a symphony concert in Saint Louis, a group of marauding vampires kill her makers and burn their house to the ground.

Barbara wanders for decades in search of a purpose. She eventually finds it with Prince Lestat. She takes control of the day-to-day goings-on of his French castle, which has also become a home to his Court of the Prince, along with thousands of other vampires. She removes all the mortal staff members and organizes groups of vampires to be the Château's clerks, housekeepers, lady's maids, gentleman's valets, chauffeurs, accountants, telephone operators, tailors, and many other important and necessary positions involved in the hospitality industry. Barbara becomes the manager of Château de Lioncourt.

Barbara appears in *Blood Communion* (2018). For more perspectives on Barbara's character, read the *Alphabettery* entries **Château de Lioncourt** and **Lestat de Lioncourt.**

Baron Van Kindergarten

• ALIAS •

In *The Tale of the Body Thief* (1992), "Baron Van Kindergarten" is an alias that Lestat takes when he stays at the Ritz near the Place Vendôme in Paris, to read David Talbot's manuscripts, sprawled out on the tapestried Directoire daybed. Baron Van Kindergarten is one of numerous pseudonyms used by the rock star Elton John.

For more perspectives on the "Baron Van Kindergarten" alias, read the *Alphabettery* entry **Lestat de Lioncourt.**

Bartola di Raniari

• MORTAL •

Born only one year after Vittorio, Bartola di Raniari is his beloved younger sister and the middle child between him and her three-year-younger brother, Matteo. After their father, Lorenzo di Raniari, denies the vampire Florian's proposal, the coven of the Court of the Ruby Grail attacks their home. Bartola and Matteo are initially captured by Ursula, but temporarily saved by Vittorio, who severs her arm. Only moments later, another vam-

pire takes hold of both Bartola and Matteo and beheads them. The last thing Bartola sees is her older brother, Vittorio, swearing vengeance.

Bartola di Raniari appears only in *Vittorio the Vampire* (1999). For more perspectives on Bartola's character, read the *Alphabettery* entries **Court of the Ruby Grail, Florian, Lorenzo di Raniari, Matteo di Raniari, Vittorio di Raniari,** and **Ursula.**

Baudwin

• VAMPIRE •

Baudwin is born in the British Isles at the beginning of the first millennium. He is turned into a vampire by the very ancient Gundesanth, also called Santh, the third vampire made by Akasha and the oldest vampire in existence in the twenty-first century, after the recent deaths of Maharet, Mekare, and Khayman.

When Prince Lestat forms the Court of the

Prince at Château de Lioncourt, Baudwin is furious with Lestat because the elders of his Court of the Prince killed Baudwin's fledgling Roland as punishment for his imprisonment and torture of the Replimoid Derek. Baudwin attacks Lestat in New Orleans but is captured by Cyril, bound in iron wrappings, and taken to the dungeon at Lestat's Château. Santh appears at the Court of the

Prince, disgusted with his fledgling. He dismembers Baudwin and gives his blood to the vampires in the Château.

Baudwin appears in *Blood Communion* (2018). For more perspectives on Baudwin's character, read the *Alphabettery* entries **Château de Lioncourt, Gundesanth, Lestat de Lioncourt,** and **Santh.**

Beatrice Mayfair

• WITCH •

Born in New Orleans, Beatrice Mayfair is the granddaughter of Remy Mayfair, sister to the notorious Julien Mayfair. She often asks her parents about their Mayfair family history, but her father cannot remember any details, and her mother will not share any. In her early twenties she marries a man who soon dies of throat cancer. A few years later, she encounters Aaron Lightner, a department head for the Talamasca, in charge of organizing the Order's records of witch families, namely the Mayfair family. As Aaron becomes acquainted with many members of the family, he and Beatrice fall in love. They wed shortly after the Talamasca excommunicates Aaron for having uncovered a nefarious plot in their ranks. When excommunication fails to end his investigation, underhanded members of the Talamasca hire an assassin who kills him by running him over with a car. Beatrice greatly mourns the loss of her second husband and finds consolation only within the sprawling members of her Mayfair family.

Beatrice Mayfair appears in *Merrick* (2000). For more perspectives on Beatrice's character, read the *Alphabettery* entries **Aaron Lightner** and **Talamasca Order.**

Bela Lugosi

• SANCTUARY •

Bela Lugosi is one of several vampire bars in the Vampire Connection, bars that vampires frequent alongside mortals, where they share secretive information concerning other vampires and even find sanctuary from the threat of stronger immortals. Located in Los Angeles, Bela Lugosi is named after the cinema actor who became known for his role as Dracula in the beginning of classic Hollywood cinema in the sound era.

Bela Lugosi vampire bar is mentioned in *The Vampire Lestat* (1985). For more perspectives on Bela Lugosi bar, read the *Alphabettery* entries **Carmilla**, **Dracula's Daughter**, **Dr. Polidori**, **Lamia**, **Lord Ruthven**, **Vampire Bar**, and **Vampire Connection**.

Beloved Boss

• SOBRIQUET •

After Lestat turns the dying witch Mona Mayfair into a vampire as a favor to his companion Quinn Blackwood, Quinn and Mona both become devoted friends of Lestat and, in particular, accompany him to the secret island of the Taltos. Quinn and Mona refer to Lestat as their Beloved Boss in *Blood Canticle* (2003).

For more perspectives on Lestat as the Beloved Boss, read the *Alphabettery* entries **Lestat de Lioncourt**, **Mona Mayfair**, **Quinn Blackwood**, and **Taltos**.

Benedict

• VAMPIRE •

Benedict is the most beloved fledgling of Rhoshamandes. Both of them are duped by Amel into becoming two of the most notorious villains in recent vampire history. Benedict appears in *Prince Lestat* (2014), *Prince Lestat and the Realms of Atlantis* (2016), and *Blood Communion* (2018).

Born during the Dark Ages, in the time of the Merovingian dynasty, a member of the royal classes and a Latin scholar, Benedict is eighteen years old when Rhoshamandes imprisons him for six months so that his monastic tonsure can grow out into long locks before he turns Benedict into a vampire. Not simply raised a Christian, he also enters the monastic life and has such a deep personal encounter with God that he becomes a mystical saint in his day.

Due to his Christian belief in the Final Judgment, Benedict fears damnation for being turned into a vampire. But his fears soon subside and he comes to love Rhoshamandes as an intimate companion, although he never forsakes his great cosmic fears of an Eternal Maker and Judge. Maintaining a childlike attitude without cunning or guile, he clings to Christ's teaching that one cannot enter the Kingdom of Heaven unless he or she becomes like a little child (cf. Matthew 18:2–4). In this way, Benedict feels a deep empathy for Louis's struggle to accept his vampire nature, particularly when he reads Louis's book, *Interview with the Vampire*. Similarly, he does not simply suffer alongside Louis but also greatly relates to the Vampire Chronicles that Lestat writes. In them, he sees how much he, too, desires to cause a wild rebellion in the vampire structure of belief and behavior, but he does not have Lestat's gall or bravery.

Before the end of the first millennium of the Common Era, Rhoshamandes makes several other fledglings, whom Benedict considers to be siblings, namely what Rhoshamandes comes to call his line of de Landen vampires, which includes Allesandra, Eleni, Eugénie, Notker the Wise (who is also a monk), and Everard. When the Children of Satan attack Rhoshamandes, the wicked coven captures Allesandra, Eleni, Eugénie, and Everard. Wanting not to fight them but rather to live in peace, Benedict moves with Rhoshamandes to the north of England, where they build a fortress castle that will stand for the next thousand years. Benedict remains with Rhoshamandes during all those centuries. Together they defend and guard their land, which comes to be known as the realm of Rhoshamandes. Despite their defenses, Benedict reveals to an acquaintance the hidden location of his daytime resting place. A mortal alchemist named Magnus discovers Benedict's lair, binds him in chains, drains Benedict's blood before draining himself of blood to the point of death, and then Magnus drinks Benedict's blood, which turns him into a vampire, making Benedict his maker without Benedict's consent. Benedict is severely humiliated by the experience and becomes a laughingstock among other vampires.

To better protect Benedict, Rhoshamandes teaches him how to use the Fire Gift and the Mind Gift in defense of any other vampires who will seek either to destroy him or take his blood again. Over the years, Benedict uses his powerful abilities against numerous foes and practice objects, such as blowing massively heavy doors off their hinges.

In the twenty-first century, when the spirit of Amel becomes very discontented living in the wounded mind of the witch twin Mekare, Amel convinces Rhoshamandes to kill Maharet and Khayman in order to devour Mekare's brain and take Amel, the Sacred Core, into himself, making Rhoshamandes the new host of vampire existence. Benedict helps Rhoshamandes decapitate Maharet and Khayman and then futilely kidnap Lestat's son, Viktor, in an effort to fulfill Amel's plan. When Lestat severs Rhoshamandes's arm and brands him with the mark of Cain, stating that no vampire is to harm Rhoshamandes for his crimes against Maharet and Khayman, Benedict retreats with Rhoshamandes back into their fortress castle, where they remain until another vampire, Roland, invites them to his compound. There, Roland shows Rhoshamandes and Benedict a Replimoid alien named Derek from the planet Bravenna. Roland then explains to Rhoshamandes and Benedict how Rhoshamandes might use Derek to regain power among the vampires. But in time, this plan fails, and when a group of vampires destroy Roland, Benedict helps convince Rhoshamandes to end his vengeance on Lestat and the other immortals and to live in peace with them.

Benedict lives for a time on Saint Rayne, a private island sanctuary owned by Rhoshamandes, but he leaves the island and his maker because of a greater attraction to Prince Lestat. He lives at Château de Lioncourt, where he learns that the Court of the Prince desires to vengefully destroy Rhoshamandes for killing Maharet and Khayman. He agrees with the judgment and feels that he, too, should be destroyed for his compliance. He kills himself in the middle of the Court and allows fledgling vampires to drink his blood until nothing remains but his husk. They burn his body and scatter the ashes.

For more perspectives on Benedict's character, read the *Alphabettery* entries **Allesandra**, **Amel**, **Children of Satan**, **Eleni**, **Eugénie**, **Everard**, **Fire Gift**, **Khayman**, **Maharet**, **Maker**, **Mekare**, **Mind Gift**, **Notker the Wise**, **Rhoshamandes**, **Roland**, **Sacred Core**, and **Viktor**.

Benjamin the Devil

• ALIAS •

During the rule of Rhoshamandes in northern France and England, the five-thousand-year-old Khayman is known as Benjamin the Devil by the Talamasca. They study him under that name, noting that he can be a mischief maker, although he is always protective of innocent mortals and vampires alike.

Khayman's alias is revealed in *Prince Lestat* (2014). For more on the "Benjamin the Devil" alias, read the *Alphabettery* entries **Khayman**, **Rhoshamandes**, and **Talamasca Order**.

Benji Mahmoud

• VAMPIRE •

Benji and his beloved Sybelle are Armand's dearest companions in the late twentieth century. Like Lestat before him, Benji uses modern media to summon all vampires together into a cohesive race. He appears in *The Vampire Armand* (1998), *Prince Lestat* (2014), *Prince Lestat and the Realms of Atlantis* (2016), and *Blood Communion* (2018).

Son of Abdulla Mahmoud and born to a Bedouin family living in Israel, Benjamin

Mahmoud is young when he is bought and imported to the United States. By the age of twelve, Benji, as he is called, becomes the live-in servant of twenty-five-year-old Sybelle and her violently abusive older brother, who is forcing her to perform concerts as their only source of income. When they come to New York City to perform a concert, Benji prays for spiritual assistance as he witnesses the escalating abuse that Sybelle's older brother inflicts upon her while she works tirelessly to perfect her piano playing. Although Benji's prayers are in fluent Arabic, they are understood perfectly by the vampire Armand, who recently tried to commit suicide by flying into New York's winter sun. Having failed, he falls under an overhang on an abandoned building and is now covered by mountains of snowfall.

Drifting in and out of consciousness, Armand telepathically summons Benji and Sybelle from the nearby hotel, who free him from the hardened ice with household tools. They secretly bring him back to their room, where Armand foresees that Sybelle's brother will eventually kill both Sybelle and Benji. With the strength of his Mind Gift, he projects an image of how he looked when Marius turned him into a vampire—an unburned, seventeen-year-old young man with a head of beautiful auburn curls. Benji prays to Armand again, referring to him as a dybbuk (the malicious spirit of a disembodied soul), begging him to protect Sybelle. Armand kills Sybelle's brother effortlessly, but he is still too weak either to heal his severe burns or leave the hotel room. To help his dybbuk, Benji goes to the hotel bar, finds a DEA officer, lies to him about a stash of cocaine under a corpse

in their hotel room, and lures the officer back to the room, where Armand drinks all his blood. Benji waits with Sybelle in the hotel room while Armand disposes of the officer's body and drinks the blood of several more victims for the next few hours until he is fully healed.

Benji and Sybelle welcome Armand to stay with them for several months. Benji accompanies Armand and Sybelle to visit Lestat, who has fallen into a peculiar comatose state. Armand introduces Benji and Sybelle to his maker, Marius, and asks Marius to care for Benji and Sybelle temporarily while he attempts to drink Lestat's blood, to gain some insight into Lestat's recent journey with Memnoch the Devil. Marius agrees, but after Armand leaves, Marius turns Benji and Sybelle into vampires, as a gift to his fledgling. At first, Armand is furious with Marius. But Marius and Daniel Malloy (Armand's fledgling) both help Armand realize that if Armand had turned Benji and Sybelle into vampires, their relationship would have deteriorated, just as Armand's relationship with Daniel deteriorated because of Daniel's inferior power, as well as because of the severed telepathic link between maker and fledgling. Furthermore, Marius's ancient blood not only makes Benji and Sybelle equal with Armand, but it also allows Armand to communicate with them on an intimate telepathic level.

Despite being limited to his twelve-year-old's body, Benji matures into a man interiorly and begins an internet radio station/website dedicated exclusively to vampires. Broadcast every night out of the coven's Trinity Gate townhouse on New York's Upper East Side, Benji's program reaches the

Undead all over the world. In the beginning, he speaks exclusively to vampires, trying to mask his voice by speaking low under Sybelle's beautiful piano playing. As the popularity of vampire fiction grows, he stops hiding his voice, broadcasting openly, not caring if mortals hear him. If anyone calls the show, he can tell by the sound of their voice if they are living or Undead. Similar to the music and lyrics of Lestat's rock band, Benji's message is a supplication to all vampires, especially the ancient ones, beseeching them for modern leadership in a modern world.

Around that same time, the spirit of Amel, the Sacred Core of all vampire existence, desiring to leave Mekare's wounded mind and enter the mind of a saner vampire, begins possessing older vampires with the Fire Gift and immolating scores of younger vampires. Inadvertently complying with Benji's wish, Armand uses Benji's radio program to summon the vampire coven to a ball at Trinity Gate. Benji endorses Lestat when he takes the spirit of Amel from Mekare. After the Replimoids move Amel from Lestat's mind to a Replimoid body, Benji becomes a loyal member of the Court of the Prince at Château de Lioncourt, supporting Lestat's regime, even though he is no longer the host carrier.

For more perspectives on Benji's character, read the *Alphabettery* entries **Amel**, **Armand**, **Daniel Malloy**, **Dybbuk**, **Fledgling**, **Maker**, **Marius**, **Mekare**, **Memnoch**, **Mind Gift**, **Sacred Core**, **Sybelle**, and **Trinity Gate**.

𝕭𝖊𝖙 𝕳𝖆 𝕾𝖔𝖍𝖆𝖗

• SANCTUARY •

Bet ha sohar has been the dungeon for Rhoshamandes's home in the Loire Valley for hundreds of years. Although his home is adapted from a Roman Catholic monastery, Rhoshamandes creates the *bet ha sohar* dungeon underneath a nearby forest. Therein he keeps his mortal and immortal prisoners. In the twenty-first century, after Benedict kills himself at Château de Lioncourt, Rhoshamandes takes his revenge by kidnapping Gabrielle, Louis, and Marius and holding them prisoner in *bet ha sohar*. When Lestat kills Rhoshamandes, the last words he hears from Rhoshamandes's lips are *"bet ha sohar."* Lestat finds the hidden dungeon with the aid of his Court of the Prince and frees his two fledglings and his beloved friend.

Bet ha sohar appears in *Blood Communion* (2018). For more perspectives on *bet ha sohar*, read the *Alphabettery* entries **Allesandra**, **Benedict**, **Eleni**, **Lestat de Lioncourt**, and **Rhoshamandes**.

Bianca Solderini

• VAMPIRE •

Bianca Solderini is one of Marius's greatest love interests, both as a mortal and as an immortal. She helps Armand become Marius's fledgling, and she eventually becomes a protector of Those Who Must Be Kept. In modern times, she participates in the development of Sevraine's Caves of Gold. Bianca appears in *The Vampire Armand* (1998), *Blood and Gold* (2001), *Prince Lestat* (2014), *Prince Lestat and the Realms of Atlantis* (2016), and *Blood Communion* (2018).

Bianca Solderini is born around the turn of the sixteenth century in Venice into a wealthy family. She is cared for by her brothers until her teens. When they die, her wealth and security are transferred to her kinsmen, and in particular a Florentine banker who has evil intentions for her. Threatening her with poverty and destitution, he provides her with a beautiful home and entertainment under the condition that she operate as his assassin. She is required to entertain numerous guests while her kinsman selects one specific guest (usually someone to whom he is indebted) for her to kill by lacing his drink with poison.

Marius first encounters Bianca when she is nearly twenty years old, a popular courtesan who has secretly murdered many people, for the sake of her safety, at the command of her wicked kinsman. Her house constantly lodges numerous artists, only upon the condition that they entertain her. Marius considers her to be a ravishing beauty who should have been the model for a Botticelli painting,

but he has difficulty using the Mind Gift on her to read her thoughts. She is so skilled at entertaining guests that, just by reading their facial expressions, she appears to have the ability to read minds. The talent only makes Marius desire her even more. Despite the fact that he cannot read her mind completely, he discerns that she possesses a secret anguish, but she conceals it so well that he almost misses it. He considers her to be as pure as a blank canvas upon which he can create a magnificent vampire. When he is finally able to read her thoughts, perceiving how murderous she is, he realizes that she is not as pure as he originally assumed and balks at the idea of turning her into a vampire.

At length, Marius comes to the conclusion that he must free her from this prison of murder. So on the very same night that he reveals himself to his young mortal ward Amadeo, who will later become the vampire Armand, Marius and Amadeo attend a banquet where Bianca's kinsmen are all drinking heavily and getting drunk, including the wicked Florentine banker. Marius sits with each kinsman individually, conversing with one merrily before subtly killing him and slumping his dead body forward to make him appear passed out. In this way, he moves from victim to victim. Finally, Marius kills the last one, and he is so full of blood that his skin looks no longer porcelain white but fresh with human ruddiness.

Following this, when the lecherous Lord

Harlech trespasses in Marius's palazzo and kills several of Marius's mortal wards and mortally wounds Amadeo, Bianca cares for the dying Amadeo until Marius turns him into a vampire. As Marius teaches Amadeo how to survive in his new immortal existence, they both maintain their affectionate relationship with Bianca. One night, not long afterward, Marius's palazzo is attacked once more, only this time by the Roman coven of the Children of Satan, who are furious at Marius for violating their Great Laws. Led by Santino, the Children of Satan burn Marius's palazzo to the ground, capture Amadeo, and almost burn Marius to death.

Badly wounded, Marius summons Bianca to him with his Mind Gift. He drinks her blood to recover his strength and offers to turn her into a vampire. She willingly accepts and helps bring him to the shrine where he keeps Akasha and Enkil. Bianca remains with Marius while he recovers from his wounds, and she assists in caring for Those Who Must Be Kept. During that time, she is even allowed to drink Akasha's blood and grow in vampiric strength. Their devotion to each other increases, yet Marius still pines deeply for his other fledgling, Pandora.

A few centuries later, after Marius is fully recovered and ready to rejoin society, when he is informed by a member of the Talamasca named Raymond Gallant that he has heard reports that Pandora is being held captive by the vampire Arjun in Dresden, Marius takes Bianca with him to Dresden to search for her. It is Bianca who first discovers that Pandora and Arjun are attending a ball at the Duke's palace. She gives this information to Marius, despite her jealousy of Pandora

for many years. Marius finds Pandora at the ball and begs her to leave Arjun for him; he even promises to leave Bianca for her. Bianca overhears this exchange and bitterly abandons Marius.

Bianca roams for many years until she finally finds a home with Sevraine, in the golden caves beneath Cappadocia, where she lives in a coven with Allesandra, Eleni, and Eugénie. These five vampires live together for many years in an all-female coven, occasionally visited by spirits and ghosts, such as the incarnate spirit of Gremt and the ghost of Raymond Gallant.

In the twenty-first century, when the spirit of Amel begins speaking to the vampire race as the mysterious Voice and threatens their existence, Lestat and Gabrielle go to Sevraine's golden caves in an effort to find Rhoshamandes, who is being coerced by Amel to commit atrocities against other vampires. Bianca is the one who first greets them, shows them around the caves that are now full of beautifully decorated rooms, as ornate as a palace, and then introduces them to the other members of the coven.

Once Amel is finally released from Lestat and in a new body, Bianca leaves Sevraine's compound in Cappadocia and goes to Château de Lioncourt, Lestat's vampire castle in the Auvergne. She reunites with many vampires she has known over the centuries, even Marius. After all that time, they feel enough of a reconciliation between each other to step out upon the ballroom floor and dance together for hours.

For more perspectives on Bianca Solderini's character, read the *Alphabettery* entries **Akasha, Allesandra, Amadeo, Amel,**

Arjun, Armand, Eleni, Enkil, Eugénie, Gabrielle, Great Laws, Gremt Stryker Knollys, Lestat de Lioncourt, Lord Har-lech, Marius, Mind Gift, Pandora, Raymond Gallant, Rhoshamandes, Santino, Sevraine, and **Those Who Must Be Kept**.

Big Ramona

• MORTAL •

Big Ramona runs the kitchen at Blackwood Farm when Quinn is a teenager. She is the mother of Little Ida and the grandmother of Little Ida's daughter, Jasmine, who will give birth to Quinn's son, Jerome. Big Ramona is called "big" not because she is overweight but because she is the grandmother on the property. Beginning in his boyhood, Quinn sleeps chastely in the same bed as Big Ram-ona's daughter, but after Little Ida dies when Quinn is thirteen years old, he begins sleeping in Big Ramona's bed. She makes him pray every night before they go to sleep.

Big Ramona appears in *Blackwood Farm* (2002). For more perspectives on her character, read the *Alphabettery* entries **Blackwood Farm**, **Jasmine**, **Little Ida**, and **Quinn Blackwood**.

Blackwood Farm

• VAMPIRE CHRONICLE •

An adventure with Lestat, this ninth book in the Vampire Chronicles is written by Tarquin "Quinn" Blackwood and how he grows up on Blackwood Farm haunted by the ghost of his long-dead twin brother, Goblin. Quinn sees a stranger on his property, living on Sugar Devil Island. After several confrontations, the stranger attacks Quinn. Needing hospitalization for his wounds, Quinn encounters Mona Mayfair at Mayfair Medical Center, and they fall in love. Before they can pursue their relationship further, Quinn is taken to Europe by his aunt Queen, where he is turned into a vampire by the same stranger living on his island, the hermaphrodite vampire, Petronia. Quinn learns how to be a vampire and returns to Blackwood Farm, where Goblin attacks him severely. Quinn seeks the help of the vampire Lestat, who employs the aid of his friend and former Talamasca member David Talbot, who in turn enlists the aid of his former Talamasca protégé, **Merrick**

Mayfair, a witch in the Mayfair family and a fledgling of Louis. Merrick performs an exorcism that banishes Goblin's soul to the light of the afterlife, yet she loses her life in the process.

For more perspectives on this Vampire Chronicle, read the *Alphabettery* entries **Aunt Queen**, **Blackwood Farm**, **David Talbot**, **Garwain**, **Goblin**, **Lestat de Lioncourt**, **Louis de Pointe du Lac**, **Mayfair Medical Center**, **Merrick Mayfair**, **Mona Mayfair**, **Quinn Blackwood**, **Petronia**, **Sugar Devil Island**, **Talamasca Order**, and **The Vampire Chronicles**.

Blackwood Farm

• SANCTUARY •

Blackwood Farm is the plantation property north of New Orleans, across Lake Pontchartrain, in the Louisiana swampland, that Manfred Blackwood purchases in the seventeenth century, where he and his first wife, Virginia Lee, build Blackwood Manor. Along with the plantation, Blackwood Farm property includes Sugar Devil Swamp and Sugar Devil Island, where Manfred Blackwood murders his second wife, Rebecca Stanford, with the assistance of the vampire Petronia. Several generations of Manfred's descendants live on Blackwood Farm into the twentieth century, when Quinn Blackwood inherits the vast property with all the ghosts that haunt the land.

Blackwood Farm is featured in the 2002 novel of the same name. For more perspectives on the Blackwood Farm plantation, read the *Alphabettery* entries **Blackwood Manor**, **Manfred Blackwood**, **Petronia**, **Quinn Blackwood**, **Rebecca Stanford**, **Sugar Devil Island**, **Sugar Devil Swamp**, **Talamasca Order**, and **Virginia Lee Blackwood**.

Blackwood Manor

• SANCTUARY •

Blackwood Manor is the house built by Manfred Blackwood in the seventeenth century on his lush Louisiana property, Blackwood Farm, in Sugar Devil Swamp. Over the past several centuries, Blackwood Manor has served as a hotel for many guests. Several generations of the Blackwoods even live in Blackwood Manor's numerous rooms. Most of the family members die in Blackwood Manor, and when their souls cannot rest in the family crypt, their ghosts can be seen by family and guests roaming the halls and rummaging through bedrooms. For instance, the ghost of Manfred's son, William, can be seen in his old bedroom, while the ghost of Manfred's daughter, Camille, can be seen tiptoeing up the stairs to the attic. In the twentieth century, Quinn Blackwood inherits Blackwood Farm and Blackwood Manor, which Lestat visits and finds enjoyable.

Blackwood Manor appears in *Blackwood Farm* (2002). For more perspectives on Blackwood Manor, read the *Alphabettery* entries **Blackwood Farm**, **Camille Blackwood**, **Lestat de Lioncourt**, **Manfred Blackwood**, **Quinn Blackwood**, **Sugar Devil Swamp**, and **William Blackwood**.

Blessed Alice

• MORTAL •

Blessed Alice is the wife of Gravier Blackwood, grandson of Manfred Blackwood, founder of Blackwood Farm. She and Gravier have one son, Thomas "Pops" Blackwood, who will be the grandfather of Quinn Blackwood, vampire, paramour of Mona Mayfair, and companion of Lestat.

Blessed Alice appears in *Blackwood Farm* (2002). For more perspectives on her character, read the *Alphabettery* entries **Blackwood Farm**, **Gravier Blackwood**, **Lestat de Lioncourt**, **Manfred Blackwood**, **Mona Mayfair**, **Pops**, **Quinn Blackwood**, and **Sugar Devil Swamp**.

Blessed Sacrament

• HONORIFIC •

"Blessed Sacrament" is a term that refers to the sacrament of the Eucharist in the Catholic Church. For Catholics, a sacrament is a sign of God's grace in the world effectively saving souls. The Eucharist is a sacrament that happens during the Mass, when the priest transubstantiates bread and wine into the real presence of Jesus Christ.

In *The Vampire Lestat* (1985), when Lestat and Gabrielle are fleeing from Armand and the Children of Darkness in the seventeenth century, they hide under an altar in a Catholic church while Mass is being celebrated. In *The Queen of the Damned* (1988), Jesse asks David if he truly believes in the presence of Christ in the sacrament of the Eucharist. In *Memnoch the Devil* (1995), Lestat tells David that if the Devils started chasing him down Fifth Avenue, he would run into Saint Patrick's Cathedral and fall to his knees before the Blessed Sacrament, asking God to forgive him.

For more perspectives on the Blessed Sacrament, read the *Alphabettery* entries **San Juan Diego** and **Veronica's Veil**.

The Blood

• IDIOM •

A phrase that does not refer to the common blood of mortals, "the Blood" most specifically refers to the supernatural blood of vampires. The Blood of immortals becomes different from the blood of mortals more than six thousand years ago, when the spirit of Amel, who enjoys the taste of blood, fuses with the mortal blood of Akasha, who is dying from multiple stab wounds. The fusion is possible because Amel was a mortal more than ten thousand years ago, but he was abducted by an alien race known as the Brevennans, who altered his genetic code to make him superior to other mortals. When he died, the material elements of his spirit still harbored that enhanced genetic code for the next few thousand years. Upon fusing with Akasha, his genetic code, along with his transformation from corporeal to ethereal, alters her blood with the same genetic enhancements, creating a supernatural metamorphosis through which she evolves into the first vampire. As she makes many fledglings over the centuries, and as those fledglings make more fledglings, her blood becomes known as the Sacred Fount and is venerated by her vampire followers as inviolable. To be made a vampire is to be brought into the Blood. And to be a vampire is to be in the Blood. Thus, the Blood becomes a sacred institution among all vampires and is by many deemed to be the greatest gift that can be given.

For more perspectives on the idiom "the Blood," read the *Alphabettery* entries **Akasha**, **Amel**, **Bravennans**, **Fledglings**, and **Sacred Fount**.

Blood and Gold

• VAMPIRE CHRONICLE •

As his fledgling Armand, his eternal paramour, Pandora, and his beloved Lestat, the vampire Marius now writes his tale, about how he begins life as a Roman nobleman at the outset of the Common Era, in this eighth book of the Vampire Chronicles. In his twenties, he seeks to marry the twelve-year-old Lydia, who will later become his fledgling Pandora. He is kidnapped by Druids and turned into a vampire by the four-thousand-year-old Teskhamen, who is badly burned and who tells Marius to discover the fate of Akasha and Enkil, the first vampires. Marius goes to Alexandria, steals Akasha and Enkil from the Elder, who is keeping them, and becomes the new protector of Those Who Must Be Kept and, by default, the protector of all vampires, who suffer when Akasha and Enkil suffer. For the next two thousand years, Marius cares for the Mother and the Father, taking them all over the world, from Rome to the Alps and even all the way to the Canadian wilderness in the north. During that time, he befriends companions, namely Mael, who was one of Marius's Druid captors, and Avicus, who is as ancient as Marius's maker, Teskhamen. When he encounters Lydia, now grown into a woman and hiding in the city of Antioch, Marius turns her into a vampire. They remain together for many centuries, but ultimately separate after a bitter argument. A few centuries later, Marius befriends the mortal Bianca and turns Armand into a vampire. But when Santino captures Armand and destroys Marius, Marius turns Bianca into a vampire, and they remain companions for the next few centuries. In the seventeenth century, Marius encounters the vampire Lestat, who awakens the Queen with his peerless boldness. Marius protects Those Who Must Be Kept until the twentieth century, when the vampire Lestat once more awakens Akasha, who kills Enkil, buries Marius under crushing ice, and rampages across the globe, immolating her children. In the end, Marius is reunited with Pandora and Armand when they defeat Akasha, and he gets his revenge against Santino with the help of the vampire Thorne.

For more perspectives on this Vampire Chronicle, read the *Alphabettery* entries **Armand, Avicus, Bianca Solderini, The Elder, Enkil, Lestat de Lioncourt, Mael, Pandora, Santino, Teskhamen, Thorne, Those Who Must Be Kept**, and **The Vampire Chronicles**.

Blood Canticle

• VAMPIRE CHRONICLE •

Following the story in the ninth book in the Vampire Chronicles, *Blackwood Farm* (2002), the tenth book, *Blood Canticle* (2003), picks up the love between Tarquin "Quinn" Blackwood and Mona Mayfair, dying in the hospital due to having given birth to her Taltos child, Morrigan. As a favor to Quinn, Lestat saves Mona's life by turning her into a vampire so that she and Quinn can be together forever. Briefly, they try to keep Mona's transformation a secret from the Mayfair family, during which time Lestat and Rowan discover deep feelings for each other. Mona desires to find her child, who has run away with the Taltos Ashlar to a secret island where the Taltos live safely away from mortals who seek to harm them. Lestat promises to help his fledgling Mona and her paramour, Quinn. Through Maharet's guidance, they discover the secret location of the Taltos' island, but when Lestat, Quinn, and Mona arrive, they learn that Ashlar and Morrigan's son Silas has

incited a civil war and incited Rodrigo and his Drug Merchants to take over the island and kill most of the inhabitants, including Ashlar and Morrigan. Lestat, Mona, and Quinn defeat the Drug Merchants and invite the remaining Taltos to return with them to New Orleans, where they can remain at Mayfair Medical Center, be a part of their family, and live in greater safety and peace. The Taltos agree. Once everyone is settled in their new life, Quinn and Mona depart with the ancient vampire Khayman, who teaches them about being vampires in the modern world.

For more perspectives on this Vampire Chronicle, read the *Alphabettery* entries **Ashlar**, **Drug Merchants**, **Khayman**, **Lestat de Lioncourt**, **Maharet**, **Mayfair Medical Center**, **Mona Mayfair**, **Morrigan Mayfair**, **Quinn Blackwood**, **Rodrigo**, **Rowan Mayfair**, **Silas**, and **Taltos**.

Blood Communion

• VAMPIRE CHRONICLE •

Even though Amel has been completely removed from Lestat, the Court of the Prince at Château de Lioncourt still desires Lestat to be their Prince. He accepts and completely

renovates the Château along with the Village de Lioncourt for his Court of the Prince. Lestat receives a letter from the vampire Dmitri Fontayne, asking for his assistance.

Lestat goes to New Orleans to assist Dmitri, but is attacked by the ancient vampire Baudwin, who despises the new Court of the Prince. Cyril binds Baudwin in iron bars, hindering his vampire gifts, before imprisoning Baudwin in the Château de Lioncourt dungeon. Meanwhile, the Court of the Prince desires to destroy Rhoshamandes for killing Maharet and Khayman. When Benedict destroys himself in the court, Rhoshamandes vengefully kidnaps Gabrielle, Louis, and Marius. Lestat destroys Rhoshamandes and saves his two fledglings and his beloved friend. Baudwin's maker Santh appears in the Court and destroys Baudwin. Santh reveals that he is the oldest vampire in the world, the third vampire made by Akasha, but he loves Lestat and vows fealty to the Prince of the Vampires. Blood drinkers from all over the world, and from various histories, appear and also vow fealty to Lestat. He gathers them all under his roof, referring to them as his Blood Communion.

For more perspectives on this Vampire Chronicle, read the *Alphabettery* entries **Baudwin, Château de Lioncourt, Dmitri Fontayne, Lestat de Lioncourt, Rhoshamandes**, and **Santh**.

Blood Communion

• IDIOM •

The "Blood Communion" is an idiom coined by Lestat, which he uses to refer to the company of vampires who live in his newly renovated Château de Lioncourt in the twenty-first century. Forming an official Court of the Prince ruled by Prince Lestat, myriads of vampires from all over the world gather in peace, as a unified race, without fear of persecution or internal conflicts. With the ancient covens and blood feuds finally ended, the Blood Communion becomes the family Lestat always desired, a community of like-minded individuals in pursuit of excellence, beauty, and truth.

The Blood Communion appears in the eponymous book *Blood Communion* (2018). For more perspectives on the Blood Communion, read the *Alphabettery* entries **Château de Lioncourt** and **Lestat de Lioncourt**.

Blood Curse

• VAMPIRE ABILITY •

Vampires have the ability to curse another vampire drinking their blood. The curse nauseates the other vampire, who is forced to stop drinking blood. The curse dissipates after several days. For more immediate healing, the cursed vampire must drink the blood of a vampire who is stronger than the cursing immortal.

This happens when Lestat tries to drink from Baudwin, but Baudwin curses Lestat, which forces him to stop drinking Baudwin's blood. The curse leaves Lestat feeling nauseated until he drinks Gregory's ancient blood, which restores his health.

Blood cursing appears in *Blood Communion* (2018). For more perspectives on the Blood Curse, read the *Alphabettery* entries **Baudwin**, **Cloud Gift**, **Crippling Gift**, **Dark Gift**, **Fire Gift**, **Lestat de Lioncourt**, **Mind Gift**, and **Spell Gift**.

Blood Drinker

• IDIOM •

More than four thousand years before the Common Era, after Akasha and Enkil become vampires, they satisfy their bloodlust by drinking the blood of countless victims. Thus, they become known as the Drinkers of the Blood. The word "vampire" will not come into existence until the latter half of the second millennium of the Common Era. As the phrase "Drinker of the Blood" is handed on to the next generation of vampire fledglings, and as vampirism spreads across the known world, the idiom shortens to simply "blood drinker." It is only in the final few centuries of the Common Era's second millennium that blood drinkers become aware of a new mortal term for them: "vampire." Marius, for instance, does not hear the term until the fifteenth century when he meets Raymond Gallant, a member of the Talamasca Order, who informs him of how the Order watches and increases their knowledge of vampires like him. Despite the widespread use of the term "vampire" into the twenty-first century, Children of the Millennia continue to refer to themselves by the old term "blood drinkers."

The idiom most often occurs in *The Queen of the Damned* (1988), *Blood and Gold* (2001), and *Prince Lestat* (2014). For more perspectives on the idiom "blood drinker," read the *Alphabettery* entries **Akasha**, **Amel**, **The**

Blood, Children of the Millennia, Drinker of the Blood, Enkil, Fledgling, Lestat de Lioncourt, Raymond Gallant, and Talamasca Order.

Blood Genesis

• LEGEND •

The Blood Genesis tells the story of how spirits lived in the Time Before the Moon, namely the spirit of Amel, who is summoned by Maharet and Mekare and who fuses with the blood of Akasha to create the first immortal blood drinker. Akasha begets Enkil and Khayman into the Blood. Khayman begets Mekare, and Mekare begets Maharet, and the three of them beget the First Brood, which fights against Akasha's begotten army, the Queens Blood. The First Brood and the Queens Blood fight for centuries until Akasha and Enkil are captured and imprisoned for so long that they become statuelike, and no one can remember why they must be imprisoned. By then, the story of the Mother and the Father is mere legend—a Blood Genesis.

The Blood Genesis can be read in *The Vampire Lestat* (1985), *The Queen of the Damned* (1988), *Prince Lestat* (2014), and *Prince Lestat and the Realms of Atlantis* (2016). For more perspectives on the Blood Genesis, read the *Alphabettery* entries **Akasha**, **Amel**, **Enkil**, **Khayman**, **Maharet**, and **Mekare**.

Blood Kindred

• COVEN •

When Gregory Duff Collingsworth and Chrysanthe welcome Flavius into their home, Gregory refers to their coven as the Blood Kindred. Unlike most covens that dissolve in a few years, the Blood Kindred lasts for centuries, all the way into the twenty-first century. During this time, the Blood Kindred welcomes many more vampires, such as Avicus, Zenobia, and Davis.

The Blood Kindred appears in *Prince Lestat* (2014). For more perspectives on the Blood Kindred coven, read the *Alphabettery* entries **Avicus**, **Chrysanthe**, **Davis**, **Flavius**, **Gregory Duff Collingsworth**, and **Zenobia**.

Blood Spouse

• IDIOM •

When two vampires decide that they truly desire to spend immortality together, they will make a solemn and moral commitment to remain Blood Spouses, a vampire bride or wife and her vampire bridegroom or husband. An example of Blood Spouses who remain together for centuries are Zenobia and Avicus, and Chrysanthe and Gregory.

Avicus and Zenobia meet in the sixth century in Constantinople, when he is more than four thousand years old, and she is less than one hundred. They fall almost immediately in love and stay together for the next six centuries.

Gregory and Chrysanthe encounter each other in the third century and live together in Carthage in North Africa, where they build a small coven of vampires called the Blood Kindred. Though he is more than four thousand years old at the time, and she is his new fledgling from that era, they continue as Blood Spouses through the twenty-first century.

Blood Spouses appear in *Blood and Gold* (2001) and *Prince Lestat* (2014). For more perspectives on Blood Spouses, read the *Alphabettery* entries **Avicus**, **Chrysanthe**, **Gregory Duff Collingsworth**, and **Zenobia**.

Blood Thief

• IDIOM •

In *Blood Canticle* (2003), the idiom "blood thief" is often used by Taltos, such as Ashlar and Morrigan's son Oberon, to describe vampires, in particular the vampire Lestat, as Oberon observes how Lestat, Quinn, and his grandmother Mona Mayfair dispatch Rodrigo and his Drug Merchants from the Secret Isle.

For more perspectives on blood thieves, read the *Alphabettery* entries **Ashlar**, **Chrysanthe**, **Drug Merchants**, **Lestat de Lioncourt**, **Morrigan Mayfair**, **Oberon**, **Quinn Blackwood**, **Rodrigo**, **Secret Isle**, and **Taltos**.

Born to Darkness

• IDIOM •

A phrase highly popular among the Children of Satan, "Born to Darkness" is a euphemism, not for being physically born, as an infant is born from the womb, but rather for being turned from a mortal into a vampire. A spiritual rebirth, a change from being a beloved child of Heaven to a minion of Hell, "Born to Darkness" essentially means that the mortal, who is a mortal no more but an immortal vampire, is inextricably in the service of Satan, damned to do dark deeds eternally, to be an instigator of suffering and torment in the world, and to continue to turn God's children away from the hope of eternal salvation and peace.

The idiom appears in *The Vampire Lestat* (1985). For more perspectives on being Born to Darkness, read the *Alphabettery* entries **Children of Darkness** and **Children of Satan**.

Boulevard du Temple

• SANCTUARY •

Boulevard du Temple is the street where Lestat begins his acting career as a mortal in eighteenth-century Paris.

Similar to modern-day Broadway in Manhattan's Theater District, Boulevard du Temple is the popular district in eighteenth- and nineteenth-century Paris where numerous theater houses entertain the Parisian populace nightly. Among theaters such as Théâtre de Nicolet, Théâtre de l'Ambigu-Comique, Théâtre des Associés, Théâtre des Élèves pour la Danse de l'Opéra, and several others, there resides the small but popular Renaud's House of Thesbians, where a young actor named Lestat de Valois becomes very popular performing *Lelio and Flaminia*.

The theater district continues to be a highly in-vogue area in Paris all the way through the nineteenth century, when it is commonly referred to as the Boulevard du Crime, due to the number of highly popular crime melodramas shown in the district's theaters every night. It is in this setting that Louis and Claudia visit the renovated Renaud's House of Thesbians, which is now called Théâtre des Vampires.

Boulevard du Temple appears in *The Vampire Lestat* (1985). For more perspectives on the Boulevard du Temple, read the *Alphabettery* entries **Lelio, Lestat de Lioncourt, Lestat de Valois, Renaud, Renaud's House of Thesbians**, and *Lelio and Flaminia*.

Brat Prince

• SOBRIQUET •

The title "Brat Prince" is meant to be a derogatory reference to the vampire Lestat, who is the Queen's new paramour. It was first coined by Marius after Lestat's music awakens Akasha, who kills her king-husband before burying Marius under an avalanche of ice and then enacts a plan of mass destruction through fire. When Lestat hears the title, he loves it and proudly owns it as his. Until he becomes Prince Lestat, host carrier of Amel, the Sacred Core, he is the unofficial Brat Prince of all vampirekind, behaving rebelliously when the opportunity suits his desire.

Occasionally others will refer to Lestat with this title, such as Amel in fury or David Talbot when he is showing a little disdain or Gabrielle teasingly, reminding him how much he loves being called the Brat Prince.

The sobriquet appears in *The Queen of the Damned* (1988) and *Prince Lestat* (2014). For more perspectives on the sobriquet, read the *Alphabettery* entries **Amel**, **David Talbot**, **Gabrielle**, **Marius**, **Lestat de Lioncourt**, and **Sacred Core**.

Bravenna

• SANCTUARY •

Bravenna is the home world of the alien race known as the Bravennans. More than ten thousand years before the Common Era, they discover that planet Earth can provide them with an invaluable source of nutrition and sustenance, as they feed on the psychic energy of human suffering. To increase this resource, Bravennan scientists abduct a mortal from Earth named Amel. They genetically enhance him to make him immortal, then they return him to Earth, with the expectation that he will aid their consumption of human suffer-

ing. Amel rebels and protects Earth. Bravenna then wages a small war against the planet, creating troops of humanoid soldiers called Replimoids to attack Amel. But he is able to stop them or convert them to help him protect Earth from Bravenna. With superior technology, Bravenna sends a meteor shower across the galaxy that pummels planet Earth, right on top of Amel's greatest creation, the great city of Atlantis, and sinks the otherworldly metropolis into the sea, and Amel along with it.

Bravenna appears in *Prince Lestat and the Realms of Atlantis* (2016). For more perspectives on the planet Bravenna, read the *Alphabettery* entries **Amel**, **Bravennans**, and **Replimoid**.

Bravennans

• MORTALS •

Bravennans are alien beings who, by trying to exploit the human race, inadvertently initiate the creation of the vampire race. They call themselves the Parents, but they could also be considered the grandparents of vampires. They appear in *Prince Lestat and the Realms of Atlantis* (2016).

With luminous eyes, like huge owl eyes, large smiling mouths with thin lips, and massive wings, the Bravennans are an alien race from the planet Bravenna, many light-years from planet Earth. They discover a way to transform the psychic energy of human suffering into physical energy, and they depend upon the suffering as a food source. To facilitate a more efficient means of supplying themselves with food, they abduct an earthling named Amel, transform him into a superhuman, and then send him back to Earth on a mission to repair their transmission stations, although he has no idea of their true plans. When he discovers that he is doing more harm to people than good, out of his own enhanced DNA he develops a substance that he refers to as luracastria and that confuses the Bravennans, who can receive no transmissions through it. Amel covers their transmission stations and his humans in vast cities made of luracastria. But the Bravennans make humanlike creatures called Replimoids. The Replimoids are taught to call the Bravennans their Parents, and the Parents teach them to distrust Amel and all humans. The Bravennans send the Replimoids to Earth in the hope of stopping Amel, but when Amel converts them to his cause, the Bravennans then send a horrific meteor shower that destroys Amel along with all of his luracastric creations. Once hindrances to their plans are eliminated, the Bravennans are free to resume gathering human suffering and transforming its psychic energy into a consumable resource.

For more perspectives on the Bravennans, read the *Alphabettery* entries **Amel**, **Bravenna**, **Luracastria**, **Parents**, and **Replimoid**.

Brittany Harrison

• MORTAL •

Brittany is the daughter of Terry Sue and the half sister of Tommy Harrison, whose father is Pops, the grandfather of Quinn Blackwood, who, after Pops dies, becomes the owner of Blackwood Farm. Brittany is often considered to be a workhorse by the staff at Blackwood Farm, always helping out in the kitchen. Although Brittany has a different father, through Tommy's connection to the Blackwood family, she and her siblings are well taken care of by Quinn and the Blackwood estate, given proper housing and an education.

Brittany appears in *Blackwood Farm* (2002). For more perspectives on Brittany's character, read the *Alphabettery* entries **Blackwood Farm**, **Pops**, **Quinn Blackwood**, **Terry Sue Harrison**, and **Tommy Harrison**.

Camille Blackwood

• MORTAL •

amille is the sister of William Blackwood and the daughter of Virginia Lee and Manfred Blackwood, founder of Blackwood Farm. Camille is a prolific writer of poetry and stories, with the determination and talent to become another Emily Dickinson or Emily Brontë. But she is betrayed by Rebecca Stanford, her stepmother, after Virginia Lee dies. She is the great-great-great-aunt of Quinn Blackwood. After Camille dies, her ghost can be seen roaming through Blackwood Manor, tiptoeing up the stairs to the attic.

Camille Blackwood appears in *Blackwood Farm* (2002). For more perspectives on Camille's character, read the *Alphabettery* entries **Blackwood Farm**, **Lestat de Lioncourt**, **Manfred Blackwood**, **Quinn Blackwood**, **Rebecca Stanford**, **Sugar Devil Swamp**, **Virginia Lee Blackwood**, and **William Blackwood**.

Carmilla

• SANCTUARY •

Carmilla is a vampire bar located in London and a part of the Vampire Connection worldwide. It is named after Carmilla, the heroine of the eponymous gothic novel by Joseph Sheridan Le Fanu, published as a serial in the London-based literary magazine the *Dark Blue* between the years 1871 and 1872.

Carmilla the vampire bar is mentioned in *The Vampire Lestat* (1985). For more perspectives on the Carmilla bar, read the *Alphabettery* entries **Bela Lugosi**, **Dracula's Daughter**, **Dr. Polidori**, **Lamia**, **Lord Ruthven**, **Vampire Bar**, and **Vampire Connection**.

Cassiodorus

• MORTAL •

Though much of his early life is spent in Rome's political arena, Cassiodorus eventually retires to the contemplative life of a monastery. He establishes a monastery at Vivarium, simply called the Vivarium, a school for the monastic life, which teaches the religious how to study the scripture through rigorous training in Latin and Greek, as well as reading commentaries of early church fathers, copying sacred texts, and meditating on the Bible.

When Cassiodorus dies in the book *Pandora* (1998), a spirit named Gremt issues out of the beehive and possesses a scarecrow, which openly mourns. When the vampire Pandora sees this, she encourages the spirit to evolve. Taking her advice, Gremt eventually evolves into an incarnate form and, with the aid of Teskhamen and Hesketh, begins the Talamasca Order, inspired by Cassiodorus's pursuit of truth.

Cassiodorus is mentioned in *Pandora* and *Prince Lestat* (2014). For more perspectives on the character of Cassiodorus in the Vampire Chronicles, read the *Alphabettery* entries **Gremt Stryker Knollys**, **Hesketh**, **Pandora**, **Talamasca Order**, **Teskhamen**, and **Vivarium**.

Castello Raniari

• SANCTUARY •

Built by the Raniari ancestors in the twelfth century, the time of the Lombards, when Germanic barbarians come down from the north to invade Italy, Castello Raniari stands occupied by the Raniari family for many generations until the middle of the fifteenth century, when Florian and his coven of vampires attack the Raniari family, ransack and destroy the *castello*, and kill everyone except for the oldest son, Vittorio, who vows vengeance for his family. Vittorio seeks out the vampires in their Court of the Ruby Grail in the northern mountains. He kills all of them except for Ursula, with whom he falls in love. She turns him into a vampire, and they spend the rest of their lives traveling around the world.

Castello Raniari appears in *Vittorio the Vampire* (1999). For more perspectives on Castello Raniari, read the *Alphabettery* entries **Court of the Ruby Grail**, **Florian**, **Ursula**, and **Vittorio di Raniari**.

Caves of Gold

• SANCTUARY •

After fleeing her captivity as Queen Akasha's handmaiden, Sevraine wanders for many centuries until she founds a coven beneath Cappadocia, in the middle of the Anatolian plain, where caves extend for many miles. Inside those underground caves, Sevraine decorates as though they were a palace, filling them with statues and ornamentation, going so far as to plate the cave walls in gold. Because of this, her coven house comes to be known as the Caves of Gold.

Sevraine's Caves of Gold are written of in *Prince Lestat* (2014). For more perspectives on the Caves of Gold, read the *Alphabettery* entries **Allesandra**, **Bianca Solderini**, **Coven**, **Eleni**, **Eugénie**, **Gremt Stryker Knollys**, **Lestat de Lioncourt**, and **Sevraine**.

Celeste

• VAMPIRE •

In *Interview with the Vampire* (1976), Celeste is a member of the coven at Théâtre des Vampires. Louis and Claudia encounter her during their visits with Armand. Along with Santiago, Celeste joins other vampires who demand Claudia's death for attempting to kill Lestat. Shortly after Louis turns Madeleine into a vampire, Celeste and other vampires of her coven capture Louis, Claudia, and Madeleine and drag them back to the *théâtre*, where they imprison Louis in a coffin and wall him in without escape, and then lock Claudia and Madeleine in a small cell exposed to the sun, where they burn to ashes at sunrise. After Armand frees him, Louis returns and burns alive nearly every vampire in the Théâtre des Vampires. Celeste is included among the dead.

For more perspectives on Celeste's character, read the *Alphabettery* entries **Armand, Claudia, Lestat de Lioncourt, Louis de Pointe du Lac, Santiago,** and **Théâtre des Vampires.**

Cemetery of les Innocents

• SANCTUARY •

Known by Parisians as Cimetière des Innocents (translated "Cemetery of the Holy Innocents"), Cemetery of les Innocents was a burial ground in Paris from the twelfth to the eighteenth century. Often called "Les Innocents" throughout the Vampire Chronicles, the name comes from Matthew 2:16–18, where Herod the Great orders the execution of many children in Bethlehem in an effort to kill the newly born Jesus of Nazareth, an event that comes to be called the Massacre of the Holy Innocents, honored in the Catholic Church as the Feast of the Holy Innocents. Over the centuries, the Cemetery of les Innocents is used to bury individuals and masses of bodies, particularly during the time of the Black Death. It was finally closed due to an overcrowding of corpses.

When Santino orders Armand to begin a new coven of the Children of Darkness in Paris, Armand takes with him several vampires from Santino's coven in Rome and establishes his new coven, the Children of Darkness, under the Cemetery of les Innocents, where they live in squalid dirt among the corpses of mortals.

Mention of the Cemetery of les Innocents can be found in *The Vampire Lestat* (1985),

The Queen of the Damned (1988), The Tale of the Body Thief (1992), The Vampire Armand (1998), Blood and Gold (2001), Prince Lestat (2014), Prince Lestat and the Realms of Atlantis (2016), and Blood Communion (2018). For more perspectives on the Cemetery of les Innocents in the Vampire Chronicles, read the Alphabettery entries **Armand**, **Children of Darkness**, **Children of Satan**, and **Santino**.

Chamber of Suffering

• SANCTUARY •

The Chamber of Suffering appears in Prince Lestat and the Realms of Atlantis (2016), not simply as a tool of the Bravennans but also as a reason for Amel to create luracastria, the substance that incites the destruction of Atlantis.

Many thousands of years ago, particular rooms are constructed either inside or adjacent to the ancient Pyramids of Egypt. These rooms are commonly referred to as the Chambers of Suffering. The chambers are places where mortals have an opportunity to contemplate their existence and all the events that cause them great disappointment, conflict, and turmoil, and where they have an opportunity to sit on benches, grieve, and lament over all their sufferings before the Maker of the world. They can weep loudly and beat their fists against the stone walls. It is a place of raw sorrow and anger.

Some chambers are guarded by strong sentries. Others have elderly guides within, who help individuals share their suffering more openly. A few chambers have fallen into neglect and ruin; they are no longer cared for yet are available to anyone—especially those living in the Wilderness—who happens to enter.

However, the reality of these Chambers of Suffering is that they are transmitters of human suffering, transferring the psionic energy of human suffering across the universe to the planet Bravenna, where the occupants, the Bravennans, consume human suffering as a natural resource of energy. Needing humans, or humanlike individuals, to maintain these Chambers of Suffering, Bravennan scientists abduct a human named Amel. Genetically enhancing him to be an immortal superhuman, they send him back to Earth, deceptively informing him that these chambers are meant for the benefit of humankind and that his work is to aid human welfare. With his enhanced intellect, Amel soon figures out the truth and attempts to either destroy these Chambers of Suffering or protect humans from them. With extracted samples of his genetic coding, he develops a new chemical compound called luracastria, which prevents the Bravennans from receiving the transmissions from the Chambers of Suffering and protects humans within the vast cities made out of luracastria, such as the city of Atlantis, which has no Chambers of Suffering and is a paradise of peace and joy.

When the Bravennans discover Amel's treachery, they send to Earth a shower of meteors that destroys Atlantis, Amel, and most of their Chambers of Suffering.

For more perspectives on the Chambers of Suffering, read the *Alphabettery* entries **Amel**, **Atlantis**, **Bravenna**, **Bravennans**, **Wilderness**, and **Wilderness People**.

Charlie

• MORTAL •

Charlie is the abusive boyfriend of Terry Sue, who becomes the mother of Tommy, whose father is Pops, the grandfather of the vampire Quinn Blackwood, whose mother is Patsy, the daughter of Pops and Sweetheart. Despite his grandfather's extramarital affair with

Terry Sue, Quinn still cares for his younger uncle, Tommy, and ensures that Charlie does no harm to Tommy or Terry Sue. Eventually, Charlie ends his life by shooting himself in the head.

Charlie appears in *Blackwood Farm* (2002). For more perspectives on Charlie's character, read the *Alphabettery* entries **Patsy**, **Pops**, **Quinn Blackwood**, **Sweetheart**, **Terry Sue Harrison**, and **Tommy Harrison**.

Château de Lioncourt

• SANCTUARY •

On one of the most isolated mountain plateaus of the Massif Central, roughly two hundred and fifty miles from the city of the Auvergne, in France, surrounded by undisturbed forests, nestled near the peaks of the mountains, Château de Lioncourt has stood for centuries. A vast castle with four towers, able to comfortably lodge more than a hundred guests, with a ballroom and many rooms to entertain any number of visitors, Château de Lioncourt is the eighteenth-century feudal home of the Marquis and Marquise de Lioncourt and their three sons, the youngest of whom is named Lestat. By the time Lestat is sixteen, the family fortune has been squandered. Lestat is the main provider for the Château, and he is looked to as a problem solver for the villagers, mostly poor families struggling daily for a loaf of bread or morsel of meat.

After Lestat goes to Paris and is turned into a vampire against his will, his mother, Gabrielle, follows, as does his aging father after the French Revolution, leaving the Château mostly abandoned. With the vast fortune that his maker Magnus willed to him,

Lestat buys the old Château and lets it sit in ruins for many years.

In the late twentieth century, he sends architects and stonemasons to rebuild it, restoring its ancient round towers from the cliff above the fields and valleys. He then returns to his old home to discover that his old village still remains at the foot of the mountain, with a reconstructed inn, a church, shops, and townhouses. Lestat commences a massive restoration of both his home and his village, hiring most of the mortal workmen in the village, as well as workmen from elsewhere who take up residence in rooms above the shops. Lestat even brings on mortal physicians to care for his workmen's health, while also paying for all their food and drink. Before the reconstruction is complete, Lestat becomes so enamored with his mortal foreman, Alain Abelard, that he takes Alain as his fledgling, after Rose and Viktor.

Lestat spends his vast fortune to recreate the Château and the village into an eighteenth-century replica of the home he had once known. Three of the four towers have collapsed; he has them all reerected. All the furniture is re-created in the eighteenth-century French style. The floors throughout the Château are the finest hardwood parquet, making the Château appear as if an eighteenth-century gentleman has restored it. Windows have double sashes and heavy glass for insulation. Lestat also has the crypt restored and enhanced far below the Château, so that he and his vampire guests can retire there during the day and sleep safely. Every room is supplied with twenty-first-century refinements, namely electric lights, heat, computers, the internet, gardens, plumbing, and all the modern luxuries of palatial accommodation. The bathrooms have modern marble, sunken tubs, and spacious showers. The banquet room becomes the new Council Chamber of the Court of the Prince. The great hall where Lestat's family once dined becomes the new palatial ballroom, large enough to comfortably hold more than one thousand vampires and a grand vampiric orchestra. Marius decorates the Château with countless beautiful murals, such as the battle of Troy, the tragic journey of Phaeton, Apollo's steeds charging across the sky, and many more, including a vast mural on the ballroom ceiling depicting a circle of vampires, beginning with Akasha and ending with Alain.

Farther beneath the crypt, a dungeon is discovered. Lestat was completely unaware of it in his mortal life. The dungeon is restored with modern prison security. The ancient vampire Baudwin is its one and only vampire inhabitant until his death, then the prison is used to keep mortal evildoers (drug dealers, assassins, murderers, and so on) that

serve to feed the Château's vampire guests. A kitchen is installed in the dungeon to feed the mortals, and a massive furnace is installed to destroy the bodies.

A one-hundred-thirty-year-old American vampire named Barbara becomes the manager of Château de Lioncourt, overseeing the hospitality of the vampire guests. Numerous other vampires work as butlers, maidservants, chambermaids, and in various other servant capacities.

The village is also restored to what Lestat knew during his mortal life, replete with all the shops from the late eighteenth century, including the tailor, butcher, baker, cheese maker, and even the draper's shop run by Nicki and his father. He re-creates the old fairground where the yearly markets were held in his youth. He also creates an inn where mortals can reside. Notwithstanding the Château's modern enhancements, it and the village remain a place of solitude and safety, completely unmarked on modern maps.

By the end of the renovation, Château de Lioncourt is so large that it can hold more than two thousand vampires. After Lestat becomes Prince, Château de Lioncourt becomes the official Court of the Prince from which he rules all vampirekind. The great hall fills every evening with vampire musicians and dancers. There are numerous rooms: some have giant flat screens dedicated to watching films; others have vast libraries for silent reading and meditation.

Château de Lioncourt appears in *Prince Lestat* (2014), *Prince Lestat and the Realms of Atlantis* (2016), and *Blood Communion* (2018).

For more perspectives on Château de Lioncourt, read the *Alphabettery* entries **Lestat de Lioncourt, Magnus, Marius, Marquis de Lioncourt,** and **Marquise de Lioncourt.**

Château de Lioncourt Dungeon

• SANCTUARY •

The Château de Lioncourt dungeon is built many years before Lestat's birth in the eighteenth century. Knowledge of its existence fades from memory. When he commences a massive reconstruction of the Château in the twenty-first century, Lestat is surprised when workmen discover the dungeon's existence. At the insistence of his council of vampires, Lestat has the dungeon updated with modern security measures, toilets, a kitchen, and a large furnace. The ancient vampire Baudwin is the only blood drinker ever imprisoned in the dungeon. After Baudwin's death, Prince Lestat and his Court of the Prince decide to keep a supply of mortal evildoers (murderers, slavers, kidnappers, and so on) in the dungeon, available for hungry vampires who reside in Lestat's newly renovated and updated Château de Lioncourt. The dungeon kitchen prepares meals for the occupants of the prison. The dungeon furnace destroys the bodies after vampires drink their blood.

The Château de Lioncourt dungeon appears in *Blood Communion* (2018). For more perspectives on the Château de Lioncourt dungeon in the Vampire Chronicles, read the *Alphabettery* entries **Baudwin, Château de Lioncourt,** and **Lestat de Lioncourt.**

Child of the Blood

• IDIOM •

The idiom "Child of the Blood" is another way for a vampire to refer to his or her fledgling. Marius, for instance, uses this term in reference to his fledgling Armand.

The idiom appears in *Blood and Gold* (2001). For more perspectives on Child of the Blood, read the *Alphabettery* entries **Armand, Fledgling, Maker,** and **Marius.**

Children of Atlantis

• COVEN •

"Children of Atlantis" is a term coined by Lestat to describe Amel and the Replimoids, namely Kapetria, Derek, Garekyn, Welf, and the clones they produce. These are the immortal beings who lived during the time that Amel built the great city of Atlantis, and they also witnessed its destruction. The Children of Atlantis become coworkers with Prince Lestat and his Court of the Prince, seeking ways to use science for the better-ment of mortals and immortals alike. The Children of Atlantis dwell in a colony in a hidden location in England.

The Children of Atlantis appear in *Prince Lestat and the Realms of Atlantis* (2016) and *Blood Communion* (2018). For more perspectives on the Children of Atlantis, read the *Alphabettery* entries **Amel**, **Atlantis**, **Derek**, **Garekyn**, **Kapetria**, **Lestat de Lioncourt**, **Replimoid**, and **Welf**.

The Children of Darkness

• COVEN •

The Children of Darkness is a vampire coven that endures for nearly a century. Also known as the Children of Satan, they feed off the blood of indigents, live in squalor, and seek to do the work of Satan as they understand it. They either destroy vampire covens that do not conform to their beliefs or capture vampires and convert them to their faith through torture. Their most prominent members are Santino and Armand. The Children of Darkness are referred to in *The Vampire Lestat* (1985), *The Queen of the Damned* (1988), *The Vampire Armand* (1998), *Pandora* (1998), *Blood and Gold* (2001), and *Blood Canticle* (2003).

Arising in Late Antiquity, a group of vam-pires develops an ideological belief that they are literally the children of Lucifer because of their demonic disposition to drink blood and murder innocent victims. In this Satanic spirituality, the group of vampires fully believes that they serve God in the same way that Lucifer serves God, by tempting, tormenting, terrorizing, and destroying the lives of mortals. Banding together into a coven, they call themselves the Children of Darkness and develop the five Great Laws that govern their particular faith.

In general, these Great Laws dictate how the coven is to be run, who in the coven is authorized to make other vampires, the kinds of mortals that are allowed to be turned into vampires, the relationship between maker and fledgling, the kinds of mortals that are allowed to be hunted, the way in which vampires ought to exist, and the necessity for absolute secrecy concerning the existence of vampires.

A central feature of the Children of Darkness is that they only hunt people who are either poor, diseased, or outcast from society, most likely because of immoral or criminal behavior. Similarly, the vampires subject themselves to an existence of poverty, wearing only rags and sleeping in dirt and filth, as if they themselves are the poor, the diseased, and the outcasts. They believe not only that this fulfills God's will but also that Satan himself must be subjected to such conditions and that wealth, beautiful clothing, art—any luxury of any kind—are all forbidden to the vampires in the coven of the Children of Darkness. They even deny themselves the possibility of entering into a church, considering it an ultimate act of desecration, sacrilege, and a threat to their existence, since the mysteries of believers in God have the supernatural authority to enact divine retribution and damnation.

One of the principal coven houses of the Children of Darkness is located in Rome. In the death and dirt of the catacombs, the coven works either to convert vampires to their cause or to destroy those vampires who disobey their Great Laws. Marius, Mael, and Avicus, who live in Rome together, guarding Those Who Must Be Kept, often have skirmishes with the Children of Darkness, whom they easily destroy or drive out of the city. After Marius, Mael, and Avicus take Those Who Must Be Kept to Constantinople, the Children of Darkness thrive once more in the streets of Rome. During the late Early Middle Ages, and the early High Middle Ages, the Children of Darkness enter France, attack Rhoshamandes's castle, and capture his coven, namely Everard, Allesandra, Eleni, and Eugénie. By capturing and converting vampires, the Children of Darkness flourish throughout Europe for centuries. During the Black Plague, the vampire Santino becomes the leader of the Roman coven. He approaches Marius in the fifteenth century, begging him to become the new leader, but Marius rejects him. Shortly after this, Santino leads a pack of the Children of Darkness to Marius's Venetian palazzo, burns it to the ground, nearly burns Marius to death, and captures Marius's newest fledgling, Amadeo. Bringing Amadeo back to Rome, Santino imprisons him without blood until he fully memorizes the Great Laws and converts to his Satanic coven. Rhoshamandes's fledgling Allesandra befriends Amadeo and helps him make the transition. After many months, once Amadeo has proved to be an exemplary Child of Darkness, Allesandra changes his name to Armand. Santino sends him, along with Everard, Allesandra, Eleni, and Eugénie, to Paris to begin a new coven house.

Making their lair in the Cemetery of les Innocents, Armand's coven rules Paris from the filth, prohibiting all vampires who live contrary to their beliefs. Everard eventually escapes, but Allesandra, Eleni, and Eugénie remain faithfully alongside Armand. When Lestat and Gabrielle move to Paris in the eighteenth century, the Children of Darkness try to either convert or destroy them. Lestat persuades Armand and his coven that their ways are anachronistic in the modern world of the French Enlightenment. Convinced that their cult of the Children of Darkness is ultimately doomed, Allesandra encourages Armand to destroy them all by throwing herself into a funeral pyre. Believing that his vampires cannot survive in the modern world, Armand throws them into the fire as well, destroying them completely, except for four—Eugénie, Eleni, Felix, and Laurent. They beg Lestat to be their new leader, and to guide them into this new era, but he refuses. Through the intervention of his fledgling Nicolas, Lestat gives them an old theater he owns on the Boulevard du Temple, which, although currently closed and boarded up, was known in its day as Renaud's House of Thesbians. After Eugénie, Eleni, Felix, Laurent, Nicolas, and Armand move into the theater and rename it the Théâtre des Vampires, it becomes their new coven, where they put on plays and pretend to be mortals who pretend to be vampires, thus snuffing out the last vestiges of the Children of Darkness.

For more perspectives on the Children of Darkness, read the *Alphabettery* entries **Allesandra, Armand, Children of Satan, Eugénie, Everard, Great Laws, Laurent, Lestat de Lioncourt, Line of de Landen Vampires, Nicolas de Lenfent, Renaud's House of Thesbians, Santino,** and **Théâtre des Vampires.**

Children of Darkness

• IDIOM •

Nearly a century after Lestat destroys Armand's coven, the Children of Darkness, sometime during the late twentieth century, the term "Children of Darkness" recurs, this time as a general reference to any and all vampirekind. Benji often calls vampires the Children of Darkness in his radio broadcasts; Everard recalls how Queen Akasha destroyed the Children of Darkness globally; even Lestat recalls the same, mourning the loss of three- and four-hundred-year-old Children of Darkness, although Gregory argues that vampires should not be called by such an idiom while they live in a world brightened by technological advances. This idiom, as distinct from the coven by the same name, occurs in *Prince Lestat* (2014) and *Prince Lestat and the Realms of Atlantis* (2016).

For more perspectives on the Children of Darkness idiom, read the *Alphabettery* entries **Benji Mahmoud, The Children of Darkness, Everard, Gregory Duff Collingsworth,** and **Lestat de Lioncourt.**

Children of Satan

• IDIOM •

The Children of Satan is an alternative name for the Children of Darkness, a vampire coven that arises in Late Antiquity and thrives until the eighteenth century. They are governed by the Great Laws of Satan, which essentially prohibit them from enjoying any of life's luxuries, convince them to drink the blood of indigents, and proselytize disciples of Satan to effect the damnation of souls. Some of the most prominent Children of Satan are Santino, Allesandra, and Armand, who create and lead two prominent coven houses, Santino in Rome and Armand in Paris. No mention of the idiom "Children of Satan" occurs in *The Vampire Lestat* (1985), *The Queen of the Damned* (1988), *The Vampire Armand* (1998), *Pandora* (1998), *Blood and Gold* (2001), and *Blood Canticle* (2003). However, the Children of Darkness coven is often referred to as Children of Satan, specifically in *Prince Lestat* (2014), *Prince Lestat and the Realms of Atlantis* (2016), and *Blood Communion* (2018).

For more perspectives on the Children of Satan, read the *Alphabettery* entries **Allesandra**, **Armand**, **Children of Darkness**, **Coven**, **Eugénie**, **Everard**, **Great Laws**, **Laurent**, **Lestat de Lioncourt**, **Line of de Landen Vampires**, **Nicolas de Lenfent**, **Renaud's House of Thesbians**, **Santino**, and **Théâtre des Vampires**.

Children of the Millennia

• IDIOM •

This title is generally applied to vampires who have lived for more than a thousand years. It is always applied to any vampire who has survived for more than two millennia. Lestat is not a part of the Children of the Millennia, since he has only lived for a few centuries; neither is David Talbot, Jesse Reeves, or even Armand, born in the middle of the second millennium.

Vampires who have lived for more than a thousand years and are generally referred to as Children of the Millennia would be Eric, Thorne, and the line of de Landen vampires, which includes Benedict, Allesandra, Eugénie, Everard, Eleni, and Notker the Wise.

Vampires who have lived for more than two thousand years and are always referred to as Children of the Millennia would be Gregory Duff Collingsworth (also called Nebamun), Cyril, Rhoshamandes, Marius, Mael, and several others, including the late Maharet, Mekare, and Khayman.

The idiom appears in *Prince Lestat* (2014), *Prince Lestat and the Realms of Atlantis* (2016), and *Blood Communion* (2018). For more perspectives on Children of the Millennia, read the *Alphabettery* entries **Allesandra, Armand, Cyril, David Talbot, Eric, Eugénie, Everard, Gregory Duff Collingsworth, Jesse Reeves, Khayman, Lestat de Lioncourt, Line of de Landen Vampires, Maharet, Mekare, Nebamun, Notker the Wise,** and **Thorne.**

Children of the Night

• IDIOM •

Children of the Night is the general term for all vampires across the world, since most vampires in their nascence are induced to sleep every day only to rise every night and hunt for fresh blood. Although the phrase is used universally, mainly by Benji Mahmoud, who broadcasts his radio program to every Child of the Night, it is specifically directed at those vampires too young to endure any sunlight lest they immolate or are severely burned.

This idiom appears in *Prince Lestat* (2014) and *Prince Lestat and the Realms of Atlantis* (2016). For more perspectives on the Children of the Night, read the *Alphabettery* entries **Benji Mahmoud** and **The Voice.**

Christine

• MORTAL •

When Lestat rises from his torpor in the twentieth century, he copes with the nuances of this new age by retaining a lawyer named Christine. Much the same way he employed Pierre Roget, his lawyer in the eighteenth century, Lestat has Christine execute all of his desires, such as ensuring the fame and fortune of the Vampire Lestat band.

The name Christine originates from Anne Rice's lawyer, Christine Cuddy.

Christine appears in *The Vampire Lestat* (1985). For more perspectives on Christine's character, read the *Alphabettery* entries **Alex, Larry, Lestat de Lioncourt, Pierre Roget, Tough Cookie,** and **The Vampire Lestat.**

Chrysanthe

• VAMPIRE •

Chrysanthe is the Blood Spouse of the ancient vampire Nebamun, who becomes Gregory Duff Collingsworth. She helps him transition into the new millennium of the Common Era and create a long-lived coven in the third century and a leading pharmaceutical empire in the twenty-first century, all of which serve a key function in shaping the future of vampirekind. Chrysanthe appears in *Prince Lestat* (2014), *Prince Lestat and the Realms of Atlantis* (2016), and *Blood Communion* (2018).

Born in the third century of the Common Era, Chrysanthe lives in Hira, a glorious Arab-Christian city, with her mortal spouse, a Hiraian merchant. Shortly after his death, a vampire named Nebamun rescues her from the city, not long before the Battle of Hira and the imminent Muslim conquest of Persia. Bringing her to Carthage in North Africa, he does not immediately confess to her his vampire nature or that he is by that time more than four thousand years old, having been turned into a vampire in ancient Egypt by the Queen herself, Akasha. He has gone into the earth, slept for centuries, and now, fully risen, he is attempting to make contact with the world that in many ways is very modern to him. After Nebamun changes his ancient name to the more modern-sounding Gregory Duff Collingsworth, Chrysanthe teaches him how to read Latin and Greek; she instructs him on the waning Roman Empire and the waxing Christian religion. She teaches him

much about the poetry, history, philosophy, and sciences of many other cultures that he has never encountered or could never have imagined in his lifetime. As she teaches him, he falls in love with her and turns her into a vampire. He makes a commitment to her, to remain with her throughout eternity, during the rest of their immortal existence, thus making him her Blood Husband, and she his Blood Wife.

While in Carthage, they create a coven together, the Blood Kindred, and welcome any vampire needing sanctuary. One of the first vampires that approach them is Flavius, fledgling of Pandora and former slave to her and Marius. Gregory is amazed that another vampire has brought Flavius into the Blood, since he has only one leg, as anyone with a disability was forbidden according to the old vampire laws of Akasha's reign. Chrysanthe is delighted for her Blood Spouse when Flavius also teaches Gregory many of the ancient Roman and Greek stories, mathematics, politics, philosophies, and sciences. Joining their coven a little later is another Blood Spouse couple, Zenobia and Avicus, whom Gregory knew in ancient Egypt. For centuries, Chrysanthe and her kindred maintain a powerful and enduring alliance. They build a castle near the Rhine and sleep in the lower levels far below the castle, safe from the daylight.

Chrysanthe and Gregory remain together for many centuries, all the way through the twenty-first century, when Gregory creates Collingsworth Pharmaceuticals, a drug company that becomes a successful international power in finance and medical advancement. She and Gregory often visit Prince Lestat's Court of the Prince at Château de Lioncourt.

For more perspectives on Chrysanthe's character, read the *Alphabettery* entries **Akasha**, **Avicus**, **Blood Kindred**, **Blood Spouse**, **Collingsworth Pharmaceuticals**, **Gregory Duff Collingsworth**, **Nebamun**, and **Zenobia**.

Clarence Oddbody

• ALIAS •

"Clarence Oddbody" is the alias Lestat has shortly before meeting with Raglan James, the Body Thief, in the book *The Tale of the Body Thief* (1992). When Lestat hands Raglan his passport, James makes a remark on the name. Lestat tells him that it is a private joke. Later, after James thieves Lestat's body, Lestat searches for the alias "Clarence Oddbody," but James has already changed it.

Clarence comes from the name of the angel in the 1946 movie *It's a Wonderful Life*.

For more perspectives on the use of aliases in the Vampire Chronicles, read the *Alphabettery* entries **Alexander Stoker**, **Baron Van Kindergarten**, **Benjamin the Devil**, **Eric Sampson**, **Isaac Rummel**, **Jason Hamilton**, **Lestan Gregor**, **Lionel Potter**, **Renfield**, **Sebastian Melmoth**, and **Sheridan Blackwood**.

Claudia

• VAMPIRE •

Claudia is one of the most memorable characters in the Vampire Chronicles. A child vampire made to keep a small coven together, she is both a child and a paramour for Louis and Lestat, as well as the cause of their ruined relationship for centuries. Claudia appears in two Vampire Chronicles, first as a vampire in

Interview with the Vampire (1976) and then as a ghost in *Merrick* (2000).

On a night when Louis can no longer resist the temptation to drink human blood, he drinks the blood of a five-year-old girl to the point of her death. He stops only when Lestat discovers him and mockingly celebrates Louis's capitulation to the blood thirst. Louis flees in shame, leaving the girl only a few feet away from the corpse of her mother, Agatha, but Lestat brings the child back with him to their townhouse on Rue Royale. There, he reveals to Louis that the child will die if they do not turn her into a vampire. Reluctantly, Louis allows Lestat to change the five-year-old girl into a vampire. Together, they adopt her as their mutual fledgling (Louis having drained her blood, Lestat having given her his own) and they name her Claudia.

As a daughter to both Lestat and Louis, Claudia learns from them how to hunt for victims. Through their tutelage, she becomes one of the fiercest blood drinkers. As she matures mentally throughout the next sixty-five years, living together with Lestat and Louis in the same townhouse, she begins to realize that human girls mature into women, but, as an inhuman vampire, that natural ability is beyond her. She will remain trapped in the body of a little girl forever. Claudia becomes increasingly angry because of her inability to grow up. When Louis reveals to her how she was turned into an immortal, she is outraged at both her makers, but she loves Louis too much to feel vengeful towards him for long, so she directs all her antipathy towards Lestat. She and he argue often, until one night she develops a cunning trap to kill him by overdosing two young boys on absinthe and laudanum, which makes them appear passed out and their blood warm; then she presents them to Lestat as a peace offering. Unwittingly, Lestat drinks their dead blood, which weakens him so much that Claudia is able to cut his throat with a knife, right before she plunges the knife

into his heart. Believing he is dead, she and Louis sink Lestat's body in the Louisiana swamps, expecting alligators and swamp life to consume him. Unaware that he is still alive, soliciting the assistance of Antoine, his soon-to-be fledgling, Claudia and Louis make preparations to leave New Orleans on a boat for Europe, in search of other vampires as well as answers to the purpose of their immortal existence. On the night that their ship is bound to sail for Europe, Lestat appears at their Rue Royale townhouse. Afraid for their lives, Louis and Claudia fight off Lestat by setting their maker, Lestat's new fledgling Antoine, and the townhouse on fire. Believing that this second attempt at killing him must have been successful, they flee to the boat in time to depart for Europe.

Louis and Claudia travel across the world for many years. They find some vampires, but they are revenants—mindless and ravenous for blood, incapable of answering any of their questions. Throughout their travels, Claudia grows increasingly furious at the fact that she is an immortal trapped in a five-year-old's body. Eventually, they come to Paris, where they first encounter another vampire like them, Santiago, who is a member of the coven at the Théâtre des Vampires. Shortly thereafter, Louis and Claudia meet the leader of the coven, Armand, who invites them to see how the coven has survived in the modern age. When Louis and Claudia discover that the coven of the Théâtre des Vampires pretends to be humans pretending to be vampires in stage plays, Claudia is immediately repulsed by them. Meanwhile, Lestat has also come to Paris, seeking Armand, whose ancient and powerful blood can more quickly help restore him to his former strength. Lestat reveals to Armand that Claudia tried to kill him, which inspires Armand to plot against Claudia, since he and Louis have been spending more time together and developing deep feelings for each other's company.

Claudia becomes aware of this and realizes that Louis is going to leave her for Armand. So she finds a new companion and guardian for herself, Madeleine, a doll maker by trade, whose daughter has died and who has been re-creating the image of her lost child in her dolls. At first Louis is reluctant to turn Madeleine into a vampire, but through persuasive arguments and guilt, Claudia convinces Louis to give Madeleine the Dark Gift because she herself does not have the strength. They remain a small coven for a while, until the

coven at the Théâtre des Vampires abducts them and holds a trial, accusing Louis and Claudia of violating one of the Great Laws—not to kill or attempt to kill one's maker. Armand promises Lestat that he will give him some of his blood if he testifies against Claudia, but because Lestat wants Louis to be with him and because of the bitterness that Armand holds against Lestat for ruining his former coven over a century earlier, Armand does not keep his agreement and pushes Lestat out a window once Claudia is found guilty. As punishment for their crime, the coven locks Louis in a coffin with large iron locks and buries him for all eternity. Then they lock Claudia and Madeleine in a prison without a roof, where they wait for the dawn. Claudia and Madeleine hold on to each other

as the sun rises. Their screams can be heard throughout the *théâtre*. All that remains of the vampire who looks no older than a little girl is ashes.

For more perspectives on Claudia's character, read the *Alphabettery* entries **Agatha, Armand, Dark Gift, Fledgling, Lestat de Lioncourt, Louis de Pointe du Lac, Madeleine, Maker, Revenant,** and **Théâtre des Vampire.**

Clem

• MORTAL •

Clem is the son of Little Ida, Quinn's nurse, and the brother of Jasmine, Blackwood Manor's housekeeper. Clem works on the Shed Men crew, along with Allen, the nominal leader. Clem serves on the Blackwood Farm plantation, taking care of all the automobiles, especially chauffeuring Aunt Queen in her car and keeping up the maintenance on Quinn's black Porsche.

Clem appears in *Blackwood Farm* (2002). For more perspectives on Clem's character, read the *Alphabettery* entries **Allen, Blackwood Farm, Blackwood Manor, Jasmine, Quinn Blackwood,** and **Shed Men.**

Clement

• MORTAL •

Clement is a Christian Roman around the fourth century and the captain of a ship that carries Marius, Avicus, Mael, and Those Who Must Be Kept from Rome to Constantinople. This happens at a time when Marius is living very close to mortals. He spends much time with Clement in particular, listening keenly to his tales of sailing voyages through the Mediterranean. Seeing the world through Clement's eyes gives Marius new hope in his new home, where he will welcome Clement as a friend.

Clement appears in *Blood and Gold* (2001). For more perspectives on Clement's character, read the *Alphabettery* entries **Akasha, Avicus, Enkil, Mael, Marius,** and **Those Who Must Be Kept.**

Cloud Gift

• VAMPIRE ABILITY •

Similar to the Fire Gift, this ability is generally acquired in one of two ways. First, if vampires reach a very great age, they develop within themselves the ability to levitate and fly. No specific age is determined as to exactly when a vampire achieves the Cloud Gift. Alternatively, vampires can acquire this gift by inheriting it after drinking the blood of a vampire already in possession of this gift. An example of this is when Lestat drinks Akasha's blood for the first time, shortly after the concert of the Vampire Lestat in the mideighties. Because the Queen is six thousand years old at that time and has already naturally developed the ability to fly, her blood bestows it upon Lestat, who is only two centuries old, giving him the ability to fly over great distances in a short period of time. Without her blood, he would have needed to age for centuries before he could have naturally developed the Cloud Gift. The only known way to prevent vampires from using the Cloud Gift is to wrap them in iron binds.

The Cloud Gift is utilized in *The Vampire Lestat* (1985), *The Queen of the Damned* (1988), *Memnoch the Devil* (1995), *Prince Lestat* (2014), *Prince Lestat and the Realms of Atlantis* (2016), and *Blood Communion* (2018). For more perspectives on the Cloud Gift, read the *Alphabettery* entries **Akasha, Blood Curse, Crippling Gift, Dark Gift, Fire Gift, Iron Curse, Lestat de Lioncourt, Mind Gift,** and **Spell Gift.**

Cold Sandra

• MORTAL •

Being of European descent, the Mayfair witching family consists mostly of lighter-skinned Caucasian women, except for Cold Sandra, who shows the darker skin of her African heritage. She has two daughters, whom she names Honey in the Sunshine and Merrick, the future vampire fledgling of Louis de Pointe du Lac. Unlike her own twelve siblings who can pass for Caucasian, Cold Sandra, who cannot hide her African heritage during a time of rampant racism, takes her two daughters to a derelict neighborhood in New Orleans, where they live together with Merrick's godmother, Great Nananne. Throughout the years, Cold Sandra uses her witch magic to attract men in the hope of finding a good husband and father. The last man she attracts is Matthew Kemp, an Olmec archaeologist. She convinces him to come to New Orleans to study artifacts and read a book belonging to Great Nananne's older brother, Oncle Vervain, a Voodoo man.

Cold Sandra and Matthew wed. Persistent in his archaeological studies, he takes Cold Sandra, Honey in the Sunshine, and Merrick on an expedition to Guatemala, where Matthew falls ill and dies while researching in a cave. Matthew leaves Cold Sandra enough money to take care of herself and her older daughter, Honey in the Sunshine. She leaves Merrick in the care of Great Nananne but promises to come back for her. Merrick never hears from her again, except in spirit after her mother and sister are murdered. The bodies of Cold Sandra and Honey in the Sunshine are found in their vehicle, which the murderer submerged in a swamp in Lafayette, Louisiana.

Cold Sandra appears in *Merrick* (2000). For more perspectives on Cold Sandra's character, read the *Alphabettery* entries **Great Nananne, Honey in the Sunshine, Louis de Pointe du Lac, Matthew Kemp, Merrick Mayfair,** and **Oncle Vervain.**

Collingsworth Pharmaceuticals

• SANCTUARY •

Owned by the ancient vampire Gregory Duff Collingsworth, who went by the name of Nebamun four thousand years before the Common Era, Collingsworth Pharmaceuticals is one of the major pharmaceutical manufacturers of the twentieth and twenty-first centuries. The company makes major investments in research and development, particularly in the areas of genetic resequencing and cloning, which are overseen by vampire scientists, such as Akasha's son, Seth, and Fareed Bhansali, who together develop a clone of Lestat, whom they name Viktor. Collingsworth Pharmaceuticals' greatest feat in the modern world is also its greatest secret: it provides the world's first and only health care for the Undead, treating vampires all over the world in recovery from wounds or fatal disease. It is in one of the research facilities of Collingsworth Pharmaceuticals that a former scientist, Dr. Karen Rhinehart, who is actually a Replimoid from the planet Bravenna named Kapetria, creates a means of removing Amel and his Sacred Core from Lestat's brain into a luracastric body grown from genetically enhanced cells from her own body.

Collingsworth Pharmaceuticals appears in *Prince Lestat* (2014) and *Prince Lestat and the Realms of Atlantis* (2016). For more perspectives on Collingsworth Pharmaceuticals, read the *Alphabettery* entries **Amel, Bravenna, Fareed Bhansali, Gregory Duff Collingsworth, Kapetria, Lestat de Lioncourt, Replimoid, Sacred Core, Seth,** and **Viktor.**

Commedia dell'Arte

• IDIOM •

Performance art developed in sixteenth-century Italy, commedia dell'arte employs a formula of familiar characters in similar circumstances. The most basic involves two lovers who want to marry, older people who try to stop the marriage, and comic-relief characters whom the lovers depend on to help them wed.

Lestat learns how to perform commedia dell'arte when, at the age of sixteen, he tries to run away with an acting troupe passing through the Auvergne village. He performs the main lover character named Lelio, while his female lover goes by the name Isabella. Years later, in Renaud's House of Thesbians, Lestat once again plays his lover character Lelio in the commedia dell'arte style, only this time his lover's name is Flaminia.

Commedia dell'arte appears in *The Vampire Lestat* (1985). For more perspectives on commedia dell'arte, read the *Alphabettery* entries **Flaminia**, **Isabella**, **Lelio**, **Lestat de Lioncourt**, **Pantaloon**, **Pulcinella**, and **Renaud's House of Thesbians**.

Corpus Gift

• VAMPIRE ABILITY •

The Corpus Gift is a regenerative facility possessed by all vampires that enables them to autonomically heal quickly and restore severed body parts.

The speed with which vampire's can heal depends on a vampire's age and blood. Older vampires heal almost instantly. Younger vampires heal slowly, unless they drink the blood of an older vampire, which bestows upon them the ability to heal much more rapidly. For instance, when Santino badly burns Marius, Marius drinks from Akasha's blood and heals swiftly.

Vampire blood can also heal mortal wounds much faster than mortal medicine: when Killer drops his blood on the bite marks of his victims, the wounds completely heal, even those on a corpse. He uses the gift to hide that those people have been killed by a vampire.

If a vampire loses a limb, that limb can be restored as long as it is not lost. For example, when Lestat severs Rhoshamandes's left arm, Rhoshamandes is able to reattach it perfectly, as if it had never been cut off. When Mael's head and arm are severed, Avicus reattaches them so poorly that Marius must remove Mael's limbs again and reattach them.

However, if a mortal loses a body part before becoming a vampire, that mortal part cannot be restored to the immortal body. The maimed vampire must steal body parts from other mortals and immortals and attach those parts to his or her body. If a vampire steals mortal body parts, the mortal tissue will eventually die and need to be replaced. Stealing the body parts of immortals produces a more permanent solution. Maharet is an example of both scenarios: Maharet's eyes are taken out before she is turned into a vampire. She can regain her sight only by stealing the eyes of mortals, but in time those eyes die and she is forced to find new ones.

Her fledgling Thorne gives her his own eyes out of a sense of duty and reconciliation after he destroys Santino under her roof.

In the twenty-first century, Seth and Fareed develop a way of restoring long-lost limbs through genetic cloning techniques, such as when they restore Flavius's leg that had been severed during his mortal lifetime, two thousand years earlier. Seth and Fareed also are able to clone Maharet's eyes and restore her sight permanently.

The Corpus Gift can be found in *The Queen of the Damned* (1988), *Blood and Gold* (2001), and *Prince Lestat* (2014). For more perspectives on the Corpus Gift, read the *Alphabettery* entries **Avicus**, **Fareed Bhansali**, **Flavius**, **Lestat de Lioncourt**, **Mael**, **Maharet**, and **Rhoshamandes**.

Council of Elders

• COVEN •

After the deaths of Maharet and Mekare, when Lestat takes into himself Amel and the Sacred Core, becoming Prince Lestat, ruler of all vampires, all vampirekind looks to him as a sovereign decision-maker. Undesirous to make widespread decisions alone, he convenes at Château de Lioncourt what he refers to as the Council of Elders, comprising mostly Children of the Millennia, vampires more than a thousand years old, vampires who are old enough and strong enough to withstand telekinetic attacks

from other vampires, namely attacks of the Fire Gift. In attendance at these councils are elders such as Marius, Thorne, and Sevraine. Also in attendance are much-younger vampires, such as David Talbot, Jesse Reeves, and Fareed Bhansali—vampires who are born in the twentieth century, yet have within them the blood of an elder, which makes them strong enough to withstand the Fire Gift, and other such telekinetic attacks.

The Council of Elders appears in *Prince Lestat* (2014) and *Prince Lestat and the Realms of Atlantis* (2016). For more perspectives on the Council of Elders, read the *Alphabettery* sections **Amel, Children of the Millennia, David Talbot, Fareed Bhansali, Fire Gift, Jesse, Lestat de Lioncourt, Maharet, Mekare, Sacred Core, Sevraine,** and **Thorne.**

Court of the Prince

• COVEN •

After Lestat restores Château de Lioncourt in the twenty-first century, a court is established to help him make decisions in his princely duty to all vampirekind. The Court of the Prince consists of Allesandra, Antoine, Avicus, Benji, Bianca, Chrysanthe, David Talbot, Davis, Eleni, Everard de Landen, Fareed, Gabrielle, Gregory Duff Collingsworth, Jesse Reeves, Lestat, Marius, Notker the Wise, Pandora, Santh, Seth, Sevraine, Sybelle, and Zenobia.

One of the decisions that the Court of the Prince helps Lestat make is the just destruction of Rhoshamandes, who killed Maharet and Khayman.

The Court of the Prince appears in *Blood Communion* (2018). For more perspectives on the Court of the Prince in the Vampire Chronicles, read the *Alphabettery* entries **Château de Lioncourt, Coven, Gregory Duff Collingsworth, Lestat de Lioncourt,** and **Santh.**

Court of the Ruby Grail

• COVEN •

The Court of the Ruby Grail is both a coven and an idiom. In the physical sense, it is the royal court of a vampire coven, located in the northern mountains of Italy. The coven master is Lord Florian, although his wife, Lady Ursula, also holds some authority. In this court they keep many mortals prisoner, keeping them alive by feeding them until they are plump and full of blood. Then, in the court, the vampires will greedily gorge themselves on a feast of blood, which seems to flow endlessly and which also inspires the euphemism "ruby grail," a reference to the abundance of blood for vampires to enjoy in excess. Before he is turned into a vampire, Vittorio is brought to the Court of the Ruby

Grail, where he vows to destroy Florian and all his vampires in revenge for them having slaughtered his entire family. Vittorio almost keeps his word, too, killing every vampire, save Ursula, who woos him into immortal life.

The Court of the Ruby Grail appears in *Vittorio the Vampire* (1999). For more perspectives on the Court of the Ruby Grail, read the *Alphabettery* entries **Coven**, **Coven Master**, **Florian**, **Ursula**, and **Vittorio di Raniari**.

Coven

• IDIOM •

In the Vampire Chronicles, the word "coven" is used to describe a gathering of vampires who coexist in a community. The origin of the word derives from two Latin words: *con* (with) and *venire* (to come); thus, "coven" literally means "come with," but figuratively it should be understood as a coming together of kindred creatures. It was originally used to describe how witches would convene to practice their supernatural craft. The term and concept likely are incorporated into the Vampire Chronicles through the influence of such witches as Maharet who are turned into immortal blood drinkers. An exception to the rule is, in the late twentieth century, with the Vampire Connection, a series of vampire bars where blood drinkers can convene safely without obligations to an immortal fellowship. Examples of famous vampire covens include Killer's Fang Gang, the Coven of the Articulate, Ursula's Court of the Ruby Grail, Armand's Théâtre des Vampires, Severain's Caves of Gold, Santino's Children of Satan, and Lestat's Court of the Prince. This idiom occurs in every Vampire Chronicle except *Memnoch the Devil* (1995) and *Pandora* (1998).

For more perspectives on the "coven" idiom, read the *Alphabettery* entries **Caves of Gold**, **Children of Satan**, **Court of the Prince**, **Court of the Ruby Grail**, **Coven Master**, **Coven of the Articulate**, **Fang Gang**, and **Théâtre des Vampires**.

Coven Master

• IDIOM •

A coven master is the head of a coven of vampires. Coven masters enforce their coven's laws internally, torturing or destroying vampires who do not conform. Coven masters also possess the right to destroy vampires whose youth or weakness prevents them from surviving major transitions, such as the collapse of a coven, like when Armand immolates most of the Children of Satan in Paris. Coven masters are not simply leaders of immortal blood drinkers; they are also intransigent protectors of a way of life, attacking and destroying all external influences that might negatively affect the coven, particularly blood drinkers who refused to join their coven or follow their coven's rules. An example of this is when Santino, as coven master of the Children of Satan in Rome, destroys Marius's Venetian palazzo in the fifteenth century. Later, Armand, as coven master of the Children of Satan in eighteenth-century Paris, attempts (and fails) to destroy Lestat and Gabrielle for not following the Great Laws. However, Armand's role as coven master changes when his coven is destroyed and the Théâtre des Vampires coven is established; he informs Louis that he is not a traditional coven master but only a leader, in the sense that he is the oldest and most powerful. In the twentieth century, Lestat refers to the term "coven master" as "old lingo," as if the fall of antiquated superstitions perpetuated by outmoded covens also felled fruitless methods of leadership. The coven master idiom occurs in *The Vampire Lestat* (1985), *The Queen of the Damned* (1988), *The Vampire Armand* (1998), *Blood Canticle* (2003), *Prince Lestat* (2014), and *Prince Lestat and the Realms of Atlantis* (2016).

For more perspectives on the "coven master" idiom, read the *Alphabettery* entries **Armand**, **Children of Satan**, **Coven**, **Gabrielle**, **Lestat de Lioncourt**, **Marius de Romanus**, and **Santino**.

Coven of the Articulate

• COVEN •

The authors of the Vampire Chronicles make up the Coven of the Articulate, namely Louis, Daniel Malloy, Lestat, Armand, Marius, and David Talbot, along with the authors of the New Tales of the Vampires, Pandora and Vittorio. Vittorio does not consider himself to be a member of the Coven of the Articulate, since he has no desire to recount the story of his adventures, but provides the reader with a tale of his beginnings as a vampire.

Louis narrates *Interview with the Vampire* (1976), while Daniel Malloy helps shape the story with his questions and dictation.

Lestat authors the majority of the books, beginning with *The Vampire Lestat* (1985), *The Queen of the Damned* (1988), *The Tale of the Body Thief* (1992), and *Memnoch the Devil* (1995).

Armand authored *The Vampire Armand* (1998).

Pandora authored *Pandora* (1998).

Vittorio authored *Vittorio the Vampire* (1999).

David Talbot authored *Merrick* (2000).

Marius authored *Blood and Gold* (2001).

Quinn Blackwood authored *Blackwood Farm* (2002).

Lestat then returns to author the remaining Vampire Chronicles with *Blood Canticle* (2003), *Prince Lestat* (2014), and *Prince Lestat and the Realms of Atlantis* (2016).

The Coven of the Articulate appears in *Prince Lestat* (2014). For more perspectives on the Coven of the Articulate, read the *Alphabettery* entries **Armand**, **Coven**, **Coven Master**, **Daniel Malloy**, **David Talbot**, **Lestat de Lioncourt**, **Louis de Pointe du Lac**, **Marius**, **Pandora**, and **Vittorio di Raniari**.

Creative Gardens

• SANCTUARY •

Many facets of Amel's planning for the city of Atlantis go into protecting the people of Earth from the exploitive appetites of the beings from the planet Bravenna. One result is a section of the city devoted to the enhancement of the city and its inhabitants. Filled with laboratories, factories, libraries, and centers of learning and artistry, such as the Creative Tower, this particular area is commonly referred to as the Creative Gardens, where every walkway and path is lined in gold and where the buildings are constructed with the beauty of the pearlescent substance known as luracastria. Amel's residence is in the Creative Gardens, where, with his superhuman intellect, he can work on the development of innovations for the betterment of humanity.

The Creative Gardens appear in *Prince Lestat and the Realms of Atlantis* (2016). For more perspectives on the Creative Gardens, read the *Alphabettery* entries **Amel**, **Bravenna**, **Creative Tower**, and **Luracastria**.

Creative Tower

• SANCTUARY •

After Amel creates the city of Atlantis out of a chemical compound called luracastria, which he develops from his enhanced genetic coding, he establishes in his luracastric city a place of inspiration, imagination, innovation, and inventiveness, a sanctuary of pure artistry that will work to benefit humankind, a sanctuary that he calls the Creative Tower, where the walls are pearlescent and the floors are gold. It is not simply an edifice of industry, but also the place where many professional administrators establish their personal chambers, including Amel, who works and rules over the city from the Creative Tower, not tyrannically, but clemently, as a friend and guardian of the inhabitants.

The Creative Tower appears in *Prince Lestat and the Realms of Atlantis* (2016). For more perspectives on the Creative Tower, read the *Alphabettery* entries **Amel**, **Bravenna**, **Creative Gardens**, and **Luracastria**.

Crippling Gift

• VAMPIRE ABILITY •

A vampire who is strong enough to destroy another vampire has the option to render the other vampire inert by snapping the vampire's neck. This causes the other vampire to enter a silent, dreamless state, wherein the being cannot communicate, not even with the Mind Gift. The strike renders the vampire paralyzed in body and mind.

This happens when Rhoshamandes kidnaps Louis, Gabrielle, and Marius. He breaks their necks, binds them in iron bars, and keeps them in the dungeon of *bet ha sohar*. After Lestat kills Rhoshamandes and frees his companions, Louis and Gabrielle need Fareed's medical assistance to return to health, while Marius is powerful enough to heal on his own once his neck is snapped back into place.

The crippling Gift appears in *Blood Communion* (2018). For more perspectives on the Crippling Gift, read the *Alphabettery* entries ***Bet Ha Sohar***, **Blood Curse**, **Cloud Gift**, **Dark Gift**, **Fire Gift**, **Gabrielle**, **Lestat de Lioncourt**, **Louis de Pointe du Lac**, **Marius**, **Mind Gift**, **Rhoshamandes**, and **Spell Gift**.

Cyril

• VAMPIRE •

Cyril is the outsider of the outsiders. A rogue vampire, he lives on the fringes of his own race until Lestat becomes the Prince; then Cyril finds his true calling as the Prince's protector. Cyril appears in *Prince Lestat* (2014), *Prince Lestat and the Realms of Atlantis* (2016), and *Blood Communion* (2018).

Long after the Blood Genesis, when Akasha and Enkil have established themselves as the gods Isis and Osiris, Cyril is born into a labor-intensive family in ancient Egypt. Miserable in a seeminly pointless existence of hard work and hunger, Cyril's desire to become a blood god is spurred by his abusive father. Eventually, the Elder, the protector of Those Who Must Be Kept, turns Cyril into a vampire and brings him to the shrine where priests guard the Sacred Fount of Queen Akasha. Cyril deplores the Queen's priests and he only consents to drink the Sacred Fount in order to gain greater power for greater independence. When he has a chance to leave, he takes it and wanders for centuries as a lone immortal.

Occasionally he makes fledglings, but their time together does not last long. He brings them to the blood temple where the Mother and the Father sit like statues. He ignores the objecting priests, who put up little challenge when he tells his children to drink from the Queen's Sacred Fount. Once his fledglings are strong enough, he leaves them and goes off on his own again.

About three hundred years before the Common Era, Cyril moves to the newly established city of Alexandria, where he takes up lodging in a three-story home that he fills with the treasures of his victims. One night, he happens upon a group of evildoers who have just kidnapped the fifteen-year-old Eudoxia. He slays each of them, but he is so stunned to discover that Eudoxia is such a beautiful young woman that he instantly, unceremoniously, turns her into a vampire. He dresses her in the clothes of her kidnappers and takes her hunting in the Alexandrian streets. He detests her long hair and cuts it short like a boy's hair every night; the first time he does it, she weeps bitterly, but he ignores her. He gives her a coffin and tells her the basic fundamentals of how to survive as a vampire. As a young woman groomed for the vocation of housewife, she quickly adapts to this lifestyle and enjoys it whenever he takes her swimming in the ocean to drink the blood of sailors on ships in the harbor. He tolerates her when she wears dresses, makes herself look beautiful, reads poetry to him, and cleans up their house by organizing a small library and setting up statues. Aware that the Elder, his maker, is keeping Those Who Must Be Kept in Alexandria's Egyptian quarter, Cyril understands that the best way to release himself from someone as young as his fledgling Eudoxia will be to have her drink Akasha's ancient blood. Like before, vampire priests in her blood temple object to him bringing his fledgling there, but no one stops him, not even the Elder, when Cyril sets Eudoxia at Akasha's feet and tells her to drink. He is satisfied when Eudoxia drinks enough of Akasha's blood to make her very powerful. Then he leaves her in the temple and abandons Alexandria.

When he grows tired of living, he goes into the earth and sleeps quietly for months or years. In the twentieth century he finds a solitary sanctuary on the side of Mount Fuji. He battles and defeats an ancient vampire for it and then sleeps until Amel, through the mysterious Voice, rouses him.

Desiring to leave Mekare and enter into a much-less-traumatized yet equally powerful vampire, Amel is able to manipulate Cyril to use his ancient abilities to destroy younger vampires in Tokyo. In time, Cyril breaks free of Amel's influence. Cyril hears the telepathic summons to the new tribe of vampires and finds himself moving towards it. By the time he arrives, Rhoshamandes has killed Maharet, and Lestat has destroyed Mekare to take Amel into himself and become the new host of vampire existence. As soon as Cyril sees the great power Lestat now possesses, the great power given to one so like himself, a vampire who continues to disregard authority, he knows he has waited all his life to vow allegiance to the Brat Prince without complaint or argument. Even after Amel is removed from his host by the Replimoid Kapetria, Lestat remains the Prince of the Vampires with Cyril by his side protectively.

For more perspectives on Cyril's character, read the *Alphabettery* entries **Akasha, Amel, Brat Prince, The Elder, Enkil, Eudoxia, Isis, Mekare, Osiris, Rhoshamandes, Sacred Fount**, and **Those Who Must Be Kept**.

Damnedest Creature

• SOBRIQUET •

amnedest Creature" is an affectionate sobriquet that Marius gives to Lestat in the eighteenth century both before and after Lestat plays the violin for Those Who Must Be Kept and awakens Akasha and Enkil, one in rapture, the other in rage. Even Gabrielle affectionately refers to her own son by this sobriquet at the end of *The Vampire Lesat*.

The sobriquet appears in *The Vampire Lestat* (1985), *The Queen of the Damned* (1988), *The Tale of the Body Thief* (1992), and *Memnoch the Devil* (1995). For more perspectives on the use of sobriquets in the Vampire Chronicles, read the *Alphabettery* entries **Beloved Boss**, **Brat Prince**, **Dazzling Duo**, **James Bond of Vampires**, **Little Brother**, **Little Grandmother**, **Old Queen**, **Ophelia Immortal**, **Ordinary Man**, **Sparrow**, and **Wolfkiller**.

Daniel Malloy

• VAMPIRE •

Daniel Malloy could be considered the spark that sets the Vampire Chronicles ablaze. His work inspired Louis to tell his story; Louis's story inspired Lestat's story; the rest is history. Daniel eventually becomes an immortal member of the Vampire Chronicles, although he does not find warmth until he meets the maker of his maker. Daniel appears in *Interview with the Vampire* (1976), *The Queen of the Damned* (1988), *The Vampire Armand* (1998), *Blood and Gold* (2001), *Prince Lestat* (2014), and *Prince Lestat and the Realms of Atlantis* (2016).

When he is a mortal eager to establish a name for himself as a noir biographer of ordinary people's lives, seventeen-year-old Daniel Malloy immediately becomes enchanted with the story of the nearly two-hundred-year-old vampire Louis de Pointe du Lac. In a sparse hotel room on Divisadero Street in San Francisco, Daniel listens attentively to all of Louis's story while recording his interview with the vampire on a tape recorder. Louis speaks of his mortal life in New Orleans, of the vampire Lestat who turns him into a vampire, of their vampire child, Claudia, of the ancient vampire Armand, who allows his coven to destroy Claudia before allowing Louis to destroy them so that he can accompany Louis into the modern world. Daniel marvels as Louis concludes the nightlong interview of his epic biography by providing the details of Lestat's last-known location. Daniel then begs Louis to turn him into a vampire.

Crestfallen that the message of his agonizing loneliness and sorrow has fallen on deaf ears, Louis reveals to Daniel the full horror of his monstrously supernatural being. The vampire moves with lightning speed, flashes his fangs, drinks Daniel's blood to the point of death, and abandons him, sprawled out on the table where the interview occurred, not knowing whether Daniel will survive.

When Daniel awakens the next morning, he listens to Louis's description of the house in New Orleans where he last saw the vampire Lestat. Despite the fact that Louis has denied his request to become a vampire, Daniel remains hopeful that he can exchange his mortal life for an immortal existence of blood drinking. He spends the next two weeks investigating the facts of Louis's story. As the puncture wounds from Louis's fangs disappear, Daniel's newfound obsession drives him to madness. He leaves San Francisco for New Orleans in search of Lestat, driving a few hundred miles a day and staying in cheap roadside motels. On the way, he makes copies of his interview with Louis and sends them to his New York publisher. Daniel investigates public records, discovers Lestat's name on a property title, and hurries to that same address. He breaks the lock on the front door, enters the house, and searches through it, room by room, with a small flashlight. He finds a pocket watch engraved with Lestat's name, adding confirmation to Louis's story. He locates in an armoire rags of black frock coats that are so old that they disintegrate to dust upon the slightest touch. He finds leather boots so timeworn that they are withered and curling, now tumbled over on the old house's cedar boards. He finds no other sign of Lestat living in that house. As he once more listens to his tapes of his interview with the vampire, Armand appears, captures Daniel, and imprisons him in the dank basement for the next three days. When Armand determines that the publication of *Interview with the Vampire* will be innocuous, he releases Daniel and then laughs at him when Daniel begs Armand to give him the immortal life of a blood drinker. Armand promises Daniel that he will release him, but he will follow him wherever he goes. As long as Daniel is interesting, Armand will not kill him.

The publication of his book, *Interview with the Vampire*, births a collection of books titled the Vampire Chronicles, most authored by the vampire Lestat, with some by David Talbot and Marius de Romanus.

Daniel flees from Armand for the next twelve years. Wherever he goes, Armand is there—in Lisbon, Madrid, Vienna, Berlin, on a bus, in a taxi, in a train, in a café, in a hotel room. Daniel shows Armand a mortal's fascination with the modern world. Sometimes Armand leaves Daniel for weeks at a time. Daniel is driven to the brink of insanity wondering when Armand might appear. Throughout it all, Daniel continues to beg Armand to turn him into a vampire; Armand continues to refuse. At first he is afraid that Armand will kill him, but in time he begins to realize that Armand will neither kill him nor turn him into a vampire. The knowledge that immortality is at his fingertips, yet can

never be touched, propels his descent into madness. To cope, Daniel starts drinking so heavily that alcoholism begins to kill him. A few nights before the rock concert of the increasingly popular band Vampire Lestat, Armand finally turns Daniel into a vampire, even though Armand is fully aware that Daniel will hate him in time and they will inevitably separate.

After the defeat of the Queen of the Damned, Daniel leaves Armand. Armand lets him go, knowing that Daniel is strong enough to care for himself with Armand's five-hundred-year-old blood coursing through his veins. Despite Daniel's great strength, he cannot flee from the madness that has been chasing him ever since Louis sank his fangs into Daniel's neck. Fortunately, Armand's maker, Marius, finds that Daniel is interiorly lost and deranged, unable to care for himself. Taking pity on him, knowing that Daniel needs him, knowing that he also needs Daniel, Marius welcomes Daniel into his home and takes care of him. Over the next few decades, Daniel's mind heals and his sanity, dreams, and ambitions are restored. Marius teaches Daniel how to paint; they travel together all over the world and eventually become fast companions. Although the relationship between Marius and Armand suffers some tension when Marius turns Armand's mortal companions, Sybelle and Benji, into vampires, the animosity between Daniel and Armand heals, particularly during the time when Amel no longer desires to live inside the damaged mind of Mekare and inspires numerous ancient vampires to immolate their weaker kin. Many vampire relationships are restored at that time. And after Lestat becomes the Prince of the Vampires with the spirit of Amel now inside him, Daniel and Armand reunite at the new coven at Trinity Gate, where they go out hunting together in the gentle warm rain, while in the sanctuary Louis rereads the opening pages of *Interview with the Vampire* in fond reminiscence of the love and goodness he sought in those bygone days, which all began with seventeen-year-old Daniel, eager to make his mark on the world.

For more perspectives on Daniel Malloy's character, read the *Alphabettery* entries **Benji Mahmoud**, **Lestat de Lioncourt**, **Louis de Pointe du Lac**, **Marius**, **Night Island**, **Sybelle**, and **Trinity Gate**.

Dark Blood

• IDIOM •

"Dark Blood" is a euphemism for the act of being turned into a vampire. Marius often uses the term; for instance, he explains that he became a vampire when his maker, the God of the Grove (Teskhamen), gave him the Dark Blood. Marius also explains that he does not want to condemn Armand to the Dark Blood by turning Armand into a creature like himself.

The idiom appears in *The Vampire Lestat* (1985), *The Tale of the Body Thief* (1992), *The Vampire Armand* (1998), *Blood and Gold* (2001), *Blood Canticle* (2003), *Prince Lestat* (2014), and *Prince Lestat and the Realms of Atlantis* (2016). For more perspectives on the Dark Blood in the Vampire Chronicles, read the *Alphabettery* entries **Armand**, **God of the Grove**, **Marius**, and **Teskhamen**.

Dark Gift

• IDIOM •

"Dark Gift" is a reference to the giving and receiving of a vampire's blood in the process of turning a mortal into a vampire. It is a process that can occur once, as when Lestat gives Louis the Dark Gift, or it can occur several times through the course of a night, such as when Teskhamen turns Marius into a vampire. Teskhamen drinks Marius's blood, and then Marius drinks Teskhamen's, not once, but over and over again throughout the night, until Teskhamen is absolutely certain that Marius has received the Dark Gift.

The only exception to this case is when Magnus captures Benedict, drains both Benedict and himself of blood, then proceeds to drink Benedict's blood and turn himself into a vampire. Magnus steals the Dark Gift with unprecedented scientific precision.

An early reference to this Dark Gift can be found in the Great Laws of the Children of Satan, specifically the second law, which states that "The Dark Gifts must never be given to the crippled, the maimed, or to children or those who cannot, even with the Dark Powers, survive on their own." Because the Children of Satan exist during the early centuries of the Common Era, before the fall of the Roman Empire, it is likely that the Dark Gift is a reference to the religious beliefs of the Children of Satan that their work must cooperate with Lucifer's work, which, in the fulfillment of God's plan, destroys God's greatest creation, a human being, by giving the person darkness as a gift.

The idiom appears in *The Vampire Lestat* (1985), *The Queen of the Damned* (1988), *The Tale of the Body Thief* (1992), *The Vampire Armand* (1998), *Pandora* (1998), *Merrick* (2000), *Blood and Gold* (2001), *Blood Canticle* (2003), *Prince Lestat* (2014), and *Prince Lestat and the Realms of Atlantis* (2016). For more perspectives on the Dark Gift in the Vampire Chronicles, read the *Alphabettery* entries **Blood Curse**, **Cloud Gift**, **Crippling Gift**, **Dark Gift**, **Fire Gift**, **Children of Satan**, **Great Laws**, **Lestat de Lioncourt**, **Louis de Pointe du Lac**, **Marius**, **Mind Gift**, **Spell Gift**, and **Teskhamen**.

Dark Trick

• IDIOM •

One of the earliest references to the Dark Trick comes from the Great Laws of the Children of Satan, an ancient vampire coven that existed long before Lestat, during the times of the Roman Empire and throughout the Middle Ages. Their first Great Law specifically states: "Each coven must have its leader and only he might order the working of the Dark Trick upon a mortal."

Essentially, the Dark Trick is a name for the process of turning a human mortal into an immortal vampire. The Dark Trick works several supernatural facets throughout the transformation process. Not only does the Dark Trick give the fledgling a ferocious bloodlust, but it also provides the superhuman abilities of telepathy, telekinesis, pyrokinesis, and levitation, along with superior strength, speed, senses, and healing, plus immortality.

The act of both giving and receiving the Dark Trick is very intimate. An ironic result of the Dark Trick is that it diminishes intimacy between maker and fledgling. While makers usually transform fledglings into a vampire out of love in the hope of creating an immortal companion, their telepathic connection is eternally severed. No longer can the maker hear the fledgling's thoughts or send psychic messages. This one facet in the process of making a vampire is both dark and a trick to maker and fledgling, since it causes between them, in most cases, a great rupture of intimacy.

In one case of the Dark Trick destroying a relationship, Armand loves Daniel Malloy so much that he dreads turning him into a vampire, knowing how they will be separated telepathically. His instincts are correct when, after he turns Daniel into a vampire, Daniel ends up hating Armand intensely. In another case, Marius does Armand a favor by turning Armand's wards, Benji and Sybelle, into vampires so that their strength will be equal to Armand's and so that they can communicate with him telepathically.

The idiom appears in *The Vampire Lestat* (1985), *The Queen of the Damned* (1988), *The Tale of the Body Thief* (1992), *The Vampire Armand* (1998), *Pandora* (1998), *Blood Canticle* (2003), *Prince Lestat* (2014), and *Prince Lestat and the Realms of Atlantis* (2016). For more perspectives on the Dark Trick in the Vampire Chronicles, read the *Alphabettery* entries **Armand**, **Benji Mahmoud**, **Children of Satan**, **Daniel Malloy**, **Great Laws**, **Lestat de Lioncourt**, **Louis de Pointe du Lac**, **Marius**, **Sybelle**, and **Teskhamen**.

David Talbot

• VAMPIRE •

David Talbot is Lestat's dearest companion in the twentieth and twenty-first centuries. Together they share many adventures, and Lestat often seeks out David's sagacious counsel. David is one of the few vampires whose mortal life positively influences his immortal behavior. David appears in *The Queen of the Damned* (1988), *The Tale of the Body Thief* (1992), *Memnoch the Devil* (1995), *Pandora* (1998), *Merrick* (2000), *Prince Lestat* (2014), *Prince Lestat and the Realms of Atlantis* (2016), and *Blood Communion* (2018).

More than twenty years before the defeat of Akasha, the Queen of the Damned, David Talbot, Superior General of the Talamasca, takes from Aaron Lightner as his ward Merrick Mayfair, an orphaned child and an extraordinarily powerful witch of the Mayfair family. David raises her in the environs of the Talamasca until she eventually graduates from the university and becomes a member of the Order herself. As mentor and pupil, and verging on lovers, David and Merrick have numerous missions together for the Talamasca. When Merrick is compelled to go to Central America, to unearth from a deadly cave a magical jade mask that reveals to the wearer ethereal spirits as if they were incarnate, David accompanies her. They are confronted by a perilous spirit resembling a priest. As a result, David becomes mortally ill, but he is eventually cured of the disease.

Following the destruction of Akasha, Lestat and Louis travel to the London Motherhouse of the Talamasca and encounter the elderly David Talbot, still the Talamasca Superior General. They demand from him the diary of Claudia the vampire. David surrenders the diary to them, but when Lestat offers to turn him into a vampire, David refuses.

Lestat is impressed with this first meeting and visits David often. The two become confidants. David grows to value Lestat's company, not simply because of his Talamasca duty to observe the ancient and powerful vampire, but also because he truly cares for Lestat. As time wears on, and as David ages, Lestat increasingly offers to make David an immortal, realizing that one day he will lose him to death. David continues to reject his offer, because he does not want or need immortality. When Lestat's failed suicide attempt in the sun leaves him wounded and weakened, he goes to David's home, where he spends time recuperating. David and Lestat soon discover that, because he has within himself the potent blood of Queen Akasha, the sun cannot harm him anymore, only bronze his skin.

Shortly thereafter, when Lestat receives Raglan James's offer to switch bodies, David advises Lestat against this. But Lestat ignores David's advice, and Raglan steals Lestat's vampire body. David helps Lestat psychically push Raglan from Lestat's vampire body and back into his former mortal body. Because this happens at sunrise, Lestat must flee and find a place to slumber throughout the day, while the elderly David must contend with the much-younger Raglan James, who switches bodies with David for the purpose of tricking Lestat into changing David's elderly body (with Raglan inside) into a vampire. When Lestat drinks his blood and discovers that it is not David in that body but in fact Raglan James, the Body Thief, he kills Raglan by crushing the skull of David's former body. When he finally finds David Talbot in Raglan's former body, Lestat turns him into a vampire, against David's kicking and screaming protests. Deeply angered by this in the beginning, David disappears for a while, but he and Lestat eventually reconnect in New Orleans. David expresses to Lestat that he secretly desired to become a vampire and that he is glad and grateful to Lestat for giving him not simply the Dark Gift but also the powerful blood within him.

Following Lestat's return from his journey with Memnoch the Devil through Heaven and Hell, David becomes one of his caretakers when Lestat falls into a catatonic state, waking occasionally but sleeping most of the time, in the New Orleans townhouse that they share with Louis. During their time together in New Orleans, David embarks on a new adventure with Merrick Mayfair, his former apprentice in the Talamasca.

After the unfolding of the events that took place when Lestat switched bodies with Raglan James, Merrick's doubts about David's death are confirmed when David contacts her and explains how he survived in the former body of Raglan James and is now an immortal vampire. David enjoins her to use her magic to raise the spirit of Claudia for Louis. Shortly after she does, Louis is so drawn to her that he turns her into a vampire. Much to David's surprise, Merrick confesses that she used her magic power to attract Louis and David to herself, because she desired to become an immortal blood drinker. David, Merrick, and Lestat form a New Orleans coven, residing with Louis, not long after they save Louis from a failed suicide attempt.

However, when Merrick performs an exorcism that aids the ghost of Quinn Blackwood's dead twin brother, Goblin, to go into the light of the afterlife, Merrick loses her own life in a self-sacrificial act. Grieving the great depth of the loss of Merrick, David pens the story of Merrick for his former brothers and sisters in the Talamasca, as well as for any follower of the Vampire Chronicles, because he loved her very much.

In the early twenty-first century, David Talbot takes up residence at Château de Lioncourt and becomes an influential member of the Court of the Prince. He consents to the vengeful destruction of Rhoshamandes and attends the first Winter Solstice Ball.

For more perspectives on David Talbot's character, read the *Alphabettery* entries **Aaron Lightner**, **Akasha**, **Lestat de Lioncourt**, **Louis de Pointe du Lac**, **Merrick Mayfair**, **Raglan James**, and **Talamasca Order**.

Davis

• VAMPIRE •

Davis is a twentieth-century vampire who joins three prominent covens: the Fang Gang, the Blood Kindred, and the Court of the Prince. He appears in *The Queen of the Damned* (1988), *Prince Lestat* (2014), *Prince Lestat and the Realms of Atlantis* (2016), and *Blood Communion* (2018).

Davis is born in New York, raised by a Caucasian father and a mother of African descent, and trained to be a classical pianist. But the strain of his parents' expectations drives him to a mental breakdown. He devolves into a drug addict and begins living on the streets. He is discovered by the vampire Killer, who turns him into a vampire and invites him to join his vampire gang, the Fang Gang.

The vampire Davis then wears a leather jacket and rides a Harley-Davidson motorcycle all over the United States. They bring in other members, Tim, Russ, and the barely teenage Baby Jenks. Davis is happy as a vampire. He loves to dance, and whenever the Fang Gang rides into a new town, they spend their nights in graveyards, where he dances on graves. When the vampires Louis and Lestat write their books *Interview with the Vampire* and *The Vampire Lestat*, Davis encourages the other members of the Fang Gang to read them, since the books reveal new insights into their history as vampires. And when the music of the Vampire Lestat rock band begins topping radio charts, he dances to the music around cemetery headstones. He urges the gang to go west towards San Francisco, where the Vampire Lestat band will be playing its one and only concert.

As they are going, Davis and the others notice how vampire coven houses are being burned to the ground all over the country, perhaps even all over the world. Davis and Killer warn Baby Jenks not to go near them because many older vampires dislike younger ones. Before the concert, the Fang Gang is separated. Unbeknownst to them, Lestat's music has awoken the Queen, Akasha, who is rampaging throughout the world, immolating her vampire children, except for a precious few. Baby Jenks already left them a few nights earlier, but Davis sees Killer fleeing through the crowd, and he believes he sees Tim and Russ destroyed. Davis is, however, saved from the immolations by the ancient vampire Gregory Duff Collingsworth, who is almost as old as Akasha herself. He takes Davis away from the carnage, flying him up into the air with the Cloud Gift, and brings him to his own coven, to be cared for by Zenobia, Avicus, and Flavius. In the end, Davis makes his residence at Château de Lioncourt and becomes a member of the Court of the Prince.

For more perspectives on Davis's character, read the *Alphabettery* entries **Akasha, Avicus, Baby Jenks, Blood Kindred, Enkil, Fang Gang, Flavius, Gregory Duff Collingsworth, Killer, Lestat de Lioncourt, Russ, Tim, The Vampire Lestat**, and **Zenobia**.

Davoud of Iran

• VAMPIRE •

Scant details have been gathered on the life story of Davoud of Iran. Speculation suggests that he might be as old as Akasha and Enkil, and may have even served in the ancient Egyptian court, perhaps in the Queens Blood alongside Gundesanth and Nebamun. He reveals himself to Lestat at the outset of the twenty-first century at the Court of the Prince at Château de Lioncourt.

Davoud of Iran appears in *Blood Communion* (2018). For more perspectives on Davoud's character, read the *Alphabettery* entries **Akasha, Lestat de Lioncourt, Nebamun, Rhoshamandes**, and **Santh**.

Dazzling Duo

• SOBRIQUET •

Because of his deep admiration for his own fledgling, the former witch Mona Mayfair, and her paramour, Quinn Blackwood, one of Lestat's closest companions, he refers to them, and their passionate love affair, as the Dazzling Duo.

The idiom is used in *Blood Canticle* (2003). For more perspectives on the Dazzling Duo in the Vampire Chronicles, read the *Alphabettery* entries **Lestat de Lioncourt**, **Mona Mayfair**, and **Quinn Blackwood**.

Dead Blood

• PHENOMENON •

When a vampire drinks the blood of the dead, the effect is a reaction opposite to that of drinking the blood of the living. The dead blood sickens a vampire to the point of paralysis, making the vampire appear corpselike. This happens to Lestat when Claudia, in an attempt to kill her maker, tricks him into drinking the dead blood of a young boy. He lies on the carpet of their Rue Royale townhouse, staring helplessly at the ceiling, shuddering, his eyes veiling, barely able to form a coherent cry for help to Louis, utterly susceptible to the kitchen knife that Claudia uses to cut his throat before plunging it into his chest.

The dead blood phenomenon appears in *Interview with the Vampire* (1976). For more perspectives on dead blood, read the *Alphabettery* entries **Claudia**, **Lestat de Lioncourt**, and **Louis de Point du Lac**.

Dead Guys

• IDIOM •

"Dead guys" is the term that the Fang Gang—Killer, Davis, Baby Jenks, Tim, and Russ—use to describe their own kind, even though they have seen the word "vampire" numerous times in the books written by the vampire Lestat and follow his eponymous rock band.

The idiom appears in *The Queen of the Damned* (1988). For more perspectives on Dead guys in the Vampire Chronicles, read the *Alphabettery* entries **Baby Jenks**, **Fang Gang**, **Killer**, **Laurent**, **Lestat de Lioncourt**, **Russ**, **Tim**, and **The Vampire Lestat**.

"Declaration in the Form of Graffiti"

• PHENOMENON •

"Declaration in the Form of Graffiti" is a hidden text in the guise of graffiti, to prevent mortal eyes from reading vampire secrets. Mortals would see the declaration as meaningless vandalism, but a vampire could read the declaration within the graffiti. And only a vampire would have written such a declaration in the form of graffiti. Written in Dracula's Daughter vampire bar in San Francisco around 1984, the declaration informs vampires of Lestat's exploits in the late twentieth century of writing an autobiography and producing rock music, both of which reveal vampire secrets. The declaration also demands that Lestat, Armand, Gabrielle, Louis, and all of Lestat's cohorts be put to death. The message spreads worldwide through the Vampire Connection. Many vampires come to the 1985 concert of the Vampire Lestat rock band seeking to fulfill the declaration's demand.

"Declaration in the Form of Graffiti" appears in *The Queen of the Damned* (1988). For more perspectives on this declaration in the Vampire Chronicles, read the *Alphabettery* entries **Akasha**, **Gabrielle**, **Great Burning of 1985**, **Lestat de Lioncourt**, **Louis de Pointe du Lac**, **Vampire Bar**, and **Vampire Connection**.

Denis

• MORTAL •

Denis is a mortal boy who resides with the vampires at the Théâtre des Vampires. Little is known of his history, but he is revealed to be an intimate companion of Armand.

When Louis and Claudia visit Armand

at the Théâtre des Vampires, Armand offers Denis to Louis hospitably, and Denis readily surrenders himself to the possibility that Louis might kill him. Through Denis, Louis experiences for the first time a mortal's willing desire to be bitten by a vampire. And through Louis drinking Denis's blood, Armand witnesses Louis's sympathy for mortal victims, increasing Armand's longing for companionship with Louis, which spurs their debate on the nature of good and evil. Claudia views Denis as nothing more than Armand's slave, but Louis views him as the image of love, not mortal love, but vampiric love, which, for Louis, culminates in the kill. As Armand's attraction to Louis intensifies, and as he contrives to part Louis from Claudia, he confesses to Louis that he has killed Denis. The news shocks Louis, but Armand gently assures him that Denis had to die because "it was best."

Denis appears in *Interview with the Vampire* (1976). For more perspectives on his character, read the *Alphabettery* entries **Armand**, **Claudia**, **Louis de Pointe du Lac**, and **Théâtre des Vampires**.

Derek

• IMMORTAL •

In the great rebellion of Amel against the Bravennans, thousands of years before the building of the first Pyramids on Earth, Bravennan scientists create humanoids, called Replimoids, that can combat Amel, a human whom they have abducted and genetically enhanced to do their bidding. Derek is among the last group of Replimoids sent to Earth to combat Amel and destroy his luracastric cities, along with three others: Kapetria, Garekyn, and Welf. Their mission to destroy Amel fails once they encounter him. Through persuasive arguments, he convinces them that the Bravennans, whom they refer to as the Parents, have been lying to them and that they have been using human suffering as a natural resource for food and satisfaction. Amel has only been trying to protect humans against the Bravennans, who send plagues and disasters upon Earth to make its inhabitants suffer more and to increase "food" production.

Once the Bravennans realize that Derek and his companions have failed, they send a meteor shower through space, which falls directly down upon Amel and his greatest luracastric creation, the city of Atlantis. As the city sinks into the boiling sea, Derek is separated from his companions. Made similar to Amel, only less powerful, Derek and his companions have the ability to survive, self-replicate, and live a potentially immortal existence.

To survive throughout the long centuries of isolation and loneliness, Derek retreats to a place of solitude, often to the isolation of the Andes Mountains, and sleeps until he is ready to reemerge and learn the customs of the modern world.

By the time of the twentieth century, Derek has lived so long that his memories of his Replimoid companions, of Amel and the city of Atlantis, are more like dreams. He awakens and is educated in the ways of the modern world by a poor Peruvian priest, teaching him Spanish and Christianity. From what he recalls of his old life, Derek discovers that Amel's spirit has lived on and has fused with an ancient Egyptian queen, Akasha, to create a new race of beings on Earth, referred to as the Drinkers of the Blood or, more commonly in the modern era, vampires. One very old vampire in Budapest named Roland realizes that Derek is not human, captures him, and feeds upon his blood. Roland learns that, because of Derek's ability to heal rapidly, he is an unending fount of humanlike blood: Roland can drink every drop of blood in his body, and the blood will replenish after an hour or two, so that Roland will begin again. He shares Derek with other vampires, such as Avicus and Rhoshamandes. They hold Derek captive for ten years. Whenever they feed off Derek, he dreams of Atlantis and passes those dreams through his blood to his vampire captors, particularly the name of Amel. Rhoshamandes is still bitter about his dealings with the spirit of Amel, and how Lestat cut off his left arm because of it. In outrage against Amel, Rhoshamandes cuts off Derek's left arm. Because Derek is a Replimoid and has the ability to self-replicate, his severed left arm grows into a perfect clone of himself, which he refers to as his son and names Derek Two, which is soon shortened to "Dertu."

Dertu helps Derek escape and reunite with Kapetria, Garekyn, and Welf, who are companions of more congenial vampires, namely Lestat, Marius, Armand, and many others in their coven. Together, Derek works with Kapetria to learn more about why Amel desires to be free of living inside a vampire host. They develop a way to re-create a clone of the body that Amel had while he lived in Atlantis. They also use genetic cells from the skin in their hands to re-create the most difficult and important scientific achievement— Amel's brain. Once they finally re-create a perfect likeness of the man he was thousands of years earlier in the city of Atlantis, they perform a delicate exercise that removes Amel from Lestat's brain, so that Amel can now live in a body all his own, without destroying the Sacred Core, the center of all vampire existence.

Derek appears in *Prince Lestat and the Realms of Atlantis* (2016). For more perspectives on Derek's character, read the *Alphabettery* entries **Amel, Atlantis, Bravennans, Dertu, Garekyn, Kapetria, Lestat de Lioncourt, Luracastria, The Parents, Replimoid, Rhoshamandes, Roland,** and **Welf.**

Dertu

• IMMORTAL •

After Derek, a Replimoid from the planet Bravenna, is captured and imprisoned by the vampire Roland for almost a decade, Roland shares Derek's blood with the vampire Rhoshamandes, who drinks Derek's blood and, through it, discovers that Derek is intimately connected with the spirit of Amel, who betrayed Rhoshamandes and caused the severing of his left arm by Lestat. In anger and retribution, Rhoshamandes severs Derek's left arm. Unbeknownst to Roland and Rhoshamandes, because Derek is a scientific creation from the planet Bravenna, able to survive immortally through self-replication,

Derek's left arm grows into a perfectly cloned likeness of him. This clone refers to Derek as his father, and Derek accepts him as his son and names him Derek Two, which is immediately shortened to "Dertu."

Dertu helps Derek escape from Roland's compound and then helps him to safely reunite with other Replimoids whom the Bravennans have sent to Earth.

Dertu appears in *Prince Lestat and the Realms of Atlantis* (2016). For more perspectives on Dertu's character, read the *Alphabettery* entries **Amel**, **Atlantis**, **Bravennans**, **Derek**, **Kapetria**, **Katu**, **Replimoid**, **Roland**, and **Welf**.

Designée of the Mayfair Legacy

• HONORIFIC •

The Designée of the Mayfair Legacy is instituted by the sixth witch in the line of thirteen Mayfair witches, which the spirit of Lasher establishes as a means of incarnating himself as a Taltos. The Designée is the Mayfair witch who inherits the fortune that the Mayfair family has been amassing for many centuries, which, by the time of the twenty-first century, is worth billions. The Designée must wear the Mayfair emerald on her wedding day, and she must keep

her Mayfair name. All Designées through the centuries have the ability to control the spirit of Lasher, until he becomes incarnate through Rowan Mayfair. By the time Lestat encounters Rowan, her cousin Mona Mayfair is the Designée, and after her comes Mona's daughter, Morrigan.

The title "Designée of the Mayfair Legacy" appears in *Blood Canticle* (2003). For more perspectives on the Designée in the Vampire Chronicles, read the *Alphabettery* entries

Lasher, Lestat de Lioncourt, Mayfair Legacy, Mona Mayfair, Morrigan Mayfair, Quinn Blackwood, Rowan Mayfair, and Taltos.

Devil's Road

• IDIOM •

A term that arises during the medieval era, the "Devil's Road" is used to describe the lifestyle of vampires. It does not mean simply drinking blood and killing people. More specifically, the Devil's Road refers to the widespread and ultimate work of vampires as agents of Satan and is used primarily by the Children of Satan, a cultish vampire coven that has many houses and followers. All of them believe that they are agents of Satan working together to corrupt humankind away from God, away from Heaven, to fill Hell with as many sinful souls as possible. The Devil's Road is the work of vampires to turn people away from believing in God and towards faithlessness, hopelessness, and lovelessness. In other words, progress along the Devil's Road in the immortal life of a malevolent vampire juxtaposes the Christian belief system for saints on a pilgrimage in the opposite direction toward the eternal life of Heaven. It is an ancient tradition on the Devil's Road for elder vampires, when they determine to end their life, to give their blood to younger vampires, so that none of the sacred blood is wasted.

The idiom appears in *The Vampire Lestat* (1985). For more perspectives on the Devil's Road in the Vampire Chronicles, read the *Alphabettery* entries **Children of Darkness**, **Great Laws**, **Lestat de Lioncourt**, **Line of de Landen Vampires**, **Magnus**, and **Those Who Must Be Kept**.

Divine Couple

• HONORIFIC •

Divine Couple becomes another name for Akasha and Enkil, the first vampires, who associate themselves with the ancient Egyptian deities Isis and Osiris. Their fledglings and disciples, and even their mortal subjects, always refer to them as divine beings. Marius keeps up the practice when he is caring for Those Who Must Be Kept, often referring to them as the Divine Couple.

The honorific appears in *Blood and Gold* (2001). For more perspectives on the Divine Couple in the Vampire Chronicles, read the *Alphabettery* entries **Akasha**, **Enkil**, **Isis**, **Lestat de Lioncourt**, **Marius**, **Osiris**, and **Those Who Must Be Kept**.

Divine Pair

• HONORIFIC •

Because the first vampires, Akasha and Enkil, establish themselves as leaders of a blood cult religion, donning the identities of Isis and Osiris, they also gain for themselves honorifics and are often called "divine" by their subjects and devotees. The word is used in numerous descriptors, such as "Divine Parents" or "Divine Couple." The vampire Marius, who cares for Akasha and Enkil, often calls them the Divine Pair, particularly when he is moving them from one shrine to another.

The honorific appears in *Blood and Gold* (2001). For more perspectives on the Divine Pair in the Vampire Chronicles, read the *Alphabettery* entries **Akasha**, **Enkil**, **Isis**, **Lestat de Lioncourt**, **Marius**, **Osiris**, and **Those Who Must Be Kept**.

Divine Parents

• HONORIFIC •

"Divine Parents" is an ancient term to describe the Mother and the Father of the vampire race, Akasha and Enkil. Marius often uses it, like many other vampires before him, as a sign of respect for the ones he cares for, Those Who Must Be Kept. Marius also often uses the term "divine" to venerably describe Akasha and Enkil's importance to the vampire race, such as "Divine Pair" or "Divine Couple."

The honorific appears in *Blood and Gold* (2001). For more perspectives on the Divine Parents in the Vampire Chronicles, read the *Alphabettery* entries **Akasha**, **Enkil**, **Marius**, and **Those Who Must Be Kept**.

Dmitri Fontayne

• VAMPIRE •

Dmitri Fontayne is the full name of Mitka, the vampire whom Lestat befriends in the early twenty-first century. Dmitri is born in Russia in the 1700s and is turned into a vampire by Pandora at the age of thirty-four. Dmitri joins the Court at Château de Lioncourt, where he becomes very close companions with Louis.

Dmitri Fontayne appears in *Blood Communion* (2018). For more perspectives on Dmitri's character, read the *Alphabettery* entries **Baudwin**, **Château de Lioncourt**, **Lestat de Lioncourt**, **Louis de Pointe du Lac**, **Mitka**, and **Pandora**.

Dolly Jean Mayfair

• WITCH •

Mentioned in *Blood Canticle* (2003), Dolly Jean Mayfair is a part of the witch family that separates during the feud between Julien and Augustine Mayfair. Before her birth, her family moves away from the Riverbend plantation and starts a new Mayfair plantation called Fontevrault. By the time Dolly Jean is living there with her granddaughter, Mary Jane, Fontevrault has fallen into ruins.

When Mona Mayfair becomes pregnant with Michael Curry's child, Dolly Jean's granddaughter, a powerful witch, senses that Mona's baby is a Taltos, so she brings Mona out to the Fontevrault plantation to give birth. Because giving birth to a Taltos is extremely difficult, especially for non-Taltos mothers like Mona, Dolly Jean assists in the delivery and observes how quickly after the birth the baby, whom they name Morrigan, becomes a Walking Baby, who grows to an adult immediately.

For more perspectives on Dolly Jean Mayfair's character, read the *Alphabettery* entries **Fontevrault Plantation**, **Julien Mayfair**, **Mary Jane Mayfair**, **Mona Mayfair**, **Morrigan Mayfair**, **Riverbend Plantation**, **Taltos**, and **Walking Baby**.

Donnelaith, Scotland

• SANCTUARY •

Discussed in *Blood Canticle* (2003), Donnelaith, Scotland, is the place of origin of the Mayfair family of witches. When the evil spirit Lasher seeks to become incarnate, he develops a plan for inbreeding thirteen generations of witches, with the thirteenth and final witch giving birth to his incarnation as an immortal Taltos.

This plan originates in Donnelaith with Suzanne Mayfair, the first witch who summons Lasher. Through her descendants, Lasher will be born. The Mayfair family moves away from Donnelaith when Suzanne is burned at the stake for witchcraft, and her daughter, Deborah Mayfair, is taken away by the Talamasca to live in Amsterdam.

For more perspectives on Donnelaith in the Vampire Chronicles, read the *Alphabettery* entries **Lasher**, **Talamasca Order**, **Taltos**, and **Thirteen Witches**.

Dora

• MORTAL •

Dora is a mortal televangelist whom Lestat is both committed to protect and deeply attracted to in *Memnoch the Devil* (1995). She helps Lestat bring Veronica's Veil to greater public attention.

Born in New Orleans and named Theodora Flynn, though she comes to be called simply Dora, she is raised by her unwed mother, Terry, a practical nurse. Dora grows up knowing her father, Roger, only by his visits from New York. He lavishes upon her gifts and money. Dora dislikes her mother and often wishes she would die. Her wish comes true when her mother threatens to take Dora away from Roger. Dora never forgets that Roger killed her mother; she never forgets seeing her mother's dead body wrapped in plastic. Roger takes Dora back to New York with him and, as she ages, she begins to understand that Roger is a major criminal, not only a murderer, but also a smuggler, a contract killer, and a very wealthy drug lord.

As Dora matures, realizing that she desires to be utterly unlike Roger, she goes to the seminary, is ordained as a Christian minister, and eventually becomes a successful televangelist. Despite her popularity, she continues to interact with Roger, rejecting his gifts yet always hoping for his salvation. Unbeknownst to her, the vampire Lestat stalks and kills Roger at the height of her popularity. Roger's ghost appears to Lestat and implores him to protect Dora from his enemies and from the harm that his reputation can do to her Christian vocation. Dora encounters Lestat as she is on her way to her chapel, shortly after she hears the news of Roger's death. Lestat goes to her, fulfilling his promise to Roger and admitting to her not only that he killed Roger but also that he is a vampire and that he will now protect her. Dora's fearlessness impresses Lestat; he feels deep love for her. They talk for some time, and their affection for each other grows. Soon Lestat begins to feel the presence of his Stalker, so he leaves Dora but promises that he will return.

When Dora next sees Lestat, he tells her how he went on a spiritual journey with Memnoch the Devil, where he wiped the face of the crucified Jesus with Veronica's Veil. Lestat reveals that he has kept the veil and then gives it to Dora. In turn, she shows Veronica's Veil to the world on the steps of Saint Patrick's Cathedral in New York, as proof of Jesus Christ's sacrificial love on the cross.

For more perspectives on Dora's character, read the *Alphabettery* entries **Lestat de Lioncourt**, **Memnoch**, **Roger**, and **Veronica's Veil**.

Dracula's Daughter

• SANCTUARY •

Dracula's Daughter is a cabaret within the Vampire Connection, a union of several vampire bars offering sanctuary for vampires seeking information and companionship. Named after the 1936 vampire horror film *Dracula's Daughter*, the cabaret is considered the most beautiful of all vampire bars. On the red wall in one of the back rooms, a vampire has penned in black felt-tip marker the "Declaration in the Form of Graffiti," which recounts the violations of the vampire Lestat as of 1985 and urges vampires throughout the Vampire Connection to destroy him and all vampires connected with him.

For more perspectives on Dracula's Daughter bar, read the *Alphabettery* entries **Bela Lugosi**, **Carmilla**, **Dr. Polidori**, **Lamia**, **Lord Ruthven**, **Vampire Bar**, and **Vampire Connection**.

1

Drinker of the Blood

• IDIOM •

The term "vampire" is of Eastern European descent, in use as early as the seventeenth century, perhaps two hundred years earlier; thus, vampires from the first millennium and older would not have called themselves "vampires" until the latter half of the second millennium.

When Amel enters into Queen Akasha, and she makes King Enkil her first fledgling— the first two vampires in existence—they call themselves "Drinkers of the Blood," a term describing their most obviously identifiable behavior that makes mortals most fearful of them.

Following their transformation into blood drinkers, they begin making fledglings, such as Khayman, Gundesanth, Teskhamen, Nebamun, and Rhoshamandes, who follow their makers' example and also refer to themselves by the term "Drinker of the Blood." During the passage of century after century, as the Drinker of the Blood race proliferates, breaking into factions of good and evil that fight against each other, they continue to keep that title and share it with their fledglings in following generations.

The idiom appears in *The Vampire Lestat* (1985) and *The Queen of the Damned* (1988). For more perspectives on the Drinkers of the Blood in the Vampire Chronicles, read the *Alphabettery* entries **Akasha**, **Amel**, **Blood Drinker**, **Enkil**, **Khayman**, **Nebamun**, **Rhoshamandes**, **Santh**, and **Teskhamen**.

Dr. Polidori

• SANCTUARY •

Dr. Polidori is a vampire bar in London, one of many in the Vampire Connection, where vampires can openly congregate with one another, share information, and find sanctuary. It is named after John William Polidori, author of "The Vampyre" (1819), the first successful fictional work on vampires in the gothic style.

Dr. Polidori vampire bar is mentioned in *The Vampire Lestat* (1985). For more perspectives on the Dr. Polidori bar, read the *Alphabettery* entries **Bela Lugosi**, **Carmilla**, **Dracula's Daughter**, **Lamia**, **Lord Ruthven**, **Vampire Bar**, and **Vampire Connection**.

Drug Merchants

• IDIOM •

When Silas the Taltos rebels against his parents, Ashlar and Morrigan Mayfair, on the Secret Isle, poisoning them and enslaving all other Taltos who will not follow his rebellion, he attacks the mortals living on surrounding islands. On one of the islands he attacks a drug cartel. In retaliation, the drug cartel comes to the Secret Isle and guns down most of the surviving Taltos, except for a small number. As one of the survivors, Oberon, who is Silas's brother, recounts this tale to Lestat, Mona Mayfair, and Quinn Blackwood, he identifies the killers of his kind simply as the Drug Merchants.

The idiom appears in *Blood Canticle* (2003). For more perspectives on Drug Merchants in the Vampire Chronicles, read the *Alphabettery* entries **Ashlar**, **Lestat de Lioncourt**, **Mona Mayfair**, **Morrigan Mayfair**, **Oberon**, **Quinn Blackwood**, **Secret Isle**, **Silas**, and **Taltos**.

Dybbuk

• ALIAS •

When Armand's suicide attempt fails in the late nineties, after he flies into the sun while listening to Lestat's fantastical tale of traveling with Memnoch the Devil and returning with Veronica's Veil, Armand falls and lands in a sheltered part of a roof on an abandoned building, not far from the hotel where Benji and Sybelle are staying.

Benji, a Bedouin servant boy from Israel, prays earnestly that some supernatural being will please save Sybelle from her violently abusive brother. Armand reaches out to both Benji and Sybelle telepathically, urging them to free him from the snow that has compacted upon him and is now hardened ice. The two mortals bring household instruments to chisel him free. Armand is horribly burned and weakened because of his exposure to the sunlight. Benji and Sybelle bring him back to their hotel room, where Armand can heal. With his telepathic powers, he projects an image of himself, the way he once looked: an adolescent boy with beautiful auburn hair, and with the capacity to viciously destroy a human being. Armand demonstrates his ferocity when he effortlessly kills Sybelle's brother, who is about to beat her to death. Believing that his prayers are answered,

Benji refers to Armand as a disembodied spirit that has the power to demonically possess mortals and is commonly called the dybbuk.

The alias appears in *The Vampire Armand* (1998). For more perspectives on the dybbuk in the Vampire Chronicles, read the *Alphabettery* entries **Armand**, **Benji Mahmoud**, **Sybelle**, and **Veronica's Veil**.

Elath

• TALTOS •

lath is one of the Taltos who live on Secret Isle, the island owned by the Taltos Ashlar, husband of Morrigan Mayfair, the daughter of Mona Mayfair, the fledgling of Lestat. Elath loves the jungles of the Secret Isle and can often be found there with the other Taltos, Releth. After Silas's rebellion coerces mortal drug dealers to attack the island, the only male Taltos kept alive are Elath, Hiram, and Oberon. Elath sees an opportunity to escape and kills one of the Drug Merchants, but he is shot dead soon after by the Drug Merchant's companions.

Elath appears in *Blood Canticle* (2003). For more perspectives on Elath's character, read the *Alphabettery* entries **Ashlar, Lestat de Lioncourt, Mona Mayfair, Morrigan Mayfair, Releth, Secret Isle**, and **Taltos**.

The Elder

• VAMPIRE •

The Elder is infamous for instigating the Great Burning of 4 C.E. when he abandons Those Who Must Be Kept under the Egyptian sun. He appears in *The Vampire Lestat* (1985), *The Queen of the Damned* (1988), and *Blood and Gold* (2001).

Thousands of years before the Common Era, after the great war between the Queens Blood and the First Brood, Akasha and Enkil are captured and imprisoned for so long that they become mute and immovable—like statues. When they are freed from this prison and once more elevated as the most honored of all vampires, they need to be cared for by a vampire almost as ancient as themselves. This caretaker vampire becomes known as the Elder.

Vestiges of the old blood religion remain. The Elder facilitates the blood rituals of the priests who continue to worship Those Who Must Be Kept. The Elder becomes the gateway for younger vampires to gain admittance to kneel before the Queen, to beseech Akasha for a taste of her powerful blood, and to clear away the remains of the young vampires she rejects. Caretaking becomes one of the principal duties of the Elder. He must wash and clean the Mother and the Father, change their clothes, and wipe away any dust that gathers over time. Throughout it all, Those Who Must Be Kept remain perpetually motionless, except on those rare occasions when they take a victim. They sit motionless, staring straight ahead like lifeless dolls, but their minds remain highly active.

To endure his eternal duties, the Elder makes several fledglings, two of whom are Cyril (Prince Lestat's bodyguard-to-be) and Avicus (Marius's eventual companion in Rome, who will help protect Those Who Must Be Kept). After more than a millennium of caring for them, the Elder grows weary of his endless and repetitive duties and no longer fully values the meaning of his life as the caretaker of the Mother and the Father of all vampirekind. Early one morning, he takes Akasha and Enkil out of their shrine, drags them to the banks of the Nile River, and leaves them lying there, exposed to the rising sun. He flees back to his sanctuary, where he remains safe throughout that day. When he rises the next night, he discovers that younger vampires have been utterly immolated, older vampires have been charred to a living crisp, but ancient vampires like himself have bronze skin, the way his mortal body once tanned under the hot Egyptian sun. Full of curiosity, he returns to the place where he left Those Who Must Be Kept and discovers to his dismay that they have not died but are tanned, with bronze flesh, like him. Understanding the profound connection between the Mother and the Father and all of their children, he also grasps the vast immensity of caring for Those Who Must Be Kept. If Akasha and Enkil suffer, all vampires suffer, in greater degrees for those with the fewest years. Moreover, he comprehends that if the Mother and the Father die, all vampires will also die. So the Elder brings Akasha and Enkil back to their shrine secretly and tells no one what he has done. But his new knowledge of the interconnectivity of all vampires sparks in him a new idea. Dreading the possibility of continuing his duties, he begins to consider ways to rid himself of Those Who Must Be Kept while also protecting them from anyone who might seek to destroy them. He comes up with the idea of dropping them to the bottom of the ocean, since in their current statuesque state, they do not appear to be breathing; and as long as they are not exposed to the sun again or any fire that might destroy them, they will remain alive while also preserving the lives of every vampire in existence.

Right at that time, Marius arrives in Egypt, having been sent by Teskhamen, who was an integral member of Akasha's blood priest cult. Marius finds the Elder in the temple library in old Egypt sitting at a desk, and he explains to the Elder how he was sent by Teskhamen, who was severely burned. The Elder tells Marius the vague and compelling legend about the Blood Genesis, but by then the stories seem too mythic to inspire the Elder's devotion to the old religion or his love for Those Who Must Be Kept. His faith in the Old Ways is dead. In his discussion with Marius, the Elder never mentions anything about the preservation of the old religion or the establishment of a new one. When Marius questions why so many vampires have been burned around the world, the Elder feigns ignorance and lies, stating that he does not know. Later, however, when the Elder stands with Marius before the Mother and the Father, Akasha uses the Mind Gift to confirm for Marius that the Elder is corrupt, evil, and a cowardly liar, and that she greatly desires Marius to take her and Enkil away from him because the Elder is once again planning to rid himself of his duties by drowning them at the bottom of the sea.

Upon Marius's inward acquiescence, Akasha rises from her throne to the great astonishment of the Elder. Stupefied, he can only stand perfectly still as Akasha crushes him under her feet. Finally, when he is nothing but a pulpy mess of flesh and bone and blood, Akasha sits back down upon her throne and uses her Mind Gift to telepathically knock over a nearby oil lamp. The oil mingles with the Elder's remains, and her Fire Gift ignites the oil to incinerate the Elder to ashes, which are subsequently trampled underfoot when Marius moves Those Who Must Be Kept to a holier shrine in Antioch.

For more perspectives on the Elder's character, read the *Alphabettery* entries **Akasha**, **Avicus**, **Cyril**, **Enkil**, **Lestat de Lioncourt**, **Marius**, and **Teskhamen**.

The Elders

• TALAMASCA •

After Teskhamen, Hesketh, and Gremt (along with Pandora, inadvertently) create the Talamasca Order in the eighth century, in an effort to more empirically understand the supernatural world, Teskhamen and his two ghostly companions oversee the development and expansion of the Talamasca, beginning with their Motherhouse in France. After many years pass, Teskhamen, Hesketh, and Gremt select mortal members of the Order who will take over leading the Talamasca, referring to these mortal leaders as the Elders.

As generations of members elapse, more Elders are selected. In time, Teskhamen, Hesketh, and Gremt become decreasingly involved, so much that, by the second millennium, they have been forgotten altogether as the founders of the Order.

Once the Elders are selected from among the ranks of the Talamasca, they withdraw and become anonymous figureheads of the Order, running the Talamasca from a distance, often communicating by letter, courier, email, fax, and any other means that maintains their anonymity. Furthermore, the location of their seat of power also remains a mystery. No one, not even the Superior General of the Order, knows the identities or the location of the Elders.

The Elders are spoken of in *Memnoch the Devil* (1995), *Merrick* (2000), and *Prince Lestat* (2014). For more perspectives on the Talamasca Elders in the Vampire Chronicles, read the *Alphabettery* entries **Gremt Stryker Knollys**, **Hesketh**, **Talamasca Order**, and **Teskhamen**.

Eleni

• VAMPIRE •

Eleni's appearance in the Vampire Chronicles is short-lived in *The Vampire Lestat* (1985), but she leaves such a lasting impression as a brief chronicler of Nicolas's tragic tale at the Théâtre des Vampires that her reappearance in *Prince Lestat* (2014), *Prince Lestat and the Realms of Atlantis* (2016), and *Blood Communion* (2018) ushers in a renewed joy for Lestat.

Shortly before the turn of the first millennium of the Common Era, in the region of modern-day France, Eleni is turned into a vampire by Everard, fledgling of Rhoshamandes, who incorporates Eleni in his line of de Landen vampires, which includes Benedict, Allesandra, Eugénie, Notker the Wise, and Everard. While they are still in that region,

Rhoshamandes and his fledglings are attacked by the Children of Satan, who capture Eleni, Allesandra, Eugénie, and Everard. Avoiding any further confrontations with the Children of Satan, Rhoshamandes and Benedict flee from that land to the north of England, shortly after the Norman Conquest, where they build a castle fortress and remain safe from any further mortal or immortal attacks.

The Children of Satan imprison, torture, and starve the four de Landen vampires until they finally agree to be indoctrinated into the coven by accepting their five Great Laws, which means that they can no longer live in luxury and are allowed to drink the blood only of poverty-stricken people of Paris and only under the filthiest of circumstances. Eleni's life is now compassed by guilt and pain, loneliness and sorrow.

A few centuries later, Armand becomes Eleni's leader of the Children of Darkness in Paris. He sends Everard to discover the fate of the Roman coven of the Children of Satan, but Everard takes that opportunity to escape, and Eleni will not see him again for centuries.

During the Age of Enlightenment, when the Parisian coven encounters Lestat and Gabrielle, Lestat convinces Armand that the norms and attitudes of the Children of Darkness are outmoded in the new era. In revolt, Eleni's de Landen sister, Allesandra, convinces Armand to destroy the coven by throwing herself into a funeral pyre. Armand proceeds to destroy all the vampires in the coven, sparing only four, two of whom are Eleni and Eugénie. Not realizing that Allesandra has survived the burning, they beg Lestat to stay with them and be their new leader. He refuses, but his fledgling, Nicolas

de Lenfent, persuades Lestat to give them Renaud's House of Thesbians. And when Nicolas and Armand join the coven, they change the name to Théâtre des Vampires, where they put on successful theater shows pretending to be humans who are pretending to be vampires. After Lestat leaves, Eleni writes to him about the fate of their endeavor, how the theater is becoming increasingly prosperous, how Armand governs them, and how Nicolas killed himself.

Eleni abandons this Parisian coven before Louis and Claudia arrive, only to eventually join Sevraine's underground coven in the Caves of Gold in the land of Cappadocia, a coven comprising only female vampires, which include her de Landen sister Eugénie, Marius's Bianca, and her other de Landen sister, once thought to be destroyed, Allesandra.

In the twenty-first century, Eleni encounters Lestat once more when he visits their Cappadocian coven in search of Rhoshamandes. After Lestat consumes Mekare's brain and takes into himself Amel, the Sacred Core, Eleni joins him along with many other vampires at Armand's coven house in New York, Trinity Gate. It is there that she is almost destroyed by the Replimoid Garekyn, who has just ingested the brain of the former founder of the Fang Gang, Killer, and destroyed him. Although he could have killed her, Garekyn ruptures Eleni's skull and leaves her for Armand and Benji to heal and save. She is eventually restored to full health at Fareed's laboratories in Paris. Afterward, she visits her old coven master, Rhoshamandes, on the island of Saint Rayne, but she takes up residence at the Court of the Prince in Château de Lioncourt.

For more perspectives on Eleni's character, read the *Alphabettery* entries **Allesandra, Amel, Armand, Bianca Solderini, Children of Darkness, Eugénie, Everard, Garekyn, Lestat de Lioncourt, Line of de Landen Vampires, Nicolas de Lenfent, Notker the Wise, Rhoshamandes, Sevraine, Théâtre des Vampires,** and **Trinity Gate.**

Emaleth

• TALTOS •

Emaleth is a short-lived Taltos who appears in *Lasher* (1993), but she is mentioned by name in *Blood Canticle* (2003) as the child of Lestat's fledgling Rowan Mayfair.

After Rowan decides to settle with Lasher in Houston, Texas, so she can study him clandestinely in the city's various hospitals and laboratories, Lasher betrays Rowan by imprisoning her and repeatedly raping her until she becomes pregnant with their Taltos child, whom Lasher desires as his bride.

The child in Rowan's womb begins communicating with her telepathically, informing her own mother that her name is Emaleth. She also speaks of ancient times that Lasher is ignorant of, as well as many other secrets that only a pure Taltos would know. Rowan telepathically tells Emaleth about New Orleans, the First Street house, and about her husband, Michael Curry. Rowan also tells her daughter that if she dies, Emaleth should go to New Orleans and inform Michael.

When Lasher discovers that Rowan is pregnant with their daughter, he lowers his guard caring for her, and she uses that opportunity to escape. Rowan heads to New Orleans, but on the way, she gives birth to Emaleth. The horrific ordeal of birthing a Taltos leaves Rowan comatose in a roadside park. Like all Taltos newborns, Emaleth matures into a fully grown adult within the hour. Emaleth feeds on her mother's breast milk until Rowan's comatose body cannot produce any more. Unable to rouse her mother, Emaleth abandons Rowan and walks the rest of the way to New Orleans.

When she finally arrives at the First Street house, she discovers that Rowan was found and is still comatose. Emaleth's own breast milk revives her mother, but Rowan rouses in such a frantic state that she grabs a gun off the bedside table and shoots Emaleth three times in the face. The Taltos child's final words ring out seconds before the first shot. "Mother, no."

For more perspectives on Emaleth's character, read the *Alphabettery* entries **First Street House, Lasher, Rowan Mayfair,** and **Taltos.**

Emily

• MORTAL •

Recently married and honeymooning in the European countryside, Emily and Morgan lodge for the night in an inn in a small village. Unfortunately, that village is located near ruins in the north where a revenant vampire lives. The vampire comes from his lair that night, feeds off Emily, and kills her. The villagers want to cut off her head to prevent her from rising from the dead as an immortal blood drinker. Shortly thereafter, the vampires Louis and Claudia appear, hear Morgan's tale, and promise to do what they can to find the vampire who did this to her and put an end to him.

Emily appears in *Interview with the Vampire* (1976). For more perspectives on Emily's character, read the *Alphabettery* entries **Claudia**, **Louis de Pointe du Lac**, **Morgan**, and **Revenant**.

Enkil

• VAMPIRE •

Enkil is the King of ancient Egypt, but he is a secondary ruler compared with his wife, Akasha. In mortality he supports her decisions for reform; in immortality he obeys her formative ruling as Queen of the Damned. Enkil appears in *The Vampire Lestat* (1985) and *The Queen of the Damned* (1988).

More than four thousand years before the Common Era, when the Queen of Egypt dies, the young Enkil succeeds her. He takes as his queen-bride the ravishing and intelligent Akasha of Uruk. Enkil is an impotent king, acting only after Akasha acts first. He is greatly jealous of her and will not allow her to keep lovers, such as Nebamun. He allows her to have great influence over Egyptian life. She brings many innovations from her unique culture to the throne, one of which is the replacement of Egypt's ritual cannibalism with her own culture's practice of wrapping corpses in shrouds and burying the dead. This causes revolt among common Egyptians, who take great comfort in their religious rites. When Enkil and Akasha hear of twin witch sisters with fiery-red hair and emerald-green eyes, Maharet and Mekare, who have the ability to commune with spirits, the Queen and King send the twins a royal message, asking them to come from their homeland in Israel south to Egypt, where they might convince the people that the spirits of the afterlife are happier when their corpses are not cannibalized but buried whole in the earth. The twins think this idea is absurd, since they, too, practice ritual cannibalism in their culture's religious beliefs; and they refuse the royal request. In response, Enkil and Akasha send the King's steward, Khayman, along with the royal army, to the twins' village, and they force Maharet and Mekare to come down to Egypt, but not before destroying their villages and massacring most of the villagers.

When the twins appear in the royal court, Akasha puts many questions to them. Maharet and Mekare try to convince the Queen that her ideas are misguided, so Akasha imprisons them. The Queen brings the twins back out to the court every day, where she continues to put the same questions to them. Frustrated, Mekare summons the spirit of Amel, who insults Enkil and Akasha. As punishment, Akasha orders Khayman to rape the twins before the entire court, after which she releases them back to their homeland. Amel's spirit does not return with the twins to Israel but remains behind in Egypt, where he haunts Khayman's house for his cruelty to the twins. Khayman complains to Enkil, who goes to Khayman's home along with Akasha. Coincidently, conspirators plotting to kill the King and Queen for outlawing ritual cannibalism take this opportunity to stab Enkil and Akasha to the point of death. Amel, who likes the taste of blood, tastes Akasha's blood, enters her wounds, and fuses with her in an unprecedented way to create the world's first vampire. With her new instincts taking over, Akasha turns Enkil into a vampire like herself.

As undead immortals, Enkil and Aka-sha can no longer go out into the sun, and the only way to endure their great hunger pangs is to drink blood incessantly. Enkil orders Khayman to dispose of the bodies in a deep pit. Their new bloodlust disturbs them so much that they summon the twins back to the royal court and question them about this strange transformation. Maharet suggests that, because spirits are such large entities, turning other mortals into vampires might spread out Amel's spiritual potency and dilute the bloodlust. Akasha tests this by turning Khayman into a vampire against his will, but it is not enough. After Mekare mocks and curses the Queen for her pride and foolishness, Akasha cuts out her tongue, plucks out Maharet's eyes, and sentences them to death. Khayman, however, seeking to overthrow Enkil and Akasha, turns Mekare into a vampire, who turns Maharet into a vampire also. Then the three escape and spend the next week turning numerous other mortals into vampires in an effort to raise an army that will eventually be called the First Brood and will fight against the King and Queen. Khayman escapes as the Egyptian army captures Maharet and Mekare. Enkil and Akasha entomb Maharet in a sarcophagus and set her adrift in the western ocean and then entomb Mekare in a sarcophagus and set her adrift in the eastern ocean.

Enkil observes as Akasha makes an army of fledglings called the Queens Blood, who war against the First Brood. To further solidify their power, Enkil and Akasha identify themselves as the gods Osiris and Isis and establish a blood cult full of blood rituals, blood priests, blood acolytes, and a discipleship of both vampires and mortals alike, yet it is the mortals who become the sacrificial blood offering to the new gods. Their reign lasts for centuries until the First Brood defeats the Queens Blood. Enkil and Akasha are captured and entombed beneath large stones too heavy for them to move, with only their necks and heads exposed so that their captors can drain their blood and drink from them.

After the passage of many more centuries, Enkil's and Akasha's skin becomes as white as marble, and they become statuesque, no longer responding to any stimulus. Their imprisonment lasts so long that their captors eventually forget the reason that the King and Queen must be bound. They understand the immensity of their power, particularly one night when their captors discover Enkil and Akasha lying on the floor, naked, embracing each other, while their stone prisons have been smashed to dust. Their fledglings then set them on altars and venerate them as the most powerful vampires. Referring to them now as "Those Who Must Be Kept," they place an elder vampire in charge of watching them.

Shortly after the outset of the Common Era, the Elder no longer desires the responsibility of keeping Enkil and Akasha, and he exposes them to the sun. But their great age makes them so powerful that the sun cannot destroy them; it only bronzes their skin. It is their fledglings who suffer the greatest consequences: younger vampires are destroyed altogether, older vampires are burned and blackened to char, while the oldest vampires, like Enkil and Akasha, are only bronzed.

Far away in the land of Gaul, the four-thousand-year-old Teskhamen turns Marius de Romanus into a vampire and sends him to Egypt to discover the fate of Enkil and Akasha. Marius and Akasha destroy the Elder, and then Marius brings her and Enkil out of Egypt into Antioch, where he becomes the new protector of Those Who Must Be Kept. Over the next few centuries, Akasha displays movement occasionally, but Enkil remains mostly motionless. One notable time he moves is when Marius brings the wounded and weakened Mael before Akasha, requesting that Mael be allowed to drink from her. Right before Mael can, Enkil suddenly rises and attempts to crush the younger vampire. Marius seats him, and Enkil does not move again until the eighteenth century, when Marius brings before the King and Queen the young vampire Lestat. The instant attraction between Lestat and Akasha arouses Enkil's ancient jealousy. He finally moves and attempts to kill Lestat, but Marius and Akasha are able to placate him. Enkil returns to stillness and remains that way until the twentieth century, when Lestat's music awakens Akasha for the last time.

Consolidating all vampiric power into herself as the sole progenitor of the vampire race, Akasha bites into Enkil's neck and drains his blood completely. The white, milky color of his marblelike skin drains away until his whole body—bones, lungs, organs, eyes—become as utterly transparent as glasswork.

For more perspectives on Enkil's character, read the *Alphabettery* entries **Akasha, Amel, Khayman, Lestat de Lioncourt, Mael, Maharet, Marius, Mekare, Nebamun, Teskhamen**, and **Those Who Must Be Kept**.

Eric

• VAMPIRE •

Eric is most known for being the long-term companion of Maharet who accompanies her transition into the Common Era. He appears in *The Queen of the Damned* (1988) and *Prince Lestat* (2014).

Eric is born almost a thousand years before the Common Era, in the region known today as India. He encounters the then three-thousand-year-old vampire Maharet, who is so beguiled by Eric that she turns him into her vampire companion. They blissfully enjoy each other's companionship for the next one thousand years, but tragedy occurs when the Elder guarding Those Who Must Be Kept sets Akasha and Enkil in the sun, which causes a terrible pandemic of vampire burnings. While older vampires like Maharet merely bronze, younger vampires are utterly immolated; Eric, however, being roughly one thousand years old, does not die but suffers severe burns. Maharet must nurse him back to health by feeding him her powerful blood.

Eric and Maharet separate sometime before the eighth century. He wanders to many places for many centuries and eventually becomes a companion to Santino in the sixteenth century. Their companionship lasts all the way until the twentieth century, when Eric and Maharet reconnect at Maharet's compound in Sonoma, but not as companions, since she has already taken a new companion, Mael, almost one thousand years younger than her fledgling and former companion. Eric is invited to sit at the council, along with Santino and Mael, when the rock music of the Vampire Lestat awakens Akasha, the Queen of the Damned, who begins burning her vampire children all over the world.

After Maharet's twin sister, Mekare, destroys Akasha by consuming her brain and heart and taking into herself Amel, the Sacred Core, Eric resumes his companionship with Santino. In the early twenty-first century, when Amel no longer desires to live within Mekare's wounded mind, he begins speaking as the mysterious Voice to vampires whose minds are susceptible to his influence, controlling them like a possessive spirit and particularly inspiring the more powerful vampires to immolate the weaker. Eric becomes a casualty. Maharet grieves bitterly over his death and blames Khayman, who cannot recall killing him, only standing over his body. Khayman professes repeatedly, earnestly, that he would not have harmed Eric or anyone of his own will, but in her deep sorrow she will not believe him. Despite the fact that Khayman has no memory of doing any harm to Eric, he is willing to offer his life as recompense for Eric's, imploring Maharet, "Kill me! . . . You do what you have to do with me. You do it!"

For more perspectives on Eric's character, read the *Alphabettery* entries **Akasha, Amel, Enkil, Khayman, Lestat de Lioncourt, Mael, Maharet, Marius, Mekare,** and **Santino.**

Eric Sampson

• ALIAS •

"Eric Sampson" is the alias employed by the Talamasca agent known as Jake, a friend and longtime collaborator with David Talbot. Under the alias, Jake helps Lestat and David Talbot acquire a cabin on the *Queen Elizabeth 2* full of everything that they will need to capture Raglan James, the Body Thief.

The alias is employed in *The Tale of the Body Thief* (1992). For more perspectives on Eric Sampson in the Vampire Chronicles, read the *Alphabettery* entries **David Talbot**, **Lestat de Lioncourt**, *Queen Elizabeth* **2**, and **Raglan James**.

Estelle

• VAMPIRE •

When the vampires Louis and Claudia first encounter their own kind in Paris at the Théâtre des Vampires, among them is the vampire Estelle. She and her companion, Celeste, fondle Claudia's beautiful dresses, as they are nothing like their own black garb, reminiscent of the forsaken coven, the Children of Darkness, that their coven leader, Armand, had been a part of centuries earlier. Estelle often demonstrates boredom in their coven. When it is decided among them that Louis and Claudia are guilty of attempting to kill their maker, Lestat, Estelle is among the party of vampires who capture Louis, Claudia, and Madeleine and drag them back to the Théâtre des Vampires, where Louis is imprisoned for all eternity, while Claudia and Madeleine are burned alive. After Armand frees Louis from his prison, Louis returns with two barrels of kerosene and burns the Théâtre des Vampires to the ground. Estelle perishes along with most of the other vampires.

Estelle appears in *Interview with the Vampire* (1976). For more perspectives on Estelle's character, read the *Alphabettery* entries **Armand**, **Celeste**, **Claudia**, **Lestat de Lioncourt**, **Louis de Pointe du Lac**, and **Théâtre des Vampires**.

Eudoxia

• VAMPIRE •

Eudoxia is Marius's first real antagonist after he steals Those Who Must Be Kept from the wicked Elder. Through her intervention, Marius and Akasha both discover that they have the Fire Gift. Eudoxia appears in *Blood and Gold* (2001).

During the reign of Alexander the Great, Eudoxia's family migrates out of Athens to help establish the new and prominent city of Alexandria. Her mother dies when she is young, and she is reared by a detestable stepmother, but her stepmother thoroughly prepares Eudoxia for marriage, teaching her to read and write so that she can write letters to her family after she is married and read poetry to her children. She is delighted that a marriage to a suitable man is arranged for her before her fifteenth birthday.

One month before the wedding, her stepmother plots for her to be kidnapped. Once the kidnappers bring her to their filthy hideout, the vampire Cyril appears, kills them, and is so smitten with Eudoxia that he turns her into a vampire. Cyril dresses her in the clothes of her male kidnappers, and together they go hunting in the streets. He teaches her how to be a vampire with rough shoves and grunts. Afterward, he brings her to his lair, which is filled with the treasures of his victims, where he continues to treat her roughly by cutting off her long hair and throwing her into her coffin. Drinking blood and killing people never bothers her, but when Cyril cuts off her hair, she weeps bitterly, as if it is the end of life as she knows it. Cyril explains to her in simple terms the limits of her new vampiric life. She is glad that her hair grows back while she sleeps, but Cyril dislikes her locks and continues to cut them off every night. She observes that he never changes his clothes until they become worn, then he will steal fresh clothes off a victim, whereas she will often buy new gowns and make herself look beautiful. She also buys books and reads poetry to him. He finds all of this humorous; he does not understand her delight in beauty. They swim in the sea and hunt on the ships in the harbor. She is with him for several years and considers Cyril to be always rough and brutish but never cruel. One night he does not cut her hair, but leaves it long, and brings her to the Elder and to Those Who Must Be Kept. Eudoxia mistakes them for statues at first until Cyril pushes her forward and tells her to drink. She sees how Akasha's hand rises ever so slightly and beckons her to drink from her neck. Akasha allows Eudoxia to drink as much blood as she likes, which makes her very powerful. Cyril's purpose in having her drink from Akasha is to make her powerful enough to be on her own. As soon as she imbibes as much as she likes, Cyril leaves.

Soon afterward, Eudoxia continues the pretense that she is a man and establishes her house as a center of learning and philosophy. She visits the Great Library of Alexandria, and she learns of the world from the many people she entertains in her home. Priests from the blood temple try to persuade her to cease living in such a profane way, but she is more powerful, and she refuses them. Eudoxia lives in Alexandria for several more years until she meets a young man who, thinking she is a young man also, professes his love for her by forsaking marriage altogether. When she reveals to him that she is a woman, he is offended and rescinds his amorous offers. Eudoxia is offended and takes revenge by turning him into a vampire. Together they leave Alexandria for Ephesus and remain there until the Great Burning of 4 C.E. Eudoxia's young paramour is burned to ashes, but the blood she drank from Akasha has made her powerful enough to withstand that Great Burning. Seeking answers, she returns to Alexandria to discover the fate of Those Who Must Be Kept, but Marius has already hidden them in Antioch.

Eudoxia seeks but never finds them. She moves to Constantinople, refers to herself as "the Vampire Empress," and establishes a coven with two young male vampires, Rashid and Asphar, as well as the beautiful Zenobia and a number of other slave vampires. Around the fourth century, when Marius, along with Avicus and Mael, moves to Constantinople to protect Those Who Must Be Kept, Eudoxia visits them and demands that they give her Akasha and Enkil. When Marius refuses, Eudoxia attempts to destroy Avicus when Marius defends him and accidentally burns Rashid to ash with the Fire Gift. He is about to destroy Asphar next, when Eudoxia retreats. Upon her next visit,

she politely requests to come before Akasha. Marius allows this, but when Eudoxia stands before the Queen, she is so emotionally overcome by the experience of being in the sacred presence of Those Who Must Be Kept that she offers herself to Akasha as a blood sacrifice. Immediately, Akasha takes Eudoxia and drains her almost completely of blood. Only after Marius's desperate pleas does Akasha release Eudoxia, mostly drained and barely alive.

Following this, Eudoxia seeks to destroy the shrine beneath Marius's house. After drinking the blood of a merchant, her vampires leave his corpse to rot in such a way that the mortals of Constantinople blame Marius. The mortals loot and burn Marius's house to the ground. Furious, Marius goes to Eudoxia's house, burns her slaves to ashes, including Asphar. Then he drags Eudoxia from her house to the ruins of his shrine. He flings her into Akasha's deadly embrace. The statuesque Queen grips her tightly and drinks from her every last drop of blood. Akasha releases Eudoxia, and Cyril's fledgling slumps to the ground. Akasha summons the Fire Gift against Eudoxia. A flame bursts from her heart and spreads throughout her veins until she is nothing but ashes. Marius kneels down like a poor scrubwoman to scour them away with his cloak. He weeps for Eudoxia, but only because she had so much learning and culture, so much potential to be better, yet failed miserably.

For more perspectives on Eudoxia's character, read the *Alphabettery* entries **Akasha, Asphar, Avicus, Cyril, Enkil, Mael, Marius, Rashid,** and **Zenobia.**

Eugénie

• VAMPIRE •

After the ruination of the Children of Darkness, Eugénie is one of the first vampires Lestat meets who do not wish to destroy him but to learn from him. She appears in *The Vampire Lestat* (1985), *Prince Lestat* (2014), and *Prince Lestat and the Realms of Atlantis* (2016).

Before 1000 C.E., when Rhoshamandes still rules the region known today as contemporary France, he sires a fledgling named Eugénie, whom he includes in a coven that he refers to as his "line of de Landen vampires," which also includes Benedict, Allesandra, Eleni, Notker the Wise, and Everard. They live together in relative peace for centuries, until the Children of Satan learn of their existence. Observing that Rhoshamandes and his fledglings live in a state of opulence, wearing the finest clothing of the time and dwelling in comfort, the Children of Satan perceive their lifestyle as completely antithetical to their Great Laws of vampire behavior, which fundamentally state that, because of the evil nature of vampires, they have to live in an abased state, existing in squalor, wearing ragged clothing, and feeding only on the poor and degenerate of cities. Thus, seeking to convert Rhoshamandes and his fledglings to their belief system, the Children of Satan attack them and capture Eugénie, Allesandra, Eleni, and Everard.

Rhoshamandes and Benedict, not wanting any further conflict with other vampire covens, flee from that region of France to the north of England around 1100 C.E., where they spend centuries building and modifying a castle fortress while abandoning the other four de Landen vampires to torture and starvation at the hands of the Children of Satan. Once Eugénie and her three vampire siblings finally convert and are indoctrinated into their new coven, they remain a part of the Children of Satan for the next few centuries, foul and feeding in the filth of Rome's growing city.

Around the middle of the second millennium, after Santino chooses Armand to start a new coven in Paris, Armand takes with him several vampires, including Eugénie and her de Landen siblings. In time, Everard escapes, and Allesandra grows increasingly mad. A few centuries later, when Lestat and Gabrielle convince Armand that the Children of Darkness represent an outmoded belief system in the era of the Enlightenment, Allesandra persuades Armand to destroy the Paris coven by burning them in a great fire that she willingly, madly, leaps into first. Only four vampires escape that initial burning, two of whom are the de Landen sisters Eugénie and Eleni. Once their coven has been destroyed, they implore Lestat to become their new coven leader. He refuses, but his fledgling Nicolas de Lenfent convinces Lestat to give them a small theater he owns on the Boulevard du Temple. Eugénie and Eleni are delighted, especially when Nicolas and Armand join them. They transform the theater into the

Théâtre des Vampires, where they perform theatrical shows pretending to be humans who pretend to be vampires.

When Lestat returns years later as Louis and Claudia are about to stand trial for their crimes against him, Lestat seeks Eugénie and Eleni among the others at the Théâtre des Vampires, but these two de Landen vampires have already left the coven. Eugénie and Eleni eventually join an underground coven, in the beautiful golden caves beneath Cappadocia, led by Sevraine, the former Blood Wife of Rhoshamandes's ancient friend Nebamun. Sevraine also gathers into her coven Marius's fledgling Bianca and Allesandra, who did not die in the fire she started in the catacombs beneath the Cemetery of les Innocents. After so many centuries of oppression and confusion, Eugénie has finally found a home where she can be with her two de Landen sisters.

For more perspectives on Eugénie's character, read the *Alphabettery* entries **Allesandra, Benedict, Bianca Solderini, Eleni, Everard, Lestat de Lioncourt, Line of de Landen Vampires, Nebamun, Nicolas de Lenfent, Notker the Wise, Rhoshamandes, Santino, Sevraine,** and **Trinity Gate.**

Evan

• TALTOS •

Evan is a Taltos who lives on a secret island owned by the ancient Taltos Ashlar, along with Ashlar's wife, Morrigan, and their four children. One of those children, Silas, decides that the reign of his father must end. He starts a rebellion, poisoning his parents, and gathering numerous Taltos to himself and his cause. Silas and his band of rebels take over the island and then invade a nearby island, killing all mortal inhabitants on it, who happen to be drug dealers. The rebelling Taltos take the drug dealers' guns and drugs and bring them back to their secret island, where they become intoxicated and kill some of their own kind. Evan is among those accidentally shot.

Evan appears in *Blood Canticle* (2003). For more perspectives on Evan's character, read the *Alphabettery* entries **Ashlar, Drug Merchants, Morrigan Mayfair, Ruth, Silas,** and **Taltos.**

Everard

• VAMPIRE •

More than seven hundred years ago, in the territory of modern-day France, Everard is a servant in a castle. One night, he thinks he hears the lord of the castle summoning him outside, but it turns out to be the beguiling voice of the ancient vampire Rhoshamandes, who turns him into a vampire and includes him in a small coven that he refers to as the "line of de Landen vampires," which comprises Benedict, Allesandra, Eleni, Eugénie, and Notker the Wise. Ever cautious of protecting his fledglings, Rhoshamandes trains Everard how to use the Fire Gift, but none of the other higher gifts, such as the Cloud Gift or the Mind Gift. Despite Rhoshamandes precautions, the vampire coven known as the Children of Satan attacks Rhoshamandes and his fledglings and captures Allesandra, Eleni, Eugénie, and Everard. Similar to the way Armand is captured from Marius and subsequently converted, the Children of Satan torture and starve the line of de Landen vampires until they become indoctrinated and willingly obey the five Great Laws of vampire vehavior of their new coven.

Seeking to avoid further confrontation, Rhoshamandes flees from that territory with his remaining fledgling, Benedict, to the north of England, where he spends the next few centuries building and modifying a castle fortress. Everard feels condemned to a miserable existence utterly contrary to the life of ease and comfort that he once enjoyed living with Rhoshamandes, since part of the Great Laws of the Children of Satan is to experience condemnation through deprivation of luxury. Miserable, dressing in filthy rags and feeding on the poor and despondent in the sordid hovels of Rome, Everard never makes much advancement in the coven, not even when the younger vampire Santino enters the coven during the Black Plague and becomes the leader or when Armand enters centuries later and becomes Santino's beloved disciple.

When Santino sends Armand to Paris to begin a new coven house called the Children of Darkness, Armand takes with him Everard and his de Landen siblings. Despite the change of scenery, Everard is still subjected to a life of misery, living under a cemetery.

During the Renaissance, the Children of Satan in Rome grow silent, so Armand sends Everard to unearth the coven's fate. Everard not only discovers that the coven has been destroyed but also learns the coven's former leader, Santino, is now living a life utterly contrary to the dictates of the Children of Satan. Observing how Santino is wearing beautiful clothing and jewelry and indulging in a very hedonistic, secular existence, Everard takes this opportunity to escape the Parisian coven. He survives the next few centuries relying on his memories of the vampiric skills that Rhoshamandes taught him. With his resurfaced ability, he is able to defend himself against much-older and -stronger vampires. He is even able to survive the Great Burning of 1985, centered around the infamous concert of the Vampire Lestat. He abandons the other three de Landen vampires to the Children of Satan, never returning to set them free. He remains in Italy into the twenty-first century, when he leaves Italy to return to France to live at the Court of the Prince in Château de Lioncourt.

Everard is discussed in *Prince Lestat* (2014) and *Blood Communion* (2018). For more perspectives on his character, read the *Alphabettery* entries **Allesandra**, **Benedict**, **Bianca Solderini**, **Cloud Gift**, **Eleni**, **Great Burning of 1985**, **Lestat de Lioncourt**, **Line of de Landen Vampires**, **Nebamun**, **Notker the Wise**, **Rhoshamandes**, and **Santino**.

Evil Doer

• MORTAL •

"Evil Doer" is a term that Marius uses for his victims. He only hunts mortals who commit evil acts, not humans of goodwill or virtue. When he is the caretaker of Those Who Must Be Kept, he never brings them any innocent victims, either, but only the Evil Doer from whom the Divine Parents can feed. For Marius, hunting the Evil Doer is how he lives at peace with being a vampire in the world; it is how he manages to endure the centuries.

The term appears in *Blood and Gold* (2001). For more perspectives on the Evil Doer, read the *Alphabettery* entries **Children of Darkness**, **Lestat de Lioncourt**, and **Marius**.

Evil Eye

• VAMPIRE ABILITY •

The "Evil Eye" is the Fang Gang's term for the Mind Gift, which can telepathically make mortals and immortals alike obey a command. In *The Queen of the Damned*, Killer urges Baby Jenks to use the Evil Eye to coerce her way into a vampire bar.

The term appears in *The Queen of the Damned* (1988). For more perspectives on the Evil Eye, read the *Alphabettery* entries **Baby Jenks**, **Davis**, **Killer**, and **Mind Gift**.

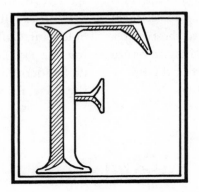

Fang Gang

• COVEN •

Founded by the vampire Killer, the Fang Gang is a vampire motorcycle club comprising mostly three other members: the black dancer Davis, Tim, and Russ. For many years, they ride their motorcycles all over the United States, going from one major city to another. In Detroit they expand their group to five when Killer happens upon the fourteen-year-old Baby Jenks, a prostitute addicted to heroin, dying on a hospital bed from a failed abortion. Killer, who was not much older than she when he was made a vampire sixty years earlier, saves her life by turning her into a vampire also. The Fang Gang avoids vampire covens in major cities, which have older vampires who often kill younger ones. The gang frequently feeds on riffraff living in small shacks on the outskirts of cities and buries their bodies far underground. If they do not have time to hide the corpses of their victims, the Fang Gang pricks a finger and drops blood on the bite marks to heal the neck wound, making it appear as if the victim has died of a heart attack. Refusing to call themselves vampires, and instead referring to themselves and other vampires as

Dead guys, they thoroughly enjoy the music and books of the vampire Lestat. When they hear of the Vampire Lestat band's concert in San Francisco, they plan to go out west and attend, to show their support for him, admiring him as an exemplary iconoclast. Lestat's music has awakened the ancient Mother of the vampire race, Akasha, who rises from her statuelike state and begins immolating weaker vampires and coven houses all over the world. The Fang Gang rides their motorcycles past coven houses burned to the ground in Oklahoma City and Dallas. While they are in Texas, before they go out west, Baby Jenks separates from the Fang Gang, desiring to return to her home in Gun Barrel City, with the intent of destroying her mortal mother and father. But the Fang Gang never meets Baby Jenks at their agreed-upon rendezvous. She backtracks their path to the coven house in Saint Louis, Missouri, which is also burned to the ground, with only one surviving member, the vampire from the Paris coven of the Children of Darkness and the Théâtre des Vampires, Laurent. He is about to ride with Baby Jenks to the concert in San Francisco when Akasha appears and immolates them both.

The rest of the Fang Gang continues on to the Vampire Lestat's San Francisco concert. While there, they are utterly unprepared for the appearance of Akasha, who begins immolating her vampire fledglings. The Fang Gang is fatally separated. Tim and Russ are seen to be destroyed. But the six-thousand-year-old vampire Gregory Duff Collingsworth, also known as Nebamun, saves Davis by carrying him up and away from the massacre. Killer flees desperately from the concert and hides in San Francisco's slums until he can escape the city with a small remnant of vampires who have also survived. The Fang Gang never reunites.

The Fang Gang appears in *The Queen of the Damned* (1988) and is mentioned in *Prince Lestat* (2014). For more perspectives on the Fang Gang, read the *Alphabettery* entries **Akasha, Baby Jenks, Children of Darkness, Coven, Davis, Dead Guys, Gregory Duff Collingsworth, Killer, Lestat de Lioncourt, Nebamun, Russ, Théâtre des Vampires, Tim,** and **The Vampire Lestat.**

Fareed Bhansali

• VAMPIRE •

Fareed is the fledgling of Seth, Akasha's mortal son and immortal fledgling. Fareed utilizes his immortal powers to develop medical science on vampires, especially cloning. He appears in *Prince Lestat* (2014), *Prince Lestat and the Realms of Atlantis* (2016), and *Blood Communion* (2018).

Born in India, Fareed Bhansali moves

to England, where he receives his doctoral degree in medical science. At a young age, he marries and moves with his new wife to Mumbai, where he conducts advanced research in medicine. In the mid-1980s, when his beautiful wife takes a lover, the two betray Fareed, steal his research, and attempt to murder him. Fareed is rushed to the nearest hospital, where he lies in a locked-in coma, fully aware of his surroundings yet unable to speak or move. His only hope for recovery comes when the six-thousand-year-old vampire Seth enters his room.

Seth, having been awakened from a thousand-year torpor by the rock music of the Vampire Lestat band, believes that Fareed is brilliant and beautiful enough to help him make contact with this modern world and all of its technological advances. He turns Fareed into a vampire, and they leave the hospital together. Seth begins explaining to Fareed the scope of his new existence. Fareed discovers that Seth is the biological son of Akasha, whom she and Enkil had in ancient Egypt while they were still mortal. With the Queen's blood in him, Seth is immensely powerful. He shares his blood with Fareed every night, which increases Fareed's own powers and abilities.

When Akasha rises from her millennia-long torpor and begins globally immolating younger vampires, Seth protects Fareed and keeps him strong with his blood. Seth and Fareed then move to West Hollywood, where they establish a medical research facility and commence scientific studies on the Undead. Fareed educates Seth on all the advances that medical science has made over the last few thousand years, particularly in the most recent centuries. Seth masters them all, as he still has a great desire to be a healer, but Fareed is the more ingenious of the two and conducts impressive experiments on vampires, utilizing skin-grafting techniques and genetic cloning.

In one experiment, Fareed and Seth successfully replace the leg that the vampire Flavius lost more than two thousand years earlier, during his mortal life. Also through their unique medical techniques, Fareed and Seth replace Maharet's eyes so that she will never need to steal eyes ever again. They even offer to replace the tongue of Maharet's twin sister, Mekare, keeper of the Sacred Core of vampire existence, but Mekare is too mentally wounded to be willing to undergo such a procedure.

Fareed and Seth also inject the vampire Lestat with an infusion of hormones that allow him to experience the sensuality of sexual intercourse with one of Fareed and Seth's colleagues, Dr. Flannery Gilman, a mortal scientist conducting medical research on vampires for more than a decade. After Lestat unknowingly impregnates Dr. Gilman, Fareed and Seth extract the fetus, enhance it with genetic-cloning techniques, and implant the fetus back inside Dr. Gilman's uterus. Nine months later she gives birth to Lestat's son, whom they name Viktor. Fareed and Seth's genetic enhancements make Viktor not a combination of the genes of Lestat and Dr. Gilman but an exact clone of Lestat. Fareed, Seth, and Flannery raise Viktor in their medical and research facilities, both in West Hollywood and in the Southern California desert, where, due to the fact that he ages like an average mortal, Viktor matures into a healthy young man.

Almost two decades later, when Viktor is around twenty years old, Fareed and Seth encounter Lestat again when Lestat's adopted daughter, Rose, is blinded and nearly killed by a would-be assailant. Fareed and Seth use their unorthodox medical techniques to heal Rose's eyes and restore her to health. While Viktor and Rose become intimately acquainted, Fareed and Seth inform Lestat that their hormonal experiment on him two decades earlier was not simply successful, but Lestat now has a mortal son. Excited at the news, Lestat begins making plans to turn his biological son and his adopted daughter into vampires also. Before that happens, through Lestat, Fareed and Seth are introduced to Gregory Duff Collingsworth, the owner of a vast pharmaceutical empire and also an old acquaintance of Seth, dating back six thousand years, when Gregory was known as Nebamun, a powerful vampire and Cap-

tain of Akasha's army, the Queens Blood. Gregory is immediately impressed by Fareed and Seth's advanced medical research on the Undead and invites them to use his own, much-more-well-funded medical research facilities. With Gregory and Seth, Fareed even establishes a new hospital and medical research center just outside Paris, dedicated exclusively to the well-being of vampires and other Undead individuals.

Fareed relocates to Château de Lioncourt, where he catalogs the immortals who stay at the Court of the Prince. He compiles their histories and creates a vampire family tree, similar to Maharet's work on the Great Family. Fareed plans to trace ancestral lines from contemporary fledglings to ancient elders.

For more perspectives on Fareed's character, read the *Alphabettery* entries **Akasha, Flannery Gilman, Gregory Duff Collingsworth, Lestat de Lioncourt, Nebamun, Rose, Seth,** and **Viktor.**

The Father

• HONORIFIC •

After Akasha becomes the first vampire, her husband-king, Enkil, becomes her first fledgling. Together they establish themselves as the god and the goddess Osiris and Isis. They are worshipped not simply as gods but also as creative progenitors and referred to as the Mother and the Father of the vampire race. Enkil's title as "Father of vampires"

lasts until his death in the late twentieth century.

Enkil is referred to as the Father in *The Vampire Lestat* (1985) and *The Queen of the Damned* (1988). For more perspectives on this in the Vampire Chronicles, read the *Alphabettery* entries **Akasha, Divine Parents, Enkil,** and **Those Who Must Be Kept.**

Father Kevin Mayfair

• WITCH •

Father Kevin is a member of the Mayfair family of witches and is himself a very powerful witch. Ordained as a Jesuit priest in New Orleans, he becomes the family confessor and minister of the Holy Sacraments of the Catholic Church. In particular, Father Kevin helps Mona Mayfair receive proper medical and spiritual attention after she gives birth to her Taltos child, Morrigan.

Along with the Old Captain in the French Quarter, Father Kevin becomes a mentor to Roger, the father of one of Lestat's dearest loves, Dora, to whom Lestat gives Veronica's Veil after he kills Roger and goes on a spiritual journey with Memnoch the Devil.

Oftentimes, Father Kevin will enter Saint Mary's Assumption Church, on Josephine Street, and contemplate Jesus's wounds, imagining himself kissing and adoring the holes in Jesus's hands and feet.

Father Kevin can be read about in *Memnoch the Devil* (1995) and *Blood Canticle* (2003). For more perspectives on Father Kevin's character, read the *Alphabettery* entries **Dora**, **Lestat de Lioncourt**, **Mona Mayfair**, **Old Captain**, **Roger**, and **Veronica's Veil**.

Felix

• VAMPIRE •

Felix is one of the four vampires who survive the transition between Armand's burning of his Children of Darkness coven and the initiation of the coven of the Théâtre des Vampires. Felix appears in *The Vampire Lestat* (1985).

After the vampire Armand goes to Paris to begin a new coven house for the Children of Darkness in the sixteenth century, Felix becomes one of its members. Unlike Armand or Laurent in the coven, who are turned into vampires when they are in midadolescence, Felix has already reached manhood when he receives the Dark Gift. In the Paris coven house of the Children of Darkness, Felix learns the five Great Laws that govern them; he lives in filth and grime among the skulls and skeletons of the Cemetery of les Innocents, and he drinks the blood of only the most poor and unfortunate souls on Parisian streets.

While Lestat and his fledgling Gabrielle are living in Paris around the year 1780, the Children of Darkness, who have been following Lestat, reveal themselves openly and attack. Although Lestat and Gabrielle escape, the Children of Darkness capture Lestat's dearest friend, Nicolas de Lenfent. Lestat returns to the Cemetery of les Innocents, frees Nicolas, turns him into a vampire, and then convinces Armand and his coven that their ways of worshipping Satan are outmoded in eighteenth-century Paris, the era later known as the Age of Enlightenment. When a member of Armand's coven, who is already more than one thousand years old and going mad—Allesandra, who has been in the Children of Darkness for many centuries, all the way back to Santino's ancient Roman coven—throws herself into a fire, Armand follows her example and begins burning the other members of the coven. Only four vampires survive: Felix, Eleni, Laurent, and Eugénie. Felix and the others beg Lestat to be their new leader, but he refuses. They confess that they do not know how to survive in the world, but Lestat tells them that they can easily take clothes and money from their victims; they can pretend to be gypsies, if they choose, or acrobats or street performers. Lestat allows them to live inside the theater he owns, Renaud's House of Thesbians,

believing that they might be able to find costumes to wear in the streets, instead of their customarily filthy clothing that they had to wear as Children of Darkness.

During that time, Lestat's fledgling Nicolas is growing madder by the night and hates Lestat for turning him into a vampire. He plays his violin in Renaud's theater. Felix and the other three vampires dance to his music. Nicolas calls it the Théâtre des Vampires, and he demands that Lestat give it to them as their new coven house. Reluctantly, Lestat agrees. He signs the deed over to them and leaves Nicolas in the care of Felix and the others.

Almost a century later, by the time Lestat's other fledglings, Louis and Claudia, come to the theater, Felix has already left the Théâtre des Vampires, disappearing into the darkness.

For more perspectives on Felix's character, read the *Alphabettery* entries **Armand, Children of Darkness, Eleni, Eugénie, Gabrielle, Great Laws, Laurent, Lestat de Lioncourt, Nicolas de Lenfent, Renaud's House of Thesbians, Santino,** and **Théâtre des Vampires.**

Felix Welf

• ALIAS •

To hide his Replimoid identity from vampires, particularly Gregory Duff Collingsworth, CEO of Collingsworth Pharmaceuticals, the organization for which he works, Welf takes the alias "Felix Welf," while his Replimoid

companion Kapetria takes the alias "Dr. Karen Rhinehart."

Felix Welf appears in *Prince Lestat and the Realms of Atlantis* (2016). For more perspectives on the alias "Felix Welf," read the

Alphabettery entries **Collingsworth Pharmaceuticals, Karen Rhinehart, Gregory Duff Collingsworth, Kapetria, Replimoid**, and **Welf**.

Fire Gift

• VAMPIRE ABILITY •

The Fire Gift can be gained one of two ways. First, once vampires reach a certain age, the Fire Gift becomes a part of their natural abilities. Alternatively, if a young vampire drinks from the blood of an older vampire already in possession of the Fire Gift, the younger vampire can gain that ability, too.

Essentially, the Fire Gift is pyrokinesis—the ability to make objects combust through the power of the mind and will. Vampires can even make other vampires burst into flames, igniting their blood and reducing them to cinders. The Fire Gift has one specific limitation: vampires must be able to physically see the object that they desire to burn. They might be able to visualize it telepathically, but if they cannot see it with their eyes, then they cannot burn the object.

An example of a young vampire gaining the ability of the Fire Gift from an older vampire is when Marius defends himself and Akasha against Rashid and Eudoxia. Marius accidentally burns Rashid to death with the power of his mind, much to everyone's surprise. Though Marius is about five hundred years old at this time, it is unlikely that he is old enough to naturally achieve the Fire Gift. Rather, it is more likely that he has received this gift from Akasha, after she lets him drink much of her blood.

An example of a vampire who ages into the ability is Akasha, who uses the Fire Gift against Eudoxia, burning her completely to ashes. Since she is the first vampire, she never drinks the blood of an older, stronger vampire to gain the power. Hers develops over thousands of years.

The only way to prevent the Fire Gift is by wrapping the vampire in iron binds.

The Fire Gift is utilized in *The Queen of the Damned* (1988), *Blood and Gold* (2001), *Prince Lestat* (2014), and *Blood Communion* (2018). For more perspectives on the Fire Gift in the Vampire Chronicles, read the *Alphabettery* entries **Akasha, Blood Curse, Cloud Gift, Crippling Gift, Dark Gift, Eudoxia, Iron Curse, Marius, Mind Gift, Rashid**, and **Spell Gift**.

First Brood

• COVEN •

After Khayman turns Maharet and Mekare into vampires, they rebel against Queen Akasha and turn an army of mortals into vampires, calling them the First Brood.

In response, Akasha also creates an army of vampires, which she calls the Queens Blood, to fight against the First Brood.

The war between the First Brood and the Queens Blood rages for centuries. By the time the war finally ends, Khayman, Maharet, and Mekare are no longer fighting in the First Brood. Their vampire descendants capture Akasha and Enkil and imprison them underneath large blocks of diorite and granite, leaving only their heads and necks exposed, so that the First Brood can drink the blood of the Mother and the Father. Once victory is achieved, the First Brood dissolves, until there are no more soldiers to warn the vampire who, after discovering that Akasha and Enkil have broken free of their prisons, erects them on thrones as Those Who Must Be Kept.

The First Brood appears in *The Queen of the Damned* (1988) and is mentioned in *Prince Lestat* (2014). For more perspectives on the First Brood in the Vampire Chronicles, read the *Alphabettery* entries **Amel**, **Akasha**, **Enkil**, **Khayman**, **Maharet**, **Mekare**, **Queens Blood**, and **Those Who Must Be Kept**.

First Street House

• SANCTUARY •

Purchased by Julien and Katherine Mayfair in the nineteenth century, the First Street house becomes the principal domicile of the Mayfair family in New Orleans, moving most of the family from the Riverbend plantation. Lestat hears many tales of the First Street house, particularly its involvement with the conception of Taltos in the incarnation of the spirit Lasher, as he becomes a principal rescuer of several Taltos imprisoned on an island, one of whom is Mona Mayfair's daughter.

The First Street house can be read about in *Blood Canticle* (2003). For more perspectives on the First Street house in the Vampire Chronicles, read the *Alphabettery* entries **Designée of the Mayfair Legacy**, **Lasher**, **Lestat de Lioncourt**, **Mayfair Legacy**, **Mona Mayfair**, **Rowan Mayfair**, and **Taltos**.

Flaminia

• CHARACTER •

When Renaud finally allows Lestat to act at his House of Thesbians, Lestat performs in the commedia dell'arte style as Lelio, the lead character in *Lelio and Flaminia*, which is very similar to his performance years earlier with a wandering troupe of actors in the commedia dell'arte play *Lelio and Isabella*. This time Flaminia is Lelio's onstage love interest. Lestat's performance as Lelio wooing Flaminia in Renaud's theater not only thrills audiences, who call repeatedly for Lelio and Flaminia to return to the stage, but also captures the attention of the vampire Magnus, Lestat's eventual maker.

Flaminia appears in *The Vampire Lestat* (1985). For more perspectives on Flaminia in the Vampire Chronicles, read the *Alphabettery* entries **Commedia dell'Arte**, **Isabella**, **Lelio**, **Lestat de Lioncourt**, **Renaud**, and **Renaud's House of Thesbians**.

Flannery Gilman

• VAMPIRE •

Flannery Gilman is one of the vampire scientists who help Lestat make a cloned son and release the spirit of Amel from his mind. Flannery appears in *Prince Lestat* (2014) and *Prince Lestat and the Realms of Atlantis* (2016).

Flannery Gilman attends the concert of the Vampire Lestat in the 1980s and is truly astounded to discover that vampires exist. She sees them and has no doubt of the reality of the supernatural world, especially when she observes vampires immolating in the parking lot during the Great Burning of 1985. As a medical doctor and scientist, she gathers samples of immolated bone fragments, skin, and teeth from the asphalt. She analyzes the numerous photographs of the scene that night. She documents how some scientists have actually captured vampires, either not knowing what they have or subjecting the vampires to cruel experiments, exposing them to the sun or starving them for blood. Sometimes powerful vampires are captured who will consequently confuse their captors with the Mind Gift and then burn their medical facilities to the ground with the Fire Gift. Flannery Gilman spends all of her money over the next two years studying all the data, analyzing her specimens, and writing a one-thousand-page book on her findings. She is ridiculed and drummed out of the mainstream scientific community and denied access to grant money and admission to medical conventions and conferences. Her license to practice medicine in California is revoked, and she has neither colleagues nor family to support her.

When she thinks she has no one to turn to, when she assumes she is all but dead to the world, Dr. Flannery Gilman is approached by two vampire scientists, the six-thousand-year-old Seth and his fledgling Fareed, both of whom are very impressed with her impartiality over the data as well as her desire to use science for the betterment of both mortals and immortals alike. Seth and Fareed invite Flannery to work with them in their facilities in Southern California. During her time with them, Seth and Fareed encounter the vampire Lestat in the 1990s and invite him to undergo a procedure in which they inject him with an infusion of hormones that allow him to experience sexual sensuality and possibly ejaculate semen to be analyzed for fertility. Fueled by her greatest desire to study Lestat himself, Flannery volunteers to be the receptive vessel of his erotic emission. Lestat has sexual intercourse with her, and she becomes pregnant with his child. Seth and Fareed remove the fetus from her uterus, then they begin manipulating it with cloning technology and Lestat's DNA. Afterward, they insert the genetically

enhanced fetus back into Flannery's uterus. Nine months later, she gives birth to a clone of Lestat, not an immortal vampire, but a human mortal.

After her brilliant work, Fareed turns Flannery into a vampire. She, Fareed, and Seth raise Viktor for the next twenty years in their Southern California facilities until Seth encounters an old acquaintance, Gregory Duff Collingsworth, whom he has not seen in six thousand years, when Gregory was known as Nebamun and was the Captain of Akasha's army, the Queens Blood. When Gregory hears of the work that Seth and Fareed are accomplishing, he invites them to work in his vast pharmaceutical empire. As a result of this merger of technology and ideas, Gregory is introduced to Flannery. Feeling an immediate connection with her, Gregory offers Flannery a job as his assistant. After being utterly rejected by the standards of the mortal world, Flannery gladly accepts and becomes one of the most influential figures among the Undead.

For more perspectives on Flannery Gilman's character, read the *Alphabettery* entries **Fareed Bhansali, Fire Gift, Gregory Duff Collingsworth, Lestat de Lioncourt, Mind Gift, Nebamun, Seth, The Vampire Lestat,** and **Viktor.**

Flavius

• VAMPIRE •

Flavius is the only known mortal to have been turned into a vampire while missing a limb. He lives for nearly two thousand years as a one-legged vampire in the Blood Kindred coven until Fareed's medical breakthroughs help him regain his amputated appendage. Flavius appears in *Pandora* (1998), *Blood and Gold* (2001), *Prince Lestat* (2014), and *Prince Lestat and the Realms of Atlantis* (2016).

An Athenian slave in Antioch, Flavius receives his Roman name from his first mortal master, a Roman citizen seeking to conform to Antioch's rising urban culture influenced by Rome. Though Flavius is a slave, his master teaches him to read and write both Greek and Latin and educates him in the Septuagint; the writings of Augustine of Hippo and Marcus Aurelius, Tertullian and Pliny the Elder; the mathematics of Euclid; and even the philosophies of Socrates and Plato. As he grows and matures physically and intellectually, Flavius becomes one of his master's most beloved servants.

At the age of twenty, tragedy befalls Flavius when, on a wild-boar hunt with his master, he loses his left leg below the knee. But his master cares for him so much that he not only saves Flavius's life from the boar attack but also hires a master sculptor to painstakingly carve a new leg from ivory, intricately detailing even the toes and the sandal. Flavius's misfortune augments when his beloved

master dies, and Flavius is sold to a miserable slave shop run by a swindler.

He languishes until a Greek courtesan named Pandora, who has recently moved to Antioch and is seeking to purchase slaves, approaches the slave shop and engages in conversation with Flavius. Impressed by his genuineness and intelligence, and discovering that he will fairly manage the female slaves that she has already purchased, since Flavius is not attracted to the opposite sex, Pandora purchases him and makes him steward over her household. Now, at thirty, Flavius serves Pandora with newfound vigor and becomes her most beloved servant. His true mettle shines forth when Pandora begins to be pursued by a monstrously burned creature, almost humanlike in appearance, with an insatiable bloodlust. Flavius tries to protect Pandora, yet he cannot. The monster reveals himself to be a vampire from ancient Egypt, Akbar, former member of Akasha's blood priest cult and severely burned in the Great Burning of 4 C.E. Akbar has come to Antioch to find Akasha, no longer kept by the Elder but by Pandora's great love interest, Marius. Akbar drains Pandora of her blood to the point of death and threatens to let her die if Marius does not take him to Akasha. Once Akbar is before the ancient Queen, Akasha destroys him, and Marius rescues Pandora by turning her into a vampire. Although she does not reveal her secret to her household,

Flavius suspects that she is no longer human, yet he continues to serve her regardless. When Pandora lives together with Marius so that they can protect Those Who Must Be Kept, she takes Flavius with her, and he serves her and Marius faithfully.

Marius shares Pandora's admiration for Flavius, valuing not only his intelligence but also his indefatigable service. When Flavius becomes mortally ill at the age of forty, Marius could turn him into a vampire but instead chooses to let him die a mortal death. Besides, the ancient laws of turning others into vampires stipulate that it is forbidden to turn disabled or infirmed mortals (especially amputees like Flavius) into immortals. Witnessing the great sorrow that Marius suffers at the possibility of Flavius's death, Pandora turns Flavius into a vampire. The decision so enrages Marius that he banishes Flavius from his house forever, and it eventually becomes the cause that divides Marius from Pandora.

Flavius thanks Pandora for the gift of his immortality and then, with his ivory leg, he journeys all the way to Carthage, where he encounters a small coven of two vampires. The first is the four-thousand-year-old vampire calling himself Gregory Duff Collingsworth, although his real name is Nebamun, who was turned into a vampire by Akasha herself to become Captain of her army, the Queens Blood. The second is Gregory's recent fledgling, Chrysanthe, from the great Arab-Christian city Hira. Chrysanthe has been Gregory's teacher of the modern world ever since he rose from his earthen torpor. Seeing Flavius's missing leg is another reminder for him that the old religion is dead in this modern world. Flavius informs Gregory of the fate of Akasha and Enkil, through relating his experience with Marius and Pandora. Then he teaches Gregory more of the Greek and Roman languages and art and literature. Gregory is so awed by Flavius's sincerity and intellect that he gladly welcomes him into their coven, which Gregory refers to as his Blood Kindred.

Flavius remains with Gregory and Chrysanthe for centuries. In time, two more vampires join their coven: Avicus, a vampire who is almost as old as Gregory himself yet cannot remember much of his early life, and Avicus's Blood Wife, Zenobia, fledgling of Eudoxia, fledgling of Cyril, fledgling of the wicked Elder who burned Those Who Must Be Kept. Gregory builds a great fortress for the Blood Kindred, where Flavius enjoys relative comfort among equals and friends, and where he also plays the lute, philosophizes on laws and mortal courts, and memorizes whole histories of long-forgotten civilizations.

Flavius survives into the twenty-first century—unfazed by the Great Burning of 1985—when he is introduced to Dr. Fareed Bhansali, a vampire who has devoted his life to practicing modern medicine on the Undead. Flavius reluctantly accepts Fareed's offer to use contemporary genetic cloning techniques and skin grafting to restore his lost leg. Amazed at the modern world, Flavius spends months growing accustomed to his new leg, hunting at night, flexing his supernatural powers, until the leg finally feels like a natural part of himself, as if he never lost it at all.

For more perspectives on Flavius's character, read the *Alphabettery* entries **Akbar, Avicus, Chrysanthe, Cyril, The Elder, Eudoxia, Fareed Bhansali, Gregory Duff Collingsworth, Marius, Nebamun, Pandora, Those Who Must Be Kept,** and **Zenobia.**

Fledgling

• IDIOM •

A vampire who transforms a mortal into a vampire is called a "maker"; a mortal transformed into vampire is called a "fledgling." Makers can create many fledglings, but fledglings can have only one maker. In some cases, fledglings refer to their makers as "mentors," as with Seth and his fledgling Fareed.

An example of the fledgling-maker relationship between vampires is Merrick, fledgling of Louis. Similarly, Louis is the fledgling of Lestat; Lestat is the fledgling of Magnus; Magnus is the fledgling of Benedict; Benedict is the fledgling of Rhoshamandes; and Rhoshamandes is the fledgling of Akasha, the first vampire.

The idiom appears in *Interview with the Vampire* (1976), *The Vampire Lestat* (1985), *The Queen of the Damned* (1988), and *Prince Lestat* (2014). For more perspectives on fledglings in the Vampire Chronicles, read the *Alphabettery* entries **Akasha, Benedict, Fareed Bhansali, Lestat de Lioncourt, Louis de Pointe du Lac, Magnus, Merrick Mayfair, Rhoshamandes,** and **Seth.**

Florian

• VAMPIRE •

Florian is Vittorio's principal antagonist, as well as the principal villain across Italy. He appears in *Vittorio the Vampire* (1999).

Florian is turned into a vampire around the age of fifteen. Quickly he ascends in the ranks of his own vampire coven and becomes a powerful leader. He establishes his coven's court in the ruins of a Gothic castle, calling it the Court of the Ruby Grail, a euphemistic reference to the superabundance of blood that continues to flow in its halls every night. Florian marries the thirteen-year-old mortal Ursula. On the night he consummates their marriage, he also turns her into a vampire. Together they rule their court as lord and lady, and they love each other for a time, until Florian grows bored with Ursula and seeks affection elsewhere. Even though he still harbors a modicum of love for her, it is not enough, and she, too, begins to seek love elsewhere.

Florian develops contractual agreements with various nearby villages and castles. The contracts state that the castles and the villages must surrender their weak, infirm, and villainous citizens to his court, otherwise his coven of vampires will come and destroy everyone and everything. Most communities agree to this, except for Lord Lorenzo di Raniari of Castello Raniari. He rejects Florian; and for that, Florian and his vampires destroy Castello Raniari and everyone inside, except for Lord Lorenzo's oldest son, Vittorio. Ursula is immediately attracted to him. She brings him to the Court of the Ruby Grail and begs Florian to spare his life, even when Vittorio swears vengeance upon Florian for murdering his family. Out of chivalric love for his wife, Florian consents and has Vittorio rendered unconscious and left in the streets of Florence. Vittorio returns, however, with the assistance of holy angels. He slays every vampire in the court, except Ursula, sparing her life, due to his great love for her. Not even Florian can escape Vittorio's wrath or divine retribution. Vittorio gashes open Florian's chest with a sword and then beheads him, leaving his head in a pile with other vampire heads to burn to ashes in the sunlight.

For more perspectives on Florian's character, read the *Alphabettery* entries **Castello Raniari, Court of the Ruby Grail, Ursula,** and **Vittorio di Raniari.**

Fontevrault Plantation

• SANCTUARY •

When Julien and Augustin Mayfair's feud ends with Augustin's tragic death, the Mayfair family divides. Julien remains the manager of the Riverbend plantation, while other members buy a large piece of property and begin a new Mayfair plantation, naming it Fontevrault.

The family that founds the Fontevrault plantation also builds the house on Amelia Street, the childhood home of Mona Mayfair, who eventually becomes the fledgling of Lestat.

By the twentieth century, Fontevrault plantation has fallen into ruins and is cared for by Mary Jane Mayfair and her grandmother Dolly Jean. When Mona's daughter, Morrigan, becomes the Designée of the Mayfair Legacy, she assigns funds from the vast wealth of the Mayfair family to help Mary Jane restore Fontevrault.

Fontevrault plantation is referenced in *Blood Canticle* (2003). For more perspectives on Fontevrault plantation in the Vampire Chronicles, read the *Alphabettery* entries **Designée** of the Mayfair Legacy, **Dolly Jean Mayfair**, **Julien Mayfair**, **Lestat de Lioncourt**, **Mary** **Jane Mayfair**, **Mona Mayfair**, **Morrigan Mayfair**, and **Riverbend Plantation**.

Fra Filippo Lippi

• MORTAL •

Fra Filippo is a brother and priest in the Order of the Carmelite friars of fifteenth-century Italy. A highly skilled and sought-after painter, Fra Filippo becomes patronized by the powerful Medici family, who commissions him to paint such works as *The Annunciation* and *Seven Saints*.

Vittorio di Raniari admires him greatly. After being abandoned on the streets of Florence by the vampire Florian's coven, Vittorio encounters Fra Filippo's two guardian angels, Ramiel and Setheus, who help him return to the Court of the Ruby Grail and slay its vampires, including Florian.

Fra Filippo is written of in *Vittorio the Vampire* (1999). For more perspectives on Fra Filippo in the Vampire Chronicles, read the *Alphabettery* entries **Court of the Ruby Grail**, **Florian**, **Ramiel**, **Setheus**, and **Vittorio di Raniari**.

Frederick Wynken

• ALIAS •

"Frederick Wynken" is an alias used by Roger Flynn ("Flynn" being another alias), who is a hitman, smuggler, and drug kingpin and who eventually becomes an important victim of the vampire Lestat, shortly before Lestat encounters Memnoch the Devil. Roger has been raised in New Orleans, where he is a devotee of the writings of Wynken de Wilde, whose first name Roger uses as the surname for his alias.

The alias is used in *Memnoch the Devil* (1995). For more perspectives on the alias "Frederick Wynken" in the Vampire Chronicles, read the *Alphabettery* entries **Lestat de Lioncourt**, **Memnoch**, **Roger**, and **Wynken de Wilde**.

Freniere Plantation

• SANCTUARY •

Up the river from Louis's Louisiana plantation, Pointe du Lac, is the Freniere plantation, a sprawling, beautiful land that grows sugar as a source crop, shortly after the sugar-refining process is invented. During Louis's time operating his own plantation, the Frenieres are a wealthy French family that has produced five daughters and one young man, their youngest brother, young Freniere, upon whom the family fortune and the plantation depends.

After Lestat turns Louis into a vampire, Louis protects the Frenieres from Lestat and develops a friendship with the oldest daughter, Babette. Lestat kills young Freniere, leaving the plantation in jeopardy due to property rights of eighteenth-century Louisiana. As Louis's hatred towards Lestat increases, the slaves of Louis's plantation grow more suspicious that their master and his companion are Devils, until one night they finally burn the Pointe du Lac plantation to the ground. Louis and Lestat find refuge at the Freniere plantation. Babette realizes that they are unnatural creatures, and believing that they are from the Devil, she locks them in her basement, which enrages Lestat. Louis calms his temper and takes him away from the Freniere plantation before he can do any harm to Babette or her surviving sisters.

The Freniere plantation appears in *Interview with the Vampire* (1976). For more perspectives on the Freniere plantation in the Vampire Chronicles, read the *Alphabettery* entries **Babette Freniere**, **Lestat de Lioncourt**, **Louis de Pointe du Lac**, and **Young Freniere**.

Gabrielle

• VAMPIRE •

 abrielle is Lestat's first vampire fledgling; he is her last mortal child. As mother and son, Gabrielle and Lestat share a deep bond in solitude. As vampire fledgling and maker, they are a ferocious pair divided only by how they revel in their immortal power. Perhaps the most enigmatic character in the Vampire Chronicles, Gabrielle appears in *The Vampire Lestat* (1985), *The Queen of the Damned* (1988), *Prince Lestat* (2014), *Prince Lestat and the Realms of Atlantis* (2016), and *Blood Communion* (2018).

Originally from a wealthy family in Naples, Italy, Gabrielle weds the Marquis de Lioncourt of the Auvergne, France, in the eighteenth century, under the reign of Louis XV, decades before the French Revolution, receiving the feudal title, Château de Lioncourt, and lands of the de Lioncourt family. Her new French family squanders their wealth, leaving Marquise Gabrielle de Lioncourt relatively poverty stricken, save for a few precious items that she received from the wealth of her Italian family and keeps hidden. Four of her children do not survive into adulthood, but three do; Gabrielle names her youngest Lestat.

During his boyhood, Lestat tries to join a monastery and a troupe of traveling actors. Both times, his father and brothers bring him back home against his will, while Gabrielle consoles him. She deeply admires Lestat because she considers him to be the man she can never become. She does not always console him, particularly when she is reading books that Lestat cannot read, as he is illiterate for much of his early life. Her reclusiveness hurts Lestat and makes him more desirous for those special moments when she gives him the kind of attention that she gives to no one else. On one of those special occasions, Gabrielle reveals to him she feels trapped and unhappy in her life, that she wants to be free of it all, and that she is dying.

After Lestat befriends Nicolas de Lenfent, Gabrielle becomes aware of their secret plan to abscond to Paris. She encourages them by giving Lestat one of her precious jewels that will fund their journey. For much of the time he is in Paris, she remains ignorant of the fact that he is now a vampire, since his letters to her speak only of the good fortune he has as an actor at Renaud's House of Thesbians. She receives from him money, books, newspapers, a harpsichord, music paper, and other such gifts that he can now easily afford, having inherited the vampire Magnus's immense fortune. She promises him that she will go to Italy in the hope of regaining her strength, but as her health decreases from consumption, she goes to Paris to be with him instead. When consumption finally brings her to the point of death, Lestat turns her into a vampire, his first fledgling. He teaches her how to hunt and how to conceal her nature

from mortal eyes. When he seeks to dress her in beautiful gowns and jewelry, she rejects such feminine accoutrements by killing the nearest young man she finds, donning his clothes, and tucking her long hair under his cap, becoming a vision of the young man she always wanted to be. To further this attitude, she often has Lestat cut her hair in the evening when they awake and burn it in the fire, but it grows back every day while they sleep. Similar to her behavior during her mortal life, Gabrielle continues to desire solitude and reclusiveness. She has a great eagerness to explore forests and jungles, while Lestat has more of a desire to be surrounded by wealth, festivities, and groups of happy mortals.

Not long after Lestat turns Gabrielle into a vampire, they are attacked by the Children of Darkness, led by the vampire Armand. Lestat and Gabrielle escape, but the Children of Darkness capture Nicolas. Lestat and Gabrielle rescue him, but now that Nicolas knows about the existence of vampires, he begs Lestat to turn him into one also. Gabrielle warns Lestat against this, but Lestat does it out of love. The process drives Nicolas mad. Lestat, Gabrielle, and Nicolas return to Armand and the Children of Darkness and convince them that their ways are utterly outmoded in this Age of Enlightenment. Armand destroys his coven, except for four: Felix, Laurent, Eugénie, and Eleni. They implore Lestat and Gabrielle to remain with them, but Lestat refuses. Since he owns Renaud's House of Thesbians, he gives it to them out of guilt for Nicolas.

Armand, Nicolas, and the four other

vampires move into the theater and turn it into the Théâtre des Vampires, where they perform theater shows as mortals pretending to be vampires. Armand warns Lestat that Gabrielle will leave him soon, before also confessing to Lestat a small story of his history, which involves the great vampire Marius. Lestat becomes obsessed with finding Marius, but Gabrielle believes that Marius is probably dead and that seeking him is a fool's errand. She remains with him, traveling around the globe for ten years. Every time they come to a new place in search of Marius, Gabrielle goes on little adventures on her own, disappearing for days, weeks, and even months. Lestat receives letters about Nicolas from Eleni, but Gabrielle is not interested in listening to any of it, until one night the news comes that Nicolas has killed himself. Gabrielle remains with Lestat for a little while longer, consoling him, but her desire for independence increases. She begs Lestat to accompany her into the depths of the African jungles, but he declines and explains that he is going to travel to the New World. Before separating, Gabrielle tells Lestat to find her if he ever considers committing suicide.

Gabrielle and Lestat do not see each other again for almost two centuries, not until the night of the Vampire Lestat concert. Lestat has taunted and angered many vampires by revealing their secrets to the mortal world. They have set about to kill him, but Gabrielle appears at the concert in a getaway car that speeds her, Lestat, and Louis to safety.

Gabrielle then goes to Maharet's Sonoma compound to unite with several other vampires who survived the Great Burning of 1985, when Akasha arose from her statuesque torpor and began killing her vampire fledglings. Gabrielle listens to Maharet's story of how Akasha became Queen and how she created the vampire race. Gabrielle stands with the other vampires as they fight against Akasha, who endeavors to enact a plan of world domination.

After Akasha is defeated and Mekare becomes the new Queen of the Damned, Gabrielle stays by Lestat's side once he visits with Memnoch the Devil and falls into a catatonic state. She remains with him until he is mostly back to his old self.

At the beginning of the twenty-first century, when vampires begin hearing the mysterious voice of Amel, the Sacred Core of vampire existence, Gabrielle accompanies Lestat to find an old Nordic vampire named Sevraine in her lair of beautifully adorned golden caves beneath Cappadocia, in order to discover the location of Rhoshamandes, the ancient vampire whom Amel is detrimentally influencing. Lestat observes how Gabrielle appears to know her way around Sevraine's golden caves, apparently having been there before. Once Rhoshamandes is defeated and Lestat takes into himself Amel, making him the Prince of the Vampires, Gabrielle remains with her son, her long-lived wanderlust apparently quelled, especially after Lestat has their old castle, Château de Lioncourt, in the Auvergne, restored to the beauty and elegance that they had never known in mortal life.

For more perspectives on Gabrielle's character, read the *Alphabettery* entries **Akasha**, **Allesandra**, **Amel**, **Armand**, **The Auvergne**, **Children of Darkness**, **Eleni**, **Eugénie**, **Felix**, **Fledgling**, **Laurent**, **Lestat** de Lioncourt, Louis de Pointe du Lac, Maharet, Maharet's Sonoma Compound, Marius, Memnoch, Marquis de Lioncourt, Marquise de Lioncourt, Nicolas de Len-fent, Renaud's House of Thesbians, Rhoshamandes, Sacred Core, Sevraine, and Théâtre des Vampires.

Gabriel the Archangel

• IMMORTAL •

Gabriel the Archangel is generally portrayed in the Bible as the messenger of God, most notably when he tells Mary and Joseph that they will be the parents of Jesus Christ.

In the book *Memnoch the Devil* (1995), Lestat writes about Gabriel, portraying him as a companion of Memnoch before Memnoch falls from grace.

For more perspectives on Gabriel the Archangel in the Vampire Chronicles, read the *Alphabettery* entries **Lestat de Lioncourt** and **Memnoch**.

Gardner Paleston

• MORTAL •

Gardner Paleston is a professor of English literature at Stanford University. The adopted daughter of the vampire Lestat, Rose, meets him during her first two weeks attending classes and begins a passionate affair shortly thereafter. But when she begins talking with him about Lestat (whom she refers to as Uncle Lestan), Gardner becomes furious with her for believing in the reality of the Vampire Chronicles, which he refers to as "foolish, pedestrian schoolgirl trash." When she ends their relationship, he becomes a jealous lover, kidnaps her, and pours a deadly concoction into her mouth and over her eyes, blinding her completely and bringing her close to death. Rose's bodyguard, Murray, discovers them before she dies and shoots and kills Dr. Gardner Paleston, before rushing Rose to Seth and Fareed's vampire clinic, where they save her life and restore her sight.

Dr. Gardner Paleston appears in *Prince Lestat* (2014). For more perspectives on Dr. Paleston's character, read the *Alphabettery* entries **Fareed Bhansali**, **Murray**, **Lestat de Lioncourt**, **Rose**, **Seth**, and **Uncle Lestan**.

Garekyn

• IMMORTAL •

Garekyn is one of the Replimoids who help Lestat free Amel from his mind and provide Amel with a new body. Garekyn appears in *Prince Lestat and the Realms of Atlantis* (2016).

For the fight in the rebellion against Amel on Earth, scientists from the planet Bravenna create humanoid beings out of the cells of every living creature from planet Earth, perfect superhumans who have the ability to regenerate immortally. The Bravennans call them Replimoids and send them to Earth in waves of raiding parties to destroy Amel. Each party fails to resist Amel's superior intellect and strength. One of the last parties to be sent consists of four Replimoids: Kapetria, Derek, Welf, and Garekyn, all of whom are created to look like the dark-skinned peoples who live on what will become the African continent.

The Bravennans inform their Replimoids that Amel is also a Replimoid who is hurting the human race and that their purpose is to stop Amel and help earthlings live in harmony. Then the Bravennans send Garekyn and the Replimoids to Earth. The Replimoids soon discover that it is the Bravennans who are hurting the human race, and it is actually Amel who is fighting to protect earthlings. Deciding to combine their abilities, they form into a group called the People of the Purpose. United, they help Amel thwart Bravennan plans for human exploitation, collaborating together in Amel's stronghold, the city of Atlantis. When the Bravennans discover that the Replimoids have failed in their mission, they send a meteor shower to Earth, which destroys Amel, sinks Atlantis into the ocean, and separates Garekyn from his Replimoid companions. Garekyn drifts in the ocean until he washes ashore and wanders throughout the land that comes to be called Siberia. Exhausted, he goes into the Siberian mountains and sleeps. Time buries him under snow and inside ice.

Almost eleven thousand years later, he is discovered by a Russian amateur anthropologist, Prince Alexi Brovotkin. He brings Garekyn out of Siberia and back to the Brovotkin palace in Saint Petersburg. Prince Alexi loves Garekyn, educates him, and even adopts him, giving him the last name Zweck Brovotkin, as well as the title "Prince," thus Garekyn comes to be known as Prince Garekyn Zweck Brovotkin.

He lives on into the twenty-first century, vaguely able to remember his past with the other Replimoids, until one night two vampires break into his home and attack him. One of those vampires, Avicus, has already encountered and drunk the blood of Derek, Garekyn's former Replimoid colleague. The other vampire, Garrick, does not survive the assault. Garekyn leaves Avicus alive while taking Garrick's head and fleeing from the house. He has never desired to harm another individual, yet he feels instinctively compelled to drink Garrick's brain fluid. Upon doing so, Garekyn receives flashes of memory from the time he lived in Atlantis, and he becomes consumed with finding more vampires, who might help him discover more of this past.

In New York, near the vampire compound at Trinity Gate, Garekyn encounters the vampire Eleni, formerly of Armand's Children of Darkness and the Théâtre des Vampires, as well as the vampire Killer, formerly of the Fang Gang, who survived the Great Burning of 1985 after Akasha awakened. Garekyn ruptures Eleni's skull and kills Killer by taking his head and drinking the brain fluid, which enables him to see more visions of his past in Atlantis with the other Replimoids.

When news of his struggle with the vampires comes to Kapetria and Welf, who are working as mortal doctors in Gregory Duff Collingsworth's research laboratories, they leave their work in search of their former companion. After finding him, they form an alliance with the vampires. Together they cooperate on finding a solution that can release the spirit of Amel from Lestat's brain. After that, Garekyn and his Replimoid compatriots live in harmony with the vampires, whom they consider to be allies in immortality.

For more perspectives on Garekyn's character, read the *Alphabettery* entries **Amel, Atlantis, Avicus, Bravenna, Bravennan, Derek, Eleni, Garrick, Great Burning of 1985, Gregory Duff Collingsworth, Kapetria, Killer, People of the Purpose, Replimoid, Trinity Gate**, and **Welf.**

Garetu

• IMMORTAL •

When Garekyn, a Replimoid from the planet Bravenna, imbued with a natural ability to replicate himself, amputates one of his appendages, his limb grows back, the way Kapetria's left foot grows back when she severs it to make Katu. Garekyn's amputated appendage grows into a duplicate likeness of himself, which he names Garekyn Two but shortens to "Garetu."

Even replicated duplicates like Garetu have the capacity to replicate themselves, which he does before his family of Replimoids meet with Lestat and his vampires concerning the spirit of Amel.

Garetu appears in *Prince Lestat and the Realms of Atlantis* (2016). For more perspectives on Garetu's character, read the *Alphabettery* entries **Amel, Bravenna, Garekyn, Kapetria, Katu, Lestat de Lioncourt**, and **Replimoid.**

Garrick

• VAMPIRE •

Garrick is a maverick vampire in California who tries to help Avicus capture the Replimoid Garekyn. Their endeavor fails miserably when Garekyn overpowers them, beheads Garrick, flees with his head, and drinks the brain fluid to gain knowledge of Amel and the city of Atlantis.

Garrick appears in *Prince Lestat and the Realms of Atlantis* (2016). For more perspectives on Garrick's character, read the *Alphabettery* entries **Amel**, **Atlantis**, **Avicus**, **Garekyn**, and **Replimoid**.

Garwain Blackwood

• MORTAL •

Garwain Blackwood is Tarquin's twin brother, who dies shortly after birth. His ghost returns, calling himself Goblin, to haunt Blackwood Farm, and most especially his brother, Quinn Blackwood.

Garwain's corpse is dug up by Merrick Mayfair, who is both a Mayfair witch and the vampire fledgling of Louis. Merrick's plan is to use Garwain's corpse in an exorcism ritual, which involves burning the corpse in a funeral pyre to exorcise Goblin from Blackwood Farm and send Garwain's soul to Heaven. The ritual is unsuccessful in exorcising Goblin and saving Garwain's soul, until Merrick takes Garwain's corpse and leaps into the fire with it. Only then does Goblin depart and Garwain go towards Heaven's beatific light.

Garwain appears in *Blackwood Farm* (2002). For more perspectives on Garwain's character, read the *Alphabettery* entries **Blackwood Farm**, **Goblin**, **Louis de Pointe du Lac**, **Merrick Mayfair**, and **Quinn Blackwood**.

Giuseppe

• MORTAL •

Giuseppe lives in Marius's Venetian palazzo along with several other boys, including Armand, before Marius turns him into a vampire. Giuseppe is the smallest of all the boys. It is likely that he is killed when Santino and the Children of Darkness burn the palazzo to the ground.

Giuseppe appears in *Blood and Gold* (2001). For more perspectives on Giuseppe's character, read the *Alphabettery* entries **Children of Darkness**, **Marius**, and **Santino**.

Goblin

• IMMORTAL •

When Garwain Blackwood dies at birth, shortly after the birth of his twin brother, Tarquin "Quinn" Blackwood, Garwain's ghost does not go into the light of Heaven but remains behind on Blackwood Farm, where he haunts his brother for the next two decades. In the beginning, they are almost like playmates, since Quinn is born with the ability to see ghosts, yet he does not understand that Goblin is the ghost of his dead twin brother. As Quinn grows and matures, Goblin becomes jealous of the fact that he cannot experience the same sensations as his living brother. The ghost becomes petulant and angry, especially when Quinn gives others more attention than him. Whenever Quinn tries to leave Blackwood Farm, Goblin tries to follow, yet the farther he gets from the plantation, the weaker he becomes. This is particularly true when Quinn, in his twenties, accompanies Aunt Queen to Europe. Goblin is furious, but he is able to keep in contact with Quinn through email and the housekeeper, Jasmine.

When Petronia captures Quinn and turns him into a vampire, Goblin is outraged and attacks Quinn so violently that Quinn seeks out the assistance of the vampire Lestat. Lestat turns to the aid of his friend David Talbot, who turns to the aid of Louis's fledgling Merrick Mayfair, who is also a member of the Mayfair witch family. She, Lestat, David, and Quinn return to Blackwood Farm, where Merrick performs an exorcism ritual, using Garwain's corpse. Merrick hopes to burn the corpse in a funeral pyre, which should dispel

Goblin by sending Garwain's soul to Heaven. But the ritual is unsuccessful until Merrick leaps into the fire with Garwain's corpse to ensure that her soul will take Garwain's soul into Heaven's light, banishing Goblin's haunting forever.

Goblin appears in *Blackwood Farm* (2002).

For more perspectives on Goblin's character, read the *Alphabettery* entries **Aunt Queen**, **Blackwood Farm**, **David Talbot**, **Garwain Blackwood**, **Jasmine**, **Lestat de Lioncourt**, **Louis de Pointe du Lac**, **Merrick Mayfair**, **Petronia**, and **Quinn Blackwood**.

God of the Grove

• VAMPIRE •

"God of the Grove" is a title given to ancient vampires in Akasha's blood cult who rule small temples as minor gods in her honor. Two minor gods are Teskhamen and Avicus. The God of the Grove appears in *The Queen of the Damned* (1988) and *Blood and Gold* (2001).

When Akasha begins making vampires in great numbers to combat the army of the First Brood, she assigns most of those vampires to serve her personal army, the Queens Blood. She uses a smaller number of her vampires in the proliferation of the blood religion that she and Enkil establish, identifying themselves as the ancient gods Isis and Osiris. Of that number, she makes some priests to administer the blood religion, while a few she identifies as minor gods who mortals worship. Although on the surface being identified as such a god might appear to be a blessing, in reality it is a curse and a punishment for many vampires. In one example, when the vampire Nebamun turns the mortal Sevraine into a vampire, Akasha punishes him by removing

him from his prominent role as Captain of the Queens Blood and imprisoning him in a temple where mortals worship him and will allow him to drink blood only on feast days, which occur as infrequently as once a month or six times a year.

Over the centuries, as Akasha's blood cult spreads across the known world, extending to every point of the compass, it makes its way as far east as the Himalayas, where Azim is worshipped as a blood god for many thousands of years. The blood cult also makes its way west, as far as Gaul, where Teskhamen is worshipped by Druids as a blood god, and even as far as pre-Roman Britain, where Avicus is also worshipped as a blood god by Druids.

Unlike Azim, who receives nightly human sacrifices in his temple, Teskhamen and Avicus live inside large oak trees, locked in small rooms behind large iron doors, and are only allowed to drink blood during certain Druid feast days. Because they still willingly follow

the command of Queen Akasha and adhere to the rules and precepts of her blood cult, Teskhamen and Avicus surrender to the worship of mortals, who do not let them leave the oak tree and insist on calling them by the title "God of the Grove."

For more perspectives on the God of the Grove in the Vampire Chronicles, read the *Alphabettery* entries **Avicus, Azim, First Brood, Nebamun, Queens Blood, Sevraine,** and **Teskhamen.**

Godric

• VAMPIRE •

Godric is the elder vampire at the Court of the Ruby Grail. Second-in-command, he makes most of the decisions for the coven, save for their coven leader, Florian, whose decision is final. Godric's decision is even above that of Florian's Blood Wife, Ursula, who pleads with Godric not to kill Vittorio, the mortal she secretly loves. In seeking ven-geance for the murder of his family, Vittorio eventually beheads Godric alongside Florian and burns their heads to ash.

Godric appears in *Vittorio the Vampire* (1999). For more perspectives on Godric's character, read the *Alphabettery* entries **Court of the Ruby Grail**, **Florian**, **Ursula**, and **Vittorio di Raniari**.

Grace Blackwood

• MORTAL •

Grace is the first wife of William Blackwood, the son of Manfred Blackwood, the founder of Blackwood Farm. Grace and William have Gravier, who becomes the great-great-grandfather of Quinn Blackwood. Although William's ghost can be seen haunting the rooms of Blackwood Manor, Grace's ghost never appears.

Grace appears in *Blackwood Farm* (2002). For more perspectives on Grace's charac-ter, read the *Alphabettery* entries **Black-wood Farm**, **Blackwood Manor**, **Gravier Blackwood**, **Manfred Blackwood**, **Quinn Blackwood**, and **William Blackwood**.

Grady Breen

• MORTAL •

Grady Breen is the Blackwood family law-yer and an old friend of Gravier Blackwood, grandson of Manfred Blackwood. Around eighty-five years old when Quinn Blackwood reaches manhood, Grady helps the Blackwoods sort out numerous affairs, such as Patsy's extravagant spending and Pops's extramarital child, Tommy Harrison. He even helps Tommy's mother, Terry Sue, earn a reasonable income from the Blackwoods, so that Tommy can receive an education.

Grady Breen appears in *Blackwood Farm* (2002). For more perspectives on Grady's character, read the *Alphabettery* entries **Blackwood Farm**, **Gravier Blackwood**, **Manfred Blackwood**, **Patsy Blackwood**, **Pops**, **Quinn Blackwood**, **Terry Sue Harrison**, **Tommy Harrison**, and **William Blackwood**.

Gravier Blackwood

• MORTAL •

Gravier is the son of William and Grace Blackwood, as well as the grandson of Manfred Blackwood, founder of Blackwood Farm. Because Gravier's father is sterile, his grandfather persuades Julien Mayfair to father children for William, making Gravier's father a member of the Mayfair family of witches and introducing the Mayfair blood into the Blackwood family. Gravier marries Blessed Alice and they have one son, Thomas Blackwood, who will come to be called Pops and be the grandfather of Quinn

Blackwood. Gravier practices law and is a local judge. When he dies, his ghost is often seen by the front door, smiling and waving his right hand.

Gravier appears in *Blackwood Farm* (2002). For more perspectives on Gravier's character, read the *Alphabettery* entries **Blackwood Farm**, **Blackwood Manor**, **Blessed Alice**, **Gravier Blackwood**, **Julien Mayfair**, **Manfred Blackwood**, **Patsy Blackwood**, **Pops**, **Quinn Blackwood**, **Thomas Blackwood**, and **William Blackwood**.

Great Burning of 4 C.E.

• PHENOMENON •

Thousands of years before the Common Era, a vampire known as the Elder is given the supreme and solemn duty of caring for Those Who Must Be Kept—Akasha and Enkil,

the Mother and the Father of the vampire race. Since they sit utterly motionless upon their thrones, with skin as white and hard as great marble statues, staring straight ahead as if in a catatonic state, the Elder's duties grow terribly tedious, century after century, constantly wiping the dust from their bodies, including their eyeballs, changing their clothes often, bathing them, overseeing certain rituals among the remnant blood priests, along with numerous other responsibilities, from which he has no relief.

At the beginning of the Common Era, while still in Egypt, the Elder can no longer endure the monotony of his role as caretaker of Those Who Must Be Kept. So just before dawn, he takes Akasha's and Enkil's statuesque bodies from their shrine and brings them to the bank of the Nile River, where he abandons them to the deadly rays of the morning sunlight. The sun's powerful rays do not destroy the Mother and the Father but only give their skin a beautiful bronze shade. But the deadly effect of the sunlight extends to all their children, every other vampire in existence, through their spiritual connection in Amel. The effect varies among vampires.

Weaker vampires are instantly immolated. Older vampires and those made by very ancient vampires with powerful blood are so severely burned that they are like charred skeletons. Only the very oldest vampires survive with little effect, their skin, like the skin of Akasha and Enkil, is deeply bronzed.

This varies among ancient vampires. For Maharet—a four-thousand-year-old vampire at the time, whose maker is her twin sister, Mekare, whose maker is Khayman, whose maker is Akasha herself—Maharet's skin only bronzes, like Akasha's. Teskhamen is also four thousand years old, but he is horribly burned, his skin almost gone and his bones sticking through the remains, all of him charred completely black. The same happens to Maharet's fledgling Eric, who, at the time, is only one thousand years old. Maharet must feed Eric her powerful blood to heal him while Teskhamen lives on for many years, a charred thing, while he heals.

When the Elder awakens on the night following the Great Burning, discovering that his skin is deeply bronzed, he goes out to the Nile River and sees that Those Who Must Be Kept also have bronzed skin. Realizing that he made a calamitous mistake, he brings Akasha and Enkil back to their Egyptian shrine and pretends as if nothing happened.

The Great Burning of 4 C.E happens in *The Vampire Lestat* (1985) and *The Queen of the Damned* (1988). For more perspectives on the Great Burning of 4 C.E. in the Vampire Chronicles, read the *Alphabettery* entries **Akasha, The Elder, Enkil, Khayman, Maharet, Mekare, Teskhamen,** and **Those Who Must Be Kept**.

Great Burning of 1985

• PHENOMENON •

When the music of the Vampire Lestat band awakens the ancient vampire Queen and Mother, Akasha rises from her wintry shrine in the north where Marius keeps safe Those Who Must Be Kept. She destroys her husband, King Enkil; abandons Marius; and flies across the world immolating her vampire fledglings with the power of her Fire Gift. Her plan is to destroy her vampire children, along with 90 percent of the world's male population, and remake the world into a vampire paradise where she will be worshipped as the goddess Queen. Many vampires are destroyed in this Great Burning, such as Baby Jenks from the Fang Gang and Laurent, whom Lestat knew in Armand's coven, the Children of Darkness, and in the Théâtre des Vampires. Akasha spares those vampires whom she cannot destroy with the Fire Gift, such as Maharet and Khayman, as well as those younger, weaker vampires whom Lestat (Akasha's new paramour) loves, such as Gabrielle, Louis, and Marius.

The Great Burning of 1985 happens in *The Queen of the Damned* (1988). For more perspectives on the Great Burning of 1985 in the Vampire Chronicles, read the *Alphabettery* entries **Akasha, Baby Jenks, Children of Darkness, The Elder, Enkil, Fang Gang, Khayman, Laurent, Lestat de Lioncourt, Maharet, Théâtre des Vampires, Those Who Must Be Kept,** and **The Vampire Lestat.**

Great Burning of 2013

• PHENOMENON •

For nearly six thousand years, the spirit of Amel remains buried in the subconsciousness of Queen Akasha, as well as in her vampire fledglings. When Mekare beheads Akasha and consumes her brain, she becomes the new Queen of the Damned and the host carrier for the spirit of Amel and his Sacred Core. But after a few decades of existing inside Mekare's traumatically wounded mind, Amel's consciousness surfaces. He begins speaking to other vampires in an effort to leave Mekare for a new suitable carrier host. Amel speaks to these other vampires as the mysterious Voice, whose persuasive influence seemingly takes possession of vampires who have the Fire Gift. Amel forces these vampires to begin burning vampire covens all over the world—in

China, in India, in France, and even in the United States. The vampires who have been repopulating their race over the last few decades are now completely immolated to ashes. The burnings do not stop until the vampires finally discover Amel's desire to leave Mekare and live inside a vampire of equal strength but greater sanity.

The Great Burning of 2013 happens in *Prince Lestat* (2014). For more perspectives on the Great Burning of 2013 in the Vampire Chronicles, read the *Alphabettery* entries **Amel**, **Fire Gift**, **Mekare**, and **Lestat de Lioncourt**.

Great Family

• MORTAL •

After Akasha separates Maharet from Mekare by setting them adrift in tombs in oceans on opposite coasts, dividing them for more than six thousand years, Maharet's tomb washes ashore on the African coast. She returns to her old home in northern Israel, near Mount Carmel, where she finds that the daughter she had when she was mortal has grown into a woman. As an immortal, Maharet watches her daughter have children, and their children have children. After two centuries of observing, she begins to chronicle her family tree, beginning on tablets. As her family grows larger over the long centuries, they disperse into numerous family units and travel to other countries, adapting to new languages and cultures. Maharet spends her centuries wandering from one family unit to another, learning the different languages of her family, and introducing herself as the family chronicler. When one generation dies, she reports to her family members that the Maharet who chronicled her family in

the past has grown old and died and that she is the new Maharet, chronicler of the family. As she ages, she also amasses great wealth, and she shares her wealth with her ever-growing family. In one sense, this is her defiance against Akasha, who has tried to take everything from her but cannot take the family generated from her only child. She is also in defiance of other vampire behaviors: when most vampires find it impossible to adapt to the new changes of a modern world, they will either destroy or bury themselves in the earth and sleep until they can rise again and make contact with a mortal who will help them transition; yet Maharet never goes into the earth and never contemplates suicide, since it is encountering her family, generation after generation, that helps her transition into each new era of human development. Her tools of chronicling also develop, with stone tablets traded for parchment, parchment for paper, and eventually paper for digital information. She keeps records of the progress of her entire family for six thousand years, hundreds of generations, all the way into the twentieth century. They are her Great Family. By the time of the twenty-first century, shortly before Rhoshamandes murders Maharet, she ensures that her family will be able to survive without her. She entrusts all of the Great Family's information to a corporation whose lawyers will handle the ongoing chronicling of her family and the distribution of her wealth to its members.

The Great Family appears in *The Queen of the Damned* (1988) and *Prince Lestat* (2014). For more perspectives on the Great Family in the Vampire Chronicles, read the *Alphabettery* entries **Akasha**, **Jesse**, **Khayman**, **Maharet**, **Mekare**, and **Rhoshamandes**.

Great Laws

• PHENOMENON •

For almost one thousand years, the Children of Darkness, a vampire coven of Satan worshippers, believe that they are an integral part of God's plan for the salvation of souls because of their own cooperation in Satan's work for the damnation of people. Denying themselves all mortal pleasures, they reject luxury, fine clothes, beautiful houses, and even drinking the blood of the innocent. Sleeping in filth, wearing rags, and feeding off the destitute, the coven of the Children of Darkness spread across Europe, having prominent houses in Rome and Paris. An important reason they thrive is because their organization, their belief in the supernatural world, and their blind obedience to the five Great Laws govern them to coexist or be mortally punished. Those five Great Laws are as follows:

LAW ONE
Each coven must have its leader, and only he might order the working of the Dark Trick upon a mortal, seeing that the methods and the rituals were properly observed.

LAW TWO
The Dark Gifts must never be given to the crippled, the maimed, or to children or to those who cannot, even with the Dark Powers, survive on their own. Be it further understood that all mortals who would receive the Dark Gifts should be beautiful in person, so that the insult to God might be greater when the trick is done.

LAW THREE
Never should an old vampire work this magic lest the blood of the fledgling be too strong. For all our gifts increase naturally with age and the old ones have too much strength to pass on. Injury, burning—these catastrophes, if

they do not destroy the Child of Satan, will only increase his powers when he is healed. Satan guards the flock from the powers of old ones, for almost all, without exception, go mad.

LAW FOUR

No vampire may ever destroy another vampire, except that the coven master has the power of life and death over all his flock. And it is further his obligation to lead the old ones and the mad ones into the fire when they can no longer serve Satan as they should. It is his obligation to destroy all vampires who are not properly made. It is his obligation to destroy all those who are so badly wounded that they cannot survive on their own. And it is his obligation finally to seek the destruction of all outcasts and all those who have broken these laws.

LAW FIVE

No vampire shall ever reveal his true nature to a mortal and let the mortal live. No vampire must ever reveal the history of the vampires to a mortal and let the mortal live. No vampire must commit to writing the history of the vampires or any true knowledge of vampires lest such a history be found by mortals and believed. And a vampire's name must never be known to mortals, save from his tombstone, and never must any vampire reveal to mortals the location of his or any other vampire's lair.

The Great Laws appear in *The Vampire Lestat* (1985). For more perspectives on the Great Laws in the Vampire Chronicles, read the *Alphabettery* entries **Armand**, **Children of Darkness**, and **Santino**.

Great Nananne

• MORTAL •

Great Nananne is Merrick Mayfair's godmother, a very powerful witch who teaches Merrick everything she knows about their witching abilities, as well as about the Mayfair family history, particularly "Oncle Julien" (that is, the legendary Julien Mayfair, who died many decades earlier). Merrick lives with her Great Nananne when her mother, Cold Sandra, and her sister, Honey in the Sunshine, die in a tragic car accident. As Merrick's abilities grow, making her a powerful witch, the Talamasca becomes aware of her. When Great Nananne dies, the Talamasca takes Merrick to live with them, where she is the apprentice of David Talbot.

Great Nananne appears in *Merrick* (2000). For more perspectives on Great Nananne's character, read the *Alphabettery* entries **Cold Sandra**, **David Talbot**, **Honey in the Sunshine**, **Merrick Mayfair**, **Oncle Julien**, and **Talamasca Order**.

Great One

• IMMORTAL •

In order to protect earthlings from the exploitation of alien beings from the planet Bravenna, in the Realm of Worlds, their own creation, Amel (a human whom they abducted thousands of years before the Common Era and genetically enhanced into a superhuman who will do their bidding) rebels against them and creates great cities, especially the city of Atlantis, out of the substance called luracastria, which confounds Bravennans and their technology. The human inhabitants of Amel's protective cities look to him as a great leader and protector, one who provides for them peace, security, and a better way of life than they have ever known. They regard him as a messiah and savior and refer to him as the Great One.

The concept of the Great One appears in *Prince Lestat and the Realms of Atlantis* (2016). For more perspectives on the Great One character, read the *Alphabettery* entries **Amel**, **Atlantis**, **Bravenna**, **Bravennans**, and **Luracastria**.

Gregory Duff Collingsworth

• VAMPIRE •

Gregory Duff Collingsworth is one of Akasha's most trusted servants. Over the many millennia of his life, he influences the shape of vampirekind through powerful covens that become billion-dollar companies and reform vampirism in the twenty-first century. He appears in *Prince Lestat* (2014), *Prince Lestat and the Realms of Atlantis* (2016), and *Blood Communion* (2018).

After going down into the earth to sleep and survive the test of time, the ancient vampire Nebamun, who is made by Queen Akasha herself, arises in the third century of the Common Era and takes the name Gregory Duff Collingsworth.

When he encounters Chrysanthe, a mortal from the great Arab-Christian city of Hira, she gives him vast and informative lessons on history, art, and the sciences. Gregory falls in love with Chrysanthe, turns her into a vampire, and takes her as his second Blood Wife, having forsaken all hope of ever finding his first Blood Wife, Sevraine, whom Akasha took from him in ancient Egypt. Gregory and Chrysanthe live together in northern Africa, in the city of Carthage, for many years, where they meet the one-legged Athenian slave, Flavius, whose maker is Pandora. Flavius informs Gregory and Chrysanthe of all he knows of the fate of Those Who Must Be Kept (Akasha and her husband-king, Enkil), since his maker's paramour, Marius, is their caretaker. Flavius also teaches Gregory much on Roman and Greek culture, artists, historians, philosophers, writers, and more. Gregory, who as Nebamun lived under Akasha's rule that no one with deformities or disabilities will be turned into a vampire, is immediately impressed that Flavius is now an immortal, despite having only one leg, which effectually shatters Gregory's superstitions of his former vampire religion. He and Chrysanthe welcome Flavius to stay with them in a coven, and the three remain together for centuries.

During the eighth century, in what is known as modern-day France, when Rhoshamandes still rules, before the Children of Satan besiege him and his realm, Gregory encounters Teskhamen and his fledgling Hesketh, and they talk about much concerning the ancient days, since Gregory (as Nebamun) was the Captain of Akasha's army, the Queens Blood, while Teskhamen was a part of Akasha's sacred blood priests.

A few centuries later, Gregory desires to expand what he calls his Blood Kindred and invites into the coven two vampires, Avicus and Zenobia. Avicus was turned into a vampire during the reign of Akasha and made to worship in her blood cult, but he has heard tales of Gregory's former identity, Nebamun, who rebels against the Queen.

Over the next millennia, Gregory builds a place of security for his Blood Kindred, a sanctuary that will not only guard them against enemies but also provide a place of advancement for the Undead. The pinnacle of his work comes in the twenty-first century, when he builds Collingsworth Pharmaceuticals, a conglomerate of pharmacies and hospitals that help mortals and secretly serve Undead clients. Through Collingsworth Pharmaceuticals, Gregory begins working with the vampire scientists Fareed and Seth, Akasha's son, whose breakthrough research makes many advances for the benefit of vampires. One such benefit is restoring Flavius's leg through a cloning procedure.

After Prince Lestat creates the Court of the Prince at Château de Lioncourt, Gregory becomes a prominent member, especially in informing the Court of the existence of the ancient vampire Gundesanth. He supports the destruction of Rhoshamandes for killing Maharet and Khayman. And he helps the Replimoids purchase a new colony in rural England.

For more perspectives on Gregory's character, read the *Alphabettery* entries **Akasha, Avicus, Chrysanthe, Collingsworth Pharmaceuticals, Enkil, Fareed Bhansali, Flavius, Lestat de Lioncourt, Nebamun,** and **Zenobia.**

Gremt Stryker Knollys

• IMMORTAL •

Gremt Stryker Knollys is a spirit who knows Amel in the spirit realm. After learning how to become incarnate, he not only teaches other disembodied spirits (many are former vampires) how to become incarnate but also is also one of the key founders of the Order of the Talamasca. He appears in *Prince Lestat* (2014), *Prince Lestat and the Realms of Atlantis* (2016), and *Blood Communion* (2018).

Gremt's existence begins as a disembodied spirit, similar to the spirit of Amel, which is an enormous entity without flesh, blood, or bone but with a small amount of matter at the core of its being. Although he has no knowledge of Atlantis, Gremt reveals that there was a time when Amel did not exist. As a spirit, Gremt knows Amel. He observes how Amel interacts with the twins, Mekare and Maharet, and how Amel enters into Akasha and then is shared from Akasha to Enkil; and from there how Amel's spirit can be spread out and shared into many other mortals. Though a spirit, Gremt can hear the voice of Amel speaking to the vampire race. By his unique amalgamation with mortals, Amel awakens in Gremt much interest in becoming more human. The principal difference between their spirit natures is that Amel's nature began as human before he became a spirit, while Gremt has always been spirit and never mortal. Amel's humanity shapes his spiritual identity, while Gremt's spiritual identity is shaped by his infinite nature.

Around the sixth century C.E., Gremt spends time with the great scholar, historian, statesman, and monk Cassiodorus. His disembodied spirit exists in the energy of a beehive near Cassiodorus's monastery, Vivarium, until his death. As the vampire Pandora happens to be passing by, Gremt's spirit emerges from the beehive and possesses a nearby scarecrow, which he causes to weep for Cassiodorus's death. Pandora recognizes that this must be a spirit and that this spirit has a great desire to be human. She encourages him to pursue that goal no matter how long it takes. Inspired and strengthened by her fearless words, he spends the next two hundred years working to become incarnate by gathering little particles of dust and other such minuscule motes and compacting them so tightly together into a tangible body of organs, skin, teeth, hair, and even blood that mortals can touch him, feel warmth from him, and even taste salt upon his skin.

Over time, the more incarnate he becomes, the less he can hear the voice of Amel in vampires, not the way the vampires will later hear it. Finally, Gremt cannot hear Amel at all. He is too much of an individual, fleshly and distinct, to access that particular power in himself. Gremt focuses on becoming a blue-eyed male with black wavy hair, Caucasian skin, broad shoulders, and slender hands. Although he is not human in the biological sense, he possesses a heartbeat and respiration, capable of fooling even modern-day airport X-ray machines. He is not omniscient, but he is able to leave his body and travel in an invisible and silent form to any location in the world instantaneously, although he forswears that power when he trains himself to behave with a human disposition. In his training, he also teaches himself to imitate human reactions flawlessly, such as smiling, laughing, weeping, coughing, yawning, and so on. No matter how human he appears to be, he often wonders what he looks like through mortal eyes, chiefly concerned with appearing too impassive, even though he can feel blood rushing to his cheeks or tears pooling in his eyes.

During those two hundred years, he encounters the spirit of a slain vampire, Hesketh. Deformed and hideous during her mortal life, she learns from him how to incarnate herself in the same way he has, by gathering dust particles and compacting them together so tightly that they shape the semblance of a living, breathing body. When she is ready to present herself, he takes her to the vampire who was her maker in life, Teskhamen. Hesketh does not reveal her form in the way he remembers her to be on the outside but the way he saw her on the inside. Her ghost form is that of a beautiful woman, as beautiful as she always wanted to be in life. At the same time, Gremt's encounter and subsequent friendship with Teskhamen are powerful enough to inspire Gremt to model his manner of life after the former God of the Grove.

Having been inspired by Pandora to become incarnate, and also inspired by Cassiodorus's pursuit of knowledge and truth, Gremt forms an alliance with Teskhamen and Hesketh. The three desire to gain knowledge about the mysteries of the world. They want to understand how red-haired witches like Mekare and Maharet can manipulate spirits. They want to fathom how a pure spirit like Gremt and a formerly mortal spirit like Hesketh can become incarnate. They are especially curious to know how Amel was able to fuse with Akasha. In effect, they want to understand every aspect of the supernatural world. Their alliance to pursue truth is the beginning of the Talamasca. Eventually, mortals join their order, their numbers grow quickly, and in no time the Talamasca flourishes so much that they have to form institutions where information can be gathered and mortals can be trained in the acquired knowledge. Institutions such as the Motherhouses and libraries are inspired by Gremt's admiration for Cassiodorus's monastery, Vivarium. Gremt, Teskhamen, and Hesketh assign mortals called the Elders to lead the Talamasca into new generations. In time, the three founders become a mystery to the Talamasca. Members often ponder the origins of their order, but David Talbot has a feeling that it all began with bees.

Afterward Gremt encounters the ghost of Magnus, Lestat's maker. Gremt teaches Magnus how to become incarnate also. This allows Magnus and Lestat to form the kind of relationship that they never could have had in Magnus's mortal life. Lestat is so profoundly grateful to Gremt for this gift that he also begins a deeply tender relationship with Gremt.

Gremt eventually settles in the Replimoid colony in rural England, where he assists Kapetria in her scientific experiments.

For more perspectives on Gremt's character, read the *Alphabettery* entries **Akasha, Amel, David Talbot, Hesketh, Maharet, Mekare, Replimoid, Talamasca Order,** and **Teskhamen**.

Gretchen

• MORTAL •

After Raglan James, the Body Thief, steals Lestat's vampire body, Lestat (in Raglan James's mortal body) begins suffering pneumonia. In a hospital, he is cared for by Gretchen, a Roman Catholic nun, who is experiencing a crisis of faith. She takes him home with her, to better care for him. He tells her his life story and promises to share his life with her. After a night of passionate intimacy, which allows Lestat to experience sexual pleasure for the first time in two centuries, he decides that he needs to find his vampire body, while Gretchen decides that she wants to return to the religious life in a South American mission.

Gretchen appears in *The Tale of the Body Thief* (1992). For more perspectives on her character, read the *Alphabettery* entries **Lestat de Lioncourt** and **Raglan James**.

Gundesanth

• VAMPIRE •

Read the *Alphabettery* entry **Santh**.

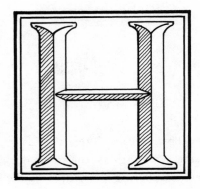

Héloïse

• MORTAL •

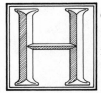 éloïse was a brilliant scholar in the twelfth century who fell in love with her tutor, Peter Abelard, one of the most famous scholars of his time. At first the love affair was kept secret, but when she became pregnant, the revelation of their relationship caused a great scandal as a violation against the precepts of their era. Héloïse entered a convent, while Peter was castrated and went to live in a monastery. Though they were divided, they corresponded with each other, and their relationship became one of the earliest and greatest romances in Western civilization.

Quinn Blackwood likens his romantic correspondence with Mona Mayfair to the romantic correspondence between Héloïse and Noble Abelard, assuring Mona that their correspondence will one day also become legendary.

Héloïse is discussed in *Blackwood Farm* (2002). For more perspectives on Héloïse in the Vampire Chronicles, read the *Alphabettery* entries **Mona Mayfair**, **Noble Abelard**, and **Quinn Blackwood**.

Hermitage

• SANCTUARY •

The Hermitage is a two-story house on Sugar Devil Island in Sugar Devil Swamp on the Blackwood Farm property. It is built by Blackwood Farm's founder, Manfred Blackwood, as a private retreat for himself. After Manfred encounters the vampire Petronia, he builds for her a gold-and-granite mausoleum where she can safely sleep during the day. With Petronia's assistance, Manfred murders his second wife, Rebecca Stanford, in the Hermitage. In time, knowledge of the location of the Hermitage becomes lost among the Blackwood family members. The house is not rediscovered until Rebecca's ghost helps Manfred's great-great-great-grandson, Quinn, find Sugar Devil Island as well as her body in the Hermitage. After Quinn becomes a vampire, he confesses to Lestat that the Hermitage is his true home.

The Hermitage is in *Blackwood Farm* (2002). For more perspectives on the Hermitage, read the *Alphabettery* entries **Blackwood Farm**, **Manfred Blackwood**, **Quinn Blackwood**, **Petronia**, and **Rebecca Stanford**.

Hesketh

• IMMORTAL •

Hesketh is Teskhamen's fledgling and ghostly spouse. She is best known for being a founder of the Talamasca. She appears in *Prince Lestat* (2014), *Prince Lestat and the Realms of Atlantis* (2016), and *Blood Communion* (2018).

When Teskhamen flees from the Druids and his oak tree, after turning Marius into a vampire, he encounters a woman living alone in a meager hut. She is badly deformed, with twisted limbs and skin full of warts and pockmarks. Many mortals cruelly call her a witch. Teskhamen sees beyond her exterior hideousness, finds a very beautiful woman deep inside, and learns that her name is Hesketh. Due to his own deformity from the Great Burning of 4 C.E., Hesketh takes compassion on him, invites him to stay with her, and the two take care of each other. With his supernatural powers, he gives her warning whenever people are approaching; he defends her whenever anyone attacks; his Fire Gift intensifies the fire beneath her cauldron to make it boil and bubble like magic; and he reads the minds of mortals and tells her their secrets.

In time, their love for each other grows. Because of her kindness, and because of his love for her, he turns her into a vampire, against all the ancient rules that he once lived by, which state that no one physically deformed can be brought into the Blood. They live together for the next six hundred years, while Teskhamen continues to heal, recover his former power, and gain new abilities that he'd never had before. They are timid at first about killing and drinking blood, drinking from thieves they find on lonely roads. But as time passes, they grow bolder and invade castles and fortresses.

Despite the fact that Hesketh is very strong and powerful as an immortal, she cannot escape the torture she feels at being immortally deformed. In the same way that mortals were frightened of her appearance before she was given the Dark Gift, mortals continue to scream in fear whenever they see her, not only because of her vampiric threat but also because of her deformity. Full of anger at her outer ugliness, Hesketh becomes argumentative with Teskhamen. Their bickering increases over time until their disagreements divide them. One night, when she is alone, she enters a village where a mob overwhelms her and burns her alive. Teskhamen hears of this, destroys the village and everyone in it, and then buries Hesketh's ashes near an old monastery in France, hoping that her soul will find rest. Mourning the loss of Hesketh greatly, he stays in the scriptorium near the monastery and rises every night to light a lamp and place it over her unmarked grave. He stays there for a long time, hoping to see Hesketh once more, not wanting to go on without her.

In the spirit realm, Hesketh encounters another spirit named Gremt, who has the ability to incarnate by gathering motes of dust and other minuscule particles to himself to shape his organs, bones, flesh, teeth, hair, and other mortal externals, to the point that this new incarnate form can wear clothing. Gremt teaches Hesketh how to do this, and when she is finally able to maintain a form that Teskhamen can see, she comes to him and reveals that she not only is able to incarnate her spirit form but is also able to remove all of her defects and reveal the true beauty that she knows that she always had on the inside in life, with flaxen hair, a tall and straight body, and skin that is soft, pale, and shimmering. She is so incarnate that Teskhamen can touch her with his hands and embrace her with his arms and even kiss her lips, all of which he does.

Inspired by Gremt's desire to more fully understand the supernatural world, Hesketh forms an alliance with him and Teskhamen. The three of them make it their mission to gain knowledge about ghosts, vampires, witches, and anything else that no mortal or immortal has been able to explain hitherto. Their alliance is the inception of the Talamasca. Mortals join their quest. Hesketh, Teskhamen, and Gremt form the anonymous Elders and select a few mortals from each generation to guide the Order into new eras of learning and growth. As time wears on, Hesketh, Teskhamen, and Gremt withdraw from the Talamasca, until the Order forgets about them.

Hesketh and Teskhamen remain together into the twenty-first century as supernatural spouses, he her Blood Husband, she his ghostly wife. They eventually resettle in the Replimoid colony in rural England, although

Teskhamen also visits the Court of the Prince in France.

For more perspectives on Hesketh's character, read the *Alphabettery* entries **Great Burning of 4 C.E.**, **Gremt Stryker Knollys**, **Talamasca Order**, and **Teskhamen**.

Hiram

• TALTOS •

Hiram is one of several Taltos who live on the secret island owned by the ancient Taltos Ashlar and his wife, Morrigan, daughter of Mona Mayfair, the vampire fledgling of Lestat. When Ashlar and Morrigan's son Silas causes a rebellion, a drug cartel invades the island, killing many Taltos and capturing several others. Ashlar and Morrigan's other son, Oberon, last sees Hiram escaping when their companion Elath is shot dead.

Hiram appears in *Blood Canticle* (2003). For more perspectives on his character, read the *Alphabettery* entries **Ashlar**, **Elath**, **Mona Mayfair**, **Morrigan Mayfair**, **Silas**, and **Taltos**.

Honey in the Sunshine

• MORTAL •

Honey in the Sunshine is the daughter of Cold Sandra and the older sister of Merrick Mayfair. As a part of the Mayfair witch family, they each demonstrate unique abilities, although Honey in the Sunshine is not as powerful as her mother or Merrick, the most powerful of them all. When her mother uses her witching abilities to attract and marry the archaeologist Matthew Kemp, he takes them all on an expedition to Guatemala, where he falls ill and dies. When Cold Sandra inherits his small fortune, she decides to leave and take Honey in the Sunshine with her, leaving Merrick in the care of her godmother, Great Nananne. Shortly after they leave, Cold Sandra and Honey in the Sunshine are murdered, strangled in their car, and submerged in the lake. Their bodies are not found until many years later.

Honey in the Sunshine appears in *Merrick* (2000). For more perspectives on her character, read the *Alphabettery* entries **Cold Sandra**, **Great Nananne**, **Matthew Kemp**, and **Merrick Mayfair**.

Houn'gan

• IDIOM •

Houn'gan (or *houngan*) is the Haitian term for a priest or priestess in Haitian Voodoo. When Great Nananne talks about Oncle Julien (Julien Mayfair), she refers to him as a *houn'gan*.

Houn'gan appears in *Merrick* (2000). For more perspectives on *houn'gan* in the Vampire Chronicles, read the *Alphabettery* entries **Great Nananne**, **Julien Mayfair**, and **Oncle Julien**.

Hybrid Creatures

• IMMORTAL •

The war of the First Brood and the Queens Blood ends when Akasha and Enkil are captured and imprisoned under large blocks of diorite and granite, leaving only their heads and necks exposed. Their captors try to make vampires using Queen Akasha's blood, but their initial attempts are unsuccessful, most likely because they do not fully drain the mortals of their blood before feeding them with Akasha's blood. The unfortunate consequence of these early experiments is the creation of strange hybrid creatures that are neither vampire nor human but a monstrous mangling of both. To their great lament, these hybrid creatures always die horribly.

Hybrid creatures appear in *The Vampire Lestat* (1985). For more perspectives on hybrid creatures, in the Vampire Chronicles read the *Alphabettery* entries **Akasha**, **Amel**, **Drinker of Blood**, **Enkil**, **First Brood**, **Khayman**, **Maharet**, and **Mekare**.

Interview with the Vampire

• VAMPIRE CHRONICLE •

t nearly two centuries old, the vampire Louis de Pointe du Lac tells the story of his vampire life to Daniel Malloy. Louis is turned into a vampire in 1791, in New Orleans, by the vampire Lestat. Louis's efforts to seek the meaning of his vampire existence are thwarted by Lestat's cavalier attitude towards life. While living in New Orleans, they both make the child vampire, Claudia, who matures into an immortal trapped in a child's body. As Lestat continues to disappoint Louis and Claudia, they grow to despise him for having turned them into vampires. Claudia and Louis attempt to murder Lestat before fleeing to Europe, where they encounter the three-hundred-year-old Armand and his coven at Théâtre des Vampires. At Lestat's prompting, Armand's coven kills Claudia while Armand and Louis form a deep friendship. Louis spends his life up through the twentieth century seeking meaning.

For more perspectives on this Vampire Chronicle, read the *Alphabettery* entries **Armand, Claudia, Lestat de Lioncourt, Louis de Pont du Lac, New Orleans,** and **Théâtre des Vampires**.

Iron Curse

• PHENOMENON •

When a vampire desires to prevent another vampire from using vampiric abilities—such as the Fire Gift, the Mind Gift, the Cloud Gift, or the Blood Curse—that vampire can wrap the other vampire in iron wrappings. The vampire must be totally wrapped in the iron wrappings like a mummy; otherwise the vampire can still send out telepathic messages or attack with pyrokinetics. Iron wrappings lock in vampiric energy.

An example of one vampire wrapping another is Cyril wrapping Baudwin in iron. Baudwin is totally incapacitated and unable to use his gifts to attack younger vampires.

The phenomenon of the iron curse appears in *Blood Communion* (2018). For more perspectives on iron wrappings, read the *Alphabettery* entries **Blood Curse**, **Cloud Gift**, **Fire Gift**, **Lestat de Lioncourt**, and **Mind Gift**.

Isaac

• TALTOS •

Isaac is one of the remaining Taltos living on a secret island owned by Ash Templeton, a successful and wealthy doll maker whose actual name is Ashlar, when he is many thousands of years old, one of the original Taltos, who lives in the Time Before the Moon. Ashlar's son Silas causes a rebellion on their island, and the rebellion spills over into nearby islands owned by a mortal drug cartel. When the Drug Merchants retaliate by invading the secret island, most of the Taltos are shot and killed. Oberon, another of Ashlar's Taltos sons, thinks he sees Isaac escaping. His body is not among the honored dead.

Isaac appears in *Blood Canticle* (2003). For more perspectives on Isaac's character, read the *Alphabettery* entries **Ashlar**, **Drug Merchants**, **Elath**, **Silas**, **Taltos**, and **Time Before the Moon**.

Isaac Rummel

• ALIAS •

"Isaac Rummel" is the alias that Lestat has in the beginning of *Memnoch the Devil* while he stays at an opulent New York hotel where he meets David Talbot. Lestat picks that hotel not because he wants it; his next victim, the hitman and drug dealer Roger, picks it because he always meets with his daughter, the televangelist Dora, in the restaurant. When Lestat desires to leave the hotel and check into the Olympic Hotel on Fifth Avenue, he wonders if David, who books Lestat's room, will keep Lestat under that name or if he will change his alias to Renfield, after the character in Bram Stoker's 1897 gothic novel, *Dracula*.

The alias appears in *Memnoch the Devil* (1995). For more perspectives on the "Isaac Rummel" alias in the Vampire Chronicles, read the *Alphabettery* entries **David Talbot**, **Dora, Lestat de Lioncourt**, and **Memnoch**.

Isabel Blackwood

• MORTAL •

After Manfred Blackwood founds Blackwood Farm, he and his wife Virginia Lee have four children, William, Camille, Philip, and Isabel. While William and Camille survive into adulthood, Philip and Isabel both die in childhood, Isabel from lockjaw.

Isabel Blackwood appears in *Blackwood Farm* (2002). For more perspectives on her character, read the *Alphabettery* entries **Blackwood Farm, Camille Blackwood, Manfred Blackwood, Philip Blackwood, Virginia Lee Blackwood**, and **William Blackwood**.

Isabella

• CHARACTER •

At the age of sixteen, when Lestat decides that he wants to run away from home and join an acting troupe, the troupe gives him the lead role in the play *Lelio and Isabella*, performed in the commedia dell'arte style. Isabella is a character performed by one of the troupe members who, after the play receives high praise from the audience, gives her own intimate accolades to Lestat as he falls asleep in her arms.

Isabella appears in *The Vampire Lestat* (1985). For more perspectives on this commedia dell'arte character in the Vampire Chronicles, read the *Alphabettery* entries **Commedia dell'Arte**, **Flaminia**, **Lelio**, and **Lestat de Lioncourt**.

Isis

• IMMORTAL •

Isis is the ancient Egyptian goddess of marriage, procreation, and motherhood. She is also an inspiration for the solidarity of Egyptian family life. Married to the Egyptian god Osiris, she is considered to be the Queen of the gods, particularly among her massive cult following.

When Akasha is transformed into the world's first vampire, she builds up around herself a cult following of blood worshippers and identifies herself as the goddess Isis, which greatly augments reverence for her among her followers.

Isis appears in *The Queen of the Damned* (1988). For more perspectives on Isis in the Vampire Chronicles, read the *Alphabettery* entries **Akasha** and **Osiris**.

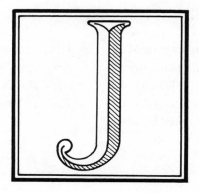

Jabare

• VAMPIRE •

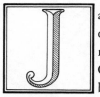 Jabare is a contemporary of Gundesanth and Nebamun. He is a servant to the Queens Blood, but he never becomes a soldier. Little is known about his history. In the twenty-first century, he becomes a member of Lestat's Court of the Prince at Château de Lioncourt.

Jabare appears in *Blood Communion* (2018). For more perspectives on Jabare's character, read the *Alphabettery* entries **Santh** and **Nebamun**.

Jacope

• MORTAL •

Jacope is one of the boys who lives in Marius's Venetian palazzo with Armand before Marius turns him into a vampire. When Lord Harlech invades the palazzo and attacks the occupants within, Jacope is stabbed by Lord Harlech's poison-tipped blade and dies.

Jacope appears in *Blood and Gold* (2001). For more perspectives on his character, read the *Alphabettery* entries **Armand**, **Lord Harlech**, and **Marius**.

Jake

• TALAMASCA •

Jake is a Talamasca investigator who has worked with David Talbot for many years. In *The Tale of the Body Thief*, Jake helps David and Lestat acquire aliases, passage on the *Queen Elizabeth 2*, and weapons as they pursue Raglan James, the Body Thief, in possession of Lestat's vampire body.

Jake appears in *The Tale of the Body Thief* (1992). For more perspectives on Jake's character, read the *Alphabettery* entries **David Talbot**, **Lestat de Lioncourt**, *Queen Elizabeth 2*, and **Raglan James**.

James Bond of Vampires

• SOBRIQUET •

"James Bond of Vampires" is the sobriquet that Lestat gives to himself at the beginning of *The Tale of the Body Thief* (1992). This is likely in reference to the multiple aliases, the high security, the globe-trotting, the limitless wealth, and even the romances constantly pervading the lifestyle of the vampire Lestat.

For more perspectives on this sobriquet in the Vampire Chronicles, read the *Alphabettery* entries **David Talbot**, **Lestat de Lioncourt**, and **Raglan James**.

Jasmine

• MORTAL •

Jasmine is the daughter of Quinn Blackwood's nanny, Little Ida, and the granddaughter of the head cook at Blackwood Farm, Big Ramona. Jasmine works as a housekeeper in the mansion. She has the peculiar ability to see ghosts, especially the ghost that haunts Quinn, the ghost of his identical twin brother, who calls himself Goblin. When Quinn becomes a man and his grandfather Pops—who had been a father figure to him—dies, Quinn turns to Jasmine for consolation. After a night of passion, Jasmine becomes pregnant with Quinn's son, Little Jerome.

Jasmine appears in *Blackwood Farm* (2002). For more perspectives on Jasmine's character, read the *Alphabettery* entries **Big Ramona**, **Blackwood Farm**, **Goblin**, **Little Ida**, **Little Jerome**, **Pops**, and **Quinn Blackwood**.

Jason Hamilton

• ALIAS •

In *The Tale of the Body Thief* (1992), "Jason Hamilton" is the alias that Raglan James assumes after he thieves Lestat's body and boards the *Queen Elizabeth 2*, staying in the Queen Victoria Suite. After Lestat repossesses his body and kills James, he also assumes the alias briefly.

For more perspectives on this alias, read the *Alphabettery* entries **Lestat de Lioncourt**, *Queen Elizabeth 2*, and **Raglan James**.

Jason of Athens

• VAMPIRE •

The history of Jason of Athens remains mostly obscure. It is rumored that he is as old as Marius, although others speculate that he might be as old as Gregory Duff Collingsworth. Jason enters into the Chronicles after the death of Rhoshamandes in the twenty-first century, when he appears at Château de Lioncourt for the first Winter Solstice Ball.

Jason of Athens appears in *Blood Communion* (2018). For more perspectives on Jason's character, read the *Alphabettery* entries **Gregory Duff Collingsworth**, **Lestat de Lioncourt**, **Marius**, and **Rhoshamandes**.

Jeannette

• MORTAL •

During his mortal life, while Lestat performs as an actor at Renaud's House of Thesbians, one of the actresses who performs with him onstage is Jeannette. Lestat fights with her and Luchina most, and loves both of them more than all the other actresses. After he becomes a vampire and receives Magnus's vast wealth, he bestows gifts upon Jeannette. His vampire cravings find their beauty and their blood almost irresistible, and he nearly reveals his vampire nature onstage. Humiliated by his behavior, he closes the theater and sends Jeannette along with the entire acting troupe to London, where they perform in a new theater.

Jeannette appears in *The Vampire Lestat* (1985). For more perspectives on her character, read the *Alphabettery* entries **Lestat de Lioncourt**, **Luchina**, **Magnus**, and **Renaud's House of Thesbians**.

Jerome

• MORTAL •

During the time of Manfred Blackwood in nineteenth-century New Orleans, Jerome becomes one of the first servants at Blackwood Farm. Jerome marries Ora Lee, who also works at the plantation, in the kitchen. Both of their parents had been free Creole people of color and artisans before the Civil War. Jerome and Ora Lee both work to keep Manfred's children, William and Camille, safe from dangers in the Louisiana swampland, as well as from their stepmother, Rebecca Stanford. Jerome eventually becomes the ancestor of many generations of servants at Blackwood Farm, in particular Big Ramona, Little Ida, and Jasmine.

Jerome appears in *Blackwood Farm* (2002). For more perspectives on his character, read the *Alphabettery* entries **Big Ramona**, **Blackwood Farm**, **Camille Blackwood**, **Jerome**, **Little Ida**, **Manfred Blackwood**, **Ora Lee**, **Rebecca Stanford**, and **William Blackwood**.

Jesse

• VAMPIRE •

Jesse is prominent in the Vampire Chronicles as a member of the Talamasca, a hereditary ancestor and witch of Maharet, and Maharet's fledgling. Jesse serves as an initial bridge between Lestat and the head of the Talamasca Order, David Talbot. Jesse appears in *The Vampire Lestat* (1985), *The Queen of the Damned* (1988), *Merrick* (2000), *Prince Lestat* (2014), *Prince Lestat and the Realms of Atlantis* (2016), and *Blood Communion* (2018).

In the twentieth century, nearly three hundred generations after Maharet begins the Great Family, Jessica Miriam Reeves's mother prematurely gives birth before perishing in a fatal car crash. Jesse's ancient ancestor, the six-thousand-year-old vampire Maharet, delivers her from the hospital to Matthew and Maria Godwin, relations in Maharet's Great Family, who care for her until she reaches the age of twenty.

Throughout her life, Jesse develops an abiding relationship with Maharet, who writes many letters and visits her often as a distant aunt, while also bestowing upon her countless gifts. Aunt Maharet introduces Jesse to the vastness of her Great Family throughout the world. Endowed with the family's gift for witchery, Jesse has the ability to see ghosts and spirits. Sometimes she even communes with her long-deceased mother. Maharet fosters that ability, even after Jesse comes to live with her for several years. Jesse immensely delights in spending so much time with her beloved aunt and her companion Mael. While she lives with them, she observes their peculiar behavior: they never appear during the day; they eat sparingly; Mael often asks her strange questions about ordinary things of modernity; and once when she descends into the cellar during the day, Jesse finds Mael lying on the ground and Maharet sitting up against a wall, both with their eyes wide open like corpses'. Her suspicions about their peculiar nature increase when she overhears Mael pleading with Maharet to do something to Jesse that will prevent her from death, and the only way for Maharet to end his relentless persistence on the matter is to backhand him so hard that he flies across the yard. Jesse has not yet suspected that Mael is pleading with Maharet to turn Jesse into a vampire.

After Jesse has lived in Maharet's Sonoma compound for several years, David Talbot, the Superior General of the Talamasca, invites her to join the Order. Against Maharet's wishes, Jesse accepts David's invitation, and he assigns her to read and investigate the early published books of the Vampire Chronicles, namely Louis's *Interview with the Vampire* and Lestat's *The Vampire Lestat*. When Jesse reads Mael's tale, she connects the possibility of this seemingly fictional Mael with her aunt Maharet's Mael, since his behavior seems so similar to the behavior described in Lestat's book. Suspecting that Lestat, Maharet, and Mael are all truly vampires, she endeavors to

prove her point by encountering the vampire Lestat at his eponymous rock concert. Unbeknownst to her, Lestat's music has roused Maharet's ancient foe, Akasha, the Queen of the Damned, who is massacring numerous vampires across the globe. Jesse is also unaware that several vampires are attending the rock concert, some of whom seek to destroy Lestat, others to destroy Akasha, yet one is there to protect Jesse. When she leaps up onstage and realizes not merely that Lestat but also that her aunt Maharet and Mael are the same kind of supernatural creature, a young vampire backstage, seeking to use his power against Lestat, uses it instead to thrust Jesse against a wall and break her neck. Mael rushes her to Maharet, who turns Jesse into an incredibly powerful vampire with her ancient blood.

At Maharet's Sonoma compound Jesse attends the council of vampires, who listen to the Legend of the Twins before they all discuss how they are going to destroy the Queen of the Damned. When Akasha appears and no vampire can defeat her, Maharet's long-lost sister, Mekare, suddenly returns and destroys Akasha by decapitating her, consuming her brain, and taking into herself Amel, the Sacred Core, turning Mekare into the new carrier host of vampire existence. Jesse joins Maharet, who takes Mekare away to a new compound in Java, Indonesia.

Jesse observes with great sadness that, although Maharet's six-thousand-year search for her twin sister has now come to an end, Mekare is not the sister that Maharet remembers. Mekare has suffered many traumas: losing her mother, being prevented from religiously caring for her mother's body, seeing the destruction of her village, being raped and imprisoned, having her tongue cut out, being turned into a vampire, turning her twin sister into a vampire, being entombed in a sarcophagus that was set adrift in an ocean, being separated from her twin sister for six thousand years, and finally taking into herself an entity that intrinsically connects her to every vampire on the earth as their principal source of life. Mekare is like a walking comatose victim. Her eyes are open, she moves and drinks blood, but there appears to be little to no sign of consciousness, little to no sign that she recognizes Maharet or the passage of time. Jesse consoles Maharet as she tries to heal Mekare, walking with her, singing to her, watching movies with her, and many other things that might bring the old Mekare back. Jesse laments how all of it proves ineffective.

A few years after Jesse becomes a vampire, Lestat turns her old mentor, David Talbot, into a vampire also. David and Jesse become excellent companions. Together they continue the scholarly practices that they learned in the Talamasca, particularly researching through Maharet's ancient archives, which mostly comprise the Great Family.

During those years, Maharet begins growing weary of her life. She dreams of throwing herself and Mekare into an active volcano and being burned alive, knowing that destroying Mekare also destroys Amel, which would also destroy the entire vampire race. Painfully aware of this, Jesse is able to talk Maharet out of her fantasy.

Mekare's deteriorated mental state also rouses Amel to consciousness, after he has lain dormant in Akasha, acting as all vampires' instinctual drive. Amel becomes aware that he is existing in the wounded mind of a traumatized soul. Also aware of Maharet's fantasy, Amel begins to seek ways of escaping before Maharet can enact her plan. He speaks to vampires as the mysterious Voice and possesses them with an animalistic drive to destroy weaker vampires and their sanctuaries. One night, Maharet briefly leaves the compound while Jesse remains behind with Khayman, Mekare, and a few younger vampires. But then Jesse also leaves briefly for Jakarta; and when she returns, she is greatly surprised to discover that the compound has been burned to the ground, libraries have been lost, the young vampires have been immolated, Khayman is bewildered, and Mekare seems aware of her surroundings for a few fleeting moments.

Maharet moves Mekare and Khayman to a new compound in the jungles of the Amazon. Jesse parts ways with them. The spirit of Amel continues to wreak havoc in the minds of other vampires, specifically the five-thousand-year-old Rhoshamandes, convincing him that vampire existence is in jeopardy and inspiring him to kill Mekare, consume her brain, and take Amel, the Sacred Core, into himself, becoming the new host carrier of vampire existence. Rhoshamandes and his fledgling Benedict go to Maharet's Amazonian compound, destroy Maharet and Khayman, and kidnap Mekare. Jesse grieves greatly over the loss of her dear ancestor, aunt, and maker, Maharet.

Lestat and other vampires retrieve Mekare, yet she greatly desires to join her sister in death. After Mekare allows Lestat to consume her brain, take Amel into himself, and become the new host carrier of vampires, Jesse weeps over Mekare's grave. She finds some small measure of solace when Maharet's body is retrieved from her unmarked grave in the Amazon and buried beside the remains of her ancient twin sister.

In the early twenty-first century, Jesse lives at Château de Lioncourt and becomes an active participant in the Court of the Prince, ruling over many decisions, especially sup-porting the lawful destruction of Rhosha-mandes for killing Maharet, which Lestat fulfills himself.

For more perspectives on Jesse Reeves's character, read the *Alphabettery* entries **Aka-sha**, **Amel**, **David Talbot**, **Great Family**, **Khayman**, **Lestat de Lioncourt**, **Louis de Pointe du Lac**, **Mael**, **Maharet**, **Maria God-win**, **Matthew Godwin**, **Mekare**, **Rhosha-mandes**, and **Talamasca Order**.

Jessica Miriam Reeves

• MORTAL •

Read the *Alphabettery* entry **Jesse**.

John McQueen

• MORTAL •

John McQueen is the husband of Lorraine Blackwood, known by Quinn Blackwood as Aunt Queen. Much of John McQueen's life remains a mystery; it is known only that he is exceedingly wealthy. When he dies after crashing his Bugatti sports car on the Pacific Coast Highway, his wife inherits his vast fortune.

John McQueen is mentioned in *Blackwood Farm* (2002). For more perspectives on John McQueen's character, read the *Alphabettery* entries **Aunt Queen**, **Blackwood Farm**, and **Quinn Blackwood**.

Jonas Harrison

• MORTAL •

Jonas is the son of Terry Sue and the half brother of Tommy. Jonas has a different father than Tommy, whose father is Pops, the grandfather of Quinn Blackwood, the owner of Blackwood Farm. Because Tommy is technically Quinn's much younger uncle, Quinn takes care of Terry Sue and her children, so that Jonas and his siblings can receive an excellent education and have a hopeful future.

Jonas appears in *Blackwood Farm* (2002). For more perspectives on Jonas's character, read the *Alphabettery* entries **Blackwood Farm**, **Quinn Blackwood**, **Terry Sue Harrison**, and **Tommy Harrison**.

Julien Mayfair

• WITCH •

Julien Mayfair is one of the most notorious characters in the Lives of the Mayfair Witches. In the Vampire Chronicles, he is very influential in the life of Lestat's fledgling Mona Mayfair, and he even appears to converse with Lestat himself. Julien Mayfair appears in *Merrick* (2000), *Blackwood Farm* (2002), and *Blood Canticle* (2003).

Born in the early nineteenth century, Julien Mayfair demonstrates powerful witching abilities from an early age. He can see ghosts and spirits and the etheric form of recently deceased individuals leaving their physical body. He is a powerful psychic who has the ability to move objects with his mind and to read people's thoughts. His sister, Katherine, would have been the eighth witch in a line of thirteen female witches in Lasher's plan for incarnation as a Taltos, but Katherine is less powerful in magic, and Julien takes her place in the plan, often demonstrating the ability to control Lasher.

Growing up with his sister on their Riverbend plantation, Julien becomes the manager of the plantation by the age of fifteen. Highly educated, able to speak and read several languages, he demonstrates a voracious sexual appetite from an early age, even developing amorous feelings for his sister, Katherine.

In time, a feud develops between Julien and his cousin Augustin, who dies as a result. His death divides the family, which results in the construction of another Mayfair plantation called Fontevrault.

Julien often takes Katherine into New Orleans dressed as a man. They frequent the taverns and enjoy the city's nightlife. They discover a beautiful, undeveloped property on First Street, in New Orleans's Garden District. They immediately purchase it and hire the Irish architect Darcy Monahan to design a lavish home. When Katherine and Darcy fall in love, Julien vehemently opposes the marriage. Katherine threatens to elope with Darcy and summons the spirit of Lasher to protect them, and Julien finally agrees to their marriage, but he will not leave Riverbend to visit her at the First Street house, not until Darcy dies many years later. After moving in at Katherine's request, he and his sister conceive a child together, Mary Beth, who becomes not simply the next in the line of thirteen generational witches but also the most powerful witch up to that time.

Julien marries his cousin, Suzette Mayfair, and they have three sons, Cortland, Barclay, and Garland, and a daughter, Jeannette. Julien goes into business with his sons, creating the law firm Mayfair and Mayfair, which oversees the family's business, legal, and financial affairs. The company also makes investments with Manfred Blackwood, founder of Blackwood Farm, where the vampire Quinn Blackwood grows up and where Louis's fledgling Merrick dies. With Lasher's help, Julien makes the Mayfair family fortune grow immensely vast.

When Julien dies, Lasher creates a storm, which he also did for the previous seven witches in the generational line prepared for his incarnation, a feat that he does not do for Katherine, the originally intended heiress.

After his death, Julien's ghost makes many appearances to both mortals and immortals alike, including a few appearances to Lestat, as well as to Michael Curry and to Mona Mayfair (Lestat's future fledgling), to trick them into conceiving a child, Morrigan Mayfair, a Taltos, who will later be sought after by Lestat.

For more perspectives on Julien Mayfair in the Vampire Chronicles, read the *Alphabettery* entries **Fontevrault Plantation, Lestat de Lioncourt, Louis de Pointe du Lac, Mayfair and Mayfair, Merrick Mayfair, Michael Curry, Mona Mayfair, Morrigan Mayfair, Riverbend Plantation, Taltos,** and **Thirteen Witches.**

Kadir of Istanbul

• VAMPIRE •

adir of Istanbul is one of the ancient vampires, perhaps one of the Children of the Millennia or older, maybe even as old as Akasha's ancient Egyptian court. Kadir has not yet recounted his tale for the Vampire Chronicles. He first appears before Lestat at the Winter Solstice Ball, celebrating the establishment of the Court of the Prince. He comes to pay his respects to the Prince of the Vampires.

Kadir of Istanbul appears in *Blood Communion* (2018). For more perspectives on Kadir's character, read the *Alphabettery* entries **Akasha, Château de Lioncourt,** and **Lestat de Lioncourt.**

Kapetria

• IMMORTAL •

Kapetria is an immortal being who quintessentially helps reshape the landscape of vampirism in the twenty-first century by freeing Amel from Lestat's mind. Kapetria appears in *Prince Lestat and the Realms of Atlantis* (2016) and *Blood Communion* (2018).

Created in the laboratories of a distant planet called Bravenna, Kapetria is the combination of every cell of life on planet Earth—plant, reptile, fish, insect, and mammal—yet she is made in the likeness of a human female, which is an abhorrence to her creators, whom she refers to as the Parents. Along with three others, Welf, Derek, and the dark-skinned Garekyn, Kapetria is informed by the Parents that she and her companions are called Replimoids and that they have superhuman abilities of regeneration, replication, and immortality. The Parents then inform them that their mission is to go to Earth and help the Bravennan purpose of maintaining peace and harmony on that distant planet. Part of their mission is to destroy a rebel Replimoid whom they have sent earlier, named Amel.

When Kapetria and her Replimoid companions confront Amel, they realize that the Parents lied to them, mainly because Amel is not a Replimoid like them but a human abducted by the Bravennans and genetically enhanced for the purpose of facilitating and increasing human suffering. The sorrow, fear, pain, and all the aspects of human torment are sent through space to Bravenna in the form of psychic energy, which is consumed as energy for the Realm of Worlds. Kapetria and the other Replimoids renounce their allegiance to the Bravennans and form an alliance with Amel, vowing never to harm another human being and to work to help humankind evolve into a fitter race. They call themselves the People of the Purpose.

Amel has developed a unique compound from his own DNA, which he calls luracastria, a substance that obstructs the Bravennans from receiving consumable psychic data on human suffering, effectively cutting off their food source. One of Amel's greatest luracastric creations is the great city of Atlantis, which is a sanctuary for human life, protecting them against Bravennan exploitation.

When the Bravennans discover that their Replimoids have failed, they send a meteor shower to Earth, which destroys Atlantis and Amel and separates the Replimoids from one another. Kapetria remains divided from Derek and Garekyn for the next eleven thousand years. She and Welf stay together and survive throughout the centuries, in the same way that vampire Blood Spouses help each other endure the difficult struggle of immortal life.

Surviving all the way into the twentieth century, Kapetria and Welf create false credentials and become Dr. Karen Rhinehart and Felix Welf, and they take up work in the research center and laboratories of the ancient vampire Gregory Duff Collingsworth, whose facilities make him one of the leading pharmaceutical manufacturers in the world and allow him to establish organizations exclusively devoted to the betterment of vampirekind. In these laboratories, they attempt to re-create Amel's luracastria compound, but fail. When they discover that Garekyn and Derek are still alive, they abandon their work to search for them.

Once they are reunited, the Replimoids join forces with Lestat and other vampires. Kapetria helps the vampires realize that what the spirit of Amel truly craves is not to drink the blood of humans to the point of their death, nor to devour the death of his victims, or to fulfill any vision of the human person dying; but rather, a vampire truly craves what the spirit of Amel craves, which is the folic acid concentrated tightly into the nutrientrich blood of Replimoids. In other words, his spirit craves being in his former superhuman body. Kapetria and the vampires collaborate on a solution that allows the spirit of Amel to be transferred out of Lestat's brain and into the brain of a Replimoid likeness of the human body Amel had eleven thousand years ago in the city of Atlantis, effectively freeing all vampires from their dependence on Prince Lestat as the host carrier of the Sacred Core. Kapetria and her Replimoid companions re-form into the People of the Purpose, promising to work with the vampire race as siblings in immortality for the betterment of humanity.

Gregory and Gremt help Kapetria and the Replimoids purchase an abandoned asylum and a stately manor in rural England. They also buy a majority share in a nearby village, where they create a health spa. Kapetria and the Replimoids live in their colony in relative peace, performing scientific experiments on cloning techniques.

For more perspectives on Kapetria's character, read the *Alphabettery* entries **Amel, Bravenna, Bravennans, Collingsworth Pharmaceuticals, Derek, Garekyn, Gregory Duff Collingsworth, Lestat de Lioncourt, Luracastria, Replimoid, Sacred Core,** and **Welf.**

Karbella

• IMMORTAL •

After Kapetria and her Replimoid companions relocate to a rural section of England and begin a colony, she conducts experiments on herself and on her Replimoid clones. She makes a clone of her clone, and a clone of that clone, and a clone of that clone, all the way to a tenth-generation clone, whom Kapetria names Karbella. With each new generation the clones have less imprinted knowledge, less ambition and curiosity, and are more easily manipulated. Karbella is absolutely subservient, with diminished intelligence, and enjoys simple comforts and peace. She is more of a slave than a servant. She will continue performing the same task happily and without resistance until told otherwise. Her docility makes her an excellent source of endless blood for Lestat.

Karbella appears in *Blood Communion* (2018). For more perspectives on Karbella's character, read the *Alphabettery* entries **Kapetria** and **Replimoid**.

Karen Rhinehart

• ALIAS •

When Kapetria the Replimoid begins working at Collingsworth Pharmaceuticals to be secretly nearer to the CEO, the vampire Gregory Duff Collingsworth, she takes the alias "Dr. Karen Rhinehart" to hide her immortal nature.

The alias "Dr. Karen Rhinehart" appears in *Prince Lestat and the Realms of Atlantis* (2016). For more perspectives on this alias, read the *Alphabettery* entries **Collingsworth Pharmaceuticals**, **Gregory Duff Collingsworth**, **Kapetria**, and **Replimoid**.

Katu

• IMMORTAL •

Before the Replimoids from Bravenna meet with Lestat and his vampires, Kapetria insists that she must understand her power better, since, as Replimoids from the planet Bravenna, they are immortals with the ability to regenerate and replicate. Kapetria amputates her left foot, which grows back shortly thereafter, while her severed left foot grows into a new version of herself, a replicate of Kapetria, who looks exactly like Kapetria, except with more obvious emotional innocence. Instead of calling her Kapetria Two, Kapetria simply shortens the name of her replicated self to Katu. After Katu's replication, Kapetria makes five more exactly like her, giving them equally unique names.

Katu appears in *Prince Lestat and the Realms of Atlantis* (2016). For more perspectives on Katu's character, read the *Alphabettery* entries **Amel**, **Bravenna**, **Kapetria**, **Lestat de Lioncourt**, and **Replimoid**.

Kemet

• SANCTUARY •

During the rule of Akasha and Enkil as King and Queen of ancient Egypt, the Egyptians do not refer to their land as Egypt but as Kemet, which is an ancient Egyptian word meaning "land of black soil." Thus, it is more appropriate to refer to the Mother and the Father of the vampire race not as the Rulers of Egypt, but as the King and Queen of Kemet.

Kemet is referred to in *The Queen of the Damned* (1988). For more perspectives on Kemet in the Vampire Chronicles, read the *Alphabettery* entries **Akasha**, **Enkil**, and **Vampire**.

Khayman

• VAMPIRE •

Khayman begins as the most beloved servant of Enkil and Akasha, but he eventually becomes the father of the rebellious First Brood and the most beloved servant of the Mother and the Father's enemies, Maharet and Mekare. He also sires Maharet's only child, who begins the Great Family. Khayman appears in *The Queen of the Damned* (1988) and *Prince Lestat* (2014).

More than four thousand years before the Common Era, when Enkil, King of Egypt, takes as his bride and queen Akasha from Uruk, the new Queen attempts to change the spiritual life of common Egyptian people by replacing their ritualized cannibalism of the recently deceased with a more humane practice of wrapping corpses in linen before burying them. When the people revolt, King Enkil dispatches his steward, Khayman, to retrieve two red-haired, green-eyed twin witches, Maharet and Mekare, who live in caves in Mount Carmel in the northern lands of Israel, and with whom Akasha desires to commune to confirm her belief that spirits are happier when their mortal bodies remain intact after death. Maharet and Mekare refuse to go to the Egyptian court. So Khayman, along with an Egyptian military contingent, is under the King and Queen's orders to destroy the twins' village, kill the villagers, and force the twins to go to Egypt. During that weeklong journey south, Khayman pities the twins. He loosens their bonds and ensures that they have enough strength for the journey. When they finally arrive at the Egyptian court and stand before King Enkil and Queen Akasha, the Queen puts many questions to the twins, who answer truthfully that Akasha is misguided in her spiritual beliefs. Enraged, the Queen imprisons Maharet and Mekare. Mekare summons the spirit of Amel, who offends the Queen. Akasha punishes the twins by ordering Khayman to rape them before the entire court. He loathes having to do this; and while he first rapes Mekare and then Maharet, he imagines that he is having intercourse with other, more willing women. After this, Akasha releases the twins back to their village, where Maharet gives birth to Khayman's daughter, Miriam.

Amel remains in Egypt and haunts Khayman's house. Khayman pleads with the King and Queen to help him. When the rulers enter his house, conspirators also enter and attempt to assassinate Akasha and Enkil. As Akasha lies bleeding to death on Khayman's floor, the bloodthirsty spirit of Amel fuses with the Queen's blood, creating the first vampire. Khayman watches all this in horror. Akasha immediately, instinctively, turns her husband, King Enkil, who is dying right beside her, into a vampire like herself. As a result of becoming vampires, they are greatly perplexed by their insatiable bloodlust and their inability to go into the sunlight. Khayman's new responsibilities include burying the corpses of their victims. Akasha and Enkil then send Khayman on the journey north once again to retrieve the twins and bring them back down to Egypt to explain the King and Queen's peculiar transformation. When Khayman delivers the twins safely, Maharet and Mekare are equally perplexed and cannot provide a satisfactory answer. Maharet suggests the possibility that, because spirits are enormously large entities,

if Akasha made more vampires, the bloodlust might dilute by also diluting the spirit of Amel. To test this, Akasha turns Khayman into a vampire against his will.

The Queen's betrayal enrages Khayman, and he begins planning his escape. Learning that Akasha has imprisoned the twins, plucked out Maharet's eyes, cut out Mekare's tongue, and sentenced them both to death, Khayman secretly goes to them and turns Mekare into a vampire, who then turns her twin sister into a vampire also. Together, the three escape from prison and for the next week flee from the royal army, which hunts them day and night. During that time, Khayman and the twins are also raising an army of their own by turning numerous mortals into vampires, who come to be called the First Brood. Khayman, Maharet, and Mekare make it all the way to the necropolis at Memphis in Egypt, where the twins are captured, imprisoned in stone tombs, and set adrift in different oceans, to be divided for the next six thousand years. Khayman is the only one who escapes.

Khayman's blood army continues fighting against Akasha and Enkil until the King and Queen are captured and kept imprisoned for so long that they become as motionless as statues and must eventually be cared for by the Elder. During the long passage of years, Khayman's mind becomes confused, and he can no longer remember his origins. His compassionate nature never truly changes. He will never feed on mortals he knows, only strangers and evildoers. He even shows great tenderness and sympathy to the Talamasca around the first millennium C.E., which refers to him simply as Benjamin the Devil.

In the twentieth century, Khayman finally encounters Akasha when she is awakened from her statuesque torpor by the music of the vampire Lestat's rock band. At that moment, he remembers everything, how he became a vampire, his name, and the anger he feels towards his former queen. Since she has already killed Enkil, Akasha now attacks him, but because of his great age and his will to survive, he is able to easily withstand her assaults. Akasha next flies across the globe to San Francisco, to the concert of the vampire Lestat, to make him her new companion. Khayman follows her and continues to resist her attacks on her children, as she is identifying them with her Mind Gift and burning them to death with her Fire Gift. At the concert, Khayman encounters Talamasca members David Talbot and Aaron Lightner; recollecting his compassion towards the Order, he cautions them on the imminent danger. Khayman also encounters Maharet's companion Mael, along with Armand, and counsels them on how to protect themselves against the Queen's attacks. Khayman is finally reunited with Maharet at her compound in the Sonoma Mountains, where they gather together with several other vampires who have survived Akasha's massacre. Khayman and Maharet tell the other vampires about their long history and about the Blood Genesis. When Akasha arrives at the compound, Khayman and the other vampires, including Lestat, fight against the Queen of the Damned, yet she proves to be more powerful. Akasha cannot be defeated until Mekare appears, decapitates her, and then consumes her brain and heart, taking into herself the spirit of Amel and his Sacred Core and becoming the new carrier host of vampire existence.

Maharet and Mekare retreat to the jungles of the Amazon; Khayman accompanies them. They live there together as a threesome coven, occasionally inviting other vampires to stay with them for a time. Khayman still experiences memory lapses and blackouts. During one such memory loss, Maharet's Amazon compound burns to the ground while she is absent; the cause of the fire remains a mystery. After they move to Maharet's Java compound, Khayman experiences another blackout and kills Maharet's fledgling and former companion Eric, which hurts Maharet deeply and causes a division between them. Lestat and the other vampires deduce that Amel has tricked Khayman into committing this crime and others because Amel desires to be free of Mekare's wounded mind and transferred to a stronger, saner vampire.

Eventually, Amel tricks the five-thousand-year-old Rhoshamandes into consuming Mekare's brain and taking the Sacred Core into himself. To do that, however, he must get past Maharet and Khayman. So Rhoshamandes and his fledgling Benedict first find and kill Maharet. Then they lie in wait for Khayman, who comes home so fatigued from his labor that he does not notice the signs of the scuffle in the house until it is too late. Rhoshamandes and Benedict attack him from behind with machetes and decapitate him. Some of Khayman's last recorded words are "It's finished. I will not continue. . . . My journey in this world is finished."

For more perspectives on Khayman's character, read the *Alphabettery* entries **Akasha,**

Amel, Benjamin the Devil, The Elder, Enkil, Eric, Fire Gift, First Brood, Lestat de Lioncourt, Maharet, Maharet's Amazon Compound, Maharet's Java Compound, Mekare, Mind Gift, Rhoshamandes, Sacred Core, and Talamasca Order.

Killer

• VAMPIRE •

Killer is the founder and leader of the twentieth-century motorcycle coven, Fang Gang. He is the maker of the tragic Baby Jenks. He appears in *The Queen of the Damned* (1988), *Prince Lestat* (2014), and *Prince Lestat and the Realms of Atlantis* (2016).

In 1925, an itinerant vampire, who no longer desires to suffer the agonizing isolation of an immortal life, wanders into a backwater Texas town and turns a thirteen-year-old boy into the vampire Killer. Similar to the way Magnus makes Lestat scatter his ashes after committing suicide by immolation, Killer's maker forces him to bury his ashes after he also commits suicide by immolation. Killer spends the next sixty years wandering throughout the United States, learning how to be a vampire. He learns how to ride a motorcycle and forms a motorcycle club by turning several others into vampires, namely Davis, Russ, Tim, and Baby Jenks. Killer calls his crew the Fang Gang.

Killer teaches his gang how to avoid the major vampire coven houses where the older vampires reside who are strong enough to kill them. He teaches his gang how it is easiest to kill isolated mortals living on the edges of cities. And he also teaches them how to prick their finger with their fangs and let their blood drop on the puncture marks on their victim's neck, which causes the wound to heal enough so that it will appear as if their mortal victim died of a heart attack or a brain aneurysm.

The Fang Gang avidly reads *Interview with the Vampire* and *The Vampire Lestat* and enthusiastically listens to the rock music of the band the Vampire Lestat. They even drive their Harley-Davidson motorcycles out west to San Francisco, to the Vampire Lestat's one and only rock concert. On the way, they observe that vampire coven houses all over the United States are being burned to the ground. Unbeknownst to them, the rock music of the vampire Lestat has awakened the vampire Queen, Akasha, who is enacting a plan of global domination by burning the majority of her vampire children.

Baby Jenks separates from the Fang Gang temporarily and is killed by Akasha. Killer and the rest of his Fang Gang thoroughly enjoy the Vampire Lestat concert, until Akasha finally appears and begins immolating hundreds of her young vampires. Killer watches helplessly that night as Tim and Russ are immolated and Davis is taken protectively into the air by the vampire Gregory Duff Collingsworth. Killer flees to the San Francisco slums, where he hides until the next night. He and a small remnant of vampires flee the city, thankful to be alive. He does not see his Fang Gang again until the twenty-first century, when he discovers that Davis has been living in Gregory's coven along with several other ancient vampires.

Killer stays near Armand's New York coven house at Trinity Gate. One night, when he and the vampire Eleni are hunting around the coven house, they encounter the Replimoid Garekyn from the planet Bravenna, who was recently attacked by Avicus and Garrick and survived that attack by taking Garrick's head and drinking his brain fluids, gaining a greater understanding of the relationship between vampires and Replimoids. Killer attempts to defeat Garekyn in a brief struggle, but the Replimoid is too powerful. Seeking more knowledge from vampire brain fluid, Garekyn ruptures Eleni's skull and tears off Killer's head, ending his nearly century-long life by quaffing down his brain fluid.

For more perspectives on Killer's character, read the *Alphabettery* entries **Akasha, Armand, Baby Jenks, Bravenna, Davis, Eleni, Fang Gang, Garekyn, Gregory Duff Collingsworth, Lestat de Lioncourt, Magnus, Russ, Tim, Trinity Gate,** and **The Vampire Lestat.**

Kitchen Gang

• MORTAL •

"Kitchen Gang" is a term describing the servants who work in the kitchen at Blackwood Manor, the grand mansion on the vast property of Blackwood Farm. Founded in the nineteenth century, the Kitchen Gang initially consists of Ora Lee and Pepper. Their descendant, Big Ramona, is still working in the kitchen, a part of the Kitchen Gang into the twentieth century.

The Kitchen Gang appears in *Blackwood Farm* (2002). For more perspectives on the Kitchen Gang in the Vampire Chronicles, read the *Alphabettery* entries **Big Ramona, Blackwood Manor, Ora Lee,** and **Pepper.**

Lamia

• SANCTUARY •

amia is one of several vampire bars in the Vampire Connection, where vampires can find sanctuary and share crucial and secretive information. Located in Paris, France, Lamia is named after a mistress of Zeus in Greek mythology who became identified in later traditions as a succubus or a vampire, capable of monstrously seducing and killing men. This Lamia vampire bar, which Lestat writes about in *The Vampire Lestat* (1985), is not the Lamia bar he mentions in *The Queen of the Damned* (1988), which is located in Athens, Greece. The Athens Lamia bar is not a part of the Vampire Connection, even though Khayman visits it, seeking two blood drinkers who suddenly burst into flames in the bar during the Great Burning of 1985.

For more perspectives on the Lamia vampire bar in Paris, read the *Alphabettery* entries **Bela Lugosi, Carmilla, Dracula's Daughter, Dr. Polidori, Great Burning of 1985, Lord Ruthven, Vampire Bar,** and **Vampire Connection.**

Larry

• MORTAL •

Larry begins his musical career as the keyboardist for the band Satan's Night Out, along with his brother, Alex, on drums and the brilliant guitarist Tough Cookie. The trio's popularity takes a major leap forward when the vampire Lestat appears in their jam room one night and offers to make them rock stars. Gladly accepting, they change their name to the Vampire Lestat, with the vampire on lead vocals.

Lestat is true to his word. He brings them great fame, throughout the mortal and immortal world alike. They play only one concert, in San Francisco, after which the vampire Lestat leaves the band, but he also provides for Larry and his bandmates enough wealth to keep them well heeled for the rest of their lives.

Larry appears in *The Vampire Lestat* (1985). For more perspectives on his character, read the *Alphabettery* entries **Alex**, **Christine**, **Lestat de Lioncourt**, **Satan's Night Out**, **Tough Cookie**, and **The Vampire Lestat**.

Lasher

• IMMORTAL •

Lasher is a disembodied spirit, similar to the spirits Gremt and Amel, although Amel began his existence as a mortal, while Gremt and Lasher have always been massive incorporeal entities. Certain mortals who have the inherent ability to communicate with spirits are referred to as witches, such as Maharet and Mekare, who communicate with Amel four thousand years before the Common Era, and Suzanne Mayfair, who communicates with Lasher in the seventeenth century. Just as Amel is fascinated with blood, Lasher is fascinated with mortal sensuality, and he develops a plan to become incarnate through a program of inbreeding among thirteen descendants of witches, beginning with Suzanne Mayfair and ending with Rowan Mayfair. A token of their relationship is the Mayfair emerald. The Mayfair who wears the emerald also wields the power of Lasher, who holds sway over the forces of nature. Lasher serves each Mayfair witch devotedly, while each generation of witch serves his plan. Every inbred generation obliviously arranges a specific genetic grouping that leads to the development of a Taltos, an ancient race of immortal beings.

When Rowan and her husband, Michael Curry (a descendant of Julien Mayfair, the only male witch to wield the Mayfair emerald), conceive a Taltos child, Lasher spiritually fuses with the fetus. Because the gestation and birthing of Taltos children are very rapid, Rowan gives birth to Lasher, who grows into an adult male within the hour. Lasher now desires to conceive a child with Rowan so that she can give birth to another Taltos who will be his mate, so he convinces her to abscond with him. They go to Houston, where Lasher binds and rapes Rowan repeatedly. She has two miscarriages before she finally conceives a Taltos child, who communicates telepathically from the womb, informing Rowan that her name is Emaleth. When Lasher learns that Rowan is pregnant, he relaxes his guard, and Rowan takes the opportunity to escape. Lasher pursues Rowan to her First Street home in New Orleans's Garden District, where he is confronted by Michael and Aaron Lightner, an agent of the Talamasca Order. Lasher learns that Rowan was found unconscious in a park somewhere between Houston and New Orleans; it appears as though she miscarried and is now in a coma. Lasher is entirely ignorant of the fact that his daughter (and hopeful mate) Emaleth was born, grew into an adult, and is on her way to the First Street house. Lasher makes an impassioned recounting of his life to Michael and Aaron, but Michael smashes in Lasher's skull with a hammer, killing him for all the abuses he heaped upon Rowan.

Lestat hears of Lasher's tale in *Blood Canticle* (2003). For more perspectives on Lasher's character, read the *Alphabettery* entries **Aaron Lightner**, **First Street House**, **Michael Curry**, **Rowan Mayfair**, **Spirits**, and **Taltos**.

Laurent

• VAMPIRE •

Laurent is one of the four vampires who survive Armand's burning of the Children of Darkness in the eighteenth century. He is also one of the few documented cases of being immolated by Akasha's Great Burning of 1985. Laurent appears in *The Vampire Lestat* (1985) and *The Queen of the Damned* (1988).

Laurent is sixteen years old when he is turned into a vampire. When Armand comes to Paris to begin a new coven of the Children of Darkness, Laurent becomes one of its members. He learns and practices the Great Laws; he dresses shabbily; he sleeps in squalor; he renounces any pleasures; he hunts only the most wretched of Parisian mortals. He is forbidden to live in a way contrary to his monstrous nature. He believes he is fulfilling God's plan for souls by aiding Satan's work for damnation.

In the eighteenth century, when the vampire Lestat and his fledgling Gabrielle begin living and hunting in Paris, Laurent and the rest of the coven try to destroy them; and when they cannot, they capture and torture Lestat's mortal friend Nicolas de Lenfent. After Lestat rescues Nicolas and turns him into a vampire, he returns to Armand and the Children of Darkness and convinces them that their way of life is outmoded in the Age of Enlightenment. Armand begins burning his coven. Only four are spared: Eleni, Felix, Eugénie, and Laurent. They beseech Lestat to become their new leader. He refuses, but his new fledgling, Nicolas, who grows insane and enraged when he becomes an immortal blood drinker, forces Lestat to give Laurent and his companions Lestat's theater, Renaud's House of Thesbians. Laurent and his companions move in, Nicolas and Armand join them, and they rename it Théâtre des Vampires, where they perform plays as mortals pretending to be vampires.

Laurent remains a part of this coven for many years, but he leaves before the arrival of Lestat's other fledglings, Louis and Claudia. Laurent then migrates to America, where he joins a coven on Central West End in Saint Louis. His coven lasts until the mid-1980s,

when the rock music of the Vampire Lestat awakens Queen Akasha, who immolates her vampire children in the Great Burning of 1985. She also burns to the ground Laurent's coven house, yet Laurent survives until the young vampire Baby Jenks rides in on her motorcycle, looking for her Fang Gang. Laurent tells her that they have to leave and find the vampire Lestat in San Francisco; he will be able to help them. But Akasha appears behind him. He pleads with her to spare his life, promising that he will do anything she wants, that he is her servant. When he sees that Akasha is not listening to him, he tries to take Baby Jenks's motorcycle and flee, but Akasha uses her Fire Gift to utterly immolate him, sending him to the ground, burning and spinning over and over, like a pathetic pinwheel.

For more perspectives on Laurent's character, read the *Alphabettery* entries **Akasha, Allesandra, Armand, Baby Jenks, Children of Darkness, Eleni, Eugénie, Felix, Great Burning of 1985, Lestat de Lioncourt,** and **Théâtre des Vampires.**

Legend of the Twins

• LEGEND •

The Legend of the Twins is a story born nearly four thousand years before the Common Era, when Akasha orders that the red-haired twins, Maharet and Mekare, be raped, imprisoned, and sentenced to death. The

King's steward and the Queen's fledgling, Khayman, has pity on the twins and turns them into vampires, so that they can cause an uprising with the First Brood. However, Akasha recaptures them, gouges out Maharet's eyes, cuts out Mekare's tongue, and entombs them in separate sarcophagi, which are then set adrift in different oceans, so that they will not be reunited for thousands of years.

However, before her tongue is cut out, Mekare curses Akasha:

"Let the spirits witness; for theirs is the knowledge of the future—both what it will be, and what I will! You are the Queen of the Damned, that's what you are! Your only destiny is evil, as well you know! But I shall stop you, if I must come back from the dead to do it. At the hour of your greatest menace it is I who will defeat you! It is I who will bring you down. Look well upon my face, for you will see me again!"

This curse is remembered among the ancient Egyptian soldiers. They witness every crime that Queen Akasha commits against the twins. The story is written down by Egyptian scribes and is handed on through the centuries, until the story of how Mekare will one day return to slay Akasha ultimately becomes known as the Legend of the Twins, which is fulfilled in 1985 of the Common Era, shortly after the rock concert of the Vampire Lestat.

The Legend of the Twins occurs in *The Queen of the Damned* (1988). For more perspectives on the Legend of the Twins in the Vampire Chronicles, read the *Alphabettery* entries **Akasha**, **Khayman**, **Lestat de Lioncourt**, **Maharet**, and **Mekare**.

Lelio

• CHARACTER •

Lelio is the name of the lead character performed by Lestat in an eighteenth-century play in the commedia dell'arte style, titled both *Lelio and Isabella*, which he performs in the Auvergne countryside with traveling actors, and *Lelio and Flaminia*, which he performs onstage at Renaud's House of Thesbians in Paris.

Lelio appears in *The Vampire Lestat* (1985). For more perspectives on the Lelio character in the Vampire Chronicles, read the *Alphabettery* entries **Commedia dell'Arte**, **Flaminia**, **Isabella**, and **Lestat de Lioncourt**.

Lelio and Flaminia

• PLAY •

Lelio and Flaminia is the play that Lestat performs in the commedia dell'arte style at Renaud's House of Thesbians in Paris, under the nom de guerre Lestat de Valois. His performance wins him great fame among the Parisian populace, as well as with the ancient vampire Magnus, who eventually turns Lestat into his fledgling. Although the actual title of the play is lost to history, Lestat's improvisational performance in the role of Lelio is so popular that the play is likely advertised according to the names of the principal innamorati, thus the eponymous title, *Lelio and Flaminia*.

Lelio and Flaminia appears in *The Vampire Lestat* (1985). For more perspectives on this play, read the *Alphabettery* entries **Commedia dell'Arte**, **Flaminia**, **Lestat de Lioncourt**, **Lestat de Valois**, **Magnus**, and **Renaud's House of Thesbians**.

Lelio and Isabella

• PLAY •

Lelio and Isabella is the play that Lestat performs in the commedia dell'arte style with an itinerate acting troupe in villages throughout the Auvergne. The title of the play remains a historical mystery. However, it is very likely that the play was titled after the two young lovers Lelio and Isabella, as plays in the Italian style concerning star-crossed innamorati have influenced numerous popular works, such as Philip Sidney's sonnet sequence *Astrophel and Stella*, John Webster's play *Appius and Virginia*, and William Shakespeare's romantic drama *The Most Excellent and Lamentable Tragedy of Romeo and Juliet*, shortened to simply *Romeo and Juliet*. Although the troupe eventually abandons Lestat and his brothers abduct him and take him back to Château de Lioncourt, the play has such a profound impact on Lestat that his experience acting in the role of Lelio becomes one of the major influences for his decision to move to Paris with his best friend, Nicki.

Lelio and Isabella appears in *The Vampire Lestat* (1985). For more perspectives on this play, read the *Alphabettery* entries **Commedia dell'Arte**, **Isabella**, **Lestat de Lioncourt**, and **Nicolas de Lenfent**.

Lestan Gregor

• ALIAS •

When Raglan James offers to switch bodies with Lestat, Lestat tries to ensure that he will still have funds as a mortal. He creates an alias for himself with the name Lestan Gregor, providing him with ten million dollars. After he switches bodies with Raglan, and after Raglan steals his vampire body, Lestat checks the accounts of Lestan Gregor, only to discover that he is penniless. Raglan has stolen that money, too.

The "Lestan Gregor" alias appears in *The Tale of the Body Thief* (1992). For more perspectives on this alias character, read the *Alphabettery* entries **Lestat de Lioncourt** and **Raglan James**.

Lestat de Lioncourt

• VAMPIRE •

Lestat is the hero of the Vampire Chronicles, which are essentially a broad biographical sketch of his life, illustrated as the centripetal force that draws all to himself, mortal and immortal alike. He is nearly two hundred and fifty years old by the time of *Blood Communion* (2018). The embodiment of a Byronic hero, Lestat has a bold nature and tortured soul that not only drive him towards numerous adventures, but also fundamentally reshape the landscape of the supernatural world. The vampire Lestat appears in every Vampire Chronicle, save one: *Vittorio the Vampire* (1999).

Lestat de Lioncourt is born on November 7, 1760, in the Auvergne, France, during the reign of Louis XV. The youngest son of Marquis de Lioncourt, Lestat is the most underprivileged of his brothers, standing to receive nothing of his father's inheritance and destined to depend upon the generosity of his eldest brother, Augustin, heir to the mostly squandered family fortune. His family is all but poverty stricken.

At the age of twelve, Lestat demonstrates a great ambition to become a religious. But his father and Augustin deny him and drag him back home from the monastery against his will. Lestat's mother, Gabrielle, is the only one who can console him, yet even in this it is not enough to quell his desire to leave his family.

A few years later, at the age of sixteen, when a traveling troupe of Italian actors in a nearby village performs the commedia dell'arte play *Lelio and Isabella*, Lestat runs

away and hides in the troupe's wagon. They allow him to join their troupe, they travel across France, and he performs the character of Lelio. Lestat is a magnificent performer, and his great passion for the arts is sparked. But his family brings him back to Château de Lioncourt against his will, where he is severely punished.

Gabrielle sells one of her heirlooms and buys him an expensive rifle and a chestnut mare. With these, Lestat spends the next two years avoiding the arts and becoming a hunter. By the time he is eighteen, he is the sole provider of his household, providing meals of hunted game for his family. And by the time he is twenty-one, the villagers look to him to solve local problems, the greatest of which are eight wolves, frightening the villagers and stealing sheep. Lestat arms himself with three flintlock guns, one flintlock rifle, his muskets, his father's sword, a very large mace, and a large flail. He goes hunting for the wolves on his mare, with two large mastiffs in spiked collars flanking him. Although the wolves kill his mare and two mastiffs, and nearly himself, Lestat kills all eight wolves. As a sign of their gratitude, the villagers go into the woods, retrieve the

wolves, skin them, and line boots and a red velvet cloak with their fur as a gift for Lestat, presented by the eldest son of the village draper, Nicolas de Lenfent. Lestat is immediately attracted to Nicolas, who studied law in Paris but ultimately quit his studies to take violin lessons from Mozart. Lestat and Nicolas (whom he refers to as Nicki) spend increasing time together and enjoy what they call Our Conversation, in which they share soul-searching secrets about their hopes for a greater life by running away together to Paris. Gabrielle encourages their friendship. When she discovers their secret plan to run away, she funds them by giving Lestat all that remains of her Italian family's fortune.

Lestat and Nicolas find employment at Renaud's House of Thesbians, a small theater on the Boulevard du Temple, at first selling tickets, helping actors dress, sweeping, and expelling troublemakers, but eventually Lestat becomes an actor on the stage and Nicolas plays his violin with the theater musicians. To hide his family's royalty, Lestat takes the stage name Lestat de Valois, and his popularity as an actor grows, drawing increasing crowds, highly praised reviews, and the attention of the three-hundred-year-old vampire Magnus.

Seeking a blond, blue-eyed young man whom he can turn into his vampire heir to inherit his massive fortune after he commits suicide, Magnus reads Lestat's mind and sees that he killed eight wolves. Impressed by Lestat's bravery, Magnus kidnaps Lestat out of the room he shares with Nicolas, turns him into a vampire against his will, and coerces Lestat into scattering his ashes after he destroys himself in a fire.

With Magnus's impressive fortune, the newly made vampire Lestat buys Renaud's theater, sends gifts of money to Gabrielle, and becomes Nicolas's patron, lavishing upon him money and an apartment. Lestat never reveals himself or his vampire secret to his friend or mother. He also begins to feel a threatening "presence" watching him, never fully realizing that it is the vampire Armand and his coven, the Children of Darkness. Eventually, Gabrielle comes to Paris, dying of consumption and seeking Lestat. Not wanting his mother to die, Lestat turns her into a vampire, which causes her to appear to grow younger. They hunt together, but Gabrielle is never interested in Lestat's preoccupation with fancy clothes and luxury. Rather, she enjoys dressing like a man and seeking solitude, much to Lestat's dismay.

Throughout this period, Lestat continues to feel "the presence" watching him, until the Children of Darkness reveal themselves by attacking Lestat and Gabrielle. Lestat fights them off, but the coven kidnaps Nicki. Lestat and Gabrielle go to the Children of Darkness's lair beneath the Cemetery of les Innocents, where they meet the vampire Armand and free Nicki, who begs Lestat to turn him into a vampire. Gabrielle warns against this, but Lestat reluctantly agrees. Becoming a vampire drives Nicki mad and fills him with hatred towards Lestat, who regrets his decision.

Lestat returns to the Children of Darkness's lair. Armand explains the coven's five Great Laws and how they worship Satan, live in squalor, and drink the blood of Paris's indigent and evildoing population. Living during the Age of Enlightenment, Lestat rejects their belief system and convinces Armand that his faith is outmoded. Armand destroys his coven, but four vampires escape—Eleni, Eugénie, Laurent, and Felix. They beg Lestat to become their new coven leader, but he refuses. Nicki convinces Lestat to give them Renaud's House of Thesbians as their new coven house. He consents out of guilt for turning Nicki into a vampire. Armand also joins them, and the new coven changes the theater's name to Théâtre des Vampires, where they put on theater productions, pretending to be humans who pretend to be vampires. Nicki writes all the plays and composes all the music.

Armand shares with Lestat a brief history of his life, partly because Lestat reminds him of his maker, the ancient vampire Marius. Compelled by an overwhelming urge to seek Marius, Lestat travels around the world for many more years. Gabrielle reluctantly accompanies him, but she has no true desire to meet Marius. Increasingly seeking solitude, she leaves Lestat for months at a time, not caring about the letters he receives from Eleni, who keeps him informed of the coven at the Théâtre des Vampires. Eleni's final letter details how Nicki committed suicide. This news deeply wounds Lestat. Another wound occurs when Gabrielle also receives a letter, describing how Lestat's brothers were killed in the French Revolution and only his father is alive. Lestat is wounded again when Gabrielle reveals that she is leaving him. Crushed by so much loss, no longer able to endure life as a vampire, Lestat finds an isolated place and buries himself in the earth to sleep.

The vampire Marius finds Lestat, exhumes him, and restores him to vampiric life by letting him drink his ancient blood. He then brings Lestat to his sanctuary island in the Mediterranean and shares with him the story of how he became a vampire, providing also a brief history of the first two vampires, Akasha and Enkil, who are called Those Who Must Be Kept. He also reveals that he is their caretaker and that Akasha and Enkil now live in a hidden shrine beneath his home, where they have been sitting enthroned in a catatonic state, looking like white marble statues, for the last several thousand years. Marius then makes Lestat promise to never reveal these secrets. Lestat agrees. But when Marius leaves Lestat alone, Lestat descends into the tomb and attempts to awaken Akasha by playing music for her. Akasha rises from her throne and allows Lestat to drink her blood. Enraged with jealousy, Enkil attempts to kill Lestat, but Marius and Akasha rescue him. Marius convinces Lestat to leave the island due to Enkil's anger.

Lestat sails to Louisiana, where he encounters a young plantation owner, Louis de Pointe du Lac, mourning the death of his younger brother. Reminding Lestat of his dead fledgling Nicolas, he offers to make Louis a vampire, who accepts, but has many questions about vampires' existence and their origin. Louis is frustrated when Lestat does not answer his questions, unaware that Marius has bound Lestat to secrecy, especially concerning Those Who Must Be Kept.

Lestat and Louis are eventually driven off the plantation by Louis's Haitian slaves, who have grown aware of their preternatural nature. They move to New Orleans, where they live in a townhouse on Rue Royale, but Louis grows increasingly depressed and no longer desires to take human life. When he can no longer resist the temptation to avoid blood drinking, he feeds on a mortal child. Guilt ridden, Louis flees, but Lestat saves the child from death by turning her into a vampire, then giving her the name Claudia. Louis cares for Claudia as if she were his own daughter. And the three vampires live together for the next sixty-five years.

During that time, Lestat becomes enamored of the mortal Antoine, who was banished from his home in Paris when his brother betrayed him. Lestat makes Antoine his ward, gives him money and musical instruments, and encourages him to compose beautiful music.

Meanwhile, Claudia becomes aware that as she ages interiorly, she remains in a child's body exteriorly. The prospect of spending eternity as an ageless child embitters her, and she grows to hate her maker. She shares Louis's frustration that Lestat never answers her questions concerning the existence of other vampires. Claudia's hatred for Lestat becomes murderous. Convinced that Lestat will never let her and Louis leave him, she tricks Lestat into drinking the dead blood of two homeless boys, which weakens Lestat to the point that Claudia is able to cut his throat and stab him in the heart with a knife. When his body is drained of blood, Claudia and Louis sink him in the Louisiana swamps, and make plans to leave New Orleans for Europe. Lestat, however, survives their attack, goes to Antoine, turns him into a vampire, and enlists his assistance against Louis and Claudia. On the night that Louis and Claudia are to set sail for Europe, Lestat and Antoine try to stop them, but Louis sets fire to their Rue Royale townhouse. Lestat and Antoine are trapped inside and badly burned, while Louis and Claudia sail to Europe.

Lestat and Antoine remain together until Lestat is well enough to follow Louis and Claudia to France, but Antoine is too afraid to make the journey. Lestat leaves him a small fortune and then sails for Paris to seek help from Armand at the Théâtre des Vampires. Lestat hopes to drink Armand's ancient blood, which will help him heal faster. But Armand has already encountered Louis and Claudia and desires to have Louis as his companion, so he tricks Lestat into admitting that Claudia is guilty of attempting to murder her maker, a forbidden act among the Children of Darkness. Armand uses this information to send his coven to kill Claudia, which frees Louis from his relationship with her. Now that he and Louis can be together, Armand lies to Lestat, telling him that Claudia and Louis are dead, before pushing Lestat from a tower window and abandoning him in his weakened state.

Lestat survives, returning to America and living much of the nineteenth century alone in a decrepit New Orleans house, feeding on vermin. After Armand and Louis separate,

Armand visits Lestat several times, informing him that Louis is still alive, but Lestat seems not to care. Later, Louis visits him, and Lestat begs him to remain by his side, but Louis abandons him once more in the New Orleans house. Eventually, Lestat can no longer bear the test of eternity and buries himself deep in the earth.

In the late twentieth century, from underground, Lestat hears the music of the rock band Satan's Night Out. Lestat exhumes himself, finds the band, and reveals that he is a vampire, only to be surprised that they know of him and show him Louis's book *Interview with the Vampire*. Eager to reveal himself and the secrets of vampires to the modern world, Lestat becomes the lyricist and singer of the band but renames it the Vampire Lestat, which later also becomes the title of his autobiography. His lyrics reveal many vampire secrets, specifically the secret of Queen Akasha and King Enkil, Those Who Must Be Kept, which breaks his promise to Marius. As his band's popularity increases, his words and music once again awaken Queen Akasha, who kills Enkil and buries Marius under several tons of ice.

On the night that the Vampire Lestat band is to perform its one and only concert in San Francisco, Akasha appears and takes Lestat as her new paramour. She brings him to the Sonoma compound of her mortal enemy, the vampire Maharet, who has been conspiring against Akasha with several other vampires—Louis, Gabrielle, and Armand among them. Akasha reveals her plan to kill 90 percent of males all over the world and then establish a new religion in which she will be worshipped as a goddess. When Lestat hears this, he rejects her and joins his companions. Together, they try to destroy Akasha, but she is too powerful for them all, until Maharet's twin sister, Mekare, appears, decapitates Akasha, consumes her heart and brain, and takes into herself the spirit of Amel and his Sacred Core, making herself the new carrier host of vampire existence and the new Queen of the Damned.

Lestat accompanies the remaining vampires to Armand's Night Island but soon leaves with Louis for London and breaks into the Talamasca Motherhouse, where they encounter David Talbot, the Superior General. Over the next few years, Lestat and David form a unique friendship. Lestat offers to turn David into a vampire, but David refuses, although he is always hospitable to Lestat, especially after Lestat grows suicidally depressed and fails to kill himself by flying into the sun. The immense strength he gained by drinking Akasha's blood prevents the sun from destroying him; he is only bronzed, the way Akasha was after the Great Burning of 4 C.E.

Following this, Lestat is approached by Raglan James, a powerful psychic and a former member of the Talamasca Order, who has the ability to switch bodies. Raglan offers Lestat the chance to live a mortal life again, if Lestat pays him ten million dollars. David and Louis both tell Lestat not to do this, but their caution only encourages Lestat's eagerness. He pays Raglan twenty million dollars but takes several precautions against trickery, even stashing money for himself with Raglan's identity. Raglan steals most of Lestat's money along with his body. Now in Raglan's former mortal body, Lestat is starving and dying of pneumonia. He is nursed back to health by Gretchen, a nun with whom he has a brief love affair. Lestat implores both Marius and Louis to turn him back into a vampire, but both refuse and abandon him.

Lestat turns to David Talbot, who helps him track down Raglan, push him out of his vampire body, and put Lestat back inside. Raglan switches bodies with David Talbot, then approaches Lestat and asks him to turn him into a vampire. Believing Raglan is David, Lestat drinks his blood and realizes that he is actually Raglan. Furious, Lestat crushes David's skull, killing the Body Thief. When Lestat finally finds David Talbot in Raglan's former body, Lestat does not want to lose David again, so he makes him a vampire against David's wishes.

Afterward, Lestat encounters two vampires in California, Fareed and Akasha's son, Seth, both of whom are scientists seeking ways to enhance the immortal life of the Undead. They convince Lestat to be the test subject of a special procedure that will allow a vampire to experience eroticism and ejaculation. They inject Lestat with an infusion of hormones, and he becomes sexually aroused by Fareed and Seth's mortal associate, Dr. Flannery Gilman. Lestat copulates with her and is unaware that he has impregnated her. Fareed and Seth extract the fetus from Dr. Gilman, genetically enhance it to become an exact clone of Lestat, and then implant the fetus back into Dr. Gilman's uterus. She carries the fetus to term and gives birth to Lestat's clone and child, a mortal, whom they name Viktor.

Not long after, Lestat saves a young girl named Rose, along with her mother, from a terrible earthquake that destroys an entire island. He flies her to safety and is so impressed by this child that he adopts her. Unable to pronounce his name, Rose simply calls him Uncle Lestan. He takes her to Florida and arranges for her to be raised by two retired schoolteachers. Over the years, he visits her and gives her many gifts, yet Rose never guesses that he is an immortal blood drinker.

While in New York, Lestat kills a man named Roger, whose ghost returns to Lestat to ask him to take care of his daughter, Dora, a Christian televangelist. Lestat agrees, but when he encounters Dora and speaks with her, they begin to develop romantic feelings for each other. Before Lestat can explore this further, Memnoch the Devil appears and takes Lestat on a journey through Heaven and Hell, as well as to the crucifixion of Jesus Christ. Jesus offers Lestat his blood to drink and then tells Lestat to take Veronica's Veil, upon which is the mystical impression of Jesus's face. Memnoch the Devil asks Lestat to serve as a prince in Hell, but Lestat refuses. Memnoch fails to steal Veronica's Veil from him and can only pluck out Lestat's left eye instead. Lestat returns to Earth and tells this story to David Talbot, Armand, and Dora before giving her Veronica's Veil. Lestat and David return to New Orleans, where Maharet gives Lestat a letter from Memnoch that also contains his left eye, and Lestat returns his eye to its socket. Memnoch's letter informs him that Memnoch has been manipulating him in a hidden plan, a notion that drives Lestat so mad that Maharet must use her own hair to bind him in the basement of Saint Elizabeth's Convent. Lestat remains catatonic in the chapel; no one can rouse him, not even his mother, Gabrielle. But when Louis's attempt to kill himself leaves him badly burned, Lestat completely awakens and heals Louis by feeding him his blood.

Upon hearing that Lestat's adopted daughter, Rose, has gotten into trouble in Florida with a criminal judge and a corrupt boarding school, Louis brings Rose and her two aunts to Lestat in New York, where Lestat gives them a magnificent apartment with a full staff on the Upper East Side and provides the means for Rose to attend the best high school.

Meanwhile, Lestat discovers the vampire Quinn Blackwood breaking into his Rue Royale townhouse to beg him to help defeat a mysterious, bloodthirsty spirit called Goblin who has been attacking Quinn. With the aid of David Talbot and Merrick Mayfair, they learn that Goblin is the spirit of Quinn's twin brother, who died in infancy. Merrick performs a ritual exorcism involving Goblin's corpse. When the exorcism fails, Merrick leaps with Goblin's corpse into a bonfire, which destroys both her and the corpse but allows her to usher Goblin's soul into the light of the afterlife. Lestat mourns Merrick's death greatly, but he cherishes his newfound relationship with Quinn Blackwood, whom he refers to as his Little Brother. Lestat and Quinn return to Blackwood Farm, where they find Mona Mayfair dying. Quinn reveals to her that he is a vampire, and Lestat turns her into a vampire so that Mona and Quinn can be together forever.

Lestat learns that Mona's Taltos child, Morrigan, has run away with another Taltos, Ashlar. He offers to help Quinn and Mona find Morrigan with Maharet's guidance. Lestat, Quinn, and Mona discover that Morrigan and Ashlar live on a secret island and have had four Taltos children, one of whom, Silas, has caused a revolt, which brought Drug Merchants to the island, who killed almost every Taltos, even Morrigan and Ashlar. Lestat, Quinn, and Mona destroy all the Drug Merchants and bring Morrigan's and Ashlar's bodies back to Mayfair Medical Center for study. Lestat also helps bring Mona's three surviving Taltos grandchildren to New Orleans, where they can live in safety among family.

Through Mona Mayfair, Lestat meets Rowan, and they develop deep feelings for each other. When Rowan learns that Lestat is a vampire, she asks him to turn her into one. Lestat refuses, reasoning that, as a vampire, she would no longer be a principal decision-making power within the Mayfair family. And he will not take that from her or them.

When Lestat's adopted daughter, Rose, attends Stanford University, she is attacked and blinded by a jealous lover. Rose is rushed to Fareed and Seth's medical facility. Through their advanced research into mortals and immortals, they are able to restore Rose's sight and save her life. As she is recuperating, she encounters Lestat's cloned son, Viktor, now in his twenties and an exact likeness of Uncle Lestan. An immediate attraction is felt between them. Rose begins to learn that her uncle is the very same vampire Lestat, hero of the Vampire Chronicles. When Fareed and Seth inform Lestat of Rose's recovery, they also inform him of the existence of Viktor. Lestat does not have long to celebrate because the mysterious Voice has begun speaking to him and other vampires, convincing stronger ones to immolate the weaker, which causes the Great Burning of 2013.

As during the Great Burning of 1985, a council of vampires convenes. Lestat and his companions discover that the mysterious Voice is the spirit of Amel, who has awakened within the wounded mind of Mekare. He desires freedom so much that he convinces the ancient vampire Rhoshamandes to destroy Maharet and Khayman, then kidnap Mekare and Viktor for the purpose of forcing the other vampires to help make Rhoshamandes Amel's new host carrier. Enraged, Lestat finds Rhoshamandes, tears off his arm, and forces him to surrender Mekare and Viktor. Saddened by the loss of her sister, and seeking to join Maharet in death, Mekare offers herself to Lestat, urging him to consume her brain and take into himself the spirit of Amel. With great reluctance, Lestat accepts her offer along with the Sacred Core, at once making himself the host carrier of the vampire race, as well as their new supreme leader, earning for himself the title "Prince Lestat."

Prince Lestat has a grand coronation attended by all of his vampire companions that he has known throughout the centuries, all paying their respects, all offering him their love. Two mortals also attend, Rose and Viktor, his special children. The crowning jewel for Lestat at this ceremony is turning both of them into his vampire fledglings before uniting them as Blood Spouses.

A few years later, a new species of immortal appears, kills several vampires, and consumes their brains. Lestat and the vampires meet with these new immortals and learn that they are Replimoids, a race of humanoid beings from the planet Bravenna. Their leader, Kapetria, shares with Lestat and his council the story of how Amel was a human mortal, abducted, and genetically enhanced by the Bravennans for the purpose of increasing and sustaining human suffering, which was the principal source of Bravennan food. Amel had rebelled and created luracastria and the city of Atlantis to stop the Bravennans and end human suffering. The Bravennans created the Replimoids to stop Amel, but Amel convinced them to join his cause. When the Bravennans discovered this, they sent a meteor shower that destroyed Amel, Atlantis, and luracastria and separated the Replimoids for thousands of years. Kapetria further explains that Amel's spirit carried his enhanced genetic code, which combines with Akasha's human genetic code when he fused with her blood to create the first vampire. The bloodlust that vampires experience is not a taste for death but a hungering to return to Amel's enhanced body.

Amel expresses to Lestat that he greatly desires to have a body of his own. So Kapetria uses her own Replimoid cells to create a clone of the body that Amel had in Atlantis. She performs surgery on Lestat that removes Amel from his brain and places Amel into his clone. When the surgery is over, the spirit of Amel and the Sacred Core of vampire existence are no longer inside Lestat. Now all vampires are free to discover the meaning of immortality without dependence on any single blood drinker. Although Lestat is no longer officially Prince Lestat, to his friends and fans he will always be the Brat Prince.

Lestat establishes the Court of the Prince in Château de Lioncourt. All of his companions join him, including Armand, Marius, Gabrielle, Louis, and David. Many more vampires join them, both very ancient and very young. Mortals rebuild the Château de Lioncourt and the village, led by foreman Alain Abelard. The mortals build alcoves for the vampires and unearth a prison beneath the Château. The prison cells are restored with modern security systems; a kitchen and a large furnace are added. Lestat's Court of the Prince still desires him to be their Prince, and they want his permission to destroy Rhoshamandes as just retribution for his murder of Maharet and Khayman. Benedict is also at Court; he agrees, but he is so distraught that he kills himself and lets young vampires drink his ancient blood.

Not wanting to kill Rhoshamandes, Lestat goes to New Orleans, where he encounters another blood drinker, Dmitri Fontayne, also called Mitka, who asks Lestat to help him fend off a vampire gang that killed his mortal servants. Lestat and his bodyguards, the ancient Egyptian vampire Cyril and the Viking vampire Thorne, destroy the gang, but another ancient and powerful vampire, Baudwin, destroys Mitka's New Orleans home and attacks Lestat for his part in the destruction of Baudwin's fledgling, Roland. Cyril binds Baudwin in iron wrappings, which prevent him from using his vampire gifts. Baudwin is the fledgling of the legendary Gundesanth, also called Santh, the third blood drinker made by Akasha and most powerful of all living vampires.

Meanwhile, Rhoshamandes takes his vengeance against the Court for the death of Benedict. He kidnaps Gabrielle, Louis, and Marius, breaking their necks to immobilize them in a dazed torpor and binding them in iron bars. Lestat kills Rhoshamandes and frees his beloved companions. Santh appears, kills his fledgling Baudwin, and joins the Court of the Prince, vowing fealty to Lestat. Lestat finally feels at peace and turns his foreman, Alain, into his latest vampire companion. All his life, Lestat has felt miserably alone, but now in this Court of vampires, in his old French home, he no longer feels so lonely. His vampire companions are his Blood Communion, his true blood kindred, his real family.

For more perspectives on Lestat in the Vampire Chronicles, read the *Alphabettery* entries **Akasha, Amel, Antoine, Armand, Augustin, Baudwin, Château de Lioncourt, Children of Darkness, Claudia, Commedia dell'Arte, Eleni, Enkil, Eugénie, Felix, Gabrielle, Great Laws, Isabella, Laurent, Lelio, Lestat de Valois, Louis de Pointe du Lac, Magnus, Marius, Nicolas de Lenfent, Quinn Blackwood, Renaud, Renaud's House of Thesbians, Rose, Satan's Night Out, Santh, Théâtre des Vampires, Those Who Must Be Kept, The Vampire Lestat**, and **Viktor.**

Lestat de Valois

• CHARACTER •

When Lestat begins to perform as an actor onstage in Paris at Renaud's House of Thesbians, he does not want his family's noble name or title to be identified, so as he grows in popularity, performing the lead role as Lelio in the play *Lelio and Flaminia*, he takes the stage name Lestat de Valois.

Lestat de Valois appears in *The Vampire Lestat* (1985). For more perspectives on this character, read the *Alphabettery* entries **Flaminia, Lelio, Lestat de Lioncourt**, and **Renaud's House of Thesbians.**

Line of de Landen Vampires

• COVEN •

When the ancient vampire Rhoshamandes settles in the land that comes to be modern-day France, he spends the next few centuries making several vampires to be not only his coven but also his children, giving each of them the surname de Landen, beginning with Benedict and progressing on to Allesandra, Eleni, Eugénie, Everard, and Notker the Wise.

The line of de Landen vampires does not last as a family unit through the first millennium of the Common Era. The Children of Satan capture Allesandra, Eleni, Eugénie, and Everard and convert them to their diabolical ways. Notker the Wise moves away and settles in a small sanctuary on the French slope of the Alps. Benedict is the only one who remains with Rhoshamandes, all the way into the twenty-first century.

The line of de Landen vampires is written of in *Prince Lestat* (2014) and *Prince Lestat and the Realms of Atlantis* (2016). For more perspectives on this coven, read the *Alphabettery* entries **Allesandra**, **Benedict**, **Children of Darkness**, **Eleni**, **Eugénie**, **Everard**, **Notker the Wise**, and **Rhoshamandes**.

Lionel Potter

• ALIAS •

"Lionel Potter" is one of Lestat's aliases when he stays in Paris. After Lestat switches bodies with Raglan James, the Body Thief, he has one of his mortal agents in Paris wire thirty thousand dollars to an agency under his Lionel Potter name. When he arrives at the agency, he has a new credit card with the name Lionel Potter as well as a wallet full of traveler's checks.

"Lionel Potter" is a reference to Lionel Barrymore playing the villain Mr. Potter in the 1946 movie *It's a Wonderful Life*.

The "Lionel Potter" alias appears in *The Tale of the Body Thief* (1992). For more perspectives on this alias in the Vampire Chronicles, read the *Alphabettery* entries **David Talbot**, **Lestat de Lioncourt**, and **Raglan James**.

Little Brother

• SOBRIQUET •

Almost from the instant he meets the vampire Quinn Blackwood, Lestat feels a deep connection to him, even going so far as to help him exorcise the ghost of his dead twin brother, Goblin. As another favor to Quinn, Lestat turns Quinn's dying paramour, Mona Mayfair, into a vampire so that they can be together forever. Lestat even helps Quinn and Mona find Mona's missing Taltos child, Morrigan Mayfair. Lestat's affection for Quinn runs so deep that he begins to refer to him as Little Brother.

The sobriquet appears in *Blackwood Farm* (2002) and *Blood Canticle* (2003). For more perspectives on the "Little Brother" sobriquet, read the *Alphabettery* entries **Lestat de Lioncourt**, **Mona Mayfair**, **Morrigan Mayfair**, **Quinn Blackwood**, and **Taltos**.

Little Drink

• IDIOM •

"Little Drink" is Lestat's expression for stealing blood from an unwitting mortal without killing them. The victims will neither feel the vampire biting their neck nor, in some instances, even know that a vampire happens to be nearby. Vampires can safely satisfy their bloodlust for the night by taking the Little Drink from countless victims and never kill anyone.

Marius's fledglings, Benji and Sybelle, demonstrate this ability by going to several nightclubs during the course of an evening and taking enough blood to satisfy themselves. No mortals are ever harmed, and both vampires are completely satiated.

The idiom appears in *The Tale of the Body Thief* (1992), *Merrick* (2000), *Blood and Gold* (2001), *Blackwood Farm* (2002), *Blood Canticle* (2003), *Prince Lestat* (2014), and *Prince Lestat and the Realms of Atlantis* (2016). For more perspectives on the Little Drink idiom, read the *Alphabettery* entries **Benji Mahmoud**, **Lestat de Lioncourt**, **Marius**, **Sybelle**, and **Thorne**.

Little Grandmother

• SOBRIQUET •

When Lestat discovers that Mona Mayfair has a Taltos child, Morrigan, who grows into a woman almost instantly, and that Morrigan has run away with another Taltos, the ancient Ashlar, to his secret island where they have four children, Lestat begins referring to his own fledgling Mona as the Little Grandmother.

The sobriquet appears in *Blood Canticle* (2003). For more perspectives on the "Little Grandmother" sobriquet, read the *Alphabettery* entries **Ashlar**, **Lestat de Lioncourt**, **Mona Mayfair**, **Morrigan Mayfair**, **Quinn Blackwood**, and **Taltos**.

Little Ida

• MORTAL •

Little Ida is one of the dark-skinned servants at Blackwood Farm. Her mother, Big Ramona, serves in the kitchen, while Little Ida is the nurse or nanny of Quinn Blackwood, and her daughter, Jasmine, is one of the housekeepers. Quinn sleeps chastely in Little Ida's bed every night throughout his childhood and early adolescence. Goblin, the ghost of Quinn's dead twin brother, sleeps there, too. Little Ida will read stories to them both. Little Ida continues caring for them both until Quinn is thirteen years old, when she dies in bed, right beside Quinn and Goblin.

Little Ida appears in *Blackwood Farm* (2002). For more perspectives on Little Ida's character, read the *Alphabettery* entries **Big Ramona**, **Goblin**, **Jasmine**, and **Quinn Blackwood**.

Little Jerome

• MORTAL •

When Quinn Blackwood's grandfather Pops dies, Quinn is grief stricken. Pops raised him and was a father to him. For consolation, Quinn shares a night of passion with the housekeeper, Jasmine, who becomes pregnant with his son. When the child is born, she names him Little Jerome, after one of her ancestors who worked for the founder of Blackwood Farm, Manfred Blackwood.

Little Jerome appears in *Blackwood Farm* (2002). For more perspectives on Little Jerome's character, read the *Alphabettery* entries **Jasmine**, **Jerome**, **Manfred Blackwood**, **Pops**, and **Quinn Blackwood**.

Little People

• TALTOS •

When the Time Before the Moon ends, forcing the Taltos to move off their island paradise to the mainland of the nearest continent, they are also forced to interact with mortals. Because the Taltos are immortals of very tall stature, mortals fear and respect them. Some mortal tribes capture Taltos and mate with them. One result of this mating is the birth of people who are very short in stature. In time, these short half-Taltos/half-mortal individuals, along with their descendants who bear the same diminutive trait, receive the designation "Little People." Unlike Taltos such as Ashlar, the Little People are not immortal, but their usual lifespan averages one thousand years. Lestat learns of the Taltos and the Little People when he helps Mona Mayfair free her Taltos children and grandchildren from the Drug Merchants.

Little People appear in *Blood Canticle* (2003). For more perspectives on the Little People characters, read the *Alphabettery* entries **Ashlar**, **Lestat de Lioncourt**, **Mona Mayfair**, **Taltos**, and **Time Before the Moon**.

Little Richard

• MORTAL •

Little Richard, who dies in childhood, is the uncle of Dora, who will become one of Lestat's deepest loves as well as the bearer of the religious icon Veronica's Veil.

Little Richard appears in *Memnoch the Devil* (1995). For more perspectives on Little Richard's character, read the *Alphabettery* entries **Dora, Lestat de Lioncourt,** and **Veronica's Veil.**

Lolly

• MORTAL •

Lolly is the daughter of Little Ida, who is the nanny of Quinn Blackwood. Lolly is also the older sister of Jasmine, the housekeeper of Blackwood Farm, who becomes the mother of Quinn's son, Little Jerome. Lolly helps her grandmother Big Ramona in the kitchen, preparing meals for the Blackwood family.

Lolly appears in *Blackwood Farm* (2002). For more perspectives on Lolly's character, read the *Alphabettery* entries **Big Ramona, Jasmine, Little Jerome,** and **Quinn Blackwood.**

Lord Harlech

• MORTAL •

When Armand lives with Marius in the fifteenth century, before Marius turns him into a vampire, Armand has a brief dalliance with the Englishman Lord Harlech. When Armand ends the relationship, Lord Harlech comes to Marius's Venice palazzo in a jealous rage. Armed with a poisoned blade, Lord Harlech kills many children in Marius's home, some as young as seven years old, until he meets Armand. Skilled with the blade, Armand slays Lord Harlech, but not before Lord Harlech's poisoned blade mortally wounds him.

Lord Harlech appears in *Blood and Gold* (2001). For more perspectives on Lord Harlech's character, read the *Alphabettery* entries **Armand, Bianca Solderini, Jacope,** and **Marius.**

Lord Ruthven

• SANCTUARY •

Lord Ruthven is a vampire bar, part of the Vampire Connection, located in New York. It is named after the character in Dr. John William Polidori's short story "The Vampyre" (1819), considered to be the first vampire Byronic hero in gothic literature.

The Lord Ruthven vampire bar appears in *The Vampire Lestat* (1985). For more perspectives on Lord Ruthven bar, read the *Alphabettery* entries **Bela Lugosi**, **Carmilla**, **Dracula's Daughter**, **Dr. Polidori**, **Lamia**, **Vampire Bar**, and **Vampire Connection**.

Lorenzo di Raniari

• MORTAL •

Lorenzo di Raniari is the lord of Castello Raniari in the fifteenth century. He rejects the offer made by the vampire Florian, who desires all the elderly, infirm, and evildoing members of his castle in exchange for the lives of the young, healthy, and good-natured. As a result, Florian and his coven attack Castello Raniari and kill everyone inside, including

Lord Lorenzo and his family, all except one—his elder son, Vittorio, who is spared by the vampire Ursula.

Lorenzo di Raniari appears in *Vittorio the Vampire* (1999). For more perspectives on Lorenzo's character, read the *Alphabettery* entries **Castello Raniari**, **Florian**, **Ursula**, and **Vittorio di Raniari**.

Lorkyn

• TALTOS •

When the two Taltos, Morrigan and Ashlar, move to a secret island owned by Ashlar, where many other Taltos also live, they have four children—two sons, Silas and Oberon,

and two daughters, Miravelle and Lorkyn. They live together in relative peace, until Silas begins secretly poisoning their mother and father. When Morrigan and Ashlar are too weak to resist, Silas causes an uprising among the Taltos, convincing many that mortals are dangerous and that the Taltos need to attack those living on nearby islands. Silas imprisons every Taltos who resists, which includes his parents and siblings. His rebellion lasts two years, until a group of mortals living on the nearby island retaliate and kill Silas along with the other rebelling Taltos. The mortals take over the island and imprison the surviving Taltos for another two years, during which time Lorkyn's parents die. The island is eventually liberated by three vampires—Lorkyn's grandmother Mona Mayfair, Lestat, and Quinn Blackwood—who kill all the evil mortals. When Mona discovers that her daughter, Morrigan, has died, she takes her and Ashlar's bodies back to New Orleans, to be studied at Mayfair Medical Center. Mona then invites Lorkyn and her other grandchildren to New Orleans, where they can be together as a family of immortals.

Lorkyn appears in *Blood Canticle* (2003). For more perspectives on Lorkyn's character, read the *Alphabettery* entries **Ashlar, Lestat de Lioncourt, Mayfair Medical Center, Miravelle, Mona Mayfair, Morrigan Mayfair, Oberon, Quinn Blackwood, Silas,** and **Taltos.**

Lorraine McQueen

• MORTAL •

Read the *Alphabettery* entry **Aunt Queen.**

Louis de Point du Lac

• VAMPIRE •

Louis begins the Vampire Chronicles with his unprecedented gothic book, *Interview with the Vampire* (1976). Louis inspires not only Lestat to write his own tale but also several others to contribute to the Chronicles. If Lesat is the antihero of the Vampire Chronicles, then Louis is the Byronic hero, who, unlike his maker, chooses to become a vampire and regrets it, whereas Lestat never chose yet regrets nothing. Louis is Lestat's dearest companion, confidant, and lover. He appears or is mentioned in *Interview with the Vampire* (1976), *The Vampire Lestat* (1985), *The Queen of the Damned* (1988), *The Tale of the Body Thief* (1992), *Memnoch the Devil* (1995), *The Vampire Armand* (1998), *Merrick* (2000), *Blood Canticle* (2003), *Prince Lestat* (2014), *Prince Lestat and the Realms of Atlantis* (2016), and *Blood Communion* (2018).

Born on October 4, 1766, to an immigrant Catholic family, Louis de Pointe du Lac grows up with his mother, sister, and younger brother, Paul, on their family plantation on the Mississippi River, very near New Orleans. Paul starts having visions of Mary, the Mother of Jesus Christ, and of Saint Dominic, who tell him to sell the family property and become a missionary in France. As the head of the family after their father's death, Louis allows Paul to explore his faith; but when Paul expresses his desire to become a Catholic religious so that he might more fully experience a mystical life in God, Louis tries to convince him otherwise. Their argument becomes so heated that Paul accidently dies. Louis blames himself and falls into a self-destructive lifestyle of drinking and gambling. One night, after engaging in a tavern brawl, Louis catches the attention of the vampire Lestat, who later drains Louis of nearly all his blood, leaving only just enough to keep his heart beating, and then offers to turn Louis into a vampire. Louis accepts.

Lestat and his blind, dying father, the Marquis de Lioncourt, move on to Louis's plantation. Even though Louis's sense of morality prevents him from killing mortals, Lestat convinces him to kill his father, the Marquis. Because of Louis's and Lestat's incessant bloodlust, the plantation slaves suspect that Louis and Lestat are Devils. Believing they are doing good, the slaves burn the plantation to the ground. Louis and Lestat escape to New Orleans, where they acquire a townhouse on Rue Royale. Lestat resumes his insatiable killing, while Louis struggles to avoid killing humans, choosing instead to drink the blood of vermin.

One night, when Louis can no longer resist the urge to drink human blood, he feeds off a small girl and leaves her for dead. Lestat discovers what he has done and eases Louis's guilt for killing the child by informing him that she is not dead, but she will die unless they turn her into a vampire. When Louis reluctantly agrees, Lestat turns the girl into an immortal blood drinker and names her Claudia.

Louis lives with Lestat and Claudia for the next sixty-five years in their New Orleans townhouse. When Claudia becomes embittered by the realization that she is an immortal trapped in a child's body, she grows to hate Lestat for what he did to her, and she begins plotting to kill him. After tricking Lestat into drinking the blood of the dead, which weakens vampires, Claudia slashes open the enfeebled Lestat's throat and gashes the knife into his heart. When the blood drains from Lestat, Louis and Claudia, thinking he is dead, sink his body in a swamp, believing that animals and reptiles will consume his remains.

Louis and Claudia make plans to leave New Orleans for Europe, in the hope of finding other vampires like themselves, unaware that Lestat has survived and turned a young musician named Antoine into a vampire. On the night that Louis and Claudia are to depart for Europe, Lestat and Antoine confront them in their Rue Royale townhouse. Louis protects Claudia by setting fire to the townhouse and leaving Lestat and Antoine inside to burn. Wondering if their maker is dead, they board the ship and sail safely to Europe.

After many years of fruitless searching, finding only mindless vampires who cannot provide them with any answers or purpose for their existence, Louis and Claudia finally come to live in Paris, where they soon encounter Santiago, Armand, and many other vampires at the Théâtre des Vampires. Louis is fascinated by those blood drinkers, who perform theater plays pretending to be mortals who pretend to be vampires, but they repulse Claudia. As Armand and Louis engage in more frequent conversations, Claudia begins to realize that Louis is going to leave her for Armand, so she asks Louis to make for her a vampire companion, because, trapped in a child's body, she does not have the power to do so herself. Loath to do what goes against his sense of morality, Louis eventually surrenders to her wishes and makes his first fledgling, the doll maker Madeleine, to be Claudia's vampire companion. While Louis and Claudia are unaware that Lestat survived the burning and has come to Paris seeking Armand's help, Armand tricks Lestat into condemning Louis and Claudia for their crime against him. Armand's coven captures Louis and Claudia and punishes them by burying Louis in a wood coffin with large iron locks and by exposing Claudia and Madeleine to sunlight, burning them to ashes. Armand frees Louis and allows him to take vengeance on the coven by burning the Théâtre des Vampires to the ground with most of its vampires trapped inside.

After discovering Lestat's betrayal, Louis intends to return to his hotel room to bury Claudia's clothes in a grave in the cemetery of Montmartre, but instead he decides to leave her clothes strewn about, as if she might return at any moment.

Louis and Armand leave Paris and travel around the world, seeing Greece, the Mediterranean, and the ancient graves of the Egyptian kings. Throughout it all, Louis pursues art and deeper meaning in life. After many years together, Armand reveals to Louis that Lestat survived the burning of the Théâtre des Vampires. Louis returns to New Orleans to seek Lestat, but Armand leaves. Lestat is miserably weak, resting in a shabby chair, yet he is delighted to see Louis. He begs his fledgling to stay with him, but Louis refuses. And instead of harboring any ill will for all the harm Lestat has caused, Louis forgives his maker before abandoning him for the next sixty years.

Louis and Lestat next encounter each other on the night of Lestat's San Francisco concert with his new rock band, the Vampire Lestat. Louis is afraid for his maker, because Lestat has been revealing vampire secrets in his music and lyrics, and now vampires across the globe want to destroy him. Louis and Lestat escape the concert in a getaway vehicle that Gabrielle is driving, but Akasha steals Lestat and immolates all his enemies in the Great Burning of 1985.

Along with several other vampires who also survive this new Great Burning, Louis and Gabrielle meet at the compound in the Sonoma Mountains owned by Akasha's ancient nemesis, Maharet. Louis listens attentively while Maharet shares her story about how Akasha became the first vampire through the spirit of Amel, how she betrayed Maharet and her twin sister, Mekare, and how Maharet and Akasha survived the many millennia in their own ways. Louis agrees with the other vampires that Akasha's quest for world domination must end in her death, even if that means their own deaths also. When Akasha arrives with Lestat, she reveals her full plan for global conquest by destroying 90 percent of the world's male population while enslaving everyone else in a religion that will worship her as goddess and Queen, a plan which even makes Lestat revolt against her. But Akasha is too powerful for them all and is defeated only when Maharet's twin sister, Mekare, appears, decapitates Akasha, consumes her brain and heart, takes into herself Amel's spirit, and becomes the new Queen of the Damned.

Louis's relationship with Lestat grows over the years. He urges Lestat not to switch bodies with Raglan James, the Body Thief, and he refuses to turn Lestat back into a vampire when James betrays him. But when Lestat regains his old body, Louis joins him in New Orleans, where they form a coven with Lestat's new fledgling, David Talbot.

When Lestat's journey through Heaven and Hell with Memnoch the Devil leaves him in a catatonic state on the chapel floor of Saint Elizabeth's Convent, Louis visits him frequently, but Lestat remains unresponsive for quite some time. Although he briefly awakens for Louis and David to take him to their New Orleans townhouse, Lestat still continues to drift in and out of a helpless stupor.

Not long after this, Louis encounters Merrick Mayfair, a member of the Mayfair witch family and the former ward and assistant of David Talbot during his mortal life as the Superior General of the Talamasca Order. Through Mayfair magic, Merrick performs a ritual that raises the spirit of Claudia from the dead so that Louis can speak with her. Merrick warns Louis that the spirit might not be Claudia but an evil spirit pretending to be her. When Claudia's spirit appears, she cruelly taunts Louis, telling him that in life she preferred him only because he was easier to manipulate than Lestat. Louis believes it is Claudia without doubt. At the same time, he also develops a deep affection for Merrick and turns her into a vampire, at which point Merrick reveals that she has used her magic to draw Louis to her just for that purpose. Meanwhile, seeing and speaking with Claudia once more affect him so profoundly that he longs to be with her in death, so he sets his coffin in an exposed place, in the hope of being immolated at sunrise. His plan fails, and he is badly burned. He only survives when he receives draughts of the healing blood of Merrick and David, but when Lestat perceives that Louis needs him, he rouses from his stupor and feeds Louis his most powerful blood.

When Louis is restored to health, he remains with Lestat, by his side as his intimate companion, the way they once were, before Claudia, when Louis was newly born into immortality with the Dark Gift. With Lestat's blood in him, Louis understands the reason that Lestat behaved as he did all those centuries ago. There is nothing between them now, nothing but reconciliation and love.

For more perspectives on Louis's character, read the *Alphabettery* entries **Akasha,** **Armand, Claudia, David Talbot, Lestat de Lioncourt, Maharet, Mekare, Merrick Mayfair, Talamasca Order**, and **Théâtre des Vampires**.

Luchina

• MORTAL •

When he is a mortal, Lestat begins his acting career in Renaud's House of Thesbians, and one of the actresses with whom he performs onstage is the beautiful Luchina. She and Jeannette often have supper with him and Nicki after their performances. He loves her greatly, partly because he often argues with her over performances. When he becomes a vampire, Luchina's beauty and blood are altogether too tempting for him. Before he can drink her blood, he nearly reveals his vampire nature onstage in front of a large mortal audience. One audience member even shoots him at point-blank range, which would have killed any mortal. As rumors spread about him, Lestat sends Luchina and the rest of the acting troupe to England, where they can perform in London in a small theater.

Luchina appears in *The Vampire Lestat* (1985). For more perspectives on Luchina's character, read the *Alphabettery* entries **Jeannette, Lestat de Lioncourt, Nicholas de Lenfent**, and **Renaud's House of Thesbians**.

Lucia

• MORTAL •

Lucia is the mother of the drug lord Rodrigo, who takes over the secret island that belongs to the Taltos Ashlar, where he lives with his Taltos wife, Morrigan Mayfair, their four Taltos children—Silas, Oberon, Miravelle, and Lorkyn—as well as many other Taltos. When Oberon and his siblings are trying to escape, Oberon woos Lucia, and they become lovers. Finally, Oberon convinces Lucia to help them escape. When Lestat, Mona Mayfair, and Quinn Blackwood begin liberating the island, and when it becomes clear to Oberon that his freedom is inevitable, he shoots Lucia three times in the face. She dies instantly.

Lucia appears in *Blood Canticle* (2003). For more perspectives on Lucia's character, read the *Alphabettery* entries **Ashlar**, **Lestat de Lioncourt**, **Lorkyn**, **Miravelle**, **Mona Mayfair**, **Morrigan Mayfair**, **Quinn Black-wood**, **Rodrigo**, **Silas**, and **Taltos**.

Lucius

• MORTAL •

The youngest son of a Roman senator, Lucius becomes jealous of his family and betrays them to the Roman authorities as conspirators against the empire. Because of his betrayal, his father and four older brothers are killed by imperial guards as traitors. But Lucius's plan backfires when he is slaughtered by soldiers. The only one of the family to escape is Lucius's sole sister, Lydia, who flees to Antioch, where she establishes herself as a Greek courtesan, takes the name Pandora, and is turned into a vampire by Marius.

Lucius appears in *Pandora* (1998). For more perspectives on Lucius's character, read the *Alphabettery* entries **Antony**, **Lydia**, **Marius**, **Maximus**, and **Pandora**.

Lucy Nancy Marie Mayfair

• WITCH •

Lucy Nancy Marie Mayfair is a member of the dark-skinned Mayfair side of the family. Her father was Caucasian, and her mother was of Creole descent. While Merrick Mayfair is still a witch, before Louis turns her into a vampire, she can occasionally feel the ghost of Lucy Nancy Marie Mayfair nearby.

Lucy Nancy Marie Mayfair appears in *Merrick* (2000). For more perspectives on Lucy's character, read the *Alphabettery* entries **Louis de Pointe du Lac** and **Merrick Mayfair**.

Luracastria

• PHENOMENON •

Luracastria is a compound Amel develops to create the city of Atlantis. Luracastria appears in *Prince Lestat and the Realms of Atlantis* (2016).

The alien race from the planet Bravenna abducts the mortal Amel and genetically enhances him into a superhuman with superior intellect, strength, regenerative powers, and more, then sends him back to Earth as their servant who will help them maintain transmission stations so that they can observe earthlings for the betterment of the Realm of Worlds. After returning to Earth, Amel realizes that the Bravennans have lied to him, and they are using their transmission stations as a means of gathering and disseminating the psychic energy of human suffering for the purpose of consumption. Horrified by this realization, and by the fact that the Bravennans are adding to human suffering by creating natural disasters and plagues, Amel takes samples of his own enhanced genetic coding, then creates from it a compound that he calls luracastria. Discovering that luracastria confuses the Bravennans and their scientific devices, Amel begins constructing sanctuaries out of luracastria to protect the people of the earth against Bravennan exploitation.

Amel can manipulate luracastria—a substance similar to a polymer or thermoplastic—into various kinds of objects, as hard as concrete for the creation of buildings and sidewalks, as durable as steel for the creation of driving pods and elevators, and as loose as woven cotton for the creation of clothing. His most impressive creation with luracastria is the great city of Atlantis, built thousands of years before the construction of the ancient Pyramids in Egypt. All the human inhabitants of Atlantis wear luracastric clothing, live in luracastric buildings, walk on luracastric surfaces, and move quickly through the city in luracastric automobiles.

When the Bravennans realize that they cannot easily defeat Amel and his luracastric creations, they send a meteor shower that batters the city of Atlantis until it sinks into the sea, destroying it completely, along with Amel and his means for creating luracastria.

No one else is able to re-create it, not even the vampire scientists of the twenty-first century, not Lestat's companions Seth and Fareed, or even Amel's Replimoid companions, Kapetria and Welf. Luracastria remains a historical mystery.

For more perspectives on luracastria in the Vampire Chronicles, read the *Alphabettery* entries **Amel, Atlantis, Bravenna, Bravennans, Fareed Bhansali, Kapetria, Lestat de Lioncourt, Seth**, and **Welf**.

Lydia

• MORTAL •

Lydia is Pandora's mortal name. She appears in *Pandora* (1998).

Fewer than twenty years before the Common Era, the only daughter of a Roman senator, whom he names Lydia, is born. The entire family deeply loves her and gives her a broad education, ranging from Roman literature to Greek philosophy.

Tragedy strikes when Lydia is age two, and her mother dies. By the time Lydia is ten years old, she has a precocious wit. Her youth, beauty, and intelligence draw the attention of a Roman nobleman nearly two decades older, Marius. He pleads with Lydia's father for her hand in marriage, but her father insists that she is too young. Lydia also begs with her father to allow this, but he is adamant in his decision. She will not marry Marius, but she never forgets her great passion for him and she continues to remember him fondly throughout the years.

Nearly a decade later, the youngest brother, Lucius, betrays the entire family to Roman guards, who come to the house and slaughter Lydia's father and her four brothers. Lucius is eventually betrayed by his own plan and slaughtered by Roman soldiers. Lydia's father has arranged for her escape. Jewish merchants steal her out of the city to Antioch, where they help her become established as a Greek courtesan under the new identity Pandora.

For more perspectives on Lydia's character, read the *Alphabettery* entries **Lucius, Marius,** and **Pandora.**

Lynelle Springer

• MORTAL •

When Aunt Queen refuses to let her nephew Quinn Blackwood receive a regional education around his Blackwood Farm home, she hires Lynelle Springer to homeschool Quinn. He explains to her how he is haunted by a ghost named Goblin, but she does not entirely believe him. The lessons she teaches Quinn also teach Goblin, who learns from Lynelle new words and new ways to communicate with Quinn. Tragically, before Quinn's eighteenth birthday, Lynelle dies in a horrible car accident. Quinn mourns her immensely.

Lynelle Springer appears in *Blackwood Farm* (2002). For more perspectives on her character, read the *Alphabettery* entries **Aunt Queen, Goblin,** and **Quinn Blackwood.**

Madeleine

 adeleine is Louis's first true fledgling. He drains her of blood and feeds her his own so that she can be Claudia's companion when he leaves her for Armand. Madeleine appears in *Interview with the Vampire* (1976).

Madeleine's happy mortal existence as the mother of a six-year-old girl and as a popular doll maker in nineteenth-century Paris crumbles into madness when her daughter dies. Her madness is exacerbated when she begins coping with her great loss by employing her doll-making talent to create realistic likenesses of her deceased child and selling them in her shop. Her grieving madness also makes her receptive to the reality of vampires when the vampire Claudia walks into her shop. Madeleine listens with hopeful attention as Claudia explains how she and her vampire companion, Louis, have come to Paris from New Orleans, and how Louis has found another vampire companion in Armand. Claudia can see that Louis will leave her soon for Armand, and she is seeking a new companion in Madeleine. Because the sixty-five-year-old vampire Claudia is trapped in the body of a six-year-old girl, she does not have the power to turn Madeleine into a vampire; she needs Louis for that. But Louis has no desire to bring another soul into an existence that he loathes. So Claudia and Madeleine plot to entrap Louis into turning Madeleine into a vampire for Claudia.

Louis is furious at Claudia for asking this of him. She and he argue about it, but Claudia finally guilts Louis into turning Madeleine into her new vampire companion. One of Madeleine's first impulses is to burn her doll shop to the ground and make Claudia her new doll. With a vampire's speed and obsessive mania, Madeleine spends the next few nights refashioning the adult furniture in Claudia's room to diminutive proportions: a child's bed, a child's chair, a child's clothes. When Madeleine is not lavishing all her affection on Claudia, she is learning how to be a vampire and feeding on human blood with rapturous delight, so much so that Louis, on more than one occasion, must pull her away from her victims, like the way Claudia had been when he and Lestat first changed the six-year-old child into a blood drinker.

When Armand's coven captures Louis and Claudia for attempting to kill their maker, Lestat, Madeleine is taken with them. Armand allows his coven to destroy Claudia for the crime because he secretly wants Louis to separate from her and be his companion. While Louis is locked in a coffin, Claudia and Madeleine are exposed to the sun and burned to ashes.

For more perspectives on Madeleine's character, read the *Alphabettery* entries **Armand, Children of Darkness, Claudia, Lestat de Lioncourt,** and **Louis de Pointe du Lac.**

Mad Manfred

• SOBRIQUET •

Read the *Alphabettery* entry **Manfred Blackwood.**

Mael

• VAMPIRE •

Mael serves as an aid to three principal characters. He helps Marius and Jesse become vampires, and he serves as one of Maharet's most beloved companions. He appears in *The*

Vampire Lestat (1985), *The Queen of the Damned* (1988), *Memnoch the Devil* (1995), and *Blood and Gold* (2001).

At the beginning of the first millennium C.E., in the forests of ancient Gaul, is a Druid religion that worships a powerful vampire called the God of the Grove, who is locked inside a large oak tree behind a heavy iron door. The god's name is Teskhamen, a vampire almost as old as the progenitors of the Blood Genesis, Akasha and Enkil. One of Teskhamen's principal disciples is a mortal named Mael.

One day, for reasons unknown to the Druids, their God of the Grove is burned so badly that he looks like a charred living corpse. Teskhamen orders Mael and the other Druids to capture a man worthy of succeeding him as the new God of the Grove. They go to Rome and capture Marius de Romanus. Mael forces Marius to learn the Druid customs and language before the ceremony of his transformation into a vampire. Teskhamen turns Marius into a vampire but then instructs him to escape, flee to Egypt, and discover the fate of Akasha and Enkil. After Marius's nascent vampire abilities enable him to evade the Druids, Teskhamen also escapes and leaves the Druids without a god. So the Druids send Mael to the location of another god of another grove, Avicus, who, like Teskhamen, is locked in a large tree in pre-Roman Britain, near present-day Yorkshire.

After Avicus telepathically reads Mael's mind and discerns how Teskhamen and Marius escape their religious trappings, Avicus also desires the same freedom. Mael helps him escape on the condition that Avicus will turn him into a vampire. After becoming a vampire, Mael loses his religious beliefs and never returns to the grove in Gaul but remains Avicus's companion for many years.

Eventually they travel to Rome, where they encounter Marius. Despite Marius's bitter feelings towards Mael for his role in turning him into a vampire, Marius befriends Avicus and makes a truce with Mael. The three of them live together for many years. They work to keep the Children of Satan out of Rome. One night, Avicus and Mael chance upon a group of drunken soldiers, who, after a brief scuffle, cut off Mael's arm and head. Mael loses much blood and becomes skeletonlike. Avicus tries to rejoin Mael's head and arm, but he does it incorrectly. Not knowing what else to do, Avicus finds Marius, who pulls off Mael's badly attached arm and head, then reattaches them properly and seals the flesh by biting into his own wrist and letting his blood mingle with Mael's wounds, which helps the severed limb and head heal correctly, back in their proper places. Through Marius's blood, Mael sees many of Marius's secrets, especially that he is the protector of Those Who Must Be Kept. Mael requests to drink the Queen's blood to help him heal, but when Marius brings him before their thrones, Enkil suddenly moves and attempts to crush Mael. Marius rescues Mael a second time from certain death, but their mutual animosity towards each other only increases. Just as Marius loathes Mael for his part in turning him into a vampire, Mael loathes Marius for keeping this secret from them, for destroying the Druid religious practice, and for keeping from Avicus the truth of his past. Despite this confrontation, the three of them remain together for several more years. In time, they move to Constantinople and collaborate in protecting Those Who Must Be Kept. Another coven in the city led by Eudoxia confronts them. After Akasha destroys Eudoxia, Eudoxia's companion Zenobia joins Marius's coven shortly before he absconds with Those Who Must Be Kept.

Avicus and Zenobia spend increasing time together, sneaking into the Emperor's palace and hunting in the shadows. She teaches him Greek and makes herself beautiful. Avicus and Zenobia develop a deep love for each other and become Blood Spouses. Zenobia has no love for Mael, which causes a deep, cold rift in the friendship between him and Avicus. In time, Avicus and Zenobia abandon Mael in Constantinople.

Mael wanders for many centuries. He stops counting how many pass.

Around the sixteenth century, he returns to Rome briefly, where he encounters Santino, the leader of the Roman coven of the Children of Satan. Santino urges Mael to join them. Mael is much older than him, much more powerful, and could destroy Santino, the way he once destroyed the Children of Satan in Rome alongside Marius and Avicus. But because he is hardly staying a day in Rome, Mael refuses and lets Santino live. Santino begs Mael to reveal the secrets of Those Who Must Be Kept; once more Mael refuses him. Before they part company, Santino reveals to Mael that Marius is now living in Venice. It surprises Marius when Mael appears at his palazzo. They inform each other of all that has happened since their parting. Mael has lived like a vagabond, never making another fledgling but existing one victim at a time. They realize that their hurtful feelings

towards each other are still very raw. Mael hardly stays the night and leaves not long after he arrives.

Mael roams until he finally becomes the unstintingly devoted companion of Maharet. He helps her raise her direct descendant, Jesse Reeves, who thinks Maharet is her wealthy aunt. When Jesse begins living with them at the age of twenty, Mael feels deep love for her. He picks her up from the airport, reads poetry to her, dances with her, and asks questions about her experiences of the twentieth century, such as the sensation of cigarettes and the taste of chocolate. Jesse observes that Mael is truly happy and cheerful, and very finely dressed, especially when he dances with Maharet, and they sing songs together and speak in ancient tongues. Jesse also observes that Mael and Maharet eat very little, that they never come out in the daylight, and numerous other hints as to their true identity, specifically their endurance and stamina in suffering great wounds. The few times Mael and Maharet fight is over Jesse. Unbeknownst to Jesse, Mael is urging Maharet to turn Jesse into a vampire, but Maharet wants Jesse to live a full mortal life.

After Jesse finally leaves them to work for the Talamasca, David Talbot assigns her to study the books *Interview with the Vampire* and *The Vampire Lestat*, wherein she learns of Mael's story and begins to believe that he is an immortal blood drinker. She later gains tickets to the Vampire Lestat concert in San Francisco with the hope of proving that Lestat, Mael, and Maharet are all actual vampires.

Aware that Lestat is revealing the secrets of Those Who Must Be Kept in his music,

Mael also attends the concert, where he recognizes the powerful vampire Khayman, who turned Maharet's twin sister into a vampire, who then turned Maharet into a vampire. Khayman has followed the newly risen Queen Akasha to the concert; Mael reveals to Khayman that Maharet sent him to protect Jesse. Meanwhile, Jesse has jumped up onstage to get a closer look at Lestat. When she is taken backstage, a young vampire throws her against a wall, breaks her neck, and crushes her skull. Mael gives her enough blood to keep her alive, and then he swiftly rushes her back to Maharet's compound, where she turns Jesse into a vampire. Several vampires who survive Akasha's great massacre, Mael included, gather together at Maharet's Sonoma compound, where she explains to them the Blood Genesis and the Legend of the Twins.

After Akasha is defeated, Mael remains with Maharet for a time, but he soon begins wandering the world once more, until Lestat returns from his journey with Memnoch the Devil. When Lestat brings back Veronica's Veil as proof of his journey, Mael's deep spiritual feelings resurface, and he believes it is time for him to end his life. He stands on the steps of Saint Patrick's Cathedral in New York, just as the sun rises upon him. Nothing more is heard of him after that. Lestat believes that Mael has survived the experience, and Marius concurs that Mael has been badly burned and has hidden himself with other companions.

For more perspectives on Mael's character, read the *Alphabettery* entries **Akasha, Avicus, Enkil, Eudoxia, Lestat de Lioncourt, Maharet, Marius, Teskhamen, Those Who Must Be Kept**, and **Zenobia**.

Magnus

• VAMPIRE •

Magnus is Lestat's maker. Although he appears only briefly in the beginning of the Vampire Chronicles as a ruthlessly powerful vampire, he returns in the later books as a sympathetic ghost. He appears in *The Vampire Lestat* (1985), *Prince Lestat* (2014), *Prince Lestat and the Realms of Atlantis* (2016), and *Blood Communion* (2018).

In the fifteenth century, while Rhoshamandes quietly rules his realm, an alchemist in Paris named Magnus seeks immortality by

becoming a vampire. Rhoshamandes denies him because by that time Magnus is already an elderly man, stooped and deformed, his body wasting away naturally; neither will Rhoshamandes allow the number of vampires in the world to grow and become unmanageable, nor will he allow anyone as grotesque as Magnus to receive the Dark Gift. Rhoshamandes's decision is not simply based upon Akasha's old law, but is also his personal preference: Rhoshamandes only desires to change beautiful mortals into beautiful vampires. But Magnus will not let that refusal stop him. When Rhoshamandes's fledgling Benedict entrusts to a mortal acquaintance the location of his daytime resting place, Magnus learns the whereabouts of Benedict's lair. He binds Benedict, drains him of his blood at sunset, drains his own blood to the point of death, and then drinks Benedict's blood. The process turns Magnus into a vampire, yet it also leaves him comatose upon Benedict's body. As far as Rhoshamandes knows, no one else has ever stolen immortal life like Magnus. Although other vampires expect Rhoshamandes to destroy Magnus for this violation, he loves and respects him instead, and he even protects him against all other blood drinkers who seek to harm him, even Magnus's unwilling maker, Benedict.

Despite the fact that Magnus has received what he wants, too much thinking about the reality of immortality drives him mad. He locks himself in his tower in Paris and spends his years accumulating wealth until he is three hundred years old and seeks to end his immortal life. Before that, he also desires to make a fledgling heir to inherit his wealth. In the process, he kills many mortals. None proves to be an acceptable heir, until one night, when he goes to Renaud's House of Thesbians and sees onstage a brilliant young mortal actor named Lestat. Magnus reads Lestat's mind, sees how he slew eight wolves, and then sends him a telepathic message, using the endearment "Wolfkiller." Magnus watches Lestat for some time before determining that Lestat will be the perfect immortal who will not only inherit his large

fortune but also fulfill his suicide plans. In much the same way Magnus turned himself into a vampire against the will of his maker, he also turns Lestat into a vampire, stealing him from the apartment that he shares with Nicolas de Lenfent, draining Lestat of his blood, and forcing him to drink down the Dark Gift. Once Lestat is a vampire, Magnus shows him the fortune that he will inherit, tells his fledgling that he is going to destroy himself in a fire, and then makes Lestat promise to scatter his ashes. Lestat obeys, but Magnus's spirit lives on.

In the spirit realm, Magnus's spirit encounters Gremt, a spirit who has learned to incarnate himself by gathering motes of dust and other particles to make himself look mortal, with warm skin and a heartbeat. He teaches Magnus how to do this, yet Magnus is not ready to reveal himself to Lestat until the twenty-first century.

At first, Magnus takes the form of a man in his midforties, with long ashen hair, who is visited by Everard, Teskhamen, and Raymond Gallant. When Lestat encounters Magnus for the first time since his maker killed himself, now in his ghost form Magnus appears to him in a shape inspired by Lestat's beauty, tall and strong, with long blond hair and blue eyes. Lestat and Magnus speak gently together for the first time, and Magnus apologizes for the wrong he did to Lestat. Moved with joy and compassion, the fledgling embraces his maker lovingly and insists that there is nothing to forgive.

The spirit of Magnus eventually resettles in the Replimoid colony in rural England, along with Gremt and Hesketh.

For more perspectives on Magnus's character, read the *Alphabettery* entries **Bene-dict, Gremt Stryker Knollys, Lestat de Lioncourt, Nicolas de Lenfent, Renaud's House of Thesbians**, and **Rhoshamandes**.

Maharet

• VAMPIRE •

Maharet is one of the first vampires ever made and one of Akasha's first enemies. She is a founder of the First Brood and the Mother of the Great Family. Through her work chronicling the Great Family tree, Maharet is the only vampire who never goes into a torpor underground like Lestat, nor does she turn statuesque like Akasha. Maharet appears in *The Queen of the Damned* (1988), *Memnoch the Devil* (1995), *Blood Canticle* (2003), *Prince Lestat* (2014), and *Prince Lestat and the Realms of Atlantis* (2016).

Maharet is born more than four thousand years before the Common Era with her twin sister, Mekare, both of whom have fiery red hair and green eyes. Their family is already ancient at the time, having lived in the caves of Mount Carmel in the north of Israel as far back as fifty generations, to the Time Before the Moon. As her family grows over the centuries, some move out of the caves and build round mud-brick houses with thatched roofs at the mountain's foot on the valley floor. Their principal profession is herding sheep and goats, yet they also produce pottery, which they trade at the markets of Jericho. Occasionally Maharet's village grows crops, some of which are hallucinogens, which the villagers regularly employ in their spiritual

practice. The women in the direct line of Maharet's family are considered to be the witches who help guide their religious belief. Maharet defines this particular vocation not as controlling nature but as presiding over the ritual cannibalism of other witches, experiencing out-of-body pilgrimages through time and space, and communicating with ghosts and spirits who help them predominate over nature and give them knowledge. Each mother instructs her daughter how to hone and perfect this gift. They divide spirits into two categories, good and evil. All spirits have the ability to influence nature, sometimes influencing the weather, other times manipulating small physical objects. The good spirits do favors for the witches, while the bad spirits are mercurial and entirely untrustworthy.

By the time Maharet and Mekare are sixteen years old, the Queen of ancient Egypt dies without a daughter to succeed her. The young King Enkil takes the throne and takes from the city of Uruk a beautiful young woman who becomes his wife and queen, Akasha. One of her first proclamations is instituting a more enlightened philosophy from her culture, which is to ban the common practice of cannibalism, but the people rebel and cause numerous revolts. To ensure that this edict is fulfilled, Akasha seeks to convince people that it is better for the spirits of their ancestors to enter the afterlife with bodies that were not divided for consumption but kept whole and unmolested by wrapping the corpses in burial cloth. To further convince the people of this practice, Akasha invites Maharet and Mekare to the royal court, because their reputation for communicating with spirits is well known. The twins laugh at the idea of not eating the dead, as if the spirits will care. But they distrust Akasha's messenger. The spirits tell them that great danger will befall them before the King and Queen, so Maharet and Mekare refuse the Queen's invitation to the royal court.

Following this, the spirit of Amel appears before them and reveals that he can wound human skin enough to cause tiny pinpricks of blood, which he enjoys tasting. Maharet's mother, a powerful witch, dismisses Amel but worries over his strange ability. When she dies a few months later, Maharet and Mekare prepare her body for ritual cannibalism. After many hours of fasting, Maharet plans to eat the heart, while Mekare plans to eat the brain and eyes. Hundreds of people from many villages come to partake of the ritual. But before the ritual can commence, more of Akasha's messengers arrive from Egypt, who desecrate their mother's body, destroy the villages, kill many villagers, capture Maharet and Mekare, and bring them back to Egypt. During their sojourn, over a week's travel on foot, the King's steward, Khayman, shows them great compassion. When Maharet and Mekare are finally brought before the Queen and King, Akasha and Enkil question them

about spirits and demons. Against Maharet's protestations, Mekare summons Amel, who torments Akasha and Enkil. The Queen punishes the twins by having them raped by Khayman before the royal court. After this, Akasha and Enkil allow Maharet to return to her village with her sister. As a result of the rape, Maharet bears a daughter, whom she names Miriam.

One year later, Khayman returns to their village accompanied by an army. He takes Maharet and Mekare back to the royal court, where they discover that the spirit of Amel has fused with Akasha's blood and transformed her into the world's first vampire, and Enkil has become her first fledgling. The King and Queen seek answers from the twins, but neither Maharet nor Mekare can explain their aversion to sunlight, their superior faculties and strength, their rapid healing ability, or their insatiable bloodlust. Maharet suggests that, because spirits are incredibly large entities, one way to reduce the bloodlust would be to make more vampires, effectively disseminating the spirit and diluting its potency. To test this, Akasha turns Khayman into a vampire against his will, but this proves futile. Mekare loathes the Queen and believes that Akasha has gotten what she deserves, referring to her as the Queen of the Damned. In bitter response, Akasha has Maharet's eyes torn out and Mekare's tongue cut off and sentences them to death on the following day. But before her tongue is severed, Mekare curses the Queen and promises to return and have her vengeance, instigating a prophecy that will come to be known as the Legend of the Twins.

Before dawn the next morning, Khayman,

who is extremely angered by what has happened to him, turns Mekare into a vampire, who then turns Maharet into a vampire. At the instant of their transformation, Maharet can see again with her mind's eye, yet her ability to communicate with spirits is cut off forever. They flee from the King and Queen. Five nights after her transformation, Maharet discovers that she can steal the eyes of her victims, place them in her own sockets, and allow her body's newfound regenerative abilities to fuse them into place, so that she can see the way other vampires see. Maharet, Mekare, and Khayman then turn numerous mortals into blood drinkers, creating a vast army, known as the First Brood, which combats Akasha's cultic forces. Unfortunately, Maharet, Mekare, and Khayman have not yet learned how to hide the bodies of their victims and leave a trail for Akasha's army to find. Two weeks after their flight, Maharet and Mekare are captured at Saqqara, the necropolis of Memphis, ancient Egypt's capital. Only Khayman escapes.

Akasha and Enkil fear harming another vampire. So instead of killing Maharet and her sister, they imprison them in stone tombs and set them adrift in different oceans. After sailing for many days and nights, Maharet finally lands ashore on the African coast. She finds a victim and takes new eyes, but she quickly learns that, because they are not vampiric eyes, they will not last long, and she must keep replacing them with fresh eyes from new victims.

Maharet searches many centuries for her twin sister, going west across Africa, traveling south, searching from one tip to another. She travels into the land that will become Europe, as high as the northernmost islands where the landscape is all ice and snow. But Mekare is nowhere to be found.

When Maharet realizes that her own daughter, Miriam, is now twenty years old, she returns to her old village at the foot of Mount Carmel. Miriam has grown into a beautiful woman who knows the Legend of the Twins, but she does not know that the younger-looking Maharet is her mother. Maharet befriends her daughter and tells her stories of their ancient ancestors, yet she warns her to avoid witchcraft, effectively breaking the traditional line of mothers teaching daughters how to communicate with spirits. Maharet takes up residence in Jericho, where killing victims is easier, but she returns to her old village often to visit Miriam, who begins to have her own children.

After two hundred years pass, Maharet begins chronicling her offspring, writing down her family tree on clay tablets. Occasionally she pauses her chronicling to search for Mekare, but she never finds her and returns to her village to continue recording her family's progress. For thousands of years, Maharet remains her family's chronicler in anonymity. In some generations, she goes to her family pretending to be a long-lost kinswoman and offering help with advice or money.

When Maharet turns three thousand years old, she returns to Egypt, shrouded in black robes. She discovers that a blood cult has grown around Akasha and Enkil. Maharet pretends to be a younger vampire and is invited to view the fate of the Queen and King, who are now referred to as the Mother and the Father. She is told by a priest vampire that if she wishes to drink from the blood of the Queen, she must present herself before the Elder and prove the purity of her fidelity to the cult. Maharet beholds that Akasha and Enkil have turned into something like statues, sitting mute and immovable on thrones. She stands before them and speaks to them, but they show no hint of recognition or intelligence. Maharet learns that the Mother and the Father have been like this for so long that the Blood Genesis and the Legend of the Twins are considered to be nothing more than myth. Even the oldest vampire in Egypt at that time does not know whether the story of the First Brood is even true.

Maharet then goes to India. She turns a twenty-nine-year-old mortal named Eric into a vampire and her companion. But at the beginning of the first millennium of the Common Era, Maharet's fledgling is nearly destroyed when, back in Egypt, the Elder puts the Mother and the Father in the sun, which causes the Great Burning of 4 C.E. Eric is charred and blackened, while Maharet has merely bronzed, like other vampires of her great age. She must let her fledgling drink from her own blood to restore him to health. Maharet discovers that Akasha and Enkil are now called "Those Who Must Be Kept" and are being cared for by a young vampire named Marius. He has taken them out of Egypt and is keeping them in Antioch. Maharet finds them easily and, with a long dagger, slices open Akasha's chest and watches the Queen's heart stop beating for a brief moment. In that moment, Maharet feels dizzy and disconnected, as if she is about to die. Maharet then understands that if anything happens to Akasha it affects every vampire, for Akasha keeps within herself Amel, the Sacred Core, the foundation of all vampire existence.

Maharet continues chronicling her family's progress. She stops using clay tablets and starts binding their stories in books. The name Maharet becomes synonymous with the family-tree record keeper. Each generation knows that this Maharet will come to them and make inquiries of parents and children. And with each new generation, an "old Maharet" dies, and a "new Maharet" takes her place. The progress of time never drives her mad, never drives her into the earth, or makes her become a statue like the Mother and the Father. Chronicling her family's progress is an anchor that keeps her sane, for she always returns to them, always learns their new language, always befriends them and dons each branch's particular customs. Out of all the vampires that have ever lived, Maharet's interest in mortals extends beyond a love for beauty or a need for blood; in the same way that deeply religious individuals can endure great suffering by looking forward to an afterlife, Maharet can always look forward to the next generation of her growing family, knowing that each new line and branch of the Great Family's tree is a further defeat of her ancient foe, Akasha.

As the centuries elapse, Maharet continues to search for her sister, Mekare, yet she never finds her. At first, she can feel a telepathic bond with her sister, at least subconsciously, in a dreamlike state, experiencing Mekare's ineffable suffering. As they continue to age into immortality, they become less human, which weakens the bond of their unique sisterhood. Feeling only silence from her sister, Maharet returns to the place of her old village, to Mount Carmel, where she paints images of their story in the mountain's caves, which eventually mortals will find, contemplate, yet never fathom the truth.

Maharet and Eric separate. In search of companionship, she turns the Viking warrior, Thorne, into a vampire. But he grows incessantly jealous of the way she behaves around other male vampires, particularly Mael. Eventually, Maharet and Thorne also go their separate ways, but Maharet remains with Mael all the way into the twentieth century.

By then, Maharet hears the tale of an archaeologist who saw Maharet's grotto images and has compared them with similar images in the jungles of Peru. Maharet knows instantly that Mekare drew those same cave paintings of their life's story. She travels with Eric and Mael to South America in search of her. They see Mekare's paintings and realize that they are nearly six thousand years old. But Maharet never finds any other trace of her twin sister.

Later that century, one of Maharet's descendants, Miriam Reeves, dies in a fatal car crash, but not before prematurely giving birth to her daughter, Jesse Reeves. Maharet identifies the newborn in the hospital and sends her to live with relatives in New York. Over the years, the ancient vampire often visits young Jesse, who knows only that Maharet is her aunt. Jesse soon shows the signs of family witchcraft, demonstrating how she can see ghosts, even the ghost of her dead mother. When Jesse turns twenty, Maharet invites her to live at her compound in the Sonoma Mountains. It is there that Jesse begins to see signs that her aunt Maharet might not

be entirely human. The Talamasca recognizes that Jesse is a powerful psychic and invites her to join the Order. Maharet objects to this vehemently, but in the end, she allows it to happen. Jesse's work for the Talamasca makes her aware that Maharet is a vampire; through Jesse's work, Maharet learns that the books and music of the vampire Lestat are revealing vampire identities and secrets. Jesse attends Lestat's concert, where she is fatally wounded. Mael rushes Jesse to Maharet, who reluctantly turns her mortal descendant into a vampire to save her life.

When Lestat's works awaken Akasha, the Queen of the Damned kills Enkil, commences the Great Burning of 1985, and takes Lestat as her new companion. Maharet summons a council at her compound in the Sonoma Mountains, consisting of herself and eleven vampires who have survived Akasha's massacre: Khayman, Mael, Marius, Pandora, Jesse, Santino, Eric, Armand, Daniel, Gabrielle, and Louis. Maharet tells them the Legend of the Twins, and the council determines that they have to destroy Akasha, only they do not know how to do so. When Akasha finally appears before them accompanied by Lestat, she reveals her plan for world domination, at which point Lestat turns on her. All the vampires now fight against Akasha, but she cannot be defeated, not until Mekare appears. Fulfilling the prophetic curse of the Legend of the Twins, Mekare decapitates Akasha, consumes her heart and brain, and takes into herself the spirit of Amel and his Sacred Core, effectively becoming the new Queen of the Damned, the host carrier for all vampire existence.

Maharet moves Mekare from her Sonoma

compound to a new compound in Java, Indonesia, where many vampires are welcome, including Jesse and David Talbot, to search through her vast library and even study Maharet's chronicles of her Great Family. Maharet learns that Mekare is severely traumatized. Her twin sister expresses the mysterious and unreachable face of a savage animal. Sometimes Mekare demonstrates love to Maharet, but beyond that the traumatized sister shows no sign of self-awareness. Maharet spends countless nights trying to help Mekare heal by speaking with her, singing to her, walking with her through the jungles, showing her all the wonders of the modern age, but Mekare never verbalizes any coherent thought. Maharet is devastated by Mekare's seemingly irreversible traumatic state. She has spent the last six millennia searching for her sister, and now that she is not the same sister that was taken from her, Maharet is utterly crestfallen.

She occasionally aids other vampires across the world, such as delivering to Lestat a message from Memnoch the Devil and then binding him with her hair when the message drives him mad. She also helps Lestat, Mona Mayfair, and Quinn Blackwood find the hidden island of the Taltos. She even welcomes to her compound the vampire scientist Fareed, whose scientific breakthroughs for the Undead enable him to permanently replace her vampire eyes. Maharet also listens for endless hours to Benji's radio broadcasts and his observations on the state of the world and of vampire existence.

Through it all, she is dying inside, and she wants to end her life, as well as the life of Mekare, which will end vampire existence altogether. She considers numerous times flinging herself and Mekare into an active volcano and letting them be burned to death. Jesse urges her not to do this. Reluctantly, she agrees to forestall her plans. But she begins the process of relinquishing her duties to the Great Family. Whereas before, she cared for the genealogical records, allocated financial support, and kept the numerous branches of the Great Family aware of one another—by then living in almost every country in the world—now she builds libraries and archives, and organizes and facilitates the distribution of her duties to law offices and bank offices, to guarantee that the Great Family can function independently of her, that it will survive without her, if anything should happen.

One night, Maharet's Java compound burns to the ground in a mysterious fire that might have been started by Mekare. So she takes her sister and Khayman to the uncharted jungles of the Amazon, where they set up a new home. Despite their newfound seclusion, Maharet continues to dream of throwing herself and Mekare into an active volcano, destroying not only themselves and the vampire race but also the spirit of Amel. Aware of this threat, Amel speaks to the five-thousand-year-old Rhoshamandes as the mysterious Voice and convinces him that they are all in jeopardy if Rhoshamandes does not destroy the twins and take the Sacred Core into himself. Thus, Rhoshamandes and his fledgling Benedict steal into the Amazon compound, pick up machetes, and attack Maharet. Although Maharet could easily destroy Rhoshamandes and Benedict, she feigns a brief fight against them before allowing them to fulfill her innermost desire. Maharet calls for Khayman. She calls for

Mekare. She speaks numerous names of her long history. And then, moments before Rhoshamandes's machete strikes the final blow, severing Maharet's head, her final words can be heard echoing through the Amazon jungles: "I am dying. I am murdered!"

For more perspectives on Maharet's character, read the *Alphabettery* entries **Akasha, Benedict, Enkil, Eric, Great Family, Jesse, Khayman, Lestat de Lioncourt, Mael, Marius, Mekare, Rhoshamandes**, and **Thorne**.

Maharet's Amazon Compound

• SANCTUARY •

After a mysterious fire burns Maharet's Java compound to the ground in the early twenty-first century, Maharet creates a new compound in the Amazon jungles, taking with her Mekare, her twin sister, who is also the Queen of the Damned, as well as her protector-companion, Khayman. Unlike her Java compound, which tolerated a thoroughfare of vampire activity, Maharet keeps her Amazon compound a secret and secluded place, known only to a few, such as her descendant-fledgling, Jesse Reeves, as well as Jesse's former Talamasca mentor, who also happens to be Lestat's fledgling, David Talbot.

When the spirit of Amel no longer desires to live in the psychologically damaged mind of Mekare, he convinces the vampire Rhoshamandes to kill Mekare and devour her brain, so that Amel can transfer to him. Amel reveals to Rhoshamandes that he is located in Mekare's mind on the grounds of Maharet's Amazon compound. In this place, Rhoshamandes and his fledgling Benedict fight and kill both Maharet and Khayman before kidnapping Mekare.

Maharet's Amazon compound appears in *Prince Lestat* (2014). For more perspectives on Maharet's Amazon compound in the Vampire Chronicles, read the *Alphabettery* entries **Amel, Benedict, David Talbot, Jesse, Khayman, Lestat de Lioncourt, Maharet, Maharet's Java Compound, Maharet's Sonoma Compound, Mekare**, and **Rhoshamandes**.

Maharet's Java Compound

• SANCTUARY •

After the battle with Queen Akasha, Maharet moves herself; her sister, Mekare; and several other vampires to her new compound in Java, Indonesia. Many vampires are welcome to come to this compound, to study in Maharet's vast library, or to have sanctuary. Maharet pays a fortune to have the technological equipment of the scientist-vampire Fareed transported to her compound so that, through his cloning technique, he can restore the eyes of both Maharet and Thorne. Also at this compound, Fareed does extensive studies on Mekare, although he is unable to regenerate her tongue. At the beginning of the twenty-first century, a mysterious fire burns Maharet's Java compound to the ground, and Maharet's descendant and fledgling Jesse Reeves notices that Mekare stands amid the rubble with a peculiar expression of awareness on her face. After the fire, Maharet moves her location to a more secret and secluded compound in the Amazon jungles.

Maharet's Java compound appears in *Blood and Gold* (2001). For more perspectives on Maharet's Java compound in the Vampire Chronicles, read the *Alphabettery* entries **Fareed Bhansali**, **Jesse**, **Khayman**, **Lestat de Lioncourt**, **Maharet**, **Maharet's Amazon Compound**, **Maharet's Sonoma Compound**, **Mekare**, and **Rhoshamandes**.

Maharet's Sonoma Compound

• SANCTUARY •

After the six-thousand-year-old vampire Maharet moves to the United States to chronicle the North American extension of her Great Family, she settles in the mountains of Sonoma, California, where she creates a vastly beautiful compound, with a large mansion that contains all the chronicled data of her family, extending back in time for thousands of years. She lives there with her vampire companion Mael. She even invites to the compound her descendant of nearly three hundred generations, Jesse Reeves, who was born prematurely when her mother died in a car crash. Calling her Aunt Maharet, Jesse visits the compound often, where she notices peculiar behavior by her aunt and her aunt's companion: how they never eat, how they avoid sunlight, and how they are supernaturally strong. Jesse learns the truth of her aunt when the rock music of the Vampire Lestat band awakens Maharet's ancient nemesis, Queen Akasha, who begins a megalomaniacal plan of world conquest through fire.

After turning Jesse into a vampire, Maharet invites several other vampires to her compound, where they discuss the Legend of the Twins. Maharet and the other vampires resolve to defeat Akasha, no matter the cost. Eventually, Akasha arrives at Maharet's Sonoma compound. Her vampire fledglings fight against her but cannot defeat her, until Maharet's twin sister, Mekare, appears, beheads Akasha, consumes her brain, takes into herself Amel, and becomes the new Queen of the Damned.

Maharet does not remain much longer in this compound but moves with her sister and the chronicles of her Great Family to Indonesia, where she builds a new Java compound as a sanctuary for all vampires.

Maharet's Sonoma compound appears in *The Queen of the Damned* (1988) and *Prince Lestat* (2014). For more perspectives on Maharet's Sonoma compound in the Vampire Chronicles, read the *Alphabettery* entries **Amel**, **Benedict**, **David Talbot**, **Jesse**, **Khayman**, **Lestat de Lioncourt**, **Maharet**, **Maharet's Amazon Compound**, **Maharet's Java Compound**, **Mekare**, and **Rhoshamandes**.

Make Contact

• IDIOM •

To "make contact" with an age is a euphemism for vampires crossing the threshold from their inability to cope with the passage of time to their understanding of new generations of human development. If vampires cannot make contact with a new age, they tend to bury themselves in the earth, be starved of blood, and enter into a state of torpidity. When vampires do make contact with an age, they feel capable of surviving into a new era of human progress.

For instance, in *Interview with the Vampire* (1976), Armand desires to make contact with the nineteenth century by befriending Louis, believing that Louis embodies the spirit of that age and can help him cope with the changes after the eighteenth century. For years, Louis helps Armand make contact until Armand leaves and eventually discovers Daniel Malloy, who helps him make contact with the twentieth century.

For more perspectives on vampires making contact in the Vampire Chronicles, read the *Alphabettery* entries **Armand**, **Daniel Malloy**, and **Louis de Pointe du Lac**.

Maker

• IDIOM •

When a vampire turns a mortal into a vampire, that first vampire is generally referred to as the second vampire's maker. In other words, vampire makers make more vampires. The act of making a vampire involves drinking all the blood in a mortal, leaving the mortal on the point of death, and then allowing the mortal to drink the vampire's blood. Once that happens, the mortal undergoes a transformation process, from life to death and from death to undeath, since a vampire is essentially an undead being. That maker has made not only a vampire but also his or her fledgling (child), whom they are often obliged to teach the ways of blood drinkers, although that is not always the case: Magnus makes Lestat and then kills himself before Lestat can learn about his new vampire nature.

Most vampires have the strength and ability to make other vampires, but there are exceptions to this rule. For example, Lestat has the power to make the six-year-old girl Claudia a vampire, but because of her diminutive proportions, Claudia, eternally trapped in a child's body, does not have the strength to make a vampire fledgling of her own and depends on Louis to make for her a surrogate fledgling, Madeleine.

One basic problem with making a vampire is that the telepathic connection between maker and fledgling is severed. This happens when Marius makes Pandora into a vampire. He enjoys a delightful telepathic connection with her while she is mortal, but

at the moment of her making, they can no longer read each other's thoughts. In another case, Marius turns Armand's mortal wards, Benji and Sybelle, into vampires as a gift to Armand, so that the telepathic connection among Armand, Benji, and Sybelle cannot be broken.

In the ancient tradition of the Children of Satan, who live by the Great Laws, it is forbidden for a fledgling to kill his or her maker. The punishment for this is death, as when Louis and Claudia attempt to kill their maker, Lestat. Santiago and other vampires at the Théâtre des Vampires punish them by killing Claudia and imprisoning Louis.

In all cases, makers give mortals not simply immortal life and bloodlust but also the great power in their blood. For instance, when Maharet turns Jesse into a vampire, she gives to her fledgling all the ancient power in her six-thousand-year-old blood, whereas if Jesse had been made by Louis, she would have been much weaker. As it stands, although Jesse is two hundred years younger than Louis, once Maharet makes her a vampire, Jesse becomes much more powerful than Louis.

Makers appear in *Interview with the Vampire* (1976), *The Vampire Lestat* (1985), *The Queen of the Damned* (1988), and every Vampire Chronicle. For more perspectives on makers in the Vampire Chronicles, read the *Alphabettery* entries **Benji Mahmoud**, **Jesse**, **Lestat de Lioncourt**, **Louis de Pointe du Lac**, **Maharet**, **Sybelle**, and **Théâtre des Vampires**.

Manfred Blackwood

• VAMPIRE •

Manfred Blackwood is the sociopathic ancestor of Quinn Blackwood. They also share the same maker. Manfred appears in *Blackwood Farm* (2002).

In the late nineteenth century, "Mad" Manfred Blackwood begins work as a saloonkeeper in the Irish Channel in New Orleans, but he makes his real fortune in merchandising. Like many Irishmen in that era, he catches the yellow fever and nearly dies, but he is saved by his nurse at the hospital, Virginia Lee, with whom Manfred falls madly in love.

Around the year 1881, he convinces Virginia Lee to quit her job and marry him. They move across Lake Pontchartrain to the Louisiana swampland, where he buys a plantation and builds Blackwood Farm. When his wife Virginia Lee dies, Manfred wanders throughout his property and discovers a delightful island in the middle of the swamp. Dubbing it "Sugar Devil Island," he builds a little hideout for himself that only he knows about and often visits alone.

The same year that his wife dies, he meets Rebecca Stanford, whom he marries and takes to Europe. While in Naples, he encounters the nineteen-hundred-year-old vampire Petronia. As they enjoy each other's company, he informs her about all the wonders of the Louisiana swampland. After returning to Blackwood Farm, he is delighted when Petronia comes to visit. He builds her a little shack in a tomb, where she can hide during the day. Understanding that she is a vampire, he strikes a deal with her: she will turn him into a vampire, and in exchange he will give her Sugar Devil Island.

Soon after, Manfred begins comparing his second wife with his first, growing increasingly angry with Rebecca, especially when she does not behave or think like Virginia. Unable to take his jealousy and cruel criticisms any longer, Rebecca tries to burn down Blackwood Farm. In vengeful retribution, Manfred abuses her savagely, before bringing her out to Sugar Devil Island, where he and Petronia torture and murder Rebecca.

Petronia eventually returns to Naples, but Manfred follows and demands that she fulfill her end of the bargain: she must turn him into a vampire. She is reluctant to do this at first, until her maker, the nearly twenty-five-hundred-year-old Arion, orders her to do so. Once it's done, Manfred, Petronia, and Arion form a small coven, and they stay together for many years.

Manfred enjoys Arion's company, and they become intimate companions, always conversing with each other on various topics or playing games, such as chess or cards.

In the twentieth century, they return to Louisiana, where they live together on Sugar Devil Island so that Manfred can watch the progress of his family and the stability of the home he built, Blackwood Farm. When Petronia seeks to turn Manfred's descendant Quinn Blackwood into a vampire, he begs her not to do it, but she disregards his pleas and does so anyway. Truly disappointed by this, but stubborn enough to move on, Manfred helps Quinn adapt to life as a vampire, explaining to him the rules that their coven lives by and teaching him how to avoid such dangerous organizations as the Talamasca.

For more perspectives on Manfred Blackwood's character, read the *Alphabettery* entries **Arion**, **Blackwood Farm**, **Petronia**, **Quinn Blackwood**, **Rebecca Stanford**, **Sugar Devil Island**, **Sugar Devil Swamp**, **Talamasca Order**, and **Virginia Lee Blackwood**.

Maria Godwin

• MORTAL •

Maria Godwin is the cousin and foster mother who cares for Jesse Reeves shortly after she survives the fatal car wreck that kills her parents. Maria and her husband, Matthew, take great care of Jesse while at the same time feeling indescribably rewarded for having such a splendid child in their home. As a dancer and teacher, Maria helps foster Jesse's love of culture, especially music, painting, and world travel, all of which are instigated and encouraged by her mysterious aunt Maharet. Jesse lives with Maria and Matthew until she is accepted into Columbia University. After that, she begins work for the Talamasca.

Maria Godwin appears in *The Queen of the Damned* (1988). For more perspectives on Maria's character, read the *Alphabettery* entries **Jesse**, **Maharet**, and **Matthew Godwin**.

Mariana of Sicily

• VAMPIRE •

Very little is known about the vampire Mariana of Sicily. Some surmise that she is as ancient as Marius; others estimate that she could be as ancient as Akasha's court in ancient Egypt. Mariana appears in the twenty-first century to join the Court of the Prince at Château de Lioncourt.

Mariana of Sicily appears in *Blood Communion* (2018). For more perspectives on Mariana's character, read the *Alphabettery* entries **Akasha**, **Château de Lioncourt**, **Lestat de Lioncourt**, and **Marius**.

Marius

• VAMPIRE •

Marius is the noble heart of the vampire clans. His sense of honor and duty guides him through every age. He is the caretaker of Those Who Must Be Kept and the sharer of vampire secrets with Lestat, who reveals those secrets in the twentieth century, causing Akasha to rise for the last time and incite the Great Burning of 1985. Marius appears in *The Vampire Lestat* (1985), *The Queen of the Damned* (1988), *The Tale of the Body Thief* (1992), *Memnoch the Devil* (1995), *The Vampire Armand* (1998), *Pandora* (1998), *Blood and Gold* (2001), *Prince Lestat* (2014), *Prince Lestat and the Realms of Atlantis* (2016), and *Blood Communion* (2018).

Marius de Romanus is born in 30 B.C., the illegitimate son of a Roman nobleman and a Celtic slave woman, in the city of Massilia (modern-day Marseille, France), in the Roman Empire, along the Mediterranean Sea between Spain and Italy. As he matures into manhood, Marius becomes a scholar and a traveler throughout the Roman Empire. In his midtwenties, he meets his future fledgling Pandora (then named Lydia) when she is only ten years old, and he desires to marry her, although his proposal is ultimately rejected by her father because she is too young. Almost two decades later, Marius is kidnapped by Mael and other Druids, who take him to the ancient vampire Teskhamen, whom they refer to as the God of the Grove. Badly burned and weakened in the Great Burning of 4 C.E., Teskhamen turns Marius

into a vampire through a very long process of blood exchanges, with the expectation that Marius will travel to Egypt to discover the fate of Akasha and Enkil.

Marius escapes the Druids and flees through the woodlands of the Celts. He travels to Egypt, where he finds the Elder who cares for Akasha and Enkil, now called Those Who Must Be Kept, since their great age has transformed them into unresponsive statues. The Elder lies when, in response to Marius's questions, he states that he does not know the cause of the Great Burning, but Akasha speaks to Marius telepathically and informs him that the Elder set them in the sun and that he is planning to sink them to the bottom of the ocean. Akasha then kills the Elder, and Marius takes her and Enkil out of Egypt to Antioch, where he reencounters his mortal beloved, Lydia, whose family was murdered, and as a result she is living in exile under the name Pandora.

Also in Antioch appears the ancient vampire Akbar, who, like Marius's maker, Teskhamen, is badly burned. Seeking to drink from the Mother and the Father, Akbar learns that Marius is their caretaker and that he loves the mortal Pandora. So Akbar drains Pandora to the point of death and threatens to kill her if Marius does not let him drink Akasha's blood. Marius acquiesces and saves Pandora by turning her into a vampire, but when Marius brings Akbar to Akasha, the Queen destroys Akbar. Marius and Pandora remain together for the next two hundred years, caring for Those Who Must Be Kept.

When Pandora begins living with her maker, she brings her one-legged Athenian slave, Flavius, to serve them. Marius grows to deeply love Flavius. When Flavius becomes deathly ill, Pandora thinks they should turn him into a vampire. Marius refuses, but Pandora does so anyway. Marius is greatly angered and exiles Flavius from his house and from the Roman Empire itself. Her disobedience plants a seed of bitterness between Marius and Pandora. He has a great desire to teach her, but she refuses to learn from him. When he can no longer live with that or their arguing, he takes Akasha and Enkil away from Pandora and will not see his fledgling beloved again for centuries.

Marius returns to Rome, where he encounters the ancient vampire Avicus, who is—like Teskhamen—a God of the Grove, but in ancient England. Marius is greatly amazed to also encounter Avicus's fledgling Mael, the former Druid who held Marius captive for Teskhamen and was sent to Avicus to take Marius's place as the new God of the Grove, Teskhamen's successor. Despite the fact that Marius begrudges Mael for forcing him to become a vampire, Marius and Avicus become friends. As the three begin living together in a small coven, Avicus and Mael soon learn Marius's secret, that he is the caretaker of Those Who Must Be Kept, and they willingly help him fulfill his duties.

At the fall of Rome, Marius, Avicus, and Mael move to Constantinople, where they continue their duties for the Mother and the Father. They discover that another coven dwells in the city, led by Eudoxia, the fledgling of the ancient Egyptian vampire Cyril, who is the fledgling of Marius's predecessor, the Elder. Referring to herself as "the Vampire Empress," Eudoxia demands to see Akasha and Enkil, but Marius refuses. With her coven of Rashid, Asphar, and Zenobia, Eudoxia attacks Marius, at which point Marius discovers that, because he has been drinking Akasha's powerful blood, he is stronger than Eudoxia, even though she is much older. He also discovers that he has the Fire Gift when he burns Rashid to ashes. Eudoxia returns later, showing greater humility and imploring Marius to let her see Akasha. Marius reluctantly agrees, but when Eudoxia stands before the Queen, she is so enraptured that she offers herself as a sacrifice. Akasha arises and drinks from Eudoxia to the point of death. Although Marius saves her, Eudoxia is greatly embittered. In a plot against Marius and Those Who Must Be Kept, Eudoxia kills a nobleman and leaves the body exposed in such a way that the mortal citizens of Constantinople blame Marius for the death. The mortals ransack Marius's house and nearly destroy the shrine. Enraged by this, Marius goes to Eudoxia's house, destroys her coven, sparing only Zenobia, and then drags Eudoxia before Akasha, who immolates Eudoxia to ashes.

Marius leaves Avicus and Mael and takes Akasha and Enkil back to Italy. He creates a secluded shrine for Akasha and Enkil in the Italian Alps, unreachable by any mortal at that time, where the vampires can rest safely while he makes a home in Venice.

He becomes a painter and a patron of the

arts. He invites many young boys to live in his house to learn an artistic craft.

Marius soon encounters the mortal courtesan Bianca Solderini. While feeling a deep attraction to her physical beauty, he marvels how her mortal mental ability prevents him from reading her thoughts. His attraction to her sours when he discovers that she is a murderer. But when he uncovers that a merciless relative is extorting her to assassinate his enemies, Marius's attraction is rekindled and he resolves to give her his powerful aid.

Marius also encounters the mortal Raymond Gallant, a member of the Talamasca Order, who provides him with news about Pandora and how the vampire from India is manipulating her, yet their whereabouts are still a mystery. Raymond promises to keep Marius informed if the Talamasca discovers any new information.

During that time, the vampire Santino, leader of the Childred of Satan, introduces himself to Marius. He reads Marius's mind, learns of Akasha and Enkil, and requests a meeting with Those Who Must Be Kept. Marius denies him, finding his Satanworshipping coven abhorrent. When Santino insists, Marius threatens to destroy him; Santino withdraws but watches from a distance the keeper of Those Who Must Be Kept.

Marius eventually finds a mortal child from Russia, Andrei, who will later become the vampire Armand. Andrei was abducted by Tartars and is now locked in the dungeon of a brothel. Marius buys the young Andrei, renames him Amadeo, and brings him to live in his palazzo. Marius and Amadeo develop a deep relationship. Amadeo doesn't learn that Marius is a vampire until the night Marius saves Bianca from her extorting relative and his malicious family. Amadeo begs Marius to turn him into a vampire, but Marius refuses. In an attempt to incite Marius's jealousy, Amadeo begins a brief affair with the Englishman Lord Harlech. When Amadeo ends the relationship, Lord Harlech storms into Marius's palazzo in a jealous rage, armed with a poisoned blade, and duels with Amadeo. Amadeo slays him, but Lord Harlech mortally wounds the boy. Bianca nurses Amadeo until Marius arrives. When Bianca leaves, Marius turns him into a vampire.

Marius and Amadeo live together happily as maker and fledgling, both developing deep feelings for Bianca, until Santino and his Satanic coven invade Marius's home, kill most of the boys, set Marius on fire, and kidnap Amadeo. Severely wounded, Marius mentally summons Bianca and receives her permission to turn her into a vampire. She takes him to Akasha and Enkil's shrine in the Alps, where Marius drinks Akasha's blood.

While his health is restored, Bianca, like Pandora before her, helps Marius care for Those Who Must Be Kept. When his wounds more fully heal and he can walk about among mortals, he goes to Raymond Gallant, who is now an old man and who informs Marius that the Talamasca has learned that the mysterious Indian vampire is still controlling Pandora and that they are likely living near Dresden.

Marius takes Bianca, Akasha, and Enkil to Dresden, where he finally reunites with Pandora and discovers that her companion and fledgling, Arjun, is not keeping her against her will after all. Marius begs Pandora to return to him, vowing that he will leave Bianca if she will leave Arjun, but Pandora rejects him and leaves. Bianca overhears Marius and leaves him also.

Nearly fifty years later, when Marius is packing up his belongings to take Akasha and Enkil to another region, he uncovers a note left behind by Pandora on the night they separated, asking him to find her in Moscow and help her leave Arjun. Marius immediately goes to Moscow in search of her, but by then she has already left. He can find no trace of either her or her fledgling lover.

Marius brings Those Who Must Be Kept to an island in the Aegean Sea, somewhere between Greece and Turkey. He remains there for years, caring for the people living on the island, until one night he begins hearing the voice of a young vampire searching for him, calling to him—the vampire Lestat. Hearing Lestat's persistence, Marius leaves his island and finds that Lestat has buried himself underground after his fledgling Nicolas committed suicide and his fledgling mother, Gabrielle, abandoned him. Marius exhumes Lestat, revives him with his own ancient vampire blood, and then takes him back to his island sanctuary. After Lestat awakens, Marius shares some of his history with him, tells him about Those Who Must Be Kept, and swears him to absolute secrecy. When Marius briefly leaves, Lestat goes to the shrine and plays his violin for Akasha. Moved by his bravado, Akasha awakens, drinks his blood, and lets him drink hers also. Full of jealousy and anger, Enkil awakens and attempts to destroy Lestat. Fortunately, Marius saves him, but warns Lestat to leave to let Enkil's anger diminish. Before Lestat

can return, Marius takes Akasha and Enkil to a new hidden location in the frozen lands of northern Canada.

He fills their shrine with every new technology, partly to show them human development but also partly in the hope that they will awaken for him. By the time of the late twentieth century, Akasha and Enkil watch on television how Lestat has returned with new rock music in a successful band that is revealing secrets of vampires and challenging Those Who Must Be Kept to arise. Impressed once again, Akasha rises from her throne for the final time. She kills Enkil and buries Marius beneath several tons of ice. He projects out mental warnings to the other vampires that the Queen has arisen, but she is already flying throughout the world, immolating most of her vampire children. When he is finally freed from the ice by Pandora and Santino, he rendezvouses with many other vampires, including his fledglings Pandora and Armand, at the compound in the Sonoma Mountains belonging to Akasha's mortal enemy, the ancient vampire Maharet. After Maharet informs Marius and the others of her version of the story of the Queen of the Damned and the Legend of the Twins, Akasha appears and offers them a choice of joining her cause for global domination as her servants, or perishing. Marius stands with Maharet and refuses to serve. So do all the others, including Lestat. They all fight against Akasha, but she is indomitable. In the end, Maharet's twin sister, Mekare, suddenly appears, beheads Akasha, consumes her brain and heart, and takes into herself the spirit of Amel, to become the new Queen of the Damned.

Now that Marius is no longer the caretaker of Those Who Must Be Kept, he keeps closer contact with other vampires, especially Armand's fledgling Daniel Molloy, who sinks into madness and bitterness towards Armand. Marius welcomes Daniel into his home, takes care of him, and helps restore his sanity; and in doing so, Marius finds a wonderful companion who also helps him make contact with the modern world.

Marius mourns when, after Lestat returns from his journey with Memnoch the Devil, Armand appears to commit suicide, but Marius's mourning turns to joy when Armand reappears a few months later, having been saved with the help of two mortals, Benji and Sybelle. Marius decides to do Armand a favor and turn Benji and Sybelle into vampires to give Armand excellent immortal companions and also to protect them from mortals seeking to destroy Armand or any vampire. In the beginning, this greatly upsets Armand, but Marius and Daniel both convince him that if Armand had turned them into vampires, they would have been weaker than him, the telepathic connection between them would have been lost, and they would have ended up hating him, the way Daniel had; but with Marius's powerful blood in them, Benji and Sybelle are Armand's equals.

Following this, when Marius is alone one night, he hears another vampire whom he has never before encountered using the Mind Gift to send out a telepathic invitation to any vampire for friendship. Marius responds and meets Thorne, an eighth-century Viking made a vampire by Maharet.

Marius and Thorne tell each other their histories. Marius is surprised to learn how Maharet abandoned Thorne for Mael, and Thorne is enraged at how Santino's injustice towards Marius has gone unpunished. Marius advises Thorne against seeking revenge against Maharet for rejecting him, but sensing that Thorne will not be dissuaded, Marius sends Maharet a telepathic warning. Marius and Thorne go to sleep that morning in Marius's home but awaken the next night at Maharet's Java compound. Much to their mutual surprise, Santino is also there as Maharet's guest. Out of a sense of honor and duty, Marius begs Maharet for vengeance for the wrongs that Santino did against him and Armand, but Maharet does not allow it. Knowing that Marius will not act without Maharet's permission, Thorne does Marius a favor and exacts the old Viking custom of wergeld—or exacting a "man price," often taking a life for a life—and blasts Santino with his powerful Mind Gift until Santino is a bloody pulp. Thorne then uses the Fire Gift to burn Santino's remains to a charred scorch on the ground. Everyone is equally surprised at Thorne's behavior, especially Marius, who, although he would never be so bold as to disobey Maharet, smiles and nods at Thorne, showing his inexpressible gratitude.

Marius relocates to Château de Lioncourt, where Lestat becomes the Prince of the vampire race. The Court of the Prince forms, and Marius is one of its most prominent figures. Arjun challenges Marius's authority by attacking him, but he easily destroys Arjun. Prompted by this event, Marius creates new laws for vampires in the new millennium and helps to guide the formation of this new Court, inspiring Prince Lestat to dub him the "Prime Minister" of all vampires.

For more perspectives on Marius's character, read the *Alphabettery* entries **Akasha, Amel, Arjun, Armand, Avicus, Benji Mahmoud, Bianca Solderini, Enkil, Eudoxia, Great Burning of 4 C.E., Lestat de Lioncourt, Mael, Maharet, Mekare, Pandora, Santino, Sybelle, Teskhamen, Thorne, Those Who Must Be Kept,** and **Zenobia.**

Mark of Cain

• HONORIFIC •

After Rhoshamandes kills Maharet and Khayman, Lestat severs his left arm and, not wanting to take a life for a life, brands him with the mark of Cain—a symbolic order from Prince Lestat to all vampires to neither harm nor kill Rhoshamandes, lest they be harmed or killed themselves. Although the mark spares his life, it is a bane, for wherever Rhoshamandes goes, vampires curse him and spit on him, so that Rhoshamandes will never be accepted into vampire society again.

The concept of the mark of Cain comes from Genesis 4:8–16, where Cain kills his brother Abel, and God makes him a wanderer in the world but places his mark on him, so that no one can kill Cain lest they suffer a sevenfold vengeance.

The mark of Cain appears in *Prince Lestat* (2014) and *Prince Lestat and the Realms of Atlantis* (2016). For more perspectives on the mark of Cain in the Vampire Chronicles, read the *Alphabettery* entries **Khayman, Lestat de Lioncourt, Maharet, Mekare,** and **Rhoshamandes.**

Mark of the Witch

• HONORIFIC •

There are three distinguishing marks that identify a Mayfair witch. The first is being born with red hair. The second is being born with a sixth finger. The third is growing taller than even above-average-height women. For instance, Rowan Mayfair has red hair. Mona Mayfair has a sixth finger. Morrigan Mayfair is very tall. A witch does not need to exhibit all three marks; one is sufficient for identification.

The Mark of the Witch appears in *Blood Canticle* (2003). For more perspectives on the

Mark of the Witch in the Vampire Chronicles, read the *Alphabettery* entries **Mona Mayfair**, **Morrigan Mayfair**, and **Rowan Mayfair**.

Marquisa de Malvrier

• ALIAS •

When Pandora and her fledgling and companion Arjun are residing in Dresden, she takes the name and title Marquisa de Malvrier as an alias to move freely as a mortal throughout the Dresden palace, among other circles of high society. The rank of marquisa is lower than princess yet higher than countess.

The "Marquisa de Malvrier" alias appears in *Blood and Gold* (2001). For more perspectives on this alias, read the *Alphabettery* entries **Arjun**, **Marquis de Malvrier**, and **Pandora**.

Marquis de Lioncourt

• HONORIFIC •

Lord of Château de Lioncourt—the castle atop the mountains in the Massif Central in Avignon, France—the Marquis de Lioncourt is the blind ruler of land falling into decrepitude. His family fortune has been squandered, except for the fortune he receives from his wife, Gabrielle, a beautiful Italian woman. He has seven sons and no daughters; three live to manhood, including the youngest son, Lestat, who matures into a restless dreamer desiring to experience all the pleasures of the world. But the Marquis denies his son's desire to become a monk, stating that the family has no fortune to buy him a cleric's profession. The Marquis later denies his son's desire to become an actor, stating that it is a denigration to the family name. By the time Lestat is a teenager, his father is completely blind; Lestat becomes the provider of the family, going into the woods and hunting for food. Gabrielle, the Marquise, gives Lestat the last of her Italian family fortune, telling him to go to Paris and live the life she dreams of living. During that time, the vampire Magnus turns Lestat into a vampire and gives Lestat his vast fortune before killing himself. Lestat shares that fortune with his family, but when the French Revolution occurs, villagers living near Château de Lioncourt rise up in revolt and kill its inhabitants. The Marquis and Marquise are the only ones to survive. Lestat takes the Marquis with him to New Orleans, to live on the plantation of his new fledgling, Louis. And when the Marquis is on the point of death, Lestat convinces Louis to drink his blood and kill him.

The "Marquis de Lioncourt" title appears in *The Vampire Lestat* (1985). For more perspectives on this title, read the *Alphabettery* entries **Château de Lioncourt, Gabrielle, Lestat de Lioncourt, Louis de Pointe du Lac, Magnus,** and **Marquise de Lioncourt.**

Marquis de Malvrier

• ALIAS •

In an effort to maintain a mortal guise, the vampire Arjun and his maker-companion, Pandora, take the name de Malvrier but add the noble titles of Marquis and Marquisa, to associate among the ranks of nobility in Dresden, particularly in the palace. The rank of marquis is lower than prince yet higher than count.

The "Marquis de Malvrier" alias appears in *Blood and Gold* (2001). For more perspectives on this alias, read the *Alphabettery* entries **Arjun, Marquisa de Malvrier,** and **Pandora.**

Marquise de Lioncourt

• HONORIFIC •

When Gabrielle, a beautiful young Italian noblewoman, marries the Marquis de Lioncourt, lord of Château de Lioncourt in Avignon, France, she becomes the lady of that land and bears for her husband seven sons (only three live to manhood), the youngest of whom is named Lestat. Gabrielle's title does not last longer than the French Revolution, for shortly after the storming of the Bastille, the farmhands living near the castle rise up in revolt and destroy the family and the title. Fortunately for the Marquise, she has already gone to Paris to find her son Lestat, who has been turned into a vampire, and who turns her into a vampire also.

The "Marquise de Lioncourt" title appears

in *The Vampire Lestat* (1985). For more perspectives on this title, read the *Alphabettery* entries **Château de Lioncourt**, **Gabrielle**, **Lestat de Lioncourt**, **Louis de Pointe du Lac**, **Magnus**, and **Marquis de Lioncourt**.

Mary

• MORTAL •

When Aaron Lightner brings Merrick to the Talamasca Motherhouse in New Orleans, Mary is one of his assistants in the Order who helps Merrick situate herself and acclimate to the hospitality of the Motherhouse's environs. Mary lives in the Motherhouse and accompanies Aaron on some of his excursions with Merrick.

Mary appears in *Merrick* (2000). For more perspectives on Mary's character, read the *Alphabettery* entries **Aaron Lightner**, **Merrick Mayfair**, and **Talamasca Order**.

Mary Jane Mayfair

• WITCH •

Mary Jane Mayfair is a character from the Lives of the Mayfair Witches. She is briefly mentioned in *Blood Canticle* (2003).

Mary Jane is born with a sixth finger, like her grandmother Dolly Jean, which is an identifying mark of a Mayfair witch, but Mary Jane's mother hires a Mexican witch doctor to cut off her extra finger to make her appear more normal and less like her witching family. Mary Jane's mother is an alcoholic and a drifter, who drags her daughter through the communes of California. Mary Jane learns how to take care of herself, learning also nursing and truck driving, and even how to kill a man, which she does in San Francisco in self-defense. As an adult, Mary Jane lives with her grandmother Dolly Jean on the Fontevrault plantation, an offshoot of the Riverbend plantation. Although very prosperous in previous centuries, Fontevrault has fallen into ruins by the twentieth century. By the time she is nineteen years old, Mary Jane is a very powerful witch and even demonstrates Julien Mayfair's financial acumen in improving Fontevrault.

Mary Jane visits the Mayfair family in

New Orleans's Garden District, and she realizes that her second cousin, Mona Mayfair, is pregnant with a Taltos child. Upon learning that the father is Rowan Mayfair's husband, Michael Curry, who had his dalliance with Mona after Rowan ran away with Lasher (the Taltos child Rowan and Michael conceived earlier), Mary Jane brings Mona out to Fontevrault where she can give birth in secret. Since Taltos births are extremely difficult and life threatening, particularly to non-Taltos like Mona, Mary Jane and her grandmother Dolly Jean not only assist Mona as she gives birth to her daughter, Morrigan, but also help Mona hide how

Morrigan grows to an adult almost immediately, like all Taltos. Mary Jane even helps Morrigan acquire a birth certificate. Later, Morrigan returns the favor when she becomes the new Designée of the Mayfair Legacy by allotting some funds from the Mayfair fortune to assist in the restoration of Fontevrault plantation.

For more perspectives on Mary Jane Mayfair's character in the Vampire Chronicles, read the *Alphabettery* entries **Designée of the Mayfair Legacy**, **Dolly Jean Mayfair**, **Fontevrault Plantation**, **Michael Curry**, **Mona Mayfair**, **Morrigan Mayfair**, **Rowan Mayfair**, and **Taltos**.

Massif Central

• SANCTUARY •

Located in southern France, this elevated region of a dormant volcano provides the beautiful atmosphere of Lestat's homeland in the Auvergne, where his centuries-old castle, Château de Lioncourt, is situated in a region conveniently hidden on modern maps. A select number of vampires and mortal workmen are privy to the location of Lestat's castle, such as Marius, who can be seen painting

murals throughout the interior of Château de Lioncourt.

The Massif Central appears in *The Vampire Lestat* (1985) and *Prince Lestat* (2014). For more perspectives on Massif Central in the Vampire Chronicles, read the *Alphabettery* entries **Château de Lioncourt**, **Lestat de Lioncourt**, and **Marius**.

Mastema

• IMMORTAL •

Unlike the guardian angels Ramiel and Setheus, who simply protect, the angel Mastema is more aggressive, wearing a suit of armor, carrying a shield and a sword, ready to be on the offensive and attack evil. When Ramiel and Setheus offer to help Vittorio slay the vampires at the Court of the Ruby Grail, they bring him to Mastema, who indeed aids Vittorio's vengeance. When Vittorio kills all but one vampire, Ursula, whom he loves, who turns him into a vampire, Mastema gives Vittorio a great insight into the dignity of human nature, warning him that each time he draws blood, he will know the sacredness of human life.

Mastema appears in *Vittorio the Vampire* (1999). For more perspectives on Mastema in the Vampire Chronicles, read the *Alphabettery* entries **Court of the Ruby Grail**, **Fra Filippo**, **Ramiel**, **Setheus**, **Ursula**, and **Vittorio di Raniari**.

Matteo di Raniari

• MORTAL •

Matteo di Raniari is the younger brother of Vittorio and Bartola di Raniari. Around the age of eleven, a coven of vampires led by Florian appears at Castello Raniari and kills everyone in the compound, family and servants alike, all except Vittorio, who escapes to seek vengeance another day. Matteo and his sister, Bartola, perish together when they are captured by a vampire and beheaded.

Matteo di Raniari appears in *Vittorio the Vampire* (1999). For more perspectives on Matteo's character, read the *Alphabettery* entries **Bartola di Raniari**, **Castello Raniari**, **Florian**, **Lorenzo di Raniari**, **Ursula**, and **Vittorio di Raniari**.

Matthew Godwin

• MORTAL •

When Jesse Reeves is birthed two months prematurely after her mother dies in a car accident, Maharet identifies Jesse in the hospital as a relative and takes her to live with cousins in a lavish, old, two-story apartment on Lexington Avenue in New York. The cousins are Matthew and Maria Godwin. Matthew is a doctor and takes great care of Jesse, providing everything she needs,

namely her English nanny, her grand education, and especially contact with her elusive aunt, Maharet. Jesse eventually leaves them to attend Columbia University.

Matthew Godwin appears in *The Queen of the Damned* (1988). For more perspectives on Matthew's character, read the *Alphabettery* entries **Jesse**, **Maharet**, and **Maria Godwin**.

Matthew Harrison

• MORTAL •

Matthew is the son of Terry Sue and the half brother of Tommy. Although Matthew has a different father, Tommy's father is Pops, who is Quinn Blackwood's grandfather. Because of Tommy's connection to the Blackwood family, Matthew and his siblings receive an excellent education.

Matthew Harrison appears in *Blackwood Farm* (2002). For more perspectives on Matthew's character, read the *Alphabettery* entries **Brittany Harrison**, **Pops**, **Quinn Blackwood**, **Terry Sue Harrison**, and **Tommy Harrison**.

Matthew Kemp

• MORTAL •

Matthew Kemp receives widespread acclamation as an archaeologist of the first major civi-

lizations in Guatemala and Mexico, known as the Olmecs. At the height of his career, he receives a message from a woman in New Orleans named Sandra Mayfair. Little does he know, her common name is Cold Sandra, and she is a member of the Mayfair witch family. She uses her magic to woo him to New Orleans to study the relics she receives from her Great Nananne's older brother, Oncle Vervain, a Voodoo man. Her magic also woos him into marriage, making him the stepfather of her two daughters, the sixteen-year-old Honey in the Sunshine and her younger sister, Merrick, the future fledgling of Louis. Matthew teaches Merrick how to read the ancient words of old spells and sparks in her

a fascination with ancient Olmec mysticism. He takes his new family to Guatemala, where they investigate a mysterious cave. It is in this cave that Matthew contracts an illness and dies shortly thereafter, in his will leaving his wife a small fortune, which she uses to try to escape her life of poverty in New Orleans with her older daughter, an escape that only leads to her and Honey in the Sunshine's murder.

Matthew Kemp appears in *Merrick* (2000). For more perspectives on Matthew's character, read the *Alphabettery* entries **Cold Sandra**, **Great Nananne**, **Honey in the Sunshine**, **Merrick Mayfair**, and **Oncle Vervain**.

Maximus

• MORTAL •

A direct descendant of pre-Romans from the time of Romulus and Remus, Maximus is born shortly before the beginning of the Common Era to a pure-blood Roman family. In time he becomes a wealthy Roman senator, marries the daughter of another wealthy Roman senator, and has five sons and one daughter, whom he names Lydia. Though his wife dies shortly after Lydia's birth, he gives all his children a well-rounded education, especially Lydia, indulging her interest in history and literature. Maximus rejects two proposals made by Marius de Romanus to wed Lydia but has no opportunity of marry-

ing her later when his youngest son, Lucius, betrays the family to Sejanus and his Praetorian Guard, accusing them of treason. *Speculatores* (Roman Army scouts) kill Maximus's sons, and Maximus slits his wrists to die as a noble Roman. But before his death, he helps Lydia escape from Italy into Greece, where she establishes herself as a Greek courtesan and takes the name Pandora; she will one day become Marius's fledgling.

Maximus appears in *Pandora* (1998). For more perspectives on Maximus's character, read the *Alphabettery* entries **Lucius**, **Lydia**, **Marius**, and **Pandora**.

Maxym

• IMMORTAL •

After Amel rebels against Bravennan exploitation of the humans on Earth, Bravennan scientists build immortal and superhuman humanoids, called Replimoids, who will combat Amel. None of the troops they send against Amel are able to defeat him because of his superior intellect and strength. Most convert to Amel's side, particularly a Replimoid named Maxym.

Maxym becomes one of Amel's greatest companions and aids him in the creation of luracastria, along with all the luracastric creations, such as the great city of Atlantis. Despite his fundamental flaws and his imperfections in comparison with the perfection that the Bravennans achieve with Amel,

Maxym serves Amel like a brother, even to the end, when the Bravennans see no other way to defeat Amel and send a meteor shower through space, which pummels planet Earth, specifically right on top of Atlantis. Many Replimoids watch as Amel is destroyed, and they assume that Maxym is destroyed along with him, although, being a Replimoid with the power of immortality, he likely survives into the twenty-first century.

Maxym appears in *Prince Lestat and the Realms of Atlantis* (2016). For more perspectives on Maxym's character, read the *Alphabettery* entries **Amel**, **Atlantis**, **Lestat de Lioncourt**, and **Replimoid**.

Mayfair and Mayfair

• SANCTUARY •

Mayfair and Mayfair is the law firm in the Lives of the Mayfair Witches, founded by Julien Mayfair and his sons, which helps to fund Blackwood Farm. The firm also traces the entire history of the secret Taltos island, finding a clear chain of title transfer from Lost Paradise Resorts to the Secret Isle Corporation, owned by Ash Templeton, otherwise known as Ashlar, a Taltos and the husband

of Morrigan Mayfair, the daughter of Lestat's fledgling, Mona Mayfair.

Mayfair and Mayfair is referred to in *Blackwood Farm* (2002). For more perspectives on Mayfair and Mayfair in the Vampire Chronicles, read the *Alphabettery* entries **Ashlar**, **Ash Templeton**, **Blackwood Farm**, **Julien Mayfair**, **Lestat de Lioncourt**, **Mona Mayfair**, **Morrigan Mayfair**, and **Taltos**.

Mayfair Emerald

• HONORIFIC •

The Mayfair emerald is an intregal part of the Lives of the Mayfair Witches. It enters into the Vampire Chronicles through references in *Blood Canticle* (2003).

When the spirit of Lasher establishes an inbreeding plan to incarnate as a Taltos through a generational line of thirteen Mayfair witches, he also gives to the second witch, Deborah, a beautiful emerald surrounded by gold filigree on a long gold chain. In time, Lasher's name becomes engraved upon the back. The emerald is a symbol of the interdependent relationship: the witch who wields the emerald also controls the spirit of Lasher. Each witch hands the emerald down to her female descendant, who is the next in the generational line of Lasher's plan for incarnation. Thus Suzanne hands the emerald down to her daughter, Deborah, who controls Lasher; Deborah hands the emerald down to her daughter, Charlotte; and so on into the twenty-first century, when the thirteenth witch, Rowan Mayfair, is the last to control Lasher, as well as the final witch in his plan for incarnation.

When the sixth witch, Marie Claudette Mayfair, creates a dynastic tradition of controlling the Mayfair family's significantly increasing income, which she calls the Mayfair Legacy, she makes the Mayfair emerald the token of the Mayfair Legacy's Designée. Whoever wears the emerald is the Designée; and whoever is the Designée controls the family fortune. Thus, after Rowan fulfills her role as the thirteenth witch in Lasher's plan, the Mayfair emerald continues to be handed down to other witches who control the Mayfair wealth. The emerald is passed from Rowan to Mona Mayfair; and from Mona it is handed down to Morrigan Mayfair.

For more perspectives on the Mayfair emerald in the Vampire Chronicles, read the *Alphabettery* entries **Designée of the Mayfair Legacy**, **Julien Mayfair**, **Lasher**, **Mona Mayfair**, **Morrigan Mayfair**, and **Rowan Mayfair**.

Mayfair Legacy

• HONORIFIC •

The Mayfair Legacy is an important facet of the Lives of the Mayfair Witches. On several occasions, the Mayfair Legacy is discussed in *Blood Canticle* (2003), bridging the Mayfairs into the Vampire Chronicles.

When the spirit of Lasher establishes his

plan to become incarnate through selectively inbreeding thirteen generations of the Mayfair witch family, he also provides the Mayfairs with a vast fortune. By the time of the sixth witch, Marie Claudette Mayfair, the Mayfair family is incredibly wealthy. When she establishes the family in Louisiana, she also establishes the Mayfair Legacy to ensure that one witch is the Designée in control of the family wealth, but on two conditions: First, she must keep the family name Mayfair on the day of her marriage and, second, she must wear the Mayfair emerald—a beautiful necklace with a large emerald. The Designée and wearer of the Mayfair emerald is a female witch (except for Julien Mayfair) and has the power to control Lasher. Rowan is the last Designée of the Mayfair Legacy to control the evil spirit. The next Designée, Mona, does not need to control Lasher, since by then he is already dead.

For more perspectives on the Mayfair Legacy in the Vampire Chronicles, read the *Alphabettery* entries **Designée of the Mayfair Legacy, Julien Mayfair, Lasher, Mona Mayfair**, and **Rowan Mayfair**.

Mayfair Medical Center

• SANCTUARY •

Mayfair Medical Center begins in the Lives of the Mayfair Witches as the philanthropic brainchild of Rowan Mayfair, but it ends crossing into the Vampire Chronicles in *Blackwood Farm* (2002) and *Blood Canticle* (2003).

Conceived by Rowan Mayfair, and funded by the Mayfair fortune, as well as by the family's legal firm, Mayfair and Mayfair, the Mayfair Medical Center is a New Orleans institution devoted to research and mostly nonprofit hospitalization. The center draws the top neurologists and neurosurgeons in the nation; it also becomes one of the most innovative centers for neurological issues. After its creation, Dr. Rowan Mayfair becomes the CEO and oversees its research projects and outreach efforts. Rowan's cousin, Mona Mayfair, is treated at Mayfair Medical after she gives birth to her Taltos daughter, Morrigan. And after Morrigan is murdered, Mona brings her body back to Mayfair Medical for research.

For more perspectives on Mayfair Medical Center in the Vampire Chronicles, read the *Alphabettery* entries **Ashlar, Designée of the Mayfair Legacy, Lestat de Lioncourt, Mayfair and Mayfair, Mona Mayfair, Morrigan Mayfair, Rowan Mayfair**, and **Taltos**.

Meditation Center

• SANCTUARY •

Meditation Centers are large auditoriumlike rooms spread throughout the vast city of Atalantaya. They are marked by relief carvings on the outside, one on each side of the entry portal, flanking figures with hands folded and heads bowed. It is the basic posture that people assume once they enter inside the vast silence of the Meditation Center. These centers are Amel's response to the Bravennans' Chambers of Suffering, which transmit human suffering psychically across the universe for consumption in the Realm of Worlds. In these Atalantayan Meditation Centers, people can find peace, despite tears and fears.

Meditation Centers appear in *Prince Lestat and the Realms of Atlantis* (2016). For more perspectives on Meditation Centers in the Vampire Chronicles, read the *Alphabettery* entries **Amel, Atalantaya, Bravennan,** and **Realm of Worlds.**

Mekare

• VAMPIRE •

Mekare is the twin sister of Maharet, Akasha's mortal enemy. Mekare kills Akasha and becomes the next Queen of the Damned until her own death, whence she surrenders Amel to Lestat, who becomes the Prince of all vampires. Mekare appears in *The Vampire Lestat* (1985), *The Queen of the Damned* (1988), *Blood and Gold* (2001), and *Prince Lestat* (2014).

In the northern lands of Israel, more than four thousand years before the Common Era, in the caves of Mount Carmel, two red-haired, green-eyed twins are born into a family of witches. The firstborn is named Mekare; her younger sister, Maharet. For the first sixteen years of their lives, the twin sisters grow up learning their family tradition of communing with spirits. They are aware that spirits are divided into good and bad. They are to avoid the bad whenever possible, yet the good spirits will do them favors, such as manipulating the weather, an integral part of their village life. The village shepherds and potters who trade in the markets of Jericho often come to the twin sisters and their mother for counsel. The witch family communes with the spirits and provides guidance for the village's religious practices. Mekare is a more powerful witch than Maharet. Considered second only to their mother in authority, Mekare leads Maharet and acts as spokeswoman for the two. One spirit they commune with is Amel, who brags how he enjoys the taste of blood.

When the Queen of Egypt, Akasha, summons Mekare and Maharet to the royal court to defend Akasha's position on outlawing ritual cannibalism, the twins refuse. Shortly after this, Mekare and Maharet's mother dies. When the twins prepare to cannibalize their mother according to their witching tradition, the King's steward, Khayman, arrives with the King's army. They slaughter most of the villagers, destroy the village, and force Mekare and Maharet down into Egypt to appear at the royal court.

The King and Queen ask them numerous questions about spirits and the afterlife. Mekare and Maharet answer truthfully, chiefly that the Queen is misguided about her spiritual beliefs and that she does not understand spirits. Enraged by their response, Akasha has them thrown into prison, yet the twins are continually brought back before the court and forced to answer the same questions. At length, Mekare grows tired of the Queen's relentless ignorance; against Maharet's better judgment, Mekare summons to the court the spirit of Amel, who is all too eager to demonstrate his prideful power. The Queen punishes the twins by having them raped by Khayman before the entire court. Afterward, Akasha and Enkil allow the twins to return to their village, where Maharet gives birth to Mekare's niece, Miriam.

The following year, Khayman returns with the royal army and brings the twins back into Egypt before the King and Queen. The twins discover that the spirit of Amel has fused with Akasha's blood, that the fusion transformed Akasha into the world's first blood drinker, and that Akasha has changed Enkil into a blood drinker also. Akasha and Enkil are confused by their unnatural and insatiable bloodlust, and they demand answers from Mekare and Maharet. Maharet suggests that, because spirits are such large entities, one possible way to alleviate the bloodlust is to turn other mortals into vampires, which might more fully dissolve the potency of the spirit's thirst for blood. To test this, Akasha turns Khayman into a vampire against his will, but that does nothing to alleviate her suffering. Mekare mocks Akasha, which infuriates the Queen so much that she sentences them both to death. Mekare then curses Akasha and promises that she will one day return for vengeance, calling her the Queen of the Damned and commencing a prophecy of the Legend of the Twins.

Akasha cuts out Mekare's tongue and plucks out Maharet's eyes. Before the death sentence can be carried out, Khayman helps the twins escape by turning Mekare into a vampire, who then turns her twin sister into a vampire. They flee from prison to Memphis's necropolis Saqqara. Along the way they turn numerous mortals into vampires in an effort to raise an army, called the First Brood, to fight against Akasha and Enkil. Less than a week later, as they are still learning how to hide their victims, the royal army follows their trail and captures the twins. Only Khayman escapes. Because vampirism is still so new, the Queen is afraid of killing another vampire. So she entombs the twins in separate sarcophagi and sets them adrift off different coasts, one to the east and the other to the west, separating Mekare from Maharet for thousands of years. Less than a century after Mekare's tomb washes ashore, she makes her way to the jungles of Peru. She climbs a mountain to a cave above the jungles where she draws cave paintings that tell the story of the Legend of the Twins.

For the next six thousand years, Mekare does not reunite with her sister, not until the twentieth century, when the music of the vampire Lestat rouses Queen Akasha from her statuesque torpor. Akasha immolates the vast majority of vampires. Some of the survivors gather in Maharet's compound in the Sonoma Mountains, where Akasha meets them for a final confrontation. After a brief battle ensues, where it seems that none can defeat the Queen of the Damned, Mekare arrives, covered in a thin layer of soil, having recently exhumed herself from the earth. Mekare clashes with Akasha and decapitates her. As the life drains from the Queen, vampire existence is also being extinguished, until Mekare, in performing their ancient ritual of cannibalizing a mother, consumes Akasha's brain and heart, effectively taking into herself Amel, the Sacred Core, and becoming the new Queen of the Damned and host carrier of vampire existence.

Mekare accompanies her sister back to the Sonoma Compound, but the two eventually relocate to Maharet's secluded compound in Java, Indonesia. Mekare is so traumatized by the past six thousand years that she resembles an impassive animal. Not even Lestat feels entirely safe around her, not knowing whether she is friendly or fearsome. Maharet spends many nights by Mekare's side, reading to her, speaking with her, walking beside her, singing to her, and doing numerous other activities to try to heal Mekare's trauma and restore the sister she loves. Mekare does show Maharet love, but not in the way she used

to, when they were living with their family at Mount Carmel. Maharet is devastated, having spent centuries seeking the long-lost sister she remembers.

When the young vampire scientist Fareed, fledgling of Seth, Akasha's son, replaces Maharet's eyes with permanent immortal eyes, Maharet has Fareed's computer equipment transferred from New York to their compound in Java. Fareed commences numerous tests and experiments on Mekare to try to restore her sanity, but all of the experiments are for naught. In the end, Fareed can only conclude that Mekare is like a waking-coma victim, alive yet unconscious. He does discover that Amel, inside Mekare, has a physical component that is possibly capable of being manipulated, like any common creature under the proverbial knife. But nothing more comes of his deductions until much later. Fareed also offers to give Mekare a new tongue, in much the same way he'd given Maharet new immortal eyes, but there is no way to communicate this to Mekare. Fareed attempts to narcotize her three times, but she is inactive only for brief intervals. Maharet tries assisting Fareed's attempts by singing and caressing Mekare, but he is able to take small samples of Mekare's hair and skin. Replacing her tongue proves impossible. Ultimately it is concluded that Mekare's unimaginable trauma is preventing her from knowing the greatness of her power, for she does not even seem to know that she has fulfilled her curse by defeating the Queen of the Damned.

Mekare's queenship only lasts for a few decades. The great damage of her mind brings Amel to consciousness. He can no longer abide living inside her traumatized mind, which is detrimentally wounded by the last six millennia of trauma. He also becomes aware of Maharet's obsessive idea to end her life and Mekare's by throwing them both into an active volcano. Seeking to escape, Amel convinces the five-thousand-year-old Rhoshamandes to destroy Mekare and take into himself the Sacred Core. Amel shows Rhoshamandes and his fledgling Benedict the location of Maharet's hidden compound. Mekare observes them arrive, but her trauma prevents her from caring about their presence. Rhoshamandes and Benedict decapitate both Maharet and Khayman and immolate their remains with the Fire Gift. They kidnap Mekare and extort Lestat and the other vampires, demanding that Fareed perform surgery that can successfully transfer Amel, the Sacred Core, from Mekare into Rhoshamandes, killing Mekare in the process. Lestat and the other vampires rescue Mekare and return her safely to their vampire sanctuary.

When Lestat is alone, Mekare approaches him. Aware that she wants to be with her sister in death, he watches her reach up and pluck out her right eyeball. As the blood drains from her eye socket down her cheek, she gives herself to Lestat. Reluctantly accepting her, Lestat destroys Mekare by sucking her brain through her eye socket, taking into himself Amel, becoming the new host carrier of vampire existence, and receiving the title "Prince Lestat."

As Mekare's remains lay at his feet, her skin, bones, and organs become as translucent as glass. The vampire coven buries Mekare's remains in the rear garden, surrounded by flowers. Two vampires return to the Amazon to retrieve the remains of Maharet and Khayman, then the entire tribe buries Khayman near Mekare before resting Maharet right beside Mekare, so that the two sisters will be together forever.

For more perspectives on Mekare's character, read the *Alphabettery* entries **Akasha**, **Benedict**, **Enkil**, **Khayman**, **Lestat de Lioncourt**, **Maharet**, and **Rhoshamandes**.

Memnoch the Devil

• VAMPIRE CHRONICLE •

In the fifth book of the Vampire Chronicles, Lestat writes how he meets a spirit who takes him on a spiritual journey. Memnoch wants Lestat to be a lieutenant angel, with the freedom to enter and exit the metaphysical existence of the afterlife. Lestat contemplates his offer while Memnoch leads his spiritual journey through Heaven and Hell, meeting God, Jesus Christ, and many angels, and they discuss morality in the Divine Plan. Memnoch even takes Lestat back in time to Jesus Christ's crucifixion. When Veronica wipes Jesus's face with her veil, Jesus takes her veil and gives it to Lestat. Memnoch attempts to take the veil from him but only snatches out Lestat's left eye as he escapes back to the natural world. Lestat shows the veil to Dora, a famous televangelist, who shows it to the world. Meanwhile, Memnoch sends Lestat a note with his eye wrapped inside. The note thanks Lestat for his assistance in Memnoch's plan, leaving Lestat to wonder if he has truly been tricked by the Devil.

For more perspectives on *Memnoch the Devil* in the Vampire Chronicles, read the *Alphabettery* entries **Dora, Lestat de Lioncourt,** and **Memnoch**.

Memnoch

• IMMORTAL •

Memnoch is the principal antagonist in his eponymous book. He takes Lestat on a Dantesque tour through Heaven and Hell, offering Lestat a choice to serve the will of a higher power. Memnoch appears only in *Memnoch the Devil* (1995), but he is mentioned in *Blood Canticle* (2003), *Prince Lestat* (2014), *Prince Lestat and the Realms of Atlantis* (2016), and *Blood Communion* (2018).

In the 1990s, after Lestat reclaims his rightful vampire body from Raglan James, the Body Thief, he encounters another individual, who says his name is Memnoch and refers to himself as the Devil of the Judeo-Christian belief system. Intrigued, Lestat follows Memnoch on a journey beyond time, into the supernatural realms of Heaven, Purgatory, and Hell. Memnoch explains to Lestat how he is the first angel that God created, how God held him in such great esteem that Memnoch became second-in-command throughout all of Heaven, and how Memnoch himself once commanded more than one-third of Heaven's angelic hosts. Memnoch then explains how, after God created human beings, Memnoch argued with God over the problem of suffering and death. Memnoch insisted that human torment and mortality are antithetical to the God of love and creation. Memnoch next attempted to empirically demonstrate the faultiness in God's creative plans by creating for himself a body of flesh and bone, into which he entered and used to interact with men and women, a defiance of God's command. For his defiant actions, God banished Memnoch from Heaven eternally. Throughout all of this, Memnoch shows Lestat the beauty of creation, the horrible facets of Hell, the penitential echelons of Purgatory, and the mystical divinity of Heaven. Memnoch even takes Lestat to Calvary, where Jesus Christ was crucified. After drinking Jesus's blood, Lestat wipes Jesus's face with Veronica's Veil and Jesus's face miraculously appears as an icon on the veil. In the end, Memnoch gives Lestat a choice: either serve the Devil, as the Children of Satan attempted to do centuries earlier throughout Europe during Late Antiquity and the Middle Ages, or serve God. With his usual bravado, Lestat refuses to serve either, serving only himself instead. Memnoch tries to take Veronica's Veil away from Lestat but only plucks out Lestat's left eye. Lestat flees from his supernatural pilgrimage and returns to the world; and Memnoch lets him go, since this is all according to Memnoch's plan. He explains this to Lestat when he sends Maharet to give him a ball of crumpled vellum, at the center of which is Lestat's eye. Unraveling the vellum and returning his eye to his socket, Lestat discovers that the vellum is decorated with beautiful ornamentation, a design of swirling shapes, which he eventually understands is writing that only he can make out. It is Memnoch's archaic writing, a mere note, simply thanking Lestat for a job perfectly well done.

For more perspectives on the Memnoch character in the Vampire Chronicles, read the *Alphabettery* entries **Dora**, **Lestat de Lioncourt**, **Maharet**, **Memnoch**, **Ordinary Man**, and **Roger**.

Mentor

• HONORIFIC •

Most often, when mortals are turned into vampires, they refer to the vampire who makes them as their maker. In some cases, fledglings will refer to their maker as a mentor. Such is the case with Fareed and Seth. Since Seth is more than six thousand years old when he makes Fareed and has studied various healing arts in his long lifetime, Fareed, who is also a medical doctor, refers to Seth as his mentor.

Mentors appear in *Prince Lestat* (2014). For more perspectives on mentors in the Vampire Chronicles, read the *Alphabettery* entries **Fareed Bhansali**, **Fledgling**, **Maker**, and **Seth**.

Merrick

• VAMPIRE CHRONICLE •

In the seventh book in the Vampire Chronicles (not including *Pandora* and *Vittorio the Vampire*), David Talbot writes the tale of his former apprentice in the Talamasca, Merrick Mayfair, a member of the Mayfair witch family, and her involvement with Lestat's fledgling Louis, who recently encountered the spirit of Claudia. Louis asks David for help, and David asks his former apprentice in the Talamasca, Merrick, for further help. David recounts how he discovered Merrick's profound psychic abilities after her stepfather died on an Olmec expedition and after her mother and sister were murdered. Merrick and David enjoy many adventures together, one of which is returning to the cave where her stepfather was killed, where they find a mask that, when worn, reveals the presence of spirits. Merrick helps Louis and David contact Claudia, but the experience is hurtful to Louis. Despite his feelings about Claudia, he develops deep feelings for Merrick and turns her into a vampire, at which point she reveals that this has been her plan from the beginning. She has summoned Claudia, she has drawn Louis and David to her, all because she wants to become an immortal.

For more perspectives on this Vampire Chronicle, read the *Alphabettery* entries **Claudia**, **David Talbot**, **Lestat de Lioncourt**, **Louis de Pointe du Lac**, and **Merrick Mayfair**.

Merrick Mayfair

• IMMORTAL •

Merrick is both a Mayfair witch and the vampire fledgling of Louis. She is the only known witch to have used her witching ability to seduce a vampire into turning her into an immortal blood drinker. She is also the only known vampire to selflessly burn herself to death in a fire to bring a soul to Heaven. Merrick appears in *Merrick* (2000) and *Blackwood Farm* (2002).

Baptized with the name Merrique Marie Louise Mayfair, Merrick is a very powerful witch, exhibiting surprisingly awesome powers from an early age, as her family is only a branch of the famous Mayfair witch family, distantly related to Julien Mayfair on her mother's and maternal grandmother's side.

Merrick never knew her father. She lives with her mother, Cold Sandra, and her sister, Honey in the Sunshine, at the house of her godmother, Great Nananne, in an older part of New Orleans. Her mother uses her witching ability to lure the affection of Matthew Kemp, an Olmec archaeologist. Matthew weds Cold Sandra and takes Honey in the Sunshine and Merrick to Guatemala to explore Olmec caves. In one cave, Matthew contracts an illness and soon dies. Cold Sandra inherits his small fortune, enough to leave New Orleans and start a new life, but only with one of her daughters, Honey in the Sunshine. Leaving Merrick in the care of Great Nananne, Cold Sandra and Honey in the Sunshine drive away but are soon after murdered; their bodies are left in their car, and the car is sunk in a Lafayette swamp.

With her witching ability, Merrick often

communicates with the ghosts of her mother and dead sister, who will sometimes possess Merrick to voice how she feels robbed of life. Merrick's powerful abilities catch the attention of Aaron Lightner, an important and knowledgeable member of the Talamasca Order. He brings Merrick to the attention of Superior General of the Talamasca David Talbot, who also recognizes Merrick's great ability. Following the death of Great Nananne, David takes Merrick into his home, makes her his ward, and gives her an unofficial education in the Talamasca.

Merrick finishes her early schooling, goes to the university, and in due course becomes a member of the Order herself. David further takes her under his wing as his apprentice. Growing in witching power, Merrick eventually learns how to resist being possessed by Honey in the Sunshine. Together, Merrick and David work on many missions for almost a decade; and on one occasion, they have a dalliance, which David ultimately regrets. One of the more memorable missions they go on together is to Central America, to the cave that infected Merrick's stepfather, Matthew, with a deadly disease. In the cave, they discover spirits protecting a sacred mask that, when worn, reveals to the wearer the presence of spirits as if they are incarnate beings. On that same mission, David also becomes deathly ill, but is eventually cured of his illness and survives to become Lestat's fledgling vampire.

Merrick and David grow apart. The last she hears is that he died helping the vampire Lestat retrieve his vampire body from the Body Thief, Raglan James. Merrick researches David's death until she learns that he switched bodies with Raglan, that Lestat killed Raglan in David's former body, and that Lestat has turned David in Raglan's body into a vampire.

Merrick uses her magic to draw the attention of both David and the vampire Louis, with the hope of tricking them into turning her into a vampire, too. David approaches, reveals to her not simply that he is a vampire but also that he needs her help because Louis desires to commune with the spirit of Claudia.

Merrick warns them that she can summon Claudia's spirit, but she has no guarantee that it will actually be Claudia herself: it might be a different spirit tricking them, or it might be the spirit of Claudia confused by her death. Regardless, Louis is determined to have Merrick perform this ceremony. The spirit of Claudia appears and behaves very cruelly towards Louis, calling him names and telling him that the only reason she liked him more than Lestat is because Louis is easier to manipulate. After Claudia's spirit disappears, Louis is convinced that what he saw was real and that all she spoke was a sad truth. At the same time, he also feels a deep love for Merrick and turns her into a vampire, fulfilling her own desire.

At first, David is furious that Merrick used her magic to trick them into giving her the Dark Gift. But his anger does not last long, since, after experiencing Claudia's remarks, Louis attempts suicide by putting his coffin in a place that will be exposed to the sunrise. Ultimately, his suicide attempt fails, but he is badly burned and is saved by the combined blood of Merrick, David, and Lestat, who gives Merrick some of his blood to make her more powerful in helping Louis recover. Merrick settles back in New Orleans, living with Lestat, David, and Louis, a small coven that will not allow any other vampires in the city.

When Lestat is contacted by Quinn Blackwood, who is bedeviled by a ghost called Goblin, Lestat enlists the aid of Merrick. She helps them discover that Goblin is actually the ghost of Quinn's twin brother, Garwain, who died at birth. Merrick informs them that the only way for Goblin to ascend into the light of the afterlife is to perform a ritual exorcism, which involves the proper text, a large fire, and Garwain Blackwood's remains. Despite Merrick's best effort, Goblin is not exorcised by the ritual alone, not until Merrick takes Garwain's cadaver and leaps into the fire, burning herself and the cadaver together, so that she can carry Garwain's spirit into the afterlife. Lestat strives to save Merrick by pulling her from the fire, but it is too late. All that remains of Merrick Mayfair is ashes.

For more perspectives on Merrick's character, read the *Alphabettery* entries **Aaron Lightner, Claudia, Cold Sandra, David Talbot, Garwain Blackwood, Goblin, Great Nananne, Honey in the Sunshine, Lestat de Lioncourt, Louis de Pointe du Lac, Matthew Kemp, Quinn Blackwood, Raglan James**, and **Talamasca Order**.

Merrique Marie Louise Mayfair

• MORTAL •

When Merrick Mayfair first encounters David Talbot, while he is still the Superior General of the Talamasca Order, before they are both turned into vampires (he by Lestat and she by Louis), Merrick introduces herself to David by her old Creole name, Merrique, and even pronounces it with a slight touch of an old French accent.

The birth name Merrique appears in *Merrick* (2000). For more perspectives on her character, read the *Alphabettery* entries **David Talbot, Garwain Blackwood, Great Nananne, Honey in the Sunshine, Lestat de Lioncourt, Louis de Pointe du Lac, Merrick Mayfair**, and **Talamasca Order**.

Michael Curry

• WITCH •

Michael Curry is a witch in the Mayfair family and the husband of Rowan Mayfair. He saves Rowan from Lasher and also becomes the father of two Taltos, Morrigan and the child with whom Lasher fuses. Although he is in the Lives of the Mayfair Witches, he crosses over into the Vampire Chronicles in *Blood Canticle* (2003).

Born Michael James Timothy Curry, he is in the direct line of descent of the affair between Julien Mayfair and the nun Sister Bridget Marie, making Michael the great-great-grandson of Julien, the only male witch among thirteen generations of female witches who control the evil spirit Lasher. Growing up in New Orleans's Irish Channel, Michael demonstrates the witching ability to see Lasher in his youth. He moves to San Francisco, where he continues his education and eventually becomes a contractor. He meets the love of his life, Rowan Mayfair, who also happens to be Julien Mayfair's great-great-granddaughter from a different line in the family, from Julien's affair with his daughter, Mary Beth, whom he'd had with his sister, Katherine. Michael and Rowan meet when he drowns in the ocean; Rowan, a medical doctor, revives him after he had been dead for an hour. Returning to life, Michael feels as if he saw a vision in death, which urges him to a higher purpose.

Shortly after the romantic relationship commences between Michael and Rowan, he is approached by Aaron Lightner, the member of the Talamasca responsible for chronicling the Mayfair family of witches. From Aaron, Michael learns more about his own Mayfair family, especially that Rowan is his family relation; but when Rowan was born, she was taken to San Francisco, where knowledge of her Mayfair family has been kept hidden from her. Impressed with Michael's psychic abilities, Aaron invites him to become a member of the Talamasca Order. Michael goes to New Orleans to investigate this further; Rowan follows him; they marry and restore the Mayfair First Street house.

For much of their courtship, Rowan keeps in contact with the evil spirit Lasher, who has planned for her to be the thirteenth witch in his three-hundred-year breeding program. According to his plan, Lasher would become incarnate by fusing with a Taltos child that Rowan would conceive with Michael. Rowan is conflicted about this, not desiring to impede her relationship with Michael, though she is also scientifically intrigued by the possibility of Lasher's incarnation through her.

Not long after their wedding, Rowan and Michael conceive a child. She attempts to hide the pregnancy from Lasher, but he appeals to her scientific mind and convinces her to allow him to combine with the fetus. Rowan temporarily incapacitates Michael by injecting him with a sedative. Like all Taltos births, Rowan carries the child to term very quickly, gives birth to him painfully, and watches him immediately grow into an adult with infant skin. When Michael awakens and discovers what has happened, he confronts Lasher and Rowan, but Lasher attacks Michael and nearly drowns him in the backyard pool.

As Rowan and Lasher run away together, Michael remains in a stupor. During that time Mona Mayfair seduces Michael, with the assistance of the ghost of Julien Mayfair. Mona becomes pregnant with Michael's child, a Taltos girl, whom Mona names Morrigan. Rowan returns to Michael in New Orleans, after Lasher betrays, tortures, and rapes her, and after she gives birth to another Taltos, Emaleth, who, like Lasher and other Taltos, grows into an adult almost instantly. Lasher eventually confronts Rowan, but Michael kills Lasher, and Rowan kills Emaleth. Afterward, Michael and Rowan remain together, having no more children.

For more perspectives on Michael Curry in the Vampire Chronicles, read the *Alphabettery* entries **Aaron Lightner**, **Emaleth**, **Lasher**, **Mona Mayfair**, **Morrigan Mayfair**, **Rowan Mayfair**, and **Taltos**.

Michael the Archangel

• IMMORTAL •

Michael the Archangel is one of the most important angels in the Heavenly Host and a prince of the first rank who defends Israel. In the war in Heaven, Michael defeats Satan and throws him into Hell along with all the other fallen angels.

When Lestat goes on his pilgrimage through Heaven and Hell, Michael the Archangel is one of the angels whom he encounters. Michael is a friend to all angels, except when they defy the plan of God. Michael always trusts God and casts out of Heaven any and all enemies of God's loving plan for creation.

In the book *Memnoch the Devil* (1995), Michael the Archangel is portrayed as being frightened for Memnoch. For more perspectives on Michael the Archangel in the Vampire Chronicles, read the *Alphabettery* entries **Lestat de Lioncourt** and **Memnoch**.

Mind Gift

• VAMPIRE ABILITY •

The Mind Gift is a general reference to the psychic abilities of vampires, which allow them to perform three principal functions: telepathy, telekinesis, and pyrokinesis. With the Mind Gift, a vampire is able to read mortals' minds, especially when the vampire is asleep in a coffin or has dug far below the earth, remaining in a century-long torpor. The Mind Gift also allows vampires to telepathically perceive the thoughts and mental images of mortals and immortals alike and telekinetically move objects, such as unlocking and opening doors, turning off car engines, pushing immortals to the ground, pulling mortals closer, rupturing a blood vessel in the brain, breaking a bone, and more.

The Mind Gift is partially hindered in the maker-fledgling relationship. After a vampire transforms a mortal into another blood drinker, the maker and fledgling lose all telepathic communication, although each can still affect the other telekinetically.

Like the Fire Gift and the Cloud Gift, the Mind Gift is an ability that develops over time, usually over the course of many centuries. Although minor abilities arise early on, such as the ability to read thoughts after a century or two, the greater abilities of telekinesis can take as long as a thousand years to develop.

The full ability of the Mind Gift can also be inherited through the blood. When an immortal is turned into a vampire with the blood of an ancient vampire (for example, Jesse Reeves by Maharet), or when a younger vampire drinks the blood of an older vampire (Lestat drinking from Akasha), that young vampire gains the full power of the Mind Gift, able to naturally employ telepathy, telekinesis, and pyrokinesis whenever needed.

Only one known method is used to prevent vampires from employing the Mind Gift, which is to wrap them totally in iron binds, the way Cyril wraps Baudwin. This completely prevents the vampire from using any form of telepathy.

The Mind Gift appears in *The Vampire Lestat* (1985), *The Queen of the Damned* (1988), *Prince Lestat* (2014), and *Blood Communion* (2018). For more perspectives on the Mind Gift in the Vampire Chronicles, read the *Alphabettery* entries **Akasha**, **Blood Curse**, **Cloud Gift**, **Crippling Gift**, **Dark Gift**, **Fire Gift**, **Iron Curse**, **Jesse**, **Lestat de Lioncourt**, **Maharet**, **Mind Gift**, and **Spell Gift**.

Miravelle

• TALTOS •

Miravelle is one of the four Taltos children of Morrigan Mayfair and Ashlar. Along with her brothers, Silas and Oberon, and her sister, Lorkyn, she lives with other Taltos on a secret island owned by her father. Her brother Silas begins secretly poisoning her parents to weaken them, as part of a plan for open rebellion to stop the threat of other mortals living on nearby islands, particularly the drug lord Rodrigo, who lives on the nearest island. When Miravelle's parents are too weak to resist because of being poisoned, Silas captures his family and any other Taltos who reject his rebellion, which lasts two years. Miravelle and Morrigan attempt to stop Silas by blinding him with a screwdriver, but Silas's rebellion is undaunted. He attacks Rodrigo, but Rodrigo retaliates by coming to the island and gunning down Silas and the rebelling Taltos.

Rodrigo then locks Miravelle's parents inside the compound's large freezer, where they freeze to death. The island is eventually liberated by Miravelle's grandmother (Morrigan's mother), Mona Mayfair, who has been turned into a vampire. Accompanying her is her maker, Lestat, and her paramour, Quinn Blackwood. After the three vampires destroy all the Drug Merchants, they find Miravelle's parents in the freezer, covered in frost, holding each other like sleeping angels. Mona takes Morrigan's and Ashlar's bodies back to Mayfair Medical for examination. She also invites her granddaughter Miravelle, along with Oberon and Lorkyn, to New Orleans, so that they can be a family together.

Miravelle appears in *Blood Canticle* (2003). For more perspectives on Miravelle in the Vampire Chronicles, read the *Alphabettery* entries **Ashlar, Lestat de Lioncourt, Lorkyn, Mayfair Medical Center, Mona Mayfair, Morrigan Mayfair, Oberon, Quinn Blackwood, Silas,** and **Taltos.**

Miriam

• WITCH •

When Akasha orders Khayman to rape Maharet and Mekare before the royal court of ancient Egypt, Maharet becomes pregnant with a daughter. She and her sister return to their village in the caves of Mount Carmel, where Maharet gives birth and names her daughter Miriam.

Many years after Maharet and Mekare are

forced to return to Egypt, where they are turned into vampires, Maharet returns to her village to discover that her daughter, Miriam, has grown into a woman and will soon have daughters of her own. Maharet introduces herself to her daughter as a distant relative, tells her stories of the Time Before the Moon, and urges her to never use her witchcraft to commune with spirits. From a distance, Maharet watches her daughter become a grandmother, then a great-grandmother. Not long after this, Maharet is inspired to begin chronicling the growth of her family, beginning with her daughter, Miriam.

Miriam appears in *The Queen of the Damned* (1988). For more perspectives on Miriam's character, read the *Alphabettery* entries **Akasha**, **Enkil**, **Khayman**, **Maharet**, **Mekare**, and **Time Before the Moon**.

Miriam Reeves

• WITCH •

Miriam Reeves is a witch in a long line of witches, cataloged in the vampire Maharet's Great Family. Maharet's cataloging shows that Miriam is the descendant of Alice, Alice is the descendant of Carlotta, Carlotta is the descendant of Jane Marie, the descendant of Anne, the descendant of Janet Belle, of Elizabeth, of Louise, of Frances, of Frieda, of Dagmar, all the way back to Maharet's own daughter, Miriam. All of them are witches, dating back four thousand years before the Common Era and even further back, to the Time Before the Moon. The generations migrated out of Palestine into Mesopotamia, then to Asia Minor, then Russia, then Eastern Europe, and finally into the United States, spreading Maharet's Great Family— and Miriam's extended family—all over the world.

While Miriam is seven months pregnant with a daughter during the late twentieth century, she dies in a car accident. Her daughter is born prematurely and hospitalized until Maharet appears, identifies the newborn as Jessica Miriam Reeves (nicknamed Jesse), and delivers Jesse to Matthew and Maria Godwin, who adopt Jesse as their own daughter. Over the years, Miriam's spirit appears to Jesse, who, as a witch, has the natural ability to communicate with spirits. But when Jesse is mortally wounded at the concert of the Vampire Lestat band, Maharet reluctantly transforms Jesse into a vampire. As the transformation into vampire effectively removes all witching abilities, Miriam will never again be able to appear to her daughter. Her spirit watches the transformation with an unmerciful expression while she also coldly hears Maharet's final words to Jesse as a mortal: "Say farewell then, my darling, to Miriam."

Miriam Reeves appears in *The Queen of*

the Damned (1988). For more perspectives on Miriam's character, read the *Alphabettery* entries **Great Family, Jesse, Maharet, Miriam**, and **Time Before the Moon**.

Mitka

• VAMPIRE •

Mitka is born Dmitri Fontayne in Saint Petersburg, Russia, in the 1700s. His father is a Parisian, and his mother is a Russian countess, providing Mitka with fluency in French, Russian, and eventually English. His parents die young, but Mitka is able to find a position in the court of Catherine the Great, serving as a translator and tutor to a noble household. At the age of thirty-four, he answers an advertisement by Marquisa de Malvrier, who is in need of a librarian, and soon discovers that the Marquis and Marquisa de Malvrier are the vampires Arjun and Pandora. She falls in love with Mitka and turns him into a vampire. Arjun is furious and banishes Mitka from Russia. Pandora sends Mitka away with a small fortune. He roams for the next two hundred years until the 1930s, when he buys a beautiful home in New Orleans, while Lestat is underground, having sunk into his second torpor.

Mitka invites Prince Lestat to his home in the twenty-first century, asking for his assistance to fend off rogue vampires who have destroyed his mortal servants. Lestat, Thorne, and Cyril arrive and kill the rogue vampires. Lestat is immediately attracted to Mitka, who desires to join Lestat's Court of the Prince at Château de Lioncourt but is worried that Arjun will not allow it. He also warns Lestat that the ancient vampire Baudwin seeks to destroy him and his Court of the Prince. Lestat returns to Court and discovers that Marius has killed Arjun in self-defense. Lestat goes back to New Orleans to speak with Mitka and is attacked by Baudwin. Cyril binds Baudwin in iron bars and ushers him to the Château de Lioncourt dungeon, where Baudwin remains until his maker, Santh, destroys him. Mitka joins Lestat's Court, where he becomes excellent companions with Pandora, Bianca, Benji, and Sybelle, but most especially with Louis, with whom he feels a special kindred.

Mitka appears in *Blood Communion* (2018). For more perspectives on Mitka's character, read the *Alphabettery* entries **Baudwin, Dmitri Fontayne, Château de Lioncourt, Lestat de Lioncourt, Marius**, and **Pandora**.

Mojo

• MORTAL •

Shortly before Lestat and Raglan James agree to switch bodies, Lestat discovers a German shepherd who lives behind Raglan's home in Georgetown. Lestat adopts the dog, partly as a means of protection after having entered into Raglan James's mortal body. After Raglan betrays Lestat by putting him in a dying mortal body before running off with Lestat's vampire body, Mojo remains one of Lestat's most faithful friends, in comparison with Louis and Marius, who will not turn Lestat back into a vampire. After Lestat regains his vampire body, he officially adopts Mojo and brings the dog back with him to live in New Orleans.

Mojo appears in *The Tale of the Body Thief* (1992). For more perspectives on Mojo in the Vampire Chronicles, read the *Alphabettery* entries **Lestat de Lioncourt**, **Louis de Pointe du Lac**, **Marius**, and **Raglan James**.

Mona Mayfair

• VAMPIRE •

Mona Mayfair is the most pivotal character to cross over between the Lives of the Mayfair Witches and the Vampire Chronicles. She is the cousin of Rowan Mayfair, the paramour of Quinn Blackwood, the Designée of the Mayfair Legacy, the mother of Morrigan the Taltos, and the vampire fledgling of Louis. Mona appears in *Blackwood Farm* (2002) and *Blood Canticle* (2003).

Born with a sixth finger, which the Mayfair family considers to be the Mark of the Witch, Mona Mayfair is one of the most powerful witches in the family, as well as a competent young woman, capable of great feats of cunning. While creating a computer program that traces the genealogy of the Mayfair family, she grows increasingly interested in family history and lineage. By the time she is thirteen years old, she begins to realize her power to seduce men, particularly the men in the Mayfair family. Despite the fact that she is in a semi-prearranged marriage to her cousin Pierce Mayfair, she dresses as an innocent child, Lolita-like, wearing baby-doll clothes with ribbons in her hair, and has many casual encounters with many members of her family. Not simply adventurous, but also highly intelligent, Mona is one of the principal driving forces in commencing construction on Mayfair Medical Center, since, after Rowan, Mona is next in line to become the Designée of the Mayfair Legacy.

When Rowan disappears with Lasher, Michael Curry, her husband, nearly dies and falls into a stupor. To rouse him, the ghost of Julien Mayfair helps Mona sneak into the First Street house and seduce Michael. After their brief affair, Michael goes in search of Rowan, and Mona becomes pregnant with a Taltos child. Like all Taltos children, the fetus grows very quickly in her womb and communicates telepathically with her. Mona can hear the sound of the fetus's voice, knows that it is a girl, that she will be called Morrigan, and that she will have beautiful red hair, like all powerful Mayfair witches.

As Morrigan continues to develop rapidly in Mona's womb, Mona's second cousin, Mary Jane Mayfair, invites Mona to the second Mayfair plantation, Fontevrault, where she can give birth in secret. Mary Jane's grandmother Dolly Jean assists in the birth, which, like all Taltos births, happens very quickly and very painfully for Mona. Mary Jane helps Mona acquire a birth certificate for Morrigan while Dolly Jean tells Mona about the legend of Taltos children, how they are called Walking Babies because of their rapid growth. Morrigan grows into an adult instantly; in an hour she looks almost exactly like Mona. Fearful that Morrigan will be treated similar to Rowan's Taltos child, Lasher, whom Michael killed, Mona declares that Morrigan will be the Designée of the Mayfair Legacy, ensuring her place by bequeathing to her the fabled Mayfair emerald.

Morrigan grows and learns quickly, and she has an increasing desire to know more about the Mayfairs, as well as other Taltos like herself. When Mona finally takes Morrigan to the First Street house in New Orleans, she discovers that Rowan and Michael have recently returned from avenging the death of Aaron Lightner with the assistance of another Taltos, the ancient Ashlar. When Ashlar unexpectedly arrives at the First Street house, he and Morrigan are instantly attracted to each other and run away together.

Before she can search for her daughter, Mona's unnatural pregnancy with Morrigan makes her critically ill, and she needs to be hospitalized at Mayfair Medical. While in treatment, Mona happens to encounter Quinn Blackwood, who is recovering from serious wounds inflicted upon him by the vampire Petronia. Mona and Quinn soon begin developing amorous feelings for each other. Their relationship burgeons into such a passionate romance that they liken one another to tragic figures of literature and history. Quinn refers to Mona as his Ophelia, from Shakespeare's tragedy *Hamlet*; and she refers to Quinn as her Abelard, from the tragic historical love of Abelard and Héloïse. Their time together is cut short when Quinn's aunt Queen requests that he accompany her on a tour of Europe, as her advanced age prevents her from any future journeys. Reluctantly, Quinn agrees, but he and Mona promise to correspond. The European tour lasts three years. Mona and Quinn correspond with each other by email, he signing off as "Noble Abelard" and she as "Ophelia Immortal." During that time, Mona's condition mortally worsens. After Quinn returns from Europe, he learns of Mona's critical state, but before he can visit her, he is turned into a vampire against his will by the very same Petronia who wounded him so severely earlier. Eventually, Mona decides that she will not die in that hospital but will die in the bed of her paramour. She orders a limousine to be filled with flowers. Then she is driven to Quinn's home at Blackwood Farm, where she covers his bed in flowers, so she can die among them like Ophelia:

There with fantastic garlands did she come
Of crow-flowers, nettles, daisies, and long
    purples
That liberal shepherds give a grosser name,
But our cold maids do dead men's fingers call
    them:
There, on the pendent boughs her coronet
    weeds
Clambering to hang, an envious sliver broke;
When down her weedy trophies and herself
Fell in the weeping brook. Her clothes spread
    wide;
And, mermaid-like, awhile they bore her up.
            —*Hamlet*, ACT 4, SCENE 7

Meanwhile, Quinn has befriended the vampire Lestat, who helps him exorcise Goblin to the light of the afterlife. Lestat accompanies Quinn to Blackwood Farm, where they find Mona lying on Quinn's bed in her death throes. Quinn reveals to her that he is now a vampire, and Lestat, desiring that the two lovers should be together forever, gives Mona the Dark Gift as a favor to his beloved friend Quinn.

Lestat learns of the disappearance of Mona's Taltos daughter and offers to help Mona find Morrigan. With Maharet's assistance, Mona, Lestat, and Quinn ascertain that Morrigan has gone to a secret island owned by Ashlar, where many Taltos now live. Morrigan and Ashlar have also had four Taltos children, two sons and two daughters—Silas, Oberon, Miravelle, and Lorkyn—all of whom have matured rapidly and are now very tall adults. Silas has caused a rebellion, poisoned Morrigan and Ashlar, and attacked a nearby island owned by the Drug Merchants. The Drug Merchants have retaliated by capturing Ashlar's island. Mona goes to the island with Lestat and Quinn. Their combined vampire powers annihilate the Drug Merchants and free the surviving Taltos. Mona finds that the Drug Merchants have locked Ashlar and Morrigan in a large freezer, where they have frozen to death, holding each other like cemetery angels. Mona takes the bodies of her daughter and Ashlar back to Mayfair Medical for research. She also invites her three Taltos grandchildren, along with all the other surviving Taltos, to New Orleans, where they can be together as a family.

For more perspectives on Mona Mayfair in the Vampire Chronicles, read the *Alphabettery* entries **Aaron Lightner, Ashlar, Designée of the Mayfair Legacy, Fontevrault Plantation, Goblin, Lasher, Lestat de Lioncourt, Maharet, Mark of the Witch, Michael Curry, Morrigan Mayfair, Petronia, Quinn Blackwood, Rowan Mayfair,** and **Taltos.**

Monastery of the Caves

• SANCTUARY •

The Monastery of the Caves, also called Kiev Pechersk Lavra, near modern Kiev, Russia, is a monastery of Eastern Orthodox Christianity. Throughout the long centuries, the monks of this Eastern tradition painted icons of sacred images.

As a child prodigy of icon painting, Andrei, who will eventually become the vampire Armand, is sent to the Monastery of the Caves to study with the monks. Andrei discovers that he has not only a talent for painting but also a deep conviction to be a monk and to spend the rest of his life in prayer, solitude, and the creation of images of God.

The Monastery of the Caves appears in *The Vampire Armand* (1998). For more perspectives on the Monastery of the Caves in the Vampire Chronicles, read the *Alphabettery* entries **Andrei** and **Armand**.

Morgan

• MORTAL •

Recently married, Morgan and his wife, Emily, honeymoon across Europe. One night in a small village where they are staying, a vampire from ruins in the north drinks Emily's blood and kills her. Morgan lays her body in a back room of the inn, where he grieves, yet the villagers are preparing to decapitate her, in the hope of preventing her from turning into a blood drinker. Morgan is frantically trying to protect his wife from desecration, when two more vampires appear posing as mortals, Louis and Claudia, having recently come from New Orleans, where they have left behind the burned body of their maker, Lestat. Louis and Claudia listen intently to Morgan's tale. Nothing can be done for Emily.

Nevertheless, Louis vows to go to the ruins in the north and find this murderous vampire, although he also hopes to find answers to questions that Lestat could not provide on the immortal nature of blood drinkers. Louis is greatly disappointed when he discovers that the vampire who killed Emily is a revenant—a mindless vampire like a walking corpse, behaving more on instinct than on rational judgment. Louis also sees that this revenant vampire is carrying Morgan over his shoulder. Louis fights the vampire, destroys him, and saves Morgan. Because dawn is quickly approaching and Louis is weak, he kills Morgan by drinking his blood, before fleeing back to the village as the sun rises.

Morgan appears in *Interview with the Vampire* (1976). For more perspectives on Morgan's character, read the *Alphabettery* entries Claudia, Emily, Lestat de Lioncourt, Louis de Pointe du Lac, and Revenant.

Morningstar Fisher

• MORTAL •

Morningstar Fisher has one daughter, Rose. She takes her daughter to an island when a natural disaster strikes. The island sinks, and Morningstar Fisher dies, but her daughter is saved and adopted by the vampire Lestat.

Morningstar Fisher appears in *Prince Lestat* (2014). For more perspectives on her character, read the *Alphabettery* entries Aunt Julie, Aunt Marge, Lestat de Lioncourt, and Rose.

Morrigan Mayfair

• TALTOS •

Due to Lasher's incestuous breeding program, Morrigan Mayfair is not simply the daughter of Michael Curry and Mona Mayfair but also a Taltos, a being from the ancient world who grows to adult size immediately after birth, looking almost exactly like Mona.

To hide her birth from her family, fearing that Rowan Mayfair and Michael Curry will kill her as they have killed two other Taltos, Lasher and Emaleth, Mona acquires for Morrigan a birth certificate and makes her the new Designée of the Mayfair Legacy by giving her the Mayfair emerald, which will make it more difficult to destroy Morrigan.

After Mona finally introduces Morrigan to Rowan and Michael, a friend of theirs appears, the ancient Taltos Ashlar, who, upon seeing Morrigan, feels an immediate attraction to her. Feeling the same for him, Morrigan runs away with Ashlar to a secret island that Ashlar owns, upon which many Taltos live.

While on the island, Morrigan and Ashlar have four children, Silas, Oberon, Miravelle, and Lorkyn, all of whom grow into adulthood in a matter of hours, as with all Taltos newborns. Silas desires to wage war against mortals living on nearby islands and causes a rebellion, secretly poisoning Morrigan and Ashlar to weaken them, then imprisoning his family and all Taltos who do not collaborate with his rebellion. For two years, Morrigan and her family are Silas's helpless prisoners. Morrigan and her daughter Miravelle try to stop him by blinding Silas with a screwdriver. But his rebellion wages war on the nearby island owned by the drug lord Rodrigo. Rodrigo retaliates by capturing Ashlar's island, killing Silas and his rebellious Taltos, and imprisoning those other Taltos who do not resist. Rodrigo then locks Morrigan and Ashlar in the large freezer in the compound's kitchen. By the time Lestat, Quinn, and Morrigan's mother, Mona Mayfair, liberate the island, Morrigan and Ashlar have frozen to death, embracing each other, covered in frost, with eyes closed like sleeping angels.

Morrigan Mayfair appears in *Blood Canticle* (2003). For more perspectives on her character in the Vampire Chronicles, read the *Alphabettery* entries **Ashlar, Lestat de Lioncourt, Lorkyn, Mayfair Medical Center, Michael Curry, Miravelle, Mona Mayfair, Oberon, Quinn Blackwood, Rodrigo, Rowan Mayfair, Silas,** and **Taltos.**

The Mother

• HONORIFIC •

When Amel fuses with Akasha, and she becomes the first vampire, she creates vampire fledglings and identifies herself as the goddess Isis. She becomes worshipped not only as a goddess but also as the Mother of all blood drinkers. This title remains with her for several thousands of years, all the way into the late twentieth century, used most often by the caretaker of Those Who Must Be Kept, the vampire Marius.

"The Mother" honorific appears in *The Vampire Lestat* (1985) and *The Queen of the Damned* (1988). For more perspectives on this title in the Vampire Chronicles, read the *Alphabettery* entries **Akasha, Amel, Divine Parents, Marius,** and **Those Who Must Be Kept.**

Mount Carmel

• SANCTUARY •

A mountain in the north of Israel, near the Mediterranean Sea, Mount Carmel has been the site of numerous religious groups and experiences for thousands of years. Hebrew prophet Elijah ascended Mount Carmel, a sacred location, nearly a thosand years before the Common Era and experienced a profoundly personal dialogue with God (cf. 1 Kings 19:10–13). Nearly two thousand years later, a Catholic religious order, the Carmelites, began here, inspired by Elijah and the Virgin Mary and dedicated to prayer, service, and the community life.

In the Vampire Chronicles, Mount Carmel serves as the site for Maharet and Mekare's village, almost three thousand years before the prophet Elijah. The twins' ancestors lived in the caves, and their village resides at the foot of the mountain. After Akasha plucks out Maharet's eyes, cuts out Mekare's tongue, and divides the twin witches for thousands of years, Maharet returns to Mount Carmel, where she paints pictographs on the cave walls, telling the story of the Legend of the Twins.

Mount Carmel appears in *The Queen of the Damned* (1988). For more perspectives on Mount Carmel in the Vampire Chronicles, read the *Alphabettery* entries **Akasha, Maharet**, and **Mekare**.

Murray

• MORTAL •

Murray is a small, muscular man who works on the San Francisco police force for ten years before the vampire Lestat hires him to be a driver and bodyguard for his adopted daughter, Rose, and pays Murray three times his salary on the police force. Murray is loyal to Rose, but is very upset when she begins a passionate affair with her college professor, Dr. Gardner Paleston. When Rose ends the relationship, Gardner kidnaps her and pours deadly poison into her mouth and over her eyes, blinding her and bringing her near death. Murray catches him in the act and shoots Gardner dead. Then he rushes Rose to a vampire clinic run by Fareed and Seth, who save her life and restore her eyesight. After Rose is turned into a vampire, Murray's services are no longer necessary.

Murray appears in *Prince Lestat* (2014). For more perspectives on Murray's character, read the *Alphabettery* entries **Gardner Paleston, Fareed Bhansali, Lestat de Lioncourt, Rose**, and **Seth**.

Nanette Blackwood

• MORTAL •

 anette is the daughter of Patrick and Regina Blackwood, the great-granddaughter of Manfred Blackwood (founder of Blackwood Farm), and the great-aunt of Quinn Blackwood, vampire and member of the Coven of the Articulate for having written the book *Blackwood Farm*. Nanette moves to New Orleans when she is young and lives her days in a cheap boardinghouse, until the night when she drinks a bottle of bourbon and eats a bottle of aspirin and dies. No one ever sees her ghost haunting Blackwood Farm.

Nanette Blackwood appears in *Blackwood Farm* (2002). For more perspectives on Nanette's character, read the *Alphabettery* entries **Coven of the Articulate**, **Manfred Blackwood**, **Patrick Blackwood**, **Quinn Blackwood**, and **Regina Blackwood**.

Nash Penfield

• MORTAL •

Nash Penfield becomes the home tutor of Quinn Blackwood after Quinn's first teacher, Lynelle Springer, dies in a horrible car accident. Nash is completing his Ph.D. in English at a university on the West Coast while he also lives and works at Blackwood Manor. Aunt Queen entices him away from a promising college career by providing him with a higher salary and a grand tour of Europe. Nash teaches Quinn how to appreciate English literature, cinema, culture, and even numerous sciences. Nash will read aloud to Aunt Queen, which she adores.

Nash Penfield appears in *Blackwood Farm* (2002). For more perspectives on Nash's character, read the *Alphabettery* entries **Aunt Queen**, **Lynelle Springer**, and **Quinn Blackwood**.

Nebamun

• VAMPIRE •

Nebamun begins as Akasha's mortal lover but soon becomes the immortal Captain of her army, the Queens Blood. Over the millennia, he evolves as a highly influential vampire, wielding more power than Akasha ever had, not through national sovereignty, but through corporate supremacy as his twenty-first-century pharmaceutical company dominates global markets. Nebamun appears in *Prince Lestat* (2014), *Prince Lestat and the Realms of Atlantis* (2016), and *Blood Communion* (2018).

Born in the ancient city of Nineveh six thousand years ago, Nebamun is nineteen years old when he becomes the lover of Akasha (before she becomes a vampire) and an important member of her special guard. At the age of twenty, he is unable to protect her when she and Enkil are mortally stabbed by conspirators. He hides in a gold-plated chest with the lid propped open and watches how Amel enters into her body through the blood and the wounds, how their fusion transforms her into the first vampire, and how she sinks her fangs into Enkil, drinks his blood, and turns him into the first fledgling. Nebamun keeps their transformation a secret. Akasha ignores him, and he returns to his post with the guards.

After Khayman betrays Akasha by turning the twin witches, Mekare and Maharet, into vampires, who then begin creating the First Brood in revolt, Akasha summons Nebamun, turns him into a vampire, and makes him the Guard of the Queens Blood, the Captain of her army. His principal responsibility is to capture Khayman, Mekare, Maharet, and their First Brood rebels. He captures only Mekare and Maharet; Khayman escapes. Akasha orders Nebamun to entomb them in two stone coffins and divide them by land and sea, Maharet on the western sea sailing in one direction and Mekare on the eastern sea sailing the opposite way. Nebamun then continues warring against the rebels bent on dethroning Akasha and Enkil.

Akasha gives him the title "Prince Nebamun." One of his closest companions is Gundesanth, the third vampire made by Akasha. Nebamun has many vampires under his command, including the vampire Rhoshamandes, who will one day betray Lestat.

During the first thousand years of Akasha's vampire rule, Nebamun meets and falls in love with a mortal slave of Nordic descent, Sevraine. Akasha forbids her subjects from turning a woman into a vampire, desiring to be the sole female blood drinker, and also because turning women into vampires is the disloyal behavior of the First Brood. Despite this, Nebamun turns Sevraine into a vampire and makes her his Blood Spouse. For this, he is accused of high treason and blasphemy. The sentence could have been death, but when Akasha beholds Sevraine, she loves her, makes her the Queen's handmaiden, and allows her to drink from her own blood. As punishment for his defiance, Nebamun is entombed in a shrine forever, where he will be a god to mortals whom he will judge by looking into their hearts, and who will worship him and bring him blood offerings on feast days; it is a torturous sentence of too much fasting and thinking.

Rhoshamandes goes to Nebamun and speaks with him through the shrine's brick walls. Nebamun's ideology of his goddess Queen, along with his religiously militant duty, has been shattered. He tells Rhoshamandes to escape, to find and join the First Brood, and to make fledglings. He recounts in detail for Rhoshamandes how the spirit of Amel fused with Akasha more than a thousand years ago on that fateful night and made the entire vampire race. Thankful for this information, yet sorrowful for abandoning his friend and former commander, Rhoshamandes escapes, but he returns fifty years later and frees Nebamun from his tomb, smashing the shrine to dust. Nebamun learns how Sevraine escaped after betraying Akasha, who now hates Sevraine as much as she hates Maharet and Mekare.

Nebamun wanders until he goes mad and can no longer bear the test of time. He goes into the earth and sleeps. When he arises from his torpor in the third century of the Common Era, he calls himself Gregory Duff Collingsworth.

For more perspectives on Nebamun's character, read the *Alphabettery* entries **Akasha, Amel, Enkil, Gregory Duff Collingsworth, Lestat de Lioncourt, Rhoshamandes,** and **Sevraine.**

New Orleans

• SANCTUARY •

New Orleans is the setting for many of the Vampire Chronicles. Lestat does not discover its enchanted beauty until after he travels to the New World and makes Louis a vampire. He adores eighteenth-century life in Louisiana so much that he sets up residence in the city for centuries, first on Louis's plantation, Pointe du Lac, and then in a townhouse on Rue Royale, where he, Louis, and Claudia live together for more than half a century, until Lestat's silence on the meaning of immortal life as blood drinkers sunders them. Louis, Lestat, and Claudia often spend time together in Saint Louis Cemetery No. 1. Lestat and Claudia often hunt in the Garden District. New Orleans serves as the backdrop for the rise and fall of Lestat's second family. Claudia plots Lestat's murder in Jackson Square. It is in New Orleans where Lestat goes into the earth for his second withdrawal into torpor, and where Daniel Malloy finds him, and where Lestat rises and forms the eighties rock band the Vampire Lestat. Even in the twentieth century, Lestat continues to live in his old townhouse on Rue Royale. In Café du Monde, Lestat first encounters Raglan James, the Body Thief. And it is in Saint Elizabeth's Convent that Maharet binds Lestat after his traumatic journey with Memnoch the Devil. He keeps New Orleans as his principal residence until he becomes the Prince of all vampires. Then he returns to his home in the Auvergne, France, and restores Château de Lioncourt, where he lodges many of his vampire friends and subjects.

New Orleans is written of in *Interview with the Vampire* (1976), *The Vampire Lestat* (1985), *Merrick* (2000), and *Blackwood Farm* (2002). For more perspectives on New Orleans in the Vampire Chronicles, read the *Alphabettery* entries **Claudia, Daniel Malloy, Lestat de Lioncourt, Louis de Pointe du Lac**, and **The Vampire Chronicles**.

Nicki

• SOBRIQUET •

Read the *Alphabettery* entry **Nicolas de Lenfent**.

Nicolas de Lenfent

• VAMPIRE •

Nicolas "Nicki" de Lenfent is Lestat's greatest mortal friend and greatest immortal tragedy. Lestat and Nicolas become beloved friends as mortals, but Lestat's turning Nicolas into a vampire drives his beloved friend towards suicidal insanity. Nicolas appears in *The Vampire Lestat* (1985).

Nicolas de Lenfent is the eldest son of a draper in the Auvergne, France. When he comes of age, his father sends him to Paris to study law at the University of Paris in the Sorbonne. During that time, Nicolas encounters a genius violin virtuoso from Padua, Italy, who is so good that rumors spread that he sold his soul to the Devil. Upon hearing his playing, Nicolas forsakes his civil education and begins studying the violin under the tutelage of Wolfgang Amadeus Mozart. Nicolas spends so much time practicing his new instrument that he eventually fails his scholastic examinations and must return to his father's house. His father, who wants his son to become an imitation aristocrat, is furious with him and breaks his violin to pieces. Nicolas immediately goes to Clermont, which is about an eight-day walk to the north, sells his expensive watch, and buys a new violin. He brings it home and continues to practice, even when his father threatens to break his hands. Nicolas is in disgrace, as is his family. His magnificent playing can be heard from his upstairs bedroom over his father's draper's shop, across from the inn, near the village church.

The attention upon Nicolas's disgrace is diverted to a problem with a pack of vicious wolves besieging the city. When the youngest son of the Marquis de Lioncourt, Lestat, goes into the mountains and slays the entire pack of wolves, the Auvergne villagers are so glad and grateful that they go into the mountains, retrieve the dead wolves, skin them, and from their pelts make a beautiful red velvet cloak and boots lined in wolf fur. Nicolas is elected to present the gifts to Lestat. From the instant these two encounter each other, they feel an immediate attraction. They spend increasing time in one another's company, their intimacy growing deeper, so much so that Lestat nicknames him Nicki. Nicolas tells Lestat all about Paris, and soon they form a secret plan to run away to Paris and start a new life there. Lestat's mother, Gabrielle, becomes aware of their plan. Desiring to live vicariously through her youngest son, she gives Lestat an expensive heirloom from her Italian family that he can sell to pay for his and Nicolas's passage to Paris.

Once there, Nicolas and Lestat find employment in a small theater on the Boulevard du Temple, called Renaud's House of Thesbians. At first they are given menial jobs, such as tearing tickets and cleaning floors, but in time their talent is revealed to Renaud. Nicolas begins performing music for the theater's productions, and Lestat begins acting. Lestat's popularity grows and draws much attention to the theater.

Lestat and Nicolas share an apartment, where they drink wine and enjoy deep philosophical conversations. While Lestat's point of view always expresses a joie de vivre, Nicolas's perspective is always formed by his Christian belief system, which, when compared with existential truths, occasionally drives him to depression. One night, Lestat is kidnapped from their apartment. Nicolas searches but cannot find him. The first word Nicolas hears of Lestat's safety comes from Lestat's mortal lawyer, Pierre Roget, who tells Nicolas vague tales of Lestat's new good fortune, then Roget gives Nicolas gifts and money from Lestat so that he can study violin with a brilliant Italian maestro and have everything he can possibly desire. To Lestat's surprise, Nicolas continues to perform at Renaud's House of Thesbians, even though Renaud is deep in debt and the theater is in jeopardy of closing. With his newfound fortune, Lestat purchases the theater house, keeps it running, and showers all its thespians with many gifts. Nicolas moves out of his and Lestat's former apartment and into a new flat.

One night, Nicolas is kidnapped from his flat by the Children of Darkness, a Parisian coven of vampires, led by the vampire Armand, who live by the Great Laws, which demand that vampires live in squalor and degradation, causing enmity between them and the well-heeled Lestat, whom Nicolas is surprised to discover is also a vampire. The Children of Darkness drink Nicolas's blood but do not kill him or turn him into a vampire. The experience drives Nicolas's occasional bouts with depression into utter nihilism. When Lestat comes to the Children of Darkness's lair in the catacombs beneath Cemetery of les Innocents, Nicolas is equally surprised to discover that Lestat has turned his own mother, Gabrielle, into his first fledgling. In the privacy of their own home, Nicolas begs Lestat to turn him into a vampire also. Initially reluctant to do this to his dearest mortal friend, Lestat acquiesces. Unlike Gabrielle, who takes to being a vampire almost more naturally than she takes to being mortal, Nicolas finds his transformation into immortality exacerbates his nihilism into insanity. Nicolas grows to hate Lestat with a burning passion. But he accompanies Lestat and Gabrielle to Cemetery of les Innocents, where they confront Armand once more and convince him that his coven's system of belief is outmoded in France's Age of Enlightenment. In response, Armand burns the Children of Darkness alive. Only four vampires are spared—Felix, Eleni, Laurent, and Eugénie.

They beg Lestat to make a new coven with them and to lead them into the new age, but he refuses. Nicolas takes up his violin and plays such beautiful music that the four vampires begin dancing in a way that was totally forbidden in their former life under the stringent Great Laws of the Children of Darkness. Moved by their performance, Nicolas demands that Lestat give them Renaud's House of Thesbians. For love of Nicki, Lestat obeys, the four vampires move in, and Nicolas joins them. He begins writing plays and composing music. The new coven performs his plays as mortals pretending to be vampires.

Lestat and Gabrielle leave Paris in search of Marius. One of the vampires who survived Armand's burning, Eleni, writes letters to Lestat informing him of the success of the theater and of their care for Nicolas, whose insanity is increasing. In time, Nicolas begins accosting strangers in the street and revealing his vampire nature. Armand must restrain him by putting him in a cell. When his insanity does not cease, Armand cuts off Nicolas's hands, but the coven ultimately restores them. In the end, when Nicolas can no longer bear the crushing weight of his existence, he writes numerous new plays and then commits suicide by leaping into a fire. Lestat laments the loss not simply of his second fledgling, but also of his only mortal friend, who became his greatest failure.

For more perspectives on Nicolas in the Vampire Chronicles, read the *Alphabettery* entries **Armand, Children of Darkness, Eleni, Eugénie, Felix, Gabrielle, Laurent, Lestat de Lioncourt, Renaud, Renaud's House of Thesbians**, and **Pierre Roget**.

Night Island

• SANCTUARY •

After the battle at Maharet's Sonoma compound, in which Mekare beheads Akasha, consumes her brain and heart, takes into herself Amel, the Sacred Core, and becomes the Queen of the Damned, the vampires gather together on an island off the coast of Miami, Florida, owned by Armand, which he calls Night Island. Armand had bought it for Daniel Malloy, where they could live together, and where Daniel could teach him how to more fully adapt to the twentieth century. Armand keeps Night Island open all night long, as a paradise resort for vampires, where they can gather together and spend time with one another, growing in their relationships and potentially forming new covens and new bonds.

On the island, Armand has a massive white villa, where vampires are surrounded by everything they want and bask in luxury. Persian carpets fill every room, and expensive paintings by master artists adorn every wall. The vampires can look out across the ocean and see the bright neon lights of Miami, with all of its waiting victims, evildoers of thievery and drugs. Inside, Armand can be seen playing chess with Santino. Pandora can be seen watching television or heard playing Bach at the piano. Marius can be seen reading in a comfortable chair by a window that looks out over the beach. Daniel can be overheard talking with Khayman about the ancient cities of Athens and Troy.

In time, this small vampire family divides and goes their separate ways (as many do). Daniel, who has grown to loathe Armand, even abandons his maker, and Armand soon after abandons Night Island, in the nineties, not many years before he flies into the sun in the hope of committing suicide.

Night Island appears in *The Queen of the Damned* (1988). For more perspectives on Night Island in the Vampire Chronicles, read the *Alphabettery* entries **Armand, Daniel Malloy, Khayman, Marius, Pandora,** and **Santino.**

Noble Abelard

• MORTAL •

As Quinn Blackwood prepares to travel through Europe with Aunt Queen, not knowing when he will return, his lover, Mona Mayfair, agrees that they will email each other often. Refusing to sign her name as "Mona," she signs "Ophelia Immortal," after Ophelia, a lead character in Shakespeare's play *Hamlet*, who, after being driven insane by her loved ones, commits suicide by drowning among flowers. Quinn likens their correspondence to that of Peter Abelard and Héloïse d'Argenteuil in the twelfth century, whose brief *affaire de cœur* was torn asunder by the precepts of their day and incited a love affair through correspondence that became legendary. Accordingly, Quinn signs his correspondence "Noble Abelard."

Noble Abelard is referenced in *Blackwood Farm* (2002). For more perspectives on Noble Abelard in the Vampire Chronicles, read the *Alphabettery* entries **Aunt Queen, Héloïse, Mona Mayfair, Ophelia Immortal,** and **Quinn Blackwood.**

Notker the Wise

• VAMPIRE •

Notker the Wise is one of two of Rhoshamandes's fledglings in the line of de Landen vampires who escape the attack of the Children of Darkness. While most of Rhoshamandes's line languish in captivity, Notker becomes the only vampire to establish an immortal music school that lasts for centuries. Notker appears in *Prince Lestat* (2014), *Prince Lestat and the Realms of Atlantis* (2016), and *Blood Communion* (2018).

Born in the late ninth century, he is the illegitimate child of a princess from Neustria in the Carolingian Empire. He is given as an oblate to the ancient monastery of Prüm, where he receives the monastic name Notker. After he gains notoriety as a musical genius and becomes the monastery's principal musician and composer, his brother monks refer to him as Notker the Wise for his liturgical acumen. Gifted with an obsession to compose songs, motets, chants, and canticles ceaselessly day and night, Notker creates glorious music that, along with his unparalleled physical beauty, attract the attention of the vampire Benedict.

Benedict begs his maker, Rhoshamandes, to allow him to turn Notker into a vampire. Rhoshamandes allows it, but only on the condition that Benedict shave off Notker's monastic coiffure, since a glabrous immortal is better than a tonsured blood drinker, according to Rhoshamandes, who demands that all his fledglings (and his fledglings' fledglings) be beautiful. Thus, Benedict follows Rhoshamandes's command and makes Notker eternally bald.

Notker remains in Rhoshamandes's coven in France, in what Rhoshamandes refers to as his "line of de Landen vampires," which includes Benedict, Allesandra, Eleni, Eugénie, and Everard. Notker then spends centuries creating beautiful music for the coven. His sacrosanct joy at becoming a vampire is often nullified by the constant attacks on Rhoshamandes's French castle by the vampires of the Children of Satan. Rhoshamandes fights for their right to live as immortals who enjoy the sensuous facets of life, while the Children of Satan demand that all vampires, because of their fundamentally evil nature, must exist as depraved monsters divesting themselves of every felicity. When at last the Children of Satan overcome Rhoshamandes's defenses and capture Allesandra, Eleni, Eugénie, and Everard, Rhoshamandes and Benedict flee to the north of England, where they create a new fortress, far away from the Children of Satan's uncompromising ideology. Notker the Wise heads into the mountains of the Alps and creates a coven on a French slope, opposite where Marius creates a shrine for Those Who Must Be Kept on the Alps' Italian slope.

Notker survives through the centuries without going underground because he is sustained by blood and music. He spends his long centuries in the Alps gathering only the finest musicians whom he turns into his own coven of musical vampires: violinists, keyboardists, composers, singers, and numerous others. Notker is even revolutionary in that, as the world celebrates the talents of castrati from the eleventh century to the eighteenth, he simply turns young soprano boys with beautiful voices into vampires instead of castrating them. In the end, Notker the Wise establishes in his alpine mountain sanctuary the one and only musical school for the Undead. His coven and court grow exponentially as he sends his musicians out into the world while gathering even more musicians to his unique academy.

In the twenty-first century, Notker remains safe in his French Alps coven while the spirit of Amel, seeking to be free from Mekare's wounded mind, commences the great Burning of 2013. After Lestat takes Amel from Mekare into himself to become the new Prince of the Vampires, Notker brings several of his musical vampires to the new coven house at Lestat's Château de Lioncourt in the Auvergne, performs at Lestat's coronation, and offers his undying devotion to the new leader of all vampires: "Oh, my Prince, I'm at your service. . . . My own humble fiefdom is only minutes away from you in the Alps."

For more perspectives on Notker the Wise in the Vampire Chronicles, read the *Alphabettery* entries **Allesandra, Amel, Benedict, Children of Satan, Eleni, Eugénie, Everard, Lestat de Lioncourt, Line of de Landen Vampires, Marius,** and **Rhoshamandes.**

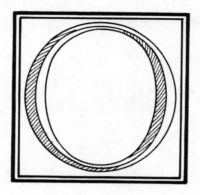

Oberon

• TALTOS •

Oberon is one of Morrigan and Ashlar's four Taltos children. Together they live with other Taltos on a secret island owned by Ashlar. Oberon feels deep affection for his sisters, Miravelle and Lorkyn. But from the moment he sees his brother, Silas, he knows he should have destroyed him, since Silas begins a rebellion on their island, poisoning their parents and attacking a drug lord, Rodrigo, on a nearby island. Oberon's parents are too weak to fight back. Silas imprisons Oberon, his two sisters, and his parents. When Rodrigo retaliates, he and his men kill Silas and the other rebelling Taltos, but Oberon and his sisters remain imprisoned, until Lestat, Quinn, and Mona Mayfair (Morrigan's mother) liberate the island by destroying Rodrigo and his Drug Merchants with their vampire powers. Sadly, they soon discover that Rodrigo has cruelly locked Oberon's parents in the compound's deep freezer, where they freeze to death. Mona takes Morrigan's and Ashlar's bodies back to Mayfair Medical in New Orleans for study, and she invites her grandchildren—Oberon and his two sisters—along with the rest of the surviving Taltos, to join them, where they will be safe on Mayfair Medical's grounds.

Oberon appears in *Blood Canticle* (2003). For more perspectives on Oberon's character, read the *Alphabettery* entries **Ashlar**, **Lestat de Lioncourt**, **Lorkyn**, **Mayfair Medical Center**, **Miravelle**, **Mona Mayfair**, **Morrigan Mayfair**, **Quinn Blackwood**, **Rodrigo**, **Silas**, and **Taltos**.

Old Captain

• MORTAL •

The owner of a small book-and-antiques shop on Royal Street in New Orleans, the Old Captain befriends and becomes a mentor to Roger, the eventual father of Dora, who will become one of Lestat's greatest mortal loves of the twentieth century. The Old Captain gives the teenage Roger passion for culture. He takes him to many libraries all over the United States and would have taken him to the libraries in Europe if Roger's mother had not declined. The Old Captain also introduces Roger to the writings of Wynken de Wilde, which teach Roger much about looking at spirituality from a new perspective. Roger helps the Old Captain sell antiques and books throughout the French Quarter, and in time he comes to realize that the Old Captain has a small dark side, since he is also a minor smuggler of rare goods. The Old Captain feels a deep attraction towards Roger, and Roger feels the same towards him, but neither he nor Roger transgress the boundary of their relationship. The Old Captain remains a father figure until Roger's senior year of high school, when the old man finally grows ill. Roger stays by the Old Captain's bedside until the dying man falls into a coma, never to wake again.

The Old Captain appears in *Memnoch the Devil* (1995). For more perspectives on the Old Captain's character, read the *Alphabettery* entries **Dora**, **Lestat de Lioncourt**, **Roger**, and **Wynken de Wilde**.

Old Faith

• IDIOM •

"Old faith" is a euphemistic reference to the belief system of the Children of Darkness (or the Children of Satan). They credit Satan as the basis of their faith, convinced that they are doing his work against God on Earth. According to the old faith, the Children of Darkness are guided in their beliefs by the five Great Laws, which state that such vampires are evil and cannot enjoy any goodness in this world, such as a luxurious lifestyle or drinking the blood of good souls. The Children of Satan in Rome lose this faith sometime before the eighteenth century, shortly after their coven master (Santino) abandons the old faith for new beliefs. The Children of

Darkness also lose this faith during the eighteenth century, when Lestat convinces their coven master (Armand) that the old faith is unreasonable during the Enlightenment.

References to the old faith can be found in *The Queen of the Damned* (1988), *The Vampire Armand* (1998), and *Blood and Gold* (2001). For more perspectives on this idiom, read the *Alphabettery* entries **Armand**, **The Children of Darkness**, **Children of Satan**, **Great Laws**, and **Lestat de Lioncourt**.

Old Queen

• SOBRIQUET •

"Old Queen" is the sobriquet that Lestat gives to Allesandra, fledgling of Rhoshamandes, when he first encounters her beneath the Cemetery of les Innocents, in Armand's coven, the Children of Darkness. In *The Vampire Lestat*, Lestat sees her perish in a fire and believes she is dead. He does not call her by her proper name until he encounters her again in *Prince Lestat*.

The "Old Queen" sobriquet appears in *The Vampire Lestat* (1985) and *Prince Lestat* (2014). For more perspectives on the Old Queen's character, read the *Alphabettery* entries **Allesandra**, **Armand**, and **Lestat de Lioncourt**.

Old Ways

• IDIOM •

"Old Ways" is a euphemism used to describe the behavior of the Children of Darkness (or the Children of Satan) for more than five hun-

dred years. The covens obey the five Great Laws, which deny luxury and excessive blood drinking—actions which Lestat fearlessly embraces. The Old Ways also enforce vampires' avoidance of the blood of innocent people and demand they drink only the blood of immoral or infirm individuals. The last vestiges of the Old Ways are destroyed by Lestat in the eighteenth century when he convinces Armand, the coven master of the Children of Darkness, that his Old Ways are superannuated behaviors in the time of modern advancements in science and philoso-phy. Later, in the twentieth century, Armand often reflects on how he once followed the Old Ways.

The Old Ways are referenced in *The Vampire Lestat* (1985), *The Queen of the Damned* (1988), and *The Vampire Armand* (1998). For more perspectives on the idiom, read the *Alphabettery* entries **Armand**, **The Children of Darkness**, **Great Laws**, and **Lestat de Lioncourt**.

Oncle Julien

• IMMORTAL •

Oncle Julien is another name for Julien May-fair. The word *oncle* is French for "uncle"—a term generally used by the Cajun side of the Mayfair family. The ghost of Oncle Julien appears to Quinn Blackwood, Mona Mayfair, Michael Curry, and many others.

Oncle Julien appears in *Merrick* (2000), *Blackwood Farm* (2002), and *Blood Canticle* (2003). For more perspectives on Oncle Julien's character, read the *Alphabettery* entries **Julien Mayfair**, **Michael Curry**, **Mona Mayfair**, and **Quinn Blackwood**.

Oncle Vervain

• WITCH •

Oncle Vervain, also known as Dr. Vervain, is a powerful Voodoo doctor who lives in New Orleans. He is the older brother of Great Nananne, who is Merrick Mayfair's god-mother, from whom she learns much of her witching heritage. Oncle Vervain's grandfa-ther is a powerful Voodoo man during the Civil War who knows the Voodoo Queen of New Orleans, Marie Laveau. Oncle Vervain has the power to see ghosts in the air around him all the time. He often tells the story of how theirs is a family of magicians, dating back four thousand years before the Aztecs, perhaps even to the Time Before the Moon.

He is a profound inspiration for Merrick Mayfair's magical and archaeological interests, especially her work for David Talbot in the Talamasca.

Oncle Vervain appears in *Merrick* (2000).

For more perspectives on Oncle Vervain's character, read the *Alphabettery* entries **Great Nananne**, **Merrick Mayfair**, **Talamasca Order**, and **Time Before the Moon**.

One Fine Blow

• IDIOM •

When Anne Rice's father, Howard O'Brien, read her first novel, he shared with her how much he enjoyed the line "one fine blow." Anne Rice has slipped it into almost every novel ever since.

Its first occurrence is in *Interview with the Vampire* (1976), when Louis fights off Lestat: "What happened then is not clear to me. I think I grabbed the poker from her and gave him one fine blow with it to the side of the head."

The idiom next occurs in *The Vampire Lestat* (1985), when Armand fights Lestat: "And he had dealt me one fine blow in the middle of the back that sent me flying out the door and onto the stones of the square."

When Lestat and David are discussing Raglan James in *The Tale of the Body Thief* (1992) Lestat says, "David, I see your point about the poor befuddled mechanic; nevertheless, why didn't his soul pop loose from the cancer-riddled body when James dealt it one fine blow to the head?"

Next it is in *Memnoch the Devil* (1995), when Lestat fights Memnoch: "I gave him one last full shove in the chest with every bit of strength I had in me, my fingers splayed out against his black armour, the stammering ornamented breastplate, my eyes so close in the first instant that I saw the carvings on it, the writing in the metal, and then the wings flapped above me as if to terrify me. He was far from me, suddenly, gigantic, yes, still, but I'd thrown him back, damn him. One fine blow that had been."

It then occurs twice in *The Vampire Armand* (1998). It first happens when Armand tries to fight off Marius: "He dealt one fine blow to my chest. I almost toppled off my feet. I was so weak, I fell forward, only at the last grasping for his cloak." The idiom next happens when Sybelle is being abused by her brother: "And the man who shook her, who pulled at her, who screamed at her, suddenly dealing her one fine blow with his fist that sent her over backwards, falling off the piano bench so that a scream escaped from her and she fell over herself, an ungainly tangle of limbs on the carpeted floor."

In *Pandora* (1998), the idiom occurs when Pandora is fighting off Akbar: "'I have you!' this creature said tenderly in my ear. 'No, you don't!' I said, and gave him one fine blow with my right elbow. It drove him off balance."

It appears again in *Merrick* (2000), when David confronts the spirit of Honey in the Sunshine possessing Merrick's body: "Suddenly she rose from the dressing table, and the left hand, free of the cigarette, swept all the bottles and the lamp off the right side of the table, with one fine blow."

And in *Blood Canticle* (2003), Lestat senses rogue vampires in New Orleans and says, "And then with one fine blow it struck me. *Their presence.*"

Its most recent appearance happens twice in *Blood Communion* (2018), when Lestat fights Rhoshamandes: "I dealt him one fine blow through the flames that struck his head from his neck" and "I dealt him one fine blow to the face with the crown of my head and blinded him as he howled like a wounded beast."

The idiom "one fine blow" does not occur in *The Queen of the Damned* (1988), *Vittorio the Vampire* (1999), *Blood and Gold* (2001), *Blackwood Farm* (2002), *Prince Lestat* (2014), and *Prince Lestat and the Realms of Atlantis* (2016). For more perspectives on the use of idioms in the Vampire Chronicles, read the *Alphabettery* sections **The Blood, Children of the Night, Devil's Road, Little Drink, Maker, Sacred Fount, Time Before the Moon, Vampiric Sleep,** and **The Voice.**

Ophelia Immortal

• SOBRIQUET •

Due to a naturally melancholy nature, Mona Mayfair often refers to herself as Ophelia, a principal character from the play *Hamlet* who is manipulated by her family and her lover—so much so that she is driven insane to the point of committing suicide by drowning herself in a brook among beautiful flowers. When Mona's lover, Quinn Blackwood, reveals to her that he is obliged to travel through Europe, not knowing when he will return, they agree to email each other. He promises to sign his emails as "Noble Abelard," and she promises to sign hers as "Ophelia Immortal."

The "Ophelia Immortal" sobriquet appears in *Blackwood Farm* (2002). For more perspectives on this sobriquet, read the *Alphabettery* entries **Mona Mayfair, Noble Abelard,** and **Quinn Blackwood.**

Ora Lee

• MORTAL •

Ora Lee is one of the first servants to be employed at Blackwood Farm by its founder, Manfred Blackwood. She works in the kitchen and marries another servant, Jerome. She and he are both children of free Creoles of color, who were artisans during the Civil War. Ora Lee and Jerome both care for Manfred's family, especially his first wife, Virginia Lee, and his children, William and Camille. Ora Lee becomes a legendary ancestor of the twentieth-century employees of Blackwood Farm, in particular Big Ramona, who works in the kitchen; her daughter, Little Ida, who is Quinn Blackwood's nanny; and her daughter, Jasmine, who is the housekeeper and mother of Quinn's son, little Jerome.

Ora Lee appears in *Blackwood Farm* (2002). For more perspectives on her character, read the *Alphabettery* entries **Big Ramona, Jasmine, Jerome, Little Ida, Little Jerome, Manfred Blackwood, Quinn Blackwood,** and **Virginia Lee Blackwood.**

Ordinary Man

• SOBRIQUET •

"Ordinary Man" is the sobriquet that Lestat gives to Memnoch the Devil when he first encounters him, not fully understanding that he is a supernatural being. When Memnoch reveals his true form with wings, talons, and hooves, Lestat no longer refers to him as ordinary.

The "Ordinary Man" sobriquet appears in *Memnoch the Devil* (1995). For more perspectives on this sobriquet, read the *Alphabettery* entries **Dora, Memnoch, Lestat de Lioncourt,** and **Roger.**

Osiris

• IMMORTAL •

In ancient Egypt, Osiris is worshipped as the god and King of the underworld. He is married to the goddess Isis, who is venerated as the Queen of the gods.

When Akasha, Queen of ancient Egypt, is turned into a vampire, her first fledgling is her husband, King Enkil. After the First Brood's rebellion, Enkil and Akasha identify themselves as the gods Osiris and Isis in an effort to build a faithful following among their subjects, both mortal and vampire alike.

Osiris appears in *The Queen of the Damned* (1988). For more perspectives on Osiris in the Vampire Chronicles, read the *Alphabettery* entries **Akasha**, **Enkil**, **First Brood**, and **Isis**.

Our Lady of Guadalupe

• HONORIFIC •

Our Lady of Guadalupe is celebrated in the Roman Catholic Church on December 12, her feast day.

In 2002, Lestat becomes fascinated with this feast day, particularly with the story behind it, how the Virgin Mary appeared to a poor peasant in Mexico named Juan Diego and told him to tell the local bishop to build a church for suffering people. In response, the bishop asked for a sign as proof of the message. The Virgin Mary produced that sign on Juan Diego's cloak (or tilma)—an image of herself. The image shows a mestiza girl wearing a pink tunic and a blue mantle spangled in eight-tipped stars, her hands are folded in prayer, she is standing on a crescent moon, which is held up by a cherub, and behind her is a bright sunburst full of pointed and wavy lines. The image has become known as Our Lady of Guadalupe, which is enshrined in the Minor Basilica of Our Lady of Guadalupe, in Mexico City.

Our Lady of Guadalupe is referenced in *Blood Canticle* (2003). For more perspectives on Our Lady of Guadalupe in the Vampire Chronicles, read the *Alphabettery* entries **Juan Diego**, **Lestat de Lioncourt**, and **Veronica's Veil**.

Pandora

Although it is in the series New Tales of the Vampires, Pandora's book can be obliquely included in the Vampire Chronicles series because of the character Pandora's membership in the Coven of the Articulate—a gathering of blood drinkers who have authored books in the Vampire Chronicles. In her tale, Pandora recounts how she is a child of the Roman Empire, how she is nearly engaged to the mortal Marius, how her family is betrayed and put to death, and how she is the only one who survives, fleeing to Antioch to begin a new life under the guise of a Greek courtesan. When the ancient vampire Akbar appears in Antioch, killing its inhabitants, Pandora's former love, Marius, also returns, this time having been turned into a powerful vampire, who also happens to be protecting Those Who Must Be Kept—the Mother and the Father of the vampire race. Akbar nearly kills Pandora to force Marius into letting him drink from the Mother's blood. The Mother kills Akbar, and Marius rescues Pandora by turning her into a vampire. Together Marius and Pandora protect the Mother and the Father until their relationship ends after a bitter argument. They do not see each other again for several centuries.

After time passes, Pandora and Marius eventually realize how much they desire to be together.

For more perspectives on this Vampire Chronicle, read the *Alphabettery* entries **Akbar, Arjun, Coven of the Articulate, Marius, Pandora, Those Who Must Be Kept,** and **The Vampire Chronicles**.

Pandora

• VAMPIRE •

Pandora is Marius's first and most beloved fledgling. Similar to Gabrielle, Pandora is one of the most independent female characters in the Vampire Chronicles. She is also among the band of rebellious vampires who fight and defeat Akasha. Pandora appears in *The Queen of the Damned* (1988), *Pandora* (1998), *Prince Lestat* (2014), *Prince Lestat and the Realms of Atlantis* (2016), and *Blood Communion* (2018).

Born around 15 B.C. in the Roman Empire under the rule of Augustus Caesar, Pandora is given the birth name Lydia. Her house is run by her father, Maximus, a wealthy senator who claims to be a pure-blood Roman, descended directly from the time of Romulus and Remus. Lydia's mother, the daughter of another wealthy Roman senator, makes the same claim, but when Lydia is two years old, her mother dies, having given birth to six children, while six more perished in the womb. Lydia's five older brothers, ranging from Antony, the eldest, to Lucius, the youngest, practice fighting with short broad swords and receive lessons from their tutors, and Lydia is always observing and learning. When she reaches the age at which she can receive tutelage on her own from Greek masters, she discovers that she loves words and adores reading.

Lydia first encounters her future maker, Marius, while he is still mortal, at the age of twenty-five. He is immediately smitten with Lydia's intelligence and character, and he begs her father, Maximus, for her hand in marriage. Maximus refuses, since she is too young. Lydia does not see Marius for the next five years, but she often thinks of him. By the time she is the common age for Roman marriage (fifteen years old), she is overjoyed to see Marius once more at the Lupercalia festival. Lydia now begs her father to allow Marius to marry her, but once more Maximus denies the request. Lydia does not see Marius again for the next two decades, not until she is thirty-five years old, a few years after the death of Augustus Caesar, when Julius Caesar was emperor of the Roman Republic. Her maturity into womanhood is plagued by blood dreams about powerful people who drink blood.

Tiberius becomes the new Roman Emperor and sets Sejanus to run the empire for him as his Roman consul, the highest office. Sejanus consolidates the Praetorian Guard and begins persecuting numerous citizens, most of whom are Sejanus's personal rivals. Lucius is jealous of his eldest brother, Antony, and promises the *delatores* (the Praetorian Guard's secret spies) that they will receive one-third of the family estate if they accuse Maximus, his father, along with his family, of treason. The Praetorian Guard sends *speculatores* (scouts) to Lydia's home, where they kill her brothers. Maximus, her father, slits his wrists, desiring to die a Roman death. When the *speculatores* try to kill him, he slays them, yet they also mortally stab him. Before Lydia's father dies, he reveals that he has arranged for two Hebrew merchants named David and Jacob to sneak her out of the city.

The two merchants set sail with her aboard a vessel heading from the Roman republic to Antioch. Upon arrival, David and Jacob give her all the money that her father bequeathed to her, they help her procure a fine house, they falsify documents to say that she is a Greek widow from Rome, and they change Lydia's name to Pandora. Once on her own, she pretends to be a Greek courtesan and buys a slave named Flavius, who lost his left leg below the knee in a hunting accident but has in its place a false leg finely sculpted out of ivory, with a perfectly cut foot, toes, and a sandal. Well educated in Greek and Roman writings, Flavius becomes her most devoted slave, trustworthy of managing not only Pandora's house but also her housemaids, since he is not attracted to women.

During this time, Pandora's blood dreams intensify: one is about a beautiful queen weeping on her throne, and another is about a man so badly burned that he looks like a monster with bones poking through his charred skin. Deeply concerned, she speaks to temple priests about her blood dreams. They confirm for her that the burned being is a reality, for they have been more fully informed of the burned blood drinker by a man who happens to be with the priest, a tall man wearing a toga that completely covers his body, except for his lips. Occasionally he speaks to Pandora aloud, but he is also able to speak with her telepathically. He reveals to her that he knows much more than she realizes, specifically about the circumstances surrounding her brother Lucius's betrayal. He also assures her that he will protect her from the burned being. After more blood dreams and more reports of a burned blood drinker killing people throughout the city, the tall man reveals himself to be her beloved Marius.

He is leaving Antioch, and he urges her to come with him. She speaks more fully of her dreams with Marius, revealing that the Queen is considered to be a primal and healing fount of blood for blood drinkers, and that numerous burned blood drinkers are desperately seeking a way to drink her pure blood for greater power and healing. Marius then describes to her how he was turned into a vampire and how he became the caretaker of Akasha and Enkil, the progenitors of all vampires, also called Those Who Must Be Kept. He also explains that the caretaker before him, a vampire called the Elder, attempted to burn Akasha and Enkil but caused the Great Burning of 4 C.E. An ancient vampire named Akbar is now badly burned because of it and seeks the blood of Akasha to heal himself.

Marius protects Pandora, but Akbar finds

her, drains her blood to the point of death, and threatens to let her die unless Marius takes him to Those Who Must Be Kept. Reluctantly acquiescing, Marius takes Akbar to them, but the Queen crushes Akbar's head, forcefully dismembers him, and burns the rest, destroying him completely. To save her life, Marius turns Pandora into a vampire, and they remain together, joint protectors of Akasha and Enkil, for many years.

Pandora invites into their home her slave Flavius. Marius is deeply impressed with him and treats Flavius as a very beloved mortal. When Flavius becomes mortally ill, Marius cannot bear the sight of him dying. Against Marius's wishes, Pandora turns Flavius into a blood drinker. Marius is furious, and he banishes Flavius from his house, and even from the empire. Marius wants to teach Pandora everything he knows, but she does not want to listen to him. A wedge grows between them. Finally, after two hundred years of arguing and heartache, Marius leaves Pandora and takes with him the Mother and the Father.

Around the sixth century, as Pandora is roaming through a Roman forest near the monastery Vivarium, Cassiodorus's monastic school that published volumes of classical literature, she encounters a spirit rising out of the energy in a beehive. The spirit possesses a scarecrow and begins to weep and mourn the recent death of Cassiodorus. Pandora is completely aware that she is observing a spirit. Utterly unafraid of it, she encourages the spirit to do whatever it can to become greater than what it is, to learn and evolve, to not be limited by what it sees but to see how far existence can go. Then she leaves,

unaware that she will encounter the spirit again in the twenty-first century.

In the interim, sometime during the fourteenth century, Pandora falls in love with an Indian prince named Arjun. She turns him into a vampire, and they remain together for many years, during which time their relationship corrupts. Arjun is with her the next time she encounters Marius, in Dresden, where he is with his own fledgling and lover Bianca. Marius hears reports that she is being held captive against her will by Arjun, but she denies it. Marius begs her forgiveness and vows that he will stay with her forever, he will even leave Bianca for her, but she denies him. Before she and Arjun leave Dresden, she writes a note to Marius in his chamber, confessing that he is right: she is Arjun's captive, and she wants Marius to find her in Moscow and take her away. But the note is lost for the next fifty years. When Marius finds it and goes to search for her, she and Arjun have already gone.

While in Saint Petersburg, Pandora hires the librarian Dmitri Fontayne, nicknamed Mitka, but soon falls in love with him. She turns him into her fledgling, but Arjun is furious. He banishes Mitka from Russia. Pandora gives her fledgling a small fortune before he leaves, but she remains separated from him until the early twenty-first century.

The next time Pandora meets Marius is in the late twentieth century, at Maharet's Sonoma compound, where they fight and defeat Akasha, who awakens at the summoning of the music of the Vampire Lestat. Marius and Pandora reconcile and remain in contact.

They meet once more in the early twenty-first century to help Lestat take the spirit of Amel into himself and become Prince Lestat, ruler of all vampires. She also reunites with the spirit that she encountered at the beehive and in the scarecrow. The spirit calls himself Gremt Stryker Knollys, and he reveals to her that, through her encouragement, he has learned how to evolve and become incarnate. Furthermore, it is also because of her encouragement that he—along with another spirit, who once was the vampire Hesketh, and Teskhamen, Hesketh's former maker and Marius's maker—is responsible for beginning the Talamasca.

Marius and Pandora remain together through Lestat's coronation ceremony, to witness and encourage the making of Lestat's son and clone, Viktor, and Lestat's adopted daughter, Rose, both of whom are united as Blood Spouses. Afterward, Pandora joins Rose and Viktor, along with Gabrielle, and even Arjun and Bianca, back at Lestat's newly renovated castle in France, where as a mortal he once killed eight wolves. They live together under the same roof as the Court of the Prince, but Arjun grows restless and tries to take Pandora away. Marius prevents him from doing so, and Arjun attacks him, but Marius obliterates him completely. Pandora is finally free of Ajun and is reunited with Mitka when Lestat brings her fledgling back to Château de Lioncourt.

For more perspectives on Pandora in the Vampire Chronicles, read the *Alphabettery* entries **Akasha, Akbar, Antony, Arjun, The Elder, Enkil, Flavius, God of the Grove, Gremt Stryker Knollys, Hesketh, Lestat de Lioncourt, Lucius, Lydia, Marius, Mitka, Rose, Teskhamen, Those Who Must Be Kept,** and **Viktor.**

Pantaloon

• CHARACTER •

Mentioned by Lestat as one of the characters in the commedia dell'arte plays he performs in the Auvergene region and in Paris, namely *Lelio and Isabella* and *Lelio and Flaminia*, Pantaloon is a stock character who can also be identified as Pantalone but can go by any name. Generally, this type of character acts as an unsympathetic antagonist to the two main characters, who are usually lovers. The name Pantaloon is synonymous with the wide pantaloon pants worn by old, doddering men, which Shakespeare marked as the final stage of life before death: "The sixth age shifts into the lean and slippered pantaloon, with spectacles on nose and pouch on side; his youthful hose, well saved, a world too wide for his shrunk shank, and his big manly voice, turning again towards childish treble, pipes and whistles in his sound" (*As You Like It*, act 2, scene 7). The Pantaloon character embodies the foolish thinking of old men, oftentimes portrayed as the father of the female lover, endeavoring to thwart the romantic ambitions of the male lover. One example of a kind of Pantaloon character can be seen in Lord Capulet as he tries to prevent his daughter, Juliet, from marrying Romeo.

This character appears in *The Vampire Lestat* (1985). For more perspectives on this character, read the *Alphabettery* entries **Commedia dell'Arte**, **Flaminia**, **Lelio**, and **Lestat de Lioncourt**.

The Parents

• MORTALS •

When the Bravennans seek to establish and maintain transmission stations across planet Earth, which provides for them the means to consume the psychic energy of human suffering, they abduct a human being named Amel, genetically enhance him into a superhuman of superior intelligence and strength, and brainwash him to believe that they are the Parents who care for earthlings. The Parents send Amel back to Earth to help their agenda. With his superior intelligence, Amel soon realizes that the Parents have lied to him, that they actually consume human suffering as a

food source. So he betrays them and creates the city of Atlantis to protect humans from the Parents. When the Parents realize that Amel has betrayed them, they create Replimoids to stop him. But the Replimoids also fail. The Parents then send a meteor shower that destroys Atlantis and Amel, although Amel's spirit and the Replimoids escape.

The Parents appear in *Prince Lestat and the Realms of Atlantis* (2016). For more perspectives on the Parents, read the *Alphabettery* entries **Amel**, **Bravenna**, **Bravennans**, and **Replimoid**.

Patrick Blackwood

• MORTAL •

Patrick is the son of William Blackwood, who is the son of Manfred Blackwood, founder of Blackwood Farm. Patrick has two siblings, Aunt Queen and Gravier, the latter being the great-grandfather of Quinn Blackwood.

Because Patrick's father is sterile, his grandfather entices Julien Mayfair to pretend to be William so that he can father children for William with both of William's wives. The ghost of Julien Mayfair confesses to Quinn that William's first wife, Grace, gave birth to his son, Gravier, before William's second wife gave birth to his daughter, Lorraine, whom Quinn knows as Aunt Queen. However, Julien does not confess to fathering any other children. The identity of Patrick's true father remains a mystery. At a young age, Patrick falls from a horse and dies of a concussion in one of the upstairs bedrooms of Blackwood Manor. Unlike his brother, Gravier, Patrick is never seen as ghost haunting the house, and everyone believes he is resting well in the family crypt.

Patrick Blackwood appears in *Blackwood Farm* (2002). For more perspectives on his character, read the *Alphabettery* entries **Blackwood Manor**, **Gravier Blackwood**, **Julien Mayfair**, **Nanette Blackwood**, **Quinn Blackwood**, **Regina Blackwood**, and **William Blackwood**.

Patsy Blackwood

• MORTAL •

Patsy Blackwood is the daughter of Thomas "Pops" and Rose "Sweetheart" Blackwood and the mother of Tarquin "Quinn" Blackwood. From a young age, Patsy shows a great desire to be a country-western singer. By the time she is sixteen years old, she is singing in a band in New Orleans and partying with men in their twenties in a flat on Esplanade Avenue. She becomes pregnant with Quinn and his twin brother, Garwain, but Garwain dies shortly after birth. Still desiring to achieve her dreams, and not wanting to be a young mother, she never seeks the identity of Quinn's father and leaves him in the care of her parents, Pops and Sweetheart. But her country-singing career never amounts to much, and she must live on Blackwood Farm, not in the mansion, but in the smaller house behind it, where workmen and guests are lodged, because she does not want to be near her family while also concealing the fact that she has contracted the HIV virus. Patsy watches her son Quinn grow up from a distance through the haze of alcoholism. If she knows that Quinn is seeing the ghost of his dead twin brother, who is calling himself Goblin, she never tells him.

She continues to perform in a band and party in New Orleans's nightlife while her HIV becomes AIDS. One of her band members, Seymour, who plays harmonica and drums, has contracted AIDS from her and eventually sues her for not informing him of his disease.

As a child, Quinn loves his mother, but as he matures, his love turns to hate. Unbeknownst to her, he often fantasizes about murdering her. His fantasy becomes a reality after the hermaphrodite vampire Petronia turns him into a vampire. When Quinn seeks the help of Lestat and Louis's fledgling the witch vampire Merrick, they perform a ritual exorcism to send Goblin's presence from Blackwood Farm to Heaven. When Patsy interrupts the ritual, Quinn grabs her neck and breaks it like a twig. Without drinking her blood, undesirous to see visions of her memory, he sinks her body in the marshes far from the house, where she is devoured by the alligators and all the other life thriving in the swampland.

Patsy's ghost returns to haunt and terrorize Blackwood Farm, especially Quinn, for whom she feels keen hatred. Quinn's companion, Lestat, helps Patsy transition from this world into the light of the afterlife, where she can have peace.

Patsy Blackwood appears in *Blackwood Farm* (2002). For more perspectives on Patsy's character, read the *Alphabettery* entries **Garwain Blackwood, Goblin, Lestat de Lioncourt, Merrick Mayfair, Petronia**, and **Quinn Blackwood**.

Paul de Pointe du Lac

• MORTAL •

The younger brother of Louis de Pointe du Lac, Paul is a young man of exceptional spirituality, even experiencing mystical visions of Saint Dominic and the Blessed Virgin Mary. These visions tell Paul to sell everything he owns and use that money to do ministerial work for God in France. These visions also inform Paul that he is to be a great religious leader in France through deeper fervor of spirituality, rejecting the world's newfound atheism during the French Revolution and the Age of Enlightenment. Louis does his best to be tolerant of Paul's profound prayer life, but he will not allow the selling of his family's plantation. Louis and Paul get into a heated argument, which results in Paul seeing a vision and then falling from a great height at the top of the stairs to his death. Paul is buried in Saint Louis Cemetery No. 1. Louis greatly mourns the loss of his brother and blames himself for Paul's early demise.

Paul de Pointe du Lac appears in *Interview with the Vampire* (1976). For more perspectives on his character, read the *Alphabettery* entries **Louis de Pointe du Lac** and **Saint Louis Cemetery No. 1**.

People of the Purpose

• COVEN •

When scientists from the planet Bravenna create humanoid creatures called Replimoids, with superhuman abilities of regeneration and immortality, the Bravennans (whom the Replimoids refer to as the Parents) teach them that their work is to use their superior powers to help the human race. With this purpose, the Bravennans send the Replimoids—Kapetria, Garekyn, Derek, and Welf—to planet Earth with the secondary purpose of destroying their greatest creation, Amel, whom they have genetically enhanced with similar superhuman abilities and who the Bravennans claim is hurting the human race. The Replimoids soon discover that the Bravennans are nefarious liars with ulterior motives. They ally with Amel and refer to themselves as the People of the Purpose, because although the Bravennans have lied to them about many aspects of their purpose, their fundamental responsibility remains the same: the betterment of humanity. Amel and the Replimoids decide that they will be the people whose purpose is to help the human race achieve splendor and security, beauty and balance. The People of the Purpose will never harm humanity but will do everything they can to ensure the survival of Earth's fragile creatures.

The People of the Purpose appear in *Prince Lestat and the Realms of Atlantis* (2016). For more perspectives on the People of the Purpose in the Vampire Chronicles, read the *Alphabettery* entries **Amel**, **Bravenna**, **Bravennans**, **Derek**, **Garekyn**, **Kapetria**, **Parents**, **Replimoid**, and **Welf**.

Pepper

• MORTAL •

Pepper is the niece of Jerome and Ora Lee, both of whom are the first servants employed at Blackwood Farm. Pepper helps Ora Lee in the kitchen and in caring for the lady of the house, Virginia Lee, Manfred's first wife and mother of Manfred's children, William and Camille. Pepper is fondly remembered by the descendants of Jerome and Ora Lee, namely Big Ramona, Little Ida, and Jasmine, the mother of little Jerome, the son of Quinn Blackwood, vampire companion of Lestat.

Pepper appears in *Blackwood Farm* (2002). For more perspectives on Pepper's character, read the *Alphabettery* entries **Big Ramona, Jasmine, Jerome, Lestat de Lioncourt, Little Jerome, Manfred Blackwood, Ora Lee, Quinn Blackwood,** and **Virginia Lee Blackwood.**

Petronia

• VAMPIRE •

Petronia is the maker of Manfred Blackwood and his descendant, the popular Quinn Blackwood. Petronia is also the only known hermaphrodite vampire. She appears in *Blackwood Farm* (2002).

Petronia is born decades before the Common Era, in Rome, during the reign of Julius Caesar. Her mother is an actress, and her father is a gladiator. Born a hermaphrodite, she is prostituted by her parents, until she is able to carry a sword and shield and be trained as a gladiator. By the age of fourteen, she is a fierce and murderous spectacle in the gladiators' arena. She continues to fight and win, with her parents charging higher and higher fees for spectators to behold Petronia's peerless strength and ability. While she is still a girl, her parents sell her for a great fortune to a master who treats her cruelly, chaining her to her bed every night and during the day sending her into arenas to fight vicious animals. Her indomitable will does not allow her to be defeated against lions or tigers. She slays them all, and the paying crowd loves her.

During all that time, one customer continues coming back to pay to see her fight and to pay to be with her intimately. It is the vampire Arion. One night, when he can no longer bear to see her enslaved to such a merciless master, he buys her freedom and gives her a purse filled with money, telling her to go wherever she desires and do whatever she wants. But she does not know where to go or what to do, except to follow after Arion and love him.

Petronia makes a home with Arion in first-century Pompeii, where they set up a shop and he teaches her how to make and sell cameos. They continue this peaceful lifestyle until Mount Vesuvius erupts and destroys Pompeii. Arion stays in the Bay of Naples while Petronia saves the shop's slaves and wares. In response to her bravery, and for his love for her, Arion turns Petronia into a vampire and teaches her how to kill only evildoers, how to hide their bodies, and how to survive the long years of immortality.

Petronia moves with Arion to Naples, where they sell diamonds for centuries. During the late nineteenth century, Petronia meets Manfred Blackwood, who has recently traveled to Naples. She is fascinated by his accounts of Louisiana's swamplands and travels to the port of New Orleans to visit. She adores Manfred's island, which he calls Sugar

Devil Island, because she can easily hunt victims and hide their bodies. Manfred makes her a tomb so she can sleep during the day. One night, she and Manfred make a deal: he will give her the island on the condition that she will make him a vampire. Petronia readily agrees to this, and even helps Manfred brutally murder his second wife, Rebecca. After Petronia receives Sugar Devil Island, she returns to Naples, but Manfred follows and demands that she keep her end of the bargain. At first she balks, but Arion commands her to keep her word, so Petronia turns Manfred Blackwood into a vampire.

They make a small coven and live together for many years. Relocating finally to Sugar Devil Island, Petronia and her coven members watch the Blackwood family mature into the twentieth century, with the birth of Tarquin "Quinn" Blackwood. Petronia has a special interest in Quinn. She visits him and Aunt Queen on Blackwood Farm, intrigued to know him more intimately. When his romance with Mona Mayfair intensifies, Petronia kidnaps him and turns him into a vampire. Along with Arion and Manfred, she teaches Quinn how to hunt evildoers, hide their remains, and keep the existence of vampires away from suspicious mortals.

Petronia soon learns that her fledgling Quinn is being haunted by the ghost of his mortal twin brother, Garwain. Motivated by

a great desire to help him, Petronia introduces Quinn to the Vampire Chronicles, in the hope that the vampire Lestat might have some way of helping her fledgling.

For more perspectives on Petronia in the Vampire Chronicles, read the *Alphabettery* entries **Arion**, **Garwain Blackwood**, **Goblin**, **Manfred Blackwood**, **Quinn Blackwood**, **Rebecca Stanford**, and **Sugar Devil Island**.

Philip Blackwood

• MORTAL •

Upon the establishment of Blackwood Farm, the founders Manfred and Virginia Lee have a small family of four children, William, Camille, Isabel, and Philip. Philip's two eldest siblings live into adulthood, and William even becomes the ancestor of Quinn Blackwood. Isabel dies in childhood of lockjaw, and Philip himself also dies in childhood, from influenza.

Philip Blackwood appears in *Blackwood Farm* (2002). For more perspectives on Philip's character, read the *Alphabettery* entries **Blackwood Farm**, **Camille Blackwood**, **Isabel Blackwood**, **Manfred Blackwood**, **Quinn Blackwood**, **Virginia Lee Blackwood**, and **William Blackwood**.

Pierre Roget

• MORTAL •

After Lestat is turned into a vampire and inherits Magnus's great fortune, which is mostly in gems, he seeks the assistance of a mortal who can help manage his finances. He finds the lawyer Pierre Roget in the Marais district in Paris. Lestat believes him to be clever and industrious but also greedy enough to assist him in accomplishing anything for the right cost. Lestat never reveals his vampire nature to Roget, but instead tells him that he is the husband of an heiress from Saint-Domingue. Roget helps Lestat exchange his highly valuable gems for currency. He also makes sure that Roget sends money back to his family in the Auvergne.

Through Roget's efforts, Lestat also becomes a benefactor to his mortal companion Nicolas "Nicki" de Lenfent, and to their old acting troupe at Renaud's House of Thesbians. When Lestat's mother, Gabrielle, moves to Paris from the Auvergne because she is dying, Roget cares for her. As the French Revolution is quickly approaching, Roget quite cunningly moves all of Lestat's finances out of France and into foreign banks. Lestat moves away from Paris after he nearly reveals his vampire nature to the audience at Renaud's House of Thesbians, and he depends on Roget to keep him informed of matters in Paris and the Auvergne. As the French Revo-lution in its nascence is beginning to sweep through the Parisian streets, Lestat hears less and less from Roget, and sometimes wonders why he stops receiving messages from Pierre Roget's little home in Marais. The fate of Pierre remains unknown.

Pierre Roget appears in *The Vampire Lestat* (1985). For more perspectives on his charac-ter, read the *Alphabettery* entries **Gabrielle, Lestat de Lioncourt, Magnus, Nicolas de Lenfent,** and **Renaud's House of Thes-bians.**

Pointe du Lac Plantation

• SANCTUARY •

Louis de Pointe du Lac inherits his family's plantation on the river when his father dies. He runs it successfully until his younger brother, Paul, dies. Louis blames himself for Paul's death and falls into a deep depression, which leads to alcoholism, gambling, and the squandering of his family's fortune. The Pointe du Lac plantation survives awhile lon-ger after the vampire Lestat turns Louis into a vampire. But the two vampires cannot hide their blood drinking for long. The plantation slaves become aware that their master and his companion are unnatural demons sent by the Devil. Shortly after Lestat convinces Louis to kill Lestat's blind father, the Marquis de Lion-court, Louis's slaves decide to burn the Pointe du Lac plantation to the ground, believing that they are righteously exorcising demons.

The Pointe du Lac plantation appears in *Interview with the Vampire* (1976). For more perspectives on this plantation in the Vam-pire Chronicles, read the *Alphabettery* entries **Lestat de Lioncourt, Louis de Pointe du Lac,** and **Paul de Pointe du Lac.**

Pops

• MORTAL •

The son of Gravier Blackwood, Thomas Blackwood comes to be called Pops and never shows any interest in leaving Blackwood Manor. He marries a young lady named Rose, whom everyone calls Sweetheart. Their daughter, Patsy, desiring to be a country-western singer, leaves Blackwood Farm for New Orleans, where she plays in a country band and parties in the city's nightlife. At the age of sixteen, she becomes pregnant with twin boys, Tarquin and Garwain, but Garwain dies in infancy. Pops and Sweetheart raise their grandson, Tarquin, whom they call Quinn, when Patsy shows no interest in being a teenage mother. Pops tries to get Quinn psychological help when he claims to be seeing his dead twin brother's ghost, Goblin. Pops suffers a massive heart attack and dies, causing Quinn deep distress. The next time Quinn sees Pops is when he is performing an exorcism ritual on Goblin. Pops appears in the light of Heaven, to Quinn's utter astonishment.

Pops appears in *Blackwood Farm* (2002). For more perspectives on his character, read the *Alphabettery* entries **Blackwood Farm**, **Blackwood, Manor**, **Goblin**, **Gravier Blackwood**, **Patsy Blackwood**, **Quinn Blackwood**, **Rose Blackwood**, **Sweetheart**, and **Thomas Blackwood**.

The Presence

• IDIOM •

After Lestat is turned into a vampire, then abandoned by his master, he lives in eighteenth-century Paris, doing his best to discover his vampire powers. With a vast fortune to support him, he lives a lavish lifestyle, which draws the attention of Armand's coven, the Children of Darkness, who follow the five Great Laws that forbid them from taking any pleasure in their vampire existence. Observing that Lestat is breaking their coven's laws, they begin to follow him around Paris. Because Lestat does not know how to sense the presence of other vampires, he perceives Armand's coven watching him as a mysterious presence. Thus, not knowing who or what they are, he simply refers to them as "the presence."

The presence appears in *The Vampire Lestat* (1985). For more perspectives on the presence in the Vampire Chronicles, read the *Alphabettery* entries **Armand**, **Children of Darkness**, **Great Laws**, and **Lestat de Lioncourt**.

Pretty Justine

• WITCH •

Pretty Justine is a Voodoo queen in New Orleans, shortly after the Civil War, who associates with Oncle Vervain (the brother of Merrick's godmother, Great Nananne), and his grandfather (the Old Man), as well as Lucy Nancy Marie Mayfair. It is reported that Pretty Justine can demonstrate so much Voodoo power that everybody is afraid of her.

Her descendants eventually move out of New Orleans to New York.

Pretty Justine appears in *Merrick* (2000). For more perspectives on her character, read the *Alphabettery* entries **Great Nananne, Lucy Nancy Marie Mayfair, Merrick Mayfair,** and **Oncle Vervain.**

Prime Minister of Vampires

• HONORIFIC •

After Prince Lestat restores Château de Lioncourt in the early twenty-first century, Marius becomes the Prince's right-hand immortal. He commands other vampires and holds sway over the Court of the Prince. He oversees the aesthetic atmosphere of the Château. He also composes a new set of laws that govern the vampire race in the second millennium of the Common Era. Lestat is so impressed with Marius's passion for the Court of the Prince that he dubs him with the unofficial title "Prime Minister" of vampires.

The "Prime Minister" title appears in *Prince Lestat and the Realms of Atlantis* (2017) and *Blood Communion* (2018). For more perspectives on the Prime Minister of vampires, read the *Alphabettery* entries **Château de Lioncourt, Court of the Prince, Lestat de Lioncourt,** and **Marius.**

Prince Alexi Brovotkin

• MORTAL •

After Garekyn the Replimoid survives the destruction of Atlantis, he drifts in the ocean until he washes ashore near modern-day Siberia. To regain his strength, he goes into the Siberian mountains and falls into a deep sleep, where he eventually becomes trapped in ice. Almost eleven thousand years later, in the late nineteenth century of the Common Era, Garekyn is rescued by Prince Alexi Brovotkin, who brings him back to Russia, educates him, and adopts him into his royal family, giving him the name and title Prince Garekyn Zweck Brovotkin.

Prince Alexi Brovotkin appears in *Prince Lestat and the Realms of Atlantis* (2016). For more perspectives on his character, read the *Alphabettery* entries **Atlantis, Garekyn, Prince Garekyn Zweck Brovotkin,** and **Replimoid.**

Prince Garekyn Zweck Brovotkin

• IMMORTAL •

After being trapped in ice in the mountains of Siberia for nearly eleven thousand years, Garekyn the Replimoid is taken to nineteenth-century Russia and educated on the royal estate of the Brovotkins. Adopted by Prince Alexi Brovotkin, Garekyn is given the title and name Prince Garekyn Zweck Brovotkin, which allows him to move more freely through the modern world, even into the twenty-first century, when he comes to discover that other Replimoids like himself have also survived the sinking of Atlantis.

Prince Garekyn Zweck Brovotkin appears in *Prince Lestat and the Realms of Atlantis* (2016). For more perspectives on his character, read the *Alphabettery* entries **Atlantis**, **Garekyn**, **Prince Alexi Brovotkin**, and **Replimoid**.

Prince Lestat

• VAMPIRE CHRONICLE •

In the eleventh book in the Vampire Chronicles, Lestat describes how the mysterious Voice is influencing powerful vampires with the Fire Gift to immolate weaker vampires, inciting a Great Burning similar to Akasha's nearly three decades earlier, when Lestat's rock music awakened her. This time it is not Akasha, but the voice of Amel, the spirit that fused with Akasha's blood in ancient Egypt four thousand years before the Common Era. Though his consciousness is suppressed in the fusion for thousands of years, it awakens now in the wounded mind of Mekare, who beheaded Akasha, consumed her brain and heart, and took Amel, the Sacred Core, into herself. Amel desires to be free of her mind and be put into the mind of a stronger vampire. He seeks out Rhoshamandes, who was turned into a vampire nearly one thousand years after Akasha's transformation. Amel inspires Rhoshamandes to kill Maharet and Khayman, so that he can consume Mekare's brain and transfer Amel into himself. But Rhoshamandes is worried that he will die before the transfer can be complete, which will destroy every vampire. So Rhoshamandes kidnaps Viktor—Lestat's clone and son, created by the vampire doctors Fareed and Seth, and Lestat and Flannery Gilman—to extort them into transferring Amel from Mekare into himself, as quickly and safely as possible. Lestat learns of this and forces Rhoshamandes to surrender Mekare and Viktor. Once they are returned safely, Mekare no longer desires to live without her sister. She gives herself to Lestat, who sucks her brain through her eye socket and takes into himself Amel, effectively becoming the new host carrier of the Sacred Core of vampire existence, as well as the new ruler of all vampires, Prince Lestat.

For more perspectives on this Vampire Chronicle, read the *Alphabettery* entries **Akasha, Amel, Fareed Bhansali, Khayman, Lestat de Lioncourt, Maharet, Mekare, Rhoshamandes, Seth,** and **Viktor.**

Prince Lestat

• HONORIFIC •

After Maharet is killed by Rhoshamandes, and Mekare the Queen of the Damned no longer desires to continue living without her twin sister, she offers herself to Lestat, urging him to consume her brain and take into himself Amel and his Sacred Core. Becoming the new host carrier of vampire existence, Lestat needs a new title. Instead of becoming the King of the Damned, and having enjoyed being given the unofficial honorific "Brat

Prince," he prefers simply to be called by the title "Prince Lestat."

The "Prince Lestat" title appears in *Prince Lestat* (2014) and *Prince Lestat and the Realms of Atlantis* (2016). For more perspectives on this title, read the *Alphabettery* entries **Amel, Lestat de Lioncourt, Maharet, Mekare, Queen of the Damned,** and **Rhoshamandes.**

Prince Lestat and the Realms of Atlantis

• VAMPIRE CHRONICLE •

In this twelfth book of the Vampire Chronicles, Lestat tells how the spirit of Amel now lives in him, making him the host carrier of the Sacred Core of vampire existence, as well as the ruling Prince of all vampires. When a new breed of immortals is discovered who

have the ability to replicate themselves, Amel begins to remember his past. The vampires meet with these replicating immortals, one of whom is Kapetria. She tells the tale of how she and her Replimoid companions were created on the planet Bravenna, informed that

Amel is a traitor, and ordered to destroy him and his creation, the city of Atlantis. When they come to Earth, they learn that Amel created the city to protect the people of Earth from being exploited by the Bravennans, who consume human suffering through a transference of psychic energy. Amel also informs them that he is originally from Earth but was abducted by the Bravennans, genetically enhanced into a superhuman, and returned to Earth to help them feed off human suffering. He created a unique substance called luracastria, which prevents Bravennans from exploiting humans. The Replimoids join Amel, but the Bravennans soon learn of their treachery and send a meteor shower to Earth, which destroys Atlantis and Amel. His spirit still possesses the genetic enhancements of his formerly corporeal state, and he roams the etheric world for thousands of years, forgetting about his former life, until he fuses with Akasha, to create the first vampire. By using her own Replimoid cells, Kapetria creates a clone of the body Amel had in Atlantis. Then she works with the vampires Fareed and Seth to extract Amel from Lestat's brain and transfer him into the cloned body. Now vampires no longer need to depend on a vampire host to sustain their existence. Lestat and Amel can finally see and speak with each other face-to-face.

For more perspectives on this Vampire Chronicle, read the *Alphabettery* entries **Amel, Atlantis, Bravenna, Bravennans, Kapetria, Lestat de Lioncourt, Luracastria, Replimoid,** and **Sacred Core.**

Pulcinella

• CHARACTER •

Pulcinella is a stock character in plays in the commedia dell'arte style developed in the late Italian Renaissance. As in old Italian *pulcinella* means "little chicken," his name embodies his tone of voice, which is often high-pitched and squeaky. The character is also portrayed as disabled or hunchbacked, who, through his own simple wisdom, does his utmost to help the main lover marry while also thwarting the older people in the play trying to prevent the marriage. Pulcinella can be best understood in contemporary terms as the character Mr. Punch in the Punch-and-Judy puppet shows.

Lestat mentions Pulcinella as one of the characters in the plays that make him popular as a mortal actor in the Avignon countryside, *Lelio and Isabella*, and in Paris, *Lelio and Flaminia*.

The Pulcinella character appears in *The Vampire Lestat* (1985). For more perspectives on this character, read the *Alphabettery* entries **Commedia dell'Arte, Lelio,** and **Lestat de Lioncourt.**

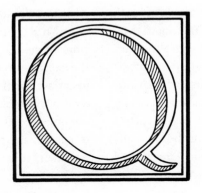

Queen Elizabeth 2

• SANCTUARY •

eatured in *The Tale of the Body Thief*, the *Queen Elizabeth 2* (*QE2*) is an ocean liner whereupon the Body Thief, Raglan James, endeavors to hide from Lestat after stealing his body. David Talbot books tickets on the *QE2* for himself and Lestat. On the ship, Lestat (in Raglan's former mortal body) and David Talbot find Raglan James (in Lestat's vampire body) and fight with him until David psychically pushes Raglan's etheric form out of Lestat's body and back into his mortal body.

David then also helps Lestat's etheric form move out of Raglan's mortal body and back into his vampire body, thus finally thwarting the Body Thief's plan.

The *Queen Elizabeth 2* appears in *The Tale of the Body Thief* (1992). For more perspectives on the *Queen Elizabeth 2* in the Vampire Chronicles, read the *Alphabettery* entries **Alexander Stoker, David Talbot, Eric Sampson, Jake, Jason Hamilton, Lestat de Lioncourt, Raglan James,** and **Sheridan Blackwood.**

The Queen of the Damned

• VAMPIRE CHRONICLE •

After the rock music of the Vampire Lestat band awakens the first vampire, the nearly six-thousand-year-old Queen Akasha, she rampages across the world, burning her children, in a plan for global domination. Akasha's ancient foe, the vampire Maharet, gathers a few remaining vampires together and tells them the story of her twin sister, Mekare, and of their dealings with Akasha in ancient Egypt. At the end of Maharet's tale, Akasha appears before them, having taken Lestat as a new companion and an imminent king, and she gives them a chance to be her servants. All the vampires reject her, includ-ing Lestat. They try to fight against her, but she is too powerful for them. Also, if they kill her, they kill themselves, for the Queen of the Damned is so connected to her vampire children that if she suffers any wound, they suffer also. Mekare appears and beheads Akasha; right before Akasha dies, Mekare consumes her brain and heart, making herself the new Queen of the Damned.

For more perspectives on this Vampire Chronicle, read the *Alphabettery* entries **Akasha**, **Lestat de Lioncourt**, **Maharet**, **Mekare**, and **The Vampire Lestat**.

Queen of the Damned

• HONORIFIC •

When the vampire Queen Akasha cuts out the eyes of the mortal Maharet and the tongue of her twin mortal sister, Mekare promises that she will one day return for vengeance and curses her as the Queen of the Damned.

The title remains throughout the long centuries, especially on the lips of the First Brood army, which rebels and fights against Akasha's army, the Queens Blood.

In the twentieth century, Mekare herself dons that same title when, after beheading Akasha, consuming her brain and heart, tak-ing the spirit of Amel into herself, and becom-ing the carrier host of the Sacred Core, she is hailed as the new Queen of the Damned—the supreme monarch of all vampires.

The "Queen of the Damned" title appears in *The Queen of the Damned* (1988) and *Prince Lestat* (2014). For more perspectives on this title in the Vampire Chronicles, read the *Alphabettery* entries **Akasha**, **Amel**, **Enkil**, **First Brood**, **Khayman**, **Lestat de Lioncourt**, **Maharet**, **Mekare**, **Queens Blood**, and **The Vampire Lestat**.

Queens Blood

• HONORIFIC •

Nearly four thousand years before the Common Era, a division arises among the inaugural Drinkers of the Blood when Khayman, Maharet, and Mekare create the First Brood, an army of blood drinkers to combat Queen Akasha and King Enkil's tyrannical rule, and Akasha creates the Queens Blood, an opposing vampire army. Each vampire in the Queens Blood drinks Akasha's blood to be more powerful than the First Brood, which is growing in number. She makes her mortal lover, Nebamun, their Captain. For decades they continue to combat the First Brood. Even Akasha and Enkil's biological son, Seth, becomes a member of the Queens Blood when she transforms him from a twenty-five-year-old healer into a great warrior.

Not all blood drinkers of the Queens Blood share the same power. Akasha gives most blood drinkers only enough blood to make them formidable fighters. To a select few, she gives much of her blood, transforming them into incredibly powerful blood drinkers, stronger than her average vampire soldier.

The Queens Blood lasts for many centuries as a powerful army, until the First Brood finally defeats these blood drinkers, captures Akasha and Enkil, and imprisons them underneath massive blocks of diorite and granite. Remnants of the Queens Blood linger throughout the centuries and become the heirs to Akasha's blood drinker religion, especially when Akasha and Enkil become statuelike and are enthroned as the Mother and the Father, Those Who Must Be Kept.

The Queens Blood is referenced in *The Queen of the Damned* (1988) and *Prince Lestat* (2014). For more perspectives on the Queens Blood, read the *Alphabettery* entries **Akasha**, **Enkil**, **First Brood**, **Khayman**, **Maharet**, **Mekare**, **Seth**, and **Those Who Must Be Kept**.

Quinn Blackwood

• VAMPIRE •

Quinn Blackwood is like Louis in that he is a native of the Louisana swamplands, but he is the one vampire whose attitude about life and love most resembles Lestat's. Lestat even goes so far as to call him his Little Brother.

Quinn appears in *Blackwood Farm* (2002) and *Blood Canticle* (2003).

Patsy Blackwood, daughter of Pops and Sweetheart, gives birth to twin boys, Tarquin and Garwain, when she is only sixteen years old. Garwain dies shortly after Tarquin's birth. Although his full name is Tarquin Anthony Blackwood, everyone calls him "Quinn." He is a direct descendant of Julien Mayfair, who impregnated his great-great-grandmother Grace Blackwood, wife of sterile William Blackwood, son of Manfred, founder of Blackwood Farm, thus making Quinn a direct relation to the Mayfair family of witches. Quinn is raised by his grandfather and grandmother, Pops and Sweetheart, in a grand southern mansion called Blackwood Farm, located in the dense, dank bayou of Sugar Devil Swamp. Quinn's mother, Patsy, still lives on the property, behind the main Blackwood house, in a small building that mostly houses workmen and occasional guests. Although he never knew his father, Quinn is told throughout his childhood that his mother, Patsy, is his sister, due to the fact that her undependable behavior makes her incapable of raising a child. Surrounded by no other children, Quinn matures in the presence of his grandparents, Jasmine the housekeeper, house servants, groundskeepers, and guests that visit Blackwood Farm.

By the time Quinn is three years old, he is haunted by a ghost called Goblin, who is actually the spirit of his dead twin brother, Garwain. The ghost has the ability to move objects and can be very mischievous. As Quinn grows older, he and Goblin communicate more, and Goblin often expresses jealousy whenever Quinn shows interest in anything besides him. Quinn also observes that Goblin ages at the same rate as himself and has similar ways of speaking and behaving. Although most people believe that Goblin is Quinn's imaginary friend, individuals with strong psychic abilities can see the ghost.

Goblin demands all of Quinn's attention, especially when Quinn encounters ghosts in an old cemetery, which are torpid and uninteresting to Quinn, as Goblin constantly haunts him. Quinn spends the next few years struggling to receive an institutional education, especially because he does not get along with other children, since all he truly wants is to live at Blackwood Farm with his family. He also goes to a psychologist who tells him that Goblin is a figment of his imagination that will eventually disappear. Around the same time, Quinn encounters Lorraine McQueen, his great-aunt, also called Aunt Queen. She spends a lot of time with Quinn and hears him talk about Goblin. Quinn begins to suspect that Aunt Queen can see Goblin, but she will not admit to this. Before returning to her home in New York, she hires a teacher, Lynelle Springer, who will teach Quinn on Blackwood Farm so that he will not have to leave it for another educational institution. Lynelle humors Quinn and pretends to speak with Goblin and eventually teaches Goblin new words to speak, although he is not as clever as Quinn. Quinn grows to be highly intelligent and articulate. He is also well traveled, mainly due to the benevolence of Aunt Queen. On his first trip to New York, Quinn notices that Goblin grows weaker the farther he moves away from Blackwood Farm. And when Quinn travels around the world, Goblin cannot go with him because the distance is too far from Blackwood Farm, but Goblin is still there when Quinn returns.

After a string of deaths in Quinn's life— Lynelle Springer who dies in a car crash when he is seventeen and his grandmother Sweetheart when he is eighteen—he goes into the attic and discovers much about the history of Blackwood Farm, especially about a woman named Rebecca Stanford. Following this discovery, the ghost of Rebecca appears to Quinn. He finds her more alluring than haunting and has a night of intimacy with her. She asks him to uncover the truth about her death. After Quinn makes several inquiries into the matter, Aunt Queen explains to him that Rebecca was the second wife of Manfred.

Quinn goes deep inside Sugar Devil Swamp in search of the place where Manfred was rumored to have murdered Rebecca. His search leads him to Sugar Devil Island, where a Romanesque tomb with the name PETRONIA stands near an old hermitage. Therein, Quinn finds Rebecca's remains. While on the island, Quinn also finds evidence that someone is still living in the Hermitage. He leaves a note telling the person living in the house to leave, but Quinn then receives a note telling him to never return to the island.

Ignoring this threat, Quinn decides to renovate the Hermitage and he invites the police to take away Rebecca's long-deceased corpse, but during the course of the renovation, Quinn's grandfather Pops dies. In his grief, Quinn enjoys a night of passion with Jasmine, the housekeeper, who, unknown to him at the time, becomes pregnant. Meanwhile, Quinn tries to convince others of the stranger living on the island, but no one believes him, until one night when the stranger appears and attacks Quinn. Saved by Goblin, who scares off the stranger, Quinn has wounds so severe that he is taken to May-

fair Medical Center, where he encounters Mona Mayfair, who is slowly dying after having given birth to a Taltos child, Morrigan.

Quinn and Mona spend much time together in the hospital and fall in love. Aunt Queen invites Quinn to travel with her to Europe, and he feels obliged to accompany her, as this will likely be her last trip, due to her great age. Quinn promises Mona that they will email often.

Unexpectedly, Quinn's travels throughout Europe last for three years, yet he and Mona continue an email correspondence. She signs off as his "Ophelia Immortal" while he signs off as her "Noble Abelard." With Jasmine's assistance, Quinn also emails Goblin, who cannot accompany Quinn that great distance away from Blackwood Farm.

Upon his return, Quinn discovers that, as a result of their night together, Jasmine has given birth to Quinn's son, Little Jerome. Quinn also discovers that Mona's condition has worsened, but the opportunity to visit her is taken from him when Petronia takes him with her vampiric power and speed to Italy, where he meets two other vampires, the twenty-five-hundred-year-old Indian, Arion, and Quinn's ancestor Manfred Blackwood. Then, against Manfred's protests, Petronia turns Quinn into a vampire.

Petronia, Manfred, and Arion explain to Quinn the confines of his new existence, namely that the Talamasca Order is now his enemy, and that Quinn can never again return to New Orleans because the vampire Lestat is guarding it from being hunted by any other blood drinker. Despite his maker and his ancestor, Quinn is truly taught how to be a vampire by Arion, who lets Quinn drink from his ancient blood, which increases his strength. After he learns how to hunt mortals and hide from them, Quinn returns to Blackwood Farm, despite Petronia and Arion's objections. Upon returning home, Quinn discovers that his mother, Patsy, HIV-positive, has now contracted the AIDS virus. When Quinn meets Goblin again, the nature of the ghost of his dead twin brother becomes altogether different. Goblin violently attacks Quinn and drinks his blood whenever Quinn drinks blood, which augments Goblin's strength. Petronia returns to Sugar Devil Island where she learns of Quinn's predicament with Goblin. She shows him the Vampire Chronicles, where he learns more about Lestat.

Eagerly hoping that Lestat can help him, Quinn goes to his townhouse in New Orleans and explains to him the situation. Lestat observes how, after Quinn drinks the blood of a victim, Goblin appears, attacks Quinn, and drinks his blood. When Goblin attacks Quinn a second time, Lestat attacks the ghost, who in turn goes and kills Aunt Queen. To rid Quinn of Goblin forever, Lestat enlists the aid of the newly made vampire, Merrick Mayfair, who is also a witch of the Mayfair family. Utilizing the etheric potency surrounding the death of Aunt Queen, Merrick plans to perform an exorcism ritual with a pyre and Goblin's long-deceased corpse, Garwain Blackwood. Before the ritual starts, Quinn sees once more the ghost of Rebecca, who desires vengeance for her death. Quinn's mother, Patsy, also comes into the house and begins saying and thinking many hateful things at him. Furious with her, Quinn breaks her neck without drinking her

blood and leaves her body in the swamp to be eaten by alligators, which satisfies Rebecca's need for vengeance, although that matters little to Quinn.

In preparation for the exorcism, Lestat lets Quinn drink some of his more powerful blood to ensure that Quinn's increased strength will be able to survive the ritual. After the exorcism ritual begins, Merrick realizes that Goblin is not going into the light of Heaven. Not knowing what else to do, and desiring to help Garwain's soul have peace in the Afterlife, Merrick holds Garwain's corpse and leaps into the pyre, which burns her to death.

Following this, Mona Mayfair arrives at Blackwood Farm to spend her final days with Quinn, the man she loves, knowing that she has wasted many years in the hospital and that she does not have much longer to live. Quinn reveals to her that he is now a vampire and he introduces her to Lestat, who instantly loves her. Knowing that she will make an excellent immortal, Lestat turns Mona into his fledgling vampire, as a favor to Quinn, so that he can be with her forever.

For more perspectives on Quinn Blackwood's character, read the *Alphabettery* entries on **Arion, Aunt Queen, Garwain Blackwood, Goblin, Héloïse, Hermitage, Jasmine, Lestat de Lioncourt, Little Jerome, Lorraine McQueen, Lynelle Springer, Manfred Blackwood, Merrick Mayfair, Mona Mayfair, Morrigan Mayfair, Noble Abelard, Ophelia Immortal, Patsy Blackwood, Petronia, Pops, Rebecca Stanford, Sweetheart, Talamasca Order, Taltos,** and **Virginia Lee Blackwood.**

Raglan James

• MORTAL •

aglan James is the second villain Lestat must confront in the twentieth century, after aiding in the defeat of Akasha, the Queen of the Damned. A kleptomaniac by nature, Raglan has the psychic ability to telekinetically move astral bodies out of their physical bodies so that he can move his own astral body inside and steal the physical body. Raglan James appears only in *The Tale of the Body Thief* (1992).

Demonstrating exceptional telepathic abilities from an early age, Raglan James becomes a prominent member of the Talamasca Order. Because of his incessant kleptomania, the Order quickly dispatches him to the secular world, where he employs his telepathic abilities to acquire dishonest wealth. Through his work in the Talamasca, he learns a procedure for astral projecting his etheric form, for detaching the silver cord from his corporeal body, for reattaching it to a new corporeal body, and then for settling his etheric form inside this new body—in other words, he learns how to be a body thief.

James coerces many people to switch bodies with him. Occasionally this process helps him prosper financially, yet his compulsiveness often leads to his capture and imprisonment by the authorities. And when his newest body is dying or in jeopardy, he switches bodies again.

Shortly before meeting Lestat, Raglan switches bodies with a mechanic, who is a drug dealer and who also recently became so intoxicated by his own narcotics that he murdered his entire family. Once Raglan switches bodies with the mechanic, Raglan kills him.

When Raglan finally encounters the vampire Lestat, he attempts to force out Lestat's etheric body so that he can live in a body that will never get sick and never die, but he quickly learns that he does not have the psychic strength to steal a vampire's body. So he begins to woo Lestat, first sending him movies with the theme of body switching and finally contacting him, offering him the chance to experience mortality once again for the fee of ten million dollars. After considering this, and taking precautions, Lestat agrees to pay him twenty million dollars, although Raglan cannot have access to it until after they switch back to their usual bodies. Despite all of Lestat's precautions, Raglan plans to never surrender the vampire body.

Stealing all of Lestat's finances, leaving him penniless and dying, Raglan eludes Lestat, the Talamasca, and other vampires, until he books passage on the *Queen Elizabeth 2* cruise ship. Lestat's mortal friend, David Talbot, Superior General of the Talamasca, uses his influence to gain passage on that same ship. When they find Raglan, David forces Raglan out of Lestat's body and helps Lestat back. But it is dawn, and Lestat must flee. Raglan and David contend throughout that day, but Raglan is much younger and stronger and forces David out of his body so that he can take possession of it. Raglan then evades David in his former body and meets Lestat later that evening after the vampire awakes from his daytime slumber. In David's body, Raglan tricks Lestat not only into believing that he is David but also into turning him into an immortal. Having longed to turn David into a vampiric companion, Lestat willingly agrees, but when Lestat bites into his neck and drinks his blood, the blood reveals to him that this is not David, but actually Raglan. Full of fury, Lestat grips Raglan's head and crushes it, thus ending the life of crime of the Body Thief.

For more perspectives on Raglan James's character, read the *Alphabettery* entries **David Talbot, Lestat de Lioncourt,** and **Talamasca Order.**

Ramiel

• IMMORTAL •

After Vittorio is abandoned in the streets of Florence by the vampire Florian, he encounters two angels, Ramiel and Setheus, who tell him that they are the guardian angels of Fra

Filippo. With the angel Mastema, the three angels help Vittorio return to Florian's Court of the Ruby Grail and slay all the vampires inside, all except Vittorio's paramour, Ursula.

Ramiel appears in *Vittorio the Vampire* (1999). For more perspectives on Ramiel's character in the Vampire Chronicles, read the *Alphabettery* entries **Court of the Ruby Grail**, **Florian**, **Fra Filippo**, **Mastema**, **Setheus**, **Ursula**, and **Vittorio di Raniari**.

Raphael the Archangel

• IMMORTAL •

Raphael the Archangel is typically known as God's healer, as his name literally means "God has healed." In the Book of Tobit (found in the Catholic and Orthodox Bible canon), Raphael the Archangel came from Heaven to help Tobias heal his wife from demon possession and to heal his father's blindness.

During Lestat's pilgrimage through Heaven and Hell with Memnoch, he encounters Raphael the Archangel, one of the most important angels in the celestial hierarchy, ranking slightly lower than Michael the Archangel. In the book *Memnoch the Devil*, Raphael is portrayed as weeping for the fallen Memnoch.

Raphael the Archangel is written of in *Memnoch the Devil* (1995). For more perspectives on Raphael the Archangel in the Vampire Chronicles, read the *Alphabettery* entries **Lestat de Lioncourt**, **Memnoch**, and **Michael the Archangel**.

Rashid

• VAMPIRE •

The vampire Eudoxia is hundreds of years old by the time she meets the young Rashid, shortly after the founding of Constantinople. Instantly attracted to him, she turns him into a vampire and welcomes him into her home, full of vampire slaves. Impressed by his talents, she elevates him above her other slaves and makes him, along with her other fledgling, Asphar, one of her constant companions.

When the vampire Marius moves to Constantinople, Eudoxia realizes that he has brought with him the Mother and the Father of the vampire race, Akasha and Enkil. Having drunk from the Queen hundreds of years earlier, Eudoxia desires to do so again. She sends Rashid and Asphar to invite Marius to her home, where she tells Marius about her past, especially about how she once drank the blood of Queen Akasha. She next reveals to Marius that she knows he is protecting Those Who Must Be Kept, and she demands that he allow her to drink from Akasha once more. When Marius refuses, Eudoxia, who thinks she is stronger than him, tries to take Akasha and Enkil by force. Rashid is the first to discover that Marius is much stronger than all of them when Marius, who has been drinking the Queen's blood for many years now, stops Eudoxia's attack with his Fire Gift and incinerates Rashid to ashes.

Rashid appears in *Blood and Gold* (2001). For more perspectives on Rashid's character, read the *Alphabettery* entries **Akasha**, **Asphar**, **Enkil**, **Eudoxia**, **Fire Gift**, **Marius**, and **Those Who Must Be Kept**.

Raymond Gallant

• IMMORTAL •

Raymond Gallant begins as an operative for the Talamasca; he is turned into a vampire shortly before he dies of old age; he is killed as a vampire and becomes a ghost until he finally learns how to become an incarnate spirit. Raymond Gallant appears in *Blood and Gold* (2001), *Prince Lestat* (2014), and *Prince Lestat and the Realms of Atlantis* (2016).

Born in fifteenth-century England, Raymond Gallant exhibits brilliant psychic abilities throughout his life that earn him a prominent place as a member of the Talamasca Order. Assigned to the Motherhouse in London, Raymond quickly learns the classical languages and becomes a master of many ancient traditions of the supernatural and the occult. One of his most passionate areas of study is the life of Marius de Romanus, who at this time is nearly fifteen hundred years old, although the exact date when Marius received the Dark Gift is still a mystery to Raymond; he only knows that Marius is very old.

In Raymond's late teens, a letter comes to the Motherhouse from a Talamasca member, informing the Order that Marius is now in Venice. Aware of Raymond's extensive study into Marius's life, the Talamasca dispatches him to Venice to confirm that the vampire seen is indeed Marius de Romanus. In Venice, on the first day Marius opens his Venetian palazzo to mortal citizens, Raymond enters among the throng of mortals. Over the course of the next few years, he observes more of Marius's life, particularly his mortal ward Amadeo. Raymond writes many letters back to his Motherhouse, describing everything he sees so that the Talamasca can grow in knowledge and understanding of the preternatural world, which so many mortals are ignorant of, while others have often persecuted creatures like Marius.

Much later, in Marius's home, Raymond approaches Marius's steward, Vincenzo, about purchasing books on magic. When Vincenzo informs him that Marius already has numerous books and a vast library, Raymond subsequently notices Marius's paintings and questions whether Marius does them himself. Later, Vincenzo expresses all of this to Marius, who grows interested in Raymond. Although Raymond is not able to purchase a painting from Vincenzo, he does find a painting that Marius has cast aside, and he takes it with him back to his modest lodgings, far away from the huge palaces of the Grand Canal.

Two months after this encounter, Raymond follows Marius, Amadeo, and Bianca to a lavish banquet. When Amadeo and Bianca stand to dance, leaving Marius alone, Raymond cordially introduces himself. He then proceeds to introduce Marius to the existence of his Order, the Talamasca, handing the vampire a gold coin engraved with TALAMASCA. Raymond speaks to Marius in fluent classical Latin and with a fearless disposition. He informs Marius of everything that he has learned, including the fact that Marius has recently turned his mortal ward Amadeo into a vampire, as well as his belief that Marius's female companion, Bianca, will most likely become his next fledgling. Marius is both intrigued and upset by how Raymond has invaded his life, simply by being aware of his existence, as well as by entering his house and approaching the steward. Raymond is courteous, civil, and also aware that Marius can kill him at any time. He promises Marius that the Talamasca has no interest either in revealing the existence of vampires or in harming them, but rather the Order offers sanctuary and knowledge. Marius permits him to live, but on the condition that he leave Venice immediately. Before departing, Raymond tells Marius that he is welcome to contact him for anything simply by writing a letter to Lorwich, a Talamasca castle, the Motherhouse for the Order in East Anglia. Marius dismisses him, but after thinking on this later that night, he goes to Raymond's lodgings and assures Raymond that he meant no harm. Once inside, Marius asks Raymond about his fledgling, the vampire Pandora, from whom he separated many centuries earlier and about whom he has thought longingly ever since.

Raymond informs Marius of all he knows, that a young vampire who despises being a blood drinker came to the Talamasca, begging for them to find some way to make him mortal again. This vampire told the Talamasca how he encountered Pandora and listened to the tale of her life with Marius, which is how the Talamasca first learned of him. The young vampire also told them how she was with a blood drinker from India and how this blood drinker was somehow manipulating her, keeping her hostage, but the vampire knew no more than that. Marius is grateful to Raymond for all this information, but he urges him to leave Venice, to return to the Motherhouse, and to write to him of any news he hears of Pandora. Then before Raymond leaves, Marius draws blood by biting into his tongue, and then he allows Raymond to taste his blood, the way he did many times with Amadeo as a mortal.

After Raymond leaves, Marius's Venetian palazzo is attacked by Santino and the Children of Satan. They burn the palazzo to the ground, kill many of its inhabitants, capture Amadeo, and almost burn Marius to death. Raymond writes to Marius whenever he has news, but he receives no reply for the next ten years, as Marius and his new fledgling, Bianca, move away and create a new shrine for Those Who Must Be Kept. At length, Raymond receives his first letter from Marius by the hand of a German monk, informing him of all that has happened over the past several years. Raymond immediately replies, informing Marius that Pandora and her Indian companion are traveling all over Europe, but never to England. Raymond also informs him that his fledgling, Amadeo, is now going by the name Armand and is the leader of a group of Satan-worshipping vampires in Paris who call themselves the Children of Darkness. Raymond also urges Marius not to go in search of either Pandora or Armand, because there are wars occurring all over Europe.

Many years pass between their exchange of letters. Marius finally travels to the Talamasca Motherhouse in East Anglia, where he meets Raymond, now an old man in his eighties, once more during his mortal life. Raymond informs Marius of all that he knows of Pandora's travels with her companion, how they gallivant all over Europe, never seeming to stay in one place, and how they are traveling under the titles "the Marquis and Marquisa de Malvrier." By the peculiar pattern in their travels, Raymond deduces that their lair must be in Dresden. Raymond also informs him that Armand is still the leader of the Children of Darkness in Paris. Marius is grateful to Raymond for all of this information, but

before Marius leaves, Raymond asks him if he has ever heard any news of the origins of the Talamasca. To Raymond's dismay, Marius confesses that he has not, but wishes him well in finding the answer.

At the age of eighty-nine, Raymond is on his deathbed, and the nearly six-thousand-year-old vampire Teskhamen comes and speaks tenderly with him about his fledgling vampire Hesketh, who has died and returned as an incarnate ghost, along with the ghost Gremt, who helped her learn how to incarnate. Teskhamen next explains how the three of them began the Talamasca many years earlier. Teskhamen then gives Raymond the Dark Gift. The ancient vampire's blood restores some of Raymond's youth, but he is unlike most other vampires, who are made at a young age; he is gaunt and thin, very delicate looking, with skin as iridescently white as mother-of-pearl.

Unfortunately, Raymond's life as a vampire does not last into the twenty-first century. After Raymond's death, Gremt (the same incarnate spirit who teaches Hesketh how to become incarnate) teaches Raymond how to transcend beyond his ghostly form and evolve into an incarnate presence capable of interacting with mortals and immortals alike, thus giving Raymond three lives, one with the Talamasca, one as Teskhamen's fledgling vampire, and one as Gremt's pupil ghost.

For more perspectives on Raymond Gallant's character, read the *Alphabettery* entries **Amadeo**, **Armand**, **Children of Darkness**, **Children of Satan**, **Gremt Stryker Knollys**, **Hesketh**, **Marius**, **Pandora**, **Santino**, **Talamasca Order**, and **Teskhamen**.

Realm of Worlds

• SANCTUARY •

The Realm of Worlds is the collection of visible worlds in the known universe. There is no exact number for the quantity of planets in the Realm of Worlds, but all of them are visible; the invisible worlds are not included. Every species on the planets in the Realm of Worlds lives in harmony with its planet. Some planets are ruled by birdlike creatures; others are ruled by intelligent insects; and many are ruled by creatures that resemble rational reptiles. Sentient life evolves out of almost every kind of species, except mammals. To the inhabitants of most individuals in the Realm of Worlds, the sentient life of mammals is an aberration and an abhorrence. One planet in the Realm of Worlds is called Bravenna. The inhabitants of the planet discover that human suffering is an invaluable resource for consumption. To most adequately consume the ethereal energy of their psionic food, they set up transmission stations on planet Earth—initially cared for by Amel—which transmit the data of human suffering throughout the Realm of Worlds and especially to the inhabitants of Bravenna, because, from the perspective of the inhabitants of the Realm of Worlds, human beings are the most savage, cruel, and inhumane creatures that ever existed in the universe.

The Realm of Worlds appears in *Prince Lestat and the Realms of Atlantis* (2016). For more perspectives on the Realm of Worlds in the Vampire Chronicles, read the *Alphabettery* entries **Amel** and **Bravenna**.

Rebecca Stanford

• IMMORTAL •

Rebecca Stanford is the second wife of Manfred Blackwood, founder of Blackwood Farm. Manfred murders Rebecca, and her ghost haunts Blackwood Farm, seeking vengeance. She appears in *Blackwood Farm* (2002).

Rebecca is born in New Orleans's Irish Channel, near Saint Thomas and Washington, in the seventeenth century, at a very low rank in society. Her Irish father and her German grandmother abuse her and her twelve siblings with a leather strap. Eventually she takes up work as a maid in a Garden District mansion, where she is raped. When her family discovers the violation, they want her to enter a Catholic convent, but she has no inclination for the religious life, so she goes instead downtown to Storyville, where she enters a house of prostitution. Soon after, she discovers that she is pregnant because of the rape, but the child never comes to term.

Rebecca finds being in a brothel very enjoyable, with its constant flow of piano playing and new gentlemen. But she has no desire to die as a prostitute in Storyville, so she pretends to be a refined lady, taking up embroidery and crocheting. The other prostitutes mock her, calling her the Countess. But when Manfred Blackwood enters the brothel, he is immediately enamored of Rebecca. He gives her beautiful jewelry and soon asks her to be his wife.

They travel to Europe and have a delightful honeymoon. Little does she know that, on their travels throughout Europe, her new husband, Manfred, encounters the hermaphrodite vampire Petronia, who is utterly fascinated with his tales of the Louisiana swampland. Rebecca returns to Louisiana with Manfred, oblivious that Petronia has accepted Manfred's invitation to visit his home.

Rebecca notices a stark change in Manfred's behavior, which is colder and more aloof towards her, particularly when he compares her with his first wife, the late Virginia Lee, who, according to others, was a saint. Rebecca's behavior becomes scandalous in the household, embarrassing many members by revealing private secrets. When Manfred can no longer bear the embarrassing behavior of his wife, he drags Rebecca out to Sugar Devil Island, where Petronia is waiting for them. Rebecca endures unimaginable torture at the hands of both Manfred and Petronia, until at last they kill her and hang her body on a hook to rot for the next hundred years.

The ghost of Rebecca Stanford lives on for decades, until one of Manfred's descendants, Quinn Blackwood, begins seeing the ghost of his dead twin brother, Garwain, who calls himself Goblin. Rebecca Stanford appears to Quinn when he turns eighteen, after he discovers her belongings in the attic. Aunt Queen reveals to him how poorly Rebecca treated other members of the Blackwood family, and how she went missing, not long before Manfred himself also went missing. Quinn finds Rebecca's ghost so very alluring that they have a night of supernatural passion, after which she asks him to uncover the truth about her murder. Agreeing, Quinn eventually discovers Rebecca's corpse in the Hermitage on Sugar Devil Island.

Rebecca's ghost appears to Quinn one last time, after Petronia turns him into a vampire, when he and the vampire witch Merrick are performing an exorcism ritual on Goblin. When Quinn's alcoholic mother, Patsy, tries to interrupt the ritual, Quinn breaks her neck and hides her body in the swamp. Satisfied that a life has been taken for a life, Rebecca's ghost leaves the world of mortals forever.

For more perspectives on Rebecca Stanford's character, read the *Alphabettery* entries **Garwain Blackwood**, **Goblin**, **Hermitage**, **Lestat de Lioncourt**, **Manfred Blackwood**, **Merrick Mayfair**, **Patsy Blackwood**, **Petronia**, and **Quinn Blackwood**.

Regina Blackwood

• MORTAL •

Regina is the wife of Patrick Blackwood, younger brother of Gravier Blackwood, son of William, who is the son of Manfred Blackwood, founder of Blackwood Farm. Regina and Patrick have one daughter, Nanette. After Patrick falls from a horse and dies, Regina lives the rest of her life in Blackwood Manor. Although she does not need to, she is always working in the kitchen, as if she were one of the Kitchen Gang, frying and slicing and chopping. After she dies, her ghost is never seen haunting Blackwood Manor; it is believed that she is resting soundly with her late husband, Patrick, in the family crypt. Regina is the great-great-aunt of Quinn Blackwood.

Regina Blackwood appears in *Blackwood Farm* (2002). For more perspectives on her character, read the *Alphabettery* entries **Gravier Blackwood, Kitchen Gang, Manfred Blackwood, Patrick Blackwood, Quinn Blackwood,** and **William Blackwood.**

Releth

• TALTOS •

Releth is one of the male Taltos who live on Ashlar's Secret Isle, where many other Taltos also live in secrecy, far away from the mortal world. Ashlar's son Silas causes rebellion, and retaliation by a mortal drug cartel ensues. When gun-carrying Drug Merchants invade the island, Releth is shot and killed.

Releth appears in *Blood Canticle* (2003). For more perspectives on his character, read the *Alphabettery* entries **Ashlar, Drug Merchants, Silas,** and **Taltos.**

Renaud

• MORTAL •

Renaud is the owner of Renaud's House of Thesbians, which employs the mortal Lestat and encourages his love for performance. Renaud appears in *The Vampire Lestat* (1985).

Coming to Paris for the first time in the eighteenth century, Lestat, along with his companion Nicolas, needs work. Nicolas is already an accomplished violinist, having studied under the tutelage of Wolfgang Amadeus Mozart, and Lestat already has some theater practice, traveling with a troupe of actors and performing a play in the commedia dell'arte style with great success: *Lelio and Flaminia*, with Lestat in the role of Lelio. They find work at a little theater on the Boulevard du Temple, Renaud's House of Thesbians. Its old manager, Renaud, allows them to perform menial tasks, such as handing out playbills or cleaning up after the show. One night in late August, Renaud gives Lestat his opportunity to perform before the audience and discovers that Lestat is an immediate success. At the insistence of one of the most prominent actresses in the troupe, Luchina, Renaud hires Lestat to perform every night and to never touch another broom or mop again.

Renaud soon loses his famous actor when Lestat is mysteriously kidnapped from his Parisian room. But several months later, Lestat returns in letters, not appearing, but revealing that he is safe and that he has inherited a vast fortune. Lestat buys the theater from Renaud and pays off all his debts. Renaud is still allowed to run the theater while Lestat maintains ownership. Renaud is delighted when Lestat pours out his fortune upon the theater, buying all new props and wardrobes. His delight turns to amazement many months later when Lestat finally returns in person. Much changed, and much the same, Lestat takes to the stage with a performance that frightens the audience. Little do they realize that he is now a vampire and that he is using his vampire power to leap and speak across the stage with superhuman strength. The entire audience flees, except one elderly member, who draws a pistol from his coat pocket and shoots Lestat at point-blank range. As a vampire, Lestat is not wounded by the bullet, but Renaud, the troupe, and the audiences of Paris now suspect that something strange must have occurred during Lestat's absence.

Mortified by his own behavior, Lestat immediately closes Renaud's House of Thesbians, then buys Renaud a new theater in London. Renaud accepts Lestat's gift and moves his entire troupe to his new theater on Drury Lane across the Channel. From there, Renaud spends the rest of his days putting on plays and taking those plays across the Atlantic, to the American theaters in New York and New Orleans.

For more perspectives on Renaud's character, read the *Alphabettery* entries **Commedia dell'Arte**, **Flaminia**, **Lelio**, **Lestat de Lioncourt**, **Luchina**, **Nicolas de Lenfent**, and **Renaud's House of Thesbians**.

Renaud's House of Thesbians

• SANCTUARY •

When Lestat and Nicolas first move to Paris in the late eighteenth century, before their transformation into blood drinkers, they begin work at a little theater on the Boulevard du Temple called Renaud's House of Thesbians. The owner, Renaud, hires Lestat and Nicolas to perform menial tasks, taking tickets and sweeping up. In time, Nicolas begins playing his violin with the orchestra. Lestat conceals his royal name, de Lioncourt, calling himself Lestat de Valois, and starts performing in the theater's shows. Quickly Lestat's stardom grows; all the people of Paris are talking about his wild performances and coming to Renaud's House of Thesbians just to watch him perform. One night in the audience sits the vampire Magnus, who, after watching Lestat's performance in reading his mind, decides that Lestat is the only one worthy to be his fledgling. After Magnus turns Lestat into a vampire and commits suicide, Lestat inherits Magnus's vast fortune, which he uses to purchase Renaud's House of Thesbians and to pay off all its debts.

One night, Lestat returns to the theater. Cajoled into performing, he allows his supernatural ability to show off and frighten the audience with his agility and speed. Then he sings his song so loudly with supernatural power that it makes the audience scream in fear. An old man with a pistol comes out of the audience and shoots Lestat, but his vampire body is impervious. The sight of this frightens the audience as well as his former acting colleagues.

Lestat flees from the theater and pays for Renaud and the actors to begin a new theater house in London. Lestat then closes his theater on the Boulevard du Temple and does not open it again until he convinces Armand to destroy his coven, the Children of Darkness, leaving only four survivors—Eleni, Felix, Eugénie, and Laurent—who beg Lestat to open the theater for them so that they can have a place to stay. They remain safe inside the theater until Lestat's new fledgling, Nicolas, joins them and demands that Lestat give them the theater as their new coven house. Reluctantly acquiescing, Lestat gives them the theater and leaves Paris. Nicolas renames Renaud's House of Thesbians as Théâtre des Vampires. One of the four survivors, Eleni, writes to Lestat and informs him of their progress. Armand has joined, Nicolas has become their playwright and composer, and the theater is growing very popular in Paris among mortals.

Nicolas is also going mad, revealing his vampire nature in the streets to ordinary mortals, frightening them, and jeopardizing the vampires at the *théâtre*. Armand imprisons Nicolas and cuts off his hands. But in time other coven members replace his hands, and Nicolas continues writing plays and music. But his madness drives him to suicide.

With Armand leading and protecting

them, the Théâtre des Vampires actors continue to perform onstage, pretending to be humans who pretend to be vampires, until the nineteenth century, when two more of Lestat's fledglings, Louis and Claudia, come to Paris. Eleni, Felix, Eugénie, and Laurent have by this time left the coven. Armand invites Louis and Claudia to the theater to watch their shows. Claudia despises them, but Louis is intrigued by Armand, who can provide for him all the answers he desires. Another member of that coven, a young vampire named Santiago, grows suspicious that Louis and Claudia have broken one of the Great Laws of their former Satanic coven by killing their maker. When Lestat appears at the theater unbeknownst to Louis and Claudia, he reveals to Armand, Santiago, and the rest of the coven that Claudia did indeed attempt to kill him, but Louis is innocent. Because Armand desires to have Louis as a companion, he allows Santiago to use this confession against Claudia, condemning her to death and freeing Louis from his companionship with her. After Claudia is burned alive, Louis vengefully burns the Théâtre des Vampires to the ground, along with most of the vampires inside it, save Armand, who spurns Lestat and takes Louis as his companion for the next few centuries, leaving behind the charred remains of what once was Renaud's House of Thesbians.

Renaud's House of Thesbians appears in *The Vampire Lestat* (1985) and in *Interview with the Vampire* (1976) as the Théâtre des Vampires. For more perspectives on this residence, read the *Alphabettery* entries **Armand, Children of Darkness, Claudia, Eleni, Eugénie, Felix, Great Laws, Laurent, Lestat de Lioncourt, Lestat de Valois, Louis de Pointe du Lac, Nicolas de Lenfent, Renaud, Santiago,** and **Théâtre des Vampires.**

Renfield

• ALIAS •

"Renfield" is a possible alias that Lestat considers in *Memnoch the Devil*. The alias is named after the character in Bram Stoker's 1897 gothic novel, *Dracula*. When David Talbot helps Lestat check into the Olympic Hotel in New York City, Lestat wonders if David will use a former alias, "Isaac Rummel," or if he will change it to "Renfield."

The "Renfield" alias appears in *Memnoch the Devil* (1995). For more perspectives on this alias, read the *Alphabettery* entries **David Talbot, Lestat de Lioncourt,** and **Memnoch.**

Replimammoid

• IMMORTAL •

Replimammoid is the first classification that Bravennan scientists give to their human mammal facsimiles that are immortal and have the power to replicate and regenerate. In time, the term is shortened to "Replimoid."

Replimammoids appear in *Prince Lestat and the Realms of Atlantis* (2016). For more perspectives on this immortal being, read the *Alphabettery* entries **Derek**, **Dertu**, **Garekyn**, **Kapetria**, **Katu**, **Replimoid**, and **Welf**.

Replimoid

• IMMORTAL •

Scientists from the planet Bravenna create human fetuses out of cells from all of Earth's life chain and grow those fetuses into humanoids. These humanoids are genetically enhanced to replicate themselves; their replicating ability is also regenerative, which grants them immortality. They have dark skin like many humanoids from the African continent. At first, these humanoids look the same, until Bravennan scientists develop ways of creating variety in their cloning procedures. The Bravennans then refer to these replicating humanoids as replimammoids, but this is soon shortened to simply "Replimoids."

Their replication occurs by severing one of their limbs so that a new appendage grows in place while the severed limb grows into an entirely new humanoid life. This happens in the case of Derek, when Rhoshamandes severs his left arm. A new arm regenerates out of Derek's torso, in the place where it had been

cut off, while the actual severed appendage grows into a perfect clone of Derek, whom he calls Dertu—a combination of "Derek Two."

The Bravennans send multiple raiding parties of Replimoids to attack a previous Bravennan experiment named Amel, who has created the city of Atlantis to thwart the Bravennan agenda for consuming the psionic energy of human suffering. Amel's superior intellect and strength either defeats the Replimoids or converts them to his cause. This is especially true with the last group of Replimoids sent to Earth, consisting of Kapetria, Derek, Garekyn, and Welf.

When the Bravennans destroy Amel and Atlantis, the Replimoids are separated for thousands of years, but they reunite in the twenty-first century to help Lestat and his vampire companions provide a Replimoid host body for the spirit of Amel.

Replimoids appear in *Prince Lestat and the*

Realms of Atlantis (2016) and *Blood Communion* (2018). For more perspectives on Replimoids, read the *Alphabettery* entries **Amel, Atlantis, Bravenna, Bravennans, Derek, Dertu, Garekyn, Kapetria, Luracastria,** and **Welf.**

Replimoid Colony

• COVEN •

After the Replimoids reunite to help free Amel from Lestat's mind by giving the disembodied spirit a new Replimoid body, Kapetria, Derek, Garekyn, Welf, Amel, and their Replimoid clones relocate to a rural section of England and begin a Replimoid colony in an abandoned asylum. Gregory and Gremt help Kapetria purchase it, along with a stately manor house and majority ownership of a nearby village. The Replimoids create a health spa in the village, where they conduct scientific experiments, endeavoring to rediscover the secret formula for luracastria, and experimenting on the replicating ability of their Replimoid clones. They even renovate the local church, invite a vicar, and attend Vespers every evening. By 2018, Kapetria has cloned herself thirty times, while Derek, Garekyn, and Welf have each replicated themselves ten times.

In time the spirits of Gremt, Hesketh, and Magnus join the colony. Teskhamen also joins the community, but he also comes to the Court of the Prince.

The Replimoid colony appears in *Blood Communion* (2018). For more perspectives on the Replimoid colony, read the *Alphabettery* entries **Amel, Derek, Garekyn, Kapetria, Lestat de Lioncourt, Luracastria, Replimoid,** and **Welf.**

Revenant

• VAMPIRE •

Similar to the hybrid creatures made from the blood of Akasha and Enkil thousands of years before the Common Era, revenant vampires are essentially mindless monsters that attack humans and vampires alike, behaving more out of instinct than from reason.

One revenant vampire is discovered by Louis after the vampire slays a mortal— Emily, the recent bride of young man named

Morgan—in a European village, and Morgan asks Louis for his assistance. When Louis beholds this revenant vampire, he realizes that it is a mindless creature with flesh barely clinging to its skin, looking almost like a zombie, newly risen from the grave.

Revenant vampires appear in *Interview with the Vampire* (1976) and *The Vampire Lestat* (1985). For more perspectives on revenant vampires, read the *Alphabettery* entries **Akasha, Emily, Enkil, Louis de Pointe du Lac,** and **Morgan.**

Rhoshamandes

• VAMPIRE •

Rhoshamandes is Akasha's servant until he runs away to form his own coven. He eventually becomes the great-grand-maker of Lestat when his fledgling, Benedict, is drained of blood by Magnus, who makes Lestat. Rhoshamandes becomes the most notorious villain of the twenty-first century when he murders Maharet and Khayman. He appears in *Prince Lestat* (2014), *Prince Lestat and the Realms of Atlantis* (2016), and *Blood Communion* (2018).

One thousand years after Amel enters into Queen Akasha, Rhoshamandes is born a mortal on the island of Crete to an Indo-European family. Living in a very poor family without a father and with only a needy mother, he is the oldest of ten mortal children. When he is twelve, his mother is murdered. He runs away from home and works as a seaman, his skin gains a creamy tan, and his arms and chest grow strong and muscular. At the age of twenty he sails up the Nile to trade with the Egyptians. His wits help him to survive many battles without violence or scars until the night Queen Akasha's vampire slaves kidnap him from his boat and bring him before her. After she and her priests thoroughly examine him for any imperfections, they determine that he is a perfect vampire, then force him to pledge his eternal fidelity to her before they drain him of his blood and make him drink Queen Akasha's blood, turning him into a vampire. Despite their efforts, Rhoshamandes never truly feels any fidelity to her and considers her to be an absolutely heartless, megalomaniacal tyrant.

Although Rhoshamandes never actually encounters Maharet, Mekare, or Khayman, he is able to telepathically glean from other vampires the history of the last one thousand years, about the war of the First Brood, which is still being waged at that time. He is given the choice either to serve under the Captain of the Queens Blood, Prince Nebamun (who later becomes Gregory Duff Collingsworth), or to be imprisoned in a shrine where he will be worshipped by mortals as a judging god between their disputes and given blood only on particular feast days. Choosing to serve under Nebamun, Rhoshamandes becomes not only Nebamun's soldier but also his friend. He will not abandon Nebamun when he takes the Nordic slave Sevraine as his Blood Wife, turns her into a vampire, and, as a result, is imprisoned by Akasha in a god shrine for his blasphemy, since it is against the Queen's command to turn a woman into a vampire; Akasha will be the only goddess blood drinker. Rhoshamandes goes to Nebamun's shrine prison and offers to set him free, but Nebamun urges him to escape before revealing to him the truth about Akasha and Enkil, that they are not the Mother and the Father of gods but that a spirit called Amel fused with Akasha and transformed her into the progenitor of their race. Rhoshamandes leaves Nebamun but returns fifty years later to smash Nebamun's shrine to dust and set him free. Rhoshamandes and Nebamun then part ways.

During the Great Burning of 4 C.E., when the Elder sets the statuesque Akasha and Enkil under the sun, which burns all vampires, Rhoshamandes's skin burns to dark brown, and he suffers great agony for months. He makes his way to modern-day France, where he sires what he comes to call his line of de Landen vampires, which includes Benedict, Allesandra, Eleni, Eugénie, Notker, and Everard, all with the surname de Landen. The Children of Satan are thriving in that same region. They attack Rhoshamandes and his fledglings and capture Everard, Allesandra, Eleni, and Eugénie; Notker escapes to the Alps. Having no desire to fight the Children of Satan, Rhoshamandes leaves France with Benedict for Northern England, around 1100 C.E., after the Norman Conquest. In order to ensure his and

Benedict's safety, Rhoshamandes spends the next hundred years building a castle in the French Gothic style. He is a kindly lord to the mortals who construct it. In the bedrock beneath the castle, he builds secret chambers for his own safety against the sun and enemies, which no mortal can access. As the years progress, he adds newer architectural styles that improve the overall stability and security of his fortress. For many centuries he rules that land, which extends even into modern-day Germany and France and which comes to be known as the realm of Rhoshamandes. He never hunts in the major cities of Edinburgh, Dublin, or London but always clings to the quiet of the countryside.

During the fifteenth century, Magnus seeks to become a vampire, but Rhoshamandes rejects him because he is too old, too humpbacked, and not beautiful enough. As a result, Magnus ascertains the secret hiding place of Benedict's daytime lair. He binds Benedict, drains his blood, drinks it, and turns himself into a vampire. By all accounts, Rhoshamandes could have destroyed Magnus, but instead he loves him, respects him, and places his seal of protection on him and vows that no vampire will harm him for his transgression against Benedict, not even Benedict himself, whom Magnus has greatly humiliated.

In the twenty-first century, when Amel begins speaking to vampires as the mysterious Voice, he reveals himself to Rhoshamandes in a plot for him to kill Mekare, drink her blood, and transfer Amel, the Sacred Core, into Rhoshamandes. Amel no longer desires to be trapped inside Mekare's damaged mind but desires rather to live inside a powerful and strong vampire like Rhoshamandes. Amel tricks Rhoshamandes into going to Maharet's secret compound, killing Maharet and Khayman, and then kidnapping Mekare. Rhoshamandes is afraid that he will die before he fully consumes Mekare's brain. Amel instructs him how to kidnap Lestat's clone and son, Viktor, to extort the vampire scientist Fareed into helping him fully consume Mekare's brain before death. Lestat learns of the plan, severs Rhoshamandes's left arm, and forces him to surrender Viktor and Mekare.

Rhoshamandes retreats to his castle in the north of England, his arm having been restored to its place. Although many vampires seek to destroy him for what he has done to Maharet and Khayman, Lestat urges everyone to forgive him, but he also places the mark of Cain upon Rhoshamandes: no one can kill him lest they receive a sevenfold punishment.

Rhoshamandes lives for a time on his private island of Saint Rayne. When Benedict leaves him and kills himself in the Court of Prince Lestat, Rhoshamandes blames Lestat and vengefully kidnaps Gabrielle, Louis, and Marius. He keeps them in his old dungeon, *bet ha sohar*, in the Loire Valley in France. Lestat offers a truce. Rhoshamandes takes Lestat to another private island, in the Pacific Ocean, where Lestat completely destroys Rhoshamandes, drains him of blood, and brings his body back to Château de Lioncourt so that the Court of the Prince can drink the remainder of his blood. Rhoshamandes's last words are *"bet ha sohar . . . bet ha sohar . . ."*

For more perspectives on Rhoshamandes's character, read the *Alphabettery* entries **Akasha, Allesandra, Amel, Children of Darkness, Eleni, Eugénie, Everard, Khayman, Lestat de Lioncourt, Line of de Landen Vampires, Maharet, Mekare, Nebamun, Notker the Wise,** and **Viktor.**

Riccardo

• MORTAL •

When Marius rescues Armand from a Venice brothel, he brings him back to his palazzo, where Armand discovers that Marius has many wards under his care. The eldest of those wards is Riccardo, who is Marius's apprentice in the arts. Despite all of Marius's peculiar behavior, Riccardo never guesses that his master is a vampire, unlike Armand, who eventually realizes his master's blood-drinking nature and begs Marius to make him a vampire also.

When Santino and the Children of Satan destroy Marius's palazzo for his heretical activities and then capture Armand to convert him to their ways, Riccardo is killed and given to Armand to drink from during his imprisonment.

Riccardo appears in *Blood and Gold* (2001). For more perspectives on Riccardo's charac-ter, read the *Alphabettery* entries **Armand** and **Marius**.

Riverbend Plantation

• SANCTUARY •

In the 1700s, when Marie Claudette May-fair, the sixth witch in Lasher's thirteen-witch breeding program, moves from Europe, she buys land in Louisiana, not far from New Orleans, upon which she develops the River-bend plantation. It is run by Mayfair witches all the way to Julien Mayfair, who eventually purchases a home on First Street.

Life at Riverbend highly impacts the May-fair family's interactions with other Louisiana families, especially the Blackwoods, two of whom become vampires, and one of which becomes the companion of a Mayfair.

The Riverbend plantation is referred to in *Blackwood Farm* (2002). For more perspec-tives on the Riverbend plantation, read the *Alphabettery* entries **Julien Mayfair**, **Mona Mayfair**, and **Rowan Mayfair**.

Rodrigo

• MORTAL •

When the Taltos Silas, the son of Ashlar and Morrigan, causes a rebellion on Ashlar's secret island, capturing his parents and siblings and any other Taltos who will not follow him, he attacks a nearby island full of mortals, who also happen to be employees of a massive drug cartel run by Rodrigo. Rodrigo retaliates by attacking the Secret Isle, killing many Taltos and capturing those who make no resistance. After gunning down Silas, Rodrigo locks Ash-lar and Morrigan in the large kitchen freezer on the compound on Ashlar's island, where the husband and wife freeze to death, locked in each other's embrace. Rodrigo controls the island for two years until the vampire Lestat arrives with his two companions, Quinn Blackwood and Mona Mayfair. The threesome attacks Rodrigo and his drug cartel, using their vampire gifts, namely the Mind Gift and the Fire Gift. Rodrigo attempts to escape as his men are being slain, and he falls from a balcony to his demise.

Rodrigo appears in *Blood Canticle* (2003). For more perspectives on Rodrigo's character, read the *Alphabettery* entries **Ashlar, Fire Gift, Lestat de Lioncourt, Mind Gift, Mona Mayfair, Morrigan Mayfair, Quinn Blackwood, Silas,** and **Taltos.**

Roger

• MORTAL •

Roger is Lestat's latest victim shortly before he encounters Memnoch the Devil. Roger is also a contract killer and a drug dealer who returns as a ghost to haunt Lestat and convince him to help Roger's televangelist daughter, Dora. Roger appears in *Memnoch the Devil* (1995).

Born in New Orleans, Roger lives with his drunken mother in a shabby yet superficially elegant boardinghouse that she owns, having inherited it from her mother. At a young age, Roger takes to the streets of New Orleans, particularly the French Quarter, where he meets the owner of a small book-and-antique shop on Royal Street. The owner, whom Roger calls the Old Captain, becomes like a father and mentor to him. Although there is an intimate attraction between them, they never act on it and maintain a familial relationship with each other. The Old Captain gives Roger a profound education on culture and life outside the city's limits. He also instills in Roger a deep love for the writer Wynken de Wilde. From Roger's freshman year of high school to his senior year, the Old Captain takes Roger across the United States, showing him various libraries and introducing him to the wider world. Roger discov-

ers many things about the Old Captain, one being that he is a cunning smuggler, which does nothing to diminish Roger's admiration for his mentor but on the contrary piques his interest. Educated by the Jesuits in New Orleans, particularly by Father Kevin, Roger can read Latin, and he begins a passionate translation of Wynken de Wilde's books into English. When the Old Captain grows ill, Roger stays by his bedside until the old man falls into a coma and finally dies. After that, Roger runs away to New York City where he also becomes a smuggler, but in that occupation in New York, he finds it necessary to delve deeper into a life of crime, becoming a notorious thief, a contract killer, and eventually a wealthy drug lord.

After making his fortune, he discovers that his mother is dying. Returning to New Orleans to care for her until her passing, he meets Terry, the practical nurse caring for his mother. Immediately attracted to each other, they have one passionate night together, which results in an unexpected pregnancy. Unwilling to have a long-term marriage to Terry, he offers her one hundred thousand dollars to marry him and then another one hundred thousand dollars to divorce him shortly thereafter, but only on the condition that she also give him their child, a daughter. At first, Terry agrees to this and marries Roger, who at that time goes under the alias "Roger Flynn." When their daughter is born, they name her Theodora Flynn, which is soon shortened simply to Dora. But after Dora's birth, Terry changes her mind and decides to keep Dora. Roger agrees to this reluctantly but visits Dora often and always lavishes upon her gifts and money.

After Terry finds a new love, she plans to run away with her paramour and take Dora with them. When Roger discovers this, he kills Terry and her boyfriend, and takes Dora to live with him. Dora matures into a woman who desires to be as much unlike Roger as possible. She studies theology, is ordained a minister, and becomes a popular televangelist. Throughout the years, she and Roger have a very rocky relationship, which ends when Roger is stalked and killed by the vampire Lestat. Roger's ghost returns to Lestat, who himself is being hunted by a presence which he calls the Stalker. Lestat listens attentively as Roger relates his story. At the end, Roger begs Lestat to protect his translations of Wynken de Wilde and also to protect Dora from Roger's enemies and his criminal reputation. He is relieved when Lestat agrees and is surprised when Lestat asks Roger to stay with them a little longer, but Roger knows he cannot. The Stalker comes for Roger and snatches away his spirit.

For more perspectives on Roger's character, read the *Alphabettery* entries **Dora**, **Father Kevin**, **Lestat de Lioncourt**, **Old Captain**, **Terry**, and **Wynken de Wilde**.

Roland

• VAMPIRE •

Roland is the fledgling of the vampire Baudwin. Roland befriends Rhoshamandes, the ancient vampire from the time of Akasha in ancient Egypt. Rhoshamandes sends Roland away. Though the parting is difficult, they both understand that their division will be best for their ultimate unity and friendship. Roland never holds the decision against Rhoshamandes and often keeps in close contact with him.

They reunite in the twenty-first century, after Amel seduces Rhoshamandes into killing Maharet and Khayman. Since then, Rhoshamandes has been in self-exile in his fortress castle, hiding away from other vampires and loathing the vampire Lestat for treating him so unfairly. Roland reveals to Rhoshamandes that he has captured a strange being named Derek. Initially, Roland was simply hunting Derek one night at the opera house in Budapest. Upon capturing him, Roland realizes that this Derek creature is neither mortal nor immortal, neither human nor vampire. Roland imprisons Derek beneath his palatial home a few blocks from the Budapest opera house. To his great delight, one of his first discoveries is that no matter how much blood he drinks from Derek, this creature regenerates more blood after about an hour, making Derek an unending fount of food, whose blood is thicker and sweeter and has greater nutrients than human blood. Roland shares Derek's blood with other vampires, including Rhoshamandes and Avicus. In the blood, they can sense a very ancient history, more ancient than that of vampires, extending all the way back to the city of Atlantis. It turns out that Derek is an artificial life-form called a Replimoid, created on the planet Bravenna. Roland holds Derek as a prisoner for

more than a decade, until Derek escapes and reunites with his Replimoid companions, who have by then befriended Lestat and his vampire coven. The Replimoids ask the vampires to enact vengeance against Roland for his injustice to Derek. Lestat and the vampires send Flavius, Teskhamen, Gregory, and others to Roland. With the Fire Gift, they utterly immolate him, with flames beginning in Roland's heart and expanding outward, until Roland is a swirl of fire and cinders, and nothing remains but a scorch mark on the carpet.

Roland appears in *Prince Lestat and the Realms of Atlantis* (2016). For more perspectives on Roland's character, read the *Alphabettery* entries **Derek**, **Replimoid**, and **Rhoshamandes**.

Rose

• VAMPIRE •

Rose is Lestat's adopted daughter and fledgling. She eventually becomes the Blood Spouse of Lestat's clone, Viktor, who is also his son and fledgling. Rose appears in *Prince Lestat* (2014), *Prince Lestat and the Realms of Atlantis* (2016), and *Blood Communion* (2018).

Rose's mother, Morningstar Fisher, dies in an island earthquake, but Rose is spared when a vampire takes her into his arms and flies her into the air with the Cloud Gift. He introduces himself as Lestat, but her young mouth can only shape the word "Lestan."

She never forgets the experience of flying high into the stars and being wrapped in the warmth of his thick coat. Learning that Rose does not know her father and that her grandparents care neither for her nor for her mother, Lestat adopts her as her uncle Lestan and takes her to Florida, where she is raised by retired schoolteachers whom she calls Aunt Julie and Aunt Marge. Her uncle Lestan visits on many occasions, giving her gifts and money. She is well taken care of and wants for nothing. In her teens, she is arrested for taking out her aunts' car and sent to a corrupt boarding school by a dishonest judge. After she endures months of torture at this school, another vampire appears, burns the school to the ground, and takes her from there to her uncle Lestan in New York City. This vampire introduces himself as her uncle's friend Louis.

Lestat gives her and her aunts a new apartment on New York's Upper East Side. She goes to a new school, and they have permanent housekeepers, cooks, and security-guard chauffeurs, her favorite being Murray, a stocky, muscular man who, before working for Lestat, was on the San Francisco police force for ten years.

She is accepted into Stanford University, where, after her first week of classes, she meets and falls madly in love with her literature professor, thirty-five-year-old Dr. Gardner Paleston. When she reveals to him how she was saved by her uncle Lestan, he turns on her angrily for believing in the fiction of *The Vampire Lestat*, which she has never heard of before. When she reads the Vampire Chronicles, she begins to believe that her uncle Lestan is truly the vampire Lestat and that the man who rescued her from the boarding school is his companion, the vampire Louis de Pointe du Lac. Rose ends her brief relationship with Gardner, which drives him mad. He kidnaps her and pours a poisonous concoction into her mouth and over her eyes, blinding her entirely. Murray finds her in time, kills Gardner, and rushes her to the medical facility of the vampire scientists Seth and Fareed.

Due to their decades of genetic research upon the Undead, Seth and Fareed are able to restore Rose's sight and health. When she awakens in her hospital bed, she is surprised to see a man who looks exactly like her uncle Lestan, only younger and more muscular. He introduces himself as Viktor, the son that her uncle never truly knew he had. In this facility, Rose begins to understand that all that she has read in the fiction of the Vampire Chronicles is true. Her uncle's name is not Lestan, but Lestat, and this powerful and popular vampire has cared for her ever since he saved her from that sinking island. To her delight, she also learns that, through another one of Seth and Fareed's medical procedures, Lestat fathered a son with one of the facility's doctors, Flannery Gilman, who was turned into a vampire after she gave birth to Viktor. Viktor is a mortal clone of Lestat and not a genetic combination of Lestat and Dr. Gilman.

Mortal like herself, Viktor teaches her about the supernatural world that exists around them. Rose and Viktor spend much time together in the vampire medical facility and grow to love each other greatly. But the five-thousand-year-old vampire Rhoshamandes kidnaps Viktor from the facility in an attempt to force Lestat and Fareed to use their skills to make Rhoshamandes the new King of the Damned. Rose beholds her uncle's full anger and strength when, after a brief struggle with Rhoshamandes, Lestat tears off his left arm and threatens to end his life if he does not release Viktor from captivity.

When Rose and Viktor are finally reunited, Lestat ensures that neither of them will ever come into jeopardy again by turning them both into powerful vampires. Delighted that they will be together for all eternity, Rose and Viktor vow their undying love by becoming Blood Spouses.

For more perspectives on Rose in the Vampire Chronicles, read the *Alphabettery* entries **Fareed Bhansali**, **Flannery Gilman**, **Lestat de Lioncourt**, **Louis de Pointe du Lac**, **Rhoshamandes**, **Seth**, and **Viktor**.

Rose Blackwood

• MORTAL •

Rose Blackwood is the birth name for Quinn Blackwood's grandmother, who raises Quinn and whom everyone calls Sweetheart.

Rose Blackwood appears in *Blackwood* *Farm* (2002). For more perspectives on her character, read the *Alphabettery* entries **Quinn Blackwood** and **Sweetheart**.

Rowan Mayfair

• WITCH •

Rowan Mayfair is the main hero of the Lives of the Mayfair Witches. She crosses over into the Vampire Chronicles shortly after Lestat turns her cousin, Mona Mayfair, into his fledgling. Rowan helps Lestat and Mona bring Mona's Taltos grandchildren back from the Secret Isle. Rowan appears in *Blood Canticle* (2003).

She grows up in San Francisco during the 1960s and '70s, unaware that she was kidnapped at birth and is an important member of the Mayfair family of witches. Her own abilities as a witch surface at the age of six, when by accident she psychically kills

a child on the playground, and again at the age of fourteen, when she unwittingly gives a would-be rapist a brain aneurysm. Her witching abilities continue to appear over the years, as several more people are accidentally killed because of her powerful psychic abilities. This eventually draws the attention of Aaron Lightner, a department head of the Talamasca, who is assigned to observe the Mayfair witch family closely.

Fascinated with genes and cellular structure, Rowan becomes a very talented doctor whose greatest feat is saving the life of her future husband, Michael Curry, after he's been dead for an hour. Rowan and Michael begin an intense romantic relationship until Aaron Lightner appears and informs them of the Mayfair family, dating back to the seventeenth century, back to Suzanne Mayfair, the first witch who formed a pact with the spirit Lasher. He serves the family, providing for them protection and great wealth, but they are a part of his systematic breeding program so that, through specialized gene formation by Mayfair inbreeding, Suzanne's twelfth direct female descendant will give birth to a Taltos, a giant immortal, with whom Lasher plans to fuse to become incarnate. Rowan is that thirteenth witch, destined to give birth to the foretold Taltos, destined to also be the Designée of the Mayfair Legacy, who will inherit the Mayfairs' great wealth as well as the responsibility of overseeing its distribution among the Mayfair family members.

Rowan and Michael return to New Orleans and introduce themselves to the Mayfair family. Accepted by the family as the Designée, she uses the family's vast fortune to create Mayfair Medical Center, a hospital committed to advanced medical research and charitable hospitalization.

Rowan begins having dreams that foreshadow Lasher's birth. She also becomes deeply concerned that if she and Michael are to conceive a child, Lasher will fuse with it. Despite her concerns, she is also greatly intrigued by the science underlying Lasher's imminent incarnation. When Michael and Rowan finally wed and conceive a child, Rowan feels deeply conflicted about her choice, either to help Lasher fulfill his plan for incarnation, or not. Lasher entices her by

appealing to her scientific mind, and he also promises that he will make her immortal.

When Rowan and Lasher are alone, Lasher reaches inside her womb and fuses with her unborn child, which begins to grow very quickly, and very painfully, like all Taltos children. Once born, Lasher rapidly matures into a fully grown man with the skin of a newborn. Rowan is terrified at first, but Lasher reminds her that he is still helpless and he needs her. Amazed at his newly incarnated form, Rowan starts taking Lasher away, but Michael confronts them. He attempts to fight Lasher, but even in his newborn form, Lasher is too powerful. He throws Michael into the swimming pool where he drowns and dies a second time, though first responders resuscitate him.

Rowan and Lasher go to Europe, where they begin wiring money out of the Mayfair legacy into private bank accounts. Lasher betrays Rowan and makes her his prisoner. He rapes her many times in the hope of making more Taltos so he can breed with them and populate the world. Rowan becomes pregnant twice, but they are miscarriages. When Rowan becomes pregnant a third time, she escapes, but, as before, the Taltos pregnancy is abnormally quick and very painful. She gives birth to a Taltos girl, Emaleth, who grows instantly into an adult and leaves Rowan in a comatose state.

Rowan returns to the First Street house, where Michael welcomes her home. Lasher follows her, but Michael kills him. Rowan's experience giving birth to two Taltos children, and having two Taltos miscarriages, is killing her. But her daughter, Emaleth, soon arrives at the First Street house to help

Rowan. Because Emaleth recently gave birth to Lasher's child, her breasts are full of Taltos breast milk, which contains superhuman nutrients that save Rowan. Fearing an overpopulation of Taltos, Rowan shoots Emaleth to death and then ravenously drinks her breast milk until she is completely healed.

Following this, Aaron Lightner is assassinated. Seeking justice for his death, Rowan and Michael unite with Yuri Stefano (Aaron's former Talamasca pupil), Samuel (a dwarflike Taltos), and an ancient Taltos named Ashlar. Together they discover that four members of the Talamasca are directly behind Aaron's murder: Anton Marcus, the Superior General of the Talamasca, along with two other members, Marklin George and Tommy Monohan. All four are trying to hide the fact that another Talamasca member, Stuart Gordon, has discovered another Taltos named Tessa, and that they have attempted to mate Lasher with Tessa, but she is too old to bear his children. To avenge Aaron's murder, Ashlar kills Anton Marcus; Rowan telepathically kills Stuart Gordon for his part in Aaron's murder and Tessa's subjugation; and the Talamasca, now run by Joan Cross as the Superior General, executes Marklin George and Tommy Monohan.

When Rowan and Michael return home, Rowan's cousin and the next Designée of the Mayfair Legacy, Mona Mayfair, reveals that when Rowan ran away with Lasher, Mona and Michael conceived a Taltos child. Like Rowan, Mona gave birth very quickly and very painfully, and her daughter is now a fully grown woman named Morrigan, whom Mona names the next Designée. Rowan and Michael accept Morrigan, but when their companion, Ashlar, appears at the First Street house, Morrigan and Ashlar are immediately attracted to each other and run away together.

Meanwhile, because of the rapid pregnancy with a Taltos child, Mona Mayfair is mortally wounded and dying. Rowan and Michael take her to Mayfair Medical Center, where they tend to her needs, but in the end, Mona does not want to spend her final days at the hospital, so she leaves and goes to the home of the man that she is in love with, Quinn Blackwood, at Blackwood Farm, where she meets the vampire Lestat, who, out of his love for her and for Quinn, turns her into an immortal blood drinker.

Lestat and Mona try to keep her transformation a secret from Rowan, but in his efforts, Lestat falls deeply in love with Rowan, and she soon feels the same for him. When she ultimately discovers the truth, Rowan realizes that she loves both Lestat and Michael and wants to be with both. But she is very tired of living her wearisome mortal life and implores Lestat to turn her into a vampire. He is greatly tempted to acquiesce, but in the end, he knows that the Mayfair family needs her, and refuses.

For more perspectives on Rowan Mayfair in the Vampire Chronicles, read the *Alphabettery* entries **Aaron Lightner, Designée of the Mayfair Legacy, Lasher, Lestat de Lioncourt, Mayfair Medical Center, Michael Curry, Mona Mayfair, Morrigan Mayfair,** and **Taltos.**

Ruby Grail

• IDIOM •

"Ruby grail" is a euphemistic term for an abundance of blood. The word "ruby" represents the color of blood; "grail" represents the ideal pursuit of all immortal blood drinkers, which also connotes the Christian seeking of a token of eternal life. The idiom is often employed by Lord Florian, Lady Ursula, and the vampires of their Court of the Ruby Grail, inside a castle where they keep mortals imprisoned and fattened for feasting upon.

The ruby grail euphemism can be found in *Vittorio the Vampire* (1999). For more perspectives on this idiom, read the *Alphabettery* entries **Court of the Ruby Grail**, **Florian**, **Ursula**, and **Vittorio di Raniari**.

Rue Royale

• SANCTUARY •

In the upper French Quarter of New Orleans, near Canal Street, lined with luxurious art galleries, bookshops, and antique markets, is the historic Rue Royale, the street where Louis and Lestat buy a townhouse in the eighteenth century, shortly after Louis's plantation is burned to the ground by slaves rioting because of their demonic master. Lestat, Louis, and Claudia live on that street for sixty-five years, but it is abandoned the night Claudia and Louis attempt to kill Lestat. In the late twentieth century, when Lestat and Louis have become close companions once again, they reside once more in that same townhouse on Rue Royale, along with two others, Lestat's fledgling David Talbot and Louis's fledgling Merrick.

Rue Royale appears in *Interview with the Vampire* (1976) and *Prince Lestat* (2014). For more perspectives on the Rue Royale residence in the Vampire Chronicles, read the *Alphabettery* entries **David Talbot**, **Lestat de Lioncourt**, **Louis de Pointe du Lac**, and **Merrick Mayfair**.

Russ

• VAMPIRE •

Russ is a member of the motorcycle group the Fang Gang and is in only *The Queen of the Damned* (1988).

Although his maker remains a mystery, Russ was likely turned into a vampire by Killer, the Fang Gang's founder, who also turned two other prominent members into vampires, Davis and Baby Jenks. Russ is a general friend to all members, but he seems most intimate with a fifth member, Tim, both of whom Baby Jenks calls "OK guys" in comparison with the more authoritative Davis and Killer.

Russ and Tim are eventually immolated by Queen Akasha at Lestat's one and only rock concert in San Francisco.

For more perspectives on Russ's character, read the *Alphabettery* entries **Akasha, Baby Jenks, Davis, Fang Gang, Killer,** and **Tim**.

Ruth

• TALTOS •

When the ancient Taltos Ashlar and his wife, Morrigan, leave the mortal world, they live on a secret island that Ashlar owns. Numerous other Taltos are also living on the island in safety from mortals. Ruth is among them. Ashlar and Morrigan have four Taltos children, one of whom, Silas, causes a rebellion, poisons his parents, and invades the nearby island owned by the Drug Merchants. Silas and his rebel companions kill several Drug Merchants and bring their drugs and money back to the secret Taltos island where they experience narcotic intoxication for the first time. They fire off their weapons in revelry. Ruth and another Taltos named Evan are accidentally shot and killed.

Ruth appears in *Blood Canticle* (2003). For more perspectives on Ruth's character, read the *Alphabettery* entries **Ashlar, Drug Merchants, Evan, Morrigan Mayfair, Silas,** and **Taltos**.

Sacred Core

• IDIOM •

he Sacred Core is the very life force of all vampires, connecting them intimately through a spiritual interdependency that permeates flesh and soul. Every vampire across the globe is interconnected by this etheric web that enhances supernatural abilities, bloodlust, and immortality.

The Sacred Core first sparks to life when the spirit of Amel—whose mortal life was genetically enhanced by the Bravennans (an alien species) and whose etheric form sustained those genetic enhancements on a spiritual plane of existence—fuses with Aka-sha's blood at the point of her death. In other words, when a spirit containing corporeal traces of Bravennan genetic enhancements made upon earthling DNA combines with the DNA of a human at the point of death, that rare act creates the life force of vampirism. And that life force comes to be called *the Sacred Core.*

This fusion creates two transformations: the spirit becomes the Sacred Core, and the mortal becomes the Sacred Core's vampire host, both intrinsically connected. In the same way that the mortal Lestat remains mostly intact after his transformation into a vampire, the spirit of Amel remains mostly intact after his transformation into the Sacred Core, only now he is intimately connected with Akasha, and she is his first vampire host. The two bodies are changed in some ways, yet they remain the same in many other ways.

After the fusion, Amel's consciousness is generally suppressed under the consciousness of the host vampire. Akasha does all the conscious thinking and feeling, while Amel behaves more like her subconscious instinct and autonomic reflexes, healing her wounds, giving her immortality, and driving her bloodlust.

In one sense, the interconnection between the Sacred Core and the entire vampire race can be compared to a massively intricate web that stretches out in every direction: each vampire is a point of connectedness in the web, like a star in relation to nearby stars as well as in relation to the center of the universe. Amel is that center. And because Akasha carries him for thousands of years, she, too, is the center of vampire existence. If Akasha is harmed, the wounds of that harm will spread throughout the connective net, hurting the weakest vampires gravely, but the stronger vampires minimally. An exam-

ple of this is when the Elder exposes Akasha and Enkil to the sunlight. Normally, the sun would immolate a vampire, but because the passage of time has strengthened their blood, the sun only bronzes their skin; yet through the interconnection with the Sacred Core, the immolating effect of the sun passes from Akasha to her fledglings—bronzing vampires of relatively equal age, charring younger vampires and burning to death the youngest and weakest.

Another example is when Mekare decapitates Akasha. As the blood drains from Akasha's severed head, all vampires in existence feel their own mortality equally threatened. If Mekare never consumed Akasha's brain, every vampire would have been destroyed. But when she consumes Akasha's brain and heart, she takes into herself Amel and his Sacred Core, making herself the new carrier host of all vampire existence.

The Sacred Core appears in *The Queen of the Damned* (1988), *Prince Lestat* (2014), and *Prince Lestat and the Realms of Atlantis* (2016). For more perspectives on the Sacred Core in the Vampire Chronicles, read the *Alphabettery* entries **Akasha**, **Amel**, **Lestat de Lioncourt**, and **Mekare**.

Sacred Fount

• IDIOM •

In the early years of her vampire existence, ruling over ancient Egypt, Akasha makes

most vampires with her own blood, particularly those who fight in her army, the Queens

Blood. After the war of the First Brood, when Akasha and Enkil are captured and imprisoned for many centuries, until they finally break free as lifeless statues, a priest cult develops around them, with the Elder in charge of caring for them. The Elder and the priests become the ones administering opportunities for vampires to drink the blood of the Mother, Queen Akasha. The priests divinize her blood, referring to it as the Sacred Fount.

An instance of one such vampire drinking from the Sacred Fount is when Cyril brings his fledgling Eudoxia to the shrine and makes her drink from the Queen, despite the protests of the priests.

The Sacred Fount appears in *Prince Lestat* (2014). For more perspectives on the Sacred Fount in the Vampire Chronicles, read the *Alphabettery* entries **Akasha**, **First Brood**, **Queens Blood**, and **Nebamun**.

Sacred Parents

• IMMORTAL •

Long after the war of the First Brood, when Akasha and Enkil have become something like living, unmoving statues, a priest cult reemerges, dedicated to the veneration of Akasha and Enkil, the Mother and the Father. The priest cult sets an elder vampire in charge of caring for the Mother and the Father, whom they also refer to as Those Who

Must Be Kept, but under more religious circumstances, they are also referred to as the Sacred Parents.

The Sacred Parents appear in *The Queen of the Damned* (1988) and *Blood and Gold* (2001). For more perspectives on the Sacred Parents, read the *Alphabettery* entries **Akasha**, **Enkil**, and **Those Who Must Be Kept**.

Saint Elizabeth's Convent

• SANCTUARY •

On his pilgrimage through Heaven and Hell with Memnoch the Devil, Lestat loses his eye. When he goes back to Earth, Memnoch returns Lestat's eye wrapped in vellum upon

which is written a note thanking Lestat for participating in Memnoch's hidden plan. The reality of this drives Lestat to madness. He can be restrained only by the strong strands of Maharet's hair and is then locked in the basement of Saint Elizabeth's Convent.

Saint Elizabeth's Convent appears in *Memnoch the Devil* (1995). For more perspectives on Saint Elizabeth's Convent in the Vampire Chronicles, read the *Alphabettery* entries **Lestat de Lioncourt**, **Maharet**, and **Memnoch**.

Saint-Germain-des-Prés

• SANCTUARY •

Saint-Germain-des-Prés is a quarter in Paris where Armand has built and maintained a beautiful home. But he does not care for it much and offers it to Louis. After Lestat takes into himself Amel and his Sacred Core and becomes Prince Lestat, he takes Armand's luxurious Saint-Germain-des-Prés home and makes it his royal residence in Paris.

Saint-Germain-des-Prés appears in *Prince Lestat* (2014). For more perspectives on Saint-Germain-des-Prés in the Vampire Chronicles, read the *Alphabettery* entries **Amel**, **Lestat de Lioncourt**, and **Louis de Pointe du Lac**.

Saint Juan Diego

• MORTAL •

A poor farmer from Mexico in the mid-1500s, Juan Diego lived in one of the Franciscan mission stations. One morning, as he was walking to church, the Virgin Mary appeared to him and told him to tell the local bishop to build a chapel in her honor, to help the suffering people who are praying for relief. Juan Diego told this to the bishop, but the bishop told him to come back the next day. On his way home, Juan Diego saw another apparition of the Virgin Mary, and he told her that she should find someone more convincing than him, but she told him that he was the one to deliver her message. When Juan Diego saw the bishop on the following day, the bishop told him to tell the Virgin Mary to make a miraculous sign. Later that day, Juan Diego relayed the message to the Virgin Mary, who had appeared to him again. She told him to return the next day, when she would appear and provide a sign for the bishop. Juan Diego's uncle fell ill the next day, and Juan Diego stayed with him to care for him. On the following day, on his way to find a priest for his uncle, Juan Diego traveled a different route, embarrassed for having missed his meeting with the Virgin Mary. But she appeared to him a fourth time, pointed to a hilltop where desert plants like cactus usually grew, and told him to gather the roses that were now growing, which was strange because it was not their season. Juan Diego gathered the flowers in his cloak (or tilma), brought them to the Virgin Mary, who rearranged them, then he took them to the bishop. When Juan Diego dropped the roses on the floor of the bishop's office, an image of the Virgin Mary had been imprinted upon Juan Diego's cloak. The image became a sign of veneration to the Mexican people, celebrated on December 12, the Feast of Our Lady of Guadeloupe. As a result, Juan Diego became the first indigenous American canonized a saint by the Roman Catholic Church. Juan Diego was canonized in 2002.

Lestat becomes fascinated with Saint Juan Diego's life, as exemplified in his opening sentence in *Blood Canticle*, "I want to be a saint."

Juan Diego is spoken of in *Blood Canticle* (2003). For more perspectives on Saint Juan Diego in the Vampire Chronicles, read the *Alphabettery* entries **Lestat de Lioncourt**, **Memnoch**, and **Veronica's Veil**.

Saint Louis Cemetery No. 1

• SANCTUARY •

In the year following the Great New Orleans Fire of 1788, Saint Louis Cemetery No. 1 is built and eventually becomes the oldest and most popular cemetery in the city.

Saint Louis Cemetery No. 1 is located not too far from Louis and Lestat's Rue Royale townhouse. It is also the site where Louis's brother Paul is buried. After the fire destroys his plantation, a headstone for Louis is also placed there, in a little niche where his sister visits and sets flowers.

Saint Louis Cemetery No. 1 appears in *Interview with the Vampire* (1976). For more perspectives on this residence in the Vampire Chronicles, read the *Alphabettery* entries **Lestat de Lioncourt**, **Louis de Pointe du Lac**, and **Paul de Pointe du Lac**.

Saint Rayne

• COVEN •

The island of Saint Rayne, located in the Outer Hebrides, is the private sanctuary of the ancient vampire Rhoshamandes. It takes him one hundred years to build his castle on Saint Rayne in the 1700s. He lives there with his fledgling Benedict until the twenty-first century, when he kills Maharet and Khayman and becomes enemies with the Court of the Prince Lestat. His fledglings Eleni and Allesandra often visit him. The island becomes abandoned when Lestat kills Rhoshamandes.

The island of Saint Rayne appears in *Prince Lestat* (2014), *Prince Lestat and the Realms of Atlantis* (2016), and *Blood Communion* (2018). For more perspectives on the island of Saint Rayne, read the *Alphabettery* entries **Allesandra**, **Benedict**, *Bet Ha Sohar*, **Eleni de Landen**, **Lestat de Lioncourt**, and **Rhoshamandes**.

Salamander

• MORTAL •

Salamander is a groupie of the Vampire Lestat band, who latches on to Larry, the keyboardist, and becomes his main love interest. No reports of Salamander's whereabouts have manifested yet.

Salamander appears in *The Vampire Lestat* (1985). For more perspectives on Salamander's character, read the *Alphabettery* entries **Larry** and **The Vampire Lestat**.

Santh

• VAMPIRE •

Santh, a shortened form of Gundesanth, is the third vampire made by Akasha after Enkil and Khayman in the fourth millennium B.C. The exact dates of his transformation remain a mystery at present, but it is likely that Akasha transforms him into her fledgling after

Khayman transforms Maharet and Mekare into vampires, not long before Akasha also transforms Nebamun into the vampire Captain of the Queens Blood. Gundesanth (as he was known then) becomes a prominent member of the Queen's blood priesthood and an excellent companion for Nebamun. He hunts every maverick vampire mercilessly for the Queen. But when he grows disillusioned with Akasha and Enkil, he defects from the priesthood and disappears from history. He changes his name from Gundesanth to Santh because, by his reasoning, Gundesanth is a name to be feared, while Santh is a name meant to inspire trust.

His blood becomes legendary. Many vampires claim to be made by him, but only one claim ever proves true, that of Baudwin.

When Baudwin attacks Lestat in the twenty-first century, his behavior so infuriates Santh that he comes out of hiding and dismembers his fledgling in Château de Lioncourt, giving his blood to the Court of the Prince's blood drinkers. Santh grows to love and admire Lestat, especially after observing him destroy Rhoshamandes. Santh vows fealty to Prince Lestat and joins the Court of the Prince.

When Akasha, Enkil, Khayman, Maharet, and Mekare all die in the twentieth and twenty-first centuries, Santh becomes the most ancient vampire in the world, with the purest blood of all vampires.

Santh appears in *Blood Communion* (2018). For more perspectives on Santh's character, read the *Alphabettery* entries **Akasha**, **Baudwin**, **Château de Lioncourt**, **Gregory Duff Collingsworth**, **Gundesanth**, **Lestat de Lioncourt**, **Nebamun**, and **Rhoshamandes**.

Santiago

• VAMPIRE •

Santiago is Louis's most villainous antagonist when he comes to Paris for the first time with Claudia. He is chiefly responsible for the death of Claudia and Louis's first fledgling, Madeleine. The vampire Santiago appears in *Interview with the Vampire* (1976).

Little is known about the history of the vampire Santiago at present, although several issues can be deduced. His name is a combination of "Santo" and "Yago," Spanish for "Saint James," the patron saint of Spain. Probably originating from a Spanish-speaking country, Santiago likely joins Armand's theatrical coven shortly after Lestat convinces Armand to destroy his former coven, the Children of Satan, in the late eighteenth century. By the time Santiago encounters Louis in the streets of Paris in the late nineteenth century, he is already one of the most prominent figures in the Théâtre des Vampires coven. Santiago is not as old as Armand, who is three hundred years old at the time, since Santiago often begs Armand to tell him stories of the old covens that once existed and of herbs that can make vampires invisible and of innocents burned at the stake. Even Armand attests that Santiago is not as old as Louis, whom Lestat turned into a vampire in 1791.

When Louis and Claudia arrive in Paris after attempting to kill Lestat, Armand sends Santiago to them with an invitation to come to the Théâtre des Vampires, but Santiago decides to test Louis first. He approaches Louis in an empty street on a lone night and mocks him by imitating his every move. Because Louis has been eagerly searching and hoping for years for any sign of an intelligent vampire, he is quickly disappointed and annoyed with Santiago and calls him a buffoon. Santiago furiously shoves Louis to the ground, and a brief scuffle occurs. Santiago flees, but Armand still gives Louis the invitation to come to him at the Théâtre des Vampires. Now Santiago hates Louis and wants him gone or dead.

As Louis continues to visit with Armand at the Théâtre des Vampires, and as their intimacy deepens, Santiago's hatred for Louis increases, and all because Louis called him a buffoon. When Louis and Claudia refuse to answer any questions about their maker, Santiago begins to suspect that they killed Lestat, and he seeks any shred of proof to jus-

tify his suspicions. Lestat arrives and accuses Louis and Claudia of attempting to kill him. Armand allows Santiago to exact retribution for their violation of the outmoded Great Laws of the Children of Satan.

Santiago leads the vampire coven; captures Louis, Claudia, and Louis's new fledgling Madeleine from their hotel; locks Louis in a wood coffin with large iron locks; and puts Claudia and Madeleine in a small courtyard where they are exposed to the sunlight and die. Armand frees Louis from his coffin and allows him to seek revenge. Louis brings two barrels of kerosene and a scythe to the theater. He splashes the kerosene on the theater's walls and beams, and even on the resting places of the vampires, then he lights the theater on fire and attacks any vampire with the scythe. Realizing what Louis has done, Santiago attacks, but Louis slays him with his scythe, decapitating him and kicking Santiago's head far down a distant corridor. As the Théâtre des Vampires burns, so does Santiago, along with all of the Paris coven, except for Armand, who welcomes Louis's companionship.

For more perspectives on Santiago in the Vampire Chronicles, read the *Alphabettery* entries **Armand**, **Claudia**, **Louis de Pointe du Lac**, **Madeleine**, and **Théâtre des Vampires**.

Santino

• VAMPIRE •

Santino is a major leader of the Children of Darkness. His leadership nearly destroys Marius and twists Armand into a viscious vampire. He appears in *The Queen of the Damned* (1988), *The Vampire Armand* (1998), and *Blood and Gold* (2001).

Santino is turned into a vampire between the years 1346 and 1349, sometime between the outset of the Black Death and its climax. In the year 1349, Santino comes to believe that vampires must be like the Black Death itself: their fate is to be a dreadful, irrational, inexplicable plague upon the human race to make mortals doubt God's love, mercy, and help. He becomes a member of the coven of the Children of Darkness, an ancient organization that has many covens and has been terrorizing vampires and mortals alike for more than a millennium. Ancient vampires such as Marius, Avicus, and Mael have destroyed many members of the Children of Darkness in Rome up until its fall. Already a part of that Roman coven are vampires like Allesandra, Eugénie, Eleni, Everard, and Benedict—each having been captured and forcibly converted from Rhoshamandes's coven. Over the next hundred years, strictly adhering to the five Great Laws that govern the Children of Darkness, Santino becomes the leader of the Roman coven, where he hears many tales of the great and powerful Marius. The coven lives in the catacombs beneath Rome. They sleep among the remains of mortal corpses surrounded by skulls and skeletons and numerous other sights that remind them of their utter depravity and their role as a plague upon humanity. The Children of Darkness fully believe that they are inheritors of Satan's role in God's plan for the world: they will hurt God's mortal creatures made in his Image and Likeness until they beg for mercy and miracles, and then they will kill them.

When Marius returns to Rome in the middle of the fifteenth century, after hiding Those Who Must Be Kept in a shrine in the Alps, Santino approaches him and promises to forswear his leadership of the Children of Darkness if only Marius will take Santino's place as their leader. Marius is disgusted with Santino and with all the Children of Darkness, for Marius adores beauty and art; he cherishes fine clothing and beautiful homes; he loves the world with all of its sensual pleasures, all of which the Children of Darkness renounce, sleeping in squalor, wearing shabby clothes, and feeding off destitute mortals on the streets. Marius could have destroyed Santino, the way he destroyed many Children of Darkness hundreds of years earlier when Rome was an empire. But detesting such violence as much as he detests Santino and the Children of Darkness, Marius rejects him utterly.

When Marius leaves Rome and makes his home in Venice, where he creates a house for young boys to study art and beauty, Santino remains in Rome for a few more years, where he encounters Marius's former companion Mael, who—feeling abandoned by Marius, Avicus, and Zenobia—is only passing through Rome as he wanders aimlessly around the world. With an invitation similar to that extended to Marius, Santino invites Mael to join him and the Children of Darkness. Mael informs Santino that, alongside Marius, he used to destroy Children of Darkness and scum like Santino and that Santino should leave him alone or else Mael will destroy him, too. Santino implores him urgently, trying to entice him by informing him of Marius's dwelling in Venice, but Mael will have none of it.

Santino and his coven go to Venice, burn Marius's palazzo to the ground, burn Marius severely, and kidnap Marius's new fledgling, Amadeo. They bring Amadeo back to Rome, where Santino and Allesandra teach him the Great Laws. When Amadeo refuses to submit to his new coven life, Santino imprisons and starves him until Amadeo surrenders. In time, Amadeo becomes Santino's apprentice and such an exemplary member of the coven that Allesandra changes Amadeo's name to Armand, and Santino sends him to Paris to begin a new coven house of the Children of Darkness. Armand leaves Santino and takes with him Allesandra, Eugénie, Eleni, and Everard.

Not long after, Santino loses faith in the Great Laws and in the religious practices of the Children of Darkness. He abandons his Roman coven and begins living a more opulent lifestyle. He wears beautiful clothing and enjoys the sumptuous delights of the mortal world. During his more lavish travels, Santino encounters Eric, the fledgling of the nearly six-thousand-year-old Maharet. More than four centuries older than Santino,

Eric has knowledge, experience, power, and beauty, which immediately attract Santino, and they become fast companions into the twentieth century.

Together they visit Maharet's compound in Sonoma, California, where the vampire Mael also resides as Maharet's companion. Santino and Eric discuss many issues with Maharet, sometimes peacefully, sometimes forcefully, but it is always clear that Maharet has the greatest power. Santino and Eric return one final time to Maharet's Sonoma compound when the rock music of the band the Vampire Lestat awakens the ancient Queen, Akasha, whom Marius has moved to the frozen lands in the Canadian north. She has risen from her throne, killed her six-thousand-year-old husband, King Enkil, and then buried Marius under many tons of ice. Santino accompanies Marius's fledgling, Pandora, to the frozen north, where they free Marius from his icy tomb and bring him back to Maharet's compound. Marius wants to destroy Santino for burning his palazzo and capturing Armand, but instead decides to spare his life.

After Maharet's twin sister, Mekare, destroys Akasha, Marius looks to Maharet and Mekare as the new leaders of the vampire nation. On numerous occasions, Marius seeks to destroy Santino, even when he and Santino cooperate to clean up the evidence left behind when vampires commit suicide by going into the sun after beholding Veronica's Veil, which Lestat brings back from his journey with Memnoch the Devil. Finally, after long-suffering Maharet refuses to allow Marius to kill Santino, Maharet brings Santino, Marius, and her fledgling Thorne to her new compound in Java, Indonesia. As soon as

Marius sees Santino, he again begs Maharet to let him kill Santino, but once more Maharet refuses. Because Marius and Thorne have recently exchanged their life stories, learning that Marius desires revenge against Santino, and Thorne seeks revenge against Maharet for turning him into a vampire and then abandoning him, Thorne takes his revenge for both of them, killing Santino for Marius and doing so under Maharet's roof. Santino first feels Thorne's vicious attack with the Mind Gift, blasting him so hard that he falls to his knees, crushing him and twisting him. And as Thorne utterly immolates him until he is nothing more than a blackened scorch mark on the earth, Santino's final cries are merely "Thorne . . . Thorne . . . Thorne!"

For more perspectives on Santino in the Vampire Chronicles, read the *Alphabettery* entries **Akasha**, **Allesandra**, **Benedict**, **Coven**, **Coven Master**, **Eleni**, **Enkil**, **Eric**, **Eugénie**, **Everard**, **Great Laws**, **Mael**, **Maharet**, **Marius**, **Mekare**, **Pandora**, **Rhoshamandes**, and **Thorne**.

Saqqara

• SANCTUARY •

Saqqara is a necropolis in Memphis, the capital of ancient Egypt.

After becoming vampires, Maharet, Mekare, and Khayman begin making the rebellious army the First Brood to combat Enkil and Akasha, but the Queens Blood, Akasha's own army, captures Maharet and Mekare at Saqqara. Only Khayman escapes.

Saqqara appears in *The Queen of the Damned* (1988). For more perspectives on Saqqara in the Vampire Chronicles, read the *Alphabettery* entries **Akasha**, **First Brood**, **Khayman**, **Maharet**, **Mekare**, and **Queens Blood**.

Satan's Night Out

• COVEN •

When drummer Alex; his brother and keyboardist, Larry; and guitarist Tough Cookie form a band and play around the bars in New Orleans, they call themselves Satan's Night Out. But that name is short-lived, since the vampire Lestat, who happens to be listening to them nearby, approaches them, reveals his vampire nature, and then offers them fame and fortune, if they would be his band. Gladly accepting, Lestat changes their name from Satan's Night Out to the Vampire Lestat, which goes on to become an international success.

Satan's Night Out appears in *The Vampire Lestat* (1985). For more perspectives on Satan's Night Out in the Vampire Chronicles, read the *Alphabettery* entries **Alex**, **Larry**, **Lestat de Lioncourt**, **Tough Cookie**, and **The Vampire Lestat**.

Savage Garden

• SANCTUARY •

Lestat describes all existence as a Savage Garden, a paradise of exquisite beauty and a Purgatory of exquisite death. In this existence, human beings have such a great capacity to achieve remarkable feats of artistry and science, of comprehending the abstract in tandem with the empirical, of being mortal yet striving for immortality, whether by reputation or through religion. And all vampires are wanderers and hunters in the Savage Garden; they are exotica, nothing more than anomalous predators in the system of human frailty, because their extraordinary nature destroys the ordinary beauty of a single human life, even if that single human life happens to be the greatest savage in the Savage Garden, for even one life possesses an inherent dignity of being a human person—a living, breathing, thinking, creating individual that always has the opportunity to become better, to grow beyond the instinctive animalism in every human heart that sparks fear, which sparks anger, which sparks war, which sparks death. The Savage Garden is the irony of the

human condition, that people are as beautiful as they are barbaric. And vampires are the epitome of that juxtaposition, railing against the cruelest adversary in the Savage Garden—*Time*—since no mortal can outrun, outthink, outgrow the passage of minutes and years. Everyone who lives eventually dies. And some who die are remembered, but even that memory is eaten by the passage of Time in the Savage Garden. Lestat's greatest place to live is the most forsaken outpost in the Savage Garden, where he will live eternally under the loveliness and lawlessness, the hedonism and heroism of timeless New Orleans.

The Savage Garden appears in *The Vampire Lestat* (1985), *The Queen of the Damned* (1988), *The Tale of the Body Thief* (1992), *Memnoch the Devil* (1995), *Blood Canticle* (2003), *Prince Lestat* (2014), *Prince Lestat and the Realms of Atlantis* (2016), and *Blood Communion* (2018). For more perspectives on the Savage Garden in the Vampire Chronicles, read the *Alphabettery* entry **Lestat de Lioncourt**.

Sebastian Melmoth

• ALIAS •

When Lestat checks into Claridge's Hotel in London, attracted by its heavy-curtained rooms that protect him from the sun's rays, he uses the alias "Sebastian Melmoth," but the desk clerk does not believe him, since Lestat has neither credit cards nor identification because of his self-described "recklessness and madness." Lestat uses the Mind Gift to persuade the desk clerk to believe his alias and accept the number of his credit account.

The name Sebastian Melmoth was Oscar Wilde's pseudonym in late life, a combination of "Saint Sebastian" and "Melmoth the Wanderer" from the 1820 gothic novel of the same name by Charles Maturin.

This alias "Sebastian Melmoth" appears in *The Tale of the Body Thief* (1992). For more perspectives on this alias in the Vampire Chronicles, read the *Alphabettery* entries **David Talbot**, **Lestat de Lioncourt**, *Queen Elizabeth 2*, and **Raglan James**.

Secret Isle

• SANCTUARY •

Secret Isle is the name that the ancient Taltos Ashlar gives to the island he owns, where he, his wife, Morrigan, their four children, and several other Taltos live in harmony, and in secret, far away from mortals, until one of Ashlar's sons, Silas, incites a rebellion among their people and attacks neighboring islands. One of those islands is owned by a drug cartel, which retaliates by attacking the island and taking it over. Secret Isle is eventually liberated when Lestat, Quinn Blackwood, and Mona Mayfair come in search of Mona's daughter, Morrigan. The three vampires kill all the drug dealers and take the remaining Taltos back to New Orleans.

The Secret Isle appears in *Blood Canticle* (2003). For more perspectives on the Secret Isle in the Vampire Chronicles, read the *Alphabettery* entries **Ashlar**, **Lestat de Lioncourt**, **Mona Mayfair**, **Morrigan Mayfair**, **Quinn Blackwood**, and **Taltos**.

Secret People

• TALTOS •

Secret People is the name that the ancient Taltos Ashlar gives to the group of Taltos living on the island he owns, which he calls Secret Isle. Some of those Secret People include Taltos, such as Ashlar's wife, Morrigan; their four children, Silas, Oberon, Miravelle, and Lorkyn; along with their Taltos companions, Elath, Releth, Seth, Hiram, Torwan, Isaac, Evan, Ruth; and several others who have thus far remained nameless in the Vampire Chronicles.

The Secret People appear in *Blood Canticle* (2003). For more perspectives on the Secret People in the Vampire Chronicles, read the *Alphabettery* entries **Ashlar**, **Elath**, **Isaac**, **Morrigan Mayfair**, **Releth**, **Ruth**, **Secret Isle**, **Seth**, **Taltos**, and **Torwan**.

Seth

• TALTOS •

Not to be confused with Akasha's son, also named Seth, this Seth is one of the few remaining Taltos who live on the secret island owned by the ancient Taltos Ashlar. Seth loves the solitude on the island, especially going off into the vast jungles with his Taltos companions, Elath and Releth. A rebellion instigated by Ashlar's son Silas ushers in a retaliatory attack by the drug lord Rodrigo and his soldiers. The Drug Merchants invade the island, and most of the male Taltos are shot and killed. Seth is among the slain.

The Taltos Seth appears in *Blood Canticle* (2003). For more perspectives on this character in the Vampire Chronicles, read the *Alphabettery* entries **Ashlar**, **Elath**, **Releth**, **Rodrigo**, **Silas**, and **Taltos**.

Seth

• VAMPIRE •

Seth is the son of Akasha and Enkil. He becomes an ancient Egyptian healer, and his passion for being a healer remains with him after his mother transforms him into a vampire. In the twenty-first century, he is one of vampirekind's leading undead healers and scientists. He appears in *Prince Lestat* (2014), *Prince Lestat and the Realms of Atlantis* (2016), and *Blood Communion* (2018).

Seth is five years old when his mother and father, Akasha and Enkil, King and Queen of ancient Egypt, go into the house of their steward, Khayman, and are stabbed to the point of death by cannibalistic conspirators. The child does not see the spirit of Amel enter into his mother's wounds and fuse with her blood; Seth only sees that something has changed about her, and about his father, Enkil. They no longer go into the sun; they no longer eat food; they are stronger, faster; their skin is very white; and they drink blood. They try to hide their bloodlust at first, but children always see the truth. Seth stands in the royal court, where he watches Akasha condemn to death twin witches with flaming-red hair and emerald-green eyes. Seth hears the witch named Mekare curse the Queen and promise to return, seeking vengeance. Seth observes the tongue cut from Mekare's mouth; he sees the eyes plucked out of her twin sister, Maharet. He hears how Khayman has betrayed the King and Queen, has helped the witches escape from prison, and has fled all the way to the necropolis at Memphis. He

hears how Khayman and the twin witches have raised an army called the First Brood to fight against Seth's mother and father. One twin witch has been captured, locked in a sarcophagus, and set adrift in the eastern ocean. The other sister has likewise been captured, locked in a coffin, and set adrift in the western ocean. Meanwhile, the First Brood wages a heavy war against the King and Queen. Akasha, realizing that Seth will not be safe in the palace, sends him away to Nineveh, where he studies to be a healer for the next twenty years. As a mortal, he journeys constantly in the Land Between Two Rivers, searching for healers who can teach him and increase his understanding of ancient Middle Eastern medicine. Thus he spends the majority of his mortal years learning how to care about the value of other people and about the world, and how to bring life and restoration wherever he goes.

Over the years he hears stories about the progress of the war between the First Brood and his parents, who have taken on the identities of the gods Isis and Osiris and have created an army called the Queens Blood. His old home now seems shrouded in mystery, and he has no desire to return. Reports reach Queen Akasha about how the First Brood is hunting for her son to capture and torture him until she surrenders, so she summons Seth back to Egypt at the age of twenty-five, and he obeys his mother's wishes only by force. Once he enters the old royal court,

Queen Akasha turns her son into her vampire fledgling and makes him strong enough to take care of himself against the First Brood rebels. Watching the affair is the Captain of her army, Gregory Duff Collingsworth, who at the time is known as Nebamun. Akasha commands Nebamun to train her newly transformed son-fledgling into a great warrior for the Queens Blood. Seth is destined to be another soldier against the First Brood, but he flees from Akasha and disappears into the desert sands, and no other blood drinker of those ancient days hears from him again for thousands of years. In all that time, his passion for healing never diminishes.

After the first millennium of the Common Era, Seth goes into the ground and sleeps and does not rise until the late twentieth century, when the rock music of the band Vampire Lestat awakens him. He goes to the hospital room of Fareed Bhansali, who, in the prime of his life, is dying in a locked-in coma. With the aid of the Mind Gift, Seth fathoms Fareed's brilliance as a medical doctor and scientific researcher; Seth turns him into a vampire so that Fareed will help him make contact with the modern world and all of its technological advances. Shortly after Fareed's transformation, Seth must use his power to protect him when his mother, Akasha, commences a second Great Burning, destroying all the weaker vampires across the world. Once she is defeated, Fareed teaches Seth everything he knows about medicine and healing, and together they begin a hitherto-unheard-of vocation as medical doctors for the Undead.

They live in West Hollywood at the medical center they own together, while also establishing a research facility in the Southern California desert. Seth allows Fareed to drink his blood every night to increase his strength. With their research and practice they make remarkable advances in human genetics and DNA cloning. In the 1990s, Seth and Fareed encounter Lestat in West Hollywood. Lestat marvels as he listens to them explain their revolutionary medical procedures for vampires, specifically one designed to inject him with an infusion of hormones that will allow him to briefly experience mortal eroticism as well as an ejaculation. Having enjoyed a sexual experience in another body due to his encounter with Raglan James, the Body Thief, Lestat now desires to have that experience as a vampire, so he agrees to be part of Seth and Fareed's medical experiment. They bring him back to their medical facility, infuse him with specialized hormones, and couple him with a mortal scientist, Dr. Flannery Gilman, who works at the facility and has been studying vampires for many years. Unbeknownst to Lestat, he impregnates her. Once he leaves, Seth and Fareed extract the fetus from their mortal colleague, operate on it with genetic-cloning techniques, and then insert the genetically enhanced fetus back inside Dr. Gilman's uterus. When she comes to term nine months later, she gives birth to Lestat's only son, a genetic clone of Lestat, whom they name Viktor. Completely mortal, Viktor grows and matures for the next twenty years, cared for by Seth, Fareed, and Flannery.

In the twenty-first century, Seth encounters his old acquaintance Nebamun, who now calls himself Gregory Duff Collingsworth and has established a vast pharmaceutical empire. Impressed by Seth's scientific work with Fareed, Gregory offers them access to his technologically advanced facilities, and they begin construction on a new facility just outside Paris committed to medical research and hospitalization for the Undead.

Seth and Fareed also go to Maharet's compound in Java, Indonesia. With their medical advances in Undead genetics, they give Maharet new eyes so that she will no longer have to depend on stealing the eyes of her mortal victims, nor use the eyes of her fledgling Thorne. Their advanced techniques are also able to replace the leg that the vampire Flavius lost during his mortal life two thousand years earlier.

Seth and Fareed continue to be the foremost scientific minds in their vampire community, as well as beloved companions, who remain together for many more years.

For more perspectives on Seth's character, read the *Alphabettery* entries **Amel**, **Akasha**, **Fareed Bhansali**, **Flannery Gilman**, **Gregory Duff Collingsworth**, **Lestat de Lioncourt**, **Maharet**, **Nebamun**, and **Viktor**.

Setheus

• IMMORTAL •

Setheus and his companion Ramiel are the two principal guardian angels of the painter Fra Filippo. To assist Vittorio's vengeance for the death of his family, Setheus, Ramiel, and the third angel Mastema all cooperate to help Vittorio into the Court of the Ruby Grail, where a coven of vampires lives, so he can slay nearly all of them and then free the mortals within. Setheus and Ramiel are upset with Vittorio when he allows the vampire Ursula to live, but Vittorio ignores them, especially when Ursula turns him into a vampire.

Setheus appears in *Vittorio the Vampire* (1999). For more perspectives on Setheus in the Vampire Chronicles, read the *Alphabettery* entries **Court of the Ruby Grail**, **Florian**, **Fra Filippo**, **Mastema**, **Ramiel**, **Ursula**, and **Vittorio di Raniari**.

Sevraine

• VAMPIRE •

Sevraine is the only female vampire that Akasha allows to live during her rule in ancient Egypt. She becomes Akasha's handmaid until she runs away, then wanders for thousands of years. In the modern era, she begins an all-female coven of vampires in the Caves of Gold. She appears in *Prince Lestat* (2014), *Prince Lestat and the Realms of Atlantis* (2016), and *Blood Communion* (2018).

Around one thousand years after Queen Akasha fuses with Amel, becomes a vampire, and turns her lover Nebamun into a vampire, Sevraine is captured and forced into slavery in Egypt. Of Nordic descent, she is very beautiful; Nebamun falls in love with her almost instantly. He turns her into a vampire and takes her as his Blood Spouse, which is forbidden at that time, because Akasha has outlawed making female vampires. Nebamun has been the Prince and Captain of the Queens Blood for nearly a thousand years, but he loses his rank and title when Akasha discovers his treachery. Instead of condemning him and Sevraine to death, Akasha is also beguiled by Sevraine's beauty and allows them both to live. Akasha imprisons Nebamun in a shrine and starves him for blood. She takes Sevraine as her handmaid and servant and permits her to drink from the Queen's Sacred Fount, sharing with Sevraine her powerful blood.

Less than fifty years later, Sevraine betrays Akasha, escapes, and flees from Egypt. Akasha is furious and compares Sevraine to the twin witches, Maharet and Mekare. Akasha puts a bounty on Sevraine's capture, but Sevraine disappears entirely.

Over the centuries, she keeps track of Nebamun's fate. Once she briefly reveals herself to him, during the second millennium of the Common Era, after he has changed his name to Gregory Duff Collingsworth and has begun a new coven with Avicus, Zenobia, and Flavius, long after he has taken a new Blood Wife, Chrysanthe, who has helped him adapt to the modern world.

In time, Sevraine begins a new coven in the middle of the Anatolian plain, beneath Cappadocia, in an underground cave that she plates in gold and decorates with beautiful tiles and statues, creating a subterranean city of beauty and art. She welcomes into her coven three of Rhoshamandes's fledglings, Allesandra, Eleni, and Eugénie, as well as Marius's fledgling Bianca. Ghosts and spirits who have evolved into an incarnate form often visit her coven, which is where Lestat first meets Gremt, when he comes to Sevraine in search of Rhoshamandes, who is being manipulated by Amel.

After Lestat takes into himself Amel, the Sacred Core, and becomes the host of the vampire race, Sevraine briefly leaves her Cappadocian coven to attend Lestat's coronation ceremony, where she is, after all the long millennia, finally reunited with Nebamun, who has also come to pay his respects. In the early twenty-first century, Sevraine becomes a permanent resident at Château de Lioncourt and a vocal member of the Court of the Prince.

For more perspectives on Sevraine's character, read the *Alphabettery* entries **Akasha, Allesandra, Bianca Solderini, Eleni, Eugénie, Gregory Duff Collingsworth, Gremt Stryker Knollys,** and **Lestat de Lioncourt.**

Seymour

• MORTAL •

After Quinn Blackwood's mother, Patsy, contracts HIV, she continues to perform her music in New Orleans with her one-man band, Seymour. In time, the two become intimate. She never tells him that she is HIV positive, and he eventually becomes infected as well. Considered by Quinn to be an obnoxious, opportunistic scum, Seymour sues the Blackwood estate, yet the matter is settled out of court. Seymour receives a large amount of money, but his disease kills him shortly after the lawsuit makes him wealthy.

Seymour appears in *Blackwood Farm* (2002). For more perspectives on Seymour's character, read the *Alphabettery* entries **Patsy Blackwood** and **Quinn Blackwood**.

Shed Men

• MORTAL •

"Shed Men" is the name of the group of farmhands who work on Blackwood Farm. For Quinn Blackwood, they also do several other jobs, such as run errands, chauffeur, and work security on the property. Their name comes from an earlier time, when men who did their jobs lived in a shed outside the Blackwood Farm mansion. Two of the Shed Men are Clem and Allen, the nominal leader.

Shed Men appear in *Blackwood Farm* (2002). For more perspectives on Shed Men in the Vampire Chronicles, read the *Alphabettery* entries **Allen**, **Clem**, and **Quinn Blackwood**.

Sheridan Blackwood

• ALIAS •

"Sheridan Blackwood" is an American alias that David Talbot provides for Lestat when they are pursuing Raglan James, the Body Thief, aboard the *Queen Elizabeth 2*. When Lestat hears his new alias, he feigns a sigh of relief that David did not pick the alias "H. P.

Lovecraft." Sheridan Blackwood is a combination of the names of the authors Sheridan Le Fanu and Algernon Blackwood.

The "Sheridan Blackwood" alias appears in *The Tale of the Body Thief* (1992). For more perspectives on this alias, read the *Alphabettery* entries on **David Talbot**, **Lestat de Lioncourt**, ***Queen Elizabeth 2***, and **Raglan James**.

Silas

• TALTOS •

Silas is one of Ashlar and Morrigan Mayfair's four Taltos children. Along with his parents and siblings—Oberon (brother), Miravelle (sister), and Lorkyn (sister)—they live on a secret island, unbothered by mortals. Unlike his other siblings, Silas desires to wage war against the mortals living on nearby islands. He rebels against his parents and starts an uprising on the island that involves numerous other Taltos. For two years, he keeps his parents and siblings hostage, while he works out his plan of attack on the nearest island, owned by the drug lord Rodrigo. During that time, he also slowly poisons his parents, bringing them close to the point of death. Silas steals guns from the Drug Merchants and openly attacks them. Rodrigo and his Drug Merchants come to the island, kill many Taltos, overrun it, and take the remaining Taltos hostage. In an effort to stop Silas's ongoing war against Rodrigo, his sister Miravelle and his mother, Morrigan, blind him with a screwdriver. As a result of his wounds and his rage, he and other rebelling Taltos try to make one last attack against Rodrigo. They charge at the Drug Merchants with guns blazing, but they are vastly outnumbered. Silas and the other rebel Taltos are gunned down as they run.

Silas appears in *Blood Canticle* (2003). For more perspectives on Silas in the Vampire Chronicles, read the *Alphabettery* entries **Ashlar**, **Drug Merchants**, **Elath**, **Lorkyn**, **Miravelle**, **Morrigan Mayfair**, **Oberon**, **Releth**, **Rodrigo**, **Silas**, and **Taltos**.

Silver Cord

• IMMORTAL •

Originally developed as an idea in the nineteenth-century parapsychology school of thought, the silver cord is the connecting tether binding the astral-projected consciousness with the biological body. The theory of astral projection asserts that when people astral project, they remain secured to their bodies through an invisible connection called the silver cord. The silver cord also helps to identify the distinction between the etheric body on the astral plane and the biological body on the corporeal plane.

As the theory goes, if an etheric body is hooked inside a different physical body, the silver cord can be severed from the individual's former biological body and tethered in the new biological body. An example of this is when Lestat and David Talbot switch bodies with Raglan James (the Body Thief). When Talbot and James switch bodies, Talbot's etheric body is hooked inside James's physical body, completely severing Talbot's silver cord from his former octogenarian body and connecting it to his newer, younger body. Thus, when his former body dies with James's etheric consciousness inside it, James dies along with Talbot's former body, while David Talbot lives in his new body (James's former body).

The silver cord also more fully defines the way in which Amel is connected to every vampire. When Amel first fuses with Akasha, his silver cord fuses with her body. When she makes another vampire, such as Enkil and Khayman, that silver cord extends from her to them. But this connection is an extension not from maker to fledgling but rather from the host carrier of the Sacred Core to all vampires; that is, from the Queen of the Damned (Akasha or Mekare) or from Prince Lestat to every creature interconnected within the web of vampiric existence.

Whenever Amel's carrier host is wounded, that wound extends through the silver cord's etheric connection to other vampires, such as when Akasha is burned by the sun, and every vampire experiences it. Also, when the carrier host's brain is ingested by another vampire, the etheric brain is also ingested, which connects the consuming vampire to Amel, the Sacred Core. Ingesting a host carrier's brain transfers the Sacred Core and the etheric brain into the new vampire, which makes that vampire the new central nexus in the web of the silver cord. Such is the case when Mekare consumes Akasha's brain, and likewise when Lestat consumes Mekare's brain: Mekare becomes the carrier host for a few decades, then Lestat becomes the carrier host for a few years, until Kapetria develops a scientific process that fully removes Amel's etheric brain from Lestat's brain and implants it inside the physical brain of a clone of Amel's genetically enhanced body—which perished with Atlantis many thousands of years ago—disconnecting the silver cord from Lestat and connecting it to Amel's new body.

The silver cord appears in *Prince Lestat*

and the Realms of Atlantis (2016). For more perspectives on the silver cord in the Vampire Chronicles, read the *Alphabettery* entries **Akasha, Amel, Bravenna, David Talbot, Kapetria, Lestat de Lioncourt, Mekare,** and **Raglan James**.

Sixth Street House

• SANCTUARY •

The Sixth Street house is the residence where Alex, Larry, and Tough Cookie rehearse in the attic as the band Satan's Night Out. Lestat lies sleeping in a vampiric torpor less than a block away on Prytania near the Lafayette Cemetery. When their music causes him to rise and make contact with the twentieth century, he goes to them in the attic and changes their lives forever by re-forming them into the Vampire Lestat band.

The Sixth Street house appears in *The Vampire Lestat* (1985). For more perspectives on the Sixth Street house in the Vampire Chronicles, read the *Alphabettery* entries **Alex, Larry, Lestat de Lioncourt, Satan's Night Out,** and **Tough Cookie**.

Sorbonne

• SANCTUARY •

From Collège de Sorbonne, the Sorbonne is the college where many men in Paris went to study law, theology, and philosophy. Nicolas de Lenfent is sent by his father to study law at the Sorbonne. But after he becomes enamored of the violin, Nicki quits his law studies and begins studying the violin under the tutelage of Wolfgang Amadeus Mozart.

The Sorbonne appears in *The Vampire Lestat* (1985). For more perspectives on the Sorbonne in the Vampire Chronicles, read the *Alphabettery* entries **Lestat de Lioncourt** and **Nicolas de Lenfent**.

Sparrow

• SOBRIQUET •

After Jesse Reeves's parents perish in a fatal car accident, leaving Jesse to survive after being aborted from her mother's womb two weeks prematurely, Jesse is taken to the hospital where she remains for two weeks as an unnamed child. The nurses dote on her and sing to her, and they give her the sobriquet "Sparrow," until the vampire Maharet identifies Jesse and brings her to live with cousins in New York.

The "Sparrow" sobriquet appears in *The Queen of the Damned* (1988). For more perspectives on it, read the *Alphabettery* entries **Jesse, Maharet, Maria Godwin**, and **Matthew Godwin**.

Spell Gift

• VAMPIRE ABILITY •

The Spell Gift is a facet of the Mind Gift that allows a vampire to have great influence over mortals and weaker vampires. Unlike the Fire Gift, which develops over time, the Spell Gift is inherent in every vampire, from fledgling to elder. Elders are generally masters of the Spell Gift, while fledglings need years to become proficient at it. Also, the Spell Gift cannot work over great distances. The vampire needs to be in close proximity with the subject in order for this power to be fully effective, because it does not cause the victim to be blindly obedient but lowers their inhibitions and influences their decision-making. In the cases of mortals, the Spell Gift is used to draw them nearer to the vampire for the blood-drinking embrace.

The Spell Gift appears in *The Vampire Lestat* (1985), *The Queen of the Damned* (1988), *Prince Lestat* (2014), and *Prince Lestat and the Realms of Atlantis* (2016). For more perspectives on the Spell Gift in the Vampire Chronicles, read the *Alphabettery* entries **Blood Curse, Cloud Gift, Crippling Gift, Dark Gift, Fire Gift**, and **Mind Gift**.

Spirits

• IMMORTAL •

Spirits are invisible, bodiless entities. A witch with the ability to summon a spirit can determine if that spirit is good or bad by the manner of its desire to aid that witch, such as spying on others, finding lost items, predicting the weather, possessing a mortal, or using any other spiritual ability. Before becoming vampires, while still mortals practicing their ancient Middle Eastern witchcraft, Maharet and Mekare observe that spirits appear to be trying to develop a sense of personal control over physical skills, a sense of independence from their current spiritual state, and a great desire for asserting mastery and power over the mortal world. When they fail to gain autonomy, Maharet and Mekare perceive that spirits can seem mercurial and childish. Spirits also exhibit a behavior like jealousy towards mortals, especially those mortals who experience a viscerally sensual reality. More objectively, however, they also observe that spirits are enormous entities, far larger than anything the human mind can truly imagine, which is how the spirit of Amel is able to stretch and dilute to enter so many flesh-and-blood creatures who are transformed from mortal humans into immortal vampires.

Spirits can be divided into two specific categories:

1. Spirits that have always been spirits and never mortal

2. Spirits that were once mortal but died to become an etheric presence, often called ghosts

Gremt and Amel, who are both present when Maharet and Mekare are mortal witches, are two examples of this particular distinction. Gremt is a pure spirit. Amel is a ghost.

Gremt has always been a spirit and was never mortal, yet he has within himself the ability to evolve into an incarnate form of his choosing. During this rare evolutionary process, he learns how to gather to himself motes of particles, such as dust motes, to create bones, blood, organs, skin, hair, teeth, eyes—an entire body that can wear clothes and appear lifelike to mortals and immortals alike, although powerful immortals can just barely see through the guise. Furthermore, Gremt can decide what he looks like, what kind of clothes he wears, with complete control over his mien, physiognomy, and the expressiveness of his visage. In his body, he also has the opportunity of developing his own unique personal identity, which is the dominant difference between his kind of spiritual essence and that of a formerly mortal spirit.

It is rare for the spirit of a dead mortal to remain behind, but when it does, its spiritual nature is generally referred to as a ghost. Amel is one example. He already shaped his own personal identity throughout his many years of mortal life. He still has the potential within him to evolve, but that potential will always be grounded in the personal identity that he already gained as a mortal human, before he was altered by Bravennan aliens into an immortal superhuman. Amel could incarnate similarly to Gremt, but he would have a greater likelihood of incarnating a body like the human form he had in Atlantis.

The vampire Hesketh and Magnus demonstrate the ability to incarnate as ghosts.

When Gremt encounters Hesketh's spirit on the ethereal plane and teaches her how to incarnate, Hesketh incarnates a vision of herself that is not the deformed body she had in life but a body that she already shaped for herself in her mind and heart, a beautiful body, willowy and beguiling.

Magnus, on the other hand, incarnates two different kinds of bodies, as if the first is a trial. When he visits Everard, he incarnates as a man in his midforties with long ashen hair. But when he meets Lestat, Magnus incarnates himself as a man who bears a striking resemblance to his fledgling, with blue eyes, long blond hair, and a powerful, well-proportioned body.

Thus, ghosts are still ghosts. But they have the option to avoid reincarnating the bodies they had in life and perfecting a body that nature never provided. Occasionally ghosts will shiver or quiver whenever mortal or immortal eyes gaze upon them. But the more a ghost perfects its incarnate form, the less it shivers or quivers, and the more it can maintain a solid, tangible form.

Whether a pure spirit or a formerly mortal ghost, these etheric beings consider themselves a fraternity of uniquely evolving entities, possessing a small core of matter at the center of their being, which can be identified as the primer or matrix upon which they build the incarnation of their noncorporeal selves. Younger ghosts who have been dead for only a short while and are still learning how to evolve into an incarnate form cannot eat, drink, or taste, but they can feel hot or cold, as well as a sense of existence. Older spirits can evolve into an incarnate form that can fully experience all the sensual delights of life.

Spirits appear in *The Vampire Lestat* (1985), *The Queen of the Damned* (1988), *Prince Lestat* (2014), and *Prince Lestat and the Realms of Atlantis* (2016). For more perspectives on spirits in the Vampire Chronicles, read the *Alphabettery* entries **Amel**, **Gremt Stryker Knollys**, **Hesketh**, **Lestat de Lioncourt**, and **Magnus**.

Stalker

• ALIAS •

In the years following Lestat's defeat of Raglan James, the Body Thief, Lestat begins to experience a presence stalking him wherever he goes, particularly into the bar where he encounters the ghost of his victim, Roger. Referring to this strange presence as the Stalker, Lestat feels it come into the bar and snatch away Roger's spirit. In the end, the Stalker is none other than Memnoch the Devil.

Stalker appears in *Memnoch the Devil* (1995). For more perspectives on the Stalker in the Vampire Chronicles, read the *Alphabettery* entries **Lestat de Lioncourt, Memnoch, Raglan James**, and **Roger**.

Stanford Wilde

• ALIAS •

"Stanford Wilde" is the alias that Lestat uses shortly before he switches bodies with Raglan James, the Body Thief. Lestat has all of his legal information and access to his money transferred from the alias "Lestan Gregor" to "Stanford Wilde," using complex code words that his agents can utilize for transferring money by verbal command.

"Stanford Wilde" is another reference to Oscar Wilde, the first being "Sebastian Melmoth."

The "Stanford Wilde" alias appears in *The Tale of the Body Thief* (1992). For more perspectives on this alias in the Vampire Chronicles, read the *Alphabettery* entries on **David Talbot, Lestat de Lioncourt**, and **Raglan James**.

Stella Mayfair

• WITCH •

Stella Mayfair is the child of Mary Beth and Mary Beth's father, Julien Mayfair, making Stella the tenth generation in the line of thirteen witches destined to incarnate the evil spirit of Lasher. Born during the Roaring Twenties, she gains a reputation, similar to her father's, as a scandalous wassailer. As the Designée of the Mayfair Legacy, she spends money incautiously. Oftentimes she throws wild parties and dresses in the most flamboyant clothing of the day. After having a daughter, Antha, with her brother Lionel Mayfair, she encounters Stuart Townsend, a prominent member of the Talamasca. When she expresses a desire to leave New Orleans and accompany Stuart to the Talamasca Motherhouse in London, Lionel pulls out a gun and shoots her twice, killing her immediately. Her daughter,

Antha, becomes not only the new Designée of the Mayfair Legacy, but also the eleventh witch in the line to incarnate Lasher.

Stella Mayfair appears in *Blood Canticle* (2003). For more perspectives on Stella Mayfair in the Vampire Chronicles, read the *Alphabettery* entries **Designée of the Mayfair Legacy** and **Talamasca Order**.

Stirling Oliver

• TALAMASCA •

A member of an order of psychic detectives, the Talamasca, Stirling Oliver becomes acquaintances with Quinn Blackwood before Petronia turns Quinn into a vampire. Stirling remains unaware of Quinn's transformation until the night Stirling breaks into Lestat's home, curious to know more about the famous vampire. Quinn also happens to be in search of Lestat that same night, hoping to have his assistance in exorcising the ghost of his twin brother, Goblin. Quinn, overcome by vampire bloodlust, feeds off Stirling and nearly kills him, but Lestat arrives and warns Stirling to leave and asks him to deliver a message from him to the Talamasca. Despite Stirling's audacity, Lestat takes an immediate liking to him.

Later, after Lestat helps Merrick Mayfair exorcise Goblin, the ghost of Quinn's twin brother, Lestat and Quinn journey to the Talamasca Motherhouse together to inform Stirling about the death of Merrick Mayfair. With tears in his eyes, Stirling closes her file with the Talamasca.

Stirling Oliver appears in *Blackwood Farm* (2002). For more perspectives on Stirling Oliver in the Vampire Chronicles, read the *Alphabettery* entries **Goblin**, **Lestat de Lioncourt**, **Merrick Mayfair**, **Petronia**, **Quinn Blackwood**, and **Talamasca Order**.

Sugar Devil Island

• SANCTUARY •

After the death of his first wife, Virginia Lee, Manfred Blackwood roams throughout his two hundred acres in Sugar Devil Swamp, fed by the West Ruby River, near his plantation home, Blackwood Farm. One day he happens upon a solitary island in the middle of the swamp. Walking around it for some time, he discovers it to be a place of delightful seclusion. After Manfred marries his second wife, Rebecca, they travel to Europe, where he encounters the vampire Petronia. Manfred regales Petronia with wonderful tales of the Louisiana swampland; she promises to visit. Manfred returns and builds the Hermitage on the island in Sugar Devil Swamp, which he dubs "Sugar Devil Island." Once the Hermitage is complete, Petronia comes from Europe to visit him. He builds her a tomb on the island where she can rest during the day. Discovering how much she enjoys the freedom of hunting the simple folk of nineteenth-century Louisiana, she desires to have Sugar Devil Island for herself. Manfred strikes a deal with her: if she turns him into a vampire, he will give her the island for free. Before this plan can be enacted, Manfred's wife Rebecca tries to burn down Blackwood Farm. Manfred drags

her to Sugar Devil Island, where he and Petronia savagely torture and kill her, leaving her corpse on the island to rot for the next century, until it is discovered by Manfred's twentieth-century descendant, Quinn Blackwood. Quinn also discovers that Petronia is living on the island and that the legend about Manfred's disappearance and death in the swamp is not true. Petronia turned Manfred into a vampire so that he would fulfill his end of the bargain, giving her his property and the Hermitage on Sugar Devil Island.

Sugar Devil Island appears in *Blackwood Farm* (2002). For more perspectives on Sugar Devil Island in the Vampire Chronicles, read the *Alphabettery* entries **Hermitage, Manfred Blackwood, Petronia, Quinn Blackwood, Rebecca Stanford,** and **Virginia Lee Blackwood.**

Sugar Devil Swamp

• SANCTUARY •

Located in northeast Louisiana, not far from the border of Mississippi, there is a dense swampland fed by the West Ruby River, having branched off from the Ruby River at Rubyville, an isolated territory called Sugar Devil Swamp. Infested with dangerous alligators, roaring bears, and bloodthirsty mosquitoes, Sugar Devil Swamp stretches on for miles without a solitary soul to be seen.

Early in the eighteenth century, Manfred

Blackwood, otherwise known as Mad Manfred, buys two hundred acres of this swampland, where he builds a vast plantation home with tall white columns, old-fashioned drawing rooms, and beautiful gardens, which he names Blackwood Farm.

Sugar Devil Swamp appears in *Blackwood Farm* (2002). For more perspectives on Sugar Devil Swamp in the Vampire Chronicles, read the *Alphabettery* entries **Manfred Blackwood** and **Sugar Devil Island.**

Sweetheart

• MORTAL •

"Sweetheart" is the sobriquet of Rose Black-wood, the wife of Pops and the mother of Patsy Blackwood. When Patsy gives birth to her son, Quinn, Patsy is too undepend-able to mother him, so Sweetheart and Pops raise him, telling him that Patsy is his sister. Sweetheart cherishes spending her days in the kitchen baking with the Kitchen Gang. She is aware of the family history and tells Quinn all about his ancestors, especially Manfred Blackwood, the founder of Black-wood Farm.

Sweetheart appears in *Blackwood Farm* (2002). For more perspectives on Sweetheart in the Vampire Chronicles, read the *Alphabet-tery* entries **Kitchen Gang**, **Manfred Black-wood**, **Patsy Blackwood**, **Pops**, and **Quinn Blackwood**.

Sybelle

• VAMPIRE •

By the age of twenty-five, Sybelle is a tremen-dously talented pianist in the classical style. To provide her with an assistant, her family purchases for her a twelve-year-old Bedouin boy named Benji Mahmoud. After her par-ents are killed in a horrible car accident, Syb-elle's older brother forces her to support the family by giving concerts.

When she fails to perform or practice per-fectly, he physically, verbally, and psychologi-cally abuses her without mercy. Benji prays for a spirit to save them, and his prayers are heard by the vampire Armand, whose burned body is stuck in an ice mound in an aban-doned building close by, after his failed sui-cide attempt. Too weak to free himself from that winter's snowfall, Armand telepathically summons Sybelle and Benji, who free him from the ice and secretly bring him back to their hotel room. With his Mind Gift, Armand projects a mental image of himself into Sybelle and Benji's mind, so that they see not his figure but the five-hundred-year-old vampire he is in a seventeen-year-old's body. Before Sybelle's older brother can abuse her again, Armand, despite his weakness, kills him and becomes Sybelle and Benji's guardian. To help him grow stronger, Benji lures a Drug Enforcement Administration officer to the room, whom Armand drains completely of blood. Then he leaves his two mortals in their hotel room for a few hours while he drinks the blood of several victims until he regains enough strength to heal himself. Armand lives with Sybelle and Benji for a few more months.

Armand then takes Sybelle and Benji with him to investigate Lestat's fate when Lestat falls into a comatose stupor after receiving a disturbing package from Memnoch the Devil. While Armand makes plans to drink Lestat's blood so that he can see through the blood what Lestat has experienced on his mystical journey, he leaves Sybelle and Benji in the care of his maker, Marius, who takes the two mortals back to his home. Marius soon realizes how much Armand has come to love Sybelle and Benji, so he turns them into vampires, much to the great anger of Armand. Marius and Daniel convince Armand that Marius has not acted out of spite but out of love for him. With Marius's ancient blood in them, which also possesses Queen Akasha's most potent blood, both Sybelle and Benji are now just as powerful as Armand, not inferior to him like Daniel. Moreover, since Sybelle and Benji are both made by Marius, and not Armand, Armand will never suffer the curse that prevents maker and fledgling from being telepathically connected. Armand, Sybelle, and Benji now enjoy deeper intimacy and companionship through their vampiric, telepathic connection. No one ever abuses Sybelle again. In time, she becomes one of the coven's most talented musicians, performing beautiful classical music at vampire balls, where her new vampire family dances together for hours.

Sybelle appears in *The Vampire Armand* (1998), *Prince Lestat* (2014), *Prince Lestat and the Realms of Atlantis* (2016), and *Blood Communion* (2018). For more perspectives on Sybelle's character, read the *Alphabettery* entries **Armand**, **Benji Mahmoud**, **Daniel Malloy**, **Lestat de Lioncourt**, **Marius**, and **Memnoch**.

Talamasca Order

• COVEN •

 he Talamasca is an organization of psychic detectives who observe, investigate, and catalog paranormal realities. They have existed for centuries. The Talamasca appears in *The Queen of the Damned* (1988), *The Tale of the Body Thief* (1992), *Memnoch the Devil* (1995), *Pandora* (1998), *Blood Canticle* (2003), *Prince Lestat* (2014), and *Prince Lestat and the Realms of Atlantis* (2016).

Near the end of the sixth century of the Common Era, at the monastery school of Vivarium, founded by the great scholar, statesman, and monk Cassiodorus, Pandora encounters a discarnate spirit residing in the collective energy of beehives. The death of Cassiodorus rouses the spirit to leave the beehives and possess a scarecrow that begins mourning and weeping. Impressed by the spirit, Pandora encourages him to become more than what he is, affirming that he has the power to achieve his goals and appear human. Inspired and strengthened by how she is not afraid of the unknown, the spirit begins evolving into an incarnate form who calls himself Gremt Stryker Knollys.

Almost two hundred years later, shortly after Teskhamen buries his fledgling Hesketh on the sacred grounds of the ruins of an old monastery in France, Gremt encounters Hesketh's spirit and teaches her how to become incarnate like him. Gremt and Hesketh then appear before Teskhamen, who rejoices at the sight of Hesketh. The three form an alliance and make a pact to devote themselves to learning about the supernatural world, in particular to gaining knowledge about the cause and purpose of vampires, to comprehending the verifiable reality and nature of spirits, to understanding why some ghosts remain on the earth after death while other spirits fly directly into a beatific light, and to more fully fathoming how witches have the ability to manipulate and command spirits. Seeking empirical proof to help them define their purpose as supernatural beings, they begin the Order of the Talamasca—a name taken from an ancient Latin word meaning "animal mask."

With the principal Motherhouse beginning at that French monastic location, they soon bring into their ranks many mortals who also ask the same questions and seek the same answers. Their numbers grow rapidly. Inspired by Gremt's love for Cassiodorus and his Vivarium, they form Motherhouses and libraries where members of the Order can gather their unique knowledge. These Vivarium-like institutions also become places where novices in the Order are trained before they become full-fledged members. In one sense, the Talamasca is a sanctuary where nobody is supposed to be misunderstood, since everyone is seeking true understanding.

As time passes, Teskhamen, Hesketh, and Gremt hide the origin of the Talamasca from its members. They establish a tradition of Elders, who are mortal members of the Order, ordinary people who the immortals believe can lead the Talamasca into a new generation of learning. For many generations, they continue to select Elders, until they bequeath that tradition to other members of the Order. By the second millennium, no mortal Talamasca member knows who really began the Order, although some, like David Talbot, suspect that the origin of the Order was instinctively shaped by a need to survive through knowledge, creativity, and endurance; for at the sound of buzzing bees, many members of the Talamasca tremble in fear, acutely aware that the creation of the Order is somehow mysteriously rooted in the energy of beehives.

For more perspectives on the Talamasca Order in the Vampire Chronicles, read the *Alphabettery* entries **Aaron Lightner, The Elders, David Talbot, Gremt Stryker Knollys, Hesketh, Jesse, Merrick Mayfair, Pandora,** and **Teskhamen.**

The Tale of the Body Thief

• VAMPIRE CHRONICLE •

In the fourth book in the Vampire Chronicles, Lestat once more recounts his adventures. Unlike his previous two books, which are set at various times in history, from ancient Egypt to revolutionary France, Lestat sets this tale completely in the twentieth century, beginning with how he no longer feels a reason to live. After a failed suicide attempt, he is restored to health with the aid of the Talamasca's Superior General David Talbot. Following this, Lestat is approached by an ex-Talamasca member, and notorious criminal, Raglan James, who possesses the psychic ability to change bodies, offering him the chance to temporarily be a mortal in James's body. Excited to experience mortal life once more, Lestat agrees, despite precautions about being tricked by Raglan. The Body Thief steals his vampire body and leaves him in a mortal body that is dying. With David's aid, Lestat regains his vampire body, but Raglan switches bodies with David. Raglan tries to trick Lestat into believing that he is David and asks Lestat to turn him into a vampire. Lestat uncovers his trick and kills Raglan, but then turns David Talbot, in Raglan's former body, into a vampire.

For more perspectives on this Vampire Chronicle, read the *Alphabettery* entries **David Talbot**, **Lestat de Lioncourt**, *Queen Elizabeth 2*, **Raglan James**, and **Talamasca Order**.

Taltos

• IMMORTAL •

The Taltos are an ancient race of immortal beings, almost twice the size of an average human. Each Taltos possesses a telepathic link with every other member of their race, at least on a level of lower consciousness, where they are able to identify with one another's memories. Despite their superhuman abilities, they have a particular aversion to loud noises.

They live on a secluded, pastoral island, where there is plenty of food, a peaceful life with very little arguing or envy, and even fewer deaths, save those by accident, rare pestilence, justified murder, or population control. Because they are immortal, they decide that there should be no monogamy and that their mating rituals must last thirty minutes, after which the Taltos couple will spend one more hour together, until their child is born. With such a rapid child-gestation period, the only real pain that develops in their Edenic paradise comes from childbirth.

When their island utopia begins sinking into the sea, many Taltos flee to new lands. Many sail off to lands that have painfully cold winters. And one settlement led by Ashlar migrates and eventually settles in ancient Britain, where they erect tall sacred stones for ceremonial coupling and childbirth.

As this immortal race begins to interact with the mortals who live around them, many mortals become fearful of these giant creatures and eventually raid their encampments, kill the young, and capture many Taltos. The Taltos defend themselves but feel incapable of attacking mortals. Mortals try breeding with the Taltos. One result of this mortal-Taltos mating is the birth of dwarves, which are soon given the name Little People. But male Taltos die after mating with mortal women, and mortal women take much longer to give birth than Taltos women.

Surviving Taltos clans flee north, even as far as the Orkney and Shetland Islands above Great Britain. Some Taltos leave and live an isolated life, away from Taltos and mortals, wandering into distant lands. Mortals who have never seen them before are so startled by the Taltos' great height that they inspire fables about giants roaming throughout the land. Other Taltos create a mortal-like clan called the Picts in an effort to blend in with

other mortals. They are a private group but still have peaceful contact with mortals.

As they roam, the Taltos' supernatural abilities can identify witches, just as witches can identify the Taltos as immortal. Although Taltos and witches can identify one another, they maintain an unspoken understanding that neither will reveal the other's secret. As time passes, the Taltos become a race dispersed throughout the world.

In the twentieth century, the ancient Taltos Ashlar buys a secret island where he invites many other Taltos to live. He marries Morrigan Mayfair, and they have four Taltos children on the island. But one of his children, Silas, incites a rebellion, which causes the death of many Taltos, including Morrigan and Ashlar; Taltos who do not die become prisoners of the Drug Merchants. Eventually, the captive Taltos are rescued by Lestat, Mona Mayfair, and Quinn Blackwood, who bring the bodies of Ashlar and Morrigan back to New Orleans for scientific research and invite the remaining Taltos to live at Mayfair Medical Center, where they will be safe from future mortal attacks.

The Taltos appear in *Blood Canticle* (2003). For more perspectives on the Taltos in the Vampire Chronicles, read the *Alphabettery* entries **Ashlar, Lestat de Lioncourt, Mona Mayfair, Morrigan Mayfair, Quinn Blackwood,** and **Silas.**

Tante Oscar

• WITCH •

Tante Oscar is one of the dark-skinned Mayfairs, related closely to Merrick Mayfair, the witch and fledgling of Louis. Before Merrick is turned into a vampire, Oncle Vervain predicts it and shares his prediction with Tante Oscar. Tante Oscar often sees Louis walking through the French Quarter at night, killing off the riffraff. It is Tante Oscar who informs Rowan Mayfair about the existence of vampires and how her family is connected with them. She has a small apartment in the French Quarter and lives to be more than one hundred years old.

Tante Oscar appears in *Merrick* (2000). For more perspectives on Tante Oscar in the Vampire Chronicles, read the *Alphabettery* entries **Louis de Pointe du Lac**, **Merrick Mayfair**, **Oncle Vervain**, and **Rowan Mayfair**.

Tarquin Anthony Blackwood

• VAMPIRE •

Read the *Alphabettery* entry **Quinn Blackwood**.

Tartars

• MORTAL •

Former cossacks, the Tartars are a Turkic group that helps shape the culture and people of present-day Turkey.

In the fifteenth century, Tartar pirates raid a ship bound for Constantinople and capture a young prodigy painter named Andrei. They sell him to a brothel in Venice, but he is later rescued by the vampire Marius and turned into the vampire Armand.

The Tartars appear in *The Vampire Armand* (1998). For more perspectives on the Tartars in the Vampire Chronicles, read the *Alphabettery* entries **Armand** and **Marius**.

Terry

• MORTAL •

A practical nurse in New Orleans, Terry begins caring for the dying mother of Roger Flynn, who is in New York. When he comes in town to be with his mother, he and Terry have a brief relationship. Terry becomes pregnant with their daughter, Theodora Flynn, who comes to be called Dora. Roger pays Terry one hundred thousand dollars to marry him and promises to give her another one hundred thousand dollars after she has the baby if she will divorce him and give him Dora. She agrees initially, but when Dora is born, she decides to keep the child. Roger reluctantly agrees.

Since Roger is in New York so much while Terry remains in New Orleans, she begins a relationship with another man. She tells Roger that she is leaving with him and taking Dora with her. Roger, who is a contract killer, shoots and kills her and her paramour before taking Dora back to New York with him, where he eventually becomes a victim of the vampire Lestat.

Terry appears in *Memnoch the Devil* (1995). For more perspectives on Terry's character, read the *Alphabettery* entries **Dora**, **Lestat de Lioncourt**, **Roger**, and **Theodora Flynn**.

Terry Sue Harrison

• MORTAL •

Terry Sue lives in the backwoods on the Blackwood Farm property. She is a young woman who enjoys being a mother and having children. In time, she has a total of six children, one of whom, Tommy, is the son of Pops, Quinn's grandfather. Pops gives her an envelope of five hundred dollars every week to send Tommy to a good school. After Pops dies, Quinn and Aunt Queen help Terry Sue

earn a respectable income from the Blackwood estate to ensure that Quinn's younger uncle receives a good education and a promising future.

Terry Sue appears in *Blackwood Farm* (2002). For more perspectives on Terry Sue's character, read the *Alphabettery* entries **Aunt Queen**, **Pops**, **Quinn Blackwood**, and **Tommy Harrison**.

Teskhamen

• VAMPIRE •

Teskhamen, also called the God of the Grove, is the burned vampire in the large oak tree who made Marius into a vampire. He appears in *The Vampire Lestat* (1985), *Blood and Gold* (2001), *Prince Lestat* (2014), *Prince Lestat and the Realms of Atlantis* (2016), and *Blood Communion* (2018).

Brought into the Blood more than four thousand years before the Common Era, Teskhamen directly receives the pure and primal blood of the first vampire, Akasha, whom all the vampires at that time refer to as the Mother. Hailing from ancient Egypt, the lands of Upper and Lower Egypt nearly two thousand years before the first Pyramid is built, Teskhamen is principally Akasha's servant along with numerous other vampires, such as Avicus and Cyril, in the priest cult of the Mother Queen, which serves Akasha for the next thousand years. Referred to as the Drinkers of the Blood, this priest cult eventually divides into two factions: the servants and the enemies of Akasha and Enkil. When the enemies defeat the servants and entomb Akasha and Enkil within prison blocks of diorite and granite, leaving only their heads and necks exposed so as to feed them and drink their blood, Teskhamen survives the war.

In time he makes his way to the land of Gaul in modern-day France, where he lives in a sacred grove, in a crypt under a large oak tree, accessed only by a heavy doorway of iron covered in large locks. In that place Teskhamen comes to be worshipped by Druids as the God of the Grove. In the Great Burning of 4 C.E., Teskhamen is horribly charred to a living crisp. Blackened all over, his skin shrivels down to his bones; he looks like a yellow-eyed skeleton covered in black. Only his white fangs and his long mane of flowing white hair are quickly restored. The Druids are deeply concerned for the life of their god and the fate of their faith. When he is strong enough to speak, Teskhamen orders the Druids to bring to him a man of intelligence, strength, and beauty, so that he might pass on to him his power and so that they might have a new God of the Grove to worship. When the Druids bring him Marius de Romanus, Teskhamen reveals to him that he has different plans. After he makes Marius a vampire, Teskhamen commands him to escape from the Druids and go into Egypt to ascertain the fate of Akasha and Enkil, to learn the reason behind such a horrific burning, and to prevent this from happening again.

After Marius escapes from the Druids, Teskhamen also flees. While still in his weakened state, he meets a woman with disfigured skin and deformed limbs named Hesketh. Unafraid of him, she protects him and helps him heal. In turn, he helps her also, using his vampire power to fool mortals into believing that she is an oracle. Teskhamen sees past her horrific exterior and falls in love with the beauty he beholds within. She falls in love with him also, and he, unable to be without her, turns her into a vampire against the ancient vampire laws, which state that no deformed person can be turned into an immortal. For him, this is the final break from his old religious precepts, and he begins to embark on an entirely new life with Hesketh. They remain together for the next six hundred years. In the beginning, while he is still weak, they are timid about drinking blood and drink from hapless criminals who happen to come along the darkened road. In time, as she grows in power and as his former power returns and as he learns to utilize newer vampire powers, they begin besieging castles and fortresses to drink the blood of the inhabitants.

Despite their love for each other, Hesketh realizes that she is going to be disfigured as a vampire forever, much the same way that Claudia realizes that she will forever age in a little girl's body. Full of anger, Hesketh quarrels with Teskhamen, and they separate. When Teskhamen hears the news that she was overcome by a mob who burned her to death, he destroys the mob's village and all of its inhabitants. Then he buries her remains on the sacred grounds of an old monastery in France. He stays in the monastery's scriptorium near her grave for many nights. He sets up a lamp over her grave and lights the lamp every night. He knows he cannot go on without her. Finally, one night Hesketh appears to him, not the Hesketh he remembers but the beautiful woman that he once saw deep inside her. She is no longer deformed but willowy and stunning. She is also a ghost who has learned how to become incarnate through the teaching of the spirit Gremt, who learned how to evolve into an incarnate form by psychically gathering countless motes of dust

into a solidified shape, complete with organs, bones, teeth, skin, hair, and even blood to color the skin. Despite the fact that she is a ghost, Teskhamen can touch her with his fingers, hold her with his arms, and kiss her with his lips. He takes her as his ghostly bride, and they have remained together ever since.

Teskhamen and Hesketh form an alliance with Gremt to gain a better knowledge of who they are as supernatural creatures. This alliance is the inception of the Talamasca. The ruins of the old monastery in France become the Talamasca's first Motherhouse. Mortals who share their desire to gain knowledge of vampires, ghosts, witches, and other supernatural creatures join them. Together, mortal and immortal alike, they gather knowledge of unexplained phenomena, and they try to understand the world from an unprecedented perspective. Inspired by Gremt's admiration for Cassiodorus's Vivarium, they establish more Motherhouses and libraries where members of the Order can study and learn and where novices can be trained. Teskhamen, Hesketh, and Gremt select mortals to be the elders of the Order. As the Talamasca grows over the years, mortals take over running the Order, and Teskhamen, Hesketh, and Gremt become less known, until one day they are forgotten altogether, and the Talamasca's origins are soon shrouded in mystery.

Teskhamen and Hesketh remain together, relocating in the twenty-first century to the Replimoid colony in England, although Teskhamen often visits the Court of the Prince at Château de Lioncourt.

For more perspectives on Teskhamen's character, read the *Alphabettery* entries **Aka-**

sha, Amel, Avicus, Cyril, Enkil, God of the Grove, Great Burning of 4 C.E., Gremt Stryker Knollys, Hesketh, Lestat de Lioncourt, and **Marius**.

Théâtre des Vampires

• COVEN •

Around the year 1780, when Lestat convinces Armand and his Parisian coven of the Children of Darkness that their ways are outmoded in this modern world of the Enlightenment, Armand destroys all but four members of the coven: Eleni, Eugénie, Laurent, and Felix. They beg Lestat to give them a place to stay and to become their new coven leader, but he refuses. Instead, he allows them to stay in a closed theater that he owns, Renaud's House of Thesbians, on the Boulevard du Temple. It still has many costumes and props, which these four vampires use to disguise themselves as mortals in eighteenth-century France. Lestat's recent fledgling, Nicolas, who now loathes Lestat for turning him into a vampire, goes to the theater where he plays his violin. The other four vampires dance to the music, and Nicolas calls it the Théâtre des Vampires and demands that Lestat give them the theater. Lestat acquiesces only because of his love for and guilt over his fledgling.

Lestat leaves them, and the Théâtre des Vampires becomes the new coven house for Nicolas, Eleni, Eugénie, Laurent, Felix, and even Armand. Nicolas is their playwright and composer. The other vampires perform theater shows for the Parisian masses, pretending to be mortals who pretend to be vampires. They live in the theater and drink the blood of their victims onstage and off. Eleni writes letters to Lestat, describing their immense success among the Parisians. Over the years, they gain new members and grow into a powerful coven. Nicolas, however, grows more insane every night. He accosts people in the street and reveals his vampire nature to the public. Armand must imprison him and even goes so far as to cut off his hands, but the coven members put them back on with their vampire power. When he can no longer bear the torture of eternity, Nicolas writes a stack of plays and then flings himself into a fire, destroying himself completely.

In time, Eleni, Eugénie, Laurent, and Felix leave the *théâtre*, and Lestat hears no more from them until the late nineteenth century, when his new fledglings, Louis and Claudia, come to Paris in search of vampires. By that time, the coven has gained new members, such as Santiago, who has never heard of the four founding members. Armand invites Louis and Claudia to the *théâtre*. It disgusts Claudia, but Louis and Armand develop a relationship. Lestat returns and accuses Claudia of attempting to kill him. In response, the coven kills Claudia. Armand, secretly desiring to have Louis as his

companion, allows Louis to burn the *théâtre* to the ground and kill all the vampires within. Armand and Louis abandon Lestat and leave the Théâtre des Vampires burning to rubble on the Boulevard du Temple.

Théâtre des Vampires appears in *Interview with the Vampire* (1976) and *The Vampire Lestat* (1985). For more perspectives on the Théâtre des Vampires in the Vampire Chronicles, read the *Alphabettery* entries **Armand, Claudia, Coven, Eleni, Eugénie, Felix, Laurent, Lestat de Lioncourt, Louis, Madeleine, Nicolas de Lenfent, Renaud's House of Thesbians,** and **Santiago.**

Theodora Flynn

• MORTAL •

Theodora Flynn is the birth name of Dora, one of Lestat's mortal love interests, who takes from Lestat Veronica's Veil, which she uses to show the world the real presence of Jesus Christ's love in the world.

Theodora Flynn appears in *Memnoch the Devil* (1995). For more perspectives on Theodora's character, read the *Alphabettery* entries **Dora, Lestat de Lioncourt,** and **Veronica's Veil.**

Thirteen Witches

• PHENOMENON •

When the spirit of Lasher develops a plan to become an incarnate entity, he also establishes a specialized breeding program, which involves thirteen incestuous witches over thirteen generations. Every witch belongs to the Mayfair family, and every witch is female, except one, Julien Mayfair, who becomes the Designée when his sister, Katherine, spurns the family tradition and proves to be a weaker magic user than her brother.

Suzanne, the first witch, and the Earl of Donnelaith beget Deborah.

Deborah, the second witch, and Petyr van Abel beget Charlotte.

Charlotte, the third witch, and Antoine Fontenay beget Jeanne Louise.

Jeanne Louise, the fourth witch, and Peter Mayfair beget Angelique.

Angelique, the fifth witch, and Vincent St. Christophe beget Marie Claudette.

Marie Claudette, the sixth witch, and Henri Marie Laundy beget Marguerite.

Marguerite, the seventh witch, and Tyronne Clifford McNamara beget Katherine and Julien.

Katherine and Julien Mayfair, the eighth witches together, beget Mary Beth.

Mary Beth, the ninth witch, and Julien Mayfair beget Stella.

Stella, the tenth witch, and Lionel Mayfair beget Antha.

Antha, the eleventh witch, and Sean Lacy beget Deirdre.

Deidre, the twelfth witch, and Cortland Mayfair beget Rowan.

Rowan, the thirteenth witch, and Michael Curry beget Lasher.

The Thirteen Witches appear in *Blood Canticle* (2003). For more perspectives on the Thirteen Witches in the Vampire Chronicles, read the *Alphabettery* entries **Julien Mayfair** and **Rowan Mayfair**.

Thomas Blackwood

• MORTAL •

Thomas Blackwood is the birth name for Pops, husband of Sweetheart, father of Patsy, and grandfather of Quinn Blackwood, companion of the vampire Lestat.

Thomas Blackwood appears in *Black-wood Farm* (2002). For more perspectives on Thomas Blackwood's character, read the *Alphabettery* entries **Pops, Quinn Blackwood, Rose Blackwood,** and **Sweetheart.**

Thorne

• VAMPIRE •

Thorne is the only known Viking turned into a vampire. He is Maharet's fledgling and companion until she abandons him. He takes his revenge on her and aids Marius by killing Santino on her property. Thorne appears in *Blood and Gold* (2001), *Prince Lestat* (2014), *Prince Lestat and the Realms of Atlantis* (2016), and *Blood Communion* (2018).

In the eighth century, during the great Viking age in medieval Scandinavia, the Viking warrior Thornevald accompanies his clan up a mountainside seeking a red-haired witch who drinks the blood of her victims and steals their eyes. Having buried his warrior father, who died with sword in hand, and having been reared on Norse mythology through poetry and a religious devotion to the boom of Thor's hammer in the thunder and Odin's Wild Hunt through raging tempests, Thornevald shows little fear when his clan finally happens one night upon the red-haired witch. She allows him to watch her fight Viking warriors, take one warrior's eyes, and place them in her own empty sockets, then allows him to observe her return to her cave, where she sits at a spinning wheel spinning golden thread. With his trusty hammer and ax, the lone Viking warrior prepares to fight this monstrous witch named Maharet, but she spreads her arms wide to receive Thornevald as her new companion. Biting into his neck, she turns him into a vampire. She has come to the north seeking companionship, and she believes that Thornevald's youth, strength, and raw courage will make him an excellent companion to accompany her throughout eternity.

Maharet groomed him by shaving off his thick beard before she gave him the Dark Gift. Once he becomes a vampire, he abandons the name Thornevald to be called simply Thorne, then listens attentively as Maharet recounts her tale, how she was betrayed by an ancient queen who plucked out her eyes before separating her from her sister for all eternity. Thorne loves Maharet with great intensity, which can only be comparable to the intensity of his jealousy as Maharet gathers to herself numerous other vampires, including the nearly one-thousand-year-old vampire Mael, who fascinates Maharet with the tales of his life, especially those recounting the years he lived with Marius, protecting Maharet's ancient foes, Akasha and Enkil. Becoming more attracted to Mael than Thorne, Maharet takes Mael as her new companion, and Thorne leaves, full of jealousy and hate.

He wanders the earth for a while until he can no longer endure his immortal existence. Then he makes his way north, near the hunting grounds of Inuits, where he buries himself in an icy cave and sleeps away the ages. In his torpor he hears the twentieth-century broadcasts of the vampire Lestat, revealing old secrets that Maharet never confided to Thorne. As he sleeps, he sees in his dreams the magnificent Queen Akasha rise from her throne after thousands of years of remaining statuesque, fly through the air with the Cloud Gift, and burn numberless fledglings with her Fire Gift. Thorne remains silent in his slumber; she never discovers where he lies. In his dreams he observes Queen Akasha fight with twin witches, and he marvels that Maharet still lives. Occasionally the thirst for blood awakens him from his slumber; he uses the Cloud Gift to fly into the air and drink mortal blood. But he always returns to his cave to sleep and dream. More dreams come to him of the vampire Lestat, how he has walked with the Devil, and how his bedeviled encounter leaves him so crazed that Maharet uses locks of her unbreakable hair to keep him enchained until his sanity is restored. Still, Thorne continues to sleep. He wants to sleep away eternity. That is not to be.

When memory leaves him not, and when sleep returns to him not, Thorne wakes and flies south with the Cloud Gift for several sunless days and nights, common to the northern winters. He suffers a great desire to have a companion and contact this modern age. With the Mind Gift, he sends out a silent invitation for friendship without revealing his name. The vampire Marius responds. Much older than Thorne, Marius invites him back to his home, where Marius and Thorne exchange the story of their lives. Sensing that Thorne is still very angry at Maharet and possesses a burning desire to attack her, Marius attempts to dissuade him from his suicidal plan by sharing with him how vengeance cannot solve this problem. Marius reveals how he greatly desires to destroy Santino for the wrong done to him in sixteenth-century Italy, when Santino burned Marius's palazzo, nearly destroyed Marius, and then stole his new fledgling, Armand. Thorne wonders why Marius will not seek to destroy Santino out of vengeance; Marius explains that the vampire race must live by rules: he will not kill Santino unless he has the permission of Mekare, the Queen of the Damned, through her spokeswoman, Maharet. When Thorne demands to see Maharet despite Marius's best efforts to convince him otherwise, Marius sends a message to Maharet with the Mind Gift.

When they awaken the next night, they discover that Maharet has transported them to her jungle compound in Java, Indonesia. Marius and Thorne are surprised by the presence of Armand, Pandora, and even Santino. Marius once again demands the right to destroy Santino, and once more Maharet denies him. Not willing to disobey her, Marius begrudgingly accepts her decision. Thorne is still full of anger towards Maharet, so he exacts wergeld—the "man price," idealizing the ancient law that often results in taking a life for a life. Thorne attacks Santino, blasting him first with all the force of his Mind Gift until blood flows from every orifice, then he immolates Santino utterly with the Fire Gift until all that remains is a black stain on the stones.

Still simmering with rage towards his maker, Thorne attacks Maharet, throttling her and trying to topple her with all of his might, which proves as fruitless as a mortal throttling and trying to topple a marble statue. Mekare pulls Thorne off Maharet easily. Maharet shields Thorne from Mekare's savage protectiveness for her sister, and Thorne then understands that everyone there is afraid of the untamed Mekare, except for himself. Maharet weeps not for the craven Santino but as a host might weep when tragedy befalls a guest under her roof. Recognizing his great transgression against her, Thorne tells Mekare to remove his eyes and give them to Maharet so that she no longer need hunt for corruptible mortal eyes but will have his own incorruptible immortal eyes forever. Once Maharet fits Thorne's eyes into her sockets, he is glad for his blessed blindness, but he begs them to bind him with Maharet's powerful hair, the same way she bound Lestat after his journey with Memnoch the Devil. Blind and bound, Thorne remains imprisoned in torment, albeit with utter joy, by the only woman he has ever truly loved.

In the twenty-first century, the vampire scientist Fareed visits Maharet's compound, sharing with her how he has made astonishing advances in the field of genetic cloning, specifically with that of vampire DNA. With her permission, using his genetic reproductive techniques, Fareed replaces the eyes she lost six thousand years earlier. Then he does the same for Thorne. With his sight restored, Thorne becomes the devoted servant of Maharet, Mekare, and Maharet's twentieth-century descendant, the vampire Jesse Reeves.

Maharet releases Thorne and gives him the

freedom to come and go from her Java compound. When the compound is destroyed by a fire and Maharet creates a new compound in the jungles of the Amazon, Thorne and Jesse are no longer invited, especially when Amel awakens in the wounded mind of his host, Mekare, and begins the Great Burning of 2013. Thorne hears Amel's voice when he is in Sweden and Norway, but he ignores it. He returns to Fareed, where he guards Lestat's clone and son, Viktor, but the vampire Rhoshamandes is too powerful for him and kidnaps Viktor. After Lestat retrieves Viktor and takes Amel, the Sacred Core, from Mekare, becoming Prince Lestat, Thorne and Cyril find delight in acting as the Prince's new personal bodyguards. Even after Amel is removed from Lestat's brain, Thorne remains Lestat's guardian, along with Cyril, at the request of the vampire council at the Court of Château de Lioncourt, which still desires Lestat as their Prince.

For more perspectives on Thorne's character, read the *Alphabettery* entries **Akasha, Enkil, Cloud Gift, Cyril, Fire Gift, Great Burning of 2013, Lestat de Lioncourt, Mael, Maharet, Marius, Mekare, Mind Gift**, and **Santino.**

Those Who Must Be Kept

• VAMPIRES •

Those Who Must Be Kept is another name for Akasha and Enkil. The name appears in *The Vampire Lestat* (1985), *The Queen of the Damned* (1988), and *Blood and Gold* (2001).

One night, two ancient vampires are discovered naked and holding each other on a cold floor. They have been imprisoned in a hidden sanctuary under large blocks of diorite and granite for so long that no younger vampires truly know their story. The legend is that they are Akasha and Enkil, the first vampires who spawned every vampire in existence, but none knows who was created first or if they were created simultaneously. Legend also has it that if they are the Mother and the Father, they are so old that they have become statuelike.

Their current vampire caretakers recognize the immensity of the power and importance in the great age of these two most ancient of vampires, and they bathe them, dress them in fine clothes, and set them on thrones, like two statues facing forward with eyes wide open.

One vampire, called the Elder, must watch over them, care for them, and protect them from harm. No longer formally referred to as Akasha and Enkil, or even as the Mother and the Father, these two mute and unmoving vampires now become known as Those Who Must Be Kept.

The Elder cares for them for centuries under the same routine of bathing them, changing their clothes, wiping the dust from the tiny crevices between their eyes, fingers, and toes. A new religious practice develops around them. Blood priests bring sacrificial victims for Those Who Must Be Kept to feed on. Also, young vampires are allowed to feed off Akasha's Sacred Fount of ancient blood to grow stronger, such as Eudoxia, fledgling of Cyril, fledgling of the Elder. No matter how much blood the Mother and the Father are given, no matter how much time passes, the two ancient vampires on their thrones rarely move and never speak. Eventually the Elder grows so weary of his burdensome task that he takes Those Who Must Be Kept out of their shrine in old Egypt and places them on the bank of the Nile River with the intent of letting them be destroyed under the sunlight. Those Who Must Be Kept have become so powerful that the sunlight can only bronze their skin. The Elder awakens from his daytime slumber and observes that his formerly white skin is now bronzed and that all younger vampires have either been immolated or charred to a crisp in the Great Burning of 4 C.E. He concludes that Those Who Must Be Kept are profoundly interconnected to every vampire in existence. Hurriedly, without revealing to anyone the great crime he has committed, the Elder retrieves Those Who Must Be Kept and brings them back to their shrine, as if nothing has happened.

While the world goes on, Akasha's mind is active. No longer trusting the Elder, she reads his thoughts with the Mind Gift and realizes that he is plotting to rid himself of his tedious duty by dropping Those Who Must Be Kept to the bottom of the ocean, where no sunlight or heat can damage them

and where they cannot damage their children. Before he can enact that plan, Teskhamen, an ancient vampire blackened by the Elder's treachery, dispatches his new young fledgling, Marius, to Egypt to discover the fate of Those Who Must Be Kept. When Marius arrives with questions about the Great Burning of 4 C.E., the Elder lies, telling him he does not know its cause. Despite the Elder's treachery, Akasha communicates telepathically to Marius with the Mind Gift, showing him images of the history of Those Who Must Be Kept—how Amel entered Akasha; how she turned Enkil into a vampire; how they created a vampire cult; how the cult was overthrown by rebels; how Akasha and Enkil were captured and imprisoned; how they became Those Who Must Be Kept; and how the Elder is now trying to destroy them. Once Marius understands, Akasha reveals to him the Elder's plot to harm them again. She begs Marius to take them away. When he agrees, Akasha then rises from her throne, crushes the Elder under her feet, and, with her Mind Gift, telekinetically knocks over the oil lamp that burns the Elder's pulpy remains to cinders.

Marius first takes them out of Egypt into Antioch. Akasha makes no mention of reestablishing the ancient cult practice of worshipping Those Who Must Be Kept as a goddess and god, so Marius keeps Akasha and Enkil in a hidden shrine beneath his house. He reveals to no other vampire the hidden location of the Mother and the Father. In response, the ancient vampire Akbar, who is as old as Teskhamen and was severely burned in the Great Burning of 4 C.E., drains the blood from Marius's beloved mortal, Pandora, to the point of death and extorts Marius to reveal to him the hidden location of Those Who Must Be Kept, otherwise Pandora will die. When Marius reluctantly acquiesces and takes Akbar to the shrine of the royal pair, Akasha refuses Akbar, crushes his skull, dismembers him, and destroys him by dropping an oil lamp on his remains and burning him to ash. Marius saves Pandora by turning her into a vampire; and for many years she helps Marius fulfill his duties. Akasha allows both Marius and Pandora to drink her blood, which increases their power and makes them a better fit to protect Those Who Must Be Kept.

Maharet discovers their secret location, steals into the shrine undetected, stands before Akasha, and plunges a dagger into the Queen's heart, taking revenge for Akasha's tyrannical maltreatment, as both mortal and immortal, of Maharet and her twin sister, Mekare. Maharet feels dizzy when the dagger causes Akasha's heart to pause ever so briefly; she knows that other vampires, especially the younger ones, must have felt an even-worse moment of suffering. Maharet understands Akasha's connection to all other vampires, so she leaves the Queen in Marius's care and never again returns.

When Marius and Pandora separate, he moves Akasha, Enkil, and himself in three large sarcophagi to Rome, where he takes into his confidence Avicus, who was a member of Akasha's blood cult, and Avicus's fledgling Mael. After the fall of Rome, Marius, Avicus, and Mael move Those Who Must Be Kept to Constantinople, where they encounter Eudoxia, who has already imbibed Akasha's ancient and powerful blood. Eudoxia

demands to have Those Who Must Be Kept. When Marius denies her, she tries to fight for them, but Marius is too powerful. Humbled, Eudoxia begs Marius to let her simply see them, and he kindly allows it. When Eudoxia sees them, she is so moved by the sight of Akasha that she offers herself as a victim for the Queen, who grabs Eudoxia and nearly drains her completely of blood. Vengeful, Eudoxia next kills a mortal and frames Marius for the murder. The citizens of Constantinople exact retribution for the murder by attacking Marius's house. Enraged by Eudoxia's treachery, Marius drags her from her home, brings her one last time to the shrine of Those Who Must Be Kept, and flings her before Akasha, who drains her completely of blood and burns her to ashes with the Fire Gift.

Marius takes Those Who Must Be Kept away from Avicus and Mael. He builds a new shrine deep inside a mountain, away from the sunlight, the interior painted with beautiful murals, all hidden in a secluded location in a series of uninhabited slopes in the Alps, so steep that mortals of that time dare not make the ascent, which is no problem for a powerful vampire like Marius.

Later, in the sixteenth century, after Marius is badly burned by Santino and the Children of Satan, he and his new fledgling Bianca move Those Who Must Be Kept to a castle dungeon in Saxony, Germany, which they transform into a beautiful shrine for the King and Queen of the Vampires. Marius and Bianca care for Those Who Must Be Kept. Akasha allows both Marius and Bianca to drink her blood, making each stronger.

After Bianca leaves Marius a few centuries later, he moves Those Who Must Be Kept to a new shrine on an island in the Aegean Sea. After becoming aware that the vampire Lestat is seeking him with an obsessed desperation, Marius brings Lestat to his island sanctuary and invites him into the shrine. Enraptured by what he sees, Lestat returns to the shrine when Marius is absent, takes a violin, and begins performing for Enkil and most especially for Akasha. The Queen, who has never before heard either that instrument or such bedeviled playing, rises from her throne, takes Lestat in her embrace, drinks his blood, and gives him her blood to drink. Marius attempts to enter the shrine, but Akasha keeps the doors barred against him, keeping him out and away from this rapturous moment. She relents and opens the doors when, after centuries of stillness, Enkil rises from his throne in a jealous rage and tries to kill Lestat. Marius and Akasha fend him off, and then Those Who Must Be Kept return to their thrones, where they resume sitting in mute stillness. Marius understands that, despite his almost two millennia of indefatigable service, Akasha desires Lestat to care for her and to love her. Marius sends Lestat away from the island and moves Those Who Must Be Kept to the unpopulated, frozen lands in the Canadian north.

Marius builds for them a technologically advanced citadel where Akasha and Enkil sit on their thrones surrounded by newer technology as the world progresses faster into the industrial age. In the twentieth century, he sets before them a television that receives satellite-transmission broadcasts. In that sanctuary, Akasha sees Lestat once more, only now instead of playing the violin, he is singing in the popular rock band the Vampire Lestat. His words and music tell the story of Those Who Must Be Kept and urge them to awaken. Reminded of the days when she was the blood Queen, not hiding from the world but exposed fearlessly and worshipped by fearful disciples, Akasha rises from her throne, bites into Enkil's neck, drains every drop of blood from his body, and destroys her old king and companion, thus ending the keeping of Those Who Must Be Kept, for Akasha will not be kept back anymore, as she seeks to rule the world once again as the Queen of the Damned.

For more perspectives on Those Who Must Be Kept in the Vampire Chronicles, read the *Alphabettery* entries **Akasha, Akbar, Amel, Avicus, Bianca Solderini, Children of Satan, Cyril, The Elder, Enkil, Eudoxia, Mael, Maharet, Marius, Mekare, Pandora, Santino, Teskhamen,** and **The Vampire Lestat.**

Tim

• VAMPIRE •

Tim is a member of the Fang Gang and appears in *The Queen of the Damned* (1988).

His history and maker remain a mystery, but because two other members of the Fang Gang (Baby Jenks and Davis) are turned into vampires by the Fang Gang's founder, Killer, Tim is likely also Killer's fledgling. While the Fang Gang is composed of only five vampires, Tim forms a more intimate attachment with a fifth member, Russ, as the two enjoy hunting together.

Tim accompanies the Fang Gang to Lestat's San Francisco rock concert, but his immortal existence ends there when he and Russ are immolated side by side at the arrival of Queen Akasha, recently awakened and enacting her plan of world domination.

For more perspectives on Tim's character, read the *Alphabettery* entries **Akasha**, **Baby Jenks**, **Davis**, **Fang Gang**, **Killer**, and **Russ**.

Time Before the Moon

• IDIOM •

When Maharet and Mekare are still mortal witches in ancient Israel, before ancient Egypt's construction of the Pyramids, nearly four thousand years before the Common Era, their family can count back fifty generations of witches, to the era of the world that they refer to as the Time Before the Moon. Totaling anywhere from seventy-five hundred years to nine thousand years before the Common Era, it is an epoch of Earth's history before the moon entered the sky. At the time, the Taltos live on a paradisiacal island, in perfect harmony with one another and with the land, and Amel has constructed the city of Atlantis from his luracastria creation to protect mortals from the exploitation of the Bravennans. When the moon finally ascends into the sky, the Time Before the Moon ends, and horrific floods, gale-force storms, and tumultuous earthquakes ensue. The Taltos flee their island, witches take shelter in Mount Carmel, Atlantis falls into the ocean, and Amel dies, though his spirit drifts on the etheric plane until fused with the blood of Queen Akasha.

The Time Before the Moon is referenced in *The Queen of the Damned* (1988). For more perspectives on the Time Before the Moon in the Vampire Chronicles, read the *Alphabettery* entries **Maharet** and **Mekare**.

Tommy Harrison

• MORTAL •

Tommy is the son of Terry Sue and Quinn's grandfather Pops, who was unfaithful to his wife, Sweetheart. Since Pops's real name is Thomas Blackwood, Tommy is named after him. Pops cares for Tommy by giving Terry Sue an envelope of five hundred dollars a week, which keeps him in Saint Joseph's Catholic School in Mapleville. Although he is technically Quinn's uncle, Tommy is a boy when Quinn is in his twenties. Because

Tommy demonstrates remarkable intelligence at a young age, he is eventually sent to a boarding school in England, but in time he returns to live at Blackwood Manor.

Tommy appears in *Blackwood Farm* (2002). For more perspectives on Tommy's character, read the *Alphabettery* entries **Aunt Queen, Blackwood Manor, Pops, Quinn Blackwood, Sweetheart,** and **Terry Sue Harrison.**

Torwan

• TALTOS •

Torwan is one of the few remaining Taltos females who live on a secret island owned by the ancient Taltos Ashlar; his wife, Morrigan; and their four children—Silas, Oberon, Miravelle, and Lorkyn. Unhappy with their state of affairs, Silas causes an uprising among the Taltos and attacks nearby islands, one of which is owned by mortal Drug Merchants. The Drug Merchants retaliate by viciously attacking Ashlar's island. Most of the Taltos

are shot and killed. A few are captured, Torwan among them. When she sees her chance, Torwan attempts to escape on a boat, but the Drug Merchants catch her and stab her to death on the pier.

Torwan appears in *Blood Canticle* (2003). For more perspectives on Torwan in the Vampire Chronicles, read the *Alphabettery* entries **Ashlar, Lorkyn, Miravelle, Morrigan Mayfair, Oberon, Silas,** and **Taltos.**

Tough Cookie

• MORTAL •

Tough Cookie and her bandmates, Larry and Alex, enjoy some success in New Orleans as the band Satan's Night Out, even with her on guitar, which is very forward thinking for an eighties rock band. Perhaps that is one of the reasons that the vampire Lestat finds their little group to be so attractive. When he appears to them, reveals his vampire nature, and informs them that he will give them the fame they desire, they immediately agree with him and change their band name to the Vampire Lestat.

Even after Lestat leaves the band shortly after their one and only concert, in San Francisco, he arranges for his lawyer Christine to compensate Tough Cookie and her bandmates so they will never have to worry about finances again.

Tough Cookie appears in *The Vampire Lestat* (1985). For more perspectives on her character, read the *Alphabettery* entries **Alex**, **Christine**, **Larry**, **Lestat de Lioncourt**, **Satan's Night Out**, and **The Vampire Lestat**.

Trinity Gate

• SANCTUARY •

Founded and protected by Armand, Trinity Gate is a coven house and sanctuary for certain elite vampires who meet certain criteria, such as the Coven of the Articulate or the Children of the Millennia. That is, vampires like Louis, Lestat, Marius, Armand, David, and Pandora (and perhaps even Vittorio) are welcome inside, as they have all written books in the Vampire Chronicles. Similarly welcomed are Maharet, Khayman, Thorne, Gregory, and any vampire of goodwill more than one thousand years old. On the other hand, younger vampires such as Killer and Davis are not initially welcome, although some young vampires are very much welcome, such as Benji, who broadcasts his internet radio program from one of Trinity Gate's rooms, and Sybelle, who accompanies Benji's radio program with beautiful piano playing.

Structurally, Trinity Gate is a grouping of three townhouses, all side by side, on New York's Upper East Side; a long glass porch along the back connects all three units. Inside is lavish furniture, a vast library and ballroom, and countless, priceless treasures collected throughout the ages.

After Lestat takes into himself the Sacred Core, making himself the new host carrier of the spirit of Amel, effectively becoming Prince Lestat, he takes Trinity Gate as his royal residence in New York.

Trinity Gate appears in *Prince Lestat* (2014) and *Prince Lestat and the Realms of Atlantis* (2016). For more perspectives on Trinity Gate in the Vampire Chronicles, read the *Alphabettery* entries **Amel**, **Armand**, **Benji Mahmoud**, **Children of the Millennia**, **Coven of the Articulate**, **Davis**, **Gregory Duff Collingsworth**, **Khayman**, **Killer**, **Lestat de Lioncourt**, **Maharet**, **Mekare**, **Pandora**, **Sacred Core**, **Sybelle**, **Thorne**, and **The Vampire Chronicles**.

Uncle Lestan

• ALIAS •

hen a vampire rescues a child named Rose from a natural disaster that kills her mother and family, he adopts her and tells her to call him Lestat. But her young mouth cannot shape the word, so instead it comes out as "Lestan." Ever since, Rose refers to her adopted father Lestat as Uncle Lestan.

Uncle Lestan appears in *Prince Lestat* (2014). For more perspectives on this alias, read the *Alphabettery* entries **Lestat de Lioncourt** and **Rose**.

Uncle Mickey

• MORTAL •

Brother of Roger (one of Lestat's most important victims in *Memnoch the Devil*) and uncle of Dora (one of Lestat's most beloved mortals), Uncle Mickey is a tout for a bookie in New Orleans. One day, succumbing to greed, instead of placing a bet for his bookie, he decides to keep the money for himself, hoping to inform the bookie that the horse lost. To his dismay, the horse wins. In a rage, the bookie sends gangsters who pummel Mickey and kick out his eye. As Mickey's eye lies on the pavement, the gangsters step on it, squashing it completely.

This story foreshadows Lestat's predicament when he confronts Memnoch the Devil and loses his own eye. Fortunately, unlike Uncle Mickey, who must wear a glass eye until he dies at the age of fifty, Memnoch returns Lestat's eye, which Lestat promptly places back into his empty eye socket.

Uncle Mickey appears in *Memnoch the Devil* (1995). For more perspectives on Uncle Mickey in the Vampire Chronicles, read the *Alphabettery* entries **Dora**, **Lestat de Lioncourt**, and **Memnoch**.

Undead

• IMMORTAL •

The term "Undead" is generally used in reference to any creature that has died and has come back to life again through unnatural means. That is, being undead is not like being resuscitated. In the Vampire Chronicles, mortals become Undead in the process of becoming vampires: the vampire maker drains them of blood to the point of death, the mortals drink their maker's blood, then their mortal body dies, and they come back to life, not as mortals, but as immortal blood drinkers. For instance, Louis's body dies and becomes undead when Lestat turns him into a vampire.

The term "Undead" appears in *Interview with the Vampire* (1976), *The Vampire Lestat* (1985), *The Queen of the Damned* (1988), *Prince Lestat* (2014), and *Prince Lestat and the Realms of Atlantis* (2016). For more perspectives on this term in the Vampire Chronicles, read the *Alphabettery* entries **Lestat de Lioncourt** and **Louis de Pointe du Lac**.

Uriel the Archangel

• IMMORTAL •

According to apocryphal tradition in both Jewish and Christian faiths, Uriel the Archangel is a protector of the human race. As his name means "God is my light," Uriel's work is to help God illumine human minds with knowledge, understanding, and wisdom.

In the book *Memnoch the Devil*, Lestat does not encounter Uriel, as he does Michael the Archangel, but he hears of Uriel through Memnoch's story. When Memnoch explains how he accuses God of sin, he reveals how Uriel watches him without emotion.

Uriel appears in *Memnoch the Devil* (1995). For more perspectives on Uriel in the Vampire Chronicles, read the *Alphabettery* entries **Lestat de Lioncourt**, **Memnoch**, and **Michael the Archangel**.

Ursula

• VAMPIRE •

Ursula spares Vittorio's life, draws him into the Court of the Ruby Grail, tricks him and makes him a vampire, and soon after becomes his beloved. She appears in *Vittorio the Vampire* (1999).

Born in thirteenth-century France, Ursula is fourteen when her father receives an offer to buy his daughter in marriage. After her virginity is confirmed, she is introduced to her new husband, the vampire Florian, who takes her to a ruined chapel, full of spiders and vermin, where she is made his bride as a mortal and made a vampire as his fledgling. Florian then introduces his bride to his vampire coven in his lair in a ruined castle in the northern mountains of Tuscany, called the Court of the Ruby Grail. Florian is new to that court but has much power and influence. They love each other initially, and they remain together for the next two hundred years, hunting mortals in nearby villages. Over the course of those two centuries, Florian strikes a deal with the surrounding towns, villages, and castles: their vampire coven is allowed to take the elderly, infirm, weak, and evil. As a result, the Court of the Ruby Grail keeps its mortal prisoners in a confinement like a large chicken coop, fattening them until they are plump and full of blood, and then they feast every night sumptuously. During those years, Florian also grows tired of Ursula as a wife and takes many other lovers. Soon, Ursula begins to pine for a new love herself.

One night, after Ursula has been in the Blood for more than two hundred years, the coven goes to Castello Raniari, south of their castle. Florian attempts to make the same deal with Lord Lorenzo di Raniari, but the lord rejects him. As a result, Ursula and the others come to the castle and slay all the servants within, and almost the entire di Raniari family. Ursula herself has the two smallest children, but the elder son, Vittorio, a beautiful knightly youth at sixteen years old, commands her to stop. She is utterly enamored of him from the moment she sees him, and she readily obeys. Vittorio takes advantage of her momentary hesitation to draw his sword and cut off her right arm, but she easily reattaches it with her vampire power. Another vampire enters and kills Vittorio's siblings. Vittorio is the only one to survive the attack.

Ursula returns with her coven to the Court of the Ruby Grail, yet for Vittorio she continues to yearn. On the next night, she discovers that he has left his castle and gone north, in the direction of her coven, and is lodging at the inn at the nearest town, Santa Maddalana. She appears before him in his room and warns him not to go farther north, lest he meet with death. Then she drinks some of his blood and fills his mind with visions of them in a romantic embrace, so much so that he becomes infatuated with her. She leaves and returns to her coven and is disappointed to discover that Vittorio has not heeded her warning.

When the coven returns to the village, they capture Vittorio and bring him to the Court of the Ruby Grail. Ursula pleads with the elder of the court, Godric, to spare his life; and when he looks to the lord of the court, Florian, his lady, Ursula, turns to her husband and pleads for him not to kill Vittorio. Reluctantly, Florian agrees, but he offers Vittorio the opportunity to become a vampire. When Vittorio refuses due to his chivalric devotion to the Christian faith, Ursula is at least glad that his life is spared, although Florian deserts Vittorio in the streets of Venice, doomed to the inevitable madness that happens to most mortals whenever they encounter a vampire. The qualities that Ursula beholds in Vittorio are his bravery and endurance.

Vittorio returns to the vampire castle and the Court of the Ruby Grail. He beheads all the vampires within, including Godric and Florian. He immolates their heads in sunlight and fire. When he comes to Ursula, she gazes upon him with such intensity that he spares her life, at the cost of a great moral struggle, for he believes that all vampires are demons. To save her life and win Vittorio's eternal love, she concocts a plan on the spot, lying to him, telling him that the only way for her to be free of the demon within is for her to drink all of his blood and then for him to drink hers as well. Tricking her love, she turns him into a vampire. But he is not upset with her duplicity. He loves her with all of his heart and takes her as his companion for the next five hundred years, all the way into the twenty-first century, ever adoring each other, an Undead Romeo and Juliet.

For more perspectives on Ursula in the Vampire Chronicles, read the *Alphabettery* entries **Court of the Ruby Grail**, **Florian**, and **Vittorio di Raniari**.

Uruk

• SANCTUARY •

Uruk becomes one of the most significant cities in ancient Mesopotamia due to its vast urbanization of the region, providing its people with safety from invaders as well as a thriving economic structure.

Before the vampire race comes into existence, when King Enkil of ancient Egypt is seeking a young, beautiful, and intelligent bride, he finds the exact woman he is looking for in the city of Uruk. Her name is Akasha. Compared with Egypt, Uruk is very forward thinking, having abandoned ritual cannibalism in favor of ritual burial, due to the pragmatic element of living within the Great Wall of Uruk. After her marriage to Enkil, Akasha attempts to graft onto her Egyptian Empire the more progressive attitudes of Uruk, particularly with regard to outlawing ritual cannibalism, which causes an uprising among many Egyptians, some of whom eventually attempt to assassinate her. That assassination attempt, when she is bleeding to death because of multiple stab wounds, is the moment when the spirit of Amel fuses with her blood and causes the creation of the first vampire.

Uruk is implicitly written of in *The Vampire Lestat* (1985) and explicitly mentioned in *The Queen of the Damned* (1988). For more perspectives on Uruk in the Vampire Chronicles, read the *Alphabettery* entries **Akasha** and **Enkil**.

Vampire

• IMMORTAL •

early four thousand years before the Common Era, when the bloodlusting ghost of the mortal Amel (who in his human life thousands of years earlier was genetically enhanced into an immortal superhuman by beings from the planet Bravenna) enters into the fatal stab wounds of the Egyptian Queen Akasha; the fusing of the genetic matter of his spirit with her blood precipitates the creation of this world's first vampire.

Amel's consciousness is suppressed in the fusing, but his subconscious urges, and the genetic enhancements still encoded into the matter tethered to his etheric being, remain a dominant instinct in Akasha. The fusion gives her superhuman speed, strength, agility, vision, immortality, and rapid healing from almost any wound, except the wounds from burning, which take longer to heal. The fusion also changes her skin pigmentation from dark to marble white, almost like a statue. The fusion also fills her with an insatiable bloodlust: no matter how much human blood she drinks, piling up one victim after another, she never feels satisfied. Drinking blood temporarily restores the color of her skin to a beautiful pinkish hue. The more she drinks, the less deathly white she looks, the more hue her skin regains, and the more mortal she appears.

Shortly after Amel's spirit fuses with her blood, Akasha discovers that she can turn other mortals into beings like herself, by drinking her victims' blood to the point of their death, then letting them drink her blood. Her first fledgling is her husband-king, Enkil. As Akasha makes more vampires—such as Enkil's steward, Khayman—the spiritual power of Amel dissipates a little, but not enough. The more vampires she makes, and the more vampires Khayman and his fledglings make, the more Amel's bloodlust in them dilutes, until there are so many vampires that Akasha and Enkil become like stone statues, hardly needing to drink any blood at all.

They also discover that vampires cannot become sexually aroused and do not have the ability to procreate. Since vampires are essentially beings who have died and become undead, their dead and undead tissue lacks the necessary functions for biological reproduction. For nearly six millennia, the only way to have children was to make vampire fledglings. However, in the late twentieth century, vampire scientists Seth and Fareed discover a method for vampire procreation. The first to try this method is Lestat, who, after copulating with Flannery Gilman, has a son named Viktor.

After biting the neck of a mortal and drinking the blood, vampires can drop a little of their own blood on the mortal's wound; the regenerative properties in their blood heals the wound, so that it appears as if the mortal has died from natural causes. Killer discovers this during the Depression era in the United States of America, and he can more efficiently hide the cause of death of his victims, as well as his vampire nature, from suspicious mortals.

Similarly, if vampires lose a limb, they can reattach the limb so that their internal natural regenerative abilities can restore the limb's full functionality, or if they lack the power to restore their limbs, a more powerful vampire's blood can be used on the wound to instigate the regenerative process. Marius uses this ability in third century Rome to reattach Mael's head and arm after they are torn off in a minor skirmish.

The blood of older, more powerful vampires also has the ability to heal the wounds of other vampires, as is the case when Santino almost burns Marius to death in fifteenth-century Venice. With the help of his fledgling Bianca, Marius returns to Akasha's alpine shrine, where he drinks her blood and is restored almost to full health.

During the first thousand years of vampires, their abilities remain constant: superior speed, strength, agility, rapid healing, and heightened senses. But in the second millennium of vampire existence, new abilities begin to emerge, such as levitation, which they call the Cloud Gift; pyrokinetics, which they call the Fire Gift; along with telepathy, telekinesis, astral projection, which vampires categorize as the Mind Gift.

The Cloud Gift allows vampires to levitate and fly into the air, up into the clouds, so that they can travel great distances across the earth in little time. Lestat demonstrates this when he uses the Cloud Gift to fly from the vampire coven at Trinity Gate to Maharet's private compound in the jungles of the Amazon, in less than a night.

The Fire Gift allows vampires to cause objects to spontaneously combust, although this gift is mostly used against other vampires. Akasha uses the Fire Gift to immolate Baby Jenks; Marius uses the Fire Gift to thwart an attacking Rashid; Thorne uses the Fire Gift to destroy Santino; and Benedict uses the Fire Gift to eliminate the remains of Maharet's beheaded body. In each case, vampires subjected to the fatal Fire Gift usually die, but they all experience the similar burning sensation that begins around their chest, as though the Fire Gift is always aimed at the heart.

With the Mind Gift, vampires have the ability to communicate with other vampires over long distances. Older vampires can communicate from the opposite side of the world. Vampires can also read mortal minds and make influential suggestions to weak-minded mortals. Teskhamen demonstrates such an ability in first-century Gaul, when he communicates with the mortal Marius telepathically. Along with telepathy, vampires also have the ability to cloak their minds from the telepathy of others. Akasha's biological son and fledgling, Seth, is able to cloak his mind from Lestat in twenty-first-century West Hollywood, so that Lestat does not recognize Seth until they are almost face-to-face. Similarly, the Mind Gift allows Akasha and Enkil to astral project themselves when their entombment for centuries under great blocks of diorite and granite thwart any other recourse to entertainment or sanity. The Mind Gift is limited, specifically with telepathy between makers and fledglings. Once a vampire turns a mortal into a vampire fledgling, they no longer have the ability to read each other's thoughts or to speak to each other telepathically. A great silence exists between them on a psychic level. Another limitation to the Mind Gift is the Iron Curse.

After vampires exist for many thousands of years, it is discovered that, because of their etheric connection through the spirit of Amel, whenever Akasha and Enkil are wounded in any way, all of their vampire children experience the same wound, only the severity increases for weaker vampires. When Maharet stabs Akasha's heart with a dagger during the first century of the Common Era, Maharet feels the effect slightly, yet she knows that younger, less powerful vampires are experiencing it to a greater degree. The most genocidal example occurs around 4 C.E., when the Elder exposes Akasha and Enkil to the Egyptian sun. The result only bronzes their skin, but the effect of the sunlight spreads throughout their children. The skin of other ancient vampires, such as the Elder and Maharet, only bronzes like that of the Mother and the Father; younger, weaker vampires are utterly immolated, while older vampires who are not as powerful as the ancient ones are burned so severely that they look like charred skeletons barely sheathed in scorched flesh.

Vampires' power does not depend on personal age but on the power of the blood they possess. During the Great Burning of 4 C.E., although at that time Teskhamen is four thousand years old and Eric is only one thousand, Eric is less burned because, as Maharet's fledgling, the blood in him is more powerful. Both are examples that show how age alone does not give a vampire power, but the blood that they receive when they are turned into vampires, and the blood that they receive from other more powerful vampires during their lifetime, are the true sources of their power: the blood gives them the ability to withstand death and to heal from deadly wounds. Maharet is essentially the fourth vampire made after Akasha, since Akasha makes Khayman, who makes Mekare, who makes Maharet, so Maharet's blood is very strong. Akasha likely transforms Santh into a vampire next in reaction to the First Brood's uprising, even before she has transformed Nebamun into the Captain of the Queens Blood, making Santh weaker than Khayman, who came before him, but stronger than Maharet and Merkare because of his blood relation to the Queen. The more vampires Akasha makes, the more diluted the blood's potency becomes. Because Teskhamen is one of hundreds of vampires that Akasha made afterward, the blood in him is less powerful than the blood in Maharet. This power in diminishing proportions can also be seen in Lestat's fledglings. His first fledgling, Gabrielle, is very powerful; yet his children become less powerful the more he makes, going from Nicolas to Louis to the weakest of all, Claudia. But his next fledgling, David Talbot, is more powerful than even Gabrielle, because between the making of Claudia and David, Lestat has drunk Akasha's blood, who had not made another vampire in thousands of years, and whose blood has had time to regenerate in potency.

The age of technology in the late twentieth and early twenty-first centuries brings with it discoveries that allow vampires to explore new facets of their nature. Seth and Fareed use their interest in medical science and research to find a way to allow vampires to experience sexual arousal and ejaculation through an infusion of genetically engineered hormones. These two doctors also learn that once a vampire male ejaculates inside a mortal female, the fetus in the uterus can be extracted, genetically enhanced, and reinserted into the womb so that the mortal female can bear the vampire's offspring, who is not so much a chromosomal composite of the vampire and the mortal but is more accurately a genetic clone of the vampire. Such is the case with Viktor, Lestat's son and clone, who is born in the late twentieth century, grows for the next twenty years into an exact replica of Lestat, and is then turned into a vampire by Lestat himself.

In contrast to the medical marvels that benefit the vampire race in the twentieth and twenty-first centuries, vampires begin to prostitute the Blood. They either take their own blood or steal the blood from other vampires and sell it to mortals, so that mortals can have a taste of the euphoria of being a vampire while still maintaining their mortality. If the price is high enough, the vampire will turn that mortal into a vampire also. Killer witnesses this behavior and condemns it, particularly during the Great Burning of 2013.

Despite the etheric connection among all vampires through the spirit of Amel, all vampires also experience the fundamental connection of loneliness. In every age, during the last six thousand years of vampire existence to the present, vampires need a purpose to survive each generation. Like any mortal, a vampire becomes connected to the wonders and delights of a particular era and then laments when those sensual wonders go out of fashion. Also like any mortal, a vampire becomes connected to other mortals of a particular generation, such as the great artists or brilliant minds of a certain time. When such mortal lights go out, the vampire begins to diminish a little also, no longer finding a reason or purpose to stay connected to the ever-changing mortal world. During such a crisis, vampires face three options: they can find a mortal of the next generation who will help them connect to the newly changed world; they can go underground and sleep until enough time has passed for them to rise again and find a new purpose in life; or they can destroy themselves. In any event, the vampire, like most mortals, must face the inevitability of change. And in themselves, however vampires face that change, despite the fact that on the outside they remain unchanged, a little something on the inside changes in them also.

For more perspectives on vampires in the Vampire Chronicles, read the *Alphabettery* entries **Akasha, Amel, Armand, Baby Jenks, Benedict, Children of Darkness, Cloud Gift, Enkil, Gabrielle, Fareed Bhansali, Fire Gift, Khayman, Lestat de Lioncourt, Louis de Pointe du Lac, Maharet, Marius, Mekare, Mind Gift, Nicolas de Lenfent, Santino, Seth, Teskhamen, Thorne**, and **Viktor**.

The Vampire Armand

• VAMPIRE CHRONICLE •

Following the fifth book in the Vampire Chronicles, *Memnoch the Devil*, Armand tells his tale about how he is born in Kiev, Russia, kidnapped at the age of fifteen by Tartars, sold to a brothel in Venice, and bought by the vampire Marius. Marius cares for him and many other young boys in his Venetian palazzo. Armand implores Marius to make him a vampire. Marius finally agrees, but shortly thereafter, the Children of Satan vampire coven burns Marius, burns his palazzo to the ground, and kidnaps Armand. Led by Santino with the help of Allesandra, they torture Armand until he agrees to become a member of their coven. After impressing Santino, Armand leaves Italy with Allesandra to begin a new coven in Paris, called the Children of Darkness. When Lestat arrives at the Children of Darkness coven in Paris, he convinces them that their way of life is outmoded. Armand burns most of his coven, leaving only a few survivors, who begin a new coven when Lestat gives them a theater, which they call

Théâtre des Vampires, where they put on plays in which they pretend to be mortals who pretend to be vampires. After a century of this masquerade, Lestat's fledgling Louis burns the theater to the ground after the coven kills Lestat's other fledgling, Claudia. Only Armand survives. He and Louis remain companions for many more years. In the twentieth century, Armand reunites with Marius to fight against Queen Akasha. Years later, after Armand fails in his suicide attempt, he is found by two mortals, Benji and Sybelle, who nurse him back to life. He cares for them until Marius changes them into vampires, which allows Armand to maintain his telepathic relationship and close companionship with them.

For more perspectives on this Vampire Chronicle, read the *Alphabettery* entries **Akasha, Allesandra, Armand, Benji Mahmoud, Children of Darkness, Children of Satan, Claudia, Lestat de Lioncourt, Louis de Pointe du Lac, Marius, Santino, Sybelle,** and **Théâtre des Vampires.**

Vampire Bar

• SANCTUARY •

A vampire bar is an establishment where mortals and immortals are free to congregate. Mortals are likely unaware that immortal vampires frequent such bars, unless a vampire informs them or they have witching or psychic abilities that allow them to telepathically glean such information. Vampires gain entry into a vampire bar by using the Mind Gift to inform the doorkeeper of their identity and intent.

Inside the bars, posters from vampire films adorn the walls. Large screens show vampire movies. When the music of the Vampire Lestat band becomes a global phenomenon, the cabaret in San Francisco, Dracula's Daughter, plays the band's music videos on large screens. Mortal customers generally drink Bloody Marys, but immortal patrons are forbidden to drink mortal blood. Vampires go to a vampire bar for information and sanctuary. No killing is allowed in any vampire bar. For instance, when Killer teaches Baby Jenks how to survive an attack from a more powerful vampire, he urges her to flee to the sanctuary of a vampire bar, where the stronger vampire is forbidden to destroy her.

Many vampire bars are destroyed by Akasha when she rises and commences the Great Burning of 1985.

Vampire bars appear in *The Queen of the Damned* (1988). For more perspectives on vampire bars in the Vampire Chronicles, read the *Alphabettery* entries **Bela Lugosi, Carmilla, Dracula's Daughter, Dr. Polidori, Lamia, Lord Ruthven,** and **Vampire Connection.**

The Vampire Chronicles

The Vampire Chronicles are interwoven novels, which as of 2018 total thirteen. If the two books from the series New Tales of the Vampires are included in the canon, the list totals fifteen books. Three Vampire Chronicles—*Merrick*, *Blackwood Farm*, and *Blood Canticle*—cross over into the series Lives of the Mayfair Witches.

The Vampire Chronicles are the following books:

Interview with the Vampire is written in 1976 by the vampire Louis de Pointe du Lac.

The Vampire Lestat is written in 1985 by the vampire Lestat.

The Queen of the Damned is written in 1988 by Lestat.

The Tale of the Body Thief is written in 1992 by Lestat.

Memnoch the Devil is written in 1995 by Lestat.

The Vampire Armand is written in 1998 by the vampire Armand.

Pandora is written in 1998 by the vampire Pandora.

Vittorio the Vampire is written in 1999 by the vampire Vittorio.

Merrick is written in 2000 by David Talbot.

Blood and Gold is written in 2001 by the vampire Marius.

Blackwood Farm is written in 2002 by the vampire Tarquin Blackwood.

Blood Canticle is written in 2003 by Lestat.

Prince Lestat is written in 2014 by Lestat.

Prince Lestat and the Realms of Atlantis is written in 2016 by Lestat.

Blood Communion is written in 2018 by Lestat.

From *Interview with the Vampire* through *Blood Communion*, the Vampire Chronicles tell the tale of a race of immortal blood drinkers—centered around the powerful figure of Lestat—all of whom seek to discover the cause of their origin, the deeper meaning of the present with beloved companions, and a reason to persevere into an unknowable future.

Vampire Connection

• PHENOMENON •

The Vampire Connection is an interconnected haven of vampire bars around the world in the twentieth century frequented by mortals and immortals alike. The principal law throughout the Vampire Connection is that no killing is allowed inside a vampire bar. Mortals are generally ignorant of the presence of vampires unless a vampire informs them of their existence or a mortal has telepathy, either as a psychic, like members of the Talamasca, or as a witch, like members of the Mayfair family. Immortals are prohibited from killing mortals and vampires here. Thus, vampire bars in the Vampire Connection are a sanctuary for the Undead. Nothing like this phenomenal truce has ever existed before among blood drinkers. The Vampire Connection is also the means by which vampires promulgate secretive information about their kind.

The majority of these bars are named after people and characters who have affected vampire culture. London's vampire bar is called Dr. Polidori; Paris's bar is Lamia; Los Angeles's bar is Bela Lugosi; New York has two bars, Carmilla and Lord Ruthven; San Francisco's vampire bar is a magnificently beautiful cabaret on Castro Street called Dracula's Daughter. There is even an unnamed vampire bar in New Orleans. As of 1985, no bars in the Vampire Connection are allowed to be named after characters or subjects from Louis's book *Interview with the Vampire* because they concern real events in cosmology of the Vampire Chronicles.

However, when the vampire Lestat breaks the ancient laws by revealing vampire secrets, another vampire writes "The Declaration in the Form of Graffiti" in black felt-tip pen on the red wall of the back room of Dracula's Daughter. The declaration states the events of the vampire Lestat's rise to fame with his autobiography and popular rock band. Copies of the declaration are disseminated to every bar throughout the Vampire Connection, urging all vampires to destroy Lestat, Gabrielle, Louis, Armand, all of Lestat's cohorts, friends, and associates.

The Vampire Connection is obliterated by Akasha when the music of the Vampire Lestat band urges her to rise and commence the Great Burning of 1985.

The Vampire Connection appears in *The Vampire Lestat* (1985) and *The Queen of the Damned* (1986). For more perspectives on the Vampire Connection in the Vampire Chronicles, read the *Alphabettery* entries **Bela Lugosi, Carmilla, Dracula's Daughter, Dr. Polidori, Lamia, Lord Ruthven,** and **Vampire Bar.**

The Vampire Lestat Band

• COVEN •

When the rock music of the New Orleans band Satan's Night Out awakens Lestat from his century-long torpor, he goes to the three members, Alex, Larry, and Tough Cookie, and reveals to them his vampire nature. Unsurprised but not entirely believing him, they show him the book that his fledgling, Louis, authored with Daniel Malloy. Inspired by his fledgling's audacity, Lestat promises Satan's Night Out fortune and fame if they will become his band. They accept his proposal, and Lestat changes the name of the band to the Vampire Lestat.

Alex plays drums. His brother, Larry, plays keyboards. Tough Cookie plays guitar. And Lestat is the group's lyricist and singer. The lyrics he writes reveal the secrets that Marius shared with him several centuries earlier, about the Mother and the Father of vampires, Those Who Must Be Kept, which angered many vampires around the world, except for the one vampire whom the lyrics are about, Akasha. Hearing the boldness of his music from her statuelike slumber in Marius's northern shrine, she awakens, kills Enkil, and flies across the world, immolating all her vampires, especially those who desire to do Lestat harm.

The Vampire Lestat band performs only one concert, in San Francisco. Many vampires come to the performance, most of whom desire to kill Lestat, except for the very youngest of fledglings, who desire to hear his revolutionary works, such as Killer and Davis and their Fang Gang, and the very ancient vampires, such as Khayman, Gregory, and Mael.

At the end of the concert, Akasha appears and immolates numerous blood drinkers. Few survive.

Lestat escapes with Louis and Gabrielle, but he never again performs with the Vampire Lestat band, although he makes sure through his lawyer that his bandmates will never want for anything, and will always be wealthy.

The Vampire Lestat band appears in *The Vampire Lestat* (1985). For more perspectives on the Vampire Lestat band in the Vampire Chronicles, read the *Alphabettery* entries **Alex**, **Christine**, **Davis**, **Gregory Duff Collingsworth**, **Khayman**, **Killer**, **Larry**, **Lestat de Lioncourt**, **Mael**, **Satan's Night Out**, and **Tough Cookie**.

The Vampire Lestat

• VAMPIRE CHRONICLE •

In the years following Louis's book, *Interview with the Vampire* (1976), in the Vampire Chronicles, the vampire Lestat writes his own eponymous book, describing how Magnus turns him into an immortal blood drinker against his will in seventeenth-century France, shortly before the French Revolution. For love, Lestat turns his mother, Gabrielle, into a vampire, as well as his best friend, Nicki. Unfortunately, Gabrielle leaves Lestat, and Nicki kills himself, but Lestat finds deeper companionship in the nearly two-thousand-year-old Marius, who teaches Lestat about the origin of vampires, the ancient Egyptian King and Queen, Enkil and Akasha. After Lestat awakens Akasha with his bravado, Marius spirits them away. Lestat sails to the New World and makes Louis and Claudia his new fledglings, who betray him and attempt to kill him. Then he goes into the earth, retreating into a torpor. He awakens in the late twentieth century, forms a successful rock band, and for the second time awakens Queen Akasha, who rampages across the world, immolating her children.

For more perspectives on this Vampire Chronicle, read the *Alphabettery* entries **Akasha, Armand, Claudia, Enkil, Gabrielle, Lestat de Lioncourt, Louis de Pointe du Lac, Marius,** and **Nicolas de Lendfent.**

Vampiric Sleep

• IDIOM •

When the sun rises every day, forcing a vampire to fall asleep, the vampire does not enter an unconscious paraplegia. The sun causes vampires to sleep because atmospheric changes trigger a cycle of essential processes that are restorative to a vampire's immortal nature. These processes cannot occur until the vampire enters a dormant state. Only very ancient and powerful vampires have the ability to stave off the atmospheric triggers and dormancy. Young vampires, however, find the urge to fall asleep every morning utterly irresistible.

The science underlining vampire sleep is discussed in *Blood Communion* (2018). For more perspectives on vampire sleep, read the *Alphabettery* entries **Amel, Kapetria,** and **Lestat de Lioncourt.**

Vampiric Torpor

• PHENOMENON •

The world changes, while vampires remain changeless. They enjoy the technology and fashion of one age but not the tastes of the following generation. This isolation can become a source of great suffering and loneliness for vampires. In *Interview with the Vampire* (1976), Armand explains this phenomenon to Louis: "All things change except the vampire himself; everything except the vampire is subject to constant corruption and distortion. Soon, with an inflexible mind, and often even with the most flexible mind, this immortality becomes a penitential sentence in a madhouse of figures and forms that are hopelessly unintelligible and without value." Most vampires perceive only three options for overcoming this circumstance: A vampire can "make contact" with a new generation by making a fledgling who will provide the older vampire with a deeper sense of identity and enjoyment in the new era, as when Armand makes Daniel a vampire in the late twentieth century. A vampire can commit suicide—Magnus kills himself shortly after turning Lestat into a vampire. Finally, a vampire can enter into torpor, a state of long-term vampiric unconsciousness. Unlike vampiric sleep that happens daily to younger vampires, torpor can last for years or centuries. During this time, the vampire stops drinking blood, becomes very weak, and shrivels to near-skeletal proportions, but the vampire also undergoes a therapeutic process of mental, emotional, and physical healing.

Examples of vampires who enter recuperative vampiric torpor are Arjun, Lestat, Marius, Nebamun, Seth, and Thorne. Lestat's fledgling Antoine enters vampiric torpor after being severely burned, during which time his body not only heals but also grows stronger. Allesandra does the same after she throws herself onto the funeral pyre for the Children of Darkness. Akasha and Enkil enter vampiric torpor after they are captured and imprisoned beneath large blocks of diorite and granite; Enkil remains mostly in this torpor state for thousands of years until Akasha kills him in the twentieth century; Akasha also remains mostly in torpor until the twentieth century, when the music of the vampire Lestat fully awakens her.

Two ancient vampires who never enter vampiric torpor are Maharet and Notker the Wise. Maharet never experiences the need to survive generational changes, because through her devotion to cataloging her Great Family, she continually makes contact with each new era. Similarly, Notker the Wise never feels the need for vampiric torpor because his devotion to music helps him keep in touch with each new generation.

Instances of vampiric torpor can be found in *The Vampire Lestat* (1985), *The Queen of the Damned* (1988), *Blood and Gold* (2001), *Prince Lestat* (2014), *Prince Lestat and the Realms of Atlantis* (2016), and *Blood Communion* (2018). For more perspectives on this phenomenon, read the *Alphabettery* entries

Veronica's Veil

• HONORIFIC •

The story of Veronica's Veil develops out of an ancient tradition in the Catholic Church. Not found in the Bible, the story describes a woman who, when seeing Jesus carrying his cross towards Calvary, removes the veil from off her head and wipes from Jesus's face his blood, sweat, and tears. The sacredness of the event leaves a miraculous imprint of Jesus's face on the veil. As the tradition tells it, the woman brings the veil to Rome, where it becomes a venerated icon for pilgrims. In time, a demand arises for true images of Christ; thus, more images of Christ similar to the icon on Veronica's Veil appear in different churches. To differentiate its veil from others, the church in Rome in possession of the original veil calls it a *vera eikōn*—*vera*, Latin for "true," and *eikōn,* Greek for "image"— true image. Throughout history, the words *vera* and *eikōn* (or "icon") gradually combined into one word: Veronica. Thus, the heart of the name "Veronica" most literally means "the true image of Christ."

In the eleventh century, a story develops that identifies Veronica as the woman who, after suffering constant hemorrhaging for twelve years, touches the tassel of Jesus's robe and is healed (Matthew 9:20–22; Mark 5:25–34; Luke 8:43–48).

Lestat's book *Memnoch the Devil* maintains that tradition when, on his pilgrimage through Heaven and Hell with Memnoch the Devil, Lestat encounters Christ's passion. As Jesus is carrying his cross, a woman named Veronica steps forward, removes her veil from her head, and wipes the blood, sweat, and tears from his face. She confesses that she is the same woman who was hemorrhaging for twelve years before being miraculously healed by Jesus. According to the novel, Jesus then takes the veil from Veronica and gives it to Lestat, who brings it back with him from his metaphysical journey. In turn, he gives it to his mortal companion Dora, who shows it to the entire world as a miraculous sign of God's love.

Lestat claims that it was kept in the crypts of the Vatican Museum for a time, and the Talamasca later acquired it, but it was destroyed shortly thereafter. Lestat has not yet revealed those details behind the destruction of Veronica's Veil.

Veronica's Veil appears in *Memnoch the Devil* (1995) and *Blood Communion* (2018). For more perspectives on Veronica's Veil in the Vampire Chronicles, read the *Alphabettery* entries **Lestat de Lioncourt** and **Memnoch**.

Viktor

• VAMPIRE •

Viktor is Lestat's clone and son. He has a natural birth in the twentieth century, grows into a man, and is turned into a vampire by Lestat. He is a perfect likeness of the Brat Prince. Viktor appears in *Prince Lestat* (2014), *Prince Lestat and the Realms of Atlantis* (2016), and *Blood Communion* (2018).

In the early nineties, the vampires Seth and Fareed, along with Dr. Flannery Gilman, who is at the time a mortal medical doctor working with her vampire companions, theorize that through an infusion of hormones, vampire males might be able to have an erection, experience the sensuality of coitus, ejaculate, and possibly reproduce like most mortals.

Sometime in the midnineties, Seth and Fareed encounter the vampire Lestat in West Hollywood, they explain to him their scientific work, and they ask him if he would test their theory of hormonal injection and vampiric reproduction. Fully recollecting his experience with Raglan James, the Body Thief, who helped him to experience sexual intimacy as a mortal in another body, Lestat readily accepts the opportunity and accompanies Seth and Fareed to their Los Angeles facility. Therein, they inject Lestat with an infusion of genetically enhanced hormones while Dr. Gilman volunteers herself as Lestat's sexual companion and the receptive vessel of his ejaculation. Lestat thoroughly enjoys his sexual encounter with Dr. Gilman, but he leaves the medical facility unaware that he has impregnated her.

Seth and Fareed extract the fetus from her uterus and enhance it with genetic manipulation so that the fetus is not a combination of Lestat's and Dr. Gilman's genes but is a clone of the Brat Prince. Seth and Fareed insert the fetus back into Dr. Gilman's uterus, and she spends the next nine months carrying the child to term. She gives birth to a boy, whom they name Viktor. As the child grows, he is identical to the vampire Lestat, but totally human. The principal difference is that while Lestat is leaner because of nutrition in eighteenth-century France, Viktor is a little thicker with muscle.

Viktor lives most of his life in the laboratory, educated by Seth, Fareed, and Flannery. Fareed turns Viktor's mother, Flannery Gilman, into a vampire as a reward for carrying Viktor to term. By the time he is twenty years old, Viktor discovers the truth about his father, the vampire Lestat. He reads the Vampire Chronicles and learns of Lestat's adopted daughter, Rose. Having grown up around vampires, Viktor has a keen interest in becoming an immortal also.

Around that same time, Rose is attacked and blinded by a jealous lover, and she is brought to Seth and Fareed's medical facility, where they save her life and restore her eyesight through methods based upon their research into the nature of immortals. Viktor spends time with Rose while she recovers, and they develop a deeply personal intimacy.

Not long afterward, the vampires Rhoshamandes and Benedict break into the medical facility and kidnap Viktor for the purpose of coercing Seth and Fareed, along with Mekare and all the other vampires, to remove Amel and his Sacred Core from Mekare, the Queen of the Damned, and implant him in Rhoshamandes. Seth and Fareed inform Lestat not only of this plot, but also that he is the biological father of his clone, Viktor, the result of their experiment twenty years earlier. Lestat is both thrilled at the news of having a son and enraged at Rhoshamandes for kidnapping him. With the help of his companions, Lestat finds Rhoshamandes, tears off his left arm, and threatens to destroy him, if Rhoshamandes does not surrender Viktor.

Once Viktor is finally released, he is reunited with Rose. They pledge their undying love to each other and seek to be married. As a wedding gift, Lestat turns them both into vampires so that they can be together forever as Blood Spouses.

For more perspectives on Viktor in the Vampire Chronicles, read the *Alphabettery* entries **Fareed Bhansali, Flannery Gilman, Lestat de Lioncourt, Mekare, Rhoshamandes, Rose**, and **Seth**.

Village de Lioncourt

• SANCTUARY •

The Village de Lioncourt is under the protection and patronage of the Marquis de Lioncourt, who resides in Château de Lioncourt, farther up the Massif Central in Avignon, France. In the mid-eighteenth century, during the life of Lestat de Lioncourt, the village consists of several shops: a tailor, butcher, bakery, cheese maker's, draper's, and several more. Shop owners reside above their stores in small apartments with their families, such as Nicolas de Lenfent, who lives above the draper's shop with his father. A Roman Catholic church is the central point of the village. Near the village is the Witches' Place, a grove where several women accused of witchcraft were burned to death many years before Lestat was born. After Lestat becomes a vampire, the village falls into ruin when the French Revolution incites villagers to revolt against the Marquis de Lioncourt and plunder Château de Lioncourt.

When Lestat returns to the village in the twenty-first century during the renovations to Château de Lioncourt, he decides to also fund the restoration of the Village de Lioncourt.

The Village de Lioncourt appears in *The Vampire Lestat* (1985), *Prince Lestat* (2014), *Prince Lestat and the Realms of Atlantis* (2016), and *Blood Communion* (2018). For more perspectives on the Village de Lioncourt in the Vampire Chronicles, read the *Alphabettery* entries **Château de Lioncourt, Lestat de Lioncourt, Nicolas de Lenfent**, and **Witches' Place**.

Vincenzo

• MORTAL •

Vincenzo is the property manager of Marius's Venetian palazzo. Marius believes him to be a mortal of great health and excellent intellect. As Marius gathers numerous boys to his palazzo, all of them apprentices, Vincenzo principally governs them. He remains in Marius's service for many years, never suspecting that his master is a vampire. In time, the Talamasca agent Raymond Gallant becomes aware of Marius's immortal existence. Gallant infiltrates Marius's palazzo and questions Vincenzo to a great extent concerning his immortal master, but Vincenzo remains a faithful servant, never revealing too much— and clearly ignorant that he is in service to a blood drinker. At length, when Santino and the Children of Satan attack the palazzo and burn it to the ground, Vincenzo is killed at the front doors.

Vincenzo appears in *Blood and Gold* (2001). For more perspectives on Vincenzo, read the *Alphabettery* entries **Children of Satan, Marius, Raymond Gallant, Santino,** and **Talamasca Order.**

Virginia Lee Blackwood

• MORTAL •

Virginia Lee is a very well-educated nurse living in New Orleans when a yellow-fever epidemic strikes. She aids in the recovery of many infirm Irishmen and buries many others. But she helps bring back to life one Irishman in particular, Manfred Blackwood, who is nearly twice her age. Once he is fully recovered, they confess their deep feelings for each other. He has already made a great fortune merchandising in New Orleans, but he struggles to convince her to quit her work and marry him. Together they have four children, William, Camille, Isabel, and Philip, but she loses the latter two to lockjaw and influenza. When she herself becomes mortally ill from malaria and galloping consumption, she refuses to show any sign of illness but continues to dress herself every morning and carry on delightful conversations with the people in her house, even until the day she dies around noon on a Saturday while lying on the sofa in the front parlor. She is buried in a beautiful sky-blue dress.

Virginia Lee Blackwood appears in *Blackwood Farm* (2002). For more perspectives on Virginia Lee's character, read the *Alphabettery* sections **Camille Blackwood, Manfred Blackwood,** and **William Blackwood.**

Vittorio di Raniari

• VAMPIRE •

Vittorio is an Italian mortal whose family is killed by vampires. Vittorio kills those vampires and falls in love with the immortal blood drinker Ursula, who turns him into her fledgling and beloved companion. Vittorio appears in *Vittorio the Vampire* (1999).

In the mid-fifteenth century, Vittorio is the son of Lord Lorenzo di Raniari, in his mountaintop castle, Castello Raniari, in the north of Tuscany during the de' Medici Renaissance sweeping through Italy. Vittorio receives his education in the towns of Santa Maddalana and Florence, learns the ways of knighthood, and, by the age of thirteen, he is able to ride on horseback in the full-battle dress of an Italian knight. Despite his uprearing in chivalry, he is traumatized by a nightmare wherein he holds in his hand the severed head of his sister, Bartola, who is one year younger than him, and in the other hand he holds the severed head of his brother, Matteo, who is four years younger. His nightmare comes true when he is sixteen years old.

A coven of vampires attacks his father's lordly estate and slays his family and all their servants. When the vampire Ursula, who appears to be barely older than fourteen, captures Bartola and Matteo, Vittorio commands her to stop. Enamored of his beauty, she obeys him. But a male vampire comes and beheads Bartola and Matteo. Ursula forbids the other vampire from slaying Vittorio, and Vittorio takes this opportunity to attack, slicing off

Ursula's right arm. Unfazed, she picks up her arm and reattaches it.

Before dawn, Ursula and the rest of the coven leave di Raniari castle, having slain Vittorio's family and every servant, leaving only Vittorio alive. Fulfilling his prophetic dream, Vittorio cradles the heads of his brother and sister in his arms before dragging his family down to the crypt, where he lays them alongside one another and crosses their arms over their chests funereally. The servants lay where they are slain. After sunrise, Vittorio takes all the money he can find in his father's coffers and flees to the nearest large town, Santa Maddalana, where he hides before nightfall and plans vengeance against the vampires who have killed his family.

At nightfall, in the inn, Ursula appears in his room and strongly urges him to leave the region and travel south towards Florence. Clearly attracted to him, she seduces him, and from then on, Vittorio finds her irresistible. Although she returns to her coven before morning, Vittorio does not heed her warning and remains in the town. He observes no infirm or elderly townsfolk; most appear to be in excellent health. When he inquires on the matter, the townsfolk, like Ursula, urge him to avoid going north and instead travel south. His oath of vengeance spurs him to keep going north in the direction of the vampires' lair. He leaves the inn and travels towards an ancient castle upon a nearby hilltop. He climbs the tower and waits there until nightfall. Then he sees that the vampires are coming from a castle on a distant mountain. The vampires descend like a swarm on the town and capture Vittorio. They take him to their lair in the ancient castle, wherein is the Court of the Ruby Grail—"ruby grail" being a euphemistic term for an abundance of blood to drink. In this court, Vittorio witnesses a banquet of vampires feasting on mortals who look weak, elderly, or infirm or who are evildoers. Vittorio recognizes some members of the town and learns that the townsfolk have struck a deal with the vampires: the vampires must leave the physically and morally strong but are welcome to take the rest.

The vampires bring Vittorio first to Godric, the elder of the coven, but Ursula begs for his life. So Godric looks to the lord of the court, Florian, for a decision. The vampires demand that Vittorio be destroyed, but Ursula begs Florian to spare Vittorio's life. Florian grants her request because she is his bride and his fledgling, and by their vows, he owes her this favor. Vittorio is given a chance to become a vampire, but, because of his faith in God, he rejects this offer, believing they are nothing more than demons from Hell. Florian abandons Vittorio in the streets of Florence, assuming that Vittorio will go mad because of having encountered such a gruesome sight as the gluttonous feasting in the Court of the Ruby Grail.

While in the town, Vittorio sees two angels, Ramiel and Setheus, in dispute. They are aware that he is aware of them. They introduce him to a third angel, Mastema, clad in radiant armor. Together they help Vittorio devise a plan for destroying all the vampires. By day, Vittorio returns to the castle and the Court of the Ruby Grail, slaying all the vampires within, beheading each one and taking particular delight in beheading Godric and Florian. Then he piles all their heads in the middle of a room where sunlight burns them to ash. Other heads he tosses through a stained-glass window into the outer courtyard, where they are also burned. When he comes to Ursula, he falters. His heart is too enamored of her, and he spares her life, much to the displeasure of the angels.

Ursula then lies to Vittorio, telling him that she can be free of the demon in her blood if she drinks all of his blood, and he drinks all of hers. Tricked into believing that this will make her mortal again, Vittorio unwittingly becomes a vampire. Her trickery does not matter. He loves her with all of his heart, and she loves him equally. They remain together for more than five hundred years, all the way into the twenty-first century, their story like an immortal *Romeo and Juliet*.

For more perspectives on Vittorio in the Vampire Chronicles, read the *Alphabettery* entries **Court of the Ruby Grail, Florian, and Ursula.**

Vittorio the Vampire

• VAMPIRE CHRONICLE •

Vittorio the Vampire is penned by the five-hundred-year-old Vittorio, who describes how, at the age of thirteen, in fifteenth-century Italy, vampires destroy his home, Castello Raniari, and kill everyone in it, including his mother, father, and younger brother and sister. Vittorio is the only one to survive when the beautiful vampire Ursula spares his life. After he flees her protection and goes to a nearby village, she comes to him under the pretense of warning him to stay away but seduces him instead. Eventually he discovers that the vampires are staying in the ruins of a nearby castle, wherein they hold their Court of the Ruby Grail, a euphemism for the abundance of blood they possess. Against Ursula's warnings, Vittorio challenges the lord of the court, Florian, who is also Ursula's husband. Lord Florian spares Vittorio's life as a favor to his wife, but abandons him in the streets of Florence, far from the vampire castle. After Vittorio encounters angels from God, who promise to help him slay Florian and all the vampires in the Court of the Ruby Grail, Vittorio returns to the coven and beheads every vampire, leaving their heads to immolate, all except his love, Ursula. Defying the angels, Vittorio and Ursula run off together, even though Ursula tricks him into becoming a vampire. They remain together for the next five centuries.

For more perspectives on this Vampire Chronicle, read the *Alphabettery* entries **Bartola di Raniari**, **Castello Raniari**, **Court of the Ruby Grail**, **Florian**, **Lorenzo di Raniari**, **Matteo di Raniari**, and **Ursula**.

Vivarium

• SANCTUARY •

When Cassiodorus retires from Rome's political life, he establishes on his property a monastery school called the Vivarium. In this school, monks and hermits have an opportunity to learn how to perfect their vocation through a rigorous study of scripture, scriptural commentaries, Latin and Greek, grammar and rhetoric, arithmetic, geometry, music, astronomy, philosophy, and even copying and contemplating both scripture and commentaries.

In the Vampire Chronicles, after Cassiodorus dies, the spirit of Gremt is so inspired by the promptings of Pandora that he, along with the vampire Teskhamen and Teskhamen's ghost-fledgling Hesketh, begins the

Talamasca Order, based on the disciplines of the Vivarium. Every Talamasca Motherhouse is very similar to a Vivarium school, where members gather information, study rigorously, and pursue absolute truth.

The Vivarium appears in *Pandora* (1998) and *Prince Lestat* (2014). For more perspectives on the Vivarium in the Vampire Chronicles, read the *Alphabettery* entries **Cassiodorus**, **Gremt Stryker Knollys**, **Hesketh**, **Pandora**, **Talamasca Order**, and **Teskhamen**.

The Voice

• IDIOM •

After the spirit of Amel fuses with Akasha to create the first vampire, Amel's consciousness is suppressed for six thousand years. But when Mekare kills Akasha and takes Amel's spirit into herself, Amel becomes conscious and desires to leave Mekare's traumatically wounded mind. Using his connection to every vampire across the world, he speaks to them as the mysterious Voice, especially to the older, more powerful vampires, influencing them to use their powers against other vampires. As if possessed by the Voice, these powerful vampires use the Fire Gift to immolate weaker vampires along with their coven houses, reminiscent of the Great Burning of 1985. Most vampires hear this Voice, and few have the power to resist its persuasive effect. Even the once-peaceful Rhoshamandes obeys the Voice, goes to the Amazon, kills Maharet, and kidnaps Mekare. It is not until Lestat and the vampires convene a council that they realize that the Voice is actually Amel seeking a way to escape Mekare's mentally damaged state.

Once Amel is finally transferred into Lestat, the Voice is further silenced. But it is not until Amel is ultimately transferred into a clone of the body he once had in the city of Atlantis that the Voice is finally silenced in the minds of vampires forever.

The Voice appears in *Prince Lestat* (2014). For more perspectives on the Voice in the Vampire Chronicles, read the *Alphabettery* entries **Amel**, **Fire Gift**, **Great Burning of 1985**, **Lestat de Lioncourt**, **Maharet**, **Mekare**, and **Rhoshamandes**.

Walking Baby

• TALTOS •

he term "Walking Baby" is a general reference to a Taltos's rapid maturation shortly after birth. Birthing a Taltos is a violent process, especially for a mortal. After the birth, the newborn has the innate ability to walk and talk, rapidly growing to full adult height in a matter of hours. An example of a Walking Baby happens when the mortal, Rowan Mayfair, gives birth to Lasher: soon after the birth, he is face-to-face with her and fully grown into a man with the clean skin of a newborn. Another example of a Walking Baby is when Mona Mayfair (another mortal) gives birth to Morrigan Mayfair, who almost instantly grows into a taller version of her mother.

The term "Walking Baby" appears in *Blood Canticle* (2003). For more perspectives on this term in the Vampire Chronicles, read the *Alphabettery* entries **Mona Mayfair, Morrigan Mayfair**, and **Taltos**.

Welf

• IMMORTAL •

Welf is a Replimoid created and sent to kill Amel. He lives for thousands of years until he helps Amel separate from Lestat's mind in the twenty-first century. Welf appears in *Prince Lestat and the Realms of Atlantis* (2016).

On the planet Bravenna, far from Earth, the alien beings, who feed on earthlings' suffering for sustenance, abduct a human named Amel, genetically enhance him to serve their purposes, and lie to him, telling him that his work for them will be for the betterment of humankind. When Amel's superior intellect discovers that the birdlike Bravennans have lied, he develops a compound called luracastria, impenetrable to Bravennan technology. Amel uses vast luracastric sanctuaries, such as the city of Atlantis, to protect humans from suffering and from being exploited by the Bravennan appetite. In response, the Bravennans develop humanoid creatures called Replimoids, which are almost as superhuman as Amel. They have the ability to replicate and instantly regenerate, and because of this they are immortal. The Bravennans send the Replimoids to Earth in the hope of destroying Amel and his luracastric creations. Amel either destroys them or converts them to his purpose. The final group that the Bravennans send consists of four Replimoids who have the look of dark-skinned Africans: Welf, Kapetria, Garekyn, and Derek.

After confronting Amel, Welf and his Replimoid companions discover that the Bravennans have also been lying to them.

Joining forces with Amel, they call themselves the People of the Purpose. When the Bravennans learn that Welf and the other Replimoids have betrayed them, they send a meteor shower to Earth, which sinks Atlantis, destroys Amel and his unique substance luracastria, and divides Welf from Derek and Garekyn. He and Kapetria live on through the centuries.

Becoming a couple, in the way vampires become Blood Spouses, such as Avicus and Zenobia, or Chrysanthe with Gregory Duff Collingsworth, Welf and Kapetria survive throughout the next eleven thousand years, never knowing what happened to their Replimoid companions.

In the twentieth century, learning that the spirit of Amel is somehow intrinsically connected to the race of vampires on Earth, Welf and Kapetria generate false identifications and become Dr. Felix Welf and Dr. Karen Rhinehart. They have the ability to learn faster than humans, processing a great quantity of data in a short amount of time, and they easily fit into any scientific surrounding. Taking work at Collingsworth Pharmaceuticals, owned by the ancient vampire Gregory Duff Collingsworth, Welf and Kapetria attempt to re-create another Replimoid like themselves and even to duplicate Amel's unique compound, luracastria.

In the twenty-first century, Welf ascertains that Garekyn and Derek are still alive. So he and Kapetria search for them. Finally reuniting with their antediluvian companions, the People of the Purpose join with Lestat and his vampire coven. They work together to discover that Amel's enhanced DNA remains a prominent factor in his etheric body, which fused with Akasha's DNA to form the first vampire in ancient Egypt, and which she has transmitted to other mortals who become vampires. Welf and the other Replimoids realize that it is Amel's desire for a human body once again that is driving the bloodlust of all vampires, not the old belief that they drink blood because they desire the death of a mortal. Collaborating in a monumental effort, Welf and his Replimoid companions remove the spirit of Amel from Lestat's brain and implant him into the brain of a Replimoid that Kapetria and Derek create. Through Welf's assistance, Lestat is finally free of being the host carrier of the Sacred Core of all vampires, and Amel is once more an equal among them, joining together in their unique coven—the People of the Purpose.

For more perspectives on Welf in the Vampire Chronicles, read the *Alphabettery* entries **Amel, Atlantis, Bravenna, Bravennans, Collingsworth Pharmaceuticals, Derek, Garekyn, Gregory Duff Collingsworth, Lestat de Lioncourt, Luracastria, People of the Purpose, Replimoid, Sacred Core,** and **Welftu.**

• IMMORTAL •

Before their important meeting with Prince Lestat and his vampire coven, Kapetria and her companion Welf believe that it is important to perfect their Replimoid abilities. Kapetria severs her left foot, which grows back, while her amputated left foot replicates into a duplicate of Kapetria, which she names Katu. Welf does likewise, but severs his right hand, which also grows back, while his amputated right hand grows into a replicated duplicate of himself, which he names Welftu for "Welf Two."

Each replicated duplicate is considered a child to its parent, but Kapetria considers them all to be brother and sister Replimoids.

Welftu appears in *Prince Lestat and the Realms of Atlantis* (2016). For more perspectives on Welftu in the Vampire Chronicles, read the *Alphabettery* entries **Bravenna, Derek, Kapetria, Katu,** and **Replimoid.**

Wergeld

• IDIOM •

"Wergeld" is literally translated from ancient Nordic as "man price." A Teutonic custom of social justice, wergeld places a price both on a man's life and on his property. If a man is murdered or his property is destroyed, wergeld is exacted upon the murderer or the property destroyer; usually that price means the offender's life.

In *Blood and Gold* (2001), Thorne exacts wergeld for Marius's sake, killing Santino for him because Santino nearly burned Marius to death when he burned his Venice palazzo to the ground and kidnapped Armand.

For more perspectives on wergeld in the Vampire Chronicles, read the *Alphabettery* entries **Maharet**, **Marius**, **Santino**, and **Thorne**.

Wilderness

• SANCTUARY •

Nearly nine thousand years before the Common Era, the genetically enhanced Amel creates luracastric cities, such as the city of Atlantis, to protect humans from the ravenous appetites of the Bravennans. A cultured civilization develops inside, which is entirely distinct from other humanoid interaction, so much so that Amel refers to everything not protected within his luracastric sanctuaries as the Wilderness, since it is in that wild world where people find the greatest suffering through the influence of the Bravennans, for whom human suffering is a source of food.

The Wilderness appears in *Prince Lestat and the Realms of Atlantis* (2016). For more perspectives on the Wilderness in the Vampire Chronicles, read the *Alphabettery* entries **Amel**, **Atlantis**, **Bravennans**, and **Luracastria**.

Wilderness People

• MORTAL •

Many thousands of years before the Common Era, before the building of the Great Pyramid in ancient Egypt, an alien race called the Bravennans consume the energy of human suffering to survive (theirs is a ravenous appetite, which serves as the basis for vampiric blood lust). They construct numerous transmission stations around the Earth to convey this energy across the universe to where they live in the Realm of Worlds. They also abduct a human, enhance his body with genetic augmentations, and send him back to Earth for the purpose of maintaining and repairing their transmission stations. When Amel discovers the truth of their plan, he uses his superhuman DNA as a template for creating luracastria, a compound that prevents the Bravennans from exploiting human suffer-

ing. Amel builds out of luracastria the city of Atlantis, a peaceful sanctuary where suffering is nonexistent. Amel's greatest desire is to help every human being on Earth, including the people who live in the Wilderness, whom the Atalantayans refer to as the Wilderness people, individuals with long hair and beards and coarse clothing and without any civilized manners. Amel wants to bring every Wilderness person into Atalantaya to learn how to live peacefully, without any need for hunter-gatherer skills.

Wilderness people appear in *Prince Lestat and the Realms of Atlantis* (2016). For more perspectives on Wilderness people in the Vampire Chronicles, read the *Alphabettery* entries **Amel**, **Atalantaya**, **Atlantis**, **Bravennans**, **Luracastria**, and **Realm of Worlds**.

William Blackwood

• MORTAL •

William Blackwood is the son of the founder of Blackwood Farm, Manfred. He has one sister, Camille. When their mother, Virginia Lee, dies during their childhood, William and Camille are raised by Ora Lee and Jerome, free Creole people of color who are the ancestors of Big Ramona and Jasmine.

William marries Grace, but he is sterile. When his father learns that there will be no heir, he convinces his friend, Julien Mayfair, to don a Mardi Gras mask and a red velvet cloak lined in gold satin and pretend to be William in the bedroom, to impregnate Grace. Gravier is the fruit of that union.

When Grace dies, William takes a second wife, whose name remains unknown at present. Julien Mayfair once again dons the mask and cloak, pretends to be William, and gets her pregnant, producing William's daughter, Lorraine, whom Quinn knows as Aunt Queen. William has a third child, Patrick, but Julien never confesses to fathering him, so Patrick's biological father also remains a mystery. After William dies, his ghost can be seen haunting his old bedroom.

William Blackwood appears in *Blackwood Farm* (2002). For more perspectives on William Blackwood in the Vampire Chronicles, read the *Alphabettery* entries **Big Ramona, Camille Blackwood, Grace Blackwood, Gravier Blackwood, Jasmine, Julien Mayfair, Manfred Blackwood, Ora Lee, Patrick Blackwood,** and **Virginia Lee Blackwood**.

Winter Solstice Ball

• PHENOMENON •

When Lestat kills Rhoshamandes, the Court of the Prince at Château de Lioncourt celebrates by throwing a Winter Solstice Ball in the Château's massive ballroom, a unique event without precedence in the long history of immortal blood drinkers. The occasion also celebrates the establishment of the first harmonious vampire court in the six-thousand-year history of the race.

More than two thousand vampires attend the ball, ancient and young alike. Because the ballroom's capacity is limited to one thousand immortals, many must dance on the terrace, in corridors, and in adjacent rooms, although it is possible that the older vampires in attendance use the Cloud Gift to dance in the air, on the ceiling, and on the walls.

The Winter Solstice Ball appears in *Blood Communion* (2018). For more perspectives on the ball, read the *Alphabettery* entries **Château de Lioncourt, Lestat de Lioncourt,** and **Rhoshamandes**.

Witches' Place

• SANCTUARY •

Ever since Lestat's mortal boyhood, he has heard the tale of the Witches' Place, a clearing in the woods of the Auvergne where women accused of witchcraft were burned at the stake, many years before Lestat was born. As a child, he weeps over the fate of those witches. As a man, he and his best friend, Nicolas, return to that clearing, where they can still find stakes planted in the ground, charred and blackened, where women were burned to death. Nicolas plays his violin while Lestat dances. Together they sing and laugh, believing that they are reconsecrating the ground to make it a better place.

The Witches' Place appears in *The Vampire Lestat* (1985). For more perspectives on the Witches' Place in the Vampire Chronicles, read the *Alphabettery* entries **Lestat de Lioncourt** and **Nicolas de Lenfent**.

Wolfkiller

• SOBRIQUET •

When the ancient vampire Magnus first encounters the mortal Lestat, he reads Lestat's mind and sees how the young blond mortal has slain eight wolves in the Auvergne wilderness. Finally believing that he has found a rightful heir to his fortune, a mortal worthy enough to be his fledgling, Magnus gives Lestat the sobriquet "Wolfkiller."

"Wolfkiller" appears in *The Vampire Lestat* (1985). For more perspectives on the Wolfkiller sobriquet, read the *Alphabettery* entries **Lestat de Lioncourt** and **Magnus**.

Wynken de Wilde

• MORTAL •

Wynken de Wilde is a sixteenth-century writer and illustrator who creates books that are both mystically devotional to belief in God and Christ and fundamentally heretical to Christendom's basic teachings on morality.

Lestat becomes aware of Wynken de Wilde's writings through one of his victims, Roger, who not only is a wealthy murderer, smuggler, and drug dealer but also, having been raised with a Jesuit education in New Orleans, one of the only translators of Wynken de Wilde's works into modern English. After dying, Roger returns to Lestat as a ghost and begs him not to let his translations of Wilde's works perish but to preserve them so that Wilde might inform a new generation of hopeful mystics.

Wynken de Wilde appears in *Memnoch the Devil* (1995). For more perspectives on Wynken de Wilde in the Vampire Chronicles, read the *Alphabettery* entries **Lestat de Lioncourt** and **Roger**.

Young Freniere

• MORTAL •

The youngest brother of five older sisters, young Freniere is set to inherit his family's property, Freniere plantation, just up the river from the Pointe du Lac plantation, owned by the vampire Louis, fledgling of Lestat, who also lives on Pointe du Lac. Young Freniere becomes embroiled in a disagreement with a man and challenges him to a duel. He wins, but Lestat captures and kills young Freniere, leaving the Freniere family in jeopardy, especially the oldest sister, Babette Freniere, whom Louis cherishes.

Young Freniere appears in *Interview with the Vampire* (1976). For more perspectives on young Freniere's character, read the *Alphabettery* entries **Babette Freniere, Freniere Plantation, Louis de Pointe du Lac,** and **Pointe du Lac Plantation.**

Yuri Stefano

• TALAMASCA •

Born to a wealthy American father from Los Angeles who dies before Yuri is two and a Serbian gypsy mother who dies before he is ten, Yuri Stefano is taken from his Serbian village by gypsy kinsmen who force him into a life of pickpocketing and other thievery, in Paris, Venice, and Florence. After a few months, he is discovered by the Englishman Aaron Lightner, a prominent member of the Talamasca, a secret order of psychic detectives. Aaron cares for Yuri as a ward and gives him an education. By the age of twenty-six, Yuri becomes a full-fledged member of the Talamasca Order. His work is limited to finding missing persons, gathering information, and operating as a spy or as a private investigator, among many other responsibilities, although he truly works only for Aaron Lightner or his director, David Talbot, Superior General of the Talamasca during the early half of the twentieth century.

Together, Yuri and Aaron study the Mayfair witch family and how the spirit Lasher has developed a plan of becoming incarnate through a secret breeding program involving thirteen witches in thirteen generations. Upon Yuri's unearthing not only Lasher's nefarious plan but also his collusion with several prominent members of the Order, those treacherous members have Aaron assassinated. Yuri teams up with Rowan Mayfair, Michael Curry, and Superior General Joan Cross to exact vengeance for Aaron's murder.

Yuri Stefano appears in *Blood Canticle* (2003). For more perspectives on Yuri's character, read the *Alphabettery* entries **Aaron Lightner**, **David Talbot**, **Lasher**, and **Thirteen Witches**.

Zenobia

• VAMPIRE •

enobia is Eudoxia's beloved and Avicus's Blood Spouse, a member of the Blood Kindred, and helps establish Collingsworth Pharmaceuticals, which aids in the separation of Amel from Lestat. Zenobia appears in *Blood and Gold* (2001), *Prince Lestat* (2014), *Prince Lestat and the Realms of Atlantis* (2016), and *Blood Communion* (2018).

Born and raised as a slave in the palace of Constantinople, Zenobia is fifteen years old when the vampire Eudoxia takes her from the palace because she is incomparably beautiful, extremely well educated, and uncommonly clever. Eudoxia then makes one of her own slaves, Asphar, turn Zenobia into a vampire to avoid the fundamental problem that prevents maker and fledgling from reading each other's thoughts and to allow Eudoxia to communicate with Zenobia telepathically, sharing her thoughts and reading Zenobia's mind. Eudoxia tells Zenobia the story of her life, how her family moved to Athens when Alexander the Great first founded it, how she was turned into a vampire by the great Cyril, who let her drink from the blood of the first vampire, Queen Akasha. Eudoxia takes Zenobia as her intimate companion, and Zenobia loves Eudoxia deeply.

Eudoxia becomes aware that the vampire Marius has moved to Constantinople from Rome, bringing with him two vampire companions, Avicus and Mael, as well as Those Who Must Be Kept: Akasha and Enkil. Eudoxia explains to Zenobia that she would normally destroy such vampires, since she has been keeping Constantinople clean of vampires for many years. But after discovering that Marius protects Akasha, whom Eudoxia yearns to drink from again, Eudoxia makes two attempts to drink the Queen's powerful blood, both of which end in disaster, when Marius destroys Asphar, and Akasha destroys Eudoxia, with the Fire Gift. Now all alone, Zenobia begs Marius to protect her, as she is still young and weak. Marius allows Zenobia to drink his blood; it increases her power considerably, since he himself has been imbibing Akasha's ancient and powerful blood. Marius welcomes Zenobia into their coven; he protects her and teaches her how to dress like a man and hunt safely in the streets. Avicus and Mael are not as welcoming, which angers Marius immensely. What disturbs him most is that Eudoxia's last assault causes a mob of mortals to threaten the safety of Those Who Must Be Kept. Greatly agitated, Marius knows he must take them elsewhere. His plan is to leave behind Avicus and Mael, and even Zenobia, who is now powerful yet still as gentle as ever. None of them wants Marius to go; and in their grief, Avicus and Zenobia discover deeper intimacy. She finds Mael to be too coarse and closed minded, while

Avicus is optimistic, gentle, kind, attractive, and ancient, with blood almost as old as Akasha's.

After Marius departs with Those Who Must Be Kept, Zenobia and Avicus spend much of their time together, leaving Mael alone and bitter. They sneak into the palace and feed off royalty and slaves, instead of hunting in the streets. Zenobia is too much in love with being a woman to continue dressing as a boy to hunt as Marius taught her. She is learning her own way to be a vampire. And she is dividing Avicus from Mael, maker from fledgling, in the process; for Avicus is also learning from her how to be a better vampire in that age. In time, when they can no longer endure Mael's bitter company, Zenobia and Avicus leave Constantinople without him, travel all over the world, and become Blood Spouses.

A few centuries later, Zenobia and Avicus come to Carthage in North Africa, where they encounter the coven of Gregory Duff Collingsworth, who was known as Nebamun several thousand years ago in ancient Egypt and was the Captain of the Queens Blood. In his coven, the Blood Kindred, is Gregory's fledgling and Blood Wife, Chrysanthe, a younger vampire from the great Arab-Christian city Hira. Along with them is Marius's fledgling's fledgling (Pandora's fledgling), the one-legged vampire, Flavius. Avicus and Zenobia join Gregory's Blood Kindred and remain with them for many centuries. Zenobia and Chrysanthe observe as Gregory and Avicus reminisce about the old days in ancient Egypt.

Zenobia and Avicus stay together all the

way into the twenty-first century, living in North Africa, near to the places where they spent their mortal youths, until they eventually move into Prince Lestat's Château de Lioncourt in the Auvergne.

For more perspectives on Zenobia's character, read the *Alphabettery* entries **Akasha, Asphar, Avicus, Blood Kindred, Blood Spouse, Chrysanthe, Cyril, Enkil, Eudoxia, Flavius, Gregory Duff Collingsworth, Mael, Marius, Nebamun, Pandora,** and **Those Who Must Be Kept.**

ACKNOWLEDGMENTS

Inexpressible thanks go to Victoria Wilson, my editor, for taking on this project and for her exceptional direction; to Father Joe Cocucci for his priestly guidance; to Naomi Davis, my agent, for advice on the manuscript and for overseeing contractual details superbly; to Mark Geyer for his perfect illustrations; to my family for their support; to the People of the Page and my Facebook family for their loyalty; to Rosy Avila and Veronica Martinez for their inspirational kindness; to Karen O'Brien for her brilliant proofreading; to Christopher Rice for his kindness and encouragements; to Anne Rice, my friend, my teacher, for asking me to write the *Alphabettery,* my homage to all the blood and tears that she herself poured into the Vampire Chronicles. I am also thankful for my wife, Stina, for her encouragement and unconditional love. Ultimately, I thank God for . . . everything I have, everything I am.